THE
GREATEST
INDIAN STORIES
EVER TOLD

In the same series

The Greatest Bengali Stories Ever Told (ed.) Arunava Sinha

The Greatest Urdu Stories Ever Told (ed.) Muhammad Umar Memon

The Greatest Odia Stories Ever Told (eds.) Leelawati Mohapatra, Paul St-Pierre, and K. K. Mohapatra

The Greatest Hindi Stories Ever Told (ed.) Poonam Saxena

The Greatest Tamil Stories Ever Told (eds.) Sujatha Vijayaraghavan and Mini Krishnan

The Greatest Assamese Stories Ever Told (ed.) Mitra Phukan

The Greatest Gujarati Stories Ever Told (ed.) Rita Kothari

The Greatest Kashmiri Stories Ever Told (ed.) Neerja Mattoo

The Greatest Telugu Stories Ever Told (eds.) Dasu Krishnamoorty and Tamraparni Dasu

The Greatest Goan Stories Ever Told (ed.) Manohar Shetty

The Greatest Marathi Stories Ever Told (ed.) Ashutosh Poddar

The Greatest Malayalam Stories Ever Told (ed.) A. J. Thomas (forthcoming)

The Greatest Punjabi Stories Ever Told (eds.) Renuka Singh and Balbir Madhopuri (forthcoming)

The Greatest Kannada Stories Ever Told (ed.) Chandan Gowda (forthcoming)

THE GREATEST INDIAN STORIES EVER TOLD

Edited by
ARUNAVA SINHA

ALEPH

ALEPH BOOK COMPANY
An independent publishing firm
promoted by *Rupa Publications India*

First published in India in 2023
by Aleph Book Company
7/16 Ansari Road, Daryaganj
New Delhi 110 002

This edition copyright © Aleph Book Company 2023.

Copyright in the individual stories vests in the respective authors/translators/proprietors.

Introduction copyright © Arunava Sinha 2023.

The Acknowledgements on p. 492 constitute an extension of the copyright page.

All rights reserved.

This is a work of fiction. Names, characters, places, and incidents are either the product of the authors' imagination or are used fictitiously and any resemblance to any actual persons, living or dead, events, or locales is entirely coincidental.

No part of this publication may be reproduced, transmitted, or stored in a retrieval system, in any form or by any means, without permission in writing from Aleph Book Company.

For sale in the Indian subcontinent only.

ISBN: 978-93-93852-87-8

3 5 7 9 10 8 6 4

Printed in India.

This book is sold subject to the condition that it shall not, by way of trade or otherwise, be lent, resold, hired out, or otherwise circulated without the publisher's prior consent in any form of binding or cover other than that in which it is published.

To the readers, writers, and translators of India.

NOTE ON STYLE

The text of most of the stories in this volume has been standardized according to the Aleph house style. However, occasionally where stylistic variants have been used by the authors, these have been left untouched.

CONTENTS

Note on Style		vi
Introduction ARUNAVA SINHA		ix
1	Two Old Kippers SIDDIQ AALAM	1
2	Gangrene AGYEYA	11
3	The Blue Light VAIKOM MUHAMMAD BASHEER	21
4	The Gravestone SHAHNAZ BASHIR	32
5	Trishanku MANNU BHANDARI	38
6	The Story of a Crow Learning Prosody SUBRAMANIA BHARATI	54
7	The Blue Umbrella RUSKIN BOND	58
8	The Madiga Girl CHALAM	75
9	Mahesh SARAT CHANDRA CHATTOPADHYAY	84
10	Of Fists and Rubs ISMAT CHUGHTAI	94
11	The Booking Counter MAMANG DAI	103
12	Countless Hitlers VIJAYDAN DETHA	108
13	Urvashi and Johnny MAHASWETA DEVI	118
14	Jumo Bhishti DHUMKETU	139
15	The Night of the Full Moon K. S. DUGGAL	143
16	The Alligator of Aligarh A. M. GAUTAM	149
17	Tale of a Toilet RAMNATH GAJANAN GAWADE	157
18	Values MAMONI RAISOM GOSWAMI	175
19	Beyond the Fog QURRATULAIN HYDER	193
20	The Governor's Visit KALKI	211
21	A Death in Delhi KAMLESHWAR	217
22	Coinsanv's Cattle DAMODAR MAUZO	224
23	The Holy Banyan BAMACHARAN MITRA	232

24	The Discovery of Telenapota PREMENDRA MITRA	241
25	The Solution GOPINATH MOHANTY	251
26	A Letter K. M. MUNSHI	257
27	Reply-paid Card DINANATH NADIM	261
28	Vision M. T. VASUDEVAN NAIR	267
29	A Horse and Two Goats R. K. NARAYAN	282
30	The Search DHEEBA NAZIR	297
31	The Flood THAKAZHI SIVASANKARA PILLAI	302
32	The Shroud MUNSHI PREMCHAND	308
33	Stench of Kerosene AMRITA PRITAM	315
34	Naadar Sir SUNDARA RAMASWAMY	320
35	Rats BHABENDRA NATH SAIKIA	336
36	Kalluri's Radio VILAS SARANG	344
37	The Gold Coin LAXMANRAO SARDESSAI	354
38	House Number KAVANA SARMA	360
39	Savage Harvest MOHINDER SINGH SARNA	368
40	Gold from the Graves ANNA BHAU SATHE	376
41	Rebati FAKIR MOHAN SENAPATI	383
42	Sharavana Services VIVEK SHANBHAG	394
43	Portrait of a Lady KHUSHWANT SINGH	406
44	The Times Have Changed KRISHNA SOBTI	410
45	The Kabuliwallah RABINDRANATH TAGORE	417
46	Elephant at Sea KANISHK THAROOR	425
47	Charlis and I SHASHI THAROOR	438
48	After the Hanging O. V. VIJAYAN	459
49	Gobyaer SADAF WANI	465
50	Bhaskara Pattelar and My Life PAUL ZACHARIA	470

Acknowledgements   492
Notes on the Authors   496
Notes on the Translators   507

INTRODUCTION
ARUNAVA SINHA

What makes the fifty stories in this volume the greatest Indian stories ever told? What criteria have been applied to make this selection? Who decides which the greatest stories are? Can there even be such a list? I will attempt to answer all these questions in the course of this short introduction.

First, what exactly is the nature of the 'stories' in the context of our book, not to mention 'ever told'? In India—today's and yesterday's—as everyone knows, stories almost predate history, with the epics having been handed down over centuries, and strong and vibrant traditions of storytelling—first oral and then written—having sprung up thereafter. The *modern short story*, learnt from Western literature, is, of course, a far younger creature, barely a couple of centuries old. It is this form of the story—and this form alone—that this volume contains—stories that were written, printed, and published in books, and read in the same form every time that they were read.

The oral story, passed on through retellings, is a shape-shifting organism, malleable to the instincts and impulses of the storyteller. Not so the written story, which has lived on in the same configuration—even when translated—since its birth. This is the kind of story we have here, taking a unique form in every reader's head and heart but not changing in the hands of those who take it to its audience.

Of course, you might ask why we have used the word 'told' in the title then. Why not 'written'? Well, every story is born as an urge to tell a tale, without which there would have been no story. And no matter that they finally took the form of written words, in spirit these are all stories told by their respective authors, to be heard—and felt, and remembered—by human beings rather than just being preserved on paper. So, our volume is a re-creation of that first experience, of having stories told to us.

Up next: how have we made the journey from 'stories' to 'greatest' and 'Indian'? The selection you hold in your hands was not put together by assembling an enormous array of stories from all over India and then selecting the fifty that appeared to be the best among them by conventional literary standards. These standards include but are not limited to factors like how compelling the storyline is, how authentic the characters appear to be, how well the language has been used, how vividly and imaginatively the story is presented, or how effectively the reader's attention is engaged. Those considerations may be useful in the next-to-impossible scenario of all the stories coming from a similar place in terms of history, culture, and opportunities, among other things. But, in practice, 'Indian stories' do not share such congruences in their origins. That would be an improbability in any country in the world, but in India it is a complete impossibility.

But what are Indian stories? And what are great Indian stories? The data about the multiplicity of languages, histories, geographies, races, tribes, and lived experiences in our land is too well-known to need reiteration. In this context, then, how do we imagine the India of our literatures? A single country by political choice, it nevertheless contains a bewildering variety of artistic traditions, cultures, and practices that defy any attempt at being framed neatly or singularly. What makes for 'Indian' stories, then, is not uniformity but precisely this variety. There can never be *one* particular kind of story that can be defined as Indian, out of which the best fifty can be chosen. So, the pre-condition that all the stories in this volume be 'Indian' implies that collectively they must reflect the diversity that is India. In fact, without this diversity, there would be nothing 'Indian' about this assemblage of stories. I will stick my neck out further and assert that there can be no one 'Indian' story, there can only be a multiplicity of 'Indian' stories. For India is many literatures, not a single one. And 'Indian', too, is of necessity an adjective that qualifies a set of stories, continuously proliferating and branching off—it can never be a single story, with a single set of themes, reflecting a single basket of reality, told in a single family of languages.

This is why this book brings you stories from every part of the country of India. In a variety of languages. In a symphony of voices. In an assortment of moods. In a potpourri of styles.

In the matter of the medium of storytelling, too, India does not talk through a monolithic language where all stories can be compared to one another because they use the same vocabulary, syntax, and grammar. Instead, we live and read and speak and write in a patchwork of languages that converge, diverge, overlap, break away, assimilate, discard, multiply, divide, and do a thousand other things to build a complex web of interrelated differences and variations.

India is a country that lives in translation, as we constantly navigate a path between the language we are born with, the language we live in, and the language we go on to express ourselves in—which are often different from one another. With the threads between our thinking and our speaking, our writing and our reading, our listening and our working frequently being arranged more like a spider's web than a neat lattice, we inhabit several languages simultaneously. A literature that operates only in one language, therefore, cannot have more than a constructed relationship with our world in India.

It is not accidental, then, that though you will read all the fifty stories in this selection in the English language, forty-three of them are in fact translations into English from the various languages of India. This is by design, for translation alone can be the medium through which the sheer linguistic variety of India's literatures can be appreciated by anyone in India. Stories from fifteen different languages are included in this selection, largely drawn from the volumes of Aleph Book Company's 'Greatest Stories Ever Told' series, along with a set of stories originally written in English.

And so, this selection of stories does not emphasize the quality of being the 'greatest' in terms of each individual story, but in terms of the complete set. It is, I would argue, the diversity and the variances that enable this selection to stake a claim to being called the greatest modern Indian stories ever told. To re-emphasize, the stories here have not made their way into the volume on their individual strengths—which are, frankly, unquestionable—alone, but also because each of them contribute a piece to the puzzle that is the literatures of India.

In reading these, you will live all the possibilities that India has to offer, possibilities that an individual cannot experience in a single lifetime. This selection is not just a representation of the multiplicity of magics that being 'Indian' can offer, it is a portal to all the universes that the 'Indian' identity can inhabit. It is not the totality of those universes, but it is a gateway into them.

And yet you may ask, dear reader, whether this vision of 'The Greatest Indian Stories Ever Told' is sufficient to put together a selection like this. After all, even within this framework, surely, there can be more than one such set of fifty stories, meeting all these requirements, and still having nothing in common with one another in terms of the specific stories. Indeed there can be, and this is where, finally, individual choice comes into the making of this volume. Or, into the first word of the title. *The.* Whose choice? Let's just say, a reader's.

Who, then, are the writers whose stories you will read in this volume? Reader, if you've cheated—and I would have—and looked at the contents page already, you know the answer by now. I will not disappoint you with pithy summaries of what is going on in each of them. That would be doing them a disservice, for I can guarantee that the only way to know these stories is to read them in their entirety and their fullness—the way their authors (and translators) have presented them for you. And when you are done, you will know why India is the greatest story ever told.

A highway somewhere in India
February 2023

1

TWO OLD KIPPERS

SIDDIQ AALAM

Translated from the Urdu by Muhammad Umar Memon

'...sleeping as quiet as death, side by wrinkled side, toothless, salt and brown, like two old kippers in a box.'
—Dylan Thomas, *Under Milk Wood*

Recently two pensioned old men in Calcutta met by chance in a public park. Six years ago, but on different dates, they had both retired from government service. Ever since, providence had been preparing for the day when they would be found sitting side by side on a single bench. Apparently, they had each lived their lives and were now trying to invest their remaining days in something useful. Having arrived at this point, they were still poles apart.

Since retirement, one of them could be seen every evening without fail—every evening, that is, unless he was out of town—on one of the wooden or concrete benches at the edge of the grassy patch in the park. He spoke very little, and when he settled down on a bench, he stuck his umbrella vertically between his legs and rested his chin on its handle. Usually, he preferred a bench that was remote and empty, but sometimes, when all of the benches were taken, he deigned to choose the one that had the least number of people and sat crouching in a corner so that if anyone tried to accost him, he could pick up his umbrella and leave without wasting a second. During these six years he had had surgery on his right eye, and most of his brows had turned grey. The crown of his head was bald, and in the last light of the evening he often looked like a corpse that had escaped from the morgue of the nearby medical college and crossed the street to come here. All in all, his face seemed to be that of the ideal government pensioner who'd left everything that was his inside the walls of his office building.

The other old geezer, because he'd retired from the railway service, was able to get two free travel passes, which he used to visit places within the country. His addiction to gambling, acquired in his youth, had nearly ruined him. But now, at the tail end of his life, he mostly went to see religious sites, such as those at Varanasi, Puri, Tarkeshwar, etc. He'd also bought a little hut in a hermitage at Puri so he could spend his last days in peace. But mentally he wasn't yet ready for that, so, instead, he spent his days leafing through newspapers, or sitting idly and dozing on the terrace outside his building, or going to the public park. Now and then while dozing, he unconsciously found himself standing on the Antipodes with the waves of the Pacific swelling up around him. But all he could see, even on the waves, were racehorses swimming, or playing-card jokers rowing boats, or whirlpools circling around him like a roulette. These Antipodes had stuck in his mind since his school days when his geography teacher had resorted to using a globe to explain the true shape of the earth.

One evening, when a tired sun was breathing its last on the kadamb and karanj trees planted outside the park's perimeter wall, a chubby-cheeked boy was seen crossing the grassy patch escorted by his nanny. Noticing the two old coots sitting side by side, the boy, for some strange reason, began laughing and kept on laughing for quite a while as he repeatedly turned around to look at them. The first old man was still trying to figure out what might have made the boy laugh when he heard the sound of another laugh. Without thinking he turned sideways to look. It was another man, about his own age, perched on the other end of the bench.

'Why was the kid laughing?' he asked the other man in spite of himself, although it was the laugh of his own peer that was bothering him more than the boy's.

'Perhaps because he thought we're so old,' the other replied and started to laugh again.

'Well now, that's not so strange that you should laugh about it. At his age, I'd have laughed too.' He came to the boy's defence for no reason at all. 'And anyway what are old-timers for?' He was pleasantly surprised at his own magnanimity.

'What for? To burn in the Nimtala crematory—what else!' The second man tittered heartily. Then he stopped, leaned towards the first and asked, 'Tell me a secret: would you allow them to perform an autopsy on you when you're dead?'

'What kind of question is that? And if they did, would I be there to stop them?'

'But you can. You can tell them in your will, I mean, if you die a normal death.'

To get off the subject the first man said, 'Oh well. We'll worry about it when we cross that bridge,' but deep inside the question had rattled him. For a while, he gazed at the immense field where giant tents and canopies were set up during the winter for the circus. The buildings outside the park rose high into the air like so many cardboard boxes, which some tiny hand might reach up and send crumbling to the ground any instant.

'But why was the kid laughing—really?' he wondered to himself.

Later, he was surprised to realize he'd blurted out a whole lot of things to that stranger—that didn't jibe at all with his reticent nature. Then, in quite a mysterious way, the two old men ran into each other the next evening, and again the following evening, and then every evening. Neither had asked for the other's name. They also avoided talking about personal matters, which was good; it helps prevent discussing many painful subjects.

One day, the second old man asked, 'Why do you always have an umbrella? Especially now when the weather is perfectly fine?'

'I feel defenceless without it,' the other replied unpleasantly. 'I've been lugging it around all my life. I can't give it up now. Impossible!'

'What kind of protection do you expect from an umbrella?'

'Why,' the other said irritably. 'There are many advantages, not counting the sun and rain. Suppose we're sitting on this bench and a snake slithers out of the grass right between our legs. We can at least defend ourselves with the umbrella. Or suppose you're late getting home one night and you take the Carmichael Hospital route where you find a body on the pavement. You can at least poke it with the umbrella tip to see whether it's alive or dead. And to tell you the truth, I can't even remember how many times I've used it to fend off attacks from stray dogs.'

'Wow! But you're forgetting one other advantage.' The other old coot was having a hard time suppressing his laughter. 'Say you're sitting on a bench and you're afraid you might have to face this man you really don't want to see, so you snap your umbrella open and hide comfortably behind it. Isn't that something? Ha-ha-ha!' He was laughing heartily, as usual.

'Have you ever been a circus clown?'

'No. But I've wallowed enough in the Hooghly mud to be a turtle,' the old man retorted.

There was a fence on three sides of the area of the park earmarked for the circus, and a row of dense and not-so-dense almond, kadamb, ashok, chatiyan, and karanj trees ran along it. Beneath the trees, at suitable intervals, wooden or concrete benches had been placed haphazardly. Around this huge area a blacktop path had been laid out for strollers. When the lights came on in the buildings outside the park, the area was submerged in a kind of semi-darkness in spite of a few halogen lamps installed by the city. Many couples came here to take advantage of the semi-darkness. They sat on the thick carpet of grass and spent time enjoying the nice cool breeze. The two old coots just looked at them indifferently, as if they had no interest in whatever strange acrobatics were going on in that darkened spot. They had stopped holding forth critically on society's many different ills a long time ago anyway.

'Life's an awfully tiring game,' the second old man said philosophically one day. 'That fellow above,' he pointed at the sky, 'is a mighty dangerous scorekeeper. No matter how many goals you score, he cancels them out in the end and you're left with a big zero.'

'Have you started thinking about dying?'

'What good would dying do? Even if a tree stops flowering or bearing fruit, even if no leaves sprout on it, it's still better that it stays put. If nothing else, at least snakes and squirrels can find refuge in it.'

In the fading daylight their eyeglasses would light up as if somebody had carried off two mannequins from the show window at the Grand Hotel and set them down next to each other. The first old man was used to wearing a dhoti and kurta, so he appeared much older than his companion, who wore old-fashioned pants and a shirt.

'Judging by your clothes, you still look quite fit. Perhaps you'll live longer than me.'

'Don't curse me,' said the second man. 'My grandfather was already bedridden at fifty, but he dragged on for another thirty years. The old coot made life miserable for everyone. So, it's kind of difficult to say.'

Then he came up with an idea: 'Why don't we toss a coin. Heads you'll live longer, tails I will.'

Before the first old man could say anything, the other had pulled out a five-rupee coin and was holding it between his thumb and index finger, looking at him expectantly.

For a moment, the first old man stared at the other. His pupils didn't move and he appeared to be immersed in thought. Suddenly he leaned towards his companion and said, 'You take heads and leave the tails for me.'

A derisive grin splashed across the lips of the second man. He tossed the coin in the air. It went up, spiralled down in front of the bench, rolled, and then disappeared into the tall grass. They both got up from the bench and started looking for it. The second man stretched his hand out under the bench and ran his fingers through the grass. The first one thought it was his duty to provide moral support and joined in. They went on searching under the bench, behind it, and on either side, but the grass was so thick and the daylight penetrating that thickness so weak it seemed impossible to ever find the coin. Even so, the two old codgers went on rummaging through the grass until their fingers became soiled. Strollers passing by gawked at the two with wonder and amusement. Some even stopped to watch a while.

'Looks like those old geezers have lost their dentures,' a teenager mockingly commented. The two stopped searching and quickly sat up. They were holding on to the edge of the bench, panting as if they had travelled a long distance. Suddenly, their eyes met and they both realized the disappearance of the coin was in perfect accord with their wishes. Suppose they *had* found it? At least they were happy now.

But the second old man wasn't satisfied. 'We can think of some other way, can't we?' he said.

'For instance?'

'You see that fellow coming toward us. We can ask him his name. If he turns out to be a Muslim you'll live long, and if he's a Hindu I will.'

'What if he's a Christian? Quite a few of them live in this part of town.'

The second old man shook his head, disappointed.

'In that case, we'll need a third party to play this game. But what's the use. This world is so divided on every issue there aren't enough coins in it to suffice.'

In spite of himself, the first oldster had started to take an interest in this game, all the while conscious that what was happening didn't sit right with him. But their meeting every second day had acquired the force of destiny. Every time he traversed the distance from his home to the park, supporting himself on his weak, spindly legs and his umbrella, he was always overwhelmed by a compelling desire to go back, but some invisible force kept pushing him to the other man and that familiar corner in the park.

'Do you realize,' the second old man brought it up again, 'we can still do a lot to make our remaining time meaningful.'

'What do you want me to do? Start working again? Or join some social movement?'

'Of course not!' the second man smiled. 'Old men like us aren't good for anything. We have to stay the way we are. I do feel, though, that a hermit's life, the fourth state in which old men live in the wilderness and practise renunciation, is about right for us. This will cure the world of many ills. The new world will belong to new people. What do you think? I've gone so far as to buy a small hut in a hermitage. All it needs is a bathroom, which will be built soon. It's right on the edge of the sea.'

'I lost my faith during the Hindu–Muslim riots of 1947, or rather, I threw it into the fire.'

'That's strange.'

'Isn't it, though?'

'And you think this will bring peace to your soul?'

'Well, at least it's made me rise above these filthy events and look at them dispassionately.'

For some reason the second old man started grinning again.

'You know what?' he whispered. 'We should try again. Maybe this time we'll succeed.'

'What difference would that make? Whoever dies first, it will be the same for the other. Sooner or later we'll all be on our pyres. But if you insist, all right....'

'Oh no, I wasn't joking. I'm quite serious. All right, let's just let it hang for a while. God knows I occasionally begin to fear you.'

Sometime during the afternoon it had rained and the smog had been cleared from the sky over Calcutta. The stars appeared large and bright in the sky. The second old man shifted uneasily on the bench. Perhaps he'd arrived at a fresh decision. He lifted his finger and pointed towards the pole star that had risen with the sunset.

'You see it, don't you, shining right between the two almond trees?

It's my guess that in half an hour it'll be over the top of the tree on the right. Let's walk around the grounds once. If the star doesn't reach there by then, you'll live longer.'

'Who wants to live longer? Even so, if you must insist....'

The two old-timers started to walk along the edge of the blacktop path. The first man was intentionally walking fast, followed by the other, who was plodding along slowly on his long, spindly legs.

'You're walking fast,' the second old man said from behind laughing. 'Looks like you're hell-bent on living long.'

'That's nonsense,' said the first old man, slowing down because his heart was beating quite fast, which made it hard to breathe. 'This nonsense is not likely to alter the course of nature.'

'Then why are you practically running? You'll ruin your heart. Remember your age.'

'You're really a pest,' said the first old man as he continued walking. 'You should have been in politics. That kind of work suits your kind of dirty people.'

Without bothering to look behind him, he kept walking and covered half the distance in the dim light. The second old man had been left far behind and was shaking his head meaningfully. The first one stopped to catch his breath.

'If you walk so slowly, you'll miss the pole star.'

He heard the other shoot back from behind, 'Shut up! Can't you stop blabbering? Your mouth stinks, dirty old man.'

He started off again, but with each step his heart pumped so hard he felt as though a hefty hammer was pounding away inside his ribcage. Time and again he would stare up at the sky. He felt as though all the stars were rushing forward, as if they too were hell-bent on defeating him. He started to walk even faster, so fast that cold beads of sweat started to sprout on his skull. He could also feel traces of muted pain in his chest which quickly grew so intense that he promptly sat down on the ground, clutching his umbrella tightly. As he drew quick, deep breaths he felt as though the people and lights around him were fusing together in the cool atmosphere pervading the area.

The second old man was standing in front of him, grinning.

'If you run so fast, this is what you have to expect. It's not good for your health. So greedy and at such an age!'

Rubbing his chest, he ignored his interlocutor. His chest pain was beginning to subside a bit. He got up, took a few steps on his wobbly legs and stopped again. The pain had returned.

'Let's drop this foolishness,' said the second old man, gently rubbing the other's back. 'Where in the world have you heard of a star moving? Why would it inch its way to the top of a tree? It's the earth that moves and gives this mistaken impression.'

The first old man was pissed off. Grabbing his umbrella, he pointed the tip at the other man, making a gesture, and mumbled something.

'Don't get mad,' the second old man said. 'Looks like you're not feeling well. Shall I take you to your house?'

'Go to hell!' the first one pushed the other's hand aside rudely. 'I don't need your help to get home. But I do feel we should rethink our acquaintance. Perhaps we're not meant for each other.'

And tap-tapping his umbrella, he started walking in the dim light of the field towards the park's southern gate. The second old man shook his head in disappointment.

'Strange! Why should it be my fault if the stars don't move?'

The next day he arrived at the park somewhat early, wondering how his companion was doing. But the old coot couldn't be seen anywhere. And he didn't appear for the next two weeks either, although the second old man went about methodically looking at every bench. A feeling of guilt began to stir in his heart: maybe the joke wasn't suitable for a man his age, he thought. One day, he simply couldn't stand it any more and set out to look for him. He'd always seen him come into the park through the southern gate, so he went out that gate and started walking along a fairly big street. He wandered in and out of the many small streets and alleys that branched off from it. He stared at the windows and balconies of buildings hoping to spot him somewhere, until night descended on Calcutta. Suddenly, a dog materialized from somewhere, lifted one of its hind legs and started to pee on his shoes. By the time he realized what was happening, it was too late. The dog was already gone. Vanquished and unsuccessful he returned home with wet feet. He washed his socks and hung them to dry on the line in the balcony.

'Oh Lord, could he have died?' he wondered, pressing his eyes.

Three days later, he suddenly saw him, but on a different bench and in a different corner. He leapt towards him, but before he could reach him the first old man snapped open his umbrella and hid himself behind it. Stopping in front of the umbrella, he smiled, cleared his throat, and said, 'I'm sorry for what happened that day.'

The umbrella didn't reply.

'Yesterday, I tried to look for you. But perhaps that was a foolish thing to do. To tell you the truth, I don't even know where you live, your street or your house number.'

The umbrella remained silent. The second old man gave a long, cold sigh.

'I've decided to go to the hermitage. That's all I'm good for now. I can give you the address if you like. It's a nice place. You would like it. You can stay as my guest for a week or two.'

The silence continued. Finally, he admitted defeat, turned around, and left the park.

Three years later, he returned to Calcutta. It was two o'clock and the park was deserted. On the grounds in front of him, a little boy was playing with a rubber ball under an almond tree. As soon as the second old man entered the park his feet carried him to the same old bench that stood in its place, somewhat skewed, as if it had all happened yesterday. He sat quietly on the bench for a long time. The trees' shadows grew longer, stretching across the field. It seemed as if the circus had just left a few days ago because potholes could be seen everywhere and there were animal droppings here and there. Remembering his old companion, the man smiled. Who knows, he might meet him again on this very bench. And if he did, he would tell him about life in the hermitage, about the tranquillity and peace he had found there. He would tell him how nice it felt to walk along the edge of the sea, with the land behind and nature's azure secret stretched out in front of his eyes. The sea from which Brahma and his progeny had emerged, from which every living creature had crawled like a fledgling just hatched from an egg. Look, old fellow, if you're listening to me, if you want to live long, if you truly believe in living, you must consider abandoning the cares and noise of the city. The city's demands gnaw a man completely hollow from the inside. I wouldn't be surprised at all if one day people began withdrawing inside themselves. God knows what kind of ribs keep them from deflating or what strings help them walk.

He remembered all the wagers he'd put to the other man. And how, despite appearing indifferent on the outside, deep inside they were both anxious to win, as if their whole life depended on some insignificant coin or the movement of the pole star. What if his companion *had* won! The sky wouldn't have fallen. If one really takes stock of a man's entire life objectively, would it be so wrong to say that he has nothing to lose or gain?

His reverie broke to find the little boy standing before him.

'You want something? What are you looking for?'

'My ball,' the boy said hesitantly, pointing with his finger under the bench. The old man turned his head and looked behind the bench where a pink ball was waiting to be rescued from the small jungle of green grass. The man stretched out his hand to pick it up when something suddenly glittered on the wet ground beneath the grass.

'Good god!' Handing the ball to the boy, he stood his frail body up on its legs, went behind the bench, and squatted in front of that shining object. It was a coin, a five-rupee coin, its Ashoka column side facing up. Wet from a recent rain, the coin was sending a shaft of cool, dim light towards him.

'Heads!' he screamed. His mind raced back to the time three years ago when the first old man had bet with him one evening about living a long life. 'So, *I* won the bet that day. What a miracle! How strange, this coin's been lying here all this time!'

He pried the coin from the wet dirt, returned to his place on the bench and started rubbing it between his thumb and index finger. The boy was kicking his ball under the almond tree. The jagged edges of tree shadows had advanced quite far and were touching the fence around the field. He realized time had flown by and he raised his slumped shoulders.

'Curse me! The one who said that in the end it's a man's character that counts was right. I'll probably remain a worthless old man till the day I die.'

He got up, wiping tears from his wrinkled face, and walked over to the grass behind the bench. He stuck the coin back in the wet dirt under the grass with its tail side pointing up.

GANGRENE
AGYEYA

Translated from the Hindi by Poonam Saxena

As soon as I stepped into that deserted courtyard, I sensed a shadow of some curse hovering over it, something in the atmosphere that couldn't be expressed in words or touched, but it was burdensome, trembling, dense and it was spreading....

At the sound of my footsteps, Malti came out. She recognized me and her weary face lit up for a second with sweet surprise before returning to its original expression. 'Come!' she said, and then without waiting for an answer, turned to go inside. I followed her.

Once we were in, I asked her, 'He isn't here?'

'He hasn't come yet, he's in the office. He'll come in a little while. He usually comes at around 1.30-2.'

'When did he leave?'

'He leaves as soon as he gets up in the morning.'

After saying 'Huh,' I was about to ask, 'and what do you do in that time?' But then thought it was not appropriate to ask this question all of a sudden. I looked around the room.

Malti brought a fan and began to fan me with it. I objected, 'No, I don't want this.' But she wouldn't listen, and said, 'Wah! How can you not want it? You've come from outside and it's so hot and sunny. Here....'

I said, 'All right, give it to me.'

Perhaps she was about to say 'No' but, just then, a baby started crying in the next room and, quietly giving me the fan, she placed her hands on her knees and with a tired 'Huunh,' levered herself up and went inside.

I watched her leave and, looking at her thin body, kept thinking—what is this...what is this shadow that has settled over this house....

We were distantly related, and by that connection, Malti was my sister, but it was more accurate to call her my friend, because we always had a relationship of mutual friendliness. Since our childhood, we had played together, fought together, been punished together, and we'd studied together quite a bit too, and this was always because we wanted it to be so, never because we were tied by bonds of familial relationship....

I had come to see her after about four years. When I last saw her, she was still a girl, but now she was married, the mother of a child. I hadn't thought about whether this would have changed her and if so, how, but now, watching her receding back, I thought—what is this shadow over this house...and especially over Malti....

Malti came back with the baby and sat on a rug on the floor a little distance away from me. I turned my chair to face her and asked, 'What's his name?'

Malti looked at the baby and replied, 'We haven't decided on any name as yet, but we call him Titti.'

I called out to the child, 'Titti, Titti, come,' but he looked at me with his big eyes, then clung to his mother and cried out tearfully, 'Unnh-unnh-uunh-oon....'

Malti looked at him again, and then looked out towards the courtyard....

There was silence for some time. For a while, the silence was natural, during which I waited for Malti to ask me something, when all of a sudden I realized that Malti had said nothing at all...she had not even asked how I was, how come I was here...she was just sitting quietly, had she forgotten the days gone by in just two years of marriage? Or was it that she wanted to keep me at a distance? Was it because that free mutual friendship was no longer possible...even so, this kind of silence shouldn't be there even with a stranger....

A little aggrieved, I turned away and said, 'It seems to me you're not exactly happy that I've come....'

She started and said, 'Hunh?'

This 'hunh' was in the form of a query, but not because Malti hadn't heard what I said, but because she was surprised. That's why I didn't repeat what I said but sat silently. Malti didn't say anything, so after a while I looked at her. She'd been staring at me unblinkingly but the moment I turned towards her, she lowered her eyes. But I saw that there was a strange emotion in those eyes, as if something inside Malti was trying to remember forgotten things, trying to awaken and set in motion once again a fragmented universe, to revive some broken thread of behaviour, and was failing in this effort…as if a person was suddenly trying to lift a limb that hadn't been used for a long time, as if it had died during a long period of forgetfulness…it could not be lifted with such feeble strength (though that strength was entirely obtainable).… I felt as if the yoke around a dead creature's neck had been put on a living human being and that being was trying to remove it and throw it away but was unable to….

Just then, someone knocked on the door. I looked at Malti but she hadn't moved. Only when there was a second knock did she put the baby aside and get up to answer the door.

It was he, that is, Malti's husband. I was seeing him for the first time but I recognized him from his photo. Introductions were made. Malti went into the courtyard to prepare lunch, and the two of us sat inside and began talking, about his job, about his life, about the place where they lived, and other such topics which usually crop up in an initial conversation after two people have just been introduced, like a sort of protective armour of expression.…

Malti's husband's name is Maheshwar. He is a doctor in a dispensary in this mountain village, that's how he lives in these quarters. He goes to the dispensary every morning at seven o'clock and returns around one or one-thirty, after that he's free the whole afternoon, he just has to go in the evening for one or two hours, to see the patients in the small hospital attached to the dispensary and give them necessary instructions…his life too follows a fixed pattern, every day the same work, the same kind of patients, the same instructions, the same prescriptions, the same medicines. He himself is bored, and in addition, the fierce heat makes him listless even in his free time….

Malti brought food for both of us. I asked, 'Aren't you going to eat? Or have you already eaten?'

Maheshwar said with a little laugh, 'She eats later….'

The husband comes home to eat at two-thirty, so the wife stays hungry till three!

Maheshwar began eating, looked at me and said, 'You're unlikely to enjoy the food, given that we're eating at such an odd time.'

I replied, 'Wah! Eating late is better because one is hungrier, but perhaps we're putting Malti behen to trouble.'

Malti interjected, 'Uhh-huh, this is nothing new for me...this is an everyday affair....'

The baby was in Malti's lap. He was crying, but nobody paid any attention to him.

I asked, 'Why does he cry?'

Malti said, 'He's become like this, so irritable, he's always like this.'

Then she scolded the child, 'Be quiet.' Which led him to cry even more; she picked him up and put him on the floor. And said, 'Okay, cry.' After this, she went away towards the courtyard to fetch rotis.

By the time we finished our meal, it was almost three. Maheshwar said he had to leave for the hospital earlier than usual, there were a couple of worrisome cases that might need to be operated on...two of them may need their legs amputated, gangrene had set in...he left after a while. Malti closed the door and was about to sit down next to me when I said, 'Now go and eat, I'll play with Titti till then.'

She said, 'I'll eat, what's the fuss about my eating,' but she left. I started swinging Titti in my arms, which quietened him down for a while.

Far away...perhaps in the hospital itself, a clock struck three. Suddenly I was startled by Malti's voice from the courtyard saying, with a long, tired sigh, 'It's three o'clock....' As if some task had been accomplished after a great deal of austere and rigorous work.

After some time, when Malti returned, I asked, 'Was there anything left for you? Everything was....'

'There was plenty.'

'Yes, there was plenty, I ate up all the vegetables, there wouldn't have been any left, don't just say so authoritatively that there was plenty,' I said with a laugh.

Malti said, as if she was talking about some other topic, 'You don't get any vegetables here, if someone is coming or going, we manage to get them from below; I've been back for fifteen days, we're still using the vegetables I brought....'

I asked, 'There's no servant?'

'We haven't found anyone suitable, maybe in a couple of days we'll get someone.'

'Do you wash the dishes?'

'Who else?' said Malti, then went to the courtyard for a second and came back.

I asked, 'Where had you gone?'

'The water hasn't come today, how will I wash the dishes?'

'Why, what happened to the water?'

'This happens every day...it never comes on time, now it'll come at seven in the evening, the dishes can only be washed then.'

'Chalo, you'll be free till seven in the evening,' I said, but I was thinking, now she will have to work till eleven at night, she's hardly going to be free.

She said the same thing. I had no answer, but Titti came to my rescue, all of a sudden, he began crying and tried to go back to his mother. I handed him over.

There was silence for a while, I took out my notebook from my pocket and started looking at notes from the last few days, that's when Malti remembered that she had not asked me why I had come, and she said, 'What brings you here?'

I said, 'So you remembered only now? I came to meet you, what else?'

'You'll stay for a couple of days, won't you?'

'No, I'll go back tomorrow, I have to go.'

Malti didn't say anything, but looked a little upset. I began going through my notebook again.

After some time, it struck me that I'd come to meet Malti, she was sitting here waiting to talk to me and I was busy reading, but what should one talk about? I felt as if the mysterious shadow over this house was beginning to exert its power over me too, I was also becoming as drab and lifeless as—yes, as this house was, as Malti was....

I asked, 'Don't you do any reading or writing?' I looked around to see if I could spot any books.

'Here?' Malti said, laughing a little. Her laughter implied, 'What is there to read here?'

I said, 'All right, I'll go back and send you some books....' And the conversation once again petered out....

After a while, Malti asked, 'How did you come? In a lorry?'

'I walked.'

'You walked so far? You have a lot of courage.'

'After all, I was coming to meet you.'

'You came just like that?'

'No, the coolie is following with my luggage. I thought, let me bring my bedding as well.'

'You did the right thing, here it's just....' She lapsed into silence, then said, 'You must be tired, why don't you lie down.'

'No, I'm not at all tired.'

'Don't say you're not tired, you must be.'

'And what will you do?'

'I'll scrub the dishes, and wash them later when the water comes.'

I said, 'Wah!' because I couldn't think of anything else to say....

After a while, Malti got up and left, taking Titti with her. I too lay down and began looking at the roof...my thoughts, combined with the khan-khan sound of the dishes being scrubbed, created a monotonous drone, because of which my limbs began feeling limp and I started feeling drowsy....

All of a sudden, the monotonous sound stopped. That's how I snapped out of my drowsiness and tried to listen in that silence....

The clock was striking four and Malti had stopped when she heard the first gong itself....

I saw the same reaction as when the clock had struck three, though this time it was more pronounced. I heard Malti say, in a dreary, involuntary, expressionless, mechanical—and that too, like a tired, exhausted machine—tone, 'It's four o clock,' as if her machine-like life was all about involuntarily counting the hours, the way a speedometer tracks the distance travelled, and in a languorous, programmed way, says (to whom!) that I have covered this much of the immense, empty road.... I don't know when and how I fell asleep.

It was well past six when the sound of someone coming in woke me up, and I saw that Maheshwar had returned and along with him came my coolie carrying my bedding. I was about to ask for water to wash my face when I remembered that there was no water. Wiping my face with my hands, I said to Maheshwar, 'You got quite late?'

He said in a slightly apologetic voice, 'Yes, I had to do that gangrene operation today, I did one and sent the other patient in an ambulance to the big hospital.'

I asked, 'How did the gangrene happen?'

'A thorn pierced the skin, that's how it happened, the people here are very careless....'

I asked, 'Do you get good cases here? Not in terms of income, but in terms of experience for a doctor?'

He said, 'Yes, I do get such cases, the same gangrene, every second day, fourth day, a case arrives, even in the big hospitals below....'

Malti, who had been listening from the courtyard, came in and said, 'Yes, how long does it take to make a case? A thorn pierced the skin, and so someone's leg had to be amputated, is this any kind of medical practice? Every other day, he cuts off someone's leg or arm, is this what is called good experience for a doctor!'

Maheshwar laughed and said, 'So, we shouldn't amputate the limb and let him die?'

'Yes, were there no thorns in the world earlier? I'd never heard that one could die because of a thorn....'

Maheshwar didn't reply, just smiled. Malti looked at me and said, 'This is what doctors are like, it's a government hospital, so who cares. I hear such things every day. Now if I hear of someone dying, I don't even think about it. Earlier, I wouldn't be able to sleep all night.'

Just then the open tap in the courtyard went—tip-tip-tip-tip-tip-tip-tip....

Malti said, 'Water!' And got up and went away. From the clinking and clanking sounds, we could make out that the dishes were being washed....

Titti had been standing, holding on to Maheshwar's legs for support, and looking at me, but now suddenly he left his father and began crawling towards Malti. Maheshwar said, 'Don't go there!' He picked him up and Titti began squirming in his arms and crying loudly.

Maheshwar said, 'Now he'll cry himself to sleep, only then will there be any peace in the house.'

I asked, 'Do you sleep indoors? It must be very hot inside?'

'There are a lot of mosquitoes too, but who will carry these iron cots outside? Next time I go down, I'll bring up some charpais.' Then, after a pause, he said, 'We'll sleep outside today. There should be some benefit to your coming here.'

Titti was still crying. As Maheshwar put him on the cot and began pulling it, I said, 'Let me help,' and, picking up the other end, helped carry it outside.

Now the three of us...Maheshwar, Titti, and I, sat on the two cots and, not finding any appropriate topic of conversation, we sought to cover that inadequacy by playing with Titti, he had quietened down after we came out but every now and then, as if remembering some forgotten duty he had to perform, he would start crying and then suddenly become quiet again...and sometimes we would laugh, or Maheshwar would say something about him....

Malti had finished washing the dishes. Now she was taking them to the kitchen in one corner of the courtyard; that's when Maheshwar said, 'I've brought some mangoes, wash those too.'

'Where are they?'

'They're on the brazier, wrapped in paper.'

Malti went inside, picked up the mangoes, and put them in her pallu. They were wrapped in a torn piece of an old newspaper. Malti kept reading that newspaper in the feeble evening light as she walked...she reached the tap but kept standing and reading. Only when she had finished reading both sides of the paper did she draw in a long breath, throw it away, and begin washing the mangoes.

I suddenly remembered...it had happened a long time ago...when we had just got admitted to school. When our biggest happiness, biggest victory was slinking out of the class after marking our attendance, running to the mango orchard a little distance away, climbing the trees, plucking the small, half-ripe mangoes, and eating them. I remembered...sometimes when I'd run away and Malti wouldn't be able to come I would return in a very glum state of mind.

Malti never read anything, her parents were fed up, one day her father handed her a book and said she had to read twenty pages every day. After one week he'd check if she'd finished the book, and if she hadn't he would thrash her within an inch of her life. Malti quietly took the book, but did she read it? Every day she would tear off ten or twenty pages and throw them away, and continue to play as before. When, on the eighth day, her father asked her, 'Did you finish the book?' she replied, 'Yes, I did,' and when her father said, 'Bring the book, I'll ask you questions on it,' she stood there without saying a word. When her father asked her again, she replied defiantly, 'I tore the book and threw it away, I won't study.'

After that she was thrashed quite badly, but that's another matter. At this moment, all I could think was that that impertinent, playful Malti had become so subdued, so quiet, so desperate for a scrap from a newspaper... was this, this....

At that moment Maheshwar asked, 'When will you make the rotis?'

'I'm just going to make them.'

But this time when Malti set off for the kitchen, Titti's sense of duty became even more acute, he stretched out his hands towards Malti and began crying and wouldn't stop till Malti lifted him in her arms, made him sit in the kitchen and patted him with one hand while picking up several small containers and placing them before her....

And both of us waited silently for the night, for the dinner, for a conversation with each other, and for numerous unknown voids to be filled.

We finished our meal, lay down on the bed, and Titti went to sleep. Malti had spread an oilcloth on the bed and put him down on it. He had fallen asleep, but sometimes woke up with a start. Once he even sat up but then immediately lay down again.

I asked Maheshwar, 'You must be tired, go to sleep.'

He said, 'You must be more tired…you've walked eighteen miles to come here.' But it was as if he added the words, 'I am tired too.'

I was quiet, and after a while, I sensed that he was dozing off.

It was around ten-thirty by then; Malti was eating dinner.

I looked at Malti for some time, she was lost in thought—not any deep thought, but still lost in thought as she ate her food slowly, then I shifted my position to make myself comfortable and gazed up at the sky.

It was a full moon, the sky was cloudless.

I saw—that government quarter, whose slate roof looked so desolate and colourless during the day, appeared to shine in the moonlight, so cool and smooth, as if the moonbeams were flowing on it, cascading down....

I saw—the pine trees in the wind…pine trees that had turned dry and discoloured in the heat…had softly, slowly started singing…some raag that was gentle but not pitiful or sad, that was restless but not agitated....

I saw—even the bats, in their soundless flight at the edge of the murky blue sky, looked beautiful....

I saw—the day's burning heat, discomfort, fatigue rising like steam from the mountains, only to get lost in the atmosphere above, and the mountains, like little babies, raising their arms—like branches of a pine tree—towards the sky....

But I saw all this, I alone.... Maheshwar was dozing off and Malti, having finished her dinner, was washing a clay pot with warm water, so that she could set the curd, and saying…'I'll just be free.' And at my saying, 'It's going to be eleven o'clock,' shaking her head a little to indicate that it turned eleven every day.... Malti didn't see any of that, her life was flowing along at its own prescribed pace, not prepared to pause for the moonlight, or for a universe to unfold....

How does a baby look in the moonlight, I thought idly, and turned towards Titti, and he suddenly, out of some childlike perversity, woke up, shifted on the bed, fell off and began crying at the top of his voice. Maheshwar got up with a shock and said, 'What happened?' As I rushed to pick him up, Malti came out of the kitchen; remembering that 'khat' sound, I said softly, in a voice full of compassion, 'The poor thing must be badly hurt.'

All this had happened in a second, in one unbroken action.

Malti put out her arms to take the baby from me and said, 'He keeps getting hurt, he falls down every day.'

For a second I was stupefied, and then my mind, my entire being, rebelled—but only my mind, not a word actually came out—'Ma, you're a young mother, what has happened to your heart that you are saying this when your one and only child has fallen down—when your whole life is ahead of you!'

And then I suddenly knew that this feeling was not a lie, I saw that a deep, frightening shadow had made a home in this family, was eating away at this first youthful phase of their lives like a worm, had become such a part of them they couldn't see it for what it was, but continued to move within its perimeter. Not just this, I even saw that shadow....

By then, everything became peaceful, as it had been before. Maheshwar lay down again and began dozing off. Titti was clinging to Malti on the bed, he was quiet but occasionally his tiny little body would shake with a sob. I too felt that my bed was quite comfortable. Malti was looking silently at the sky, but was she looking at the moonlight or the stars?

The clock struck eleven. I lifted my heavy eyelids to abruptly look at Malti with an inarticulate expectation. As the first of the eleven gongs sounded, Malti's chest suddenly rose and then slowly fell, like a blister on the body, in unison with the sound, and then she said, in a voice that faded away into silence, 'It is eleven o'clock....'

3

THE BLUE LIGHT

VAIKOM MUHAMMAD BASHEER

Translated from the Malayalam by O. V. Usha

This story is about an extraordinary, no, miraculous event in my life. That I call it miraculous...well, what else can I say?

This is what happened.

No need for the date, month, or year.

I was on the lookout for a house. Nothing new about that. Those days I was always looking for a house. I never came across a house or even a room to my liking. As far as the place, which called itself a hotel, where I stayed, a hundred flaws, more, had come to light there. But to whom to complain? Leave? And go where?

And so it went, hating where I stayed, constantly looking for a place and finding only those that I hated even more. I lost count of the number of houses I looked at and disliked. And, as is the way with rented houses, someone who liked them took them.

Still, it was a time when there was a dearth of houses for rent. What could be had at one time for ten rupees was not available now for even sixty.

So I spent my days, roaming the town daily, until, suddenly, one forenoon, there it stood—a house, no, my house! It was a small, two-storeyed building. 'Bhargavinilayam'. Far from the bustle and noise of the town. Yet, close to the municipality border. A decrepit board on the gate said 'For rent'.

I liked the place instantly. It was an old house. There was something strange about it even at first glance. Didn't matter; it was perfect for me. Two rooms and an open veranda upstairs. Four rooms downstairs. Also, there was a bathroom, a kitchen, and a pipe with running water. The only thing missing was electricity.

In front of the kitchen there was an ancient well with a stone wall around it. A small way off, in a corner of the walled compound around the house, stood a toilet. Trees in abundance. The public road ran right before the property.

I was surprised and delighted! Why had no one snapped up this house yet? A lady of great beauty she was. Ah! She shouldn't be seen by anyone. Should hide her behind purdah! Such unusual thoughts and feelings that old house evoked in me. I was in a happy daze; I was entranced.

I quickly made whatever arrangements needed to be made, borrowed money from various friends, paid the two months' advance rent and got the keys in my hand. Wasting not a moment, I moved into the upstairs of the old house. I bought a hurricane lamp and kerosene. I swept the rooms myself, upstairs and downstairs, kitchen, bathroom and all. I ritually cleansed the place, sprinkling water. There was a good deal of accumulated waste; there was plenty of dust. After the sweeping, I thoroughly washed all the rooms until they were spotless. I saw one room downstairs that was locked. I did not try to open it.

I had a bath, and felt a great sense of relief and well-being. I came out and perched myself on the wall around the antique well. Such bliss! One could sit and daydream here, or walk or run or whatever in complete privacy inside the walled compound around the house.

There should be a garden in the front yard, I thought, mainly of beds of roses. Jasmine too. A cook? No, that would be a bother. I could fill the thermos with tea from the tea shop when I went for breakfast after my morning bath. Lunch could be arranged from the old hotel. Hopefully, they would send me dinner as well.

The postman had to be informed about the change of address, and tipped not to reveal my whereabouts to anyone. Nights of lovely solitude; days of lovely solitude: I would be able to write a lot! Borne along by these and other happy thoughts, I peered down into the well. The tangle of plants growing across its mouth and from its walls made it impossible to see if it had any water. I threw a pebble into the well.

'Bhlllum!' it rang after a moment. There was water.

All this by eleven in the morning.

The previous night I hadn't slept a wink. I settled my account with the hotel. I met the houseowner. I folded the canvas cot and secured it. Gramophone, records—all neatly packed. Boxes, papers, armchair, shelf, everything—all my assets had been set in order. At the crack of dawn, I set out with my luggage loaded on to a pair of pushcarts. The men who brought my luggage left it outside the gate...as if they were frightened to come into the place.

Arriving at my new residence, I brought my possessions in myself, then, elated, locked the house, walked humming to the gate, fastened it, and went out on to the road with a fine new sense of pride, walking on air.

As I went along, I wondered: with whose song should the new house be inaugurated? I had more than a hundred records in my possession. English, Arabic, Hindi, Urdu, Tamil, Bengali. Nothing in Malayalam. There are talented singers. They have cut records. But the music direction and finish of all of them is poor. But good directors and singers are coming up. Yes, I must buy some Malayalam records.

Whose song should I play first today, I wondered. Pankaj Mullick, Dilipkumar Roy, Saigal, Bing Crosby, Paul Robeson, Abdul Karim Khan, Kanan Devi, Kumari Manju Dasgupta, Khursheed, Juthika Roy, M. S. Subbulakshmi...some twenty names passed through my mind. Finally, I decided: there is a song which says that someone from a distant land is here. It begins with '*Door desh ka rehne wala aaya*'. Whose voice was it? Male or female? I could not remember. I would find it when I got back home.

Thus, I went on my way, happily. First of all, I met the postman. Talked to him. When I told him which house I had moved into, he looked unnerved.

'Ayyo, sir! There was an unnatural death in that house. That's why it's been lying empty for so long. No one will stay there.'

An unnatural death? I was a little flustered. I asked, 'What unnatural death?'

'Did you see the well in the backyard? Someone jumped into it and died. After that there is no peace in that house. Many tenants came but none stayed. At night doors would bang shut on their own. Taps would open by themselves and water would gush out.'

Doors banging shut on their own. Taps opening by themselves. Startling indeed. I'd seen that both taps were secured with locks. Travellers scaled the compound wall and bathed at the taps, that was why they were locked— that was the houseowner's version. But what was the need for a lock on the bathroom tap inside the house—it did not occur to me to ask.

The postman continued, 'Some invisible thing or person would try to choke anyone sleeping inside that house! Did no one tell you, sir?'

I thought, oh, good! And I've paid two months' rent in advance. Putting a brave face on it, I said, 'All that doesn't matter. The whole thing will just take a mantra to settle. Whatever it is, bring my letters and other mail there.'

Though I spoke evenly, I did feel a ripple of anxiety, as any other man might. Call me a coward, if you will. My pace on the road slackened. What could I do? I do not usually court eerie experiences. But if they happen anyway, what does one do? But what could really happen?

I went to the hotel and drank some tea. I did not feel hungry. It was as if a strange fire had been lit in my gut, driving out my appetite. I spoke to the man in the hotel about sending regular meals to my house.

When I told him where I was living, he said, 'I can arrange to send you food during the day. At night none of the boys will come there. A woman killed herself by jumping into the old well in the yard. She still hangs around the place. Aren't you afraid of ghosts, sir?'

It was a woman; half my fear melted away.

I said, 'Oh, nothing to all that. Moreover, there's the mantra.'

I had no idea what the mantra was. But it was a woman...some softness there. I walked into the bank nearby. I had a few friends among the clerks there. I talked to them. They were furious with me: 'How foolish could you be?! It's a haunted house and it's mostly men that are harmed.'

She hated men! That was nice to know.

One of my friends said, 'Couldn't you have told us you were planning to take Bhargavinilayam on rent?'

I said, 'Who knew it was like this? Let me ask you a question—why did that woman jump into the well?'

'Love!' said another friend. 'Her name was Bhargavi. She was twenty-one. She passed her BA. Before that she was in love with someone. Big love. Then the fellow married another woman. And Bhargavi jumped into the well and died.'

Most of my fear was gone. So this is why she hated men.

I said, 'Bhargavi will not harm me.'

'And why is that?'

I smiled, 'Mantra! Mantra!'

'We'll see about that. You're going to howl in your bed at night.'

I did not say anything more.

I went back to the house. Opened doors and windows. Went downstairs and walked to the well.

'Bhargavi kutty!' I called softly. 'We don't know each other. I have come to stay in this house. I believe that I am a good man. I've been celibate all my life, you know? I have already heard many rumours about you, Bhargavi kutty. That you do not allow anyone to live here. That you open the taps at night. That you bang the doors shut. That you strangle men, especially, with invisible hands. Yes, I've heard a lot. What do I do now?

'I've already paid two months' rent as advance, and I have very little money. Also I like this house, this house that belongs to you, Bhargavi kutty, I like it so much! It's named for you, isn't it? Bhargavinilayam!

'I need to stay here and work. I must write some stories. Bhargavi kutty, do you like stories? If you do, I'll read everything that I write to you. I have absolutely no quarrel with you, Bhargavi kutty. No cause for that either, is there? A while ago I did drop a pebble into the well. I did it without thinking. Nothing like that from me in future, I promise.

'Listen, Bhargavi kutty, I have a first-rate gramophone. Some two hundred excellent songs, too. Are you fond of music?'

I fell quiet after saying that much. Who was I talking to? To the well, ready with its mouth open to swallow anything? To whom—the trees, the house, the air, the universe? Was it to the disturbance in my mind? I was talking to an idea, an abstraction—Bhargavi! I had not seen her. A young woman of twenty-one. Deeply in love with a man. She dreamt of a life as his wife, his life partner. But that dream...yes, it passed as a dream. Despair gripped her, and shame, disgrace, and betrayal, too.

'Bhargavi kutty!' I said, 'you needn't have done what you did. Don't think I am blaming you. The man you were fond of did not love you enough. He loved another woman more.

'Life turned bitter for you. That much is true. However, all of life is not full of bitterness. Forget about it! And, for you, now history will not repeat itself.

'Bhargavi kutty, don't think for a moment I am blaming you. Was it really for love that you died? Love is only the golden dawn of eternal life. Silly girl! You didn't know a thing about it. That's what your hatred of men proves. Consider that you knew just one man. Also, let's accept, for argument's sake, that he wronged you grievously. But is it right to view all men through the tinted glass of that one experience? Had you lived instead of killing yourself, you would have known through experience that your extreme reaction was not right. There would have been someone to love you, to adore you, to call you "my goddess!" Now, didn't I say for you history will not repeat itself? Bhargavi kutty, how can I get to know your whole life story?

'Whatever it is, don't harm me, I beg you. No one will question you if you were to choke me to death tonight. Not that it's anyone's business to question you. All I mean is that there is no one to do it. You know why? I have no one.

'Now you know how things stand. We, you and I, are living here. That is, I mean to live here. Having paid rent, legally, the house, well and everything else is mine. But let that be. You use the well and the four rooms downstairs. We share the kitchen and the bathroom equally. What do you say? Do you like my idea?'

Night fell. I came back with a tea-filled thermos after having eaten dinner at the hotel. By the light of my electric torch, I lit the hurricane lamp. The room was flooded in yellow light.

I went downstairs with the torch. I stood still in pitch darkness for some time. My intention was to turn the taps off tightly. I opened all the windows wide. I approached the kitchen, near the well. Suddenly, I had the strong feeling that I must not tighten the taps.

I closed the doors, climbed the stairs, and had some tea. After that I lit a bidi and sat in my armchair. I was just beginning to write, when I had the feeling that Bhargavi was behind my chair.

I said uneasily, 'I don't like anyone watching while I write.'

I turned my head; no one there.

I'm not sure why, but I didn't want to write any more. I drew up another chair in front of mine.

'Sit down in this, Bhargavi kutty.'

The chair stayed empty. I got up and began strolling through the two rooms. No breeze. The leaves of the trees outside didn't stir. I looked down through the window: a light!

Blue, red, or yellow—I couldn't tell. It was gone in a second.

Just my imagination, I told myself. I can't swear that I saw that light. Still, how could one think one sees without actually seeing? Was it a glow-worm perhaps?

I spent a long time pacing the rooms. I spent a long time standing at the windows. There was nothing unusual. I tried to read something but couldn't concentrate. The chair remained empty.

Let me go to sleep early, I thought. I made my bed and turned off the lamp. Then I wanted to play a song! I lit the lamp again. Opened the gramophone. Fitted a new needle into the playing arm, and then I wound up the machine.

Whose song should I play? The world was still and silent. Then, an uncanny whooshing filled both my ears! Like the wind, like the sea. And then absolute quiet again. Fear seized me. I must shatter this ominous silence into a thousand pieces. Whose song would best serve that purpose?

I looked through my collection, and chose a record of the black American singer Paul Robeson. The gramophone began playing. A man's voice rich and majestic:

Joshua fit the battle of Jericho....

That song ended. Pankaj Mullick was next:

Tu dar naa zaraa bhi....

You don't be afraid at all!

The next was a sweet, soft, and alluring voice:

Kaatrinile varum geetam....

The song that arrives on the breeze....

And in time, M. S. Subbulakshmi finished that song.

Somehow, after these three songs, I was at peace. I sat quietly, for quite a while. Finally, I invited Saigal in. He sang in his languid voice, full of melancholy and sweetness:

So jaa raajkumaari, so jaa....

Go to sleep, princess; may beautiful dreams visit your sleep.

That also ended.

'That's all for now, the rest tomorrow,' I said aloud, and lowering the lid of the gramophone, lit a bidi, turned off the lamp and went to bed. Next to me I had the torch, a watch and a dagger. Also the empty chair.

I closed the doors to the veranda before getting into bed. It must have turned ten now. I lay alert, my ears strained to the night.

There was no sound other than the tik-tik of the watch. Minutes passed, and hours. There was no fear in my mind. What there was... was a cold wakefulness. This was not new to me. I'd had some unusual experiences in my life over the years, in many lands, many places, during my lonely life of twenty years, none of which I could find the meaning of. Because of this, my attention constantly shifted between the past and the present.

Would there be a knock at the door? Would there be the sound of water flowing from the taps? Would I be throttled in my sleep? I stayed awake and vigilant till three in the morning.

I heard nothing, felt nothing. Finally, I fell into a deep and tranquil sleep. I did not have a single dream. I woke up at nine the next morning.

Nothing had happened.

'Good morning, Bhargavi kutty, thank you so much! I have understood one thing for certain—people are spreading false rumours about you. Let them talk, no? Who cares?'

My days and nights passed in this manner. I would think of Bhargavi kutty...her mother, father, siblings, there must be so many unknown stories.

I wrote most nights. When I got tired, I played records. I would announce the singer, the content, the mood, and so on, before the song began. I would say, 'Here, Pankaj Mullick, the great Bengali singer. The song is filled with sadness, and invokes memories. These are bygone times, you know. Listen carefully.'

Guzar gayaa voh zamaana kaisa, kaisa....

How wonderful were those days that are now gone.

Or else I would say: 'And now Bing Crosby. *In the moonlight*—it means.... Oh, I beg your pardon, you must know, you're a graduate!'

I would talk like this, to myself. Two and a half months passed. I planted a garden. When flowers appeared, I said: 'All the flowers are for Bhargavi kutty!'

In the meantime, I finished writing a short novel. Many of my friends visited me. At times, some stayed overnight. Before going to bed, I would go downstairs without their knowing it. And I would look into the darkness and whisper, 'Bhargavi kutty, listen! Some friends of mine are here. Don't strangle them. If you do, the police will arrest me. Be careful. Good night!'

Usually before going out, I would say: 'Bhargavi kutty, take care of the house. If any thieves get in, you can strangle them. Don't leave the bodies here, though. Dump them some miles away, or we will be in trouble.'

When I returned from the cinema after a late show, I would announce, 'It's me!'

All this I said in the newness of the first days. As time passed, I forgot Bhargavi. Well, my long chats to her stopped. I would still remember her occasionally, but that was all.

I will tell you what sort of remembering that was. Millions have died since human life began in this world...haven't countless men and women died? All of them have mingled with this earth as smoke or dust. We know this. Bhargavi was reduced to a memory of that kind.

Then, as life went by without any great event, something happened. That's what I am going to tell you about now.

One night. It was ten o' clock. From around nine I had been writing a story. It was emotionally charged and I was developing it briskly. I became aware that the light was getting dim.

I lifted the lamp and shook it gently to check the oil. There was no kerosene. Still, I thought, let me write one more page. I was entirely absorbed by the story I was writing, and in the meanwhile the light had faded. What could one do at a time like that? Check if there was oil in the lamp. That was what I did. I raised the wick a little; I continued writing. After a while, the light faded further. I raised the wick again, resumed my writing. The light dimmed again; again, I raised the wick. Eventually, the wick turned into a smoking red ember four inches long.

I turned on my torchlight and lowered the wick completely. The lamp was snuffed out.

I said to myself, 'How can I get some light?'

I needed kerosene. I could borrow some kerosene from the bank clerks' stove.

I locked the door and went out with my torch and kerosene bottle. I went down and out of the house, locking the front door behind me. I went down the path and out of the gate, latching it. I walked along the deserted road. A faint moon lit my way. There were heavy clouds above, too, so I strode along quickly.

I came to the bank building and, from the street, called out the name of one of the bank clerks. I called twice or thrice before one of them came down and opened the side gate. We went up using the staircase behind the building. I found that the three of them were playing a game of cards.

When I talked about kerosene, one of them asked with a laugh, 'Couldn't you have asked your girlfriend to get you kerosene? Have you finished writing her life story?'

I didn't say anything. Must write, I thought. As one of them was pouring kerosene into the bottle, it began to pour outside.

I said, 'Give me an umbrella also.'

They said, 'One? There is not even a quarter of one. Let's play cards for a while. You can go when the rain lets up.'

So we played cards. My partner and I did three rounds of salaam. Mostly because my mind was on my story and I was distracted while playing. The rain stopped at about one. I got up and picked up the torch and kerosene bottle. By now, my friends were also ready to sleep. After I went down to the street they switched off their light.

There was neither movement nor light in the street as I walked back home. When I took the turning towards my house the world lay immersed in mist and hazy moonlight. I didn't remember what thoughts ran through my mind then. Perhaps I was not thinking at all. I continued walking along the dark road, empty and silent, flashing my torch. No living thing stirred anywhere.

I reached my house, opened the gate, shut it, and then opened the front door. I entered the house and latched the door from inside. I had no cause to think that anything unusual would have happened upstairs. But something had.

For no reason whatever, a vast sorrow abruptly filled my heart and I felt like crying. I can laugh easily but never shed a tear. Tears just don't come to me. When sorrow overwhelms me, a divine exaltation takes hold of me, as it did now—a great compassion!

In that state of mind, I climbed the stairs. And what I saw when I arrived on the upper floor was extraordinary, no, it was miraculous.

When I locked my room and left, you remember, there was no oil left in the lamp; the flame had gone out and I had withdrawn the wick into the base of the lamp. Darkness had filled the room. Later, while I was out, it had rained and some hours had passed. Now, I saw light shining clear through the chink below my door. Well, my eyes saw the light but my mind did not yet register or believe what I saw.

Out of sheer habit, I took out my key and flashed the torchlight on the lock. The lock shone like silver; why, it seemed to smile.

I opened the door and went in. And now, what I saw before me struck me with full force. An indescribable sensation surged through every atom of my being. No, I did not quake with fright. Rather, as I stood transfixed, my mind was flooded by a tide of tenderness.

Blue light!

White walls, the whole room, drenched in ethereal blue light. That light came from the lamp in which a blue flame blazed.

Who had lit this blue light in Bhargavinilayam?

4

THE GRAVESTONE
SHAHNAZ BASHIR

As soon as the mist lifts, which happens in the evenings these days, he'll dash straight to the graveyard. It promises to be a really chilly evening in the wake of the April rain. He is sure the drug-addicted gamblers, for whom the graveyard is a favourite place to play whist, won't be around today.

He's scared of the idea of doing it in the night. He can't sneak out in the presence of his vigilant family members. He usually goes to get his cheap Panama cigarettes from the village market in the evening. That's the time he can do it.

He lights a filterless cigarette and paces the short, narrow, flaking cement pathway outside his small mud-and-brick house. Cacti and dead geraniums, potted in discarded paint cans and small empty Fevicol buckets, are arrayed against the walls of the house. He finishes his cigarette, then slips back into the house, ascends the creaky wooden flight of stairs, and reaches for his old cobwebbed toolkit under the tin roof where the gable makes it difficult for a person to stand upright. His workman's fingers are calloused, the fingertips bristle with cracks, the fingernails are deformed. He rummages through the dusty tools, panting with the effort of climbing the stairs.

Shortly afterwards, he finds himself running towards the graveyard, a kilometre away from the house. The pale light of dusk falls on the drenched asphalt road riddled with muddy, water-filled puddles. The roofs and leaves still drip.

The mist is all gone and the snow-shrouded mountains opposite him appear closer than they actually are. A gust breathes through the village and shakes the groves, orchards, mustard crops, and grass. Scattered plastic bags balloon into the air.

Each wrinkle and crease on his pale and weathered face with its sunken cheeks tightens as he rushes on. Each strand of his grey hair stands on end.

The pits in the road make him watch where he places his plastic-shod feet. His left hand, almost dysfunctional, trembles badly. He grabs the underside of his pheran to keep the hand steady.

His worn-out pheran smells of rain and stale smoke. He scurries on. The sound of dull clanking comes from under his pheran as the rusty hammer comes into contact with the blunt chisel. Plumes of smoke-stained breath burst from his nostrils. Occasionally, a bus or a scooter passes, tooting its horn.

Today he is welcomed again by the same stubborn clumps of nettle and thistle that are sprinkled throughout the graveyard. And beyond—there, near the graves—are assorted irises, their stamens powdering the white petals with yellow pollen dust on the insides. He traces the path to a grave whose epitaph in Urdu reads: SHAHEED MUSHTAQ AHMAD NAJAR

Muhammad Sultan was a talented carpenter before he fell from a roof while working and permanently injured his left arm. And just when the injured arm had begun to heal, against the doctor's advice, he went back to work. He had to take care of three daughters and an adolescent son, which is why he couldn't afford to rest the injured arm. The internal soft-tissue injury worsened to a haematoma. After a failed surgery, his arm was declared unfit for carpentry or any manual work.

He was a master khatamband, or lattice designer. Before cutting wood for use, he would smell it to gauge its quality. He specialized in mixing the classical with the modern, producing something that both old and new generations of Kashmiris liked. None in the entire village could rival his truss work. He was an expert on doors and windows—the thick part of work in carpentry. With each drag on the hookah, he came up with a new idea.

But Sultan had a shortcoming, too: he was not a diligent worker. He took on projects on a whim. He would hardly ever take on partners or apprentices. He liked to work alone. He normally worked for two days a week and took the rest of the days off. Sometimes he would disappear for days and later compensate for his absence by working overtime. His second romance, after carpentry, was accompanying the local militants around the village. He'd help them with anything, fetch them cigarettes, and even lavish money on them.

Carpentry was not only work or a source of livelihood for him, but an art form too. Art through which he expressed himself. Once at work, he would passionately sink into it. Sometimes he worked through the night. He would even work on Fridays, against custom, when all the carpenters and masons took the day off. He never cared for money until he really needed it. He was more of a dissolute artist than a mere time-bound carpenter. His hands are worth their weight in gold, that is what almost all his customers would say after marvelling at his work. It was because of his talent that people tolerated his truancies and wild habits.

The situation with his arm depressed him. It became impossible to work, or hold tools in his left hand. Then he started taking on projects on a contract basis, employing other carpenters and directing them. But their designs and work neither impressed nor satisfied his customers. Though his employees took all his directions, they never really followed them to the letter. They even cheated him of his share of the commission. And eventually his financial situation deteriorated.

His fate grew worse—his eldest daughter was returned by her in-laws, for the sixth time in four years of her marriage, for not fulfilling the demands of dowry. The last time she had returned with a swollen wrist and her snivelling, sick one-year-old baby daughter. Her husband, the driver of a bus that somebody else owned, had wrung her wrist during an argument and thrown her out of his house. But at her father's house, the eldest daughter behaved as though she was just on an occasional visit. She even waffled on to her sisters about her in-laws, praising them as if they were good people and as if nothing had happened. She talked about the 'generosity' of her in-laws' neighbours. She described her brother-in-law, his tastes in food. These details bored and irritated her sisters.

Without work and with his broken arm, Sultan was struggling to deal with his two other daughters at home. His middle daughter was in her late thirties, a spinster, an almost illiterate woman, who, after her father's injury, had been supporting the household with her needlework skills. She worked well into the nights, tortured her eyes, strained and overburdened herself, and gained weight and premature wrinkles on her face. She was the most beautiful among her sisters, but there was an unattended fuzz of hair over her upper lip that made her look ugly at the same time. Lately, she was running short of work, and had taken to secretly begging at the shrine of Makhdoom Sahib on Fridays. She would slip on a long, dirty black burqa and leave home saying that she was visiting the shrine to pray to God to take away their hardships and grievances. But Muhammad Sultan had begun to suspect that her veiled expeditions were for another reason altogether—that she was out hustling to earn some money. He was furious about this but tried not to show it, especially as he never wanted to follow her to confirm his suspicions.

His youngest daughter had left school at the secondary level when Sultan's wife died of a colon haemorrhage. Since her mother's death, it was she who looked after the household, cooked and cleaned. Her presence in the house was the only presence Muhammad Sultan didn't feel. She almost didn't exist for him. She was just like the family cow she fed, washed, milked, and cleaned. Whenever she cried, she didn't make a sound, not a single snivel or sob, just tears, which quietly streamed down her cheeks like melting pearls. She was born just before Mushtaq, her brother, Muhammad Sultan's only son, who died in adolescence.

Mushtaq distanced himself from school and books and instead followed a group of local militants like his father did. One day Mushtaq stayed behind with an armed group in a hideout—a posh house in Nishat. In the middle of the night, the hideout was raided, and he was the only one who was unable to escape. He was killed in the kitchen of the house. Next morning, Muhammad Sultan managed to go to the spot and see his dead son for the last time. After looking at the bullet-riddled body lying face down on the kitchen floor, he fainted. When he regained consciousness, he found that Mushtaq was being placed on a bier. The funeral was attended by the militants with whom the boy had fallen in. Wearing masks, they mixed with the funeral procession, and later also directed the graveyard management committee to get a quality marmoreal headstone chiselled for their friend. They wanted to have the headstone inscribed with an Urdu epitaph with the title 'Shaheed' before the boy's full name, which would signify that he was a full-fledged militant and had died for the cause of Kashmir's freedom. The outfit will be proud to bear all the costs, the area commander of the militants assured the graveyard management committee.

After the burial, some days later, a shiny black granite gravestone was erected at the grave, with a beautifully calligraphed Urdu epitaph in sparkling golden paint.

It was some months after his son's death that Muhammad Sultan suffered the accident in which he damaged his left arm. Soon after the accident, his elder daughter was returned and the middle one lost her work. All possible sources of income disappeared. Vexed, he ate away at himself between sips from endless cups of salty nuun tea and puffs from filterless cigarettes.

He had often heard people mention how Sataar Wagay, one of his neighbours, whose son the army had tortured to death and dumped in the river, managed to get an ex-gratia compensation of one lakh rupees sanctioned by the government. In the beginning, when he was not burdened by his own tragedies, Muhammad Sultan hated Sataar Wagay for accepting the compensation. He even called him a traitor for 'selling his son's sacrifice to the government'. But then Muhammad Sultan became confused when Rahman Parray, another of his neighbours, who had even been an active member of a separatist organization, distorted the facts surrounding his younger brother's killing by the army and accepted compensation of one lakh rupees.

Who was right, Wagay or Parray or himself? Baffled, Muhammad Sultan remained indecisive until his own condition forced him to think about applying for compensation too. Initially he hated himself for even thinking about asking the government for money. He wrestled with himself day and night.

He was already heavily in debt. Each morning the local grocer had begun to come to the house and threaten to take away Sultan's cow to settle his account. He even owed the neighbourhood baker and barber. He had stopped passing by their shops and now took longer routes, back and side paths, whenever he had to leave the village. But when his baby granddaughter was diagnosed with acute pneumonia, he gave up. Finally, he threw off the guise of commitment to the cause of freedom, ignored his guilt, and applied for compensation. He tried as much as possible to hide this from Gul Baghwaan, one of his close childhood friends, who had vehemently rejected an offer of compensation from the government after his son was killed in a crossfire incident.

Now, the only hurdle that came between Muhammad Sultan and his compensation was the word 'Shaheed', conspicuously engraved on his son's gravestone. If discovered anytime later, the word could ruin his chances.

∽

The graveyard is a plateau studded with gravestones and clumps of irises. It is away from the village houses and nestled on the edge of a vast expanse of paddy fields. As Muhammad Sultan sees the irises in the cloud-dimmed evening, the first stray thought that crosses his mind is how much better it would be to replace the cacti at his home with the irises.

He waits for the darkness to grow thicker. With the darkness comes a drizzle. Soon the voice of the muezzin from a nearby mosque floats into the air and mingles with the hissing rain. The wet mud of the graveyard sticks to the soles of his shoes, exposing patches of ochre under the upper layer of earth.

A few minutes later, when the rain stops, he holds the blunt chisel with his trembling left hand against the word Shaheed. He repeatedly strikes the head of the chisel. The sounds of metal clanking and the hammer's whumping travel through the earth and reach down to Mushtaq Ahmad Najar. At one strike the pointed end of the chisel slips, misses its mark, and scrapes off Mushtaq instead.

5

TRISHANKU

MANNU BHANDARI

Translated from the Hindi by Poonam Saxena

'The four walls of a house provide security to a person but also confine him. School-college develop a person's mind but, at the same time, in the name of rules, regulations, and discipline, his or her personality also gets blunted. The thing is, brother, everything has its opposite within itself!'

I'm not giving these examples from some book. I don't have the ability to read such weighty tomes. These are snatches of the conversations and arguments that take place in our home day and night. Our house, the wrestling ground of intellectuals. Here, in the midst of cigarette smoke and coffee cups, there is big talk, and major rhetorical revolutions come to pass. In this house there is more talk, less action. I haven't read this anywhere but, looking at my home, it certainly seemed to me that working was perhaps forbidden for intellectuals. Mother dear, after amusing herself with a light three-hour job, was free for the day. The time left after reading and writing was spent in talking and arguing or lying down. She was of the view that the mind becomes active only when the body is inactive, and so for twelve hours out of the twenty-four hours in a day, she wanted to keep her mind active. Father dear was two steps ahead! If he had his way, he would bathe at his table.

The topic that is discussed the most in our home is modernity! But, wait, don't interpret modernity in the wrong way. This modernity is not about cutting your hair or eating with a knife and fork. This modernity is the modernity of real, genuine intellectuals! What that is exactly, even I don't know for sure, but, yes, there's always a great deal of talk about abandoning established practices and customs. You should kick such customs aside, if you embrace them, you are the one who will get a kick.

Every subject in the world is the focus of discussions and arguments but there's one topic that is especially dear to everyone: marriage. Marriage, that is, ruin and destruction. Conversations that begin on a light note all of a sudden reach an intellectual plane—the institution of marriage has become utterly hollow...the husband–wife relationship has become so artificial and forced...and then marriage is made fun of with much vigour and spirit. Often, in these arguments, the women are ranged on one side and the men on the other, and things sometimes became so heated I thought some of the couples would end up divorcing. But that never happened. All the friends continued in their neat and securely organized marriages. But, yes, the tone and manner of the arguments continue to be the same even today!

Now think about it, if they curse marriage, then it is necessary to support free love and free sex. In this, the men were the most enthusiastic and at the forefront—as if they could experience half its pleasure by just talking about it. Papa himself was a big supporter! But it so happened that when a young, quiet, and retiring distant female relative who stayed in the house and never participated in such discussions acted on these principles, all that modernity went dhummmm! It was Mummy who took care of everything in an easy, natural way, and by tying her down in a meaningless marriage, gave meaning to her life. Though this is a very old story and I heard it mentioned only in hushed tones and muted whispers.

Actually Papa-Mummy also had a love marriage. It's another matter that from the time I was old enough to understand things, I never saw them being affectionate with each other, instead I only saw them arguing constantly. Mummy had had to fight with Nana, and for a long time. Despite this, theirs was not a marriage of argument but a marriage of love and Mummy used to mention this with great pride. Pride not because of the marriage itself but because of the way she had battled Nana for it. She'd repeated the conversations between Nana and herself so often, I knew them by heart. Even today when she talks about it, there's a flash of contentment on her face, that she did something outside of established norms.

So, this is the kind of house I'm being brought up in—in a very free, independent way. And one day, suddenly, I grew up. I didn't feel the fact of my growing up as much from the inside as from the outside. There's an entertaining incident connected with this. It so happened that right opposite our house was a barsati—a single room with a sprawling terrace.

Every year, a few students would come and stay there. They would walk up and down the terrace as they studied, but I never noticed them, perhaps because I was not of the age to have any interest in them. This time, I saw that two boys had moved in. They were just two, but in the evening a big crowd of their friends would gather, and not just their terrace, the entire neighbourhood would come alive! Fun, laughter, music, song, and the passing of sharp comments and jokes on the girls who lived nearby and happened to come into their sights. But their real focus was our house...to be clear, me. If I came out on the veranda to do anything, some remark or the other would fly and land there and I would quiver to my core. For the first time I became aware of myself...and that I was the centre of someone's attention. If I were to be honest, I found this first awareness very thrilling and I felt new in my own eyes...new and grown-up!

It was a strange situation. When they would pass those remarks, I would burn with anger, though there was nothing rude or uncouth about the remarks. They were more in the nature of light-hearted fun. But when they became busy with each other or if they were absent, I would keep waiting...and wrestling with an unknown restlessness. My attention was forever fixed in that direction and I was always hanging around outside my room, in the veranda.

But the neighbours were fed up of the boisterous, loud behaviour of these boys. Our neighbourhood was inhabited by the lalas of Hathras-Khurja. Those who had adolescent girls at home would threaten to break teeth and legs, because for them, the future of their daughters was in danger. The neighbourhood was all aflame but my parents had no idea what was going on. The fact is, they lived as though they were on an island. Away from everyone, despite living in the midst of everyone.

One day I told my mother, 'Mummy, these boys who live opposite us, they keep passing remarks at me. I'm not going to stay quiet; I'll answer back.'

'Which boys?' asked Mummy in surprise!

Amazing! Mummy didn't know anything. My tone a mixture of irritation and delight, I told her everything. But there was no reaction from her.

'Tell me who these boys are...' she said calmly and went back to her reading. I didn't like her indifference to what, for me, was a scandalous matter. If it had been any other mother, she would have taken them to task with the utmost severity. But not my mother.

As the afternoon waned and the boys gathered on the terrace, I told Mummy, 'Look, these are the boys who keep looking and passing comments.' I don't know if there was something in the way I said this, but Ma kept looking at me unblinkingly, then smiled gently. After sizing up the boys on the terrace, she said, 'They look like college boys but they're like little kids.'

I felt like saying: if kids won't tease me, then who will, old people? But at that moment, Mummy said, 'We'll call them for tea tomorrow evening so you can make friends with them.'

I was speechless!

'You'll call them for tea?' I couldn't believe what Mummy was saying.

'Yes, why, what happened? Arre, all this happened in our time that boys and girls couldn't meet each other, and you had to be content with passing comments from far away. Times have changed now.'

I was ecstatic at the thought. I felt my mother really was someone very exalted. These people will come to our house and make friends with me. All at once I began feeling I was very alone and that I desperately needed to make friends. I didn't really know anyone in the neighbourhood and the only people who came home were Mummy–Papa's friends.

I went through the next day with great anxiety. Who knows if Mummy will keep her word or whether she said it impulsively? And if that were the case, then that was the end of the matter! In the evening, just to remind her, I said, 'Mummy, will you really call those boys?' These were my words, but the emotion was actually Mummy, please go and call them!

And, indeed, Mummy did go. I don't remember Mummy going to anyone's house in our neighbourhood more than three or four times. I waited for her to return with bated breath. I experienced an unfamiliar thrill in every part of my body. What if Mummy brings them with her? Suppose they behave rudely with Mummy? But, no, they didn't seem like that. Mummy returned after about an hour! Very happy!

'They were struck dumb when they saw me. They thought that till now people were sitting in their homes and threatening to come and break their arms and legs, and I had actually turned up to give them a good hiding. But the poor things looked after me so well! They are very sweet kids. They've come from outside—they couldn't get space in the hostel, so they've taken up this room. We'll call them over when Papa comes home in the evening!'

I learnt for the first time how ponderously time passes when you're waiting for something. When Papa came, Mummy elatedly explained the whole story to him. Pride and gratification that she was doing something quite out of the ordinary overflowed from every word. Papa was scarcely going to hold back either. He too was delighted.

'Call the boys! Arre, let them come and have fun, let the kids enjoy themselves.' Mummy-Papa were pleased that they had got such an excellent opportunity to display their modernity.

The servant was sent to bring them over and the whole lot of them appeared in the very next instant! Mummy introduced them properly and there was an exchange of hi-hellos.

'Tanu bete, make tea for your friends!'

Oh crap! When Mummy's friends come, it is 'Tanu bete, go and make tea,' and when it's Tanu's friends, then too Tanu should make the tea! Glumly, I got up.

Everyone had tea. There was much laughter and bonhomie. They kept defending their reputation by saying that everyone in the neighbourhood was after them for no reason. They hadn't done anything to annoy anyone. Whatever they may have done was just for fun.

Papa said encouragingly, 'Arre, this is the age for all this. If we got a chance even at this age, we wouldn't hesitate.'

A wave of laughter surged from one end of the room to the other. After about two hours, they got up to leave and Mummy said, 'You should think of this as your home. Come over whenever you feel like it. Our daughter, Tanu, will have pleasant company. Sometimes she can study with you. Also, if you feel like eating anything in particular, let me know, I'll have it cooked for you.' Bowled over by Papa's openness and Mummy's warmth and affection, they went away. But they had actually been called to become friends with someone and that poor someone ended up becoming a mere spectator to the whole show.

There was a great deal of discussion about them long after they had left. Calling those very boys who had been teasing your adolescent daughter to your house for tea so that they could become friends with her, why, the whole thing was so thrilling. From the very next day, Mummy began recounting what had happened to everyone who dropped in. Mummy was an expert at making even the dullest thing seem interesting, but here, this story itself was riveting. Whoever heard it said, 'Wah, this is wonderful. You have such a healthy outlook on such matters. Otherwise, people talk big but suffocate their children and don't hesitate to spy on them if they have the slightest suspicions about them.' And Mummy would bask in the praise, and say, 'But of course. Be free and keep your children free. When we were young, there were so many restrictions on us. We were told: don't do this, don't go there. At least our children shouldn't be suffocated in this manner.'

But at that moment, Mummy's child was becoming the victim of another kind of suffocation because though she was supposed to be the heroine of the play, it was Mummy who had become the heroine.

Anyway, the outcome of the entire affair was that the behaviour of those boys changed completely. They had no choice but to live up to the mantle of decency that Mummy had thrown on them. Now when they saw Mummy-Papa on the roof, they would greet them with a namaste and when they saw me, they would throw a 'hi' and a smile in my direction. Instead of those mocking remarks, now we actually had conversations…very open and free conversations, and there was just enough distance between our veranda and their roof that we could talk to each other if we spoke a little loudly. It was another matter that the entire neighbourhood heard our conversations and listened to them with a great deal of interest. As soon as we'd start talking, four or five pairs of ears and bodies would attach themselves to each window. It wasn't as if girls had never had romantic liaisons in the neighbourhood. There had even been incidents of girls running away from home. But all that had happened furtively and in utmost secrecy. And when the people of the neighbourhood discovered such a secret, they felt intense gratification. The men, twirling their moustaches with smug satisfaction, and the women, gesticulating dramatically with their hands, would broadcast the news, adding generous amounts of salt and spice to it. Their attitude was: we have seen the world, no one can make a fool of us. But here the situation was the opposite. Our conversations were so open that people listened by hiding behind windows but even then they couldn't find anything that would give them any inner gratification.

But things had to get out of hand and they did. What happened was that the gathering on the roof slowly started moving to my room. Every day, sometimes two, sometimes three or four boys would install themselves in my room and there would be long hours of chatting, joking, laughing about everything in the world. There would be music and singing and rounds of tea and other refreshments. When Mummy and Papa's friends would come in the evening, one or the other of the boys would still be hanging around. When all those people who had initially praised the idea of 'be free and let others be free' saw this type of freedom, you could see the doubt in their eyes. A couple of Mummy's friends even said to her, sotto voce: 'Tanu is moving very fast.' Mummy's enthusiasm began waning and then the thrill of doing something against established norms completely dissipated. Now she had to face the naked truth that her very naïve, inexperienced daughter of tender years was always surrounded by three or four boys. Mummy's situation was such that neither could she fully accept the situation, nor was she able to reject what she herself had started so eagerly.

Eventually one day she called me, made me sit next to her and said, 'Tanu bete, these people come here every day and stay for so long. After all, you have to study too. I've been noticing that your studies are getting affected. This can't go on.'

'I study at night,' I said carelessly.

'I don't think you study anything at night, how much time do you get anyway? In any case, I don't like these noisy gatherings on an everyday basis. They can drop in once in a while after every five or six days for some chit-chat, but right now, someone or the other is parked here every single day.' The tinge of displeasure in her voice became more pronounced.

I didn't like Mummy's tone, but I stayed quiet.

'You've become very friendly and frank with them, tell them they should go and study, and let you study too. And if you can't say it, I will.'

But it didn't come to that. Because of the pressure of studies and because of the lure of Delhi's other attractions, the hostel boys started coming over less and less often. But Shekhar, who lived in the room in front, would turn up every day, sometimes during the afternoon, sometimes in the evening! I hadn't noticed many things about him when he was part of the group, but those aspects of his personality came out clearly when he was alone. He spoke little, but tried to say a great deal without words and all of a sudden, I began understanding his language of silence...not just understanding it, but replying as well. Soon I realized that something like love was growing between Shekhar and me. I would probably not have realized this in the normal course but after watching Hindi films, I found no difficulty in understanding it.

As long as there was nothing to hide, everything was very open, but the moment that 'something' happened, so did the desire to hide it from everyone's eyes. When the other boys came, they would make a racket from the stairs itself, talking in loud voices. But whenever Shekhar arrived, he would slink in and we would talk in whispers. They were ordinary conversations—about school, college. But they became special because they were conducted in whispers. When love is clandestine and hush-hush, it becomes very thrilling, otherwise it's plain vanilla! But Mummy had a sixth sense that could ferret out every secret of the people in the house. Even Papa was afraid of it. She lost no time in figuring out what was going on. No matter how noiselessly Shekhar walked in and no matter which corner of the house she was in, she would instantly appear or call out from wherever she was: 'Tanu, who is in your room?'

I noticed a strange look of worry on Mummy's face at Shekhar's behaviour. That Mummy would be worried by it had never crossed my mind. In a household where there were discussions about all kinds of romantic liaisons—between unmarried youngsters, married people, love affairs of people with two or three lovers—for such a household, this should've been a very ordinary matter. When you're friendly with boys, it's possible that love can happen. Perhaps Mummy thought this whole situation would unfold like the present-day art films—of which she was an admirer and supporter—where, from beginning to end, nothing sensational ever happened.

Whatever it was, I was definitely perturbed that Mummy was worried. Mummy was not just my mother but also my friend and companion. We talked about everything under the sun, laughed and joked with each other like two close friends. I wanted her to talk to me about this business but she didn't say anything. But whenever Shekhar came, she would abandon her customary indifference and hover around my room in a vigilant manner.

One day I came downstairs, ready to go out with Mummy when I bumped into a gracious-looking woman from the neighbourhood. After the namaskars and enquiries about each other's well-being, she came to the real purpose of her visit.

'Are these boys who stay on the roof opposite your house related to you?'

'Not at all.'

'Really? They are always at your place in the evenings, so we thought they must certainly be related to you.'

'They are Tanu's friends.' Mummy threw this at her with such indifference and lack of hesitation that the woman's attempts to fire an arrow at her target failed and she had to leave, crestfallen.

She left and I felt that now Mummy would pick up the topic and scold me a little. The neighbour hadn't achieved what she set out to do but she did place a weapon in Mummy's hands which could make things difficult for me. Mummy had been grappling with some internal conflict for quite a few days now, but all she said was: 'It seems as if...always busy poking their nose into someone else's house.'

Not only was I reassured, I took this as a green signal from Mummy and speeded things up in my life. But I made sure that of the three hours I spent with Shekhar, at least one was devoted to studying. He taught me with great earnestness and I studied very diligently too. Yes, in between, he would pass me little notes where he'd write the kind of lines that would thrill me to the core. Even after he left, those lines, the emotion behind those words, would make every vein in my body sing and I would be lost in them.

Another world, a big, full, colourful world was taking shape inside me. I didn't feel the need for anybody else. It was as if I was complete in myself. Even Mummy, always with me, was fading away and maybe that's why I'd stopped paying attention to her. Everyday conversations did happen, but just that—nothing else.

The days were passing and I was lost in myself, sinking deeper and deeper into my own world—quite oblivious to the outside world!

One day I came back from school and changed my clothes. I clamoured for my food, ate it, cribbing all the while and when I went to my room, Mummy, who was lying down, called me: 'Tanu, come here.'

It was only when I went closer that I noticed for the first time that Mummy's face was flushed with anger. The penny dropped. She picked up a book from the side table, pulled out five or six pieces of paper from it and showed them to me. Tauba! I wanted Mummy's help with studying so I had given her this book when I left. Shekhar's notes had got left behind in the book by mistake.

'So this is how your friendship with Shekhar is going? This is the studying that happens sitting here...this is why he comes here?'

I was silent! I knew it was the height of foolishness to answer back when Mummy was angry.

'I let you be...gave you freedom, but this doesn't mean you misuse it!'

I remained silent!

'A slip of a girl but look at her exploits! The more leeway you give, the more she keeps grabbing! One slap and all this romance will vanish in two minutes....'

I suddenly flared up at this remark. I looked up at Mummy angrily—but wait, this was not my Mummy. This was not Mummy's manner, nor was the language hers. But the sentences sounded very familiar. I felt as if I'd heard all this before and it suddenly struck me like a flash of lightning—Nana! But Nana had died so many years ago, how had he suddenly come to life? And that too, inside Mummy...who had fought him ceaselessly ever since she'd begun making sense of the world...she had opposed every single thing he'd said.

Mummy's 'Nana-type' lecture continued for quite a while, but I remained completely unmoved. If there was one thing bothering me, it was this: how come Nana had installed himself inside Mummy?

And then a strange, tension-filled silence settled on the house, especially between Mummy and me. No, Mummy wasn't even in the house, it was between Nana and me. I can explain myself to Mummy, I can understand her views, but Nana? I couldn't understand this language, this attitude, so there was no question of talking or discussing anything. Yes, Papa is also my friend, but of a different kind. Playing chess, arm-wrestling, extracting favours that Mummy hadn't agreed to.... As a child, I always clambered onto his back and even today, I do the same unhesitatingly and get him to agree to whatever I want. But despite being 'my dear friend' I always confided my personal feelings only to Mummy. And there was utter silence on that front—having knocked Mummy down, Nana was fully in command of her.

I had discreetly shown Shekhar the red flag so he'd stopped coming over and the evenings stretched interminably.

Many times I thought of going to Mummy and asking her in a forthright way why she was so angry. You know about my friendship with Shekhar. I never hid anything from you. And if there is friendship, then all this is inevitable. Did you think that we'd be like brother-sister? But then the thought came.... Mummy isn't even around, so I can't go and tell her all this.

It's been four days, I haven't seen Shekhar. Just a slight indication was enough for him to stop coming to the house, indeed, stop coming to the roof altogether. Even his friends who stayed in the hostel couldn't be seen on the roof, nor did they come to the house. If one of them had come I could have at least asked after him. I knew he was emotional to the point of foolishness. He didn't even know what exactly had happened here. It seems as if the mere possibility of Mummy's anger had crushed all of them.

But since yesterday, the tension on Mummy's face had definitely relaxed a little. It was as if the sternness that had frozen over her face had melted. But I decided that Mummy should be the one to break the ice.

In the morning, bathed and fresh, I was ironing my uniform behind the door. Outside Mummy was making tea and Papa was buried behind the newspaper. Mummy didn't realize that I had finished my bath and come out. She said to Papa: 'Do you know what happened last night? I don't know, I've been feeling bad since then—I couldn't even sleep.'

Hearing the softness of Mummy's tone, my hand froze and my ears pricked up.

'I woke up to go to the bathroom in the middle of the night. In front, the roof was in pitch darkness. Suddenly, a reddish, star-like light shone. I was startled. I looked carefully and slowly made out a silhouette. Shekhar was standing on the roof smoking a cigarette. I came back quietly. I went again after two hours and saw he was still pacing the roof in the same way. Poor thing, I don't know what to think. Tanu is also so subdued these days....' Then, as if reproaching herself, she said, 'First, give them liberty, then when they move forward, pull them down. Is this fair?'

A deep sigh of relief came from within me. An indescribable sensation surged in my heart and I felt like running to Mummy and flinging my arms around her. It felt as if Mummy had returned after a long absence. But I didn't do anything. Yes, now I would speak freely. In the last four days, so many questions had been swirling about in my head. But now... now Mummy is here, and with her at least everything can be discussed.

But when I came home I was taken aback by what I saw! Shekhar was sitting in a chair, his head in his hands, and Mummy was sitting on the arm of the chair, gently stroking his forehead and his back. Seeing me she said in a very natural, normal way: 'Look at this crazy boy. He hasn't gone to college for four days. Nor has he had anything to eat or drink. Set a place for him also to eat along with you.'

And then Mummy sat next to him and very lovingly entreated him to eat. But despite pressing him to, Shekhar didn't stay on after he finished the meal. Full of gratitude towards Mummy, he went away and such a tide overflowed inside me that all the questions I'd thought of vanished inside it.

The entire situation took time to return to normal, but it did. Shekhar began coming after every couple of days and when he did, we mostly spoke about study-related things. Expressing remorse at his behaviour, he promised Mummy that he would never do anything that would give her cause to complain. On the days he didn't come I would talk to him two or three times a day, for a short while, from the veranda itself. This love story, conducted in the open, with the permission and cooperation of everyone in the house, lost its novelty for the neighbours and after cursing these dangerous times, they abandoned their interest in the matter, till such time as some scandal might emerge.

But there was one thing I did notice. Whenever Shekhar stayed a little later than usual in the evening or if he came in the afternoon as well, Nana would start stirring within Mummy and you could see that reflected on Mummy's face. Mummy would attempt with all her might not to let Nana speak, but she didn't have the power to banish him totally.

Yes, this entire business did end up becoming the subject of everyday conversations between Mummy and me. Sometimes she would joke, 'This Shekhar of yours, he's a very limp sort of fellow. Arre, at his age boys should want to loaf about, have fun. What is this constant hanging around on the roof like some lovelorn Majnu, staring in this direction?'

I would just laugh.

Sometimes she would get very emotional and say, 'Why don't you understand, bete, I have so many ambitions for you! I have so many dreams for your future.'

I would laugh and say, 'Mummy, you are too much. You dream dreams about your life and you have dreams about my life as well...leave some dreams for me!'

Sometimes she would say, as if trying to explain something to me: 'Look, Tanu, you are still very young. All your focus should be on your studies and you should banish all these unnecessary obsessions from your mind. When you're older, fall in love and get married by all means. In any case I'm not going to find a boy for you—find someone yourself, but you should have enough sense and maturity to make a proper choice.'

I understood she didn't approve of my choice right now, so I asked, 'All right, tell me, Mummy, when you chose Papa, did Nana approve of him?'

'My choice! I made a choice at the age of twenty-five, after having completed my education—intelligently, after thinking over everything, understand?'

Mummy would say this, hiding her agitation under her anger. Age and education—these are the two points on which Mummy always pin me down. I was good at studies and, as for age, I felt like saying, 'Mummy, what your generation used to do at twenty-five, my generation will do at fifteen, why can't you get this?' But I would remain quiet. Nana's name has already cropped up, what if he awakens?

The mid-term exams were coming up and I was completely focused on my studies. No more comings and goings, and all the music and singing was at a standstill. I studied so hard that Mummy was delighted. Maybe a bit reassured too. After the last exam, I felt as if a burden had lifted. Light of mind, I wanted to have some fun. I asked Mummy: 'Mummy, Shekhar and Deepak are going for a movie tomorrow, can I go with them?' I had never gone out with them but after studying so hard, I deserved at least this much of freedom.

Mummy looked at my face for a few seconds, then said: 'Come here, sit! I want to talk to you.'

I went and sat down but couldn't understand what there was to talk about—either say yes or say no. But Mummy had an incurable habit of talking. Her yes-no wouldn't emerge until it had been wrapped in 50–60 sentences.

'Your exams are over. I myself was making a plan to go see a movie. Tell me, what movie do you want to see?'

'Why, what's the matter if I go with them?' My voice was so full of irritation that Mummy stared at me.

'Tanu, I have given you full liberty, bete, but walk only so fast that I can keep up with you.'

'Tell me plainly, will you let me go or not? This is all useless talk…I can also walk with you—where did this business of walking with you come from?'

Stroking my back, Mummy said, 'I will have to walk with you. If you fall face down, there has to be someone to pick you up, isn't it?'

I understood that Mummy was not going to let me go, but by refusing so lovingly, I couldn't even fight with her. Arguing with her meant listening to an elaborate philosophical lecture—that is, a fifty-minute class. But I couldn't understand what, after all, was the objection to going with them. Everything was a 'No'. She always said that when they were growing up, they were scolded and told 'Don't do this, don't go there', and now she herself is doing it. I'd had enough of all this big talk. I got up and stormed off to my room. Yes, I did toss this line out before flouncing off: 'Mummy, the one who walks will fall, and the one who falls will get up and get up by themselves, they don't need anyone else.'

I don't know if my words had an effect on her or whether something nagged her from within but that evening she called Shekhar and three or four other boys who were visiting him to our place and set up a proper party in my room with plenty of hot food. The mood of the evening was such that all my resentment of the afternoon washed away.

The exams were over and the weather was pleasant. Mummy's behaviour was in accordance with it and so the whole friendship saga, which had come to a standstill, picked up again. It was as if there was no space for anything else these days. But then again, a shock.

That day when I returned from a friend's place I heard Mummy's stern voice: 'Tanu, come here!'

Her voice was enough to indicate danger. For a second, I was unnerved. When I went in, her face was hard, like before.

'Do you go to Shekhar's room?' Mummy fired a salvo at me. I understood that someone from the back alley had tattled on me.

'Since when have you been going?'

I felt like saying that the person who gave you this news would no doubt have told you everything else as well...and would've probably embellished the story too. But the way Mummy was boiling with anger, it was prudent to remain quiet. Though I couldn't understand why Mummy was angry. What was the big deal if I'd gone to Shekhar's room a few times for a short while? What sin had I committed? But everything Mummy does doesn't necessarily have a reason...bas, it all depends on her mood.

It was a peculiar problem—there was no point talking when Mummy was angry but my silence fanned her rage even more.

'Remember I had told you in the beginning itself that you should never go to their rooms. He sits here for hours at a stretch, that's not enough for you?'

The lines of distress, rage, and panic on her face kept getting deeper, and I didn't know how to explain everything to her.

'It's a good thing those people who stay in front came and told me—do you know, this head hasn't bent before anyone till today, but today I couldn't raise my eyes in front of them. I won't be able to show my face to anyone because of you. Everyone in the lane is doing thoo...thoo...to us. You've disgraced us.'

Disaster!

This time the entire neighbourhood was talking from within Mummy! It was astonishing that Mummy, who till today, had kept herself aloof from the neighbourhood, in fact, used to make fun of them—today, she was singing their tune.

Mummy's lecture was in full flow but I had switched off. When her anger cools down, when Mummy is back to being herself again, then I will explain to her—Mummy, you're unnecessarily making such a big deal of a small thing.

But I don't know what kind of dose she'd taken this time that her anger showed no signs of cooling down, and her anger started making *me* angry.

Then a strange kind of tension grew in the house and this time perhaps Mummy told Papa everything. He didn't say anything. From the beginning he had stayed out of the whole affair but now there was an unspoken tension on his face.

When a similar incident had occurred around two months ago, I'd been cowed down but this time I vowed that if Mummy was going to behave like Nana, I too would have to open a front against him just like Mummy had...and I'll do it. Let me show her that I am your daughter and I'm following your lead. You broke away from established norms, all my life you fed me this tonic, but no sooner did I take my very first steps in this direction, you began making strenuous efforts to drag me back to the line you had drawn.

I thought up a whole lot of logical points with which I would one day have a proper argument with Mummy. I'd tell her clearly: Mummy, if you had to impose all these restrictions on me, you should have raised me accordingly right from the start. Why did you talk of giving freedom, why did you teach me about freedom if it was all going to be lies? But this time I was so upset, it was as if my heart had burnt and turned to ashes, I just stayed listlessly in my room, silent, lost in myself. If I felt too overwhelmed, I would cry! I'm usually all over the house, chattering and laughing, but now I turned absolutely silent and withdrawn. Yes, there was one sentence I kept repeating: 'Mummy, you should understand that I too will do what I please.' Though I had no clear idea of what it was I wanted to do.

I don't know what happened in these three or four days. Cut off from the world outside, shrunk inside myself, I was thinking of ways I could open a front against Mummy.

But this afternoon I couldn't believe my ears when I heard Mummy yelling from the veranda: 'Shekhar, tomorrow all of you will leave for home for your holidays, come over this evening with your friends for dinner.'

I don't know what internal struggles Mummy had to go through to arrive at this moment.

And that night, Shekhar, along with Deepak and Ravi, was busy tucking into the food at the dining table. Mummy was feeding them as lovingly as before. Papa was joking with them as openly as he always had, it was as if nothing had happened in the interim. A few heads poked out from the windows of nearby houses. Everything was as easy and natural as it had been before....

I was the only one looking at the whole situation with an objective eye and thinking that Nana was in every way Nana—a hundred per cent—and that's why it was easy for Mummy to fight him. But how can one fight with this Mummy who is Nana one second and Mummy the next?

THE STORY OF A CROW LEARNING PROSODY
SUBRAMANIA BHARATI

Translated from the Tamil by P. Raja

Quite close to Kutraalam a massive banyan tree stood on a hill. One evening, a sad crow was sitting on one of the branches. The crow's wife moved a little closer to her husband and asked in an affectionate tone: 'What's worrying you, dear?'

'This morning I ate more than what my stomach could hold. Now I don't feel the need to hunt for food. But I can't afford to sit still. My friends too have not yet returned from their search. If they were here, it would be easy for me to while away the time by chit-chatting with them. I thought of wandering in the sky and enjoying the scenes below...but my wings, legs, body, and head are heavy and painful. I'm sure I have a fever. My throat too is hoarse and unbearably painful. I have a severe cold. Both yesterday and the day before I didn't get enough to eat in the woods nearby. And so, I had to fly east for a long distance into areas populated by humans, all for the sake of food. Yet, until sunset, there wasn't enough to fill even half my stomach. It rained night and day without a break. It was summer rain and I was drenched to the bone. This may be the reason for my ill health. Indigestion is added to it from this morning. And I don't know how to kill time. This is why I am sad.'

The crow's wife said, 'Years ago when you married me you cooed to me that nothing on earth was more pleasurable than speaking to me intimately. You said that the time you spent with me was very productive. I recall that you said so over and over again. But now, even while I am beside you, you say you find it difficult to pass the time. By saying this you are insulting me. Every day I look at my image in the water in the spring.

My face looks more beautiful than when we married. I also consulted my friends. They also agree that I'm more beautiful now than before. I don't know why you have turned away from me.'

'Who said you are more beautiful than before? Was it your girlfriends? Or your boyfriends?' asked the crow.

'My dear friends are the ones who told me. I don't have "boy" friends,' replied the crow's wife.

The crow reacted by fluffing its wings. He took off from the branch of the tree and started flying southwards. 'Caw...caw....' The crow heard the sound from behind him. He turned his head and saw it was his wife. 'Why are you following me?' he asked.

'You are not well...yet you are going all alone. If your head reels in pain, you may fall. If I am there with you, I'll be able to avert your fall at the right moment. This is why I am following you.'

'Oh! I see! So you are here to safeguard me, are you?' asked the crow.

'Yes! Of course,' replied the wife.

'If that is so, you don't have to go with me. I am hale and hearty now. All my ailments are gone. I will neither feel giddy nor fall to the earth and become food for a fox. So you don't have to escort me. Please stay at home.'

'Where are you going?'

'Quite nearby...Vikrama Singha Puram.'

'Huh! Vikrama Singha Puram? It is near Papanasam...Quite a distance.'

'But I can cover the distance in a jiffy. You don't have to worry about it. Go home now,' instructed the crow.

'Why are you are going there? Tell me,' said the wife.

'I know of a man named Veera Maagaala Pulavar who lives in Vikrama Singha Puram. He is a king of poets. He chooses this time to teach his children the art of Tamil prosody. And you know that I understand the spoken language of man, even though I can't speak it. So I will go there, perch on the roof of his house, and learn from him all the nuances of the language. I will then apply it to our crow language to formulate our own prosody. My main purpose is to compose songs and epics in our language. Is it appropriate to call a crow a crow if it has no love for its native land and tongue? It can only be called a little living black carcass. No wood in the world is as clean and fertile as our wood in Kutraalam. It is deathless. No other language is as great as our crow language. As I am born in this wood, I should contribute my share to the growth of this wood and my language. If I happen to die before my desire is fulfilled, I will have to die with regret. Hence, I have decided to prepare our crow language and develop its potential for poetry.'

'What?' retorted the wife, 'Just a few seconds ago you said no other language is as great as our crow language. But now, you say you want to adapt the nuances of the Tamil language into ours to compose songs. So you support the view that our language is inferior to Tamil?'

'Tamil is the language of human beings. Don't be so stupid as to compare our bird language with that! What I meant was our crow language is superior to all other non-human languages. All right, it is getting late. I should leave now. You go home,' said the crow.

The wife tried another argument 'You don't have to go all the way to Vikrama Singha Puram for this! Let us go home. I will teach you, because I know.'

'What do you know?' demanded the crow.

'All the rules for composing poetry.'

'Where did you learn them?' asked the crow in astonishment.

'You may think you were the first to whom such an idea occurred. Not so! My father too nurtured such an idea. He sat on the roof of a master-poet's house and learnt the nuances when the master taught his students every day. He never missed a single one of the classes which ran for six months. At the end of the course, my father mastered Tamil poetics and prosody. Following those rules of grammar, he formulated several strict rules for composing a thousand variations of poetry. Unfortunately, he did not live to present his work for acceptance in the learned assembly hall of the crow king. And so, the new theory of poetry in our language languished in our home itself. I am my father's only daughter. He had no other child, male or female. Our law forbids the female from presenting this new theory before the learned assembly and give a new outlook to our language. But I am ready to teach *you* the theory. You can learn it from me and then present it before the assembly. You will be rewarded for that in the king's court. You will become world famous. So come home and I will teach you for two hours every day. In two months you will receive the highest honours from our crow king,' said the wife.

'I am a supporter of the Republic Party. I do not care for the honours and awards of the king,' said the crow curtly.

'So let it be...' replied the wife, 'as you said earlier you can contribute to the growth of our language and you will be remembered even after your death. For the sake of that at least, come with me. I will teach you the art of writing poetry.'

As the crow couple flew back home, that is to say, towards their nest, Manmadhan was moving in the sky, a little distance away from them. It was drizzling on the Western Ghats, a command from nature to compel the male and the female to unite in love.

In such weather and in such a place, the god of love would be extremely busy. And so, he had already spent most of the arrows from his quiver and was rushing to his own world to unite in love with his beloved Rathi Devi. There were only two arrows left in his quiver. He drew out both of them and sent the love darts to the crow couple, one for each.

Before the crow couple could reach their nest, they began fondling and kissing each other. No sooner did they enter the nest than they, unable to control their passion, began to make love. The very thought of learning the art of poesy left the crow's mind. They were so deeply immersed in their passion that they were awake till daybreak. Then they slept like logs and woke up only on the morning of the next day. Before the thought of hunting for food flashed across the minds of the crow couple Manmadhan passed that way again. All that had happened in the nest a day earlier began to repeat itself. Several days passed in this manner.

The male crow completely forgot all about learning the prosody in crow language. He did not study the art of poesy. He began, instead, to study the art of love.

7

THE BLUE UMBRELLA

RUSKIN BOND

I

'Neelu! Neelu!' cried Binya.

She scrambled barefoot over the rocks, ran over the short summer grass, up and over the brow of the hill, all the time calling 'Neelu, Neelu!' Neelu—Blue—was the name of the blue-grey cow. The other cow, which was white, was called Gori, meaning Fair One. They were fond of wandering off on their own, down to the stream or into the pine forest, and sometimes they came back by themselves and sometimes they stayed away—almost deliberately, it seemed to Binya.

If the cows didn't come home at the right time, Binya would be sent to fetch them. Sometimes her brother, Bijju, went with her, but these days he was busy preparing for his exams and didn't have time to help with the cows.

Binya liked being on her own, and sometimes she allowed the cows to lead her into some distant valley, and then they would all be late coming home. The cows preferred having Binya with them, because she let them wander. Bijju pulled them by their tails if they went too far.

Binya belonged to the mountains, to this part of the Himalayas known as Garhwal. Dark forests and lonely hilltops held no terrors for her. It was only when she was in the market town, jostled by the crowds in the bazaar, that she felt rather nervous and lost. The town, five miles from the village, was also a pleasure resort for tourists from all over India.

Binya was probably ten. She may have been nine or even eleven, she couldn't be sure because no one in the village kept birthdays; but her mother told her she'd been born during a winter when the snow had come up to the windows, and that was just over ten years ago, wasn't it?

Two years later, her father had died, but his passing had made no difference to their way of life. They had three tiny terraced fields on the side of the mountain, and they grew potatoes, onions, ginger, beans, mustard, and maize: not enough to sell in the town, but enough to live on.

Like most mountain girls, Binya was quite sturdy, fair of skin, with pink cheeks and dark eyes and her black hair tied in a pigtail. She wore pretty glass bangles on her wrists, and a necklace of glass beads. From the necklace hung a leopard's claw. It was a lucky charm, and Binya always wore it. Bijju had one, too, only his was attached to a string.

Binya's full name was Binyadevi, and Bijju's real name was Vijay, but everyone called them Binya and Bijju. Binya was two years younger than her brother.

She had stopped calling for Neelu; she had heard the cowbells tinkling, and knew the cows hadn't gone far. Singing to herself, she walked over fallen pine needles into the forest glade on the spur of the hill. She heard voices, laughter, the clatter of plates and cups and, stepping through the trees, she came upon a party of picnickers.

They were holidaymakers from the plains. The women were dressed in bright saris, the men wore light summer shirts, and the children had pretty new clothes. Binya, standing in the shadows between the trees, went unnoticed; for some time she watched the picnickers, admiring their clothes, listening to their unfamiliar accents, and gazing rather hungrily at the sight of all their food. And then her gaze came to rest on a bright blue umbrella, a frilly thing for women, which lay open on the grass beside its owner.

Now Binya had seen umbrellas before, and her mother had a big black umbrella which nobody used any more because the field rats had eaten holes in it, but this was the first time Binya had seen such a small, dainty, colourful umbrella and she fell in love with it. The umbrella was like a flower, a great blue flower that had sprung up on the dry brown hillside.

She moved forward a few paces so that she could see the umbrella better. As she came out of the shadows into the sunlight, the picnickers saw her.

'Hello, look who's here!' exclaimed the older of the two women. 'A little village girl!'

'Isn't she pretty?' remarked the other. 'But how torn and dirty her clothes are!' It did not seem to bother them that Binya could hear and understand everything they said about her.

'They're very poor in the hills,' said one of the men.

'Then let's give her something to eat.' And the older woman beckoned to Binya to come closer.

Hesitantly, nervously, Binya approached the group.

Normally she would have turned and fled, but the attraction was the pretty blue umbrella. It had cast a spell over her, drawing her forward almost against her will.

'What's that on her neck?' asked the younger woman.

'A necklace of sorts.'

'It's a pendant—see, there's a claw hanging from it!'

'It's a tiger's claw,' said the man beside her. (He had never seen a tiger's claw.)

'A lucky charm. These people wear them to keep away evil spirits.' He looked to Binya for confirmation, but Binya said nothing.

'Oh, I want one too!' said the woman, who was obviously his wife.

'You can't get them in shops.'

'Buy hers, then. Give her two or three rupees, she's sure to need the money.'

The man, looking slightly embarrassed but anxious to please his young wife, produced a two-rupee note and offered it to Binya, indicating that he wanted the pendant in exchange. Binya put her hand to the necklace, half afraid that the excited woman would snatch it away from her. Solemnly she shook her head.

The man then showed her a five-rupee note, but again Binya shook her head.

'How silly she is!' exclaimed the young woman.

'It may not be hers to sell,' said the man. 'But I'll try again. How much do you want—what can we give you?' And he waved his hand towards the picnic things scattered about on the grass.

Without any hesitation Binya pointed to the umbrella.

'My umbrella!' exclaimed the young woman. 'She wants my umbrella. What cheek!'

'Well, you want her pendant, don't you?'

'That's different.'

'Is it?'

The man and his wife were beginning to quarrel with each other.

'I'll ask her to go away,' said the older woman.

'We're making such fools of ourselves.'

'But I want the pendant!' cried the other, petulantly.

And then, on an impulse, she picked up the umbrella and held it out to Binya.

'Here, take the umbrella!'

Binya removed her necklace and held it out to the young woman, who immediately placed it around her own neck. Then Binya took the umbrella and held it up. It did not look so small in her hands; in fact, it was just the right size.

She had forgotten about the picnickers, who were busy examining the pendant. She turned the blue umbrella this way and that, looked through the bright blue silk at the pulsating sun, and then, still keeping it open, turned and disappeared into the forest glade.

II

Binya seldom closed the blue umbrella. Even when she had it in the house, she left it lying open in a corner of the room. Sometimes Bijju snapped it shut, complaining that it got in the way. She would open it again a little later. It wasn't beautiful when it was closed.

Whenever Binya went out—whether it was to graze the cows, or fetch water from the spring, or carry milk to the little tea shop on the Tehri road—she took the umbrella with her. That patch of sky-blue silk could always be seen on the hillside.

Old Ram Bharosa (Ram the Trustworthy) kept the tea shop on the Tehri road. It was a dusty, unmetalled road. Once a day, the Tehri bus stopped near his shop and passengers got down to sip hot tea or drink a glass of curd. He kept a few bottles of Coca-Cola too, but as there was no ice, the bottles got hot in the sun and so were seldom opened. He also kept sweets and toffees, and when Binya or Bijju had a few coins to spare, they would spend them at the shop. It was only a mile from the village.

Ram Bharosa was astonished to see Binya's blue umbrella.

'What have you there, Binya?' he asked.

Binya gave the umbrella a twirl and smiled at Ram Bharosa. She was always ready with her smile, and would willingly have lent it to anyone who was feeling unhappy.

'That's a lady's umbrella,' said Ram Bharosa. 'That's only for memsahibs. Where did you get it?'

'Someone gave it to me—for my necklace.'
'You exchanged it for your lucky claw!'
Binya nodded.
'But what do you need it for? The sun isn't hot enough, and it isn't meant for the rain. It's just a pretty thing for rich ladies to play with!'

Binya nodded and smiled again. Ram Bharosa was quite right; it was just a beautiful plaything. And that was exactly why she had fallen in love with it.

'I have an idea,' said the shopkeeper. 'It's no use to you, that umbrella. Why not sell it to me? I'll give you five rupees for it.'

'It's worth fifteen,' said Binya.
'Well, then, I'll give you ten.'
Binya laughed and shook her head.
'Twelve rupees?' said Ram Bharosa, but without much hope.
Binya placed a five-paise coin on the counter.
'I came for a toffee,' she said.

Ram Bharosa pulled at his drooping whiskers, gave Binya a wry look, and placed a toffee in the palm of her hand. He watched Binya as she walked away along the dusty road. The blue umbrella held him fascinated, and he stared after it until it was out of sight.

The villagers used this road to go to the market town. Some used the bus, a few rode on mules, and most people walked. Today, everyone on the road turned their heads to stare at the girl with the bright blue umbrella.

Binya sat down in the shade of a pine tree. The umbrella, still open, lay beside her. She cradled her head in her arms, and presently she dozed off. It was that kind of day, sleepily warm and summery.

And while she slept, a wind sprang up.

It came quietly, swishing gently through the trees, humming softly. Then it was joined by other random gusts, bustling over the tops of the mountains. The trees shook their heads and came to life. The wind fanned Binya's cheeks. The umbrella stirred on the grass.

The wind grew stronger, picking up dead leaves and sending them spinning and swirling through the air. It got into the umbrella and began to drag it over the grass. Suddenly it lifted the umbrella and carried it about six feet from the sleeping girl. The sound woke Binya.

She was on her feet immediately, and then she was leaping down the steep slope. But just as she was within reach of the umbrella, the wind picked it up again and carried it further downhill.

Binya set off in pursuit. The wind was in a wicked, playful mood. It would leave the umbrella alone for a few moments but as soon as Binya came near, it would pick up the umbrella again and send it bouncing, floating, dancing away from her.

The hill grew steeper. Binya knew that after twenty yards it would fall away in a precipice. She ran faster. And the wind ran with her, ahead of her, and the blue umbrella stayed up with the wind.

A fresh gust picked it up and carried it to the very edge of the cliff. There it balanced for a few seconds, before toppling over, out of sight.

Binya ran to the edge of the cliff. Going down on her hands and knees, she peered down the cliff face. About a hundred feet below, a small stream rushed between great boulders. Hardly anything grew on the cliff face—just a few stunted bushes, and, halfway down, a wild cherry tree growing crookedly out of the rocks and hanging across the chasm. The umbrella had stuck in the cherry tree.

Binya didn't hesitate. She may have been timid with strangers, but she was at home on a hillside. She stuck her bare leg over the edge of the cliff and began climbing down. She kept her face to the hillside, feeling her way with her feet, only changing her handhold when she knew her feet were secure. Sometimes she held on to the thorny bilberry bushes, but she did not trust the other plants, which came away very easily.

Loose stones rattled down the cliff. Once on their way, the stones did not stop until they reached the bottom of the hill; and they took other stones with them, so that there was soon a cascade of stones, and Binya had to be very careful not to start a landslide.

As agile as a mountain goat, she did not take more than five minutes to reach the crooked cherry tree. But the most difficult task remained—she had to crawl along the trunk of the tree, which stood out at right angles from the cliff. Only by doing this could she reach the trapped umbrella.

Binya felt no fear when climbing trees. She was proud of the fact that she could climb them as well as Bijju. Gripping the rough cherry bark with her toes, and using her knees as leverage, she crawled along the trunk of the projecting tree until she was almost within reach of the umbrella. She noticed with dismay that the blue cloth was torn in a couple of places.

She looked down, and it was only then that she felt afraid. She was right over the chasm, balanced precariously about eighty feet above the boulder-strewn stream. Looking down, she felt quite dizzy. Her hands shook, and the tree shook too. If she slipped now, there was only one direction in which she could fall—down, down, into the depths of that dark and shadowy ravine.

There was only one thing to do; concentrate on the patch of blue just a couple of feet away from her. She did not look down or up, but straight ahead, and willing herself forward, she managed to reach the umbrella.

She could not crawl back with it in her hands. So, after dislodging it from the forked branch in which it had stuck, she let it fall, still open, into the ravine below.

Cushioned by the wind, the umbrella floated serenely downwards, landing in a thicket of nettles.

Binya crawled back along the trunk of the cherry tree. Twenty minutes later, she emerged from the nettle clump, her precious umbrella held aloft. She had nettle stings all over her legs, but she was hardly aware of the smarting. She was as immune to nettles as Bijju was to bees.

III

About four years previously, Bijju had knocked a hive out of an oak tree, and had been badly stung on the face and legs. It had been a painful experience. But now, if a bee stung him, he felt nothing at all: he had been immunized for life!

He was on his way home from school. It was two o'clock and he hadn't eaten since six in the morning. Fortunately, the kingora bushes—the bilberries—were in fruit, and already Bijju's lips were stained purple with the juice of the wild, sour fruit.

He didn't have any money to spend at Ram Bharosa's shop, but he stopped there anyway to look at the sweets in their glass jars.

'And what will you have today?' asked Ram Bharosa.

'No money,' said Bijju.

'You can pay me later.'

Bijju shook his head. Some of his friends had taken sweets on credit, and at the end of the month they had found they'd eaten more sweets than they could possibly pay for! As a result, they'd had to hand over to Ram Bharosa some of their most treasured possessions—such as a curved knife for cutting grass, or a small hand-axe, or a jar for pickles, or a pair of earrings—and these had become the shopkeeper's possessions and were kept by him or sold in his shop.

Ram Bharosa had set his heart on having Binya's blue umbrella, and so naturally he was anxious to give credit to either of the children, but so far neither had fallen into the trap.

Bijju moved on, his mouth full of kingora berries. Halfway home, he saw Binya with the cows. It was late evening, and the sun had gone down, but Binya still had the umbrella open. The two small rents had been stitched up by her mother.

Bijju gave his sister a handful of berries. She handed him the umbrella while she ate the berries.

'You can have the umbrella until we get home,' she said. It was her way of rewarding Bijju for bringing her the wild fruit.

Calling 'Neelu! Gori!' Binya and Bijju set out for home, followed at some distance by the cows.

It was dark before they reached the village, but Bijju still had the umbrella open.

∽

Most of the people in the village were a little envious of Binya's blue umbrella. No one else had ever possessed one like it. The schoolmaster's wife thought it was quite wrong for a poor cultivator's daughter to have such a fine umbrella while she, a second-class BA, had to make do with an ordinary black one. Her husband offered to have their old umbrella dyed blue; she gave him a scornful look, and loved him a little less than before. The pujari, who looked after the temple, announced that he would buy a multi-coloured umbrella the next time he was in the town. A few days later he returned looking annoyed and grumbling that they weren't available except in Delhi. Most people consoled themselves by saying that Binya's pretty umbrella wouldn't keep out the rain, if it rained heavily; that it would shrivel in the sun, if the sun was fierce; that it would collapse in a wind, if the wind was strong; that it would attract lightning, if lightning fell near it; and that it would prove unlucky, if there was any ill luck going about. Secretly, everyone admired it.

Unlike the adults, the children didn't have to pretend. They were full of praise for the umbrella. It was so light, so pretty, so bright a blue! And it was just the right size for Binya. They knew that if they said nice things about the umbrella, Binya would smile and give it to them to hold for a little while—just a very little while!

Soon it was the time of the monsoon. Big black clouds kept piling up, and thunder rolled over the hills.

Binya sat on the hillside all afternoon, waiting for the rain. As soon as the first big drop of rain came down, she raised the umbrella over her head. More drops, big ones, came pattering down. She could see them through the umbrella silk as they broke against the cloth.

And then there was a cloudburst, and it was like standing under a waterfall. The umbrella wasn't really a rain umbrella, but it held up bravely. Only Binya's feet got wet. Rods of rain fell around her in a curtain of shivered glass.

Everywhere on the hillside people were scurrying for shelter. Some made for a charcoal burner's hut, others for a mule-shed, or Ram Bharosa's shop. Binya was the only one who didn't run. This was what she'd been waiting for—rain on her umbrella—and she wasn't in a hurry to go home. She didn't mind getting her feet wet. The cows didn't mind getting wet either.

Presently she found Bijju sheltering in a cave. He would have enjoyed getting wet, but he had his schoolbooks with him and he couldn't afford to let them get spoilt. When he saw Binya, he came out of the cave and shared the umbrella. He was a head taller than his sister, so he had to hold the umbrella for her, while she held his books.

The cows had been left far behind.

'Neelu, Neelu!' called Binya.

'Gori!' called Bijju.

When their mother saw them sauntering home through the driving rain, she called out: 'Binya! Bijju! Hurry up, and bring the cows in! What are you doing out there in the rain?'

'Just testing the umbrella,' said Bijju.

IV

The rains set in, and the sun only made brief appearances. The hills turned a lush green. Ferns sprang up on walls and tree trunks. Giant lilies reared up like leopards from the tall grass. A white mist coiled and uncoiled as it floated up from the valley. It was a beautiful season, except for the leeches.

Every day, Binya came home with a couple of leeches fastened to the flesh of her bare legs. They fell off by themselves just as soon as they'd had their thimbleful of blood, but you didn't know they were on you until they fell off, and then, later, the skin became very sore and itchy. Some of the older people still believed that to be bled by leeches was a remedy for various ailments. Whenever Ram Bharosa had a headache, he applied a leech to his throbbing temple.

Three days of incessant rain had flooded out a number of small animals who lived in holes in the ground. Binya's mother suddenly found the roof full of field rats. She had to drive them out; they ate too much of her stored-up wheat flour and rice. Bijju liked lifting up large rocks to disturb the scorpions who were sleeping beneath. And snakes came out to bask in the sun.

Binya had just crossed the small stream at the bottom of the hill when she saw something gliding out of the bushes and coming towards her. It was a long black snake. A clatter of loose stones frightened it. Seeing the girl in its way, it rose up, hissing, prepared to strike. The forked tongue darted out, the venomous head lunged at Binya.

Binya's umbrella was open as usual. She thrust it forward, between herself and the snake, and the snake's hard snout thudded twice against the strong silk of the umbrella. The reptile then turned and slithered away over the wet rocks, disappearing into a clump of ferns.

Binya forgot about the cows and ran all the way home to tell her mother how she had been saved by the umbrella. Bijju had to put away his books and go out to fetch the cows. He carried a stout stick, in case he met with any snakes.

∽

First the summer sun, and now the endless rain, meant that the umbrella was beginning to fade a little. From a bright blue it had changed to a light blue. But it was still a pretty thing, and tougher than it looked, and Ram Bharosa still desired it. He did not want to sell it; he wanted to own it. He was probably the richest man in the area—so why shouldn't he have a blue umbrella? Not a day passed without his getting a glimpse of Binya and the umbrella; and the more he saw the umbrella, the more he wanted it.

The schools closed during the monsoon, but this didn't mean that Bijju could sit at home doing nothing. Neelu and Gori were providing more milk than was required at home, so Binya's mother was able to sell a kilo of milk every day: half a kilo to the schoolmaster, and half a kilo (at reduced rate) to the temple pujari. Bijju had to deliver the milk every morning.

Ram Bharosa had asked Bijju to work in his shop during the holidays, but Bijju didn't have time—he had to help his mother with the ploughing and the transplanting of the rice seedlings. So Ram Bharosa employed a boy from the next village, a boy called Rajaram. He did all the washing-up, and ran various errands. He went to the same school as Bijju, but the two boys were not friends.

One day, as Binya passed the shop, twirling her blue umbrella, Rajaram noticed that his employer gave a deep sigh and began muttering to himself.

'What's the matter, babuji?' asked the boy.

'Oh, nothing,' said Ram Bharosa. 'It's just a sickness that has come upon me. And it's all due to that girl Binya and her wretched umbrella.'

'Why, what has she done to you?'

'Refused to sell me her umbrella! There's pride for you. And I offered her ten rupees.'

'Perhaps, if you gave her twelve...'

'But it isn't new any longer. It isn't worth eight rupees now. All the same, I'd like to have it.'

'You wouldn't make a profit on it,' said Rajaram.

'It's not the profit I'm after, wretch! It's the thing itself. It's the beauty of it!'

'And what would you do with it, babuji? You don't visit anyone—you're seldom out of your shop. Of what use would it be to you?'

'Of what use is a poppy in a cornfield? Of what use is a rainbow? Of what use are you, numbskull? Wretch! I, too, have a soul. I want the umbrella, because—because I want its beauty to be mine!'

Rajaram put the kettle on to boil, began dusting the counter, all the time muttering: 'I'm as useful as an umbrella,' and then, after a short period of intense thought, said: 'What will you give me, babuji, if I get the umbrella for you?'

'What do you mean?' asked the old man.

'You know what I mean. What will you give me?'

'You mean to steal it, don't you, you wretch? What a delightful child you are! I'm glad you're not my son or my enemy. But look, everyone will know it has been stolen, and then how will I be able to show off with it?'

'You will have to gaze upon it in secret,' said Rajaram with a chuckle. 'Or take it into Tehri, and have it coloured red! That's your problem. But tell me, babuji, do you want it badly enough to pay me three rupees for stealing it without being seen?'

Ram Bharosa gave the boy a long, sad look. 'You're a sharp boy,' he said. 'You'll come to a bad end. I'll give you two rupees.'

'Three,' said the boy.

'Two,' said the old man.

'You don't really want it, I can see that,' said the boy.

'Wretch!' said the old man. 'Evil one! Darkener of my doorstep! Fetch me the umbrella, and I'll give you three rupees.'

V

Binya was in the forest glade where she had first seen the umbrella. No one came there for picnics during the monsoon. The grass was always wet and the pine needles were slippery underfoot. The tall trees shut out the light, and poisonous-looking mushrooms, orange and purple, sprang up everywhere. But it was a good place for porcupines, who seemed to like the mushrooms, and Binya was searching for porcupine quills.

The hill people didn't think much of porcupine quills, but far away, in southern India, the quills were valued as charms and sold at a rupee each. So Ram Bharosa paid a tenth of a rupee for each quill brought to him, and he in turn sold the quills at a profit to a trader from the plains.

Binya had already found five quills, and she knew there'd be more in the long grass. For once, she'd put her umbrella down. She had to put it aside if she was to search the ground thoroughly.

It was Rajaram's chance.

He'd been following Binya for some time, concealing himself behind trees and rocks, creeping closer whenever she became absorbed in her search. He was anxious that she should not see him and be able to recognize him later.

He waited until Binya had wandered some distance from the umbrella. Then, running forward at a crouch, he seized the open umbrella and dashed off with it.

But Rajaram had very big feet. Binya heard his heavy footsteps and turned just in time to see him as he disappeared between the trees. She cried out, dropped the porcupine quills, and gave chase.

Binya was swift and sure-footed, but Rajaram had a long stride. All the same, he made the mistake of running downhill. A long-legged person is much faster going uphill than down. Binya reached the edge of the forest glade in time to see the thief scrambling down the path to the stream. He had closed the umbrella so that it would not hinder his flight.

Binya was beginning to gain on the boy. He kept to the path, while she simply slid and leapt down the steep hillside. Near the bottom of the hill the path began to straighten out, and it was here that the long-legged boy began to forge ahead again.

Bijju was coming home from another direction. He had a bundle of sticks which he'd collected for the kitchen fire. As he reached the path, he saw Binya rushing down the hill as though all the mountain spirits in Garhwal were after her

'What's wrong?' he called. 'Why are you running?'

Binya paused only to point at the fleeing Rajaram.

'My umbrella!' she cried. 'He has stolen it!'

Bijju dropped his bundle of sticks, and ran after his sister. When he reached her side, he said, 'I'll soon catch him!' and went sprinting away over the lush green grass. He was fresh, and he was soon well ahead of Binya and gaining on the thief.

Rajaram was crossing the shallow stream when Bijju caught up with him. Rajaram was the taller boy, but Bijju was much stronger. He flung himself at the thief, caught him by the legs, and brought him down in the water. Rajaram got to his feet and tried to drag himself away, but Bijju still had him by a leg. Rajaram overbalanced and came down with a great splash. He had let the umbrella fall. It began to float away on the current. Just then Binya arrived, flushed and breathless, and went dashing into the stream after the umbrella.

Meanwhile, a tremendous fight was taking place. Locked in fierce combat, the two boys swayed together on a rock, tumbled on to the sand, rolled over and over the pebbled bank until they were again thrashing about in the shallows of the stream. The magpies, bulbuls, and other birds were disturbed, and flew away with cries of alarm.

Covered with mud, gasping and spluttering, the boys groped for each other in the water. After five minutes of frenzied struggle, Bijju emerged victorious.

Rajaram lay flat on his back on the sand, exhausted, while Bijju sat astride him, pinning him down with his arms and legs.

'Let me get up!' gasped Rajaram. 'Let me go—I don't want your useless umbrella!'

'Then why did you take it?' demanded Bijju. 'Come on—tell me why!'

'It was that skinflint Ram Bharosa,' said Rajaram. 'He told me to get it for him. He said if I didn't fetch it, I'd lose my job.'

VI

By early October, the rains were coming to an end. The leeches disappeared. The ferns turned yellow, and the sunlight on the green hills was mellow and golden, like the limes on the small tree in front of Binya's home. Bijju's days were happy ones as he came home from school, munching on roasted corn. Binya's umbrella had turned a pale milky blue, and was patched in several places, but it was still the prettiest umbrella in the village, and she still carried it with her wherever she went.

The cold, cruel winter wasn't far off, but somehow October seems longer than other months, because it is a kind month: the grass is good to be upon, the breeze is warm and gentle and pine-scented. That October, everyone seemed contented—everyone, that is, except Ram Bharosa.

The old man had by now given up all hope of ever possessing Binya's umbrella. He wished he had never set eyes on it. Because of the umbrella, he had suffered the tortures of greed, the despair of loneliness. Because of the umbrella, people had stopped coming to his shop!

Ever since it had become known that Ram Bharosa had tried to have the umbrella stolen, the village people had turned against him. They stopped trusting the old man, instead of buying their soap and tea and matches from his shop, they preferred to walk an extra mile to the shops near the Tehri bus stand. Who would have dealings with a man who had sold his soul for an umbrella? The children taunted him, twisted his name around. From 'Ram the Trustworthy' he became 'Trusty Umbrella Thief'.

The old man sat alone in his empty shop, listening to the eternal hissing of his kettle and wondering if anyone would ever again step in for a glass of tea. Ram Bharosa had lost his own appetite, and ate and drank very little. There was no money coming in. He had his savings in a bank in Tehri, but it was a terrible thing to have to dip into them! To save money, he had dismissed the blundering Rajaram. So he was left without any company. The roof leaked and the wind got in through the corrugated tin sheets, but Ram Bharosa didn't care.

Bijju and Binya passed his shop almost every day. Bijju went by with a loud but tuneless whistle. He was one of the world's whistlers; cares rested lightly on his shoulders. But, strangely enough, Binya crept quietly past the shop, looking the other way, almost as though she was in some way responsible for the misery of Ram Bharosa.

She kept reasoning with herself, telling herself that the umbrella was her very own, and that she couldn't help it if others were jealous of it. But had she loved the umbrella too much? Had it mattered more to her than people mattered? She couldn't help feeling that, in a small way, she was the cause of the sad look on Ram Bharosa's face ('His face is a yard long,' said Bijju) and the ruinous condition of his shop. It was all due to his own greed, no doubt, but she didn't want him to feel too bad about what he'd done, because it made her feel bad about herself; and so she closed the umbrella whenever she came near the shop, opening it again only when she was out of sight.

One day towards the end of October, when she had ten paise in her pocket, she entered the shop and asked the old man for a toffee.

She was Ram Bharosa's first customer in almost two weeks. He looked suspiciously at the girl. Had she come to taunt him, to flaunt the umbrella in his face? She had placed her coin on the counter. Perhaps it was a bad coin. Ram Bharosa picked it up and bit it; he held it up to the light; he rang it on the ground. It was a good coin. He gave Binya the toffee.

Binya had already left the shop when Ram Bharosa saw the closed umbrella lying on his counter. There it was, the blue umbrella he had always wanted, within his grasp at last! He had only to hide it at the back of his shop, and no one would know that he had it, no one could prove that Binya had left it behind.

He stretched out his trembling, bony hand, and took the umbrella by the handle. He pressed it open. He stood beneath it, in the dark shadows of his shop, where no sun or rain could ever touch it.

'But I'm never in the sun or in the rain,' he said aloud. 'Of what use is an umbrella to me?'

And he hurried outside and ran after Binya.

'Binya, Binya!' he shouted. 'Binya, you've left your umbrella behind!'

He wasn't used to running, but he caught up with her, held out the umbrella, saying, 'You forgot it—the umbrella!'

In that moment it belonged to both of them.

But Binya didn't take the umbrella. She shook her head and said, 'You keep it. I don't need it any more.'

'But it's such a pretty umbrella!' protested Ram Bharosa. 'It's the best umbrella in the village.'

'I know,' said Binya. 'But an umbrella isn't everything.'

And she left the old man holding the umbrella, and went tripping down the road, and there was nothing between her and the bright blue sky.

VII

Well, now that Ram Bharosa has the blue umbrella—a gift from Binya, as he tells everyone—he is sometimes persuaded to go out into the sun or the rain, and as a result he looks much healthier. Sometimes he uses the umbrella to chase away pigs or goats. It is always left open outside the shop, and anyone who wants to borrow it may do so; and, so in a way, it has become everyone's umbrella. It is faded and patchy, but it is still the best umbrella in the village.

People are visiting Ram Bharosa's shop again. Whenever Bijju or Binya stop for a cup of tea, he gives them a little extra milk or sugar. They like their tea sweet and milky.

A few nights ago, a bear visited Ram Bharosa's shop. There had been snow on the higher ranges of the Himalayas, and the bear had been finding it difficult to obtain food; so it had come lower down, to see what it could pick up near the village. That night it scrambled on to the tin roof of Ram Bharosa's shop, and made off with a huge pumpkin which had been ripening on the roof. But in climbing off the roof, the bear had lost a claw.

Next morning, Ram Bharosa found the claw just outside the door of his shop. He picked it up and put it in his pocket. A bear's claw was a lucky find.

A day later, when he went into the market town, he took the claw with him, and left it with a silversmith, giving the craftsman certain instructions. The silversmith made a locket for the claw, then he gave it a thin silver chain. When Ram Bharosa came again, he paid the silversmith ten rupees for his work.

The days were growing shorter, and Binya had to be home a little earlier every evening. There was a hungry leopard at large, and she couldn't leave the cows out after dark.

She was hurrying past Ram Bharosa's shop when the old man called out to her.

'Binya, spare a minute! I want to show you something.'

Binya stepped into the shop.

'What do you think of it?' asked Ram Bharosa, showing her the silver pendant with the claw.

'It's so beautiful,' said Binya, just touching the claw and the silver chain.

'It's a bear's claw,' said Ram Bharosa. 'That's even luckier than a leopard's claw. Would you like to have it?'

'I have no money,' said Binya.

'That doesn't matter. You gave me the umbrella, I give you the claw! Come, let's see what it looks like on you.'

He placed the pendant on Binya, and indeed it looked very beautiful on her.

Ram Bharosa says he will never forget the smile she gave him when she left the shop.

She was halfway home when she realized she had left the cows behind.

'Neelu, Neelu!' she called. 'Oh, Gori!'

There was a faint tinkle of bells as the cows came slowly down the mountain path.

In the distance she could hear her mother and Bijju calling for her.

She began to sing. They heard her singing, and knew she was safe and near.

She walked home through the darkening glade, singing of the stars, and the trees stood still and listened to her, and the mountains were glad.

8

THE MADIGA GIRL

CHALAM

Translated from the Telugu by Dasu Krishnamoorty and Tamraparni Dasu

It was December vacation when, without telling anyone, I travelled to my wife's village to see how she was doing after I'd impregnated her for the sixth time in the eight years of our marriage. People in the village give the impression that they have nothing more to do on earth other than wait for their end. The fragrance of dew-drenched hay, the greenness of the crop, the freshness of grass underneath, and the music of the carefree birds hold you in thrall, like the memories of your ancestors who've left you behind.

I spent a sleepless night, ruing the thirty-five years I'd wasted, cooped up in wobbly office chairs or lounging in the sagging string cot in my wife's village. A village that seems to have an unfair share of glossy-skinned beauties bursting with life. Those girls, the village belles, with sinewy muscles undulating under their ebony skin! When I see them, unable to rein in their voluptuous charms behind their flimsy saris, I'm tempted to prostrate and pay obeisance, ignoring the risk of being flattened by an oncoming lorry, or the call of pending files, or the shrivelled visage of my supervisor.

Just as you can't help but caress a cool, smooth marble surface, or the mane of a freshly groomed thoroughbred, or the hackles of swan-like doves, I've an irresistible longing to stroke the nubile bodies of the village damsels. No matter that they're not beautiful, or decked in gold, or draped in snow-white Uppada or gossamer Benares saris, or that their hair is undone, or that they have rustic forms, or that they lack the delicate complexion of their sophisticated counterparts. What man wouldn't give his life to get lost in those mesmerizing curves? And to gawk at the gait that animates their hourglass waists and the pure sheen of their bodies?

They don't flee at the sight of a stranger, or peep from behind doors, or shy away mumbling inaudible invective when you greet them. They laugh all the time, their pearly teeth gleaming pure white, like the perfectly set seeds in a tender pomegranate. They are not laughing at you. I think it is the sheer joy of living that courses through their bodies, the thrill of enjoying the God-given light and air. It is difficult to say whether the caprice in their eyes is the glint of the setting sun or the burden of the grace of their bosom.

My very first evening in my wife's village revived an acute desire that had been killed by kitchen smells, wailing kids, remonstrating supervisors, and visitors baiting me with bribes. It is not the mundane desire that familiarity and a home-cooked meal arouse in you. Nor is it the hurried act and the stealthy exit after a promiscuous rendezvous that make you vow never to see the face of the wayward bitch again. It is the call of the cowherd beckoning the straggling herd home, the tingling when the cool breeze scatters her hair and caresses the back of her neck. Then I want my love to sit by my side, smile, and, pressing her young bosom into my flesh, look into my eyes.

Such a desire is natural in any living, breathing human being; I could never conquer it despite my best efforts. I'm timid. In my village, such thoughts would never cross my mind. Toiling, eating, going to bed, making love, and loafing about with fellow clerks are the things that make me happy. But the breeze here, in my wife's village, is so intoxicating that I can't rein in unruly thoughts. Even God, my creator, couldn't have suppressed them. Not even those worthies who invented morality to deny men and women their due could accomplish this.

You've seen the coastal highway, haven't you? The road runs sandwiched between the canal and the plantations. The sun fills the canal waters with twinkling images of swaying orchards. It was on this road that one day my heart skipped a beat at the sound of a giggle that had the melody of a gurgling stream. I stood in the middle of the road, enchanted by words falling to the ground like rose petals. A song filled the air. 'Does she, the source of this music, have a care in this world?' I wondered. That laughter merged magically with the morning light, the limpid water, and the birds' love songs. 'Did this same laughter stir the flowers, the air, and the coconut fronds?'

Fifteen minutes later, she appeared before me like a nymph, emerging from inside the orchards, talking to an old Muslim man and singing. She was in her early twenties and wore a red sari. She approached the canal, hitched up her petticoat and stepped into the water to wade through. My searing scrutiny failed to dent her equanimity. I'd never seen such a resplendent complexion. She wore no blouse. Her sari covered her bosom. One glimpse of her velvety body conjured up a new moon in a sky lit up by stars; all those poetic descriptions you read in the epics fail to do justice to the radiance of her body. A speck of dust has no choice but to slide off her marble-smooth skin. The sun played hide and seek on her shoulders. The mere thought of the curves of her shoulders…oh my lord, ignited the body with desire. The dark thighs radiated a blinding light under the hoisted hem of her petticoat.

My wife, with her distended abdomen, reedy arms, and the elongated neck of a stork, greeted me when I returned home from that visit to paradise.

'Where did you go, so early in the morning?'

I ignored the question and fled inside, afraid to meet her eyes. By all accounts, my wife is a beautiful woman. She has all the attributes of beauty mentioned in the ancient scriptures. She has an hourglass middle when she is not pregnant. She is fidelity personified. I think she would spit at the nymph, were she to see her. But my infatuation with the rustic damsel was such that I'd have readily strangled my wife that night. If I had to choose between the damsel and the office of a governor, I'd be the first to sign a document relinquishing the office.

Restless, I ventured out again that afternoon. The rain had spoilt the day but the evening after the rain was magnificent. The roads were puddled. The trees and birds were busy flicking off raindrops. The breeze romped with joy. The desire to see her had become acute, like a school-going child wanting to skip classes. 'What more would I want in life, once I have her friendship? How about caressing her hand, her curves!' My thoughts hit a low. In my mind, I could see the water flow under the fickle shade of the coconut palms, the grass flanking the cool, moving waters, and a strong wind fluttering her sari. The furtive glances of her love-filled eyes intoxicated me.

If this dream comes true, does it matter if I slave as a clerk for the rest of my life, or face an abusive supervisor? I would ask everyone, 'Miserable fellows, what do you know about the sensual pleasures of rasa and happiness?'

I arrived at the orchard and settled down for a long wait. No trace of life. Half an hour later, I saw my swaying beauty returning from some unknown rendezvous. It didn't take long to start a conversation with the simple girl. We start trading pleasantries.

'It's slushy here. Let's find a better spot,' she said, and guided me to the veranda of a factory next to the orchard. We stood there chatting. I was happy to stand close to her, close enough to read the thoughts that animated her face. Isn't it enough for me if her eyes meet my gaze, enough to look at her as she stealthily watches the road for fear of detection, pulling back the inconstant sari onto her shoulder?

'What will the passers-by think of us? They are foul-mouthed. Come stand here,' she said and pulled me aside.

'I first mistook you for the mailman. He often passes this way like Brahma,' she giggled.

That laughter erased my jealous thoughts about the mailman and disarmed me. What was I to do? Could I be content with appropriating that laughter, kissing those smiling lips, touching her tremulous neck, and pressing against her swaying bosom? Why is this silly mailman spoiling the fun? Should I slaughter him, burn him, or simply trample him?

'Why are you chatting with me for so long...don't you have important matters to take care of?' she asked me.

'Because I have a crush on you.'

'What a joke! We're poor folk. No nice clothes or ornaments. Only darkness and crudeness,' she said and stretched her arms forward. A raging desire to grab her hands and taunt her to free herself swept over me, but I held back, afraid of scaring her away. In those ten minutes, I longed several times to touch her but fear stood in my way.

An inner voice told me to act fast before someone showed up and time ran out. But courage failed me. A passer-by might notice!

To prolong the conversation, I asked her if the orchard belonged to her family.

'Oh, you want to see the orchard? Come,' she said and led the way.

I trailed her, watching her swaying behind. Ah, the curves. I realized what I'd missed until now and rued my barren life.

'Watch for carpenter ants, come this side,' she said and pulled me aside. Was it intentional? I was not sure.

We stood behind the dense hibiscus growth. She plucked two flowers and tucked them into her serpentine braid. That tug lifted her bosom and chased my fears and reticence away. I clasped her hands. The firm flesh of her arms resisted my touch. Such delight! Such warmth and smoothness! How different from the married ones who give in too readily, and then act coy. Depressing, my god!

What a contrast those five minutes were! How can I explain my delightful plight? The more she tried to free herself the tighter I held her. But my hands kept slipping. My strength ebbed. The natural scent of her body was making me feel faint—the perfumes arrayed in the attar vendor's shop are no match! Neither is the fragrant rosemary that homeless urchins sell on passenger trains. Her presence exuded a feral scent, a commingling of the scent of the scorched earth after rain and of the fragrance of the musk deer. I would gladly spurn divinity and immortality in exchange for these few moments.

She pushed me away and in mock anger said, 'Please, don't touch me.' Then she ran off to the riverbank, laughing. Was she amused by my shock and disappointment?

I followed her, admiring her loping gait, like a heifer. Letting me move closer, she leant in towards me.

'I'm not that type,' she said, and laughed in an odd way.

My head began to reel. I was having difficulty keeping my eyes open. Her eyes, her entire body were mocking me now.

'The sun barely sets before couples sneak into those rooms.' She laughed again pointing to some shacks not far from us. 'They've no shame, nothing,' she said.

I was intrigued. Who is this woman? Is this a charade or genuine innocence?

'Men like you think I'm that type. We're respectable folks. Now, hands off...no more mischief. Who do you think I am?'

What does she see in my eyes, despair, or resignation? As I stare stupidly, she comes close to me. She nudges my shoulder with her bosom and passes her hand across my pocket.

'There's no rice for the night. If you can give me....'

I averted my face; I couldn't look her in the eye. That statement shattered my dreams. My heart bled at the loss of the beauty and romance I'd imagined. I couldn't believe that she was of the same ilk as the jewellery-crazed, mansion-inhabiting city vampires. But I was not ready to shun her. Perhaps she really needed money for the night meal. Before I could answer, an old woman spotted us.

She asked the girl, 'Who is this fellow? What are you doing here?'

Oh my god, would she complain that I was trying to molest her? Or, is she just playing with me? I regretted having met her. I began imagining terrible things—public humiliation, my in-laws discovering their son-in-law messing around with a Madiga girl.

'Nothing, he wanted to see the garden,' the girl said.

'What business do you have with these men? Go home, girl! Ha, wanted to see the garden!' the old woman scoffed.

The girl hesitated.

'Why aren't you leaving? Do you want me to tell your father to thrash you?'

'Don't be angry. This man is a gentleman, don't you see? You're angry for no reason.'

'Hmm, everyone is a gentleman. There is no rice for the night. Go get some. Will chatting with gentlemen fill your stomach?' the old woman barked and left.

'My mother,' the girl said.

'Do you really have no food? Whose orchard is this, then?'

'We leased it, but it is always losing money. This year is no different.'

I pulled out a five-rupee note.

'Come inside,' she said.

'Not now, I have to go.'

'Not now? Then when?'

'I won't come again.'

'Why?'

'I have nothing to do here.'

'Then why did you come today?'

The question rattled me.

'I never thought you were this type.'

'What type do you think I am?'

'You'll do anything for money.'

She bit her lip and looked at me with tear-filled eyes.

'Why did you pay me, then?' Her voice shook.

'Because you need something to eat.'

She stood silently as two tears rolled down her chest. A cuckoo warbled incessantly. A humid breeze floated in. The dying rays of the sun kissed her hands. Stray strands of hair fell over the flowers in her braid. Her beauty beckoned me again. Spontaneously, my lips brushed her tear-filled eyes. I was happy to be with her but the matter of money still irked me. I made a move to leave.

'You may go but listen to me for a moment,' she pleaded.

'I'm listening,' I said, rooted to the spot.

'Will you come inside that room with me?'

'All right, let's go,' I said.

She steered me into the room and bolted the door. In one corner of the room were a cot covered with a cotton mat, a soiled pillow, and many bidi stubs on the floor.

'What?' I asked her, confused.

She let her sari drop down deftly and placed my hand on her bare bosom. Would I have pulled my hand back were it not for the smelly room, the dirty bed, and the bidi stubs? Would I not feast on that body? Would I not greedily take in that neck, that belly button? Just their sight gave me all the bliss I needed in this birth.

'No,' I said, retrieving my hand with some effort.

'Why did you touch me a while ago when we were in the garden?' she said combatively, adding, 'I'm not as cheap as you think.'

Her eyes filled again, her lip trembled, and she drew back. I did not know what to do.

She stretched out her hand and pressed the five-rupee note into my palm and closed it.

'Where will you find food for the night?' I asked her.

The look she gave me would have reduced any mortal to ashes.

'Are you angry with me?' I asked.

'What does it matter? The anger of lowly people like us does not count.'

'Look, you're angry.'

'Not at all. You may go now.'

'Please accept this,' I said stretching out the note.

'Not if it is charity.'

'Is it worse than the way you make money?'

Silence.

'I'm your friend. This is a gift; I can't see you go hungry. Please accept.'

I touched her cheek with affection and gazed at her. She slumped onto the bed, covered her eyes with her palms, and cried. I knew this would happen. I wiped the tears and kissed her eyes and sat by her side.

'Why do you cry?' I asked.

She did not reply, but I knew she wanted to tell me something. I waited.

'You think I asked you for money for myself? But it has become my job, my living, whether I like it or not. We've always lived beyond our means. I guess my mother used to raise extra money in this manner. One day, she gifted me to Venkayya, a man of our caste.

'We owed him a few hundred rupees. He tried to take me when I was asleep. I shouted for help but Mother had already left. My father too.

'I ran all over the orchard and hid behind a jujube bush, gasping. It was a full moon night. He found me and threw me down. I fought him till my strength failed. I collapsed. I closed my eyes and awaited the worst. But I don't know what came over him. He bashed my head against the ground, spat, and left, cursing my parents. I was lying there like a corpse when my mother came and began beating me and complaining that I hadn't pleased him. I told her I wasn't going to allow him to enter me. That angered her more and another round of thrashing followed. "Who'll repay the debts; your husband?" she yelled.'

'What happened then?' I asked.

'Oh, what a night that was! He returned the next day. "I'll kill you if you touch me,"' I told him. My mother threw me out again.

'There was no one to help me. My husband, whom I had never seen after I came of age, had migrated to Rangoon.'

'You must have been in quite a difficult spot,' I said.

'I was. There was hardly a man who didn't ogle me whenever I stepped out. I was too innocent and didn't understand the meaning of those looks. Over time, I began to fear my beauty. I realized why Muslim women wore the burqa. The lecherous looks of these men bothered me more than their touch or illicit caress. I wanted to spit in their faces.'

'Then?' I asked her.

'One day, the owner of the factory asked me to report for the night shift. I refused. "You won't get any wages, then," he said. How do we repay our mounting debt? So, I reported for the night shift. There was no one else in the factory. He grabbed my hand. I told him not to touch me. "I'm a Madiga and you're a Brahmin. It doesn't befit you," I told him. I managed to slip out and ran to his house, not far from the factory, and fell at the feet of his mother and wife. "Don't touch us, you Madiga," they shouted. "What about your son who is stalking a Madiga?" I asked them.'

She paused for a minute to catch her breath.

'They hurled a sickle at me. The owner came and tried to molest me regardless of the presence of his wife and mother. I picked up the sickle and threw it at his face and fled. Soon, the police caught me and locked me up in jail. A constable came by and said he could get me out if I agreed to sleep with him. I didn't. He beat me till I became unconscious. Then he had me. Then others followed.'

She sighed.

'That was it. After I'd lost my chastity, there was no point in virtue, I thought. I agreed to become Venkayya's concubine. He gave me good clothes, jewellery, good food. When he died, I was back on the streets again. This is the only way I know to save my family from starvation. Tell me, is there any other way?'

I had no answer.

MAHESH

SARAT CHANDRA CHATTOPADHYAY

Translated from the Bengali by Arunava Sinha

I

The village was named Kashipur. An insignificant village, with an even more insignificant zamindar, but such was his authority that his subjects were in awe of him.

It was the birthday of the zamindar's youngest son. Having performed the holy rituals, Tarkaratna, the priest, was on his way home in the afternoon. The month of Boishakh was drawing to a close, but there was not even a trace of clouds anywhere, the searing sky seemingly pouring fire on everything below. The field stretching to the horizon before him was parched and cracked, with the blood in the veins of the earth escaping constantly through the crevices in the form of vapour. Gazing at it coiling upwards like flames made the head reel with drunkenness.

Gafoor Jolha lived on the edge of this field. The earthen wall surrounding his house had collapsed, merging his yard with the road. The privacy of the inner chambers had all but surrendered itself to the mercy of the passer-by.

Pausing in the shade of a white teak tree, Tarkaratna called out loudly, 'Are you home, Gafra?'

Gafoor's ten-year-old daughter came to the door. 'What do you need Baba for? He's got a fever.'

'Fever! Call the swine! Monster! Godless creature!'

The screaming and shouting brought Gafoor Mian to the door, shivering with fever. An ancient acacia stood next to the broken wall, with a bull tethered to it. Pointing to it, Tarkaratna said, 'What's all this? Have you forgotten this is a Hindu village with a Brahmin zamindar?' Red with rage and the heat, his words were fiery, but Gafoor, unable to understand the reason for the outburst, could only stare at him.

'When I passed this way in the morning he was tethered there,' said Tarkaratna, 'and now on my way back he's still tethered the same way. Karta will bury you alive if you kill a bull. He's a devout Brahmin.'

'What can I do, Baba Thakur, I have no choice. I've had this fever for several days now. I collapse every time I try to take him to graze.'

'Then turn him loose, he'll find food on his own.'

'Where can I turn him loose, Baba Thakur? The winnowing isn't done, the grain is still lying in the fields. The hay hasn't been sorted, the earth is burning, there's not a blade of grass anywhere. What if he eats someone's grains or hay—how can I turn him loose, Baba Thakur?'

Softening, Tarkaratna said, 'If you can't let him loose at least give him some straw. Hasn't your daughter made any rice? Give him a bowl of starch and water.'

Gafoor did not answer, only looked at Tarkaratna helplessly and sighed.

Tarkaratna said, 'No rice either? What did you do with the hay? Did you sell your entire share without keeping anything for your beast? You butcher!'

Gafoor seemed to lose his power of speech at this cruel accusation. A little later he said haltingly, 'I did get some hay this year, but Karta Moshai took it away to pay for taxes left over from last year. I fell at his feet, I said, "Babu Moshai, you're the supreme authority, where will I go if I leave your kingdom, give me at least a little hay. There's no straw for the roof, we have just the one room for father and daughter, we can still manage with palm leaves this monsoon, but my Mahesh will die of starvation."'

With a mocking smile, Tarkaratna said, 'Really! What a loving name, Mahesh. I'll die laughing.'

Paying no attention to the taunt, Gafoor continued, 'But the lord had no mercy on me. He allowed me some rice to feed us for two months, but all my hay was confiscated and the poor thing got nothing at all.' His voice grew moist with tears. But this evoked no compassion in Tarkaratna, who said, 'What a man you are. You've eaten up everything but don't want to pay your dues. Do you expect the zamindar to feed you? You people live in a perfect kingdom, still you bad-mouth him, you're such wretches.'

An embarrassed Gafoor said, 'Why should we bad-mouth him, Baba

Thakur, we don't do that. But how do I pay my taxes? I sharecrop four bighas, but there's been a famine two years in a row—the grains have all dried up. My daughter and I don't even get two meals a day. Look at the house, when it rains we spend the night in a corner, there's not even enough space to stretch our legs. Look at Mahesh, Thakur Moshai, you can count his ribs. Lend me a little hay, Thakur Moshai, let the creature feed to his heart's content for a few days.' Still speaking, he flung himself to the ground near the Brahmin's feet. Leaping backwards hastily, Tarkaratna exclaimed, 'My god, are you going to touch me?'

'No, Baba Thakur, I'm not going to touch you or anything. But give me some hay. I saw your four huge haystacks the other day, you won't even know if a little of it is gone. I don't care if we starve to death, but this poor creature cannot talk, he only stares and weeps.'

Tarkaratna said, 'And how do you propose to repay the loan?'

A hopeful Gafoor said, 'I'll find a way to repay it somehow, Baba Thakur, I won't cheat you.'

Snorting, Tarkaratna mimicked Gafoor, 'I won't cheat you! I'll find a way to return it somehow! What a comedian! Get out of my way. I should be getting home, it's late.' Chuckling, he took a step forward only to retreat several steps in fear. Angrily he said, 'Oh god, he's waving his horns, is he going to gore me now?'

Gafoor rose to his feet. Pointing to the bundle of fruit and moistened rice in the priest's hand, he said, 'He's smelt food, he wants to eat....'

'Wants to eat? Of course. Both master and bull are well-matched. Can't get hay to eat, and now you want fruits. Get him out of my way. Those horns, someone will be killed by them.' Tarkaratna hurried away.

Gafoor turned towards Mahesh, gazing at him in silence for a few moments. There was suffering and hunger in the bull's deep black eyes. Gafoor said, 'He wouldn't give you any, would he? They have so much, but still they won't. Never mind.' He choked, and tears began to roll down from his eyes. Going up to the animal, he stroked his back and neck, whispering, 'You are my son, Mahesh, you've grown old looking after us for eight years, I can't even give you enough to eat, but you know how much I love you.'

Mahesh responded by stretching his neck and closing his eyes in pleasure. Wiping his tears off the bull's back, Gafoor murmured, 'The zamindar took away your food, leased out the grazing ground near the crematorium just for money. How will I save your life in this year of starvation? If I turn you loose, you'll eat other people's hay, you'll spoil their trees—what do I do with you! You have no strength left, people tell me to sell you off.' No sooner had Gafoor said this in his head than his tears began to roll down again. Wiping them with his hand, he looked around surreptitiously before fetching some discoloured straw from behind his dilapidated house and placing them near Mahesh's mouth, saying, 'Eat up quickly, if not there'll be....'

'Baba?'

'Yes, Ma?'

'Come and eat,' said Amina, appearing at the door. After a glance she said, 'You're giving Mahesh straw from the roof again, Baba?'

This was just what he was afraid of. Reddening, he said, 'Old rotten straw, Ma, it was falling off anyway....'

'I heard you pulling it out, Baba.'

'No, Ma, not exactly pulling it out....'

'But the wall will collapse, Baba....'

Gafoor was silent. The house was all they had left, and no one knew better than him that if he continued this way it wouldn't survive the next monsoon. But how long could they go on?

His daughter said, 'Wash your hands and come, Baba, I've served the food.'

Gafoor said, 'Bring the starch out, Ma, let me feed Mahesh first.'

'No starch left today, Baba, it dried in the pot.'

No starch? Gafoor stood in silence. His ten-year-old daughter knew that when the times were bad even this could not be wasted. He washed his hands and went in. His daughter served him rice and vegetables on a brass plate, taking some for herself on an earthen plate. Gafoor said softly, 'I'm feeling cold again, Amina, is it safe to eat with a fever?'

Amina asked anxiously, 'But didn't you say you were hungry?'

'Maybe I didn't have a fever then, Ma.'

'Then let me put it away, you can have it in the evening.'

Shaking his head, Gafoor said, 'Eating cold food will make things worse.'

'What should I do then?' asked Amina.

Gafoor pretended to think before solving the problem. He said, 'Why don't you give it to Mahesh, Ma? You can make me some fresh rice at night, can't you?'

Amina looked at him in silence for a few moments before lowering her eyes, nodding, and saying, 'Yes, Baba, I can.'

Gafoor reddened. Besides the two actors, only someone up there observed this little charade between father and daughter.

II

Five or six days later, Gafoor was seated outside his front door with an anxious expression on his face. Mahesh had not been home since yesterday morning. He himself was too weak to move, so his daughter Amina had searched high and low for the bull. Returning home in the late afternoon, she said, 'Have you heard, Baba, Manik Ghosh's family has taken our Mahesh to the police station?'

'What nonsense,' said Gafoor.

'It's true, Baba. Their servant said, "Tell your father to look for him in the Dariapur pen."'

'What did he do?'

'He got into their garden and destroyed their trees, Baba.'

Gafoor sat in silence. He had imagined all manner of mishaps that might have befallen Mahesh, but had not anticipated this. He was as harmless as he was poor, which was why he had no apprehensions of being punished so severely by any of his neighbours—Manik Ghosh, in particular, for his respect for cows was legendary.

His daughter said, 'It's getting late, Baba, aren't you going to bring Mahesh home?'

'No,' answered Gafoor.

'But they said the police will sell him in the cattle market after three days.'

'Let them sell him,' said Gafoor.

Amina did not know what exactly a cattle market was, but she had noticed her father becoming agitated whenever it was mentioned with reference to Mahesh. She left without another word.

Under cover of the night Gafoor went to Bansi's shop, and said, 'Khuro, I need a rupee,' and deposited his brass plate beneath the raised platform on which Bansi sat. Bansi was familiar with the exact weight and other details of this object. It had been pawned some five times in the past two years, for a rupee each time. So, he did not object this time either.

Mahesh was seen in his usual place the next day. Beneath the same tree, tethered to the same stake with the same rope, the same empty bowl with no food in front of him, the same questioning look in the moist, hungry black eyes. An elderly Muslim man was examining him closely. Gafoor Mian sat nearby, his knees drawn up to his chin. When the examination was over, the man extracted a ten-rupee note from the knot in his dhoti and, smoothening it repeatedly, went up to Gafoor, saying, 'I don't need change, take the whole thing—here.'

Holding his hand out for the money, Gafoor remained sitting in silence. But just as the old Muslim's companions were about to untie the bull, he suddenly jumped to his feet, saying belligerently, 'Don't you dare touch that rope, I'm warning you.'

They were startled. The old man said in surprise, 'Why not?'

Still furious, Gafoor said, 'What do you mean, why not? It's mine to sell or not. And I'm not selling.' He threw the ten-rupee note on the ground.

They said, 'But you took an advance yesterday.'

'Here's your advance.' Retrieving two rupees from the knot in his dhoti, he flung the coins at them, and they fell with a clatter. Realizing that a quarrel was imminent, the old man said gently with a smile, 'You're putting pressure on us for two rupees more, aren't you? Go on, give his daughter two rupees more. That's what you wanted, isn't it?'

'No.'

'Are you aware that no one will give you a better price?'

'No,' said Gafoor, shaking his head vehemently.

The old man said in annoyance, 'What do you think? Only the skin is worth selling. There's nothing else in there.'

'Tauba! Tauba!' A terrible expletive suddenly escaped Gafoor's lips, and the very next moment he ran into his house threatening to have them thrashed within an inch of their lives by the zamindar's guards unless they left the village at once.

The possibility of trouble made them leave, but soon Gafoor received a summons from the zamindar's court. He realized that word had reached the landowner.

There were people both refined and unrefined in court. Glaring at Gafoor, Shibu Babu said, 'I don't know how to punish you, Gafra. Do you know where you live?'

Bowing, Gafoor said, 'I do. We're starving, or else I would have paid whatever fine you think fit.'

Everyone present was astonished. They had always considered him an obstinate and bad-tempered man. And here he was on the verge of tears, saying, 'I'll never do it again, Karta.' He proceeded to box his own ears, rubbed his nose into the ground from one end of the court to the other, and then stood up.

Shibu Babu said indulgently, 'All right, enough. Don't do all this again.'

Everyone was shocked when they heard the details. They were certain that only the grace of the zamindar and the fear of punishment had prevented the abject sinner from committing worse transgressions. Tarkaratna was present, and provided the scriptural analysis of the word 'go' for cow, enlightening everyone as to why it was forbidden to allow this godless race of heathens to live within village limits.

Gafoor did not respond to any of this, humbly accepting all the humiliation and vilification and returning home cheerfully. Borrowing the starch from the rice pots of neighbours, he gave it to Mahesh to eat, murmuring many endearments as he stroked the bull's back and horns.

III

The month of Joishtho was drawing to a close. The sun was still harsh and severe in the sky. There was no trace of mercy anywhere. People were afraid to even hope for change, hope that the skies could again be moist and pleasurable with the weight of rain-bearing clouds. It seemed that there would be no cessation to the flames burning constantly across the entire fiery earth—that they would not die down till they had consumed everything.

Gafoor returned home on such an afternoon. He was not used to working as a labourer on someone else's fields, and it had been only four or five days since the fever had subsided. He was as weak as he was exhausted. Still, he had gone out in search of work, but all he had got was the unforgiving heat and sun overhead. He could barely see for hunger and thirst. Standing at the door, he called out, 'Amina, is the food ready?'

His daughter emerged slowly and stood grasping the post without an answer.

Gafoor shouted, 'Not ready? Why not?'

'No rice at home, Baba.'

'No rice? Why didn't you tell me in the morning?'

'But I told you last night.'

Contorting his face and mocking her, Gafoor said, 'Told you last night! How can anyone remember if you tell them at night?' The harsh tone he was using stoked his anger. Contorting his face even further, he said, 'How will there be any rice? Whether the sick father gets any or not, the grown-up daughter will eat five times a day. I'm going to lock up the rice from now on. Give me some water, I'm dying of thirst. Now tell me we have no water either.'

Amina remained standing with her eyes downcast. When Gafoor realized after waiting a few moments that there was not even any water to drink at home, he could control himself no longer. Striding up to his daughter, he slapped her resoundingly, saying, 'Haramjaadi, what do you do all day? Why can't you die?'

Without a word his daughter picked up the empty pitcher and went out in the heat, wiping her eyes. Gafoor felt heartbroken as soon as she was out of sight. He alone knew how he had brought up his daughter after her mother's death. He remembered that it was not the dutiful and affectionate girl's fault. Ever since they had run out of the paltry amount of rice he had received for his work in the fields, they had not had two meals a day. On some days, just one—or not even that. His accusation that Amina was eating five times a day was as impossible as it was untrue. Nor was he unaware of the reasons for the lack of water to drink. The two or three tanks in the village were all dry. The little water there was in the pond behind Shibcharan Babu's house was not available to ordinary people. The water that could be collected by digging a hole or two in the middle of the tanks was fought over by a crowd of people.

Being a Muslim, the young girl was not even allowed near that water. She had to wait for hours, pleading for some water, and only if someone took pity on her, and poured her a little could she bring it home. He knew all this. Perhaps there had been no water that day, or no one had had the time to take pity on his daughter during the battle. Realizing that something like this must have taken place, Gafoor found his own eyes filling with tears. At that moment the zamindar's footman appeared like a messenger of death, screaming, 'Gafra, are you home?'

Gafoor answered bitterly, 'I am. Why?'

'Babu Moshai has sent for you. Come along.'

Gafoor said, 'I haven't eaten yet. I'll come later.'

Unable to tolerate such audacity, the footman swore and said, 'The Babu has ordered me to flog you and force you to come.'

Gafoor forgot himself a second time, uttering an unprintable word in retaliation, and said, 'No one is a slave in the kingdom of the empress. I pay my taxes, I won't go.'

But for such a small man to give such a big reason was not just futile but also dangerous. Fortunately, such an insignificant voice would not reach the ears of the important man it was meant for—or else he would have lost both his home and his livelihood. There is no need for an elaborate account of what ensued, but when he returned from the zamindar's court an hour later and lay down in silence, his face and eyes were swollen. The primary cause of such severe punishment was Mahesh. After Gafoor had gone out, Mahesh had broken free from the post, entered the zamindar's yard, eaten his flowers, spoilt the paddy put out in the sun, and, when about to be caught, had made his escape after knocking the zamindar's youngest daughter to the ground. This was not the first time it had happened, but Gafoor had been pardoned earlier on the grounds of being poor. He might have been pardoned this time too had he begged and pleaded as in the past, but what he had said—that he paid his taxes and was no one's servant—was the kind of arrogance from a subject that Shibcharan Babu, being a zamindar, could not tolerate. Gafoor had not protested in the slightest against the thrashing and the humiliation, bearing it all in silence. Back home, too, he sat coiled up in silence. He had no awareness of hunger or thirst, but his heart was burning just like the noonday sky outside. However, when he heard his daughter's stricken cry from the yard, he leapt to his feet and ran outside to find Amina lying on the ground and Mahesh lapping up the water trickling out of the shattered pitcher. Gafoor lost his mind. Picking up the plough-head he had brought home yesterday to repair, he smashed Mahesh's head with it repeatedly.

Mahesh tried to lift his head just once, then his starving, skinny body slumped to the ground. A few tears rolled down his eyes, along with a few drops of blood from his ears. His entire body trembled once or twice, after which, stretching out his front and hind legs, Mahesh died.

Amina sobbed, 'What have you done, Baba, our Mahesh is dead.'

Gafoor had turned to stone, neither moving nor speaking, only staring at a pair of unblinking, bottomless dark eyes.

Within an hour or two, a group of cobblers from one end of the village arrived, and slinging Mahesh up on a pole took him to the dumping ground. Gafoor trembled when he saw their shining knives, but closing his eyes, he didn't say a word.

The neighbours said that the zamindar had sent someone to Tarkaratna to find out what should be done next, 'You may have to sell your house as penance.'

Gafoor did not reply to any of this, burying his face in his knees and not moving.

Late that night he woke his daughter up, saying, 'Amina, we must go.'

She had fallen asleep outside the front door. Rubbing her eyes and sitting up, she said, 'Where will we go, Baba?'

Gafoor said, 'To work at the jute mill in Phulbere.'

His daughter looked at him in astonishment. Despite all their troubles her father had never been willing to work at the jute mill. She had often heard him say that it was impossible to maintain one's faith there, that women had neither honour nor protection.

Gafoor said, 'Hurry up, Ma, we have to walk a long way.'

Amina was about to take the tumbler and the brass plate her father ate from, but Gafoor stopped her. 'Leave them here, Ma, they will pay for my penance for Mahesh.'

He left in the dead of night, holding his daughter's hand. He had no family in this village, no one to inform. Crossing the yard, he stopped abruptly beneath the familiar tree and suddenly burst into tears. Raising his eyes to the star-studded black sky, he said, 'Allah! Punish me as you will, but my Mahesh died with a thirst. There was no land he could graze on. Do not forgive the sin of whoever it was who did not let him eat the grass you gave us, or quench his thirst with the water you gave us.'

10

OF FISTS AND RUBS

ISMAT CHUGHTAI

Translated from the Urdu by Muhammad Umar Memon

There was quite a crush of people at the polling station, as if it was the premiere of some movie. A long line stretched out to infinity. Five years ago, too, we'd formed such endless lines, as if we'd come to buy cheap grain, not to cast a vote. Wisps of hope flitted across our faces: regardless of how long the lines, our turn was bound to come sometime. And then you just watch, we'll be raking in piles and piles of money. He's our trusted man; the reins of good fortune will be in the hands of one of our own. All our miseries will vanish.

'Bai, oh Bai! How are you?' The woman wrapped in a dirty-looking kashta bared her filthy yellow teeth and grabbed my hand.

'Oh, it's you, Ganga Bai....'

'No, Ratti Bai. Ganga Bai was the other one. She died, poor woman.'

'What a pity! Poor woman....' And my mind zoomed back five years. 'Rubs or fists?' I asked.

'Rubs,' Ratti Bai winked. 'I kept telling her not to, but why would she listen, the blasted woman. Who are you voting for, Bai?'

'And you, who for?' we asked each other casually.

'Our caste-wallah, of course. He comes from our area.'

'Five years ago, too, you voted for a man of your own caste, didn't you?'

'Yes, Bai. But he turned out to be a real scrap. He did nothing for us,' she said, making a long face.

'And this one, he's also from your caste?'

'But he's really first class. Yes, Bai. You'll see, he'll get us our farmland.'

'And then you'll go back to your village and thresh rice.'

'Yes, Bai,' her eyes flashed.

Five years ago, when I was in the hospital giving birth to my Munni, Ratti Bai said that she was on her way to the polling station to vote for her caste-man. He'd made a solemn promise before a crowd of tens of thousands gathered at Chowpatty that the second he came into power he would change everything. Milk would flow in rivers, life would become as sweet as honey. Today, five years later, Ratti Bai's sari was even shabbier, her hair even more grey, and her eyes twice as dazed. Hobbling on the crutches of promises made again today at Chowpatty, she'd come to cast her vote.

'Bai, why do you talk to that slut so much?' Ratti Bai opened her bundle of exhortations and advice as she pushed the bedpan under my cot.

'Why? What's the harm?' I asked, acting as though I didn't know.

'Haven't I told you? She's a very bad woman. Downright wicked, a slut.'

Before Ratti Bai came on her rounds, Ganga Bai had used exactly the same words to let me know her opinion of the former: 'Ratti Bai's a first-rate tramp.' The two hospital workers were always at loggerheads. Now and then they didn't even hesitate before coming to blows. I heartily enjoyed talking to them.

'That bum Shankar, he's not her brother.' Ganga Bai told me. 'He's her lover. Why, she sleeps with him!'

Ratti Bai's husband lived in a village near Sholapur. He had a small piece of land and was stuck to it. The entire yield was sucked up by debt and interest payments. Just a little bit was left; before long it too would be paid up. Then she would go and live with her children, happily ever after threshing rice to separate it from the husk. Both women dreamed with such longing of living happily pounding rice in their homes, the way a person dreams of Paris.

'But, Ratti Bai, why did you come to Bombay to earn money? It would have made more sense to have your husband come instead.'

'Oh, Bai, how could he? He works in the field. I couldn't have managed farming.'

'And who looks after the children?'

'Oh, there's a slut,' she said, calling her every bad name in the book.

'He hasn't married another woman, has he?'

'The bastard, he hasn't got the guts. No, she's a keep.'

'What if she becomes the mistress of the house in your absence?'

'How could she? Wouldn't I beat her hollow and stuff her with hay?

Once we've repaid the debt, I'll go back.'

It turned out that Ratti Bai had herself chosen the poor helpless woman left to care for her husband and children. Once the field became theirs, she would return home as a proper housewife and thresh rice. And what would become of the keep? Oh, she would find another man whose wife has gone to Bombay to earn money and who had no one to look after the kids.

'Doesn't she have a husband?' I asked.

'Why, of course.'

'So why doesn't she live with him?'

'The little land he had owned was gobbled up. He works as a farm labourer, but for eight months of the year he steals and pilfers, or wanders into big cities and supports himself panhandling all day long.'

'Does she have children?'

'Of course, she does. Four, at least she used to. One was lost right here in Bombay. Nobody ever found out what became of him. The two girls ran away and the youngest boy lives with him.'

'How much money do you send back to the village?'

'The full forty-one.'

'How do you get by?'

'My brother supports me.' The same brother Ganga Bai had said was her lover.

'Doesn't your brother have a family of his own?'

'Of course, he does.'

'Where do they live? In the village?'

'Yes. It's a place near Poona. His elder brother takes care of the farming.'

'You mean *your* elder brother,' I said just to tease her.

'Come on now. Stop it! Why would he be *my* brother? Oh, Bai, do you really take me for that kind of woman? I'm not like Ganga Bai. Do you know, hardly four days go by in a month that she doesn't receive a beating. Bai, if you've got any old, worn-out clothes, don't give them to that vile woman. Give them to me instead. Okay?'

'Ratti Bai.'

'Yes, Bai.'

'Does your "brother" whack you?'

'That tart Ganga Bai, she must have told you that. No, Bai, not very much. Just sometimes, when he's had too much to drink. But then he also shows affection.'

'He shows affection, too?'

'Why wouldn't he?'

'But, Ratti Bai, why do you call that scoundrel a brother?'

She started to laugh. 'Bai, that's just how we talk.'

'But Ratti Bai, when you earn forty rupees, why whore around?'

'How else would I manage? Three rupees for renting the kholi, the rathole where I live, and then I have to pay five to Lala.'

'To Lala, whatever for?'

'All the chawli women have to, otherwise he would throw us out.'

'Because you carry on this business?'

'Yes, Bai,' she seemed somewhat embarrassed.

'And your "brother", what does he do?'

'Bai, really I shouldn't say, but selling drugs is a nasty business. If someone doesn't bribe the police, they chase him out.'

'You mean throw him out of Bombay?'

'Yes, Bai.'

Meanwhile a nurse barged in and scolded her, 'What are you doing here jabbering away. Go, the bedpan needs to be removed in No. 10.' Ratti Bai promptly left the room, grinning, flashing her yellowed teeth.

'What's with you, you spend hours talking to these loose women. You need rest, otherwise you'll start bleeding all over again.' The nurse picked up my baby girl from the hammock and left the room.

Ganga Bai was on duty in the evening. She walked into my room without bothering to ring the bell first.

'Bai, I've come for the bedpan.'

'Oh no, Ganga Bai. Sit.'

'The sister will start hollering. The slut. What was she telling you?'

'Sister? Oh, she was telling me to rest.'

'No, not the sister. I mean that Ratti Bai.'

'Just that Popat Lal beats Ganga Bai black and blue,' I teased her.

'That son of a bitch, forget it. He wouldn't dare.' Ganga Bai started pounding slowly on my legs with her fists.

'Bai, you promised to give me your old chappals.'

'Okay, take them. But tell me whether you got a letter from your husband.'

'Of course.' Ganga Bai promptly pounced on the chappals. 'If that whore of a sister saw it, she would kick up a ruckus. She makes too much fuss.'

'Ganga Bai.'

'Yes, Bai.'

'When will you return to your village?'

Ganga's shining black eyes drifted off to the lush green haze of fields far away. She took a deep breath and said softly, 'May Ram give us an abundant crop this time. And then, Bai, I will go back. Last year the flood ruined all our rice paddy.'

'Ganga Bai, does your husband know about your "friends"?' I probed.

'What are you saying, Bai?' She became deathly quiet. I sensed she was feeling somewhat embarrassed. She immediately tried to change the subject, 'Bai, you had two girls in a row. The seth will be mighty angry, won't he?'

'Seth—who?' I asked, confused.

'Your husband. What if he got himself another wife?'

'If he did, I would also find myself another husband.'

'Your people do that? Bai, I thought you come from a high caste.' I couldn't help feeling that she was making fun of high-caste people. I tried my best to make her understand, but she firmly believed that by giving birth to a second girl I really would be thrashed. If my seth didn't beat me black and blue, then he must be an absolutely third-class seth.

Staying in a hospital is nothing less than solitary confinement. Friends and acquaintances visited me for two hours in the evening, the rest of the time I spent chatting and gossiping with Ganga Bai and Ratti Bai. Had it not been for them, I would probably have died long before then from boredom. A little bribe was all it took to get them to spill all kinds of things about each other, whether true or false. One day I asked Ratti Bai, 'You used to work in a mill, so why did you give that up?'

'Oh Bai, the blasted mill was a racket.'

'Racket?'

'Oh Bai, for one thing, it was awfully hard work. Still that would've been bearable, but the bastards kicked you out after a couple of months.'

'How so?'

'They would hire other bai log.'

'Why would they do that?'

'Why? Because if a person stayed for six full months, the Factory Law kicked in.'

'Oh, now I get it.'

In other words, the entire staff changed every few months. If any worker stayed longer in her job, she would be entitled to sick leave, maternity leave, the works, to comply with the Factory Law. So they kept switching workers every couple of months. That way a worker was employed for hardly four months a year. In between, women often returned to their villages. Those who couldn't afford to would run around to other factories looking for work. Some would roost along the sidewalks selling piles of rotten old vegetables. Swearing matches and fights broke out over turf. And since they carried on without a licence, they had to cough up some dough to 'feed' the policeman at the corner. Still, when an unfamiliar officer wandered that way now and then, there would be a veritable stampede. Some would quickly bag their merchandise and slither into a side street; some would get caught and start crying and wailing. But the police kept dragging them to the station. When the situation cleared up, they would swarm back, spread their tattered pieces of cloth and put their wares on display. The clever ones threw a few limes and ears of corn into a shoulder bag and walked along pretending to be shoppers themselves. When someone passed by, they would utter softly, 'Hey, brother, buy some corn. Just one anna a piece.' Buying vegetables from one of them was to practically invite cholera.

The totally wretched ones resorted to begging, and if the opportunity presented itself they weren't above a quickie on the run. Perfectly primped, at least in their opinion, with a wad of paan stuffed in their mouths, they strolled up and down in the dimly lit area by the railway station. A customer walked in, glances were exchanged, and the deal was struck. The customers were mostly milkmen from Uttar Pradesh, or homeless labourers with wives back in villages, or eternal bachelors who only had these squalid streets and sidewalks to call home.

One morning a brawl broke out between the two bais on the veranda. Ratti Bai plucked out Ganga Bai's topknot. In return, Ganga Bai broke Ratti Bai's mangalsutra—her marriage necklace of black glass beads—an assurance that her husband was still alive. The poor woman started sobbing inconsolably as if she'd been widowed. The cause of the fight was the cotton pads that were used for cleaning wounds or for pregnant women and then discarded. According to the city ordinance, they had to be carefully burned, but it turned out that the two bais would remove the soiled cotton from the containers, wash it clean, roll it into a bundle, and take it home. Since their relationship had become quite tense lately, Ganga Bai snitched about it to the supervisor. Ratti Bai started swearing at her, which quickly turned into fisticuffs. Both of them would have been fired but they whined and pleaded so much that the supervisor kept the matter under wraps.

Ratti Bai was a bit flabby and older. Ganga had really let her have it. When she came in to return the bedpan with a swollen nose, I asked, 'What do you do with the dirty cotton, Ratti Bai?'

'Wash it and dry it. It's perfectly clean.'

'And then?'

'Then we sell it to the cotton merchant.'

'Who would buy such germ-filled cotton from him?'

'The mattress man—the one who makes cushions for rich people's furniture.'

'Oh my god!' I bristled with revulsion. I remembered that when I had the cotton removed from a wicker sofa so that it could be re-fluffed, it had turned out to be completely dark. Oh no, was it the same cotton that was used for cleaning and dressing wounds! Is my daughter's mattress made from that too? My daughter, as delicate and fair as a flower, and this pile of germs! God curse you, Ganga Bai! God take you away, Ratti Bai!

Because they had gone after each other with their shoes today, Ratti Bai was writhing inside. And since Ganga was relatively younger, Ratti Bai considered her a greater sinner than herself. To add more fuel to the fire, a few days ago she'd managed to snatch Ratti Bai's standing customer. All those abortions Ganga Bai had had over time, and the live baby she had dumped in the gutter that still kept breathing even after she stuffed the umbilical cord in its mouth! A whole crowd had gathered near it. If Ratti Bai had wanted to, she could easily have spilled the beans and got her caught, but she buried the secret in her chest. And look at the cheek of that vile woman, the way she sits on the sidewalk selling piles of unripe jujube and guava, as though nothing had happened.

'Friendship is one thing, but what if something went wrong, Ratti Bai? Isn't it better to go to the hospital?'

'Why should we? We've got plenty of bais among us who are as good as any doctor. Absolutely first class.'

'Do they give you medicine to get rid of the foetus?'

'Of course they do. What did you think? Then there is this fists method, but rubs work best.'

'What is this "fists", "rubs"?'

'Bai, you won't understand.' Ratti Bai blushed a little and started to laugh. She had been eyeing my powder case for some days now. Whenever she dusted me with it, she would put a pinch on her palm and rub it on her own cheeks. I thought the box would be enough to get her to talk. When I offered it to her, she took fright.

'No, Bai, the sister would kill me.'

'No, she won't. I'll tell her I didn't like the smell of the powder.'

'Why it smells fine, very fine. Oh Bai, you're crazy in the head.'

After a good deal of prodding, she described the details of 'rubs' and 'fists':

'Rubs' work perfectly during early pregnancy—like a doctor, absolutely first class. The bai makes the woman lie down flat on the floor, then holding herself with a rope suspended from the ceiling or to a club, she stands on the woman's stomach and works it with her feet real well, until the 'operation' is performed. Or she makes the woman stand against the wall and after combing her own hair she ties it tightly into a topknot. Then, after dousing it with a fistful of mustard oil, she bangs it against the woman's legs like a ram. Certain young women, used to hard labour, don't respond to this. Then it's time for 'fists'. After dipping her unscrubbed hands with their grimy nails in oil, she just pulls out the throbbing life from the womb.

Most of the time the operation goes off without a hitch on the very first assault. If the performing bai happens to be a novice, sometimes one of the hands is broken off, or the neck comes out dangling, or even a part of the woman's own body that needed to stay inside spills out.

Not too many die from the 'rubs', but the woman generally falls prey to all kinds of disease. Different parts of her body swell up. Permanent wounds form and never heal, and if her time's up, she dies. 'Fists' are used sparingly—only when everything else fails. Those who survive aren't able to walk. Some drag on for a few years and then croak.

I threw up. Ratti Bai, who was describing all this with relish, panicked and ran off. I felt overwhelmed in the dreary silence of the hospital. Oh god, such a dreadful punishment for bringing life into this world—I thought, drifting off into a haze.

My throat was stinging from pure horror. My imagination began colouring in the pictures Ratti Bai had drawn for me and then breathed life into them. The shadow of the window curtain was trembling on the wall. Soon it began to flail like a blood-soaked corpse on which Ganga Bai had applied her 'rubs'. A horrific iron clamp in the shape of a fist with filthy nails sank its teeth deep into my brain. Tiny fingers, a drooping neck, in a sea of blood—the prize of the first assault. My heart sank, my mind felt dazed! I tried to scream, to call someone, anyone, but my throat jammed. I tried to reach for the bell, but my hand wouldn't move. Silent cries were stifled inside my breast.

It was as if the screams of someone murdered suddenly shot up in the impenetrable silence of the hospital. They rose from my own room, but I was unable to hear them, unable to hear anything that was spilling from my own mouth unconsciously.

'You must have had a dreadful nightmare,' said the nurse as she stabbed me with the syringe of morphine. I tried to tell her, 'Sister, please, don't. Look, there, the dead body covered with blood from Ganga Bai's rubs is writhing on the cross. Its cries are piercing my heart like a poker. The feeble sobs of the child dying in some gutter far away are pounding in my brain like a hammer. Don't give me morphine to dull my senses. Ratti Bai has to go to the polling booth. The newly elected minister is her caste-man. Her debt will be paid up with interest now. Ganga Bai will happily thresh rice. Please lift this mantle of sleep from my mind. Let me be awake. The spots left by Ganga Bai's blood are swelling on the white sheet. Let me be awake.'

I woke up when the man sitting behind the desk looking like a clerk stamped one of the fingers of my left hand with blue ink.

'Vote for *our* caste-man, okay,' Ratti Bai admonished me.

The ballot box of Ratti Bai's caste-man rose like a massive fist and came down with all its awesome power on my heart and mind. I didn't drop my vote into that box.

11

THE BOOKING COUNTER
MAMANG DAI

The queue was a very long one. I stood somewhere at the centre-front and knew if I stuck it out, I would reach the counter in, maybe, another nine hours or so. One by one people stepped up and were disposed of briskly. No one said a word. Perhaps conversation is not allowed, I thought. I tried a small cough. No one reacted. But I noticed a tall man about two bodies ahead of me turn his head around to give me a shifty, sliding glance.

At last! The tall man had reached the counter. I saw him bending forward with his shoulders hunched up as if to hide what he was saying to the man behind the counter. He needn't have bothered because the man at the counter rapped out loudly: 'This is reserved for APST!'

'But I have a right!' the tall man shouted. His voice boomed out over our heads. 'We are brothers!'

'Move aside,' said Counter Man.

'Okay, okay, don't shout,' said the tall man. 'I represent a group who want to book a day to call a bandh! We also have a grievance. Ha! Hah!' He laughed, but as he backed away he looked at me. His eyes had turned hard and expressionless as if he had died.

I stepped forward.

'Yes?'

'I want to make a booking,' I said.

'Go ahead.'

'I want to book a bandh.'

'Tell me the date.'

I smiled. I had made my calculations. 'For Tuesday, 11 October.' It was May. I was booking early.

'Sorry, all booked up,' said Counter Man. His eyes were black and spiteful.

'Oh! What about the next day....'

'Nothing. Nothing.'

'What about....'

'No WAat...about...TAat about... Move!' Counter Man was very rude.

I grabbed the metal bars between him and me and shouted, 'Don't tell me to move aside. Why should I move aside? I have every right to be here. Who do you think you are to shout at people left and right?'

Counter Man jumped up from his chair. 'I said MOVE!' he roared.

I was furious. I tried to punch him in the face but he was agile as a cat and parried the blow. 'You come out!' I yelled. 'Why are you hiding behind this metal box?'

'Hiding, huh?' said Counter Man. He pushed his face up close against the bars, pulled out a long rod and zapped my wrist. A stinging pain shot through my body.

'Stop it!' someone cried.

Counter Man was laughing.

'Cruel beast,' I yelled.

People were pushing behind me. A woman clutching a red coin purse whispered: 'They are all the same, these people hiding behind iron bars. They think they are safe but just you wait. The day will come when they will rot in their hi-fi cages!' She laughed wildly.

I felt emboldened by these angry words. 'Just you wait!' I yelled some more. The crowd took up the roar. Then something happened. Counter Man clapped his hands. The small room where he was sitting expanded, and I realized that he was not alone. There were more people with black, beady eyes lined up behind him. I think they were armed because just then a shot rang out and a cloud of smoke covered everything. I sensed people running, falling, pushing past me, but I could see nothing.

When the smoke cleared, I was lying on my stomach—not exactly in a pool of blood, but in a field of filth and stench. I felt the iron taste of hatred and rage, but the silence was eerie.

'Hey,' someone was nudging me. I tried to raise myself up on my elbows and crawl away. 'This is how an insect feels,' I thought. Bodies were strewn all around me. Were they dead?

'No, they are zapped. It's a trick. They are in a state of inertia. You are lucky. My colleague saw you. Here, let me help you....'

'Aaah...' Now I could turn around to face my helper. I saw a well-rounded, bullet-headed man with dark, burning eyes and straight hair that fell like a black mane on to his shoulders.

'Who are you?'

'I am in charge here,' he replied. He smiled at me showing big, yellow teeth and I felt a shadow pass over my heart.

'Come,' he continued, 'we have something to discuss.'

I hesitated, but only for a fraction. I followed Bullet Head straight up to the booking counter. Perhaps I was nearing my goal! But Bullet Head marched right past the counter into an interior room. The first thing I noticed was that the walls were of glass. A few chairs were placed in a semi-circle and a dozen people were already there checking an enormous bound register with a green cover. A woman hailed me. She was the same woman with the red money purse. I joined the circle.

'We are scrutinizing the list of bandhs,' she told me. 'This is a landmark decision.' She looked up at Bullet Head.

Bullet Head said, 'From henceforth this committee will decide which bandhs will be legal and which not.'

'Hear, hear,' there was a rap-rap of agreement and someone patted me on the shoulder like a comrade.

I gulped. This was what I had stood so long in line for to protest. I thought it was great idea to call an all-out massive bandh to end all bandhs and other irregularities. I had friends. Each bandh call had affected them in different ways. Our lives, times, business, communication, and work had been burned out and eaten up by bandhs, and the very idea of food, shelter, welfare, and friendship—everything—had changed because of bandhs. What angered me most was the death of my black dog on a bandh day because the vet could not be in his clinic. There was no protection for bandh breakers and though the poor man would have come I did not want to risk a human life. Instead, I had watched in silence as my dog, friend, and protector of my house for seven years had tried to look at me and then let his head fall.

A sharp knock jolted me. Every one turned their heads towards the sound. It was the tall man waving his hands. He wanted to come inside.

'No, no, go away!' Bullet Head dismissed him peremptorily.

'We are all insiders now,' someone shouted in glee.

Fear gripped my heart. I looked through the glass walls. How strange!

I felt I wanted to be outside. Everything was closed in here—tight, compartmentalized. But a small breeze was drifting in from somewhere.

'It is only a glass wall,' I thought, hope suddenly rising up unbidden in my heart like a magic bird. Perhaps there is a chink somewhere, a translucence that will show a reflection of ourselves in another light—a landscape of love and beauty and wonder of wonders—happiness in this land!

∞

The small breeze seemed to be gaining in force. The Bullet Head group was fading. I felt my soul had been thrown out like a stone into a high, open field outside the glass box. I sat up feeling refreshed, as if my life was being redesigned by the scent of grass. I saw a figure of a man looking at something in the distance. He did not turn around and I was content to sit still and watch him. Every time I peeped at him his visage seemed to change. At one time he looked tall and sturdy. When I looked again he seemed more elderly, even a little sad. Who is this man? I wondered. I had the feeling that I was looking at the great Mr Abo Tani, father of my fathers and blood of my blood. He wore a long cloak of dyed wool and he was very statuesque, like a god.

It was dusk when I finally found my voice and whispered: 'Who are you?'

The legendary figure turned and looked at me. A dark mass of clouds moved over his head but his eyes shone bright like the sun.

'Why did you come here?' he asked.

'I was thrown here. I don't know how I got here.'

Abo Tani smiled. 'The path creates itself. But this is not the place for you.' he said.

'I don't want to go back!' the words shot out of my mouth.

'You have to go back.' he said gently. 'I am the past. There is a place called the future. But it is something even I cannot see. All my life I have worked and undergone great upheaval to create the present moment where earth and sky nourish you and give you breath and life.'

'I know everything,' I cried. But I don't want to go back!' I beat the ground with my fists.

Abo Tani raised one hand. It was as long as a green bough reaching from earth to sky. His shoulders merged with the steep slope of the mountain.

'Look closely,' he said. 'Whatever you do, don't deceive yourself.' Bright sparks of flint flew through the air. I saw pillars of air and water gathering force swirling around a bowl of light cupped in his hands. The breeze that had pushed me out of the glass box was pushing me back in. I was nothing but a spinning speck of mud, a drop of ocean, a sun seed trying to find a foothold.

∞

'What are you staring at? Come on, let us finish our business.' Bullet Head's voice brought me back to reality. Everyone was looking at me. The glass walls reflected a circle of people who looked outrageously large and distorted. But I felt calm now. I stared back at the group. I saw Bullet Head and the woman exchange glances, and suddenly, in their hard, angry faces I saw vestiges of the dream I had just dreamt.

'Where were we?' I said.

'Here, about the bandhs. We have a list now,' said Bullet Head.

'These will be allowed,' said the woman, tapping her red purse and closing the book with a sharp thud. She smiled. 'We are a constituted organ of the government.'

'Hear, hear! It is the will of the community.'

I nodded, feeling I had nothing more to say. I had been to a place I prayed I could return to. It was a narrow space no bigger than the width of a crack in the wall but it was enough. It had offered me nothing but a piece of flint. I embraced it.

'Come on, move, move,' cried Bullet Head just like Counter Man had said to me on the day when the sun was rising over the hill.

We trooped out of the room. It was a sad, lonely evening. The field where so many people had been standing in queue was empty.

A signboard had been nailed over the booking counter. I read the big, bold words: COUNTER CLOSED. BOOKING FULL FOR 100 YEARS.

COUNTLESS HITLERS

VIJAYDAN DETHA

*Translated from the Rajasthani by
Christi A. Merrill and Kailash Kabir*

The five were only men. Some younger, some older, all between thirty and fifty. The eldest was beginning to grey here and there, but the others had heads of hair as black as bumblebees. They looked like men: eyes where eyes should be, noses where noses should be, teeth where teeth should be. Arms and legs where arms and legs should be. Copper-coloured complexions. White turbans, some old, some new. Cholas of white muslin, like their dhotis. Knotted gold earrings in their ears. Gold pendants around their necks hung from black cords. Each man spoke like a man. Each man walked like a man.

All were farmers. They worked the land and reaped the yields. The dry womb of the earth turned green with their wheat and fennel, mustard, cumin, and fenugreek. After Independence, these mighty farmers had done well. They cast seeds in the dirt with their eyes closed, and then gathered up the fruits. The five looked as if they had been born not of woman's flesh but from the earth's own womb. As if they had grown up and blossomed among the kareel, aak, khejari, and acacia trees. As if the grass, the trees, the shrubs, the flowers were their kin.

The five were brothers, cousins of near about the same stock. They were going to Jodhpur to buy a tractor. Each had bundles of rupee notes stashed in the undershirt pocket at his breast. The heat of it made their faces glow. The roots of wealth may lie deep in the heart, but the sheen of such invisible fruits shines clear for all to see.

They stepped off the bus with their hands in their pockets and headed off, their strides long and brisk, towards the tractor showroom as arranged. If it were in their power, they wouldn't have let their feet even touch that pavement black as rot. Once they reached the showroom, they recognized the owner through the window. As soon as their eyes fell on his shiny bald pate they cried, 'We're in luck! Omji himself is here today.'

A blast of ice-cold air rushed over them as soon as they pulled open the door. They walked into the shop, and one sighed, 'Here he's enjoying heaven, while we toil like beasts of burden.'

Omji smiled a thin smile and said in a delighted voice, 'If you want to exchange your farm for my shop, I wouldn't object.'

'Hah! You'd regret it!'

'That remains to be seen.'

The eldest cousin scolded them, 'We've only just walked in the door and already you're talking about regrets. Each person must follow his own fate, and do the work that suits him best.'

Sitting on those cushiony chairs felt like sitting on nothing. They poked and prodded the soft cushions two, three times to make sure the seats would hold their weight. Satisfied, they settled into the chairs, elbows on the armrests. After the perfunctory duas and salaams one of the cousins began, 'Somehow or the other our number has finally come. We need to have the tractor today. We started out this morning at an auspicious hour. We need to return to our village before the day is done. We would consider it a favour if you could arrange for it somehow.'

'Every customer I meet makes the same demand. You have waited more than two years and now you cannot even wait two more days?'

The youngest cousin said, 'Two days would be too long. At this point we cannot wait another two hours. Our women have been standing at the doors ever since we left this morning watching for our return to bless the tractor. Charge a little extra if you have to, but you must deliver it today!'

Omji smiled at their impatience, then said, 'I know how you rustics are. I made sure the tractor was ready yesterday. Take it whenever you wish.'

Their joy knew no bounds. It was as if they had suddenly been handed the whole world to rule! The middle cousin looked at Omji's head shining like the moon and said, 'How could a man with such a lucky brow ever shirk his work? May you live long.'

The cousins were familiar with Omji. One or the other would visit him from time to time to check their number on the waiting list. He became as friendly with them as business demanded. His manner was easy, his words pleasant. Every bit of him looked like it had been manufactured in a factory, like the parts of the tractor. There was a bald spot where a bald spot should be, fringed on three sides with thinning hair. A neck where a neck should be. A smile as the occasion required.

He scanned the five faces before him and said, 'You must be relieved. You've spent your whole day bouncing up and down inside a bus. Now sit back and relax, have some cold water,' and he reached for his buzzer as he continued to make polite conversation. A man came in at once. Omji asked him to bring some lassis. When the man disappeared, he began apologizing, 'I will not be able to offer anything to rival what you have in your village. The milk here is water-thin. The curds will turn your stomach. All you get in cities is cooled air, icy water, soft cushions, and bright lights. The grandiosity of the adulterated and the ostentation of the fake. You cannot find good grain and spices at any price. I am ashamed to offer you anything at all.'

One of the cousins laughed and said, 'If you really mean to offer, there are plenty of luxuries to be had around here. The envy of the gods above. Otherwise, we'll just have to cool down with a lassi instead.'

The hint was clear enough. Omji laughed loudly and said, 'No, we cannot have any of that here in the store. But if you can wait till evening, I will be able to offer you real hospitality at my home.'

'Your invitation alone is enough, Omji! Where's our tractor? Let's just take a quick peek.'

'First, have your lassis and then we'll go down and have a look.'

'The lassis aren't going to run away, are they? The sight of the tractor will cool us down. Then the lassis will taste sweeter.'

Omji went with them himself. The tractor stood ready in the workshop. A blood-red Massey Ferguson, vivid as a mound of birbahuti bugs. The sight of it made them flush in their hearts. They patted the tractor and inspected it closely. Then they all went back to the office. Their glasses of lassi were sitting on the table, carefully covered.

Omji eased himself back into his chair and began musing, 'How times have changed! There used to be just one thakur who ruled over the area. But now you big peasants have become the new thakurs. You are the ones who have really taken advantage of Independence. Where before people used to dream of having buttermilk, now they order all the luxuries as if they were water. In the old days people couldn't even afford a plough and a spade but now no one even gives a second thought to spending thousands of rupees on a tractor. Yaar, enjoy this independence, have as much fun as you can, don't even think twice.'

The fourth cousin interrupted him. 'I wouldn't call this khak fun! Nothing to eat but grain and you barely fill your belly. We've suffered for a thousand generations. Now the one-eyed lady puts on make-up and you begrudge her airs? Thanks to Gandhi baba we actually live like human beings now. How else would our villages have got all those motors, tractors, and radios?'

'And soon we'll have to fill our stomachs with paper notes. Before too long we won't even be able to buy grain.'

'You just keep giving us tractors and we'll keep giving you grain. Draw up a contract if you like.'

The eldest cousin spoke up. 'No one gives anything to anyone just like that. The water buffalo grazes only to fill its own belly. Everyone everywhere wracks his brain just to find a way to meet his own needs. One does it by selling a tractor, and another by buying it.' When his words reached his own ears the eldest cousin realized his talk had gone down the wrong path and he tried to steer the conversation back to better terrain by adding, 'Still, what you say is true. Due to Gandhi baba's grace, we're better off since Independence. Heaps of grain in every home, milk and curds flowing freely....'

Omji began shaking his bald head and cut in, 'No, not in every home, that's not true. It's only a small number of you big farmers who have all you could want.'

The youngest cousin had been to college. He said, 'What do you mean *all* we could want? The best you can say is that the jaws of misery's grip have loosened a little. Just enough to give us room to breathe. But happiness is still as distant as the moon.'

Wanting to put an end to all this nonsense the middle cousin said, 'What's the use of wishing for the moon? Let's get down to business. Take the money out of your pockets to give it to Omji so we can get our goods and return. We're wasting time talking.'

Suddenly they remembered why they had come. A moment later their hands were in their pockets, pulling out rupee notes, piling them on the table. A 50-horsepower, foreign-built tractor with trolley, harrow, and plough.

A sixty-thousand-rupee transaction.

Omji got busy counting the money and putting it away in his drawer while the five cousins all stood up at the same time and went down to the garage for their merchandise. The eldest cousin sent the youngest off to the bazaar for garlands, mounds of gur, rum, and bright red gulal powder. The four cousins helped to load the plough and harrow on to the trailer. They had just caught their breath when the youngest returned. They celebrated by passing around the gur and festooning the tractor's hood with marigold garlands. Then they painted a gleaming red swastika on the front of the hood in gulal. The youngest three were able drivers.

The day had passed quickly. The sun was just about to slip behind its western veil. From the Ajmer–Jodhpur toll gate the road looked clear, smooth, and wide. The garlands fluttered in the breeze to the rhythm of the engine's roar. Sitting atop the tractor the five cousins felt as if heaven itself were gliding beneath their wheels. And the earth curving towards the horizon before them seemed punier than a coconut shell. As if the sinking sun had paused in the sky just to gaze at them. As if the thrumming wind were trying to sweep away any inauspiciousness. All the happiness in the world tossed inside their hearts. Even the long journey of the setting sun's rays seemed to be made worthwhile at the touch of the goddess sparkling in their pendants. The tractor's clanging sent birds hidden in roadside thickets and trees flying in all directions. But, to the cousins, it was their own happiness taking wing.

Suddenly, a shrill cry broke into their reverie. They looked around, startled. A hawk was swooping down, wings spread wide, on a baby hare it had spotted hiding in the brush. It seized the trembling body in its talons and soared upwards, back into the sky. The cousins smiled and looked at one another. The eldest observed, 'One's fate can never be postponed. It was destined that his death should take place in this very bush, by this very hawk, at this very moment.' They gazed into the sky until the hawk faded away. The tractor continued to roar along the road. They were approaching a small overpass. The fourth cousin urged the driver on, 'As much as we're hurrying, we're still running late. So far everything has been auspicious—there were good omens when we left the village.'

A steep slope lay just ahead. As they came over the crest they noticed a cyclist riding on the road, a few furlongs ahead. The cyclist heard the roar of the engine and turned to look behind him. A tractor coming. He turned back and began pedalling furiously. The men sitting in the tractor noticed him speed up, and watched as the gap between them widened. The youngest cousin was at the wheel. He muttered, 'Fool! Pedal as fast as you like, you'll never beat a tractor!' He gave the throttle a little tug, and it roared even louder.

The engine's roar rattled louder in the cyclist's ears. He pedalled faster, and the gap widened again. The driver couldn't stand to see the distance between them. He accelerated even more, saying, 'Little mother-lover! He'll tire out in the end, let him enjoy his little triumph while he can.' The middle cousin added, 'You never know what's going on inside the skulls of those bareheaded punks.'

The tractor was racing along by now. The garlands began flapping even more wildly. The eldest cousin agreed, 'Of course, he'll wear out. Why bother speeding up? A poor cycle can't compete with a tractor!'

A piercing shriek struck their ears as a hawk swooped down from the sky and pounced on a mouse scurrying desperately to get to his hole underground. A moment later, the shrieks faded away. The sun was half-sunken. Now the sun would also disappear for the night. Scarlet light radiated from the setting sun, red as gulal, as if reflecting the tractor's red gleam. The brothers turned from the setting sun and looked at the road ahead. Arre! He was even further ahead! The same thought pinched everyone inside: a two-hundred-rupee cycle against a sixty-thousand-rupee tractor. No match! Does a mouse dare to wrestle an elephant?

The second cousin spat out, 'If he pumps those pedals till his lungs burst, it's his family he'll be leaving behind.' The fourth cousin said, 'Ram only knows when he'll leave his family behind; all I can see is that he's leaving our tractor in the dirt.' The youngest cousin eased out the throttle a little more. The tractor was brand new. It wasn't good to race along at full throttle.

The cyclist looked back. He had quite a lead now. And his exhilaration made him pedal even faster. His feet were spinning round and round like reels. The cycle slipped down the road as easy as water down a mountainside. As if the cyclist had turned into a whirlwind, or even that he were riding a whirlwind.

All the eyes on the tractor were riveted on the cyclist. Quite a gap lay between them now. And it was only growing wider. A foreign tractor. Worth sixty thousand rupees. Festooned with marigold malas. And a two-paisa cycle! A college punk. Head bare. Wearing shorts.

A sharp gust of wind snapped one of the garland threads. The garland began to flap around. Doubling up, unfurling straight. Another garland snapped. The tractor driver felt every thump of the marigold garland on the hood like a thorny cane beating against his breast. He ground his teeth together and pulled the throttle out to the limit. The tractor catapulted forward like a shot from a cannon. The sound of the revving engine echoed in the air. The sky that moments ago seemed to be falling beneath their wheels now seemed to be rising higher and higher over them.

The gap began to close. Even more. Ah, now they were really close.

The world seemed as small as a coconut, reduced to two little dots. The tractor. The bicycle. A sixty-thousand-rupee machine. And a two-paisa piece of junk.

As it happened, two army trucks came bumping down the road from the other direction just at that moment and the tractor was forced to slow down. The cyclist saw his chance and slipped ahead.

The middle cousin said, 'These city punks are worthless! Taking advantage of a chance like that!' The eldest cousin said, 'If the poor fellow wants to show off for now, then let him. How long can he carry on like this? He's bound to run out of breath. Pagla, squandering his energies like this. Once his internal piping starts sagging, he won't even be able to do it with his woman. Were such drives meant to be spent on a cycle?'

Now that the road was clear the youngest cousin opened up the throttle. Like gunpowder suddenly touched with a spark. The tractor was like a dust storm trying to catch the wind. And gradually the gap began to diminish.

The cyclist heard the tractor just behind him and looked around. He snapped his head forward in a fury. And his feet began to spin like reels. They became speed itself, speed and nothing else.

Now he had begun to sweat. He was the fastest cyclist in all of Rajasthan. And, yes, he was also a man. Arms where arms should be, legs where legs should be. Breath where breath should be. Dreams where dreams should be. He had been working out on his bicycle, sixty or seventy miles a day for the past two months. If he came first in the All India Bicycle Championship next month, then he might get to go to Paris. He felt confident enough after two months of dedicated training. But today's little contest would prove it for certain. He clenched his teeth and poured all his strength into spinning the pedals.

He went to college with a young woman who had fallen in love with him the first time she saw him race and proposed to him. But he had not been able to reply with a forthright 'yes' or 'no'. They kept meeting and talking and spending time together, and once they had begun to know each other in their souls, it became clear what they had to do. He had promised to marry her as soon as the All India Championship was over. He had been raised in tight circumstances. And she had grown up in a house of plenty. But they lived only for one another. They ate as if with the same mouth. And on their priceless wedding night the moon would smile on their bridal bed.

Suddenly, her face appeared before his eyes. As if she had turned into the breeze to watch the race. His vigour increased tenfold. As if his feet had grown wings. What power did that lifeless tractor have compared to the shimmery image of his beloved? The cyclist pulled further and further ahead. Before long, the distance between them had doubled.

Now the tractor was at full throttle. They could do no more. Their insides started writhing. The whistling wind was being swallowed up by the roar of the engine. Their reign over the whole world had been grabbed from their hands in a dash. The new tractor shot down the road like a cannonball. It looked as if a whirlwind had taken over that bareheaded boy's feet. His beloved's face shone before his eyes. The distance grew and grew. His lungs didn't quaver, and his breath didn't break.

Half of the marigold garlands had snapped and fallen. But what could the cousins do?

No one can see what the ephemeral future holds. Suddenly the feet fast as a whirlwind were spinning emptily. The chain had come off. Still the boy didn't worry. He figured his feet could match the tractor's speed. Images of his beloved's face surrounded him. There could be no greater power than this in the world. He stopped the cycle and quickly dismounted. He leaned the bicycle on the kickstand and patiently began putting the chain back on.

Slowly the distance was decreasing. The air could not contain the tractor's roar, nor the five cousins' happiness. Well, who knows when luck will smile on you? It didn't matter how, but this sixty-thousand-rupee matter of honour was saved. If people want to deceive themselves into believing in fraudulent victories, then who would stop them?

The tractor's roar sounded closer. It was taking much too long to get the chain back on in the flurry. Before long the tractor was right there. And still he had confidence in his strength, and the power of his beloved's face before him.

The tractor roared past. All five cousins shouted out words typically human as they sped by. A flock of crows began cawing overhead as if in one voice. The voices of the humans couldn't be heard over the cawing of the crows and the roar of the engine.

The tractor was already one or two farm-lengths ahead when the cyclist got the chain back in place and started off again. Four of the cousins turned back to watch him. They thought to themselves, the bastard was just pretending his chain came off! Maybe the race was too much for him.

But the chain was back on and he had turned into a tornado again. The distance between them slowly began to decrease as he came closer and closer.

The scenery was beginning to merge with the darkness. The four cousins were straining to see the boy behind them. He was gaining ground!

Now it was an all-out race. The tractor couldn't go any faster. They gnashed their teeth. The red of the tractor began to dissolve in the fading light. The youngest cousin asked, 'Where is that haraami now?'

The fourth cousin said through clenched teeth, 'Looks like he's going to pull ahead.'

'Hah! Even his father wouldn't have dreamed of it!' As he said this, the youngest cousin started to hear first the hawk's shrieks, then the mouse's squeals, echoing in his ears in turns. After a moment the shrieks were in one ear, the squeals in the other, and wouldn't stop. It seemed as if the entire universe were about to rip apart. The tractor's roar got swallowed up in that echo.

A whole different world was glittering in the eyes of the cyclist. Everywhere he looked, images of his beloved's face were twinkling—in the soft scattering of stars, in the trees and shrubs, in the sand dunes, in the tractor's trolley up ahead. Today would be the test. If he could get ahead of the tractor, then he would get married as soon as possible. Tomorrow, if she agreed. If not, then the day after. Or the day after that. Whenever she wanted. Why wait to pass them? All the world was in the palm of his hand. The warp and woof of golden dreams was being woven in front of his eyes.

Meanwhile, the hawk's shrieks and the mouse's squeals were smothering every particle of air. The four cousins shouted through clenched teeth, 'That bare-headed fellow is making us lick the dirt off our turbans!'

Then they came up with a new plan. 'Make the tractor swerve as soon as he gets close. What will the little haraami have to say to that....' The hawk's shrieks and the mouse's squeals had now found human voices.

And meanwhile the images of his beloved's face began growing brighter and brighter. Each image became more and more distinct.

Now he had moved up, beside the trolley. The shrieks and squeals hid themselves away in the driver's head and assumed a posture of silence.

The next moment the speeding cyclist crashed into the tractor. Lightning flashed before his eyes and the lights of his beloved's faces extinguished one by one. The tractor's rear tyre passed over his bare head, mashing it into chutney. The rest of the faces were snuffed out.

A human voice hissed once more in the wind, 'Mother-lover, he had nerve trying to overtake a tractor!'

The youngest cousin had been to college. He pulled the tractor over, grabbed a bottle out of a sack and said, 'Let's give the poor guy some rum!'

Then he went over to him, walking on two legs like a man. Opened the bottle above the cyclist. Emptied half the bottle of rum into the boy's mouth. Then he broke the bottle near the boy's head and ran back to the tractor. The tractor roared as he took off. The women must be standing in the doorway waiting for them. How happy they would be to see them return!

Human laughter echoed in the wind.

A picture was left behind them on the road, waiting for expert appraisal. Brain-white smudges on a blood-red background. Shards of broken glass. A man's dead body. White shorts. Bloodied sky-blue undershirt. Mashed dreams. Streams of love. The painting wasn't bad!

But...paintings of the two World Wars, pictures of Hiroshima and Nagasaki, of Vietnam, of Bangladesh...those are the true masterpieces. Compared to this one, those are so much more refined, so much more complex and nuanced. This one doesn't compare. Still, considering it was done by a band of rustics, it wasn't so bad.

Yes, the five were only men. Each man spoke like a man. Each man walked like a man.

13

URVASHI AND JOHNNY

MAHASWETA DEVI

Translated from the Bengali by Arunava Sinha

Johnny was sitting with Urvashi in his lap, for she wouldn't sit anywhere else. If she was asked to sit elsewhere, she would just flop dramatically on the floor. What sort of coquetry was this? Was Urvashi going to sit in Johnny's lap in full view of the doctor? The doctor wasn't pleased at all. Eventually, he said, 'Get up, come this way.'

Settling Urvashi in the chair carefully, Johnny got up. The doctor talked to him while keeping an eye on Urvashi. As usual, Urvashi didn't answer the doctor's question. The only person she spoke to was Johnny.

'What was the problem with the throat at first?'

'Sore throat, hoarseness.'

'And then?'

'Coughing.'

Johnny's eyes turned yellow with jealousy whenever the doctor looked at Urvashi. The doctor ignored this and said to Urvashi, 'Didn't you realize earlier? Didn't you see a doctor?'

Johnny said with a smile, 'This woman, you see, Doctor, is eating me up. You know what a bitch is like, she won't tell you when something's wrong. Look at that face, she still makes your head spin. I did go to a doctor.'

'Which doctor?'

'Kaviraj, hakim, the lot.'

'Have you brought a letter from Dr Husain? Did he check?'

'He was the one who sent me. I don't like what I'm seeing, Johnny, he said. This Urvashi is killing you. Your life will be hell because of her.'

'Did he say what's wrong?'

Johnny's face fell. As though a familiar figure—a doll or an ancient statue—had suddenly cracked and faded from constant exposure to rain and storms. Johnny said, 'You know very well, Doctor, that without Urvashi all the shows will flop. She will sing, chat, dance, sway her hips, laugh. The public will say, how are you, Urvashi? She will say, I'm so happy. I'm the queen of happiness. Johnny keeps me in such comfort.'

'Get to the point.'

Johnny whispered, 'What Dr Husain told me has scared the shit out of me, Doctor.'

'What did he say?'

'He said it'll all come to an end, Johnny. Your Urvashi will no longer laugh or sing or speak.'

'Do you know why he said that?'

'Something wrong with the throat.'

'What's wrong?'

'Something.' Johnny twisted his neck from side to side, like a sacrificial lamb who knows the blade is about to fall.

'It's throat cancer, Johnny.'

'Give us medicines, injections.'

'It's too late, Johnny. You went to the cancer hospital, too, didn't you? Didn't they tell you?'

'They did.'

Johnny's voice broke, sobs welled up. 'That's what they said, saar,' he said. 'I beg of you. If Urvashi can't sing or dance we'll starve to death.'

Johnny wept. Urvashi kept sitting without turning a hair. Suddenly the doctor felt a stab of fear. Of what, he couldn't say. He was delivering a death sentence. There were so many different kinds of death. *End of life. Being killed. Ceasing to be. That object which has ceased to be is dead.* Urvashi is dead, deceased, rejected. For everywhere in the throat from which Urvashi spoke and sang and laughed, the windpipe, the food pipe, the membrane, the vocal cords—cancer has claimed all of them as its kingdom. The throat was the cancer's throne. When its term ended, the cancer would take its throne and depart.

But Urvashi was detached, alluring, exquisite, her breasts arrogant, her lips reddened, her eyes still. Only Johnny wept. His despair and Urvashi's indifference chilled the young doctor to the bone. As though it was he who had died and frozen. But why the fear? After death there could be neither fear nor courage.

'Say something, Doctor.'

'Johnny, at the hospital, the cancer hospital...'

'They know nothing at the cancer hospital, Doctor, you can have stomach cancer, lung cancer, have you ever heard of throat cancer?'

'Getting admitted there might...'

'Urvashi can't be left alone.'

'This is madness, Johnny. What harm can Urvashi come to?'

'You won't understand.'

Johnny got to his feet with a sigh. Wiping his eyes, he said, 'Let's go home, Urvashi.'

'Johnny, I've known you a long time, I'm giving you good advice. You can't do at home what can be done at the hospital.'

'Will going to the hospital make Urvashi dance again, sing again, talk again?'

'No, Johnny.'

'The voice with which she sings Kar le muhabbat Lolita...will it be repaired?'

'No, Johnny.'

'Then why?'

Johnny lost his composure. 'All the "bastards" have signed up with that one-eyed Kani Moti,' he said. 'You want to separate me from Urvashi. Shut up, you swine, say the word hospital again and I'll stick a dagger up your arse.'

Johnny began to shout. A flood of invective, starting with bastard. The nurses and orderlies and hospital staff came running. All of them scared stiff.

'Get away, all you bastards—yes, fuck off. I'll kill the lot of you. All you motherfuckers have joined hands with Kani Moti. You think I don't know. Come on, Urvashi, I'm not letting you go. Shaala thinks he's a doctor. Wants to separate you and me.'

The doctor said, 'Let him go, he's gone mad.'

'YOU have gone mad. Weren't you staring at her all this time? If you're talking about illness, motherfucker, why were you looking at her tits? You think I don't understand?'

The doctor rose to his feet. Placing his hand on Johnny's shoulder, he said, 'Don't shout, Johnny. Not another word. Speak softly, then leave.'

'You're telling me Urvashi won't talk or sing any more, and you expect me not to shout?'

'No, you won't.'

Johnny lowered his voice fearfully. 'I won't shout?'

'No.'

Johnny began to cry. In his patched and floppy trousers, bright T-shirt, the bandanna around his neck, the oversized shoes, and the feathered cap, the old man looked like a weeping monkey. Like a sobbing clown on a poster stuck on a wall. Still weeping, he gathered up Urvashi tenderly in his arms and left.

Outside the hospital, where bottles of medicine were sold, Ramanna, the cripple, was selling tea. Johnny squatted in front of him, helping Urvashi take a seat on a packing box.

'Well, meri jaan?' said Ramanna. 'A cup of tea? A red skirt today, I notice.'

'Shut up, you cripple,' said Johnny.

'You have some, then.'

'Give me a cup.'

'Ginger?'

'Yes.'

'What did the doctor say?'

'Cancer.'

'Where?'

'Throat.'

'Huh!'

Pouring scorn into his voice, Ramanna said, 'Who gets throat cancer? Don't show me cancer, Johnny. I've grown up with death. If it's cancer there's a rotten smell even when alive. Don't you remember that fellow? When they were lowering him from the ambulance the stench was everywhere. When he died, you know, Johnny, they doused him in perfume, still the fucker didn't stop smelling.'

'I remember.'

'When he died everyone scattered coins, the bastards.'

'You slipped when you tried to pick them up.'

'And you ran away with my money, you fucker. Two rupees sixty paise.'

'Who paid for the drinks the next day?'

'Did I say you didn't?'

Johnny drank his tea. Then he said, 'What do you think I should do?'

'Go to Lengri.'

'Why?'

'Because Kani Moti can't handle this. Lengri will tell you.'

'Why do you say that?'

Scratching his belly with his amputated arm, Ramanna said, 'I went to Lengri. She's greedy. Says, get me good cigarettes, some fries. She wanted a pillow from a dead body. The corpse of a married woman. I told her I'd get her one. So I brought her cigarettes and fries....'

'With your own money?'

'Who owns money? Whom do you belong to, money? Whoever I'm with. No, not my own money. Do you know what happened that day?'

'What?'

'Bhagirath had sold the medicines. Meant for the patient. When the patient died the family went to fetch a cot. Bhagirath disappeared with the medicines and Horlicks, everything. He paid.'

'What did Lengri say?'

Ramanna looked grave. 'You're blaming Kani for nothing, Johnny,' he said. 'She loves you.'

'Fuck off! Kani, that hag. Who wants her love?'

'No, Johnny. True love is a very good thing. She gives you food, doesn't even take rent every month. Just the other day she was sitting with me in tears. She said, "Johnny just has to ask once, I'll support him for life. But, yes, he has to leave Urvashi".'

'What did you say?'

'I said, forget it, Kani. Johnny won't leave Urvashi, talk about other things.'

'What did Lengri say?'

'She said, someone else wants Urvashi. So he's done some black magic. You can't get throat cancer otherwise. So I said, Johnny is my closest friend. I know everything about him, Lengri. Tell me.'

'What did she say?'

'She said, "Tell him to come to me tonight".'

'Should I go to her today?'

'No, it's that man's chautha today. Lengri is a boss at gathering leftovers. She'll be there with her people. So much fucking trouble everywhere. There are rules. Lengri and her people will get the leftovers from all the feasts on the left of the Lakka field, and Magandas on the right. But now these fucking beggars have abandoned all principles, you know? Lengri never goes to the right, but Magandas and his gang have begun targeting the left and creating trouble. They don't know Lengri. She's taking Badri and Hamiza with her today. If Magandas creates trouble they will fuck him all the way to hell and back.'

'Badri and Hamiza are going?'

'Bloody right, they will! They manage their own areas, no problem. Who allotted the Lake Market pavement to Badri and the Kamlavilas pavement to Hamza? Lengri, of course. Do you know how much Badri collects from the market? Meat and fish entrails, vegetables, Badri has a lot of clout. So he said, Mashi, as long as Badri is around, Magandas will not be able to collect food from your dustbins.'

'Big feast tonight, then.'

'Fuck off. It's not Bengalis doing their last rites, there's no meat or fish or anything. But then Lengri said this is a battle for our rights. I'll lose face if I give in. Lengri knows what it is to fight. Even after she's gone, her reputation as a fighter will remain. We'll fucking name a pavement for her.'

'Then I shouldn't go today?'

'Go tomorrow. Full moon, a good time.'

'Will she give medicines?'

'Of course! Lengri never goes back on her word. But don't go in the morning. She cleans taxis in the morning, in shorts. Making lots of money. Go at night. Take a bottle.'

'Kani Moti is innocent?'

'Yes, Johnny.'

'Call for a rickshaw.'

'You'll go home?'

'Yes. If I take Urvashi out in the sun she....'

'Johnny.'

'Yes?'

'Do you consider me a close friend?'

'Of course.'

'From naked butt days.'

'Of course.'

'Leave Urvashi.'

Johnny's heart froze in fear. Ramanna, Ramanna! Such an old friend of his. And here he was, saying the same thing. The icy coldness of a morgue settled in Johnny's heart. Was he to die of fear? What if he did? But what was all this fear, this terror, even after death? Surely, man went beyond fear and courage when he died? At least, he was supposed to.

'Why are you saying this, Ramanna?'

'She will eat you up.'

'I know.'

Johnny looked mournful. As though the clown on the posters stuck on the walls had decided not to show a smiling face to the city any more. Like a melancholy aged ape he said, 'I know, Ramanna. But you know how I've spent so much of my life in joy and in sorrow with my love. I'll die if I cannot see her eyes, her face, her smile.'

'I know.'

'Would anyone survive, you tell me. You know how beautiful life is, everyone wants happiness. People ask her, how are you, Urvashi? She says, I'm very happy. People say, and how are we? She says, you're very happy too. People say, then sing a song of happiness. She laughs and sings: O jeenewale. Jeena. Living.'

'I know.'

Ramanna grew sorrowful too. He said, 'Urvashi is a witch, a prisoner of the devil, a djinn. She has finished everyone she's been with. She will finish you too. And no one knows who'll be next.'

Johnny said, 'I'll kill her before that.'

'You!'

'Yes, me.'

Ramanna sighed. He said, 'Go to Lengri at night. Take her something to eat and drink. She won't talk otherwise.'

'Of course, I will. Urvashi will dance, she'll sing Bareilly ke bazaar mein jhumka gira re. Lengri will give medicines. Or else I will plunge a dagger into my heart and in hers too.'

Ramanna clucked. 'A knife through those breasts? Fuck off then, I won't organize your chherad.'

Winking with one clouded eye, Johnny chuckled. 'That comes later, first you have to decide whether to burn me or to bury me. Do you have any idea?'

'To hell with you, as if you have any religion.'

'Bury me and burn me too.'

'Will be there two corpses, you fucker?'

'Me and Urvashi, got it? Get a band with bagpipes, get acetylene lamps, cover us with flowers, buy all the flowers in the city. Then light the pyre. And then bury the ashes. Have a grand chherad. Lengri's gang, Magandas's gang, Badri's gang, Hamiza's gang...give all of them a feast on the pavement. Get uniformed bearers from the canteen.'

'Who'll pay for all this?'

'Oh, everyone will do everything for free. Johnny's dead, Urvashi's dead, everything's free. Fuck it, Laila and Majnu are leaving us. Who will ask for money? When we're dead, you'll see, no one will fly pigeons, no one will sing. They will die too, beating their breasts and chanting, hamein gam dil, hamein gam dil. We'll take all the joys with us when we die, fuck everything.'

Ramanna, the cripple, and Johnny began to laugh. Still laughing, Johnny helped Urvashi into a rickshaw. He lit a bidi, taking care not to burn Urvashi's silky tresses. Winking at Ramanna, he blew out a mouthful of smoke.

The miraculous light of the moon bathed Calcutta in love. As though the moonlight was Laila herself, and the city, her lover, Majnu, filthy because he was mad with passion for the moonlight, which was why the amorous Laila had to bathe him.

It was very late at night. Hours made no difference to the night any more. No one but a few street dogs, maddened by the moon, were taking advantage of the flood of passion. Everyone else was either asleep, or wandering around in the hope of getting drunk, or searching for flesh without love after closing the windows through which the moonlight could have entered.

Under such a moon, drenched in this deluge of love, Johnny leant against a pillar, crying. He was very sad. Now he was both Laila and Majnu. Asmaanwaale teri dunia hamein ghabra diya, saare dunia men chandni kyun mere liye badal ho gaya?'

He was plunged in despair. Even Lengri had clucked sympathetically. When Lengri realized at the age of seventy that she would have to become a warrior goddess to retain control over the footpaths, she gave up her sari and began to dress in shorts and T-shirts, swapping her flowing white hair for a bob. She kept a cloth bag tied at her waist and a mirror hanging from a black wire around her neck.

Mirror in hand, she pulled out and examined the patterns made by the nail of a new-born baby, the beak of a hornbill, the hair of one pregnant corpse, and the vermilion of another. Then she said, 'No hope, my darling. Someone has done some black magic, a demon. I no longer have the power to do any counter magic. My heart is breaking at your misfortune. If you did have to come, why couldn't it have been when the trouble had begun with Urvashi's voice?'

Johnny was crying brokenly. He was dressed in his floppy trousers, bright T-shirt, and bandanna. Oversized shoes and feathered cap. He didn't look like a man, but like a clown who had walked out of a poster stuck on a wall. Determined not to smile, or to make others smile. Rebelling, because his heart was broken.

The pain of a cracked, damaged heart is unbearable. A burning in the breast. The flames of anxiety blaze stronger than the funeral pyre. Johnny was weeping, transformed into the clown on the poster. What did he have to laugh at, after all? The flood of love in the moonlight could not heal him. Where was he to go now with his broken heart? Yeh dil kahan le jaaun?

The voice with which Urvashi—seductive like a swaying skirt, unpredictable like lightning, beautiful like dawn, always alluring, woman of the forest—sang dukhia ziara rote naina, sang love me darling, sang tomar golay gaan chhilo, amaar golay shur, sang banska khirki banska duara aao banaye gharwa pyaara, would now be stilled. The glorious moon would set—mujhe bhi le chalo sapno ke paar. And so Johnny was weeping.

The moonlight laughed at his tears, the dogs copulated. Lengri gazed at the full moon with her clouded eyes, weeping. 'You're Ramanna's closest friend, darling. I don't have the power to stop the black magic, my son. I can't even see clearly any more. That is why I cannot see his reflection in the mirror.'

'It's not Kani Moti then?'

'No, my son. She loves you very much.'

'I'm afraid of her love.'

'Afraid of what? Leave Urvashi. Set up home with her. She will cook for you, feed you, don't forget you're getting old.'

'But how can I leave Urvashi? What will happen to her?'

'Someone will buy her.'

'Who?'

'That I couldn't see, darling. Someone who wants her has done black magic.'

'That's what I suspect. Everyone is jealous.'

'You've gone mad, my boy.'

'I wasn't mad, Mashi, she made me mad. I was young then. I travelled all over in a coach with her on my lap. Dholpur, Banda, Khani, Lalthapur, Hasirpur. What performances those were, Mashi. When she sang ankhia milake jia bharmake chale nahin jaana, I would say, kabhi nahi pyare. She would sing jaanse na jaane doongi, jaake raasta tokh loongi, saiyan ke paiya par par jaoongi, roke kahoongi, aankhiya milake.'

'I know everything, darling.'

'But all dead, Mashi. The throat from which her songs come—it's got cancer.'

'Not cancer, sweet, someone has done black magic.'

'Do you know anyone?'

'Know whom?'

'Someone who can stop the black magic.'

'No, my boy. There was Ansari at Tiretti Bazaar....'

'Dead.'

'Now ask for the lord's mercy.'

'Lord!'

Johnny walked off with a glance at the moon, his head bowed. Kani Moti loved him? Pyaar? Mohabbat? Pyaar se phir kyun darta hai dil? Because of Urvashi, because of Urvashi. Suddenly, he felt that Urvashi was alone. Kani Moti leered at Johnny and despatched Urvashi to the crematorium twice a day. Johnny began to run. And as he ran, he changed into little Johnny fleeing the orphanage.

Who had left him at the orphanage door? He didn't remember anything. The orphanage belonged to Puranchandji. Along with all the other boys, Johnny too would sing deene daya karo on the train to Bandel and back. It was his singing that made Dalip Singh lure him away.

'I'll show you the world,' Dalip would say.

Johnny had not realized that Dalip was another Puranchandji, who used to take away all the alms they would get, and had the children's limbs amputated. It was he who had turned Ramanna into a cripple. Johnny was spared because he could sing well.

Ramanna and Johnny had run away together. Dalip had given Ramanna a clay pot. He would use his amputated arm to hold the pot against his body and drum on it with the other hand. Johnny would sing. In train compartments.

Johnny had learnt in childhood that people loved pleasure. He could see the sheer effort made to give people pleasure. Horse-drawn coaches would pass, distributing handbills about royal astrologers, non-surgical cures to injuries, and films. Musicians played on the roof. Happy songs, all of them.

The coaches would race along, happy tunes wafting from them, and young boys would run behind them, collecting the confetti that Johnny scattered in the breeze. Johnny knew that everyone loved big pleasures. Puranchandji from the orphanage used to love them too. He would distribute sweets on his parents' birthdays. Those whom he had crippled were not left out. Puranchandji would climb on to a large table and sit cross-legged. He wouldn't even drink a glass of water till he had performed his puja to Shiva; he had a permanent trident drawn on his forehead with sandalwood paste. From a huge basket he would toss the sweets to the boys, and order them, 'There! Pick them up! Eat! Laugh, sing, dance.'

Johnny and his companions would laugh and sing and dance uninhibitedly. The cripples and the one-eyed among them would laugh the loudest. Johnny had discovered that people loved pleasure. Pink handbills would turn the air of the city pink. Some of them would say that the astrologer was the storehouse of happiness. Some would say the most terrible wounds could be cured without pain. Abdalla would sit with his parrot on the pavement, distributing happiness. The movies offered 200 per cent happiness. The heroes would always get the heroines at the end.

Even when Dalip turned into another Puranchandji and took away the money that Johnny and Ramanna made from singing in trains, Johnny used to sing songs of happiness. He knew people went to the movies in search of pleasure. All these Bengali clerks, salesmen, peddlers, middlemen, shopkeepers, hawkers, all of them went to the movies for happiness. They tolerated the sad scenes and sad songs because all sorrows would ultimately be converted to joy.

So Johnny would sing a sad song, yeh dil kahan le jaoon, first, followed by main ban ki chidiya, to make everyone happy. People could become happy quite easily. Those who did not watch films because they had no money got their pleasure from the queues at the cinema halls. The penniless people who could not afford sweets got their pleasure from licking the pots thrown into the street. Legless and armless beggars who rolled on the melting tar of Chowringhee to collect money for Puranchandji got their pleasure by staring at the apple-like foreign women.

He had realized right then that he would have to escape from Dalip's reach. He would peddle happiness all by himself, all over the country.

Ramanna did not leave, staying on in Calcutta instead. Kani Moti had not become blind in one eye yet. She was the landlady's niece at the time. Ramanna and Johnny had pimped for Chandni and Reshmi and Bedana and other women for some time.

Johnny would also sell film tickets on the black market. He slept on the pavement. When he came into some money, he ate seekh kebab at Habib's. Johnny was one of those beggars who felt Calcutta was in their pocket when they had twenty-five paise to call their own. Eternally happy, independent. Which was why he ignored the landlady. Marry Moti, start a family—he didn't care for such advice. Who was going to marry Moti? Who wanted to become another Puranchandji, another Dalip, and become rich on the money earned by Chandni and Reshmi with physical labour?

Pleasure was to be found in the air in Calcutta.

Johnny had said, 'You can stay here.'

'What will you do?'

'I'll pick up pleasure from the world, phir sab ko de dega—it'll be the biggest charity, motherfucker. I'll give everyone all the pleasure they want. I'll tell them, you bastards, sleep on the pavement, eat on the pavement, dress up and leer at women. Sing, laugh. Happiness is the greatest jewel of life. I'll put the jewel in everyone's hand.'

'And am I just going to die here, you fucker?'

'Not at all. Let me find my pleasure first, then I'll take you along.'

'So you won't marry Moti?'

'Never, motherfucker.'

'She won't marry me.'

'You're a cripple.'

'My heart will break if you leave.'

'But you're my closest friend. Even if I leave I'll send for you.'

'You must go.'

'You're sure?'

'My word.'

'You remember everything we decided?'

'Ev...erything.'

'You'll take care of my chherad if I die. If you die, I'll take care of yours.'

'Sign in blood.'

'Okay then, bastard. Here.'

They had sliced their skin open with the same knife. Laughed in unison. Watched a film with their arms around each other's shoulders. Had seekh kebab at Habib's. Then Johnny had gone off to Howrah Station, climbing into the first train he could see. He hadn't bought a ticket—he had just curled up on the floor.

He was in Ranchi before dawn.

That was when Johnny had planned his life. Master Johnny's One-man Show.

Ranchi, Daltanganj, and then, going further north, westward through Benares, Allahabad, Lucknow.

Different lives, different performances. Like the patterns of performances, the patterns of life also varied. When the film ran, Johnny could see the pattern.

At the market, on the street, at the crossroads. As Majnu he would sing chalti hai karvan. As Laili he would sing aasmanwale teri dunia mujhe ghabra diya. As the villain he would say, bachho, mere chakku se tere kalije nikal dunga. As the joker he would stuff a pillow into his pants and dance.

The coins would rain into his bowl. Those who were in the greatest need of pleasure had no money. All of them would crowd around to watch Johnny's performance. Johnny would say, 'People of the world! Pleasure is a bird in this world. It flies around. I've captured it to give it to you.' As Tansen he would sing like Saigal, bina pankhe panchhi hoon main. As Akbar he would say, Tansen! Tumne yeh gaana kyun gaaye, Tansen?' As Tansen he would say, 'Yeh gaana nahi, Shahenshah! Yeh tute huye dil ka pukara hai.' Still as Tansen, he would lie down and say, 'Mera pyaas bujhao!' Back on his feet, he was the singer again, raising his arms to the sky and singing, Barso re! Kaale badaria, piya par barso.

Johnny would return to the station platform after vending pleasure to the public, and lie down by himself on a bench. Every life had its own pattern. The sahibs and memsahibs went to Shimla with their dogs. He was very keen to have a street dog as a pet in this lonely life of his. He would name it Rover. Rover would walk around with him on a leash. He would tell people it was an *alchechhian*. Stunted because I can't afford meat.

He had many other desires. Of travelling in a coach with Phulkalia from the Nautanki troupe. Of putting up dance shows with Anar from the bazaar. Of spending the night with Panna from the tea shop.

But the pattern of life was strange. Phulkalia and Anar and Panna had heard richer people than Johnny talk of the same dreams, and spent themselves trying to fulfil them. All that the women would say was, will you marry me, make a home with me?

Johnny would say, 'Never. Free men don't become slaves. Only donkeys get married. I'm saying I'll bring you happiness from all over the world.'

The women would roll with laughter. 'You can't get happiness free, Johnny.'

'What do you mean free? I'll give you bangles, clothes, meat for dinner every day.'

'Everyone makes the same promises. Who keeps them?'

Phulkalia's aunt was a fortune teller. She said, 'You're wasting your time trying to bind him down. There's just the one Laili for him who will find him and make him her Majnu.'

The arrogance of youth made Johnny eternally free. He would laugh with joy. 'The girls aren't willing, Mausi. You come with me. Will you be my Laili?'

'Die like a dog.'

'You'll be the one to die.'

'You'll die first.'

'If I do my best friend will organize my chherad. We've sworn in blood. There will be gas lanterns all around my corpse, a band will play, all the people I've given pleasure too will beat their breasts and lament, hai! gam-e-dil! hai! dunia ke khushi ki roshni bujh gailo. They will weep all the way. When you die the cleaners will take your body away.'

The old woman would try to slap him. Johnny would run away, laughing. But one day Phulkalia threw herself at his feet. 'I've fallen in love with you, Johnny. I can't think of anyone but you. I don't want you to marry me or give me a home, just take me with you.'

'Take you where?'

'Wherever you go.'

Phulkalia was a voluptuous woman. She had pockmarks on her face, her complexion was shiny, she sported a tattoo on her forehead. Her body was like a pitcher brimming over with milk, spilling as she walked.

When Johnny looked into Phulkalia's eyes he realized that a dagger had been plunged into her heart. Imagine a woman who wasn't willing even to take a coach ride with Johnny unless they were married now saying she was ready to go wherever he wanted to take her.

Was Johnny afraid? What was the woman saying? He was a vagabond, a nomad, wandering from place to place. Johnny did not dream of freedom. He had been free since birth. He knew that happiness was a bird. Its iridescent feathers flashed in the sunlight. Johnny kept capturing the bird to offer it to penniless, naked men. How was he to take responsibility for Phulkalia's full and desirable body, of her bleeding, passionate heart?

Johnny had run away. Phulkalia's aunt's curse may have followed him. Why else would he have ended up in Mumbai? Why would Hamid have told him at Bhuleshwar Chowk, 'What is this one man show of Master Johnny's? Have you seen my Urvashi's performance?'

'I will if you show me.'

'Put on an amulet with the pir's blessings before you do, Johnny. Or Urvashi will make you mad for her.'

'Hmmph, I've seen hundreds of Urvashis.'

'Not like her.'

'What does she have?'

'Name the one thing she doesn't have.'

'Hah! Everyone says the same thing.'

That evening Urvashi had dressed in a peshwaz and blouse with a churni. Hair ornaments, necklace, earrings. Urvashi was singing on Hamid's lap. Talking. Her complexion was like an apple's, her breasts were like ripe pears, her eyes like lotus petals, her eyebrows flying hawks, her lips a blooming rose....

Johnny was thunderstruck. Why did people flock to his performance when there was Urvashi? She was singing huskily, speaking, telling the audience jokes.

After the show Hamid told Johnny, 'Come with me.'

'Why?'

'Urvashi will sing so sweetly.'

'Will she sit on my lap?'

'On my lap and on yours.'

It was Johnny who had added new acts to the show. He had been educated a little at the orphanage. Then, in his quest to capture the bird of pleasure, he had picked up a working knowledge of Hindi, English, Marathi, and Gujarati during his travels. He used to buy film magazines all the time. 'You bloody Hamid, there's no *bichhnechh* unless your *invess*.'

He would say, 'The show must finish with *comedy*. Happy ending. Look, start with the happiness of the hero and the heroine in the rain. Second part, *tajidy*. But if it ends in *tajidy* people feel sad. A *comedy* ending puts the bird of happiness within their reach. *Comedy* endings are best.'

Now, half asleep next to Urvashi, Johnny could still see Hamid. Hamid was crying. 'I sold her to you when I was drunk, Johnny. Don't take her. I'll die if I don't see her. I'll sell my tent and pay you. Don't take her.'

'Fuck off, who wants money?'

'I'll stick a dagger in your chest, Johnny. She's an enchantress, a djinn. I got her from a Lahori. Now you're taking her from me? The witch will finish me and then punish you.'

If only Johnny had known. Oh god, how beautiful she was. Tere gore badan mein gori kaale kaale ankhiyan.

Johnny fled Mumbai the same day with Urvashi.

Kanpur, Jhansi, Agra, Delhi, Peshawar, Lahore, Karachi, Bhopal—so many different cities. Everywhere at the crossroads and markets and on the pavements penniless, naked people wanted the bird of happiness in their hands. All of them traders in a currency of no value. When they got money they drank, they smoked hash after Johnny's performance. If they didn't have money they died on the streets without taking the world to court.

But times change. Back then, at the height of his youth, Johnny had asked Ramanna to join him. Ramanna would play his music with one hand, gripping the instrument with his amputated arm. Johnny and Urvashi would ride around the city in a coach. Johnny would throw pieces of pink paper up in the air, colouring it with the pink feathers of the bird of pleasure. By then everyone had come to know that Johnny was madly in love with Urvashi. Urvashi was the rose, and Johnny her nightingale. The penniless, pleasure-hungry boys would run behind the coach to grab the coloured sheets.

Johnny began to grow old racing along the desolate streets under the passionate moonlight. Like a gooseberry branch which had lost all its leaves in winter. Just as the leafless branch is all that's left behind when all the green has been shed, so too had the good days fallen away from Johnny's life, leaving him bereft.

The good times hadn't disappeared overnight. Gradually, Johnny's shows stopped drawing people. He had to leave the glittering big cities and start touring Bardhaman, Krishnagar, Suri, Bolpur, Baharampur, Rampurhat, and other small towns. Tattered tents, out of tune music. Johnny's floppy pants, bright T-shirt, oversized shoes, and feathered cap saw him through.

But this was a performance of love. Johnny had loved Urvashi for thirty years and become her Majnu, mad for her. The things that Laili wanted were imitation-pearl necklaces, glass bangles, satin skirts. Then to Calcutta. Come into the tent, pay nineteen paisa, watch the performance. At every fair and festival in the city, wherever they were held.

Moti had sacrificed one of her eyes to the goddess, Sheetala, to become Kani Moti, one-eyed. She had fallen on bad days. Reshmi and Chandni and Bedana had been carted off the crematorium, one by one.

It was Kani Moti who settled them into a slum behind Beckbagan.

'You too?' asked Johnny sympathetically.

'Naturally.'

'Did it have to happen?'

'It did.'

With Kani Moti's help Ramanna set up a tea shop on the pavement outside the hospital. The shop was a packing crate, the bench for customers to sit on was a plank raised on bricks. Hot tea and country biscuits. Drink from your little cup, throw it away.

Kani Moti gave Johnny and Urvashi a home. Three rooms, partitioned with pieces of cardboard and rotting wooden crates. 'Pay me ten rupees as rent, Johnny,' Kani Moti told him.

A slum. Putrid living. A single hole in the ground masquerading as a toilet for twenty-two families. There were many other landladies like Moti in this slum. Little children and old men and women sat in the doorways. The air was heavy with the stench of garbage.

Johnny's heart grew heavy. Would Urvashi have to live in a room like this? There was no reaction from Urvashi. Kani Moti had made things worse.

After the performance Johnny began to cough till he almost died.

Kani Moti brought him a concoction to drink. Medicines from a hakim, an amulet from a pir.

'Why do you do all this for me, Moti?'

Kani Moti said, 'That Urvashi's going to eat you up, Johnny. Leave her.'

'Why? What's your plan?'

'Live with me.'

'Get away from me, you witch.'

Kani Moti left, weeping. But she hadn't asked Johnny to pay his rent for the past seven years, taking it only when he offered. She brought him tea and biscuits and bread and sweets. Johnny called her a witch. Moti said, 'I'm going to set that witch on fire one day.'

Johnny wasn't afraid when Kani Moti spoke in anger. But sometimes her heart broke so much that her tears were converted to song. On those nights she sat with her legs splayed out, giving people medicines and singing. Just as Johnny's songs were old, Kani Moti's songs were ancient, primal. The heartfelt lament of all fallen men and women. She croaked, out of tune:

I was as beautiful
As the moonlight
Just like all of you
At home I wore the best clothes
Coaches lined up at my door
The men came
To love me so
And to call me
Darling moon

Johnny's heart broke too at such songs. Kani had lived in Calcutta all her life. Had she not realized the need for pleasure?

Johnny came home.

A foul odour. Sunlight and moonbeams were forbidden from entering the slum. Johnny lit a lamp. Urvashi was sitting on the bed, looking at him, leaning against a pillow. Johnny alone could tell her eyes were heavy with sadness from being neglected.

'I'm back, my love.' Johnny kissed Urvashi loudly. Urvashi did not respond. Absolutely quiet.

Johnny interpreted the question in her eyes correctly.

'Lengri knows nothing. Says someone's doing black magic on you. To hell with all this nonsense. We have a show tomorrow. We'll make love tonight.'

Uncorking the bottle that Lengri had returned, Johnny raised it in Urvashi's direction. 'Cheers! Only love tonight. Love with you.'

He lit a bunch of incense sticks, and then put on his red trousers and green coat. He was emptying the bottle down his throat. The universe was spinning inside his head. Putting his cap on, Johnny winked. 'What does Lengri know? What does the doctor know? My coat and pants are old, it's been so long since I bought you a skirt to replace the torn one. How do I buy new clothes?'

Caressing Urvashi's breasts, Johnny said, 'Everything will change from tomorrow. The show you'll put up, the songs you'll sing will have everyone asking for more.'

Urvashi did not reply.

'Let's rehearse today. The whole city will be in our pocket again tomorrow, Urvashi, promise me you won't leave me.'

Urvashi was silent.

'We'll do that song tomorrow. I'll start with Urvashi ka khel. She's my Laila, I'm her Majnu. All of you are her Lakshmi. She will answer any question you ask. She will sing any song you want. She will do whatever anyone asks her.'

Urvashi was expressionless.

Everything had turned misty. The universe was whirling inside Johnny's head. Puranchandji, Dalip, Ramanna, Hamid, Phulkalia, Moti, Lengri, the doctor—they were all laughing. Pointing at him and saying, 'You lost, Johnny.'

'Never,' Johnny roared. Dressed in his bright coat and trousers, his oversized shoes, and his feathered cap, Johnny said, 'Who dares defeat me. Show me. Main Johnny hoon. Bastards, swine. Did I or did I not bring you the bird of pleasure?'

Everyone was laughing, the laughter of cynics.

Johnny said, 'Who am I anyway? Urvashi is my mistress, I'm her servant. Urvashi sings aayega aanewala. Don't you people know? Don't you ask her at the end of the show, how are you, Urvashi? Doesn't she answer, I'm happy? Johnny keeps me like a queen. Don't you ask, how are we, Urvashi? Doesn't she say, you're well, all of you are happy?'

They left. Suddenly Johnny found himself alone in the room with Urvashi. He put his arms around her. He said, 'Promise me that you won't leave me? Promise me, I'll die if I don't see you.'

Urvashi was silent.

'Should I turn out the light? You can talk to me in the dark. I can hear everything. Shall I turn out the lamp?' Urvashi did not reply.

Johnny began to cry. A putrid room, filled with smoke from the lamp and the incense. Urvashi was smiling, the smile she enchanted the world with.

Johnny sobbed.

Urvashi's show. Johnny and Urvashi's show. The last show of the season.

Nineteen paise for a ticket. Buy and enter.

The curtain parted. Johnny entered and sat on a chair, with Urvashi on his lap.

Johnny had made up his face today, put fresh feathers in his cap.

Today Urvashi was dressed in a shiny silk sari, with a crown of imitation pearls on her head and wearing costume jewellery.

Johnny said, 'You've never seen the kind of show that Urvashi has for you today. Urvashi, say hello to the people.'

'Hello hello hello people. I am Urvashi. Aami Urvashi. Main Urvashi hoon.'

'What can you do?' asked the people.

'I sing, I dance, I talk.'

'Why do you sound hoarse?'

'Because you came as my lover and got me ice cream.'

A wave of laughter.

'Will you sing a song, Urvashi?'

'Kya gaana? Ki gaan? Which song?'

'One Hindi, one Bangla, one English.'

Urvashi smiled and bowed her head. Then she tilted her neck and said something to Johnny. Johnny nodded in agreement.

Urvashi said, 'One lover got me ice cream, another got me thandai. My voice doesn't feel right. Can I sing soft and warm?'

'No, sing hard and hot.'

Urvashi sang in three languages: Chalte chalte alvida mat bolo, Jhilimili kancher churi shohag rani go, Do re mi.

'Listen to her. Her voice has cracked.'

'Lovers' torture.'

'Then talk instead.'

'Ask me questions.'

'Oye Urvashi! What will you do if you get a thousand rupees?'

'Johnny and I will have fun.'

'If you get a lakh?'

'Johnny and I will have fun along with all of you.'

'Ten lakh?'

Urvashi whispered, 'I'll catch all the birds of pleasure and put them in your hands.'

'What is it, why don't you answer?'

'Why don't all of you tell me instead?'
'Why so soft today? Are you shy?'
'I'm shy.'
'Why is Johnny crying?'
'Stupid, randy old man.'
'How are you, Urvashi? How are we? Tum kaise ho? Hum kaise hai? Speak up, like you used to. We've paid, do you realize we can't hear you speak?'

Urvashi was silent. Johnny had a terrified look in his eyes. Why wasn't Urvashi speaking?

'What's happened, Urvashi?'

Urvashi didn't answer.

'What is it? Is the show over?'

Urvashi forgot her usual soft and sweet tone. Suddenly, she screamed. Urvashi screamed in a discordant, harsh, tearful, desperate voice.

'I'm not well. My voice has been silenced. I won't laugh any more, I won't sing any more. I won't talk to you any more, people. The Urvashi who used to catch the birds of happiness for all of you, that Urvashi is no longer happy. Do you know why? My voice has fallen silent, there will be no sound any more. Everything has ended, people. I'm not well, I'm not happy, how will any of you be well? Your happiness has taken away my voice.'

The audience was dumbstruck.

Urvashi grated, 'My voice is gone, I am not well any more. Not well any more. Not well any more.'

'Not happy any more.' Urvashi shouted at the top of her voice. But suddenly her sobs, her screams, stopped. The curtain fell. The frightened, terrorized audience began to shove and yell. Everyone shouted, 'What is it, what's happened?'

Something behind the curtain was breaking, falling apart, loud sounds. The bewildered, curious public rushed onto the stage, tearing away the curtain. And then all of them fell silent.

Silence, silence, silence.

In fear, the audience watched Johnny tearing his talking doll apart, sobbing loudly.

Johnny's eyes and face and chest were soaked in tears. His lips kept moving. They said, 'I'm not well, because my voice has been silenced.'

But not a sound came from his throat.

JUMO BHISHTI

DHUMKETU

Translated from the Gujarati by Rita Kothari

Anyone who passed by Anandpur noticed the three identical squalid structures that stood in a corner, with an ancient, tired-looking tamarind tree casting its shadow over them. Here, the stink of sewage mingled with the dust in the air. The three hovels were patchwork constructions—made of tin, wood, and jute bags—and the entrance to the structures remained permanently open. Inside, Jumo Bhishti sat on a tattered mat, smoking his hookah. Throughout his life, Jumo had witnessed the sharp vicissitudes of fortune—from food being served in golden vessels to nibbling from chipped pots, he had seen it all. He had been born into wealth, the cherished child of well-to-do parents with everyone doting on him. He probably still remembered how, at the age of ten, he had sat atop an elephant for his wedding procession. This was around the same time he had been gifted a buffalo as a pet. Now, after experiencing all the vagaries of life, Venu, the buffalo, and Jumo lived together. Venu was an unusual name for an animal. In more prosperous times, Jumo had many friends, one of them being a Hindu who had a weakness for literature. He had affectionately christened the buffalo Venu, and the name had stuck.

Once wealthy, today all his possessions fit into the three ramshackle hovels. Venu occupied one of them, and Jumo, another. The third structure was used to store grass. Jumo and Venu gazed at each other all day long through the opening between their structures. Friends had come and gone. Now the only ones who remained were Jumo and Venu, bound to each other since childhood.

Every morning at five o'clock, Jumo loaded the large mashaq on Venu's back and set out. The bell around Venu's neck would tinkle gently and Jumo would follow, singing a ghazal. After delivering water from door to door, master and servant would make their way back home. Jumo would buy carrots for a few paise, and, at times, tomatoes and greens for his sabzi, and an armful of fresh fodder for Venu, which the buffalo would nibble on the way as he followed his master home. This was their daily routine. Jumo would never haggle for more than what he was offered, and he never sought a new customer if he lost an existing one. From noon till evening, Jumo would pull at his hookah. Venu, lost in the hum of the hubble-bubble, would languidly flap his ears to drive away flies and drift in and out of slumber. Later in the evening, the two friends would take a walk to the banks of the river. Occasionally, if the workload was light, they went to the riverbank in the morning as well.

One day, at five in the morning, they set out for the river. Jumo thought it would be a good idea if the buffalo chose to graze on the plants that grew by the river, but Venu disliked eating out in the open. Every time Jumo encouraged him, he would stop and bellow, as if saying, 'No, I will not eat.'

Finally, Jumo gave up, 'Very well, you can eat once we reach home. I think you enjoy being spoilt.'

The buffalo mooed victoriously, swished its tail, flapped his ears at Jumo, and turned around. He was so pleased by his triumph that he scampered a little on the way back.

'There, there...stop running, or I'll not take you home,' Jumo scolded. But Venu had already clambered onto the main road. It so happened that a railway line cut across the road. In his haste, Venu got his foot stuck between the tracks. He tried to free himself in vain and collapsed on the tracks. The more he struggled, the more firmly he was stuck. Jumo rushed to him. He held the buffalo's foot and tried to pull it out, but to no avail. In the hazy light of dawn, Jumo saw that the semaphore arm of the signal had been lowered. Terror gripped him as he wondered, what if the train....

Before he could complete the thought, he began rushing towards the road. He saw two young men out for their morning stroll. Each one had a walking stick in his hand which they swished about. They had removed the hats from their heads to enjoy the morning breeze.

Jumo ran up to them like a madman.

'Bhaisahib...my Ve...my buffalo will be cut to pieces right now. Look, he's trapped in the tracks.' The two young men looked in the direction Jumo was pointing. They could make out a dark form struggling.

'What is that?'

'My Venu...my buffalo'

'Oh ho, go quickly, run, run to the gate, man.'

'If you honourable people help me, we can save him.'

'Us? No, no, you run. Inform the gatekeeper,' they said and walked away.

Jumo ran towards the gatekeeper's hut, but there was no one around. All he could hear was the sound of someone working a grinding stone inside the hut. Just then, the distant whistle of an approaching train could be heard. Jumo cast a despondent glance around him, but there was no sign of anyone. He ran up to the signal post and pulled the chain and kept yelling for help. The hut beside him was deaf to his cries, which were drowned out by the clamour of the grinding stone. Jumo now kicked the hut door.

'Who is it?'

'Bhai-ben, please change the signal. My animal will be crushed.'

'There's no man in the house.' With that indifferent response, the grinding resumed.

The sound of the approaching train grew closer and closer.

'Run, run, my animal will be cut to pieces,' Jumo cried out as loudly as he could, but except for the harsh echo of his own voice, there was not a sound to be heard.

Jumo looked up at the sky. The last star was about to disappear. Soon, dawn broke, not with light, but with the haziness of a fog. The train was getting closer. He flung his stick away.

'Ya parwardigaar,' he called out loudly and ran. Venu lay panting from his efforts to free himself. Jumo sat by his side and gently scratched Venu's back.

'My friend, my brother, my Venu, we are together, okay?' Jumo said, and lay down by him.

With each passing moment the pounding of the train grew louder, its whistle shriller, and the clatter of its wheels came closer. Jumo hugged Venu tightly. But before the train could run over them, before he lost all his senses, Venu suddenly raised his head and struck at his master, flinging him away from the tracks!

The train ran over Venu. Jumo's clothes were soaked in Venu's warm blood. When he recovered and sat up, the only sign of his beloved friend were disjointed parts of his body lying in a pool of blood.

∽

To this day, every morning, Jumo returns to the spot where Venu had died, holding a flower in his hand. Calling out desperately for his friend, he places the flower on a stone before making his solitary journey back.

15

THE NIGHT OF THE FULL MOON

K. S. DUGGAL

Translated from the Punjabi by Khushwant Singh

No one believed that Malan and Minnie were mother and daughter; they looked like sisters—Minnie was quite a bit taller than her mother. People said, 'Malan, your daughter has grown into a lovely woman!' They never stopped gaping at the girl. She was like a pearl and as charming as she was comely.

When Malan looked at her daughter she felt as if she was looking at herself. She too had been as young and as beautiful. She hadn't aged much either. And there was somebody who was willing to go to the ends of the earth for her even now.

Why had her mind wandered to this man? He must be a dealer in pearls because every time she thought of him pearls dropped from her eyes! Her daughter was now a woman; it was unbecoming of her to think of a man. She had restrained herself all these years; why did her mind begin to waver? She must hold herself in check. Her daughter was due to wed in another week; she must not entertain such evil thoughts—never! Never!

'My very own, my dearest,' he had written only yesterday, 'do not forget me.' But every time he came to the village she sent him away without any encouragement. She shut her eyes as fast as she shut her door against him. He had refused to give her up. She was his life; without her he found no peace. He had spent many years waiting for her, pleading with her, suffering the pangs of love and passion. An age had passed and now the afternoon shadows had lengthened across life's courtyard.

Malan knew in her heart that he would come that night. Every full moonlit night he knocked on her door. And tonight the moon would be full. The night would be cold, frosty, and still. She had never unlatched her door for him. Would she tonight? She recalled a cold, moonlit night of many years ago. She was dancing in the mango grove when her dupatta had got caught in his hand. She had come to him bare-headed with the moonlight flecking her face with jasmine petals. He had put the dupatta across her shoulders—exactly the way it lay across her shoulders now. A shiver ran down Malan's spine.

Minnie came down the lane, tall and as slender as a cypress. Fair and fragile, she looked as if the touch of a human hand would leave a stain on her. Modestly, she had her dupatta wrapped around her face, and her eyes lowered.

Minnie was returning from the temple. She had prayed to the gods, she said softly to her mother, to grant her wish. She had prayed to the gods to grant everybody all their wishes.

Malan smiled. Something stirred her fancy. If her wish could be granted, she thought to herself, what would she ask for?

'Father has not returned!' complained Minnie.

'He is not expected back today; it will be a thousand blessings if he gets back by tomorrow. He has a lot of things to buy. At weddings and feasts it's better to have a little more than to run short,' explained Malan.

Minnie took off her sequinned dupatta and spread it on her mother's shoulders. She took her mother's plain dupatta instead, and went into the kitchen.

The light of the full moon came through the branches and sprinkled itself on Malan's face. The full moon always did something to her. It made her feel like one drunk. In another four days women would come to her courtyard to sing wedding songs. They would put henna on the palms and the soles of her daughter's feet. They would help her with her bridal clothes; load her with ornaments. How would her daughter look in bright red silk? And then the groom would come on horseback and take her to his own home and make love to her. He would kiss the henna away from the girl's palms and the soles of her feet.

It wasn't so very long ago that all this had happened to her, Malan. But Minnie's father had not once kissed the soles of her feet, nor ever pressed her palms against his eyes. He always came home tired; he ate his meal and fell fast asleep. Only the desire to have a son would occasionally arouse him at midnight. And then it was over so quickly that Malan had to spend hours counting the stars to cool down and get back to sleep. These midnight efforts had produced a daughter every year. The girls came to the world uninvited and departed without leave. Only one, Minnie, remained. She was a replica of her mother; like the fruit of a tree that bears only one. Minnie had large gazelle eyes—the eyes of Malan. Her long black hair fell down to her waist. And she had a full-bosomed wantonness that often made Malan think that all her frustrated passions had been rekindled in her daughter's body.

Minnie scrubbed the kitchen utensils, bolted the door of the courtyard, and went to bed in her own room. Malan was left alone.

It was late. The moon was so dazzlingly bright that it seemed to be focussing all its light in that one courtyard. Was it cold? Not really. Just pleasantly cool. Malan asked herself why she sat alone in the courtyard under the night of the full moon. Was she expecting someone? Minnie had gone to bed and her father had gone away to the city. Why was he away on a night like this? On full moon nights she used to keep herself indoors, away from temptation. But tonight she had her daughter's sequinned dupatta wrapped about her face. The sequins glistened in the silvery moonlight; it seemed as if the stars were entangled in her hair; they twinkled on her eyelashes, on her face, and on her shoulders. A nightjar called from the mango grove: *uk, uk, uk*. It would call like that all through the night: *uk, uk, uk*.

Her thoughts carried her with them. Her daughter would be married in a week's time. Then she would be left alone—all alone in the huge courtyard. A shiver ran through her body. The empty courtyard would terrify her. She would have to learn to live by herself. Her husband was too occupied with the pursuit of money; his moneylending and debt-collecting. He came back late in the evening only to collapse on his charpai. She had often asked him why he involved himself in so many affairs, but it had not made any difference.

Malan went indoors and saw her daughter fast asleep—dead to the world as only the young can be. Her red bangles lay beside her pillow. Silly girl! She had only to turn in her sleep and they would be crushed. Malan picked them up to put them on the mantelpiece. Before she knew it, she had slipped them on to her own arms; six on one, six on the other. They glistened even in the dark. They were new; her daughter had only bought them the day before from the bangle seller.

Malan came out into the moonlit courtyard—the sequinned dupatta on her head and her arms a-jingle-jangle with bright red glass bangles. She felt like a bride—warm, lusty. Blood surged in her veins.

There was a gentle knock on the door. It was he. It was the same knock—a nervous, hesitant knock. He was there as he had written in his letter he would be: 'On the full, moonlit night of December, I will knock at your door. If you are willing, open the door; if you are not willing, let it be. I will continue to knock at your door as I have always done.'

Knock, knock, knock—very soft, very sweet, a very inviting knock. Who could it be but he! The prowler on moonlit nights. Suddenly, the moon went behind a cloud and it was absolutely dark.

In a moment, Malan's feet took her across the dark courtyard. With trembling hands she undid the latch. Another moment and she was in his arms. Their lips met; their teeth ground against each other. Passion that had been held in check for over twenty years burst its banks and carried them on the flood.

Malan did not know how they went to the bo tree outside the village. She did not remember how they went into the field beside the bo tree— nor how long they stayed there. She was woken by the train that passed by the village in the early hours of the dawn. She extricated herself from her lover's embrace, covered her face with her dupatta, and hurried back to her home.

She slipped off the bangles from her arms and put them back beside her daughter's pillow. She folded her daughter's sequinned dupatta, took her own back and went to her charpai. She fell asleep at once and slept as she had never slept before—almost as if she were making up for a lifetime of sleeplessness.

When she woke, the sun was streaming into the courtyard.

'How you slept, like a little babe!' teased Minnie. Minnie had swept the rooms and the courtyard and cooked the morning meal. She had bathed and was ready to go to the temple. She had tied jasmine flowers in her dupatta to offer to the gods.

As soon as Minnie left, Malan stretched herself lazily on a charpai in the courtyard. She was filled with sleep and her head was filled with dreams.

A soft breeze began to blow. Warm sunshine spread in the courtyard. Malan felt like a bowl of milk, full to the brim—with a few petals of jasmine floating on it. It was a strange, heady intoxication. Her eyes would close, open, and then close again.

'O Malan! Where's that slut?' cried a voice suddenly. Malan felt as if someone had slapped her face.

'Never heard of such goings on!' said another voice, 'and only four days to her wedding!'

'What has my daughter done?' shrieked Malan, rising up in anger. 'She is as innocent as a calf.'

There were derisive exclamations. Then someone sneered, 'Your little calf has been on the dung heap all night.'

Malan's body went cold, her lifeblood draining from her veins; a deathly pallor spread over her face.

Lajo, her neighbour, was speaking. 'It was barely dark when the bitch walked off with a stranger. I had got up to relieve myself when I saw them go away into the fields, with their arms entwined around each other's waists. I didn't get a wink of sleep. We have to watch the interests of our daughters. I've never heard of anyone blacken the faces of her parents in this way.'

Malan sat still as if turned to stone. She did not seem to hear what was being said.

The village watchman took up Lajo's story.

'Sister-in-law Malan,' he said, trying to attract her attention.

'What is it, Jumma?' Her voice seemed to come out of the depths of a deep well.

'Bhabhi, this is not the sort of thing one can talk about easily. An awful thing happened in the village last night. My hair has gone grey with the years I've been watchman of the village, but never have I known such a scandal. Your daughter blackened her face with someone under the bo tree. Twice I passed within ten paces of them. There they were locked together, limb joined to limb; oblivious of all but each other. I kept guard over your house. I said to myself, "The wedding is to take place in another four days; the house must be full of new dresses and ornaments and the door wide open!" I left at dawn. I don't know what time your daughter came back after whoring. If she were my child I would break every bone in her body.'

Malan gazed at the watchman, stunned.

Jumma was followed by Ratna, the zamindar. He was in a rage.

'Where is that slut?' he roared. 'Couldn't she find another field for whoring?' Ratna leapt about as he spoke. The neighbours came out of their homes to watch and listen. Ratna continued. 'I was on my way to the well when I saw her come out of the field with her face wrapped in the sequinned dupatta. I thought that the girl had come out to ease herself; but then her lover emerged from the other end of the same field. I saw them with my own eyes.'

At that moment, Minnie tore her way through the crowd. She had heard all that had been said about her. 'You are lying, Uncle!' she shrieked.

'You dare call me a liar, you little trollop! You ill-starred wretch! And how did a broken red bangle happen to be in my field?' He untied the knot in his shawl, took out a piece of red bangle and slapped it on Minnie's palm. Minnie ran her eyes over her arms and counted the bangles; there were only eleven. The world swam before her eyes and then darkened.

The women exchanged glances. They had seen Minnie buy the bangles. Yes, there were ten and then two more. And she had especially asked for red ones.

The courtyard was full of babbling men and women. Minnie's fiancé's father edged his way through; his wife was behind him. They flung all the presents they had received in front of Malan: clothes, money, and rings. The crowd gaped. Women touched their ears; young girls bit their fingernails. This was drama indeed. A broken engagement was a broken life. What would Minnie do, now that she would never find a husband? It served her right, shameless harlot!

Over the sound of their angry droning, there was a loud splash. For a moment the crowd was petrified. Then someone shouted, 'The well!' and understanding dawned.

Minnie was nowhere to be seen. Gentle Minnie who never raised her voice against anyone, who was as pure as the jasmine she wove into garlands. Minnie, who never tired of praying to her gods for the happiness of everyone she knew.

Suddenly sobered, people ran to the well. Only Malan sat where she was, numb with horror, unable to move. Her courtyard was empty—emptier than it ever had been, as empty as it always would be now.

16

THE ALLIGATOR OF ALIGARH

A. M. GAUTAM

Kalua listened to his belly groan with hunger. He mopped at the beads of sweat on his forehead with a gamcha and peeked over his wife's shoulder into a pot in which she was cooking some nameless concoction the colour of mucus, with a few pieces of onion here and there trying to drown themselves. The sight of it was enough to dull his appetite a little. To make things worse, there wasn't nearly enough of it to sneak some off to Safeda. His friend would just have to go hungry again.

He looked at Gudiya, his little sister, reading a scrap of a newspaper in a corner, and felt guilty about thinking of Safeda when he was failing to provide enough even for his family. Only last month, Gudiya had fallen sick and the doctor had advised Kalua to include meat in her diet at least once a week to make up for protein deficiency.

Despite this guilt, however, Safeda was also important to Kalua. Like many other people in the world, Kalua had found his best friend at his workplace. Only, the workplace happened to be a gutter, and the best friend happened to be an alligator.

Kalua didn't know how Safeda came to be there, only that the creature was hurt and starving when they first met. Kalua fed it his own lunch and applied cool mud to its bruises. Because of the whitish grey colour of its skin, which Kalua thought unusual, he named the alligator Safeda. The absence of sunlight in the creature's life might have had something to do with its unusual pigmentation. Or maybe it was just an anomaly. Whatever the cause, the contrast between the alligator's pale hide and his own had amused Kalua to no end.

A few days later, Kalua heard someone in the nearby market talking about a man arrested for smuggling exotic reptiles to Indian connoisseurs. The police were forced to release him from custody soon afterwards; apparently he had flushed his specimens down the toilet to remove all incriminating evidence. Kalua knew now where a part of that evidence had ended up, but not intending to get mixed up with the police, he kept his suspicions to himself.

That was twelve years ago.

Kalua had not been married then and Gudiya hadn't even been born. In those days, he used to go into the sewers only when his father's cough was exceptionally bad. He hated every second of it and swore daily to himself that he would become anything but a jamadaar.

That, of course, was before the world had explained the inescapability of his caste to him, and before his parents had died of tuberculosis, leaving him to bring up his baby sister all alone.

'Ae, Gudiya, what are you doing reading in this bad evening light? You'll ruin your eyes,' he called out to the girl whom he had managed to keep away from the sewers, and had even sent to school.

Up until now, at least.

Gudiya was now almost ten years old, but looked like she was only six or seven. This wasn't unusual in their neighbourhood, though—malnutrition made the kids all look younger than they actually were, and the adults older.

Gudiya looked at him and threw aside the newspaper scrap she was reading. 'Went to the butcher in the afternoon, but he had already gutted and skinned everything. He asked me to come only when my cut had healed completely.'

After school, Gudiya often went to help the neighbourhood butcher in his shop, and he tossed her a few coins for her labour every now and then. Two days ago, she had cut her hand while slicing a piece of meat.

It was an ugly gash, and Kalua had tied a clean piece of cloth around it, hoping that it would not get infected. The butcher, Kalua knew, had sent Gudiya away not out of concern for her but because he did not want to risk her blood making the meat impure for his customers.

'It's okay, beta, don't worry about it. This is just a temporary situation. Things will go back to normal soon,' Kalua told her with a conviction he did not possess himself. His wife joined them and put the cooking pot between them, holding it carefully with rags in her hands. She rotated it a few times, as though trying to pull off some magic trick that would turn that mixture of water, flour, and salt into real food. There were only two spoons in the pot.

'Aren't you eating, Bhabhi?' Gudiya asked.

'I'll eat later. You two eat now, and please make sure you wipe the pot clean.'

But, there was nothing to be had later, Kalua knew that well enough. Tomorrow it would be a week since either of them had gone to work. This muck in the pot, this was the last of their rations.

He got up so quickly that his head swam a little and his stomach growled in protest.

'I am sorry, I remembered just now—Varshneyji had asked me to visit his house today. He wants me to help unload some stuff from his terrace. I'll just go there and come back in a while, okay?'

'But your dinner?' his wife asked, not meeting his eyes.

'You two finish it off. I'll have some chai–nashta with Varshneyji.'

Kalua did not wait for her response, but at the door he paused for just a moment to look at her moving slowly to sit beside Gudiya. After he emerged from the hut, he took a few steps to the right so that they wouldn't see him standing there. Then, he let out a long, heavy sigh, the sort that can crush those who hear it and must, therefore, only be released once you are at a safe distance from the people you love.

His wife must have seen through his lie. She knew full well that he wouldn't even be allowed to sit on the curb outside a baniya's house, let alone be invited inside and asked to handle his possessions. Not in a million years—a pamphlet of Swachh Bharat Abhiyan fluttered near his feet and Kalua spat at it in disgust—not after a thousand more Swachh Bharat Abhiyans had come and gone could that happen in their world.

The only place Kalua, or anyone from his caste, could go to in the house of someone from an upper caste, like Varshneyji, was the latrine. Straight in, straight out, and a few coins dropped on their palms at the door without a word exchanged. Kalua and his kin were like elves. Shit-scooping, latrine-scraping elves. Invisible and inaudible to everyone.

Still, even while wading through all the literal and figurative shit in their lives, they had kept going, one way or another. Until a fortnight ago, when a saffron-robed rally had snaked its way through the jamadaar basti where they lived, holding up bright posters that most of the residents couldn't read.

Fat government men with sweat-shined faces, saccharine smiles, and noses scrunched up against the smell of Kalua and his people. They declared proudly through their loudspeakers that no one would be required to lower themselves into a sewer any more. If anybody asked them to do so, the government would penalize that person.

They were told that the credit for all this went to their chief minister and the prime minister, both of whom cared deeply for all Hindus, including Dalits like Kalua and his neighbours.

Once they had finished making their speeches, the fat men got in their vehicles and waved to Kalua and the other shanty dwellers; they were careful not to shake hands with them or touch them in any way. Amidst much fanfare, with satisfied smiles, they departed the same way they had arrived and breathed freely once more in the clean air outside the slum.

It was only a couple of hours later that Kalua, his wife, and their friends realized that the government men had forgotten to mention what jobs they would be doing now that their present employment had been declared illegal.

And so it was that the slum had begun to crawl towards starvation.

They had held up until now by dipping into their meagre savings. A few of them had managed to get odd jobs here and there, but no one really wanted to employ a jamadaar in their shop or house, or anywhere that there would be a chance of being touched by them.

Kalua wondered where he could go to pass the time while his family had their dinner and decided upon the only place that felt a little like home.

A horrible home, true, but still a home, with the comfort of an old friend.

Maybe he would also be able to catch a few rats down there and feed them to Safeda.

∽

'Do you think Bhaiya will be able to get some work today?' Gudiya asked her bhabhi, back in the house.

'Yes, yes, of course, he'll find some work. Don't you worry about it.'

But Gudiya did worry about it.

She worried that her brother had not been able to feed his pet for the past two weeks and it was making him even sadder than usual. Gudiya had never met this pet, but she knew its name was Safeda; it had slipped out of Kalua once, though he had not noticed it.

Gudiya liked to imagine that Safeda was a fluffy white dog like the pet one of her classmates had. Only, her bhaiya kept his pet in a sewer instead of at home. This didn't seem strange to her ten-year-old mind because she knew that Bhabhi would never have allowed Bhaiya to keep the dog in the house, not when they never had enough food or money for the three of them.

Like most kids in the neighbourhood, Gudiya knew that the last couple of weeks had been especially bad for everyone. It was evident in the way that people she had known all her life to wake up at dawn and go to work now spent their days sitting despondently in front of their shacks, waiting for something to happen. The desperate wait reminded Gudiya of the days when she was a toddler and would keep looking out anxiously for the ice-cream man, who never came to their gully. The worst of it was the change that had come over her bhaiya. No matter how bad things had got in the past, he would always have a joke tucked away somewhere in his head, ready to be summoned and released to laughter all around when things began to look too grim. He was a doer who liked to make things happen, rather than wait passively for situations to resolve themselves for better or for worse. Like, when Gudiya had waited, and waited, and waited, for the ice-cream man day after day, one day Bhaiya had just brought back three orange-flavoured ice creams from god knew where. These past few days, however, he hardly talked to her at all.

Some days, while taking a bath, Gudiya would move her fingers slowly underwater in the bucket and watch them for minutes on end. That's how her brother looked these days. Like a man living underwater in his head; walking around in a bubble of empty space where no one could really reach him. Except for his pet, maybe. It might cheer him up if Gudiya brought it to the house and surprised him. Anyway, she was sure that it would cheer her up!

So, after her bhabhi had put her to bed, and gone to sleep herself, Gudiya put on the robe that Kalua wore when he went into the sewers. He had made it by stitching together discarded polythene bags. It was too large for her, of course, and fluttered behind her like a superhero's cape. In the weak light leaking into the hut from a street light, the multicoloured robe of polythene bags shimmered like an undisciplined rainbow. She then put on Kalua's yellow safety helmet and his brown leather boots.

Quietly, Gudiya stole out of the hut and closed the door behind her.

She walked up to the open manhole down which she had seen her bhaiya disappear many times. Then, with a look at the moon overhead, she lowered herself down into the darkness, down the iron rungs of the sewer.

☙

This manhole into which Gudiya had lowered herself was connected to other manholes in the city through large pipes constituting Aligarh's sewage network. As Gudiya descended further down the hole, she could hear the water splashing at the bottom and her guts contracted a little with the inherent fear of invisible damp things.

The stench of sewage was overwhelming and made her feel a little faint.

To steel herself, she looked up at the circle of the night sky through the open manhole, but it looked so far away suddenly that she thought it better to concentrate on her descent.

Finally, after a few moments, or minutes, or millennia, her boots found mushy ground.

A small part of her mind wondered how a dog could live in a place where the water came up to her ankles. But before she could give it a thought, there was a sound of water splashing nearby.

It sounded like she wasn't alone. Someone else was also taking a night walk here. Or maybe it was just the sound of her heart tumbling out of her mouth and falling into the sewer.

Gudiya moved forward, putting one foot in front of the other, like a little soldier in large boots. Her polythene robe made an almost-but-not-quite-silent slithering sound behind her.

A few more steps and the darkness would be absolute. Gudiya pressed a little wire in the helmet and the bulb–battery combination that Kalua had taped together came to life. The feeble light threw long shadows on the sewer's walls and Gudiya saw that the pipe turned sharply to the left a little way off in the distance.

Again, she heard the sound of water splashing. Despite an instinctive urge to run back, she kept walking in the direction of the sound. And then, as she stood at the bend in the pipe she saw in front of her a man tossing something into the water at his feet.

No, not into the water. Tossing something to a creature on the ground.

A creature that definitely was not the fluffy white dog that she imagined Pinky's pet looked like. Sharp white teeth glinted in an evil grin at her.

A pair of dull green eyes with black slits for pupils measured the flesh on her bones. In the wavering light of Gudiya's helmet-bulb, she thought she saw a ripple of excitement pass through the monster's dirty rubbery-white body.

The man standing beside it, startled by the light, turned to face Gudiya. It was her bhaiya, of course, and how shocked he looked! Dead rats dangled by their tails in his hand like the balls of the neighbourhood butcher, who had shown them to Gudiya last week and had given her twenty rupees just for touching them.

She looked from her brother to the monster at his feet and opened her mouth to scream but found the sound missing. She closed her fists so tightly at her sides that the cloth Kalua had tied as a bandage came off and two tiny drops of blood dropped down from the open cut into the water. The starving alligator, half-blind, but no less a predator for it, caught the whiff of fresh blood and lunged towards it.

Kalua's mind tried to make sense of the situation and failed irrevocably. His thoughts came to him only as snatches of the self-evident truth. Must do something. Quickly. His friend, whose primary trait in the last twelve years had been laziness, was now paddling furiously towards his sister, who stood rooted to the spot.

A large piece of stone, dislodged long ago from the sewer's wall, was lying near where Safeda's tail was thrashing around in the water, and Kalua picked it up.

'Gudiya! GUDIYA! Run. NOW!'

But Gudiya's eyes were locked on Safeda, as though hypnotized, and she looked like she could not even hear Kalua.

Kalua moved towards Safeda, stumbling in the water and almost falling down. He righted himself and was near the alligator's head in a couple of strides. Safeda turned to look at him and, for a moment, Kalua thought he could see a trace of human intelligence in the green eyes, a hesitation in moving towards Gudiya.

But hunger is hunger.

It turned again towards Gudiya and with a flick of its tail almost hit Kalua, as if warning him not to meddle with its dinner.

Kalua raised the stone high above his head, stepped forward, and brought down its jagged corner into Safeda's left eye. He wanted only to buy enough time to send Gudiya away, but it was as if the violence had unleashed something inside him which he did not know existed.

Before Safeda could turn towards him, he straddled the creature and brought the stone down once again with all his strength. And then again, and again, until there was no movement left in the body and the light had gone out of Safeda's eyes. It felt a little like the final cleaning away of the shit that other people had flushed his way. Regular work, nothing odd. A frightened little giggle escaped Kalua's mouth at this thought.

He did not know what made him stop finally. Maybe it happened when Gudiya managed to find her voice again.

'Bhaiya, please. Enough.'

Her face looked so small, so fragile, in the half-light-half-shadow of the bulb in her helmet. It reminded him, strangely enough, of how little Safeda had been when he had found it starving in the sewer.

'Come, let's go.'

Kalua got off Safeda's lifeless body and took Gudiya by her hand.

He took one last look at his friend before turning away. An eyeball, dislodged from its socket, dangled from the destroyed face by a thin string of flesh. Even as he watched, the eyeball fell into the sewer water...Plop!

Kalua bent down for Gudiya to climb on to his back and like that they walked to the manhole's ladder. Slowly, Kalua climbed out.

∽

In her cot, tucked in by her brother, the monster in the sewer seemed little more than one of her regular nightmares to Gudiya.

With half-closed eyes she watched Kalua put on the polythene robe she had taken off—he had thrown his own on the street, blood-stained and grimy as it was—and picked something up from the kitchen shelf before going out again.

Fear crept back into her heart. 'Where are you going, Bhaiya? Come to sleep, please?'

As he put the thing that he had picked up from the shelf into his pocket, Gudiya saw that it was the knife she took with her when she went to work at the butcher's shop.

'Don't you worry, I'll be back up in no time at all,' he said with a tired little smile. Then, with a little hesitation, he added, 'And maybe tomorrow, we will have meat again for lunch. It'll be good for you, the doctor said.'

TALE OF A TOILET
RAMNATH GAJANAN GAWADE

Translated from the Konkani by Vidya Pai

'Arre, what's going on here?' the Sarpanch demanded as soon as he set foot in the panchayat office. Many of those who were just milling around drew back, while the ones who were seated sprang to their feet respectfully for he was not only the Sarpanch of the village but also a man with immense clout, one whose word carried weight.

'What's happening here? Who is making such a noise?'

'Bhau, I've made at least ten trips to the panchayat office, why haven't I been allotted a toilet even now?'

'What? You don't have a toilet? What do you do, then?'

'What can I do? Nothing.'

'Nothing? You just hold it in?'

A ripple of laughter spread through the room and the man who was demanding a toilet was confused. 'No, no, I go like all the others go....' he stammered.

'So...you go. Every day. What do you need a toilet for, in that case?'

'Others have been given a toilet. I want one too.'

'All right. Others have been given a toilet, so you want one too. You don't really need one, do you?'

'Of course I do! That's why I'm making the request.'

'You are making a request. Then why are you raising your voice and fighting with people?'

'I'm not fighting. I just asked the Secretary why my application was rejected and he started giving me a lecture.'

'My god! He started lecturing you, did he? Arre, Secretary, why don't you see what he wants, don't make the poor fellow hold it all in!'

The Sarpanch walked into his room and sat down. The Secretary smiled his crooked smile and followed him into the room carrying a file. He showed the Sarpanch some papers and began to explain something which must have been of serious import because the Sarpanch asked the peon to shut the door of the room.

The Sarpanch and the Secretary were closeted in there for a long while and those who had come to meet the Sarpanch had to cool their heels in the outer room. The man who wanted the toilet kept telling everyone about the problems he was facing and instead of listening to him, people told him how they had gone about the process.

'We didn't want a toilet, even then they gave us one. How can you use that tiny space? We keep our hens there at night. At least they are safe now, the foxes would have made off with them otherwise.'

When he couldn't bear to listen to their stories any longer, the man sidled up to the Gram Sevak whose job it was to look after the welfare of the villagers.

'The government makes these schemes for the poor, but these officials give them to people who have no use for such schemes. The whole purpose is ruined. The hungry man gets nothing. But they heap food on the plates of those whose bellies are full. Do you think we don't know why all this is being done?' he spluttered.

'Now wait a minute, will anyone come to your house and build a toilet just because you make a ruckus here?' the Gram Sevak asked mildly. 'There is a procedure that must be followed. Your income must be within the prescribed limit, only then can you avail of this scheme.'

'Saiba, we have no income. I have no job, but we don't get a toilet. And those who roam around in motor cars get toilets under this scheme.'

'Didn't you apply to the Panch who is in charge of your area?'

'The Sarpanch is the Panch in our part of the village. Doesn't he know that there is no toilet in my house?'

'That's not how it works. There is a fixed quota of toilets. And those have to be distributed in the whole village.'

Just then the Secretary emerged from the Sarpanch's room. Two or three people pushed their way in and the man tried to follow them, but the Sarpanch sent him back. 'Why are you in such a hurry, you don't have to come here to meet me. You go past my house three or four times a day. Come and see me some time,' he said.

The man couldn't say anything to this, so he waited outside till everyone finished their work. He had decided that he would get the toilet allotted to his name today, come what may. He was tired of making these endless trips to the panchayat office and listening to excuses; his patience was wearing thin. People who didn't apply for a toilet were granted one under the scheme. Officials went to their homes and made them sign the forms. And people like us, who submitted the application forms more than once, got nothing. They don't say yes or no. How is it that only our application forms go missing? Do these people remove them from the list? He would get to the bottom of this matter today, he decided, standing with his arms crossed across his chest, waiting to meet the Sarpanch. It was a long while before the Sarpanch finished all his work and emerged from the room. The man rushed up to him, 'Bhau, you are the Panch in our area, you should allot a toilet to us under the scheme,' he said.

'Panch? I am the Sarpanch. I have to look after the interest of the whole ward.'

'But you are the Panch in our section. So you must get it allotted in my name.'

'Now, who told you that?'

The Sarpanch cast an eye around the room and the Gram Sevak bent his head over his work, writing busily while the others remained silent as though to show that they were not responsible.

'Don't listen to what people say. You want a toilet? You'll get one. Don't walk away from us. I know you think you don't need us now as you have latched on to important people. Tell me, do they give you beer and mutton?'

'Bhau, many of them came to my house, but I didn't follow any of them. I didn't accept anything either.'

'I don't know if you followed them or took what they gave, but I know that you let us down.'

'No, Bhau, I'm telling the truth... I voted for you!'

'Sheee shee! Don't say that. It's a crime to disclose who you voted for. You'll get me in trouble too.'

'How can I assure you, Bhau?'

'I'd summoned you the other day to repair the broken fence in my field. But you said you had other work.'

'How could I leave that work half done, Bhau?'

'So, how can we rely on you? What happens to the cows that graze in the field with the broken fence?'

'I'll come, Bhau, I'll come.'

'And look here, there's no need to come and shit on the embankment by our house just because you haven't been allotted a toilet. We have to pass that way every day and the stench is overpowering. I'll throw stones at you if I see you squatting there again.'

'No, no, Bhau. I don't go there. I take my tin can and go up the hill.'

'Don't tell lies.'

'It's the truth, Bhau. And even if I do go that side I don't squat on the embankment. I go down to the area by the stream.'

'No, no. Don't go down there. That stream waters our fields.'

'But there's no water in that stream now. It's dry.'

'I know. But it's full of water in the rainy season. You people only know how to dirty your surroundings. God knows when you'll learn something better.' The Sarpanch strode off briskly, muttering to himself.

The man felt as though he had been slapped publicly. The others in the room were immersed in their own work but he felt that they were laughing at his boorishness. Why did I ask the Sarpanch for a toilet, the man rued as he made his way home.

His mother was groaning loudly and calling his name aloud when he got home.

'What's the matter, why are you yelling like that?' he snapped.

'What else can I do? Come, come. Take me out at once. I can't hold on any longer, my son!'

'I've told you so many times. Lean on your stick and make your way slowly behind the house but no! You insist on waiting for me!'

'Look at my swollen fingers and my knees. Why would I wait for you if I could manage on my own?'

'Get up now. Quick. Or you'll mess up the whole place, right here.'

'Yes, yes. Give me that stick.'

'What do you need that stick for now?' He picked her up like a bundle of clothes and strode towards the hill.

'Set me down. I'll walk slowly, just give me some support,' she insisted but his patience had worn thin. Anger and frustration had set off a variety of thoughts loose in his brain and his body surged with strength as he strode up the hill.

He would usually make her squat close to the house but his neighbour Aku's words resounded in his ears. 'Our children play here. Take her somewhere that side,' Aku had said in front of the others, so he had moved ahead.

'Arre, why are you taking me so far?' the old woman protested.

'I'll take you up the hill and toss you down!'

'Do that. Do what you want. At least I'll be free of this fate worse than death!'

'The neighbours can't bear the stink, they say.'

'But I can't hold on any longer,' she whined and the man dumped her on the ground.

'Why do you go and shit near his house?' he burst out angrily as she made her way behind a clump of bushes. He didn't wait there any longer, and on his way down the hill he saw the large number of toilets that had been built beside people's houses under the government scheme. His eyes fell on the toilet next to Molu's house and he was filled with hope. Molu was close to them, almost like a family member, maybe he would let the old woman use their toilet for a few days till they could get one for themselves. He hoped Molu would agree and wanted to ask him at once, but he remembered his mother would be waiting on the hill, so he filled a tin can with water and began the climb again. He was surprised to see that he was growing short of breath. How heavy this little can is, he thought.

He didn't have the confidence to carry his mother down the slope, so he held her hand and helped her down. He told her of his plan to approach Molu but she didn't think Molu would agree.

'You know what they are like. Why will they listen to you?' she said.

'Let's see. If he says yes, things will be easier for you and for me too. You'll just have to pour water when you are done.'

'I don't think....'

'Why won't he agree? He was like Baba's brother, wasn't he?'

His mother didn't say anything after that. She merely plonked down on the veranda when they got home, as though she had accomplished some huge task. The man, however, rushed to Molu's house. 'Kaka, Kaka!' he called.

'What's the matter, Somlya?' Molu's wife, who was working in the garden, asked.

'Isn't he home?'

'He was here just a while ago.'

Suddenly the door of the toilet in the yard opened and Molu emerged. 'What's the matter, Somlya? Why are you here?'

'I was wondering if Aai could use your toilet for a few days....'

'Of course. Whenever she wants. Just see that she pours a bucketful of water once she's done.'

'No, no! We'll have to keep it shut for some time. The rains will start soon, we'll store firewood in there,' Molu's wife said, all of a sudden.

'Aggo, is the toilet meant for storing firewood?' Molu asked.

'Fix a place for the firewood, then.'

'What about the shack behind the house?'

'That shack is full of junk. And I'm scared that it will collapse with the first showers.'

'But it's just for a few days....'

'No, no. The septic tank is very small. It'll get filled quickly.'

'Bu—but....'

'Somlya, our toilet is new, we haven't started using it regularly. The children will get upset if we let others use it. Ask someone else. I'm sure they won't refuse if they know it's your mother who needs it.'

Somlo realized that there was no point in continuing the discussion, so he returned home. There were a couple of toilets outside some of the other houses in the neighbourhood but he didn't think the owners would agree to his request.

Instead, he asked his mother, 'Avai, when will Dada come? It's been a while since he came home.'

'Why? Let him come when he wants to.'

'I've been thinking, we don't want anyone's toilet. Let us build a small one for ourselves. I spoke to a mason who said it would cost about thirty thousand rupees. But if we build a simple structure close to the house, it could be done in twenty.'

'What about the money?'

'If Dada can give ten thousand, I'll dig the pit for the septic tank. We'll have to buy stone slabs and cement.'

A scooter came to a halt outside the house.

'Avai, Dada will live for a hundred years! I just took his name and here he is!'

The old woman seemed to forget her ill health as she pulled herself up eagerly, delighted to also see her daughter-in-law and granddaughter.

'What have you been up to, Avai, have you been well?' her elder son asked, and at once she lay back as though she was very ill. 'We were just talking about you,' she said.

'Me? Why?'

She remained silent and it was left to Somlo to explain the circumstances.

'Dada, Avai can't move about very easily these days. We need a small toilet near the house.'

His sister-in-law chimed in all of a sudden, 'Yes, yes. I was thinking of that, too. The government has built toilets for the whole world, why not for us? We find it very difficult when we come to the village. Bai isn't used to squatting in the open.'

'So, get one allotted to us, then.'

'That's not happening. That's why I'm saying let's build one ourselves.'

'Not happening? Why? The big houses have toilets allotted to them, but we don't. Why don't you ask Bhau?'

'How many times will I ask him? I went there again today and the Secretary gave me a big lecture.'

'You must have tried to act smart.'

'All right, I act smart. Why don't you go and ask him right now? I'm telling you, I've submitted not one, but three application forms in Avai's name.'

'Weren't you talking of building a toilet just now?'

'Yes. Instead of begging this one and that one for favours, let's build a small toilet ourselves. You give ten thousand rupees and I'll manage the rest.'

'Ten thousand rupees! Do you think I earn in lakhs just because I have a regular job? There are instalments to be paid for the scooter and other things. Life in the village is simple and cheap, you can cook and eat anything. And Bai has to be admitted to kindergarten this year. The fees for this KG class are twelve thousand rupees. Maybe it is you who can give me ten thousand now....'

Somlo, who was staring at his sister-in-law while listening to his brother's litany of woes, noticed the new gold bangles on her wrists. She grew aware of his scrutiny and quickly drew the end of her sari about herself and walked into the house.

This wretched toilet has ruined my whole day, Somlo fumed, as he lay down for a while after lunch. He had missed out on being hired for work that morning and had done nothing productive all day. He suddenly remembered the broken fence in the field and made his way to the Sarpanch's house. The Sarpanch, who was lying on the porch, opened his eyes to see who was approaching and quickly shut them again.

'Bhau, the fence....'

'Yes, yes. The fence!' The Sarpanch sat up hurriedly and called out to someone.

'Aggo, Paru, show him the broken fence.'

'The fence can wait. What about the problem with our toilet?' Paru asked.

'Yes, yes. Someone was supposed to come and check that. He hasn't come yet. I'm glad you're here, Somlya. The water in the toilet just doesn't recede. I don't know if the septic tank is full.'

'But Bhau....'

'Don't pull a long face. I'm not asking you to empty the septic tank. Just open the cover and see if it's full. Paru, show him where the pickaxe and crowbar are kept. This must be done right now. The stench is overpowering.'

'Bhau, let your man come, I can help him....'

'He'll come, he'll come. But you take a look right now. I can't bear the stink. The Secretary was supposed to bring him but god knows where he's gone. And yes, Somlya, I've included you in the list for the new set of toilets that will be sanctioned. Get an application form from the Secretary and make it out in your name.'

'Not in my name. In my mother's. The house stands in her name.'

'That doesn't matter. I'll take care of all that. You should have been allotted one from the last set but they sanctioned only two hundred toilets while there were four hundred applicants. What could we do? But this time we have asked for eight hundred toilets. Now we know that everyone needs a toilet, the MLA has said that everyone should have a toilet by their home. You go to the Secretary tomorrow and fill in the application form.'

'All right, Bhau.' He followed Paru as she led the way to the toilet and the septic tank.

He went to the panchayat office early the next morning, but the office was closed. It was a long while before someone at a nearby kiosk told him that the office would remain shut because it was the second Saturday of the month. It was past eleven, well past the time when he could be hired for any work that day. He had lost out on another day's wages, he thought angrily, as he made his way home.

Baburao, the Panch from the Opposition party, who was riding past on his scooter, drew up by his side.

'Arre, Somlya, where are you off to? Are you free today?' he asked.

'Yes...I mean no....'

'Forget what you were going to do. Come with me. There are two wells that need to be emptied and cleaned. You'll get double the usual wages.'

Somlo thought it was a good idea, he could make up for the wages he had lost on both days.

'Arre, say something. If you want to come, come at once. You'll get lunch there,' Baburao said.

Somlo knew that Baburao was the Sarpanch's sworn enemy and anyone caught hobnobbing with him was considered an enemy too. Perhaps it would be better to steer clear of this man, he thought.

'You people don't want to work, just to loaf around all day. You can earn something instead of wasting time. Now, hop on if you want to come or I'm going alone,' Baburao snapped.

Somlo felt his resolve crumble as he perched on the pillion behind Baburao, but his mind was filled with misgivings. What he had feared soon came to pass as he saw the car that belonged to the Sarpanch approach in their direction. Somlo shrank into himself, trying to seem inconsequential. The car hurtled past and he was relieved to think that he hadn't been seen.

The labourers ate and drank and worked till sundown cleaning the two wells. The others in the team were also from the village, but they belonged to Baburao's party, so he learnt a lot from the gossip that was exchanged.

The panchayat had been sanctioned two hundred toilets on two occasions in recent times, he was told. The Sarpanch had kept the major share for himself and the Panchs in his party, allotting a few toilets to those in the Opposition who were favourably disposed towards him. The application forms of the people in the Opposition who were in dire need of this facility went missing, they said. Somlo began to suspect that the Sarpanch had deliberately misplaced his application form too, but there was nothing to be gained in ranting against the powers that be.

The next day was a Sunday and there was a host of work that had to be done before the rains, but he couldn't concentrate on anything. He visited some friends who had been allotted toilets in the past and asked them what they had done. Some of them told him about the procedure, but many said they had only signed the application form, while the Panch and the Sarpanch had handled everything else, forcibly erecting the kiosks in their yards despite their protests.

Early on Monday, Somlo gathered all the necessary information and went to the panchayat office but the Secretary had not arrived. The Sarpanch showed up after a while and assured Somlo that he remembered his case, even before the man could open his mouth.

'Somlya, you looked very grand riding that scooter that day,' he added.

'Scooter? No, Bhau, who will let me ride their scooter?'

'I don't know about that. But you were sitting on a blue scooter....'

'Blue? Oh! I was on the pillion on Baburao's scooter. He took me across the river to clean two wells.'

'Don't tell lies. I saw you partying there.'

'No, Bhau. They gave us lunch that day.'

'So who was that guzzling beer?'

'No, no, Bhau. That's not true.'

'All right, then. Did you people remove all the debris and clean the wells properly? Or did you just waste panchayat funds?' The Sarpanch asked as he cast an eye over the others gathered there.

Somlo's anger and frustration grew as thoughts of the toilet hovered like an immense weight on his head. His body seemed on fire and he wanted nothing more than to move away from all this and immerse himself in silence.

The Secretary arrived and those who were seated got up and those who had moved away crowded around his desk again. Everyone wanted him to attend to their needs at once. Someone wanted a signature, another wanted a receipt. Someone wanted this, someone else wanted to submit something. Each man had a different set of needs.

Many of those who surged forward managed to get their work done. Those who were well connected to the powers that be got their needs attended to quickly. Those who held back out of deference or because they wanted to avoid the jostling crowd, like Somlo did, had to wait.

'Sahib....'

'Arre, you were the one making a big fuss the other day. Did you get the toilet?'

'Sahib, I've come for that only...the Sarpanch has sent me.'

'Arre, baba, getting a toilet allotted to someone is not in my hands. The Sarpanch has to do that. Go and speak to him.'

'I did. He told me to collect the application form from you.'

'All right. Let me tell you the old process has changed. There are new application forms which require an income certificate, land-holding proof, and an affidavit to be attached.'

'All right, sahib. Where will I get that done?'

'I'll explain all that later. I have just received this letter, I must see what it says.'

'But, sahib, we need to get the toilet this time.'

'Look, I don't provide toilets. The government does that and the panchayat allots them to people.'

'Panchayat? Isn't this our panchayat office?'

'Yes. But the Sarpanch and the other Panchs have to pass the application.'

'The Sarpanch said he had passed the application.'

'All right. Get the documents I asked for, then we'll see.'

'But, sahib, I submitted all those documents. Twice.'

'Those forms have been cancelled.'

'No. The Sarpanch said he had passed them.'

'All right. You can go, now. It's half past one. I must have lunch.'

'All right. I'll come in the evening.'

He hesitated for a long while but he was hungry too. The desire to get the toilet allotted in his name made the hunger pangs seem unimportant, so he debated whether he should go home and have lunch or wait there for the Secretary to finish.

The Gram Sevak, who had gone to a nearby restaurant for lunch, was returning to the panchayat office. 'What's the matter? Isn't your job done?' he asked.

'No. It seems we must fill some new forms.'

'Yes. What happens now is that anyone can erect a toilet anywhere once it has been sanctioned. The Sarpanch issues a certificate saying someone he favours is a needy person, even if he is wealthy. So, the poor people are sidelined while the wealthy ones get the allotments. According to the new rules, the Secretary has to first issue a certificate of income.'

'But we had submitted the forms earlier.'

'Those would have been valid if they had been passed at that time. Now they have been cancelled. If you want a toilet now you must follow the new procedure.'

There was a rush for the new application forms soon and Somlo managed to get a copy too. He got the application and affidavit ready and returned to the panchayat office in four or five days.

'In whose name is the house registered?' the Secretary asked.

'In my mother's name.'

'Then get the application done in her name.'

'But the Sarpanch told me to apply in my name.'

'All right. Just don't blame me if this application is rejected and you don't get a toilet.'

Somlo didn't say another word. He felt that the Gram Sevak was the one he could trust, so he made his way to his room. The Gram Sevak echoed the Secretary's words, but if Somlo could take his mother to the taluka revenue office and get an affidavit issued by the Mamlatdar, the other matters could be handled in the panchayat office.

Somlo dragged his ailing mother to the revenue office and rushed to the panchayat with the Mamlatdar's affidavit but the Secretary was going out somewhere. He asked Somlo to deposit the documents with the clerk, he would look at them later, but Somlo wanted him to take a look right then, so he didn't budge. Suddenly a man rushed in with a file and the Secretary returned to his desk. He spent a long time going through the file's contents, handed the man a signed receipt, and told him to come the next day.

He was getting up to go when Somlo shoved his application before him, 'Sahib, take a look at this also,' he pleaded.

'Don't you understand anything that you're told? Give it to the clerk. I have to go. It's getting late.'

'It's not late, sahib. It's not even four.'

'So you're keeping a tab on the time, are you? Go...complain to whomever you want.'

'No, no, sahib. Just give me five minutes...please.'

'Do you think I'm your servant, you're going on and on like this! No. I won't do your work. Go, complain if you want.' The Secretary picked up his bag and stomped out of the room.

Somlo stared after him for a long time. His body seemed drained of strength as he stood rooted to the spot. He walked with leaden footsteps to the clerk's desk and placed all the papers before him with a woebegone expression.

'Arre, Somlya, why do you get so excited? Why do you irritate sahib? He's not very efficient,' the clerk said.

Somlo wanted to say that it was not he who was excitable, it was the Secretary who was bad-tempered, but the clerk's comment made him hold his tongue.

'Bhau, please see if all the papers are in order. I must get the toilet this time,' he said.

'Everything seems to be in order. Come tomorrow, meet the Secretary and give him an estimate of your annual income. I will draw up an income certificate which will have to be signed by the Secretary and the Sarpanch. Then you must get it signed by the Block Development Officer.'

'All right, I'll come tomorrow.'

'Be careful this time. We'll get only a hundred toilets and there will be at least two hundred applications.'

'Only a hundred! I must latch on to the Sarpanch then!'

Somlo arrived at the panchayat office early the next morning but there was no sign of the Secretary till the afternoon. He must have bunked duty since it's a Saturday, someone said and Somlo was left tearing his hair in frustration. He arrived at the panchayat office early on Monday morning and the Secretary walked in at the usual time but Somlo didn't want to irritate him, so he stood at a distance and watched while he did his work. Then, when there was no one around, Somlo walked in and stood before his desk but the Secretary seemed immersed in the documents before him, and didn't raise his head.

'Sahib....'

'Wait. Let me finish this.' The Secretary remained immersed in the file for a long time. Somlo was about to address him again when the Sarpanch swept in with four or five men in tow.

'Arre, Secretary, these men want toilets. Fill up the forms for them and see what they need. And you, Somlya! Hasn't your problem been solved? Secretary, give him what he wants, he's Baburao's man. This time Baburao has demanded fifteen toilets. Give Somlo one from that quota.'

'But Bhau, you said you would give me one.'

'Did I? Then we'll see if one is left over.'

'No, no, Bhau. I must get a toilet this time.'

'I said we'd see. Just make sure that your papers are in order.' The Sarpanch escorted the group of men to the clerk's desk.

Somlo was overcome by anxiety. 'Sahib....' he said.

'What? Are you getting late now?'

'Sahib, I have to serve lunch to my mother....'

'All right. What have you brought?'

'Income certi....'

The Secretary took a close look at the papers and began to question him.

'What does this Somnath do?'

'I'm Somnath, sahib. I do whatever work I get.'

'And Shivnath?'

'He's my elder brother. He drives vehicles belonging to the electricity department.'

'Oh, so he is a government servant. But you haven't shown his income.'

'He doesn't live here. He is in Margao.'

'He can live wherever he wants. His name is on this ration card, so his income must be listed in the total family income.'

'But sahib....'

'How much does he earn?'

'I don't know, sahib.'

'A driver must be earning twenty thousand or so...that would be two lakhs annually. Shall I write that?'

'But the toilet will be allotted only if the annual income is less than twenty-five thousand rupees, sahib.'

'Yes. Your family income exceeds that limit. So you can't get a toilet.'

'How do the others get toilets, sahib? They earn much more than us.'

'You can get one, too. Just remove your brother's name from the ration card.'

Somlo turned away, disappointed. An official told him what he had to do to get a new ration card. He returned home and told his mother all that had happened but she was furious.

'You pay for my needs, but that doesn't mean you can break up the family like this. Your brother has as much of a right to this house as you do. His job makes him stay far away, but he takes part in all religious and family functions,' she ranted.

'Why doesn't he help build a toilet then?'

'Only he can answer that. But don't let people lead you astray, don't break up the family....'

'No, Avai....'

'I don't want your toilet. I'll do my best to control the urge. I'll lie down in a corner and die. But as long as I live, I won't let you remove his name from the ration card!' His mother worked herself up into a frenzy drawing on random incidents from the past to buttress her claim till Somlo walked out of the house in frustration.

He knew that many government servants had already built toilets in their backyards and irregularities such as these would continue. The husband had a government job, but the toilet was allotted in the wife's name. An unmarried son, living with his parents, cannot have a separate ration card. How does an unmarried young man with a government job manage to get a toilet allotted in his name, then?

Somlo thought long and hard and decided that it was the Secretary who would ultimately decide his fate, so he hurried back to the panchayat office, but the Secretary brushed him off. Someone told him that the Secretary would be more accommodating if he received a gift, but Somlo had nothing to offer. Suddenly, his eyes fell on the bunch of plantains dangling from the tree in the garden. He brought down the bunch, packed it neatly, and set off for the nearby village where the Secretary had recently built a house.

The Secretary hadn't reached home, but his wife ushered him in urgently. 'Sahib has sent you, hasn't he? Come in, come in,' she said. She took him to the toilet, 'This flush isn't working, we are having so much trouble. Set it right at once,' she said.

'I'm not the plumber, I can't repair toilets. I've come to meet sahib.'

'I saw the bag in your hand and thought you were the plumber.'

The Secretary arrived at this moment with the plumber in tow. 'What are you doing here?' he asked angrily on catching sight of Somlo.

'Sahib, I came to request you to please do something....'

'You must come to the panchayat office. Not here.'

'Sahib, I have some bananas for you....'

'We have plenty of bananas. Take a look at the garden behind the house.'

'Sahib, please...'

'Not another word. Meet me at the panchayat office.'

Somlo realized that it was pointless saying anything further, so he quietly slunk away. His eyes strayed to the garden behind the house and he stopped in his tracks. Two government-allotted toilets stood side by side for the exclusive use of the Secretary's tenants. Controlling his anger with great effort, Somlo returned home.

Many of those who had submitted the application forms were wealthy persons with considerable influence in the village. Yet Somlo, who lived in a mud-walled house, couldn't get a toilet sanctioned in his name. The time for submitting forms was running out, so Somlo phoned his brother, informed him about the situation and met the official who issued new ration cards. His head seemed to spin in dismay when the official told him that nothing could be done now as new ration cards were only issued in February and August.

The Secretary was nowhere to be seen, so Somlo rushed to the clerk, 'Bhau, what can I do now?' he asked.

'What can I say? I have one hundred and thirty applications here. I shall take them to the public works department tomorrow morning. Do whatever you can today.'

A cloud of darkness seemed to settle before Somlo's eyes and he began to tremble in rage. If the Secretary had appeared before him at that moment, Somlo would have hacked the man to pieces, but he had gone home for lunch and no one knew when he would be back. Somlo could feel his patience wearing thin, so he sprang to his feet and rushed to the Secretary's house.

The front door was shut and no one responded to his call. Somlo began to bang on it in a frenzied manner till the Secretary emerged angrily. 'What's wrong with you, you son of a dog?' he cried.

'Don't abuse me. Who do you think you are? Will you sanction that toilet or not?'

'Let go of my shirt. Or I'll call the police and have you locked up.'

'Call the police. I'll tell them everything too.'

'What will you tell the police? Tell me, what will you say?'

'We poor people don't get a toilet sanctioned, but you get to build two toilets in your yard.'

'I'll build two toilets or I'll build four. It's none of your father's business!'

'Don't drag my father into this. I tell you, I'll bury you right here!' Somlo grabbed the man by his collar and the two came to blows. The

Secretary's wife rushed out of the house screaming loudly and threw herself into the fray forcing them apart. Some more women and children rushed to the scene on hearing the ruckus and the Secretary's wife, realizing that Somlo was more than a match for her husband, began to plead with him, 'Baba, don't fight. I beg of you, don't fight!'

'Tell your husband not to mess with me. I don't care if I die, but I won't die without finishing him off. We poor people don't get a toilet, but you get to build two in your backyard. Who does he think he is, the son-in-law of the ruling powers? I'll raise this in the village council…I'll file a case…!'

'Calm down, brother…don't do this. I'll see that you get a toilet sanctioned,' the woman pleaded.

'Do that. Or I'll finish him off.'

'I will, I will….' The woman turned to her husband frantically. 'Why do you behave so childishly? Give him a toilet and get this over with.'

'Do you want me to get suspended from my job?'

'No, but what if he does something terrible? For the children's sake, don't mess with him!'

A large crowd had gathered by this time and there was a lot of discussion. Some people found fault with Somlo, others thought the Secretary was in the wrong. The Secretary finally asked him to come to the office the next day and take the income certificate.

The Secretary had finished the paperwork and the certificate was ready by the time Somlo got to the panchayat office the next morning. But a new problem had arisen overnight. Only a hundred toilets had been sanctioned this time but the list of applications was continuing to swell, so the Sarpanch had taken whatever forms had been submitted already and deposited them in the PWD office the previous day. The forms that were being submitted now were languishing on his desk.

The Secretary was filled with fear on hearing of this development. He hastened to explain what had happened to Somlo and assured him that he would personally deliver his application to the PWD office at once.

A few days passed and masons employed by the government began to erect toilet sheds by the houses of the first hundred names on the list. Somlo rushed back to the panchayat office on seeing that his name was not on the list.

'Somlya, the government is introducing a new toilet allotment scheme only for Scheduled Castes and Scheduled Tribes. You don't have to submit any income certificate or anything. That's why all SC and ST names were withdrawn from the last list. You will automatically be allotted a toilet now,' the Secretary assured him.

Somlo turned away without another word. His mother passed away soon after that and Somlo's need for a government allotted toilet began to wane. He has been waiting for news about this new scheme for the last five or six years. The Sarpanch looks away when he sees him and avoids eye contact but Somlo has become very resolute these days. The little stream and its banks are government property, so he takes his tin can and squats on the embankment in front of the Sarpanch's house every morning. The Sarpanch doesn't have the nerve to shoo him off. So the messy patches continue to spread and a foul stench hangs over the embankment in front of the Sarpanch's house all day.

VALUES

MAMONI RAISOM GOSWAMI

Translated from the Assamese by Gayatri Bhattarcharyya

Pitambor Mahajan, the merchant, sat dejectedly on a tree stump in front of his house. He had still not taken off his muddy shoes. At one time, Pitambor had been a fit and well-built man. Now he was about sixty years old and although that was not an age that could be said to be old for a man, all kinds of worries and discontentment had taken their toll on him. His face sagged and he had a haggard look about him. His head always hung low; he could never look directly at the person he was talking to. The way he held his head, it seemed as though he was scrutinizing the ground, searching intently for something.

A big teak tree had recently been cut down, and Pitambor sat on its stump looking at the children with their improvised fishing rods, trying their luck in the gutters that lined both sides of the road. The incessant rains of the last few days had made the entire village muddy and slushy. The sides of the dirt road had become covered with all kinds of vegetation, both edible and useless, and the frogs were having a great time jumping from one ditch to the other.

Pitambor was looking intently at one particular boy who was trying to untangle his fishing line from an arum plant, when a deep voice suddenly caught his attention. He looked up to see the priest, Krishnakanta, standing near him. 'Pitambor,' said the priest, 'you have been sitting there looking at those children for a long time. You were sitting exactly like this when I passed by some time ago, and you are still sitting in the same place in exactly the same way, staring intently, and with a peculiar longing, at those children. Is it because you do not have any children of your own? "Whose beloved child is being chased to the waters? Call out and bring him back so that I can kiss him!"—Is that what you are thinking? By the way, is your wife any better? Is she able to leave her bed and do some work now?'

'No. How can she move about when her hands and feet have become swollen? I have already taken her to the hospital in Guwahati at least twenty times, but she is no better.'

'There seems to be no chance of your ever having any children of your own, then? So your family will become extinct,' said the mischievous and malicious priest.

Pitambor sighed dejectedly. What else could he do?

Krishnakanta stood there silently for a while. He was dressed in an old knee-length dhoti, a tattered and worn-out kurta, and an equally old endi sador. His cheeks were hollowed out as he had only two front teeth left—all the others had fallen out—so that when he spoke, his face took on an odd and twisted shape. His eyes had a malicious glint, and a sly look, and his balding pate only intensified his cunning look. He leaned close to Pitambor and whispered, 'Have you given any thought to what you will do if something happens to your wife? Have you thought about marrying again?'

Pitambor was about to answer when he happened to look up, and his eyes fell on Damayanti. She was the widow of the priest, Shambhu, who had died not too long ago. Everyone knew that she was a dissolute woman, and after her husband died she had become the centre of attraction for all the young men of the village.

Krishnakanta called out to her, 'Where are you coming from, Damayanti?' he asked.

'Where do you think I am coming from?' she replied. 'Don't you see the endi silk worms in my hands?'

'So, you have started hobnobbing with that Marwari businessman, have you?'

Damayanti did not reply and instead started to squeeze out the water from the bottom of her sopping wet mekhela. As she bent down to do so, her blouse rode, exposing her slim, soft, and fair waist. Neither man could resist looking at this attractive spectacle, but the priest quickly averted his gaze. After she had squeezed out the water from her clothes, she calmly walked away, without even bothering to look towards the two men.

'They say that she has no inhibitions and even eats fish and meat,' said Pitambor.

'Yes, I've heard that too,' replied Krishnakanta. 'She has put all the Brahmins to shame. She does and eats whatever she likes, and does not care for any traditions or rules. In the beginning, after Shambhu died, when she cooked fish for her two daughters, she used to go down to the river and bathe and then cook separately for herself. But now, I am told, she does not bother and even sits with the girls and eats the fish.'

'Yes,' replied Pitambor. 'I have seen her taking fish from the fishmonger in exchange for paddy.'

'Dear me!' exclaimed Krishnakanta. 'What is the world coming to! A widow buying fish in exchange for some paddy!'

'Softly, Purohit, softly,' said Pitambor. 'You do not need to publicize the fact that a Brahmin widow is eating fish. Such things are common these days, even in orthodox places like Dakhinpaar and Uttarpaar. And I do not really think it is such a sin. These old rules should be abolished.'

Staring at the departing figure, Pitambor asked, 'Bapu, what is the condition of your clients these days? Has it changed at all?'

'What a surprising question, Pitambor! You know everything and yet pretend not to know! Don't you know that it is because of the quarrel between my brother and myself over our clients that I am in this poverty-stricken condition?'

'It is mainly because your brother went around telling everyone that you do not know how to read Sanskrit,' replied Pitambor.

Krishnakanta said angrily. 'Tell me,' he shouted, 'how many priests are there these days who can recite the mantras as clearly and correctly as Narahari Bhagabati? He and I studied at the "tol", the school for priests, together. He was the one who got the caning, not me. No, no. The main reason for our poverty-stricken condition is the attitude of the clients—of those people who ask us to go and conduct their pujas for them. We priests who know how to conduct the rituals and pujas should not have been in such an impoverished condition. In the olden days, there was no problem getting at least one sacred thread, a pair of dhotis, and some money from each of our clients every month. But nowadays everything is different. People want to perform the rites and pujas, but are unwilling to pay the priests. Only the other day, instead of utilizing our services, Mahikanta Sarma, one of your oldest clients, took his two sons to the Kamakhya temple for their upanayan, the sacred thread ceremony. One of my clients in Maisanpur, Surja Sarma, held the shraddha ceremonies of his mother and father together on the same day. People are gradually starting to ignore the Nandimukh shraddha, the shraddha ceremony of nine ancestors which is such an essential part of the wedding ceremony. And, of course, the smaller rituals and pujas, like the naming ceremony, house blessing puja, Basanti puja, purifying a house by holding a hom, organizing a purifying and sanctifying holy fire if a vulture happened to roost on the house...these have become things of the past. Time was when a man had to undergo a purifying ritual if he lost his sacred thread. But how many Brahmin boys today even chant the Gayatri mantra!'

Pitambor had been listening to the priest's rant without saying a word.

His mind was still on Damayanti, and her lovely, silky-smooth back which had been exposed when she bent down to squeeze the water from her mekhela. He thought that he had never seen such a beautiful woman's waist or back. And it was not as though he had not seen or touched a woman's body. He had married his second wife just two months after his first wife had died, mainly because his first wife had died childless. But this second wife was a sick woman. Soon, she became almost completely bedridden due to acute rheumatism. Pitambor had taken her to doctors in Guwahati many times, but to no avail. Ultimately, the woman had become thin, more like a skeleton than a living woman. She lay in her bed all day, quietly watching her husband's behaviour. The man seemed to have almost lost his mind, longing for a son to carry on his family name. People said that he was waiting impatiently for his sick wife to die. After a few years, he had given up going to the hospitals in Guwahati, and had given up all hope for a son and heir. The priest continued to lament his lot in life, but Pitambor hardly heard him. His wife had signalled to one of the servants to give the priest a mora to sit on, but Pitambor was not even aware of the coming and going of the servant!

'You are so absent-minded, thinking all the time only of the fact that you don't have a son and heir. In fact, many people belonging to our satra (an Assamese socio-religious institution) have started saying that you are becoming unbalanced, that you are on the verge of insanity,' said Krishnakanta. 'There are hundreds of people in the world who do not have children. It is nothing so terrible. And why don't you think of what our gurus have said—that families, sons, and so on are, after all, transitory things, and hence valueless—simply manifestations of maya.'

Pitambor simply lowered his head in dejection. The priest noticed that his hair was greying, that his eyes were circled with small cobweb-like wrinkles. The man had become completely unmindful of how he dressed and his shoes were caked with layers of mud.

Krishnakanta was overwhelmed by a sense of pity and compassion for Pitambor. Just a few years ago, many of the older villagers had called him the 'gora soldier', he was so well-built, fair, and fit. Now, even though there was no dearth of money or means, the poor man had no peace of mind. His granary was full, but there was no one to enjoy it.

Then, Krishnakanta said something quite shocking. Before saying it he looked all round to ensure that there was no one nearby. But the door of Pitambor's bedroom was wide open, and he could see the skeletal body of Pitambor's wife lying on the bed. Her sharp eyes, he noticed, were shining with a peculiar brightness—as though she was trying to find out what the priest was saying to her husband. Krishnakanta was astonished to see that a single glance, even from a distance, could be so keen, and could express such heartfelt sadness. Even so, he whispered to Pitambor, 'If you think that you can help me with some money, I too will help you to get what you so desire.'

'How?' asked Pitambor. 'How will you arrange things?'

'Don't worry about the arrangements. There will be no problems,' said the priest.

'What do you mean?' Pitambor asked curiously.

'What I mean is that I will arrange matters so that when you meet her, there will be no question of her not conceiving. I have found out that she has aborted and buried the results of her illicit and guilty pregnancies four times!' Krishnakanta said with confidence.

Pitambor almost shouted, 'Bapu, are you talking about Damayanti?'

'Yes, yes. I am talking about Damayanti,' replied the priest. 'Our Brahmin girls have started going across the Dhanasri River to marry Sudra boys. Don't you know that the Gosain of Mukteswar Satra's son has gone and married a Muslim girl? It seems that our Gandhi Maharaj has shown this path—that caste and community do not matter. That is why I am thinking about Damayanti for you.'

Pitambor jumped up in excitement. 'What are you talking about?'

'If you so desire, you can make Damayanti your own woman.' Krishnakanta glanced towards the open bedroom door again. The eyes of the woman lying on the bed were wide open and it seemed as though they were burning with a fierce fire. She was staring at Krishnakanta.

Pitambor got up and tried to clutch the priest's hands, but the latter hastily stepped away. He had just bathed and was on his way to the Adhikaar's house. He had been asked to bathe the image of Murulidhar in the Adhikaar's temple, because the regular priest there had gone to Guwahati. It was a very important duty and he had to be clean and untouched by any other person, particularly one who was not a Brahmin. But the priest's words had opened an unthinkable world for Pitambor and he did not know how to thank the man.

'So, Pitambor,' said Krishnakanta, 'it seems that you have been thinking about this for some time.'

A happy smile played over Pitambor's lips. Once again, Krishnakanta glanced towards the bedroom. The woman's eyes were now shut, but it seemed as though she was undergoing some terrible suffering and pain. Touching the priest's feet, Pitambor spoke humbly and pleaded, 'Bapu, do this for me. Everyone knows that she goes out at night to bury the things she aborts. I know it too. But she is a Brahmin woman and I am a Sudra. If she comes to me, I will place her on a pedestal and worship her.'

A sly smile spread across Krishnakanta's toothless mouth. 'It will not be easy. I will have to negotiate, I will have to get the two girls to agree to it, and for that I will have to bribe them with sweets.'

Pitambor got up hurriedly and went inside. The eyes of the woman lying on the bed flew open. She had probably just shut her eyes and was not asleep. She saw her husband go to the small wooden box that was placed on top of a stool and open it; she also saw him going out to Krishnakanta again after a while.

'You will let me know everything soon, won't you?' he said to the priest.

Taking the twenty rupees from the merchant, the wily priest went away with a mischievous smile....

Seven days passed without any word from Krishnakanta, while Pitambor waited eagerly every day for him. He had seen Damayanti a number of times; making her way to and from the Adhikaar's house to deliver the sacred threads she spun from the finest cotton. It was only now that he began looking at her properly that he thought he had never seen a woman as beautiful as her. Her mother, they said, was from the village of Routa situated on the banks of the Dhanasri River. After seeing Damayanti now, Pitambor came to the conclusion that the Brahmin girls from near the

Dhanasri River must be among the most beautiful women in the whole country. Her father, the priest Purnananda, had once lost a couple of his ploughing bullocks. At that time he had had many clients in comparatively distant places like Maisanpur, Gargora and so on. Searching for his precious bullocks, Purnananda had gone to the village of Routa by the Dhanasri River side. No one seemed to know why he had had to go so far to find his cows. But it was then that he had seen and married the beautiful daughter of Bhagawati of Routa village. No priest of the area had ever before married a girl from so far away....

It was the month of June, and the rivers and wetlands were overflowing with water. Both sides of the dirt road were full of shrubs and climbing plants that invariably came with the season. The road running in front of Pitambor's house was now covered with mud and slush. One day in spite of the mud and slush on the road, Pitambor saw Damayanti walking along, plucking the edible greens such as the tasty 'kolmou' or water spinach which grew in abundance on the roadsides in the wet weather. She had lifted her mekhela up to her knees, and was accompanied by her six-year-old daughter, who was completely naked. Damayanti's legs and hands were soft and shiny, and healthy, like a new mango plant. Her hair, which cascaded down her back, was a reddish bronze colour, very much like the colour of rusted cannons, he thought. Oh, yes, the exact tinge of an old, rusted iron canon! Pitambor remembered the huge iron cannon that was found when they were digging a well. It was said that the Burmese soldiers had left it behind when they had to retreat. He remembered that a group of students had come after some time and hauled it away.

After looking at her for a while, Pitambor plucked up the courage to speak to her. 'You will get sick if you walk about in this foul weather, on this dirty, muddy road,' he said. She turned and looked at him, her face and eyes expressing a surprised curiosity. But, as earlier, she did not utter a word in reply. 'If you had only asked me I would have sent my servant to get you all....' But before he could complete his sentence, she turned to look back at him again. Her eyes were blazing. Pitambor felt her fiery look would burn him to ashes. He walked rapidly away and sat down on his usual seat on the stump of the teak tree. He glanced towards his house and saw that his wife had taken to her bed again. She had tried to get up that morning after a long time. Her wasted limbs creaked with a ghastly sound when she tried to lift herself up, and she felt dizzy, so she had to take to her bed again. Now she lay there staring at her husband. Pitambor gazed at her with a heartless and, at the same time, somewhat embarrassed look. It was time for him to go and give her one of her medicines, and he was quite aware of it. But he did not get up—he simply sat where he was, looking down, contemplating his shoes. There were only four people in their satra who wore shoes—the clerk of the satra office, the two sons of the Adhikaar, and he himself. He bent down and tried to clean his mud-caked shoes with his handkerchief, and then again looked up at the road to see if Krishnakanta had arrived. But there was still no sign of him. As he sat waiting impatiently, a bullock cart came creaking into his compound. His tenant farmers were bringing his share of the paddy they cultivated. On any other day, Pitambor would have rushed over enthusiastically and counted the baskets of paddy. But today, seeing that his master was absent-minded and indifferent, the servant came and counted the baskets and stored them inside the granary. After some time, having rested and having some refreshments, the tenants came up to Pitambor to take their leave. As always, they had some complaints about Pitambor's tight-fisted attitude. But nothing moved him today; he sat where he was, silent and indifferent.

Glancing towards the bedroom of his house, he saw that his wife was lying with her eyes open. He noticed that someone had replaced a tumbler of water near her, and he remembered that the time for her medicine was past. But he got up anyway and was about to go and give it to her when he heard Krishnakanta's voice. Forgetting about his wife's medicine, he hurried to the gateway where the priest was waiting for him.

His wife's eyes, he noticed, seemed to be unusually weak—the fire that normally gleamed in her eyes whenever she looked towards him seemed to be slowly dying out. 'Mahajan,' the priest called out.

'Yes, Bapu. Tell me, have you any news?' asked Pitambor.

'You will have to go to meet her on the coming full moon night in the dhekal (a room containing the dheki, a wooden instrument used for pounding and cleaning rice),' he said. 'It's located behind her house.' The priest looked furtively all around, and continued. 'I have found out that she is not pregnant at the moment. Her daughter told me this after I had bribed her with sweets. It seems that it hasn't even been a month since she terminated her last pregnancy. The girl is too young to understand these things. It seems that she had helped her mother by holding an oil lamp while the woman finished her job. She also told me that on this occasion her mother had used a spade belonging to a Brahmin boy from Chataraguri. This boy used to come cycling from his home to study in the college near here. He is a boy from a well-to-do family, but of loose character. Instead of going to college, he hid his books inside a basket of rice in Damayanti's hut and spent his time with her. He would spend the money for his college fees buying things for Damayanti. The foetus she buried this time was this Brahmin boy's....

'Listen, Mahajan,' the priest continued, 'I have spoken to her about you. At first she was quite angry, "That Sudra man," she said. "How dare he even think about such a thing! Does he not know that I am the daughter of a good Brahmin priest?" I replied that everyone knew that she was a Brahmin woman. But now that she had taken the sinful path, there could be no difference between castes. I also told her that no Brahmin would stoop to marry her now. They would simply exploit her body and then cast her aside like the useless husks of sugar cane stalks. I told her that you would marry her with all due rituals, as soon as your ailing wife died, that your wife is even now as good as dead. After you marry her, she would live a good and prosperous life, I told her. Do you know, Mahajan, when she heard all this, she went into her hut and cried her heart out, I do not understand why.... She came out after some time, wiping her tears and said, "I do not keep well these days, and it would be a relief if I could lean on someone's shoulders." I replied that it was not surprising that she did not feel well, after having had no less than five or six abortions within a short time; that if her case happened to come up in a panchayat meeting, no one would even consider going near her, because anyone found to be giving her even a tumbler of water would be fined a sum of twenty rupees!

'"What other option did I have?" she wept. "My daughters were starving. The Adhikaar's wife used to ask me to do small jobs for her in the kitchen. But now she says that I am not fit to work in her kitchen, that whatever I touch will become impure and contaminated. Before I used to be asked to spin and make the sacred threads, the laguns. But now the Brahmin families of this area will not allow me to make the laguns, the sacred threads. They say that I am corrupted. The tenant farmers know that I am all alone with no one to look after me or my interests. So they too have started behaving like monsters. What do they care that I am a lonely

Brahmin widow with two small daughters? How can I fight them? I own some acres of farmland in Satpakhila, but I have not been given my share of five maunds of paddy ever since my husband died. I have not been able to pay the revenue tax for that land for three years, and the land could be auctioned off any day now. What was I to do? I had to think of feeding my two daughters...."'

Pitambor was getting more and more impatient. He almost yelled, 'Yes, yes, I understand all that. But what about me, my case?'

'Yes, I am coming to that,' replied the sly priest.

'She said, "He is a Sudra belonging to the fourth caste. Having relations with him...." But finally, she told me that she would meet you on the full moon night in the dhekal behind her house.'

Pitambor could hardly contain his joy. And taking advantage of that Krishnakanta said, 'But you will have to give me about one hundred rupees.... Damayanti says that she needs a mosquito net, and the two girls will have to be given sweets from Bhola's shop....'

Pitambor hurried into his house and went to his bedroom. He walked up to the small wooden chest he kept in a corner of the room. His sick wife opened her eyes and followed his every move. Suddenly he shouted at her, 'What are you staring at? One day I will come and pluck your eyes out!'

From where he sat outside the house, Krishnakanta could hear everything that was being said in the bedroom. He was a sly fox. When Pitambor came out and handed him one hundred rupees, he whispered, 'If necessary, give your wife a small pill of opium that night. She lies on that bed listening to everything, and understands everything. It is better to be careful.' And laughing meaningfully, the sly Brahmin priest left. The woman on the bed simply shut her eyes.

Moments later, Krishnakanta returned, 'Damayanti is very keen on money. She acts like a tigress where money is concerned.... Never mind, you will be able to hold her hands intimately.'

The Mahajan felt rather guilty, and looked back at his wife. No, she had heard nothing. She was asleep. But her forehead glistened with perspiration.

It was the full moon night of the monsoon month of Ashaar. Pitambor wore an endi kurta and a fine Santipuri dhoti. Across his shoulders he had thrown a sador of fine cotton. After a long time he had brought out the mirror with the wooden frame and scrutinized his face. He had shaved that morning, and now out in the sunlight, he could see fine wrinkles covering his face, and he was somewhat disturbed. It seemed to him that the wrinkles were a net and he was the fish trapped in it.

At the appointed hour, he walked towards Damayanti's house. It was located near the bridge on the Singra River, beyond the forest of teak trees. Very few people of the satra lived here, and it occurred to Pitambor that Damayanti was able to live as she did only because she lived in an almost deserted area. He looked up to see some mushroom-coloured clouds floating in the sky, looking for all the world like cannons. And that round moon! As though it was a deer shorn of its skin. As though someone had come and wrapped her dotted skin around the cannons. A skinned deer—her meat shaking uncontrollably without the skin to bind it in place! Lovely fresh vigorous meat! This skinned deer suddenly transformed into Damayanti. A completely nude Damayanti! There were her lovely breasts—like a pregnant goat's stomach. Her body was the colour of tender bamboo stalks, and her lips? They were soft and lovely like freshly-cut mangoes oozing sweet nectar.... Pitambor could not stand there any longer looking up at the sky, weaving fantasies about the woman. It was deathly quiet and completely deserted. It was the night of the annual bhaona performance, and the entire village had gone to see it, which was why she had chosen this night for their first assignation.

He heard some jackals howling from the thorny shrubs nearby, as he walked rapidly to Damayanti's hut. He took off his shoes and sat on the plinth. A heady fragrance of champa flowers floated in the air. Damayanti lay with her younger daughter on a small cot set between a basket meant to store rice and a heap of ripe jackfruit. The girl was drowsily writing the letters of the alphabet on a slate in the light of a dirty old lamp with a broken chimney. From where she lay, Damayanti was watching the man. After a while, she beckoned to him to come inside, and sit on a mora. A small earthen lamp filled to the brim with mustard oil burned nearby. For some reason, Pitambor was afraid to look at her body in the pale light of the lamp—he had a peculiar feeling that everything might be over if he did.... It was all a land of illusion, he felt. Was this Brahmin widow in front of him a real woman?

'Have you brought any money with you?' Pitambor was startled into reality. He had not expected her first question to be so very materialistic.

'Whatever I have is yours,' he replied and handed her a cotton bag. She took the small bag and put it inside a cane basket that was hanging on one of the posts of her dheki ghar. In the meantime, the girl who was writing the alphabet went and lay down with her sister and instantly fell asleep. There was a very low cot in one of the rooms that was used to store baskets of rice. Damayanti's dead husband, a priest, had been given those baskets during the shraddha of the Adhikaar's brother.

Pitambor followed Damayanti and sat down on that cot. After a while, she came to him....

∞

Two months passed by. One day, after the Mahajan had left her, Krishnakanta happened to see Damayanti bathing in the river, and made fun of her, 'Why Damayanti, I never saw you coming to the river to bathe after you spent the nights with the Brahmin boys of Dudhnoi Bongora!'

Damayanti did not reply. But the sly priest was not put off. 'I suppose it is because this one is a Sudra...?'

Again she did not reply, but she suddenly jumped up out of the water and began to vomit violently on the riverside.

For some moments, the priest stood where he was, dumbfounded. Then he said, 'This must be Pitambor Mahajan's child then?'

Again she was silent. But Krishnakanta continued, 'That is very good news. Poor Pitambor will be very happy; he was almost going mad at not having any children! Then I will go and give him the good news.' After a pause he said, 'Listen, you must not worry or feel bad. Our Gandhi Maharaj did not believe in all this business of caste. He said that all men are equal and the same. Just you wait and see, Pitambor will marry you with all the proper rituals as soon as his wife is dead. I am sure that you are aware that the villagers were getting fed up of your way of life, and were thinking of having a Panchayat meeting about it. I don't think you know that some time back one of the things you aborted and buried beneath the clump of bamboos was dragged out by a jackal and deposited in one of the priest's courtyards. Have you any idea how much that poor man had to spend to get himself purified—and for no fault of his own!'

Damayanti started vomiting again.

'Be careful, Damayanti,' warned Krishnakanta. 'Do not do anything this time. Even after knowing all about you and your repeated abortions,

Pitambor is willing to accept you. If you do anything this time to damage the child within you, I tell you, you will go straight to hell. No one and nothing can save you.'

Krishnakanta then went to give the Mahajan the best news he had ever heard. 'Pitambor, if she does not go and abort this child, you can be sure that she will not be unwilling to marry you.'

As usual, Pitambor was sitting on the stump of his favourite tree. He had not even bothered to take off his mud-caked shoes. Hearing the priest's words he started trembling in sheer excitement. He would be a father! Could it be true? Would he really be a father at long last? But of course it must be true. The Brahmin priest himself had told him so.

He stood up, deeply agitated, and started walking about aimlessly.

Krishnakanta said, 'What is the matter with you! Why are you walking up and down like a monkey! But of course you have more than enough reason to be happy and excited! It is not a small matter to become a father after thirty years of waiting! Great good fortune indeed!'

Suddenly, Pitambor came and knelt down in front of the other man. 'Bapu,' he pleaded, 'please see that she does nothing to frustrate the dearest desire of my life. You well know what kind of men my father and grandfather were. Only a sufferer can understand the despair of a childless man! Besides, she is a Brahmin woman from a priest's family and now she holds my life in her hands! What will I do, Bapu, what will I do?'

Krishnakanta lifted one hand as if in blessing and said, 'I will keep track of her and what she does, like a vulture keeping track of a corpse. Do not worry. I will also warn the old woman who helps in these dreadful things. But I will need some money to bribe her too.'

This time Pitambor did not have to go to his small box to get the money. That morning he had sold all the fruits from his seven jackfruit trees, and the proceeds were still in his pocket. He took out the entire bundle of notes and handed it to the priest. Extremely pleased at the way his plans were going, Krishnakanta put his hands on Pitambor's head and blessed him.

Later, when Pitambor went to the bedroom, his eyes met his sick wife's eyes. And in spite of himself, their sad and desolate expression moved him to compassion. But the next moment he regained his composure and forced himself to anger. 'Oh, you sick and barren woman! How dare you stare at me like that?' And he yelled out to his servants, 'Come, come! Lift this bed. Take it to the small room next to the dhekal. Come, hurry up!' Along with four of his servants, Pitambor carried the bed with his wife still lying on it, and put it inside a small, dark room without any sort of ventilation, near the room where the paddy and the dheki were placed.

Since his affair with Damayanti, Pitambor seemed to have almost forgotten that his wife needed at least some looking after, and had to be given medicines regularly. She was just skin and bones now, and seeing that their master did not bother about her, the servants too had started to neglect her. They were even careless about bringing her food on time, and often did not bother to bring her a glass of water with her meals let alone give her the required medicines on time. The poor woman's throat would often become parched and dry with thirst, but she would not utter a word of protest. People said that she looked more like a corpse than a living woman. Even now, when her husband brought her to this small, dark room and left her there, she kept quiet. But surprisingly, even in the dank darkness, her eyes shone brightly, and it seemed as though she saw, and understood, everything that was going on, more clearly than if she was out in the open.

The very thought of fathering a child made Pitambor delirious with joy. He lived in a world of joyful imaginings—the child in Damayanti's womb seemed to him to be already a boy, then a young man. In Pitambor's imagination, the boy walked along the banks of the Dhanasri River, holding his father's hands! The ever joyous and sparkling golden thread that binds fathers to sons seemed to stretch happily far into the distant horizon, where all was sheer happiness, where the ties and traditions of family were an unbroken celebration of joy....

Pitambor got a couple of his trusted servants to bring down an old wooden box from its perch near the roof of his room. When he was sure that he was alone, he opened the box and took out a bundle tied in an old gamosa. In the bundle were a few pieces of half-burnt bones, the 'ashthi' of his long dead father, and entwined in the dried up bones was a chain of the precious poal or coral beads that were so much a part of the traditions of Assam. Pitambor remembered how, his father, as he lay on his deathbed, almost choking with the effort to speak, had said, 'Keep this chain of my poal beads carefully. Your son will wear it, and then his son, and then his son's son, and so on. It will be the living symbol, the everlasting flag of our clan....' The old man died before he could complete the sentence. Pitambor took out this chain now, then wrapped the pieces of ashthi in the gamosa again, and put the bundle back in the old box. Finally, he called in his servants and had the box put back in its place on the shelf.

Days turned into weeks, and weeks into months, and Pitambor became more and more impatient to hear some news. He had heard that a foetus that was five months old could not be aborted and he calculated that it was now three months since she had conceived. As he waited each day without any news, the tension grew more and more unbearable. Each passing day loomed in front of him like a mountain he had to cross in order to gain access to his happiness and survive.

Almost every moment he seemed to hear the Brahmin woman's footsteps approaching him, and he imagined that she was whispering to him, 'Mahajan, hurry up and prepare for the wedding rituals. I can no longer hide my condition. Do you not see how big my stomach is? Hurry up. Get the wedding preparations ready.'

Again, 'All those things about Brahmins and Sudras, about Hindus and Muslims, are just a lot of nonsense. We are all human beings, and you will find that the same red blood flows inside all of us.... Get the rituals for the wedding ready.'

She seemed to walk with ghungroos (small bells) tied to her feet and she came to him with tinkling feet. He imagined her lovely, fair, and slim legs.... 'Mahajan,' she seemed to whisper, 'nowadays I do not bother to go and bathe in the river after I sleep with you. Go, get ready for our wedding....'

Three months passed by uneventfully, and the Mahajan still dreamt of walking along the Dhanasri riverbank with his hands on the shoulders of a handsome youth—his son!

It was the late monsoon month of Bhadra and violent storms often lashed the villages. A storm had been steadily gaining force since that afternoon. Going inside to shut the door of his wife's room, he noticed that her eyes today burned more brightly, more malevolently than usual. As the storm raged, the lamps were blown out, and all other sounds were drowned out by its sheer ferocity. Pitambor shouted for his servants, but no one could hear him. The only sounds to be heard were the rumblings and thundering of the storm and of trees being felled, either by being struck by lightning, or being uprooted by fierce winds.

There, another tree had crashed down. Which tree was it, Pitambor wondered. Somewhere in the distance, he saw a streak of lightning that had definitely struck another tree! He could hear the frightening sounds of the tree being split down the middle and crashing to the ground. He went outside to see which tree had fallen and how much damage this terrifying storm had caused.

In a corner of the grounds, the fruits of seven of his coconut trees had been heaped up waiting to be sold. Now he saw his servants running about trying to salvage them and store them inside the dheki ghar. Some of the fruits which were still on the trees thudded to the ground, having been blown down by the wind. No one could hear anyone else, but gradually the storm began to calm down, the rumblings and thunder died down, and a heavy rain lashed the village. Lighting a lantern, Pitambor could now see the heavy raindrops; he imagined he could hear the tinkling sounds of Damayanti's anklets as her feet came towards him....

Suddenly amidst the rain, Pitambor heard someone calling him by name. Picking up the lantern, he hurried outside, and saw the priest coming towards him, completely drenched and shivering. Pitambor was frightened. Only some emergency could have prompted the man to come out in this terrible weather. Krishnakanta held an umbrella over his head, but it had so many holes that it afforded no protection whatsoever. His dhoti had been drawn up to his knees, and only a thin sador that was dripping wet covered his bare body.

Holding up the lantern, Pitambor shouted, 'Bapu! What brings you out in this foul weather, so late in the night?'

Krishnakanta sat down on the plinth of the house. Leaning the torn umbrella against a post, he took off his sador and tried to wring it dry, and wiped his wet face with it. Then, pointing a shaking finger at Pitambor, he said in a choking voice, 'Pitambor, when your first wife died, were there three inauspicious stars in the ascendant, three puhkars. Three or four?'

'I do not remember,' replied the Mahajan. 'Why?'

'When three puhkars are found at the time of death of a person in the house, even the dubari grass dries up and dies. When your first wife died, there were three puhkars. And, as a result, the ill effects are still there. Everything is dead and gone!'

'What has happened, Bapu? What is wrong?'

'She has destroyed it, Mahajan, she has aborted! She refused to carry the seed of a Sudra man! She belongs to the highest Brahmin clan, a woman from the Sandilya gotra! She has spoiled your seed, Pitambor, she has finished off her pregnancy!'

As these words crashed into him, the youth holding Pitambor's hands let go and fell into the depths of the Dhanasri River. Who was it who had fallen? Was it Pitambor, or the young man? Dear god, who was it that tumbled and fell headlong into the deep waters of the river!

∞

Soon after this encounter between the priest and Pitambor, Damayanti heard a sound near her house in the dead of the night. Someone was digging something beneath the clump of bamboos behind her dekhal. She shouted, 'Who is it? Who is there?' and woke her elder daughter. The six-year-old girl and her mother stood near the window, listening. The sounds of digging came from the same place where the two of them had gone in the dead of night two days ago and buried that thing the woman had ruined. Mother and daughter had gone out that night and dug a hole with the spade the Brahmin boy from Chataraguri had given them. The young girl had shivered in fright when she heard the jackals howling nearby. And today, the unmistakable sound of digging came from that very same place. Thud, thud! Thump, thump! Standing near the window, the two of them saw a lantern burning on the spot. In the light of the lantern they saw the figure of a man, a strong, well-built man digging away at the very spot where Damayanti had dug just two days ago. Indeed, he was digging up the same hole!

Damayanti's entire body and soul trembled at the sight. The man was Pitambor Mahajan. He had hung his lantern on a bamboo, and was digging away furiously. The man had assumed a terrifying aspect and he was hacking at the earth like a madman. She trembled in fear and terror. Should she shout? Yes, of course she must. Such a terrible thing was happening outside her own house—of course she must shout!

'Mahajan! Mahajan!' she shouted. But there was absolutely no response. He simply kept on digging.

'Mahajan, why are you digging up my ground?'

Pitambor looked up towards the window, but did not utter a word.

Damayanti said in a state of great agitation. 'Yes, I buried it. But what will you find there now? It was just an unformed lump of flesh.'

Pitambor lifted his head and looked at her. 'It was my child! I will at least feel the flesh of my flesh! I will feel my child, my son and heir, with my own two hands!'

BEYOND THE FOG

QURRATULAIN HYDER

Translated from the Urdu by Muhammad Umar Memon

1

Throughout the day English sahibs, memsahibs, and their baba log cross the bridge on mules and horses or riding in rickshaws and dandis. In the evening, the same bridge becomes the site of milling crowds of Indians. The swarm of rushing humanity going up and down the slopes huffing and puffing looks like the surge of a massive tidal wave. Movies starring Esther Williams, Joan Fontaine, Nur Jahan, and Khursheed are playing in the local cinemas. Skating continues in the rinks. In the ballroom of the Savoy the Anglo-Indian crooner and his band will soon start 'Enjoy yourself, it's later than you think'. Drums will be struck; maharaja and maharani log, nabob log, burra sahib, and burra mem log will start dancing.

At this hour, while the whole of Mussoorie is absorbed in merrymaking, a poor man stands quietly on this bridge near the bazaar—'*Kabira stands in the bazaar praying for everyone's well-being*'.

In his tattered khaki jacket, a cap coming down to his ears, he looks very much like a sweeper out of work. Holding a little English girl in his arms, he often wanders into the bazaar and stands there silently until dusk or sits on the low protective wall of the bridge.

Why does this sweeper Fazl Masih look so destitute and run down if he is entrusted with the care of some sahib's daughter? Strange!

And this fellow also looks a bit cuckoo. The likes of him were called holy fools in czarist Russia, and majzub in our culture. God knows whether this poor man is a majzub or was merely born an idiot. Anyway, most of the time he just stands quietly. The little girl with curly blonde hair is so incredibly pretty that she attracts the attention of passers-by who stop spontaneously to look at her. Now and then babu log will smile broadly and utter a 'Good evening, Missy Baba' to her. Even recent English arrivals in Mussoorie look at Fazl Masih with a smile, but the local English just pass by totally indifferent to his presence. The one-and-a-half-year-old girl, nestled in Fazl Masih's lap or riding on his shoulder, laughs, cries, or becomes absorbed in her teddy bear or her lollipop. Fazl Masih gazes at the Himalayas in the distance, beyond which lies the invisible 'valley of flowers'.

When it gets dark, he hoists the girl atop his shoulders and sets out for Vincent Hill with his head hung low. Just once, when some Lukhnavi passer-by stopped briefly and asked, 'Ama, whose daughter is she?' He replied with irritation, 'My sister's, sahib.'

'What do you think, miyan, that Hindustan's Anglo-Indians just dropped from the sky?' another passer-by retorted with a resounding laugh. 'Well, this is just how they came into being.'

Perhaps the sound of that laugh reverberates in Fazl Masih's ears, but he never opens his mouth. He just plods along the uphill track to Vincent Hill with his head bent low, the little girl mounted on his shoulders.

The residents of the Vincent Hill area know that Katto ayah is the real mother of the little white girl whose father was a gora, a white man who played the drum in the army band, and that she is being brought up by Miss Celia Richmond, the white landlady of Richmond Guest House. Katto, a shapely and graceful sweeper woman with a delightfully sallow complexion, originally from Gorakhpur district, whose parents had been made Christians by Miss Celia's missionary father, was now Miss Sahib's nurse. Her real name was Martha, but she was called Katto because she went up and down the neighbouring hills with the speed and agility of a squirrel. Miss Richmond received the guest house as an inheritance from her uncle. The entire Richmond family is buried here in Mussoorie's English cemetery. Miss Richmond has spent her whole life running this guest house. Circumstances have made her quite irritable, and because she makes a lot of noise, like a lapwing, the domestics and coolies of Vincent Hill have given her the nickname Chunchuniya Mem, the Rattle Ma'am. Hers is a second-class 'Europeans Only' facility where run-of-the-mill English, poor white missionaries, or fair-skinned Eurasians come to stay. With her keen, hawk-like sight, Miss Richmond can immediately see who has what percentage of English blood. If an Anglo-Indian with even the slightest trace of sallow shows up, she has Katto tell him that all the rooms are taken.

During the last days of World War II, a young Tommy came to stay at Richmond Guest House. He was in Mussoorie on two months' leave recuperating from a recent illness. (During the war, out of sheer patriotism, Miss Celia Richmond had offered her guest house to the British government for the use of soldiers.) Before the war, Corporal Arthur Bolton, the white Tommy, used to be a drummer in the orchestra of an ordinary restaurant in London. He wanted to earn himself a name among world-class musicians, but lack of better opportunities, the fate of many artists, kept him anonymous and poor. When the war broke out, he enlisted in the army as a drummer and was packed off to India. Like other soldiers in the British army, he was given instruction in romanized Urdu. But he also liked Indian music. In short, Arthur Bolton was an extraordinary Tommy, quite different from other whites of his ilk.

Because he wasn't a Sahib Bahadur of any consequence that would allow him to stay at the Savoy, he flopped down at poor Chunchuniya Mem's. He strolled in the hills all day long or wrote poetry. He'd have Katto nanny sing kajris for him and keep time as she sang. When she sometimes swirled her bellowing white lehenga-skirt and jingled her bunch of keys with a jiggle of her hips singing, '*Mirjaapur men oaran-thhoran Kashi hamaaro ghaat*' Arthur would become overjoyed, clap like a child, and start dancing with her. He liked Katto nanny a lot and had also struck up quite a close friendship with her crazy brother, Fazl Masih. The two would set out for the valleys at the crack of dawn to roam around and stare at the fog floating across the mountains. What lies beyond that fog?

2

When the time came for Arthur Bolton to return to the Meerut Cantonment he said, 'I'm used to speaking the truth, so I always end up losing. Our regiment will probably leave for Germany. A fierce battle is going on there. I may not be able to write to you at all, or if I do write a letter, I might not write any others. I'm pretty sloppy when it comes to correspondence. And what can a person write in a letter anyway?' But, as courtesy required, he did drop Miss Richmond a note of thanks from the Meerut Cantonment, in which he also sent his greetings to Katto and Fazl Masih and said that he was leaving for the European front in a few days.

When a daughter as white as snow and resembling Arthur Bolton in every last detail was born to poor Katto, Miss Richmond, unexpectedly, didn't grill Katto about the matter at all. She knew that Katto was not dissolute. And furthermore, she'd been born in her own house and had been a loyal domestic all along. With the birth of the child, Miss Richmond's otherwise quite dreary existence became somewhat animated and no longer felt so empty. She often wondered why on earth she was killing herself over the guest house. For whom was she piling up all this money? Now God had sent her such a lovely girl.

Miss Richmond also indulged in absurd fancies and theatrics now. And very much like her kind, ordinary middle-class English ladies, she was a perfect snob. She cooked up quite a story about the little girl to tell to the erstwhile residents of the guest house. 'Her father, Colonel Arthur Bolton, was lost in action on the Berlin front. Poor Arthur...' she would say heaving a deep sigh while serving guests their breakfast. 'Poor Arthur was my first cousin. Before coming to India he married the daughter of some Irish lord. Both of them were stationed at the Peshawar garrison. Soon after Arthur left for the front, poor Bridget died giving birth to the girl in the military hospital. Arthur had given my address as "next of kin" so the Red Cross sent the girl to me.'

Even at the girl's baptism at an English church in Mussoorie she had put down the name of the father as Colonel Arthur Bolton and crossing her heart with two fingers said under her breath, 'So help me God.'

India gained her freedom and suddenly Mussoorie began to empty of its English, except for Miss Richmond, who was not about to return to Britain to work as a dishwashing and cleaning lady. Unexpectedly, her hotel, its 'European Only' sign now removed, picked up business, because Indians took great pride in staying in an 'English guest house'. Where earlier quite ordinary English stayed there, it now became the haunt of upper-class wealthy Indians.

Catherine Bolton, nicknamed Katy, who was now called 'little Katto' because of her frisky, wanton behaviour, went to a convent school. Here, they had started teaching Hindi and Sanskrit after Independence. The teacher was a wily young local man. Katy took Hindi lessons from him, and her fair colour left the free children of free India in a state of awe.

The English priest who had baptized Catherine left India and settled in Australia, but he kept up a correspondence with Miss Richmond. On Katy's fifteenth birthday he wrote about his concern for the girl. What kind of future would she have in India? Surely Miss Richmond didn't wish for her to marry some Hindu heathen? It would be far better if she brought the girl over to Australia.

Miss Richmond gave the matter serious thought: really, what future could such a beautiful Anglo-Indian girl have in India? Telephone operator, office secretary, or, god forbid, a call girl or cabaret dancer? Already Katy Bolton had become the talk of the town throughout Mussoorie for her geniality. The day the shifty Hindi teacher tried to get fresh with her and, when she tried to fend off his advances, outright called her 'a coquette, a mongrel', she went home in a rage and told Miss Richmond everything that had transpired. There and then on that cold evening Miss Richmond made up her mind. She spent the whole night awake in her bed. It wasn't easy to leave home for good. What might become of her in a foreign land? But Catherine's future was at stake, it took precedence over everything. Come morning she sent for Katto and Fazl Masih. They came and stood in the doorway. Miss Celia sat by the fireplace busily knitting. Katy stood by the radiogram. In a grave tone of voice Miss Celia Richmond began, 'Katto, we're going to Australia. Katy Baba will go with us. Start packing our stuff.'

Both Katto and Fazl Masih were stunned. The two white women before them seemed to have gone off their rockers. They burst out crying. After a while, Katto sniffled and said firmly, 'Memsahib, I gave birth to Katy; I won't let her go. My brother too, this girl is his entire life, Miss Sahib. The only reason I didn't marry was the fear of how a stepfather might treat her.'

'Be quiet!' the old hag yelled. 'Don't forget your place, Katto. What proof do you have that Katy is your child? How dare you say that?'

Katto was stupefied. She never expected that. Miss Sahib had never said such a cruel thing before. Falling to the floor, she cried her heart out.

Katy went into the other room. She could hardly wait to go to Australia. The prudent and far-sighted Miss Richmond had already told her a few days ago that Colonel Arthur Bolton was an imaginary being. Corporal Bolton and Katto were her real parents. But her entire well-being lay in keeping this secret under wraps. Katy, who had an instinctive understanding of the rules of survival, had taken this advice to heart.

In an attempt to reason calmly with the distraught woman, Miss Richmond now said, 'Katto, you're crazy, altogether crazy. You really ought to think a bit...with a cool head. What will be Katy's future after I die? A smattering of Mussoorie natives still knows that she's your daughter. What if the news spreads all over? The caste system is rampant in India. Who will marry her? What is the value of an Anglo girl here after all? People regard her as no more than a tart. Do you really want your daughter to become a striptease dancer in some hotel? Or do you plan to marry her off to some municipality sweeper? Something to think about, isn't it?'

Katto was speechless.

Miss Richmond sold her establishment to a Sindhi who lost no time in expelling Jesus and Mary from the lounge, installing Guru Nanak and Shankar Parvati in their place, and replacing the 'Richmond's' sign outside with 'New Himalayas Vegetarian Hotel', but he let the old staff, Katto included, stay on. A bereft Fazl Masih and Katto came all the way to Dehra Dun station to say goodbye to Miss Richmond and Katy. The train left the station, leaving behind a forlorn Fazl Masih in his kantop and a light brown quilted vest staring vacantly into space, as was his wont.

3

At the Sydney airport Miss Richmond swept her glance over the place and smiled with satisfaction. She had made it to a white country...finally. (Although she was pure white on both sides, she was born in Gorakhpur. Only once in her whole life had she been to England, and for no more than a few months.) Both she and Katy waited for some coolie to rush to pick up their baggage, but no one paid any attention to them. Finally, taking their cue from other travellers, they found themselves a trolley and started to load their bags. When Miss Richmond started to push the cart, her heart suddenly broke a little.

Reverend Sigmore was waiting outside in the hall and took them to his house. He helped Miss Richmond buy a small grocery shop in the market adjacent to his church and also a flat. Within two weeks, Miss Richmond found herself sitting in her shop by the scales. She had made her entry into Sydney's working class.

Catherine was enrolled in a school. It didn't take her long to unfurl her wings. She went on 'dates' now, returning late in the evening. Miss Celia

Richmond, brought up on Victorian and Indian values, would admonish and rebuke her. Heated arguments would follow. The lives of both women had become miserable. A sixty-five-year-old uprooted English spinster and a sixteen-year-old girl of mixed blood with no clear background to speak of. A tragic pair of fake aunt and niece.

In Sydney, Miss Richmond couldn't cope with either her self-imposed exile or her loneliness for very long and died while Catherine was still in her eighteenth year. Reverend Sigmore assumed guardianship of the girl. He had her admitted into the school's boarding house. Within a few months she ran away. Not even in a blue moon did she deign to drop a letter to her mother or uncle. A few months later the priest also died. Catherine's boyfriends knew she had come into a lot of money. When she attained legal majority they started to play fast and loose with it. A ravishing beauty, her life's ambition was to become an actress, but back in those days Australia boasted neither a regular theatre scene nor a movie industry. Some rake advised her to take off for Hollywood, or if she wanted to enter London showbiz, the best place to start was the nightclubs there. She took cabaret lessons. In the meantime, she sold her grocery shop and had pretty much spent her entire inheritance. Money just slipped through her fingers like sand.

And so, wandering through Hong Kong and Singapore, she ended up in the Kuala Lumpur nightclub circuit, dancing cabaret here, working as a hostess there. But there she had to suffer the fierce competition of slant-eyed Anglo-Chinese prostitutes, and she was not, at any rate, a call girl, but the daughter of 'Colonel Arthur Bolton'. This imaginary colonel ensured, at every step, that she maintained her dignity. At times, she remembered her overly strict, fake Aunt Celia Richmond and, on occasion, the image of her own mother and uncle sailed before her eyes. She would wipe her tears and light another cigarette wondering about all the upheavals her life had gone through. The South Asia nightclub circuit had made her quite wise and equally melancholy. She had danced in the stag parties thrown by the high-living, pleasure-seeking sons of corrupt politicians and knew well enough the political and moral state of this part of the Third World. In every city in every country, she found the same Bible on the side table in the hotel suites, and found the sacred text to be utterly useless. The mysterious old Chinese hags with incredibly small feet who sat in the back rooms of Chinese restaurants amid the blue haze of incense smoke and told fortunes were never able to solve even one of her problems.

In one Jakarta Chinese restaurant she ran into a delightful Dutchman, about forty, with a toupee pasted on his head and wearing something resembling a robe over his suit. He told her that he was a Dutch Sufi and a disciple of the Paris Sufi preceptor Inayat Khan. 'I've come from Amsterdam to gain knowledge of the mysteries of Indonesian Sufism,' he told her. 'I'm one of those who are referred to as "Dutch Sensitives". We possess a heightened sixth sense.'

'Your father is alive,' he abruptly said, digging into his chop suey.

She was jolted.

'You'll certainly meet him one day. He's a great man.'

'Really? What kind of great man?'

'I can't tell you. But he *is* a great man.'

Did this mean he really was a colonel and, by now, maybe a general in the British army? The thought made her incredibly happy. Half of her miseries vanished there and then. She felt herself quite safe.

The Dutch Sufi's nearness gave her a sense of profound comfort. Swept away by Sufism, ESP, and her own desire for some sense of security in her life, she followed this mysterious man all the way to a mosque in Jakarta, where a slant-eyed, scraggly-bearded Indonesian 'Shaikh' had her recite the kalima. She was given the name Halima and she was married to the Dutch Muslim Muhammad Moeen Koot. As she signed her name 'Catherine Halimawati, daughter of Colonel Arthur Bolton' on the marriage register, she couldn't resist feeling an immense exhilaration flooding her soul.

That new Dutch Muslim was a staunch momin. He ordered Halimawati to cease her dancing and singing forthwith. But here was the problem: if she didn't dance in the Jakarta hotel where she did her floor show she would have to pay for her room and all her bills. Since Muhammad Moeen's money orders from Amsterdam wouldn't be in for quite a while yet, Catherine Koot was once again obliged to dip into her savings.

They had been living in the hotel for a fortnight when one morning she woke up and found that her Dutch Sufi was clean gone. And gone too were the diamond rings, the genuine pearl necklace, and the earrings Celia Richmond had left for her, along with her remaining cash. The lofty Bible on the side table still remained, untouched, with an empty plastic cup on top of it. Just last night, her Dutch literature-loving spiritualist had repeated a line from some American short story writer, which went something like:

'You may wander through the whole world but a day comes when you realize that the world is full of Holiday Inns and plastic cups and that you must go back home.' So Catherine Koot, stumbling about, returned from Jakarta to her home in Sydney. She was getting along in years, her ravishing beauty dangling precariously on the edge of evanescence. All she could find there was a job as a bus conductor.

A peculiar feature of the struggle for survival is that humans never admit defeat. Distributing tickets to the bus riders, she still daydreamed. Maybe at the next stop she would find the prince of her dreams, for who knows what lies beyond the fog?

4

Raja Sir Narendranath's great-grandfather was a poor Brahmin fortune-telling astrologer from Kannauj. Pleased by some of his auspicious predictions, Shahenshah Jahangir bestowed on him a jagir by the edge of the Kali River. The present Raja Sahib is a staunchly religious man who firmly believes in sadhus and sants. After the government abolished princely states, he moved into a gorgeous mansion in New Delhi and started a big business. It was in this connection that his eldest son (who earlier went by the name of Yuvraj Shailendranathji, but now is merely Mr S. N. Bajpai) took a business trip to Japan, Singapore, and Australia. This was the first trip out of the country for this rather naïve youth, so he was left quite dazed and fazed in Australia.

It was the Christmas season and a boisterous hustle and bustle had gripped Sydney. That day, as he was getting ready to go to the Opera House, he suddenly remembered the test match that was to take place in the afternoon between Australia and India, so he hopped aboard a bus for the cricket stadium instead and found himself a seat next to the window. The bus was a veritable portrait gallery of faces, one more beautiful than the next: Lebanese girls, Italian immigrants, round-faced Australians. When the bus conductor's hand came abreast of his face, he lifted his head and his eyes were dazzled: such a lustrous face, as beautiful as the full moon. Is such beauty possible! Seeing an Indian, the fairy-face smiled with a trace of fellowship.

The rajkumar had once heard someone say: if a white woman smiles at you, she's as good as hooked. He looked into her eyes a little less afraid and fell in love with her, heart and soul.

Those who visit a white country for the first time and fail to marry a mem within the first six months escape, otherwise not. Rajkumar Shailendra had been in Australia hardly ten days.

The conductor handed him his ticket and moved on smiling. Afterwards she gave him no more attention, but he was a man of firm resolve and nothing if not steadfast. The next day he boarded the bus at the same time. He succeeded, but only on the fourth attempt. He introduced himself: Prince Shailendranathji of India.

'Prince' did seem to make an impression on the earthly houri, because she had been watching princes and the sons of royalty all her life in Mussoorie, right from childhood, and if someone on a bus in Sydney was introducing himself as a rajkumar, her experienced cabaret dancer's eyes could easily see that he was no fake.

The magic began to work on the fairy. Appointment for the evening, candlelight dinner, ballroom dancing, a leisurely stroll, shopping, high-placed family, English girl, a colonel's daughter, granddaughter of some lord—well, what's the harm?

It was a standing practice among our nabobs and raja log that they got themselves a junior begum or a junior rani of European blood, most of whom had been mere London barmaids in their earlier incarnations. But the headline news of free India was that all the rajwaras had been folded up, harems put paid to, and the law of single marriage had been slapped on the people. All the same, the snob value that an English or an American wife still had in free India was not something that Shailendranathji was unaware of. His first wife was a princess, a rajkumari, but the poor thing died within two years of marriage.

So when he proposed to Catherine she found herself in a Sydney ashram the very next day. Her nikah had been performed at a mosque in Jakarta. Here, the pundit recited Vedic mantras. She was given the name Shailaja Devi, to accord with Shailendra—the Bengali pundit explained with a smile.

'Akhand Sobhagyawati, Yuvrani Rajyalakshmi Shailaja Deviji—may she prosper and fructify!' Her nitwit of a husband, several years her junior, shook hands with her, beaming. On the marriage register her father's name was inscribed as 'Colonel Arthur Bolton of London and Peshawar Cantonment'.

5

From Meerut Cantonment, Corporal Arthur Bolton had straightaway headed to Berlin. The war ended shortly thereafter and he played his drum in the army band to celebrate the victory in different parts of England. Later, he was let go of his temporary employment in the army.

Arthur Bolton's father, a shoeshiner who worked in Piccadilly Circus, had died during the bombardment of London. His mother had died too. Arthur found himself a job with a dance band in the West End. He didn't marry. Why get into that mess? Years passed. After paralysis disabled one of his arms, he had to give up drumming. When he got out of the hospital he started working as a doorman. By now age had caught up with him. He still wrote poetry, which never got printed. He attended church regularly—churches, that is, that had somehow escaped being turned into Sikh gurdwaras. Since he knew Urdu he was able to hit it off quite well with Pakistani and Hindustani labourers. Actually, it was a Sikh watchman friend who had got him his present job in one of the stores of a major Punjabi businessman, Mr Khosla. It was a gorgeous showroom in Knightsbridge. There, everyone liked this soft-spoken, loveable, slightly eccentric old man.

That day, after arriving at the showroom, he did his cleaning and dusting in the hall. As he was arranging the scattered periodicals on the table his eyes fell on the cover of a women's magazine published from Bombay. The face of the girl on the cover caught his attention. Inside there was a photo essay on the interior decoration of this beauty's house. Arthur Bolton plopped down on the sofa, took out his eyeglasses, and began reading it:

> Yuvrani Shailaja Deviji is English and a member of British aristocracy. Her father, Colonel Arthur Bolton, was lost in action in the last World War. Her grandfather was an Irish lord. Rajkumariji has spent her childhood in Mussoorie. Later she left for Australia with her aunt, Lady Richmond, where she trained in ballet dancing, piano, and interior decoration.

Old man Arthur was dumbstruck. He closed his eyes and remained in a state of quiet immobility for some time. Then he got up, walked over to a corner, dropped down on his knees and immersed himself in prayer.

For some strange reason he felt certain that Katto was still in Mussoorie and that if he wrote to her at the same old address, she would reply.

And so she did. When he got her letter he asked the manager of the showroom for a month's leave which was granted. He went to India House to obtain a visa. Next, he withdrew his life's savings from the bank, bought himself a return plane ticket, and spent the rest on gifts for Katto and Catherine. Carrying the heavy bag of gifts in his working hand, he would get tired, catch a brief rest in some doorway, and start walking again. With the money saved by walking, he bought a tie for his son-in-law.

Exactly a week later he found himself standing in front of the servants' quarters at the New Himalayas Vegetarian Hotel.

Katto nanny told him plainly, 'Sahib, my daughter didn't send me a letter and got herself married. What does this mean? Just one thing: she doesn't want me to ruin her new life.'

Katto was sitting on a rock outside the quarters working mustard oil into her hair. As ever, Fazl Masih sat under a pine tree staring quietly at the Himalayas. The valleys in the distance had become filled with purplish fog.

Old man Arthur lit his pipe with his working hand and pondered how incredibly peaceful this poor, illiterate, and heartbroken woman was.

'Katto, you're not angry at all?' he said, in a voice genuinely surprised.

'Angry—whatever for, sahib?' she said. 'In whatever I had to go through, I lived up to the fate assigned by Chhati Ma.'

'Chhati Ma? Who is this lady?'

'A Bohri memsahib of Bombay once came here. When she heard how angry I was, she told me, "Katto Bai, the sixth day after a child is born, Chhati Ma appears at midnight and inscribes its fate on its forehead." Here we call it the "karm ke lachhann", the signs of fate.'

Arthur listened attentively. Raising his eyebrows, he rubbed his forehead and started laughing.

Katto continued, 'In the front room of these very servants' quarters, Chhati Ma came at night and inscribed on my Katy Baba's forehead that she would become a queen. Listen to me, please, sahib. Don't go to meet her.'

'Why?'

'Because I'm telling you.'

'No, Katto. Chhati Ma has also written down that both you and I will go to Delhi to visit her. I've brought so many gifts for her from England.' Arthur sat down beside her on the rock and started to open the bags with longing and eagerness.

6

A small, nicely manicured lawn was visible at the front of the grand mansion and right across from the gate stood the window of the bedroom which was featured in that English-language women's magazine. It was a pleasant Sunday morning in early spring. Out on the lawn Raja Sahib, his middle son, and a few European men and women were immersed in listening to the discourse of a Swamiji. This was some relatively new Swamiji who had just recently joined the international guru circuit and was now staying at Mouriya, having returned only a few days ago from France with a slew of his millionaire French and German disciples. After breakfast with Raja Sahib, he was holding forth on sat and a-sat when a taxicab pulled in at the gate and a threesome got out: a grubby old Englishman holding a Selfridges shopping bag, a poor native woman in an ordinary sari, and a crazy-looking man in a kantop and faded quilted vest with a matted salt-and-pepper beard who cringed and huddled behind one of the columns of the gate. The shabby Englishman held the hand of the boggled, fearful woman and started walking towards the lawn.

Raja Sahib lifted his eyes and looked at the new arrivals with extreme annoyance and wondered: how in the world did his Gurkha gatekeepers ever allow this riffraff in!

Maybe this clumsy bunch was from the horde of Jehovah's Witnesses, harmless crazy missionaries. Early on Sunday mornings they just descend on the homes of decent people and tell them doomsday is right around the corner. Oh, how they make life miserable!

Coming near the chairs, the old Englishman stopped. When the Swamiji raised a silver glass to drink some water, the Englishman said cheerfully, 'Good morning friends!' Both he and the native woman stood there for some time. Everyone remained absolutely silent. The Swamiji was apparently quite irritated by this intrusion in the middle of his bhashan. In utter disgust he picked up a flower and started inhaling its sweet aroma. The Maharaja signalled with his eyebrows for them to sit down, and both promptly did.

'Maharaj, please go on,' Raja Sahib, a staunch believer in sadhus and sants entreated by humbly joining his hands.

Swamiji picked up where he had left off in his discourse on sat and a-sat. Old man Arthur craned his head and started to listen carefully. After a few minutes Swamiji paused to allow his French female disciple to change the cassette.

The old Englishman addressed him, 'Mister Guru! Your thoughts about truth and nontruth have affected me greatly. I too have come from England to make manifest a truth.' Then turning to the Raja Sahib he said, 'Your Highness, I'm the father of your dear daughter-in-law Catherine…' he took out the clipping from the women's magazine, 'Akhand Sobhagyawati Rajyalakshmi Shailaja Deviji.'

'Oh, what a pleasant surprise, Colonel!' The Raja quickly thrust his hand forward for a handshake smiling warmly. 'Colonel Bolton! Why didn't you inform us that you were coming? Ahead of time?'

'Your Highness,' old man Arthur cleared his throat, glanced around, and said with an angelic smile, 'there hasn't been a single colonel in my family in the past seven generations. My father was a shoeshiner, my mother a cook; I joined the army as a drummer. Now I'm just a doorman.'

Everyone present had turned into statues of solid ice. Arthur threw a sweeping glance around him and shook his head regretfully. 'All my life this has been my problem. I've always spoken the truth, nothing but the truth. And when I arrive here, what do I see but that Swamiji is talking about the essence of truth. This made me very happy. I've spent my entire life's savings just to see my daughter. I'm a poor man. All the same I've brought her some things as a dowry.' He bent over, picked up the Selfridges shopping bag from the lawn and then put it back down. The people remained as frozen as before.

Arthur started again, 'I'm sure Catherine would be delighted to meet her mother, too. After all, she's been away since she was fifteen years old.'

Arthur stopped to catch his breath. Katto just looked at him, aghast, dumbfounded. Suddenly the atmosphere had turned entirely surreal. Such episodes don't happen in real life. Arthur started again, 'This foolish woman was afraid to come here. I told her, "Martha, are you afraid of the light? Don't be afraid of the light of truth. Truth is God. And we are His children. Aren't you eager to see your lovely child? So let's go to Delhi and meet our daughter. How could it be that parents and their children would hesitate to meet each other? How can they go against the law of nature? There's nothing to fear." And Your Highness, it is mentioned in your mythology that when Lord Shiva arrived at his in-laws, his arrogant and haughty father-in-law scorned him…' Arthur paused and cleared his throat, 'Forgive me, I gave the wrong example. What I meant was…'

The old coot, he's really insane, Raja Sahib thought. He was gaping at this weird stranger with wide eyes and his face was quickly changing colours, but Arthur Bolton went on with his introductory harangue with perfect calm.

'So, Your Highness, just now as I arrived at the gate I thought for a minute you might turn out to be as arrogant and haughty as Lord Shiva's father-in-law, but then your words struck my hearing. You were expressing your agreement with Mister Guru's utterance that man must speak the truth in all circumstances and have the courage to face it. Indeed it is siddhant and gyan. And Raja Sahib, you'll be pleased to know that my Saviour Jesus Christ has also said exactly the same thing. Actually, it is His truth-speaking that brought Him to the cross—quite a well-known event, you must surely have heard of it.'

The middle prince sensed that Raja Sahib, an irascible man, was just about ready to lose his temper and god knows what he might do. To smooth things over, he quickly asked, 'Would you like coffee or tea?'

Arthur looked at him with a smile. 'Martha, coffee?'

Meanwhile Swamiji had started to stroll on the grass. The middle prince poured some coffee and offered it to Katto nanny. Old man Arthur shook his head and said excitedly in Urdu, 'I'm very pleased to see that you don't practise untouchability. We are all children of God the Father. Jesus said that there is room for everyone in My Father's palace. Your Highness, my daughter's mother was never married to me. I didn't even know that Martha had given birth to Catherine. Thirty-five years later I saw her picture in a magazine. This is all God's work. Martha is a very courageous woman; she still works as a nanny in Mussoorie. She is a righteous woman, a true Christian. Her mother and father were also true Christians, and they were also very poor. They worked as sweepers, cleaned bathrooms. Jesus said that the poor shall truly inherit the Kingdom of God. Your Mister Gandhi says the same thing too. He used to live in the Bongi colony in Delhi. My Katto is also a Bongi. She will also inherit the Kingdom of God, no doubt about it.'

Raja Sahib, who was glaring at the old man, dropped his head between his hands, and bellowed at the top of his voice. Raja Sahib was ill-tempered but no one had ever seen him shout like that before. Everyone stood up and rushed to him. He felt dizzy and closed his eyes, letting his head droop. He was beginning to faint. He had a weak heart.

7

Catherine, standing by the bedroom window, was watching this whole scene, which looked like a stage set from that distance. Life couldn't be more unbelievable! In the morning, when she was introduced to Swamiji at breakfast, both had instantly recognized each other. Swamiji was none other than the former Hindi and Sanskrit schoolteacher at Mussoorie who had tried to get fresh with her, leading to Miss Richmond's sudden decision to leave for Australia. Just as they were about to leave, it had come to light that he had siphoned off a considerable amount of school funds and dropped out of sight with some girl from the hill country. Back then too he was quite engaging and a sweet-talker.

After breakfast, when the opportunity offered itself, he told his former student, 'Now look here, Katto Junior, it has taken me twenty long years and a lot of hard work to fashion this career for myself in the West, which is teeming with swamis nowadays and a cut-throat competition is raging among them. Even so, I've got no less than eighteen ashrams in Europe and America, not to mention disciples numbering in the thousands, so don't you go spilling the beans! In the bargain, I'll keep mum to your in-laws, conservative royal family that they are, about your being the daughter of Mussoorie's Katto nanny.' The blood had drained from Catherine's face and her colour faded when she heard those words whispered to her. She'd left right away and hidden herself in her bedroom.

Meanwhile, Swamiji had returned to the lawn and resumed his bhashan, but what had to happen, happened. A taxi stopped at the gate and she saw her mother getting out, followed by her half-crazy uncle, and an eccentric-looking English codger. They walked in and sat down on the lawn, and Catherine heard every word of this unbelievable father of hers.

One time a Delhi Begum Sahib had taught Miss Celia Richmond how to cook 'baoli handia'—crazy dish. Life too was a crazy handia which, having simmered for some time, now suddenly came to a boil.

Shaking from sheer terror, she looked at what was in front of her. Her uncle stood like a pillar by the gate, staring into space, while on the lawn her insane father diligently went about destroying her life. How fervently and how much she had always yearned to meet him. How many stories of this man's innate goodness and innocence her mother and her aunt Celia had recounted—the man who had stayed barely two months in the guest house and left after winning everyone's heart. Perhaps god had created him just for that: wander in suddenly from somewhere, change the course of lives, and wander out just as swiftly. Unbelievable! Impossible! Are goodness and truth in their essence destructive forces?

Transfixed, she watched the players on the stage in front of her in what might well have been a scene from some comic opera had it not been so horrific: discovering that his oldest daughter-in-law was the child of a sweeper woman caused the Brahmin Raja Sahib to faint on the spot; the four Europeans, in order to escape the tentacles of the arch swindler Maya, had walked straight into the trap of the arch swindler Swami; the bogus holy man was now mouthing mantras to revive the unconscious Raja Sahib; her poor mother, who had shed tears all her life, still couldn't do anything but shed more; and her destitute father, paralysed in one arm, who had saved every penny with so much thrift to bring her something for her dowry from across the seven seas, was now looking at everyone, dumbfounded, like some foolish angel who had walked into the wrong place. A sudden wave of compassion and love washed over Catherine and she was overwhelmed by an instinctive desire to rush out and hug her half-mad, eccentric father, her suffering mother, and her dear uncle, to give up this palace, this aristocratic Brahmin family and her well-heeled husband, and leave with these loving, penniless, naïve, and crazy people, because her real home was where they lived, because ultimately the world is filled with Holiday Inns and plastic cups, three-storeyed Heinz-style houses with red sloping roofs, and nowhere had she found her place, her home. Was she really Akhand Sobhagyawati Rajyalakshmi Shailaja Deviji? Inside her skin she was just plain Catherine Bolton, and the conflict between Colonel Bolton and Corporal Bolton that had always left her exhausted and worn out was finally over. She would go outside and announce: Daddy, Mummy, here, I'm back. I'm coming with you.

She summoned up her courage and made for the door. Just as she was opening it, her eyes fell on her diamond bracelet. Her personal Mercedes gleamed in the sunlight up ahead in the driveway, and she suddenly recalled that she was expected at the golf club at eleven o'clock. Would all this disappear in the blink of an eye?

The sound of the shower rose from the marble bathroom and another thought crossed her mind: might her husband throw her out after this dreadful denouement? Much better if I leave honourably with these people on my own.

Her head swirled, as though she was standing on a sinking ship. She tried to grab on to the door. She must do everything to save herself. Such was the law of survival. Her nitwit husband emerged from the bathroom in his robe. 'What's all this noise outside?' he asked, walking towards the window.

Catherine heaved a deep sigh and said in a clear, firm voice, 'Darling, that magazine which had a pictorial essay about our interior decorations, remember? It seems to have created havoc. Some wicked gang has barged in to blackmail us. They're claiming to be my parents. Your father is running for election. I wonder whether this has something to do with that. Looks like your father's opponents have sent an Untouchable woman with some English geezer to say that she is my mother, just to turn the Brahmin vote against your father. The old coot might just as well be a CIA agent. You must call the police.., right now.'

Rajkumar Shailendra was a moron all right, but perhaps not an absolute moron. He lifted his face and looked at his fairy-faced yuvrani somewhat suspiciously. Catherine turned pale. She was shaking from fear. Pushing her out of his way, Rajkumar Shailendra rushed to the door and out to his father who had by now regained consciousness. Catherine ran straight to the bathroom and locked the door.

Outside at the gate her crazy uncle was asking after the well-being of everyone with his hands raised in prayer.

Kabira stands long wishing everyone well.

20

THE GOVERNOR'S VISIT

KALKI

Translated from the Tamil by Gowri Ramnarayan

Sriman Sivagurunathan Chettiar relaxed on his easy chair after lunch as usual and picked up the newspaper. As he scanned the headlines he was startled by the announcement, 'Poikai Dam: Governor to lay foundation stone'.

Chettiar had goosebumps all over. His heart began to race. Controlling himself with some effort, he read on. The report gave details of the Governor's arrival at the railway station on the twentieth at 7 a.m. He was to take a car to the site of the dam.

Chettiar at once summoned his clerk, Jayarama Iyer, and asked him, 'Have you heard the news?'

'No, sir, anything special?'

'How is it that you always seem to know nothing? Haven't I told you again and again to read the papers? Why do we spend 250 rupees every year on their subscription? What would have happened if I hadn't followed the news carefully?'

'Sir, please give me the news.'

'The Governor is visiting our town on the twentieth.'

The clerk gaped in wonder. He was too astonished to do anything except break into incoherent exclamations.

'All right, what do we do next?'

'We must get everything organized.'

'I must be at the railway station on the morning of the twentieth. Make sure our car is shining and spotless.'

'Didn't I insist you should buy a motor car? Wasn't it an excellent suggestion?'

'My good man, it is that foresight which makes you so valuable to me.... Well, shouldn't we get our house decorated for the occasion?'

'Why, is the Governor going past our home?'

'I'm not sure. He may go straight to the site from the station. I must persuade the Collector to take him through our street.'

'It doesn't matter. In any case, the fact that our house is being decorated will be reported in the papers.'

'True enough. But will the news of the Governor's arrival escape the eyes of Kurmavataram Iyengar? Doesn't he read the papers as keenly as I do?'

'Don't worry. Even if he gets to know, there is nothing much he can do about it. First of all, he has no motor car, only an old-fashioned coach. Don't you remember how the whole durbar burst into laughter when Iyengar accepted the Rao Bahadur title from the Collector, dressed like a clown and bowing as if he would never stop? The same thing will happen again.'

Chettiar chuckled as he recalled that scene. 'Still, he must not know our plans. Keep everything ready and put up the festoons on the night of the nineteenth after 10 p.m. Let Iyengar get up and blink in the morning.'

Chettiar and Iyer held long discussions about the necessary preparations. Finally, they were struck by a bright idea. Chettiar sent a message to the president of the town council saying that at their next meeting he would propose the presentation of a citation to the Governor. After that the clerk went about his usual business.

Sivagurunathan Chettiar was a prosperous businessman. He owned the only three-storeyed mansion in his little town. He had started life as a poor clerk in a hardware store. But soon the goddess Lakshmi glanced at him from the corner of her eye, and Chettiar opened his own shop and business. His wealth increased day by day. His large pre-war stock of iron doubled and tripled in value during the World War. Chettiar became a millionaire overnight.

He began to crave social recognition. His next-door neighbour, the advocate Kurmavataram Iyengar, became his role model in social graces and sartorial style. Chettiar engaged a tutor to teach him English. He adopted all the ostentations of high living. He threw frequent parties for government officers. He squandered an enormous sum to become town councillor. Presently, his entire ambition was focused on obtaining the Rao Bahadur title.

A sneaking fear plagued him. What if Iyengar became Dewan Bahadur before that? He intended to overtake Iyengar by hook or by crook in securing the Governor's favour. That was the reason the advocate figured repeatedly in his conversations with his clerk.

The next day Chettiar attended the council meeting with a beaming face. His well-prepared proposal to present a citation to the Governor was tucked into his shirt pocket.

His speech was divided into three parts. Part one described the benefits of British rule in India. Part two traced details of the Governor's ancestry, family history, character traits, and individual merits. The third part listed all the contributions of the Governor, real and imaginary, to the welfare of the state.

At the end of his peroration, Chettiar drew the kind attention of the esteemed Governor to the single regrettable act of omission in his regime. Loyal subjects of the crown were not given sufficient recognition or reward. He humbly prayed that the Governor show discrimination in the conferment of titles on deserving persons.

The clerk sent copies of the proposal to all reporters with the assurance that Chettiar would bear the cost of telegraphing the whole speech to their respective headquarters. The reporters were also invited to Chettiar's home the day after the Governor's visit.

But alas! The moment he took his seat in the council Chettiar's joy turned to grief and anger. He came to know that Rao Bahadur Iyengar had sent his claim to make a similar proposal before Chettiar had. He would therefore get precedence in the matter. But Chettiar was not a man to be stumped by reversals. Life had taught him that determined effort achieved results. He successfully manoeuvred the right to second Iyengar's proposal. After that it was but an easy step to read the entire speech in the guise of seconding the proposal. Poor man, how could he know Iyengar had made arrangements to prevent his speech from reaching the newsrooms?

As Chettiar cursed God and man, his clerk brought him information which consoled him a little.

'The Governor arrives at the station at 7 a.m. He has to travel fifty miles to be at the river Poikai by 9 a.m. to lay the dam's foundation stone. He has no time to receive the citation at the town council or at the railway station. This message came just now from the Governor's personal secretary.... Good thing you did not propose the citation. You have been spared a loss of face.'

Chettiar was very glad. 'Ah, Kurmavataram Iyengar got what he deserved. Didn't he try to steal a march over me?'

'All the same, shouldn't you be at the station on the twentieth morning?'

'Of course. All our other plans stand as before.'

∞

At last, the appointed day arrived. Chettiar was up at dawn. After his bath and breakfast, he stood before the mirror for a good half-hour making his toilette. His beloved wife was beside him, smoothening the folds in his garments and polishing his ornaments. As soon as he was ready, he sent the clerk to fetch the car from the garage. Chettiar's wife took a look at the street outside to check if the signs favoured her husband's trip. When the omens and the time were deemed auspicious, Chettiar stepped out of the house and entered his car. A big flapping Union Jack graced the car's bonnet.

Chettiar felt a pang when he saw his neighbour's house. Iyengar too had played a waiting game through the previous day and had put up flags and festoons in the dark. The car began to move and there was little time for more speculation.

It took five minutes to reach the station. Chettiar saw that Iyengar was there before him, ready for action. Their fierce competitiveness remained strictly hidden. To the world they were the best of friends.

'What brings you here so early?' Chettiar enquired.

'A small errand. I heard you were leaving for Madras. Is that why you are here?' Iyengar asked mischievously.

'Never mind. But tell me, your house has been festooned with decorations overnight. Any special occasion?'

'I saw festoons in your house too. Is it true that you are celebrating your sixtieth birthday?' Iyengar's query had a sarcastic ring to it.

Chettiar wished to give him a severe set-down but suddenly the station was filled with people. There were members of the town council, taluk and zillah board; graduates and those who were struggling to become graduates; advocates, officers, members of the security force; volunteers who had come to stage a political protest and watch the fun at the same time; representatives of the secret police who shadowed the volunteers. All of them stood cheek by jowl, their eyes straining to remain unblinkingly fixed on the railway track.

Finally, the Governor's special train arrived. Police officers strode up and down to establish peace. The honourable Governor disembarked. A path was cleared for him. All those who had come with manifold dreams stood breathless in adoration—with pounding hearts and earnest eyes. They trembled lest the honourable Governor leave without a single glance at them. Later it was learnt that an ardent soul among the multitude had fainted in rapture, but so great was his loyalty to the crown that, determined to cause no disturbance, he stood upright even in such an extreme condition, clutching the pillar which hid him.

Meanwhile, the Governor took off his hat as a mark of civility and held it in his hand. His sweeping glance surveyed the crowd from one end to the other. Everyone present knew it was the moment of fulfilment of their lifetime ambition.

Petrified by the thought that the Governor might miss their salute at the precise moment his eye rested on them, they continued to salute him until he left the station. For five whole minutes their hands kept touching their foreheads and dropping down, like forest branches swaying incessantly in the west wind.

Having brought everyone under his royal glance, the Governor swiftly strode out and got into the waiting car. And those who had come to be exalted by the 'gracious sight' returned to their respective homes.

Sriman Sivagurunathan Chettiar reached home safe and sound. He was immediately surrounded by an excited group of wife, children, clerk, and staff. Chettiar was a kind man. He did not wish to disappoint so many eager souls.

'We must call the priest to arrange a special thanksgiving puja to the temple deity. Things went very well today.'

'Did the Governor speak to you? What did you say to him? What actually happened?' Everyone wanted to know every detail.

'As soon as he got off the train, the Governor spoke to one or two officials like the zillah collector and came straight to me,' Chettiar told them. 'Do you think I felt the slightest fear? Not at all! He shook my hand and said, "Chettiar, I have heard a lot about you. How do you do? Are your friends and relatives doing well?" You know me. Once I start talking I cannot stop. I said, "Your Excellency, under your rule we have no complaints. But I am forced to express my discontent over the fact that your government shows no discrimination in awarding titles."'

'Ayyayyo! That was quite severe! Didn't the Governor get angry?' the clerk asked with concern.

The words gushed forth from Chettiar's lips. 'Angry? What do you mean? As soon as I said this, the Governor shook my hand again and said, "Chettiar, thank you very much for bringing this to my attention. I will take steps to rectify the matter." The crowd broke into applause. But you should have seen our Rao Bahadur Iyengar. He was dumbstruck. He was standing in an obscure corner. No one took the slightest notice of him.'

At that very instant, if anyone had eavesdropped in the women's quarters at Rao Bahadur Kurmavataram Iyengar's house, he would have heard Iyengar say to his beloved spouse, 'But the Governor did not waste a single glance on Sivagurunathan Chettiar. Poor thing! He stood in an obscure corner and slunk away quite unnoticed.'

A DEATH IN DELHI

KAMLESHWAR

Translated from the Hindi by Poonam Saxena

The fog is everywhere. It is nine in the morning, but all of Delhi is enveloped in mist. The streets are damp. The trees are wet. Nothing is clearly visible. You can make out the bustle of life only by the sounds. These sounds are lodged in our ears now. There are sounds coming from every section of the house. Vasvani's servant has lit the stove, like he does every day, and the hissing sound can be heard through the wall. In the room next door, Atul Mavani is polishing his shoes. Upstairs Sardarji is putting Fixo on his moustaches. The bulb outside his curtained window is glowing like an enormous pearl. All the doors are closed, all the windows have curtains, but every part of the house resonates with the clink and clatter of life. On the third floor, Vasvani has shut the bathroom door and opened the tap....

Buses are speeding through the fog. The joon-joon sound of heavy tyres comes closer and then fades away. Motor-rickshaws are speeding recklessly. Someone has just pushed down the taxi meter. The phone is ringing in the house of the doctor next door and some girls are walking to their morning shift in the lane behind.

It is bitterly cold. The streets shiver and honking cars and buses slice through the fog and hurtle away. The streets and footpaths are crowded, but each person, wrapped in the mist, looks like a restless lost spirit.

These spirits are quietly growing in the sea of mist...the buses are crowded. People are huddled on the cold seats, some are hanging in the middle of the bus, as if they have been crucified, Christ-like, arms upraised, no nails in their hands, just the shiny, frigid metal bars of the bus.

And amidst all this, from far away, comes a funeral procession.

The newspaper has a report of this funeral. I just read it. It must be news of this particular death. It's printed in the newspaper—Seth Diwanchand, a renowned and well-liked businessman from Karol Bagh, died in Irwin Hospital tonight. His body has been brought to his kothi. Tomorrow morning, his funeral procession will pass through Arya Samaj Road on its way to the Panchkuian cremation ground where it will be ritually consigned to the flames....

This must be the funeral procession coming down the street right now. Some people, wearing caps and mufflers, are quietly walking behind the bier. They are walking very slowly. I can see a little, I can't see everything, but it seems to me that there are some people behind the bier.

There is a knock on my door. I put aside the newspaper and open the door. Atul Mavani is standing outside.

'What a hassle, yaar, no ironwallah has turned up today, just give me your iron,' he says and I feel relieved. For a moment, I was scared that he might suggest joining the funeral procession. I immediately give him the iron, secure in the knowledge that Atul will now iron his pants and depart for his embassy rounds.

∞

Ever since I had read the news of Seth Diwanchand's death, I was on tenterhooks every second: suppose someone comes and says we should join the funeral procession despite the bitter cold. Everyone in the building knew him and they're all decent, worldly people.

At that moment, Sardarji's servant comes racing down the stairs noisily and opens the door to go out. To reassure myself some more, I call out to him, 'Dharma! Where are you going?'

'To get butter for Sardarji,' he answers from the door and, taking advantage of the situation, I hand him some money to get me cigarettes.

Sardarji is getting butter for his breakfast, this means he isn't going to join the funeral procession either. I feel a little relieved. If Atul Mavani and Sardarji have no intention of going, there's no reason for me to go. Both of them and the Vasvani family were better acquainted with Seth Diwanchand than I was. I had just met him four or five times. If these people are not going to participate, there's no question of my having to go.

I spot Mrs Vasvani on the balcony. There is a strange pallor on her beautiful face, and on her lips, a faint redness from last evening's lipstick. She has come out wearing her gown and is now tying her bun. She is saying, 'Darling, just give me the paste, please....'

I feel even more relieved. This means that Mr Vasvani is not going for the funeral either.

Far away, on Arya Samaj Road, the funeral procession is moving forward, ever so slowly....

∽

Atul Mavani comes to return the iron. I take it and want to close the door, but he walks in and says, 'Did you hear, Diwanchandji died yesterday?'

'I read it in the newspaper.' I give a direct reply, to prevent any further talk of this death. Atul Mavani's face has a white tinge, he has already shaved. He goes on, 'Diwanchand was a good man.'

Listening to him, I get the feeling that if the conversation proceeds further, there will be a moral responsibility to join the funeral procession, so I say, 'What happened to that work of yours?'

'Just waiting for the machinery, that's all. As soon as that happens, I'll get my commission. This commission work is so crass. But what can be done? If I can get eight or ten machines passed, I will start my own business,' says Atul Mavani. 'Bhai, when I first came here, Diwanchandji helped me a lot. I got some work only because of him. People really respected him.'

My ears prick up on hearing Diwanchand's name again. At that moment, Sardarji pokes his head out of the window and asks, 'Mr Mavani! What time should we leave?'

'The time was nine o'clock, but perhaps because of the cold and fog, it might get a bit delayed,' Atul says and I guess that they're talking about the funeral procession.

Sardarji's servant, Dharma, has given me the cigarettes and is upstairs, setting the tea on the table. Just then Mrs Vasvani's voice can be heard, 'I think Premila will definitely be there, isn't it, darling?'

'She should be there...you should get ready quickly,' says Mr Vasvani, crossing the balcony.

Atul is asking me, 'Coming to the coffee house this evening?'

'I might,' I say, wrapping my blanket around me, and he goes back to his room. In just half a minute, his voice can be heard again, 'Bhai, is there electricity in your place?'

I answer, 'Yes.' I know he is heating water with an electric rod, that's why he asked.

'Polish!' The boot polish boy calls out in his usual polite manner, as he does every day, and Sardarji beckons him upstairs. The boy sits outside and begins polishing while Sardarji gives instructions to his servant: Bring the lunch at one o'clock sharp, roast the papads, make the salad....

I know that Sardarji's servant is a scoundrel. He never reaches on time with the food, nor does he cook what Sardarji likes.

∞

Outside, on the street, the fog is still dense. There is no sign of the sun. Vaishnav, the kulcha-chholawala, has put up his stall on the street. He is arranging the plates like he does every day, and their clink and clatter is audible.

Bus number 7 is leaving. Many Christs, hanging on crosses, are in the bus and the conductor is distributing tickets in advance to the people in the queue. Every time he returns change to the passengers, the tinkle of small coins can be heard till here. The black-uniformed conductor looks like the devil in the midst of the fog-enveloped, ghostly forms.

And the bier has reached a little closer by now.

∞

'Should I wear the blue sari?' asks Mrs Vasvani.

Vasvani's reply is muffled, it sounds as if he's adjusting the knot of his tie.

Sardarji's servant has cleaned his suit with a brush and draped it on a hanger. And Sardarji is standing in front of the mirror tying his turban.

Atul Mavani appears again, portfolio in hand. He's wearing the suit he got made last month. His face looks fresh and his shoes gleam. As soon as he arrives, he asks me, 'Aren't you coming?' And before I can ask him where he calls out to Sardarji, 'Come, Sardarji! It's getting late. It's already ten.'

Sardarji comes down the stairs. Vasvani looks at Mavani from upstairs and asks, 'Where did you get this suit stitched?'

'From Khan Market.'

'It's very well stitched. Give me the address of your tailor.' Then he calls out to his missus, 'Now come along, dear.... All right, I'll wait downstairs.' He walks down to where Mavani and Sardarji are standing, feels the fabric and asks, 'The lining is Indian?'

'English!'

'Excellent fitting!' he says and notes down the address of the tailor in his diary. Mrs Vasvani appears on the balcony—the damp, chilly morning is making her look even more beautiful than usual. Sardarji sends a discreet message to Mavani with his eyes and lets out a soft whistle.

∞

The bier is right below my room now. It is accompanied by a few men and a couple of slow-moving cars. People are busy talking to each other.

Mrs Vasvani comes down, fixing the flower in her bun and Sardarji starts adjusting the handkerchief in his pocket. Before they leave, Vasvani asks me, 'Aren't you coming?'

'You go ahead, I'm coming,' I say, but in the next second I wonder—where is he asking me to go? I am still standing there, thinking about this when the four of them leave the house.

The bier has moved a little further by now. A car comes up from behind and slows down as it reaches the procession. The driver has a brief conversation with one of the people walking in the funeral procession, then the car speeds ahead with a whoosh. The two cars behind the bier also streak forward.

Mrs Vasvani and the other three go towards the taxi stand. I keep watching them. Mrs Vasvani is wearing a fur collar and the Sardarji is either showing her his leather gloves or giving them to her. A taxi driver comes forward, opens the door and all four get inside. Now the taxi is heading this way and I can hear the sound of laughter from inside. Vasvani is saying something to the driver, while pointing to the procession....

I'm watching everything silently and I don't know why, but now I think that the least I could have done is participated in Diwanchand's funeral procession. I know his son quite well and at such a time, one shows sympathy even to an enemy. I couldn't bring myself to go because of the cold...but the thought that I should go keeps bothering me.

The taxi with the four of them slows down near the bier. Mavani pokes his head out and says something; then the taxi cuts across to the right and moves ahead.

I get a bit of a jolt and, putting on my overcoat and chappals, go downstairs. My feet automatically take me towards the bier and I start walking behind it silently. Four men are carrying the bier on their shoulders and seven men are walking alongside—I am the seventh. And I think, everything changes when a man dies! Last year Diwanchand got his daughter married and there were thousands of guests. There was a line of cars outside his kothi....

Walking alongside the bier, I reach Link Road. The Panchkuian cremation ground is at the next turn.

As the bier turns the corner, I see a throng of people and a line of cars. There are a few scooters, too. A group of women is standing to one side. I can hear their loud voices. Their posture, their bodies have the same suppleness you see in Connaught Place. Everyone's hair has been styled differently. Cigarette smoke is rising from the crowd of men and dissolving in the mist. The red lips and white teeth of the women talking to each other are shining and their eyes have a certain arrogance....

The bier has been placed on a raised platform outside. A hush descends on the gathering. The scattered groups of people move closer and stand around the body and the chauffeurs holding floral bouquets and garlands wait for a signal from their employers.

I happen to glance at Vasvani. He is trying to signal his missus with his eyes to go and stand closer to the body, but she is busy chatting to another woman. Sardarji and Atul Mavani are also standing there.

The face of the body has now been uncovered and the women are placing flowers and garlands around the body. The chauffeurs, their duty done, are standing near the cars smoking cigarettes.

One of the women, after placing a garland, takes out a handkerchief from her coat pocket, dabs her eyes with it, starts sniffing, and then steps back.

Now all the women take out their handkerchiefs and make sniffling sounds.

Some men have lit incense sticks and placed them near the head of the body. They stand quite still and motionless.

From the sounds it seems as if the women have suffered a more severe shock.

Atul Mavani has taken a paper from his portfolio and is showing it to Vasvani. I think it's a passport form.

Now the body is being taken into the cremation ground. The crowd is standing outside the gate, watching. The chauffeurs have either finished their cigarettes or stubbed them out and are standing, alert, next to their cars.

The body has gone inside.

The men and women who came to mourn are leaving. There is the sound of car doors opening and slamming shut. Scooters are starting and some people are moving towards the bus stop on Ring Road.

∞

The fog is still thick. The buses are going by and Mrs Vasvani is saying, 'Premila has called us this evening, we'll go, won't we, dear? The car will come. That's all right, isn't it?'

Vasvani nods, indicating his acceptance.

The women leaving in their cars smile at each other in farewell. Some 'bye-byes' can be heard. The cars are starting and leaving.

Atul Mavani and Sardarji have moved towards the Ring Road bus stop and I stand and think, if only I'd got ready and come, I could've gone straight to work from here. But it's half past eleven now.

The pyre has been lit and four or five men have sat down on a bench under a tree. Like me, they too seem to have just come along. They must have taken leave from office, otherwise they would have got ready and come.

I can't decide whether to go home, get ready and go to work or to make this death an excuse and take the day off—after all, there has been a death and I did join the funeral procession.

COINSANV'S CATTLE
DAMODAR MAUZO

Translated from the Konkani by Xavier Cota

Driving his cattle before him, Inas herded them into the shed where he tethered them for the night before entering the house through the back door. Bent over the fireplace, Coinsanv was coaxing the fire to life by patiently blowing on the embers. Hearing Inas come in, she asked in surprise, 'Haven't you tied the cows yet, Inas?'

'I've just come in after tying them,' mumbled Inas, sitting down on the box by the wall. Retrieving the butt of the viddi stuck above his ear, he struck a match to it and drew in the smoke, deeply.

'Strange! Then, why aren't they lowing today?' Coinsanv asked in wonder. Invariably, the cows would set off a continuous mooing after being tied up in the shed. And here was Inas, back in the house after tying them and they were still silent!

'They dare not open their mouths!'

'Why? What happened?' Coinsanv asked with a stab of apprehension. 'Did they enter someone's garden or....'

'Not in anybody's garden. They got into Paulu bhatkar's coconut grove. They chewed some of his saplings, it seems. He threatened to impound them unless I paid him fifteen rupees. Only after I pleaded with him and promised to work on his plot did he let them go.'

Coinsanv heard him out in silence. Warming the tea that she'd brewed in the afternoon, she poured out a mug and placed it in front of Inas. The cattle were still quiet.

'Bitter...like poison!' muttered Inas, grimacing distastefully after taking a sip of the smoky, stale black tea.

But Coinsanv was too preoccupied to pay attention to his grumbling. Why are the cattle still not mooing? How could they still not be hungry!

'Did the cows destroy many coconut saplings?'

'Nonsense! Not a single one! I doubt that they even touched a single leaf!' In that case.... In a trice Coinsanv realized what had happened. 'Inas, did you by chance vent your anger with the landlord on the cows?'

Inas's sullen silence was answer enough.

Leaving whatever she was doing, Coinsanv rushed to the cow shed. Both the cow and the bull were standing mutely. Normally, they would both lick her with their sandpaper-like tongues as soon as she walked into the shed. Today, they made no such move. For a moment, Coinsanv imagined that they were averting their gaze from her! Could they be angry? Coinsanv laid both her hands on each of their backs. Immediately, they both started trembling. The cow started mooing first, followed immediately by the bull. Coinsanv started stroking the cow's neck with one hand and, with the other, she gently scratched the bull's forehead. The cow responded by licking her hand. Coinsanv's glance roved over the animals minutely. Though there were no definite welts on their bodies, Coinsanv's experienced eyes could tell exactly where each stroke of the lash had landed. The animals were now continuously lowing in unison. They were famished. Patting them, Coinsanv coaxed them gently, 'Okay, okay, quiet now.' She then went to the house. Inas was outside readying the coconut fronds for thatching.

'Inas, is there any oilcake in the house?'

Inas maintained a stoic silence. In any case, what could he do? Whose stomach was he supposed to fill? Three children. With their precarious hand-to-mouth existence, all they could think about was getting through each day. As long as the cow was yielding milk, they could afford to buy oilcake. Last year they had a pair of bullocks which they used for ploughing. But at Christmas, the black bull had died. Had it not died, they would have earned something from ploughing. Now, how could they afford oilcake for a cow gone dry and an idle bull?

'There's a little bran in the house, Inas. I'll go and collect some dhonn. Don't go out.'

By the time she made the rounds of their four Hindu neighbours, collecting the slop that they kept for her, the Angelus bells were ringing. She had barely entered the house, balancing the earthen pot on her head, when the cows set off an insistent bellowing.

Lowering the pot, Coinsanv put her hand in a bag and drew out some bran that she'd saved. She distributed the bran equally between two kodhim. Pouring the slop into both the earthen vessels, she stirred it with her hand till the bran was soaked.

The cattle were still lowing ceaselessly. Inas came out. Flicking the butt of his viddi, he got to work. Taking an old broom, he quickly cleared away the area in front of the cows. As soon as Coinsanv had finished stirring, he lifted the feed containers and placed them in front of the cattle. They began to feed greedily. Coinsanv went to the well and drew a pitcher of water. By this time, the cattle had licked the containers dry. Pouring water into them, Coinsanv went inside. Outside, the children could be heard raising a ruckus. The pot was bubbling on the fire. Inas must have kept the rice water to boil while she'd gone to collect the slop. Mentally thanking him for his thoughtfulness, Coinsanv resumed her interrupted chores.

She roasted some dried sardines on the embers. After removing them from the coals, she sprinkled the last few drops of coconut oil from the bottle. The aroma that wafted up was appetizing.

'O, Inas!' somebody from outside called out.

'Coming!' Inas replied from the back as Pedru made himself comfortable on the balcão. Catching a whiff of the roasted salt fish, he joked, 'Coinsanv, I'm inviting myself to dinner tonight!'

'Please join us! We have excellent fish today!' retorted Coinsanv.

'That's obvious from the aroma!' Pedru laughed, lighting up a viddi. By then Inas came out.

'Where are the cattle, Inas?' Pedru's question made Coinsanv's heart skip a beat. What now? Had their cattle got into somebody else's compound too? Pedru's next remark allayed the fear.

'Day after tomorrow is the Purument fest in Margao. I'll be taking my buffalo heifer to sell at the fair. I've come to see if you're planning to go too.'

After a moment's hesitation, Inas replied, 'No. You carry on.'

His logic was telling him to sell the cattle. A single bull was useless for ploughing and a cow that yielded no milk was expensive to look after. But his prudence was warning him not to do anything without consulting Coinsanv. She loved the animals dearly.

'Don't be foolish! Your bull is getting old. What will you do if he too dies?' asked Pedru, exhaling smoke.

Inas remained quiet. Inside, Coinsanv listened intently. Pedru continued, 'I'm selling my heifer. If I get a good crop this year, I may buy another one next year. You decide about yours. But do remember that you'll get the best price only at this fair. In my opinion, you'd better sell both the cow and the bull. You can always buy one later.'

Pedru left, yet Inas did not go back in. Coinsanv must have heard every word that Pedru spoke. But he did not dare broach the subject with her. Coinsanv called the children in to eat. She served them bits of the roasted salt fish along with the kanji.

'Coinsanv, I'll be back soon,' said Inas.

Coinsanv knew exactly where Inas had gone.

Reflecting on what Pedru had said, Coinsanv squatted in front of the fireplace. One cow and a pair of bulls. How Coinsanv had doted on them! There was nothing that both she and Inas wouldn't do for them. They had even deprived themselves to feed the cattle. Despite this, one bull had died of snakebite exactly on Christmas day. During Carnival, the cow had stopped yielding milk. And now....

When fending for three children and two adults was itself an overwhelming task, can one afford to be emotional about animals? The spiralling prices.... They were already in the last days of May and had not even thought about the transplanting of paddy which had to be done before the monsoon broke out in June. Others had already germinated their seedlings. Some had already been transplanted, hoping for early rains. Both Coinsanv's paddy plots were still fallow.

The neighbours kept asking her, 'When will you be sowing?' But where would she get so much money from? Seedlings, fertilizer, weeding—for all this she needed...yes. It was essential that they sowed their field. It was only because they had cultivated last year that their children could at least have kanji this year. Otherwise they would...! They must sow...the rains were nearing...day after tomorrow was the Pentecost fair where one had to stock up on provisions for the rainy season!

Inas trooped in after a tot at the taverna. Coinsanv served Inas some kanji. Inas glanced into the kanji buddkulo. As Coinsanv readied to ladle out some more for him, Inas said he'd had enough. Coinsanv guessed that he'd said that because there was very little kanji left in the pot. But Coinsanv was not hungry and said, 'I've already eaten, Inas. You eat well. You have to work tomorrow.'

'Don't lie to me. Have that kanji!' said Inas, getting up.

Coinsanv sipped her rice gruel and got up. She cleaned up the fireplace and came out of the kitchen. The kids were fast asleep. Inas had squatted on the box and was puffing away.

'Inas, day after tomorrow is the Purument feast.'

Inas dragged on the viddi and exhaled, but remained silent. He was bothered by the same thoughts.

'You're taking the cattle, aren't you?'

Inas stiffened. Was Coinsanv goading him? Testing him? Inas shook his head vigorously.

'What do you mean by no? Are you mad?' She was speaking to Inas but was obviously trying to convince herself. 'How will we manage if we don't sell the cattle? Don't we have to sow the fields? Where will the money for the fertilizer, the seedlings, come from? From your father?'

Inas heard Coinsanv out in wonder. He had been thinking along the same lines but hadn't said anything because of Coinsanv's feelings. Now Coinsanv was herself telling him this!

'Are you serious?' Inas croaked in disbelief.

'Is this the time for jokes? There's only tomorrow. On the day after, you take them at dawn. Do you want me to come along?'

'There's no need.' Inas was relieved. All along, he'd been hesitating to broach the subject but now Coinsanv was herself urging him to sell the cattle. He slept soundly. After Coinsanv blew out the light and went to bed, Inas wasn't awake to hear her sobbing bitterly.

Getting through the next day was hell. Early in the morning, Mari-Santan called out, 'Coinsanv, have you seen the sky? It looks like the monsoon is coming soon!'

'Maybe.'

'Aren't you transplanting?'

'We're transplanting after the feast.'

'You'd better hurry up! The rains are around the corner! Some people have already transplanted. And haven't you heard, people are queuing up for fertilizer? You better reserve yours fast!'

If in the morning it was Mari-Santan, Caitan came by at noon. 'Have you bought your paddy seedlings?'

'Not yet.'

'Do you want some?' Caitan asked.

'Do you have stock?'

'Not me. But Bebdo-Santan, the drunkard, has some for sale. If you need it, you better tell him now.'

'I'll speak to Inas about it.'

The cows had not been put out to pasture that morning. Coinsanv herself took them to graze in the evening. Taking out some money that she'd saved, she bought a kilo of oilcake. Earlier, with one rupee you could get a kilo of oilcake and a small tablet of bathing soap besides. Now soap has become precious and a rupee would not even buy a kilo of oilcake! Mentally cursing the greedy shopkeeper, Coinsanv soaked the cake in water. Asking Inas to remain in the house, she went to the houses of the neighbouring Hindus. At each house, she collected the slop and, barely controlling the tears welling up in her eyes, she told them, 'From tomorrow, we won't need the slop. We are selling the cattle in the morning!'

Ladling out a generous portion of feed for the cattle, Inas and Coinsanv went in. Both were heavy-hearted. They had brought up these two dumb animals like their own children. And now they had to sell them for the sake of their own stomachs.

It was a terrible night, full of turmoil for them both.

Coinsanv got up at the crack of dawn. She lit the fire and put the kettle on for tea. She went into the cow shed and sitting with the animals, she cried her heart out. She got up when she sensed that Inas had woken up. Coinsanv poured out the tea and both of them sipped it in silence by the fireplace. Outside, the world was stirring. Filip, Hari, and Pedru were supposed to be taking their cattle for the fair. As he was putting on his shirt, Inas told her, 'Coinsanv, go to our field and straighten out the ridges. And send a message to Bebdo-Santan that we'll need his seedlings. If it rains tomorrow, we can transplant the day after.' But Coinsanv was hardly listening. Her other ear was in the cow shed.

Pedru arrived noisily. 'Hoi there, Inas!'

Inas went out through the back door, untied the animals, and herded them out of the shed. Coinsanv couldn't restrain herself. Rushing out of the house, she hugged the cow. The bull came up to her and started licking her calves. With that, the dam burst and Coinsanv cried a flood of tears.

'You get inside now!' muttered Inas gruffly.

Her leaden feet would not move and Coinsanv remained rooted to the spot she was standing upon. Inas tugged at the cattle. Since Pedru was almost out of sight, he stepped up his pace, straining at the ropes. Coinsanv sensed that the cow's feet had become heavy and the cattle didn't want to go. Inas was actually having to drag them away. What Coinsanv wanted to say was, 'No, Inas! Don't take them!' but the words did not come. What broke out instead were uncontrollable sobs. She sank down to the ground and squatted on her heels.

As the sun came out brightly, Coinsanv got a grip on herself. It was over. She served breakfast to the children and went to the fields. With a hoe, she softened the soil and levelled it. She then straightened the ridges. Having spent half a day there, she went home. After lunch, she went to Santan's and booked some seedlings. She next went to the fertilizer shop and found out which was ideal. 'I'll collect it tomorrow, keep some for me,' she told the shopkeeper. When she reached home again, she remembered her cows. She became uneasy. Her feet took her to the cow shed. She entered the shed; its emptiness oppressed her. Such wonderful animals! We should never have sold them. Where did we get this awful idea? Our cattle were so loving, so gentle. If that stupid Pedru weren't to come that day, we wouldn't even have thought of it! Hurling two curses at Pedru, a couple at Inas, and cursing herself, too, Coinsanv got up. She then put rice in the pot boiling on the fire for kanji. As she put it in, she consoled herself. Never mind; let the cattle go! At least we won't go hungry next year. The sun had set and the lengthening shadows of darkness were casting their gloom in the house. Misgivings started assailing Coinsanv once again. It was this same cow's milk that nourished my children. By selling her milk, we could manage to buy provisions. This very bull helped maintain our household with his ploughing. And today we have decided to sell them! Our lovely cattle! God help us! I hope nobody buys our cow! I hope our bull comes back! Coinsanv consoled herself with these fervent pleas.

It was past Angelus, time for Inas to be back. But Coinsanv did not allow herself to go out and sit. Without even lighting a lamp, she squatted inside in the dark.

Quite often, many cattle come back unsold. But those cattle are quite different. Our animals are so loving; anybody will grab them. We should never have sent them! As she sat there with these thoughts tormenting her, she heard the distant tinkling of cowbells. Coinsanv stepped out.

Pedru was in front. Inas was trailing him. In the darkness she felt she could make out Pedru returning with his buffalo. But she had forgotten that Pedru's buffalo did not have a bell. Surmising that Coinsanv would be pleased even if the cows were not sold, Inas was coming back with the cows with a spring in his step.

A stunned Coinsanv was motionless for a moment. That fallow field, those seedlings, that fertilizer—everything began swimming before her eyes. The cow had barely started licking her hand affectionately when Coinsanv began screaming and flailing her arms at the two dumb animals. 'You whore! You wretched animals! How the hell are we to manage now? How are we to sow the field? What are we going to eat next year? Go—and die!'

THE HOLY BANYAN

BAMACHARAN MITRA

*Translated from the Odia by Leelawati Mohapatra,
Paul St-Pierre, and K. K. Mohapatra*

If you've ever passed through Naripur, you would've sat and rested for a while in the shade of the holy banyan. (The tree is no longer, alas; bedevilled by humans, it gave up the ghost leaf by leaf—branches, roots and all.)

For a long time, the holy banyan was a well-known landmark. Spreading well over an acre, it once stood at the edge of the village; its hanging roots had become mighty trunks. The ground underneath it was clean, polished like a cement floor. The roads connecting Naripur to the surrounding villages—Dihasahi, Daitapur, Dhanua, and Gamara to the east, and Nuagaon, Nuapatna, and Ahmedpur to the west—all passed the tree.

To the north lay the village cremation grounds, littered with human skulls big and small, discarded torn mats, mattresses and pillows of the dead. It resounded now and then with cries of Haribol, and the sobbing and wailing of women. They threw their clay cooking pots and pans into the growing heap of rubbish, took a dip in the pond, and returned home. The blazing cremation fires died down, silence and darkness surged back in again. After the period of mourning, everything returned to normal; life went on as before. But the dead remained dead, their flesh and bones enriching the soil, nourishing the grass and the weeds. What became of their souls? Christians believe they wait until Judgement Day and then, according to their karma, are sent either to heaven or to hell. Hindus believe in rebirth, the day after someone dies or two hundred years later. Atheists, of course, dismiss everything: once dead and turned to ashes, all is over! But doesn't the Bhagavad Gita say the soul endures forever? But no matter what the pandits say, the people of Naripur believed—and had reason to believe—that when a rebirth was delayed, many a soul, unable to get over their attachment to their former homes and families, chose to take shelter under the holy banyan. Even those who'd normally have found a place in heaven. Only the other day, Anta, a robust young man in the prime of life, passed away after an attack of cholera. His young widow cried so bitterly she fainted on the cremation ground. As Anta's relatives were returning home after the cremation, a fat branch of the holy banyan broke off and crashed to the ground. No whiff of a breeze, let alone of a hurricane or whirlwind. Unable to get over his love for his young wife, Anta's ghost had obviously settled in the big tree. No matter that within a month the young widow eloped with Ram Pradhan to Calcutta. This led to tongues wagging, and it came to light the young woman had poisoned her husband at the instigation of her lover. Anta's ghost was often sighted; it never left the tree.

No one could keep count of all the ghosts inhabiting it. Not only those of Naripur but the ghosts of several surrounding villages had chosen the tree as their nesting place. People claimed to have seen them climbing up and down the tree and roaming the roads.

Not a drop of rain nor a ray of sunshine could penetrate the holy tree's foliage. The ground beneath it stayed warm in winter, like a mother's lap, and dry in the monsoons. When it threatened to rain, cowherds would shelter their cattle, goats, and sheep under it. The animals would sprawl on the smooth surface and chew their cud in peace. The boys would climb up and prance about on branches as wide as roads, while some stretched out on their backs belting out snatches of a song: '*Tell me, oh sweet damsel, whose daughter or wife are you, and who has reduced you to tears?*' Others swung from the hanging roots.

A weary traveller, longing for a short rest on a hot summer day, would choose the shade of the mighty tree. Some said it gave forth a cool breeze to welcome visitors as soon as they came near. The traveller would take off his turban, wipe away his sweat, and lean back against the trunk to catch his breath. A while later he'd swig a bellyful of cool rice water, delicious with salt and crushed chillies, lie at the foot of the tree, and pass into deep, contented sleep. He'd awaken by late afternoon, when the shadows had grown long and, with a reverential bow to the tree, resume his journey. In winter, merchants would stop there for the night, accompanied by thirty or forty bullock carts piled high with merchandise. With the bullocks fed after being unyoked and tethered to the hanging roots, dinner cooked and eaten, everyone would drop off to sleep. The place, snug and warm as if under a blanket, kept the biting cold at bay. In the morning, after paying their respects to His Holiness, they'd go on their way.

The holy banyan had been planted by Banabehari some four generations ago. A quiet, honest, and truthful man, he felt disturbed by the bad blood between the two villages and went away to the high Himalayas to pray and meditate. In those days, community leaders did not have recourse to politics to solve problems; no, they considered all discord their personal failure and would undertake fasts and meditations, after which they would try with redoubled ardour to establish the rule of virtue. Quite unlike the leaders of today who advocate the rejection of religion and spirituality. There's apparently no place in modern, scientific society for such concepts, considered figments of the imagination. The only true aim of life these days is making money, creating wealth, through industry, through commerce; money alone matters. Well, time will tell who is right. Maybe imagination makes a god out of a human being, while science turns him into a demon.

A year of penance and meditation in the Himalayas later, Banabehari returned with a tiny banyan sapling and planted it at the edge of the village in a ceremony enthusiastically attended by people from nearly twenty-five nearby villages. The feasting went on for seven long days.

The sapling grew into a gigantic tree. Burying their differences, the villagers met and mingled in peace, harmony, and brotherhood under its vast canopy.

When Banabehari died, his ghost settled on its branches, instead of pushing off to heaven. Until recently, generations of his descendants had distributed rice water to thirsty passers-by under the tree during the summer. Whenever Batasundar, a descendant of Banabehari, recited the Sivastaka or the Siva-tandav stotra by Ravana, not only the temple in which the mantras were chanted but the mighty tree, too, seemed to vibrate. Batasundar could not get over his attachment to Naripur, and when his mortal remains returned to the dust of the cremation ground, his ghost, too, decided to nest in the holy tree.

Every year, on the occasion of the dwitiya-osha, the tree was given a ceremonial bath. This was an important occasion, marked by the sound of drums, conch shells, and ululation. The tree was draped in new clothes, the main and the larger trunks were dabbed with vermilion. Incense sticks were lighted, their fragrance enveloping the place, and the feasting began. The Hindus from twenty-five villages even sat and ate with the Muslims of Ahmedpur. Shops sprung up, folk opera and pala troupes performed day and night.

Apart from this great annual celebration, there were smaller functions all around the year: offerings made when a wish came true—whether it was a child begotten, or that child getting a job. The tree had brought together people over a vast area. For four generations, it had been the centre of their existence.

The village of Haldia was to the north, bordering the Naripur cremation grounds. A large village, its inhabitants were richer and more educated. The children of Naripur went to work in the fields from an early age, minded cattle and picked up swear words instead of learning nursery rhymes like 'There goes Kanhai, the dark-complexioned, with Rohini's son....' No wonder the Naripur upper-primary school never grew into a middle school, while the middle school of Haldia had long since blossomed into a high school, and was all set to become a college. Haldia villagers were in business and government service, quite a few in high positions, too; the local MLA came from the village, as did the panchayat chairman. While Naripur was full of dingy little houses—its cow sheds bigger than its living rooms—Haldia had many brick-and-mortar buildings.

But Naripur's greatest pride was its mighty banyan tree, before which, no matter how big or important the other villages were, all had to bow their heads. It was the Kalpataru, the wish-fulfilling tree, a living god.

But times began to change. The Panchayati Raj came to stay. More and more people became educated. The economy changed. Like Bhagiratha bringing the Ganga to earth from the heavens, the architects of the country's destiny got funds from abroad, which then flowed from the centre to the states to the panchayats. These modern-day Bhagirathas even tried to direct the flow directly to their own states. Some funds disappeared in transit, just as the waters of the Ganga had—a crafty Lord Shiva or a Jahnu Muni could reroute the stream in their matted locks! But that made little difference. As long as the torrents jetted in full force, a little stealing here, a little pilfering there made no difference, did it? Well, who cared!

But the trouble started when those who had been deprived awoke and suddenly turned patriotic. Their attire changed overnight: white cap on the head, cloth bag slung from the shoulder, and coarse white dhoti down to the knees.

Naripur's Batakrishna was seen dressed like this one fine day. He had been working in a jute mill in Calcutta, but once he got the scent of what was cooking in the village he rushed there like a vulture to a carcass. It took him less than a moment to figure out how to divert the flow of funds from Haldia. The first thing he did was set up the Divine Banyan Development Committee and call for a meeting. People from the twenty-five villages attended. They decided that, henceforth, every village would contribute an anna a month to the Development Committee. Individuals wanting special services would have to cough up two rupees. The washerwomen could no longer carry away for free the mountains of dry leaves and twigs they swept up from under the tree; they'd have to pay a paisa for every bundle; and so on and so forth.

Batakrishna became the secretary of the committee. Funds were collected, and quite a handsome amount they added up to. Around the principal trunk of the tree a huge cement platform was built; smaller platforms came up around lesser trunks. A brick ashram was put up for Batakrishna, and he came up with ever new ideas to increase collections.

He recognized a brilliant opportunity in the poetic excellence of Jaan Mohammed of Ahmedpur. Jaan, a popular bard, wrote slim books of verses on subjects like 'The Quarrel between Mother and Daughter-in-law' and 'The City-smart Daughter-in-law from Cuttack' and sold them out of his bag, trudging from village to village. It was he who had earlier versified the story of Anta's wife poisoning him and then eloping with Ram Pradhan to Calcutta. That book had done quite well; the village women had snapped up copies. Batakrishna commissioned Jaan to pen *Miracles of His Holiness the Sacred Banyan*. When the book was ready, the name of Batakrishna appeared as its humble author. The stories of miracles spread, the number of pilgrims grew. Not only did the fame of the holy tree grow, but so did Batakrishna's too. More and more money flowed into the committee's coffers, and some of it found its way into Batakrishna's.

Batakrishna then made a foray into the village panchayat committee, becoming an ordinary member. Shortly afterwards a rumour began to circulate that a no-confidence motion against the president of the panchayat committee—Batuk from Haldia—was in the offing.

The roof on Batuk's second floor remained to be cast. He saw trouble approaching, but he wasn't one to take it lying down. A compulsive litigant, he always wreaked vengeance through the law courts. On his payroll could be found a phalanx of witnesses swearing to speak nothing but the truth and then proceeding to speak anything but. For just two rupees and a free meal, they could casually tell the most outrageous lies, even as they tripped miserably during cross-examination. Poor judge! What could he be thinking while reading the transcripts? The truth completely eclipsed by lies, like the moon by dark clouds.

Batuk was naturally much feared. Before the panchayat meeting convened to push through the no-confidence motion against him, he slapped four or five false cases on Batakrishna, with charges ranging from molestation and rape to cheating and committing burglary—involving all the important sections of the Indian Penal Code.

Batakrishna appealed to His Holiness and went on a fast, stepping up the sales of *Miracles of His Holiness the Sacred Banyan*. The cases were fought using the Banyan's funds, the false witnesses were bought off. Batuk lost the presidency. Batakrishna took his place, but he claimed it was a victory for His Holiness, not for himself.

As the flames of fights between Naripur and Haldia leaped higher, the cracks between Naripur and the other villages surfaced too.

But Batuk became more determined than ever, hatching plans to bring a no-confidence motion against Batakrishna. He bribed the members, piled them into a truck and drove them to Bhubaneswar, where they were made to swear their loyalty and allegiance not only in the presence of the minister but before Lord Lingaraj in his temple over consecrated mahaprasad, before returning to their homes. All this before the night was over. The whole operation was carried out as stealthily as the silent movements of the sly murrel fish; not even their next-door neighbours got whiff of it.

But Lord Lingaraj's influence apparently did not extend as far as Naripur, which was under only the fiat of the holy Banyan. Groups of pala singers, daskathia and jatra troupes, in addition to Jaan Mohammed, fanned out to the villages to spread the gospel of His Holiness and, in the process, the stories of Batakrishna's greatness. Neither Lord Lingaraj nor the minister was enough to pierce the wall of propaganda. Batakrishna eyed the position of the chairman of the panchayats, and seemed to inch closer to his goal by the day. He adopted the banyan tree as his election symbol.

It was then that it struck Batuk that the myth of the sacred Banyan had to be shattered once and for all.

A couple of days afterwards, an ascetic was found in the cremation grounds of Haldia deep in meditation. His name was Batia Baba. The news eddied around that he was a worshipper of Goddess Kali, that he honed his spiritual powers on corpses at the dead of every new moon night. He had harnessed evil spirits and could destroy anyone by letting them loose, or just as easily could rid anyone of a chronic disease, or dogged ill luck, with a pinch of ash from his sacrificial firepit. Like lightning the news spread and soon there started an unending stream of people to the Baba.

A few days later, a new panic gripped the villagers all around: their homes were being bombarded with stones and excrement at midnight. No one could figure out what was happening. Terrified, people went to Batia Baba to find out the cause and the cure. So Batia Baba went into a trance, and what he revealed after his puja stunned everybody. The issue was the ghosts of all twenty-five villages, who until now had lived in perfect peace and harmony in the branches of the sacred Banyan, like the members of a large joint family, were having problems. The ghosts of Naripur, cussed as always, were suddenly trying to evict all others to have full run of the tree, and their evil designs were being supported by the Muslim ghosts of Ahmedpur. So, naturally, the homeless ghosts of the other villages were up to all sorts of mischief, including pelting homes with stones and faeces. What was the remedy? Let every village plant a banyan tree of its own to shelter its own ghostly population. A bright idea, it appealed to all. Dhulia, the chief of Batuk's lackeys, accosted him in private and suggested: 'Sir, why not slap the Naripur ghosts with Sections 17, 447, 426, 323, 500, 504, 325, 354, and 379 of the Indian Penal Code? We have a doctor who can issue medical certificates to order, though his graphic account of bruises can be misleading. And witnesses? Not only am I myself available, I can easily round up several others.' For once, Batuk was supposed to have lost his cool and told the lackey to bugger off.

The decision was taken that Batia Baba would plant the first banyan sapling in the Haldia cremation grounds and name it His Majesty the Mighty Banyan. The preparations afoot, Batuk left for Gaya to bring back a sapling of an ancient holy tree.

Batakrishna caught on to Batuk's plans and swung into action. It didn't take a lot of work. He caught hold of Naripur's Widow Bati. Although no great beauty, she had felled many a mighty man, just as she had saved some from doing time. She did not tolerate any opposition, if she was properly cajoled and appealed to.

Three or four days after she paid nocturnal visits to Batia Baba's ashram, the Baba left Haldia to set up an ashram in Naripur.

When Batuk returned from Gaya, he found his wits deserting him. He had been outsmarted and was left gnashing his teeth. Asked why he had returned empty-handed, he spoke of the dream he had on the way. It was revealed to him that if the new banyan trees were not the offshoots of the holy banyan, the homeless ghosts would refuse to roost in them. Every village had equal rights over the banyan, and was free to break off branches and grow them into new trees. 'Besides,' he added, 'to tell the truth, the holy banyan is really my property. I own the land he stands on; I bought it from Sapani for five hundred rupees. I have paid the land rent for the last five years and have the receipts to show for it. But I'm donating the holy tree to the people of all twenty-five villages. You all are welcome to cut a branch, take it to your village, and grow your own holy banyan trees to save yourselves from the menace of your brood of ghosts.' Batuk Pradhan's generosity surprised everyone; they were in a hurry to act upon his suggestion. But the whole thing was kept under wraps for some time.

One day, at midnight or thereabouts, Batakrishna awoke to the sound of axes falling on the banyan tree. People from Haldia and a few from other villages were hacking off branches. It took minutes for the news to swirl through Naripur. Armed with knives, axes, sickles, spears, and sticks, its denizens came rushing out. A mighty branch came crashing down. It echoed eerily in the temple of Bateswar, sounding like the last gasp of Time Eternal.

The two sides promptly came to blows. The holy tree trembled. Volleys of deafening laughter issued from the temple. Doomsday had arrived. Into the fray jumped the Muslims of Ahmedpur, brandishing swords. Batuk had kept them on standby. The Muslims had borne a grudge against Naripur people, ever since Batakrishna had banished them from the communal worship of the holy tree.

The combatants scattered at the sight of the naked swords. Before running for his life, Dhulia buried, as instructed by Batuk, a large quantity of the deadliest poison under the main trunk of the sacred Banyan.

The next morning the bodies of eight men and fifteen severely wounded were found at the foot of His Holiness. The ones who had sustained minor injuries had managed to crawl away.

The police arrived on the scene. Section 144 was imposed on and around the holy banyan. About a hundred arrests were made. Both Batuk and Batakrishna were handcuffed and taken into custody. All the sections of the IPC Dhulia had once suggested using against the ghosts were now cited against the two, with Section 302 for murder thrown in for good measure. Just as vultures and dogs arrive in droves to clean up carrion, touts and lawyers descended upon the villagers to make money. The wealth Batuk and Batakrishna had amassed seemed to vanish in a bonfire.

A few days afterwards, the holy banyan began to droop and wilt. The mighty tree seemed sunk in sorrowful meditation. Thinking about the past? Worrying about the future? Lord Shiva, the embodiment of eternal Time, had swallowed poison during the churning of the oceans to save mankind. Perhaps the sacred tree had decided to give up the ghost to save the people of Naripur?

But, of course, it was a plain case of murder. But could a tree file a case against its assassins under Section 302? If you are a tree you have no recourse, and nobody laments your passing.

The government auctioned off the wood. The people of Naripur and Haldia, their resources burnt up in court cases, didn't have money enough to bid. The ones who did were the Muslims of Ahmedpur. They logged away the big trunks and branches. The Naripur folks bribed them to leave a little something behind—the smaller branches and twigs. In two days flat, the holy tree had completely vanished; not a vestige remained.

A civilization had come to an end. Another had begun. Nothing to worry about of course. Nothing remained forever, except eternal Time.

Even to this day many people swear to have seen the ghost of Banabehari wandering about, lost, and to have heard the sound of his sighs and his wooden clogs slapping against the ground.

THE DISCOVERY OF TELENAPOTA
PREMENDRA MITRA

Translated from the Bengali by Arunava Sinha

If Saturn and Mars—it must be Mars—are in conjunction, you, too, can discover Telenapota someday.

In other words, if a day or two of leave can be obtained unexpectedly, just when you are gasping from work and multitudes of people, and if someone tempts you with the information that in a lake of miracles somewhere, the most simple-minded fish in the world are waiting eagerly to have their hearts impaled on a hook at the end of a rod for the first time in their lives, and if you have never had the good fortune of extracting anything but small fry from the water, then you too might unexpectedly discover Telenapota one day.

To discover Telenapota you must board a bus packed with people and their possessions in the waning sunlight one afternoon, suffer jabs from other passengers' elbows every time there is a bump on the road, and then, in the August heat, drag your sweaty, dust-caked body off the bus without warning, somewhere along the road. In front of you, you will see the road running over a low swamp like a bridge. After the bus passes along it with an eccentric rumble and disappears around a bend, you will notice that although the sun has not set yet, darkness has descended on the thick jungle all around you. You will not see a soul anywhere. The birds, too, will seem to have forsaken this place. You will become aware of the damp, sultry weather. A cruel, coiled source of venom will rise up slowly from the swamp, its invisible hood poised to strike.

You will have to step off the highway, walk down to the swamp, and wait next to it. It will seem as though someone has dug a muddy canal running through the dense jungle stretching out before you. But even its line has petered out in the distance amidst the bamboo groves and tall, shaggy trees on both sides. You should have two companions for your discovery of Telenapota. They may not be drawn to fishing as you are, and yet they have come with you on this journey—no one knows why.

The three of you will gaze eagerly at the canal in front of you. From time to time, you will stamp your feet to prevent the mosquitoes from getting too intimate, while you exchange questioning glances.

A little later, you will no longer be able to see one another's face in the gathering darkness. The chorus of the mosquitoes will grow sharper. Just as you are wondering whether to return to the highway and wait for a return bus, you will suddenly hear an exquisite sound, wondrous to your senses, from the point where the muddy canal has vanished into the jungle. Someone will seem to force even the silent forest to emit unworldly sobs.

The sound will make your wait restless. But be patient, and your patience will not be in vain. You will see, first, a pinpoint of light swaying in the darkness, and then a bullock cart will emerge slowly from the jungle, rolling from side to side as it moves along the canal.

The cart will match the bullocks—it will seem as though this minuscule version of the bullock cart has come from an underground land of the dwarves.

Without wasting words, the three of you will squeeze yourself beneath the hood on the cart, somehow solving the problem posed by three pairs of arms and legs and three heads—how to place the largest of objects in the smallest of spaces.

The bullock cart will then return the way it came, along the canal. In utter wonderment, you will see how the dense and dark jungle reveals the way forward little by little, like a narrow tunnel. At every moment, the wall of darkness will seem impenetrable, but the cart will move ahead slowly, unperturbed, as though clearing a path with its wheels.

For some time, you will be uncomfortable and discomposed as you try to position your arms, legs, and head suitably. At every moment, there will be inadvertent collisions with your friends, and then you will gradually realize that the last island of consciousness has been submerged in the dense darkness surrounding you. You will feel as though you have left the familiar world somewhere far behind. There is another one here, shrouded in fog, devoid of sensation, where the current of time is stilled, silent.

With time standing still, you will not know how long you have been sunk in this mist. Woken up suddenly by a cacophonous music, you will realize that the stars are visible from beneath the hood, and the driver is beating a tin canister at intervals with great enthusiasm.

Curious, you will ask why, whereupon the driver will inform you indifferently, 'To get rid of the damned wild animals.'

Once you have grasped this properly, the driver will reassure you before you can ask, your voice trembling, whether beating a canister is sufficient to keep tigers at bay, that he is referring to leopards, and unless the beast is famished, this sound will be enough to keep it at a distance.

While you wonder how a place infested by leopards can exist a mere thirty miles from the metropolis, the bullock cart will cross an enormous field. The delayed waning moon will have risen in the sky by then. Dimly, silently, a succession of giant men on guard will appear to pass slowly on either side of the cart. The ruins of ancient palaces—here a pillar, there the arch of a gate, elsewhere a fragment of a temple will be standing with the futile hope of offering their testimony to eternity.

Sitting as upright as you can in the circumstances, you will feel a shiver run down your body. Something will make you feel you have gone beyond the living world to enter a murky realm of memories from the past.

You won't know what time of night it is, but it will seem the night never ends here. Everything will be sunk in a deep silence without beginning or end, just like carcasses preserved in formaldehyde at the museum.

After two or three bends in the road, the bullock cart will finally stop. Reclaiming your limbs with great effort from the different places you have deposited them, you and your friends will disembark stiffly, one by one, like wooden marionettes. A foul stench will have been welcoming you for some time. You will realize it is the stink from rotting leaves in a pond. Just such a small lake will catch your eye by the light of the half moon. Next to it there will be a decrepit palace, standing like the ramparts of a fort with a crumbling roof, collapsed walls, and shutterless windows like empty eye sockets.

It is in a relatively habitable part of this ruin that all of you will have to make arrangements to stay. The driver of the cart will fetch a cracked lantern and set it in the room. With it, a pitcher of water. When you enter, you will realize that you are the first representatives of the human race to set foot in this room in a long, long time. Maybe someone has made a vain attempt to clear the cobwebs and the dust and the grime. A slightly musty smell will be evidence of the fact that the resident spirit of the room is unhappy. The slightest movement will cause the worn-out plaster to flake off the walls and ceiling, falling on you like the curses of an angry soul. Two or three bats will fight with you all night for possession of the room.

To discover Telenapota, one of your two friends must be partial to the bottle, and the other, a soulmate of Rip Van Winkle. The moment you enter the room, no sooner will a sheet be laid out on the floor than one of them will stretch himself out on it and proceed to snore, while the other will immerse himself in a glass of whisky.

The hours will go by. The glass chimney of the cracked lantern will get progressively blacker with soot and eventually go blind. Having been informed by a mysterious wireless message, each and every adult mosquito in the neighbourhood will arrive to welcome the newcomers and establish a blood relationship with them. If you are wise, you will surmise from their manner of perching on the wall and on your body that they are the most aristocratic among mosquitoes—the one and only mount for Lady Malaria, the anopheles. Your companions will by then be unconscious to the world, each for his own specific reason. Therefore, you will abandon your bed slowly to rise to your feet, and then, in a bid to get some relief from the humidity, you will try to climb up the ruined stairs to the roof by the light of a torch.

The danger of plummeting to the ground at any moment, in case a brick or a tile loosens itself beneath your feet, will thwart you for a moment, but some irresistible attraction will make it impossible not to ascend to the terrace.

Up on the roof, you will discover that the railing has crumbled to dust in most places, and the fifth column of the forest has conspired to plant its roots in the cracks to make considerable progress on the task of demolishing this edifice. And yet, everything will appear mesmerizing by the faint light of the waning moon. If you gaze at all this for a while, you will sense that, in a secret cell somewhere in this enchanted palace under the pall of the sleep of death, an imprisoned princess is sunk in the deepest and longest of slumbers with magic wands of gold and silver at her side. At that very moment, you may see a thin line of light through the window of what had originally appeared to be a ruin across the narrow street. An enigmatic, shadowy figure will appear between you and the light. You will wonder about the identity of this woman at the window at the dead of night, and why she is not asleep, but the answer will elude you. A little later you will think it was a mistake, for the figure will have disappeared, and the light will no longer be there. You will conclude that a dream had momentarily bubbled up to the surface from the depths of the sleep of this ruined palace, appearing fleetingly in the living world before exploding.

You will return downstairs gingerly. And you won't know when you will make space for yourself next to your two friends and fall asleep.

When you awake, you will be surprised to see that even in this land of the night morning does appear, and the call of birds can be heard everywhere.

Surely, you will not have forgotten the objective of your visit. Sometime later, having made complete arrangements for your act of worshipping the fish, you will settle down at one corner of the moss-covered, dilapidated flight of shallow stairs leading into the lake and lower your hook, complete with suitable divine offerings, into the green water.

The sun will climb higher in the sky. From the tip of a bamboo stalk leaning low over the water on the opposite bank, a kingfisher will repeatedly dive into the lake with an iridescent flash of colours, as though to mock you, and will return to its perch euphoric with its successful hunt to taunt you in an unintelligible tongue. To terrorize you, a long and plump snake will slither out of a crack in the flight of stairs to swim across the lake at a leisurely pace and climb up the bank on the other side. Beating their thin, glassy wings, a pair of dragonflies will compete to alight on the float of your fishing rod, while your mind wanders every now and then at the wistful cry of a dove.

Then, a sound in the water will break your spell. There will be waves in the still water, and your float will bob up and down gently on them. Turning your head, you will see a young woman pushing aside the hyacinth to fill her shiny brass pitcher with clear water. There is curiosity in her eyes, but no bashfulness or stiffness in her movements. She will look at you directly, observe the float on your fishing rod, and then look away before balancing her pitcher against her hip.

You will be unable to gauge her age. The serenity and compassion in her expression will suggest that her journey through life has been long and cruel, but her lean, tall, and undernourished frame will give the impression that her passage from adolescence to youth has been postponed.

As she leaves with her pitcher, she will suddenly turn back towards you to say—'What are you waiting for? Reel it in.'

Her voice will be so steady, sweet, and composed that it will not seem remotely abnormal that she is spontaneously talking to a stranger. Only, your sudden surprise will make you forget to reel in the line. When the submerged float rises to the surface, you will discover that the bait is no longer on the hook. You will have no choice but to throw her a rueful glance. She will turn away and leave with measured footsteps, but it will seem to you that in that instant before she turned away, her serene, compassionate face had glowed briefly with the hint of a smile.

Your solitude will not be disturbed any more. Unable to embarrass you, the kingfisher on the opposite bank will have abandoned its efforts and flown away. Probably full of contempt at your abilities, the fish will not be desirous of another round of competition. The recent incident will seem unreal to you. You will be unable to accept that there really can be a woman like her in this desolate place.

Eventually, you will have to pack up your equipment and leave. When you return you may discover that your prowess at fishing has somehow become known to your friends. Upset at their derision, when you ask who told them this story, your tippler friend may say—'Who do you think! Yamini, of course, who saw it for herself.'

You will have no choice but to ask in curiosity who Yamini is. Perhaps you will discover that the unreal woman with tragic eyes at the lake is a relation of sorts of your friend who loves his whisky. You will also learn that arrangements for lunch have been made at this woman's house.

Seen in daylight, the hideous decrepitude of the ruined building, where the fleeting appearance of a shadowy form had given you cause for wonderment last night, will pain you considerably. You would not have imagined that the retreat of the enchanted veil of night would make its bare, dilapidated form so very ugly.

You will be surprised when told that this is where Yamini and her family live. Arrangements for your meal have probably been made in one of the rooms in there. A frugal repast, perhaps Yamini herself will serve all of you. You have already observed that there is no superfluous reserve or awkwardness about her, but her tragic quietude will be even more conspicuous. The unarticulated anguish of this derelict, forgotten, and abandoned locality will be reflected on her face. Even though she has seen everything, her eyes are submerged in the depths of exhaustion. As though she too will disappear within these ruins one day.

Still, you will see her looking uneasy and anxious once or twice while serving the three of you. Someone will be calling faintly from a room upstairs. Yamini will hurry out. Every time she returns, the agony on her face will seem a little deeper—and, with it, a helpless, distracted look in her eyes.

Perhaps, you will take a short rest after your meal. Hesitating near the door, Yamini will finally say in desperation, 'Just a minute, Mani Da.'

Mani Da is the tippler friend of yours. The conversation that will ensue when he goes up to the door will not be in voices low enough to prevent you from hearing.

You will hear Yamini say in a stricken, imperilled tone, 'Ma simply refuses to listen. I can't tell you how restless she has become since she heard you're here.'

'Still the same thing?' Mani will ask in irritation. 'She thinks Niranjan is here?'

'Yes, she keeps saying, I'm sure he's here. Just that he's too embarrassed to see me. I know. You must be hiding it from me. I don't know what to do. She's become so impatient since she went blind that she refuses to understand anything I tell her. She flies into a rage and creates such a scene that sometimes I think she'll die.'

'This really has become a problem. If she could at least see she would know for herself that neither of them is Niranjan.'

Now all of you will be able to hear the faint but sharp, angry call from upstairs. A distressed Yamini will plead, 'Come with me, Mani Da, maybe you can explain things to her and calm her down.'

'Very well, you go along, I'll come in a while.' Re-entering the room, Mani will mutter to himself, 'Such an annoyance. She's blind and practically paralysed, but she's vowed not to die.'

Perhaps you will now ask, 'What's going on?' An irked Mani will reply, 'What do you suppose? When Yamini was still a child, her mother had arranged her marriage to a distant nephew of hers named Niranjan. Four years ago, the fellow had turned up to tell her that he would marry Yamini when he returned from his job abroad. Since then the old woman has been sitting here, in this godforsaken house, counting the days.'

You will not be able to stop yourself from asking, 'Has Niranjan not returned from his job abroad?'

'He would have had to go abroad first. He lied to her only because the old woman was so insistent. Why should he be interested in rescuing a pauper's daughter? He's long been married. But who's going to tell her? She won't believe it, and if she does, she'll die on the spot. Who wants to carry a burden of sin?'

'Does Yamini know about Niranjan?'

'Of course she does. But she can't tell her mother. Let me go pay for my sins.' Mani will proceed towards the staircase.

At that moment, you will also rise to your feet, not entirely of your own volition. Perhaps you will say, 'I'll come too.'

'You!' Mani will look at you in surprise.

'Yes, do you mind?'

'No, why should I?' A perplexed Mani will lead the way.

The room you will reach after climbing the narrow, dark, and broken-down staircase will appear to be situated in an underground tunnel rather than on an upper floor. Just the one window, and closed, at that. Coming in from broad daylight, everything will appear blurred at first. Then you will become aware of an emaciated, skeletal figure lying on a dilapidated cot, wrapped in a torn quilt. Yamini will be standing by the bed, turned to stone.

Your footsteps will stir the cadaverous figure into showing signs of animation. 'Is that Niranjan? You've finally remembered your unfortunate aunt. My heart's been in my mouth waiting for you all this time. I couldn't even die in peace. You won't run away again, will you?'

Mani will be about to say something, but you will interrupt him to say, 'No, I won't run away again.'

Even without raising your eyes you will sense Mani's bewilderment and the shock and astonishment on the face of the young woman standing like a statue. You will be staring at the sightless eyes, holding your breath. Two black flames will appear to emerge from the empty eye sockets to lick at your body enquiringly. You will feel the stilled moments falling like dewdrops on the ocean of time. Then you will hear: 'I know you couldn't have stayed away. That's why I have been guarding this haunted house and counting my days.' The old woman will begin gasping for breath after this long speech. Flashing a glance at Yamini, you will wonder whether something is melting slowly behind her hard mask. It will not be long before the foundations of her stern vow against destiny and existence, fired by hopelessness, begin to crumble.

The old woman will continue, 'You will be happy with Yamini. It's not because she's my daughter, but there isn't another girl like her. My sorrows and suffering and illness and old age have made me a mad woman, I make her suffer endlessly with my constant nagging—I know only too well I do, but she doesn't say a word. This is a land of the dead, you'll have to scour a dozen homes to find a single man, only corpses like me live here, gasping for life and clinging to the ruins, and yet there's nothing she leaves undone, she's man and woman rolled into one.'

Despite an ardent desire, you will not have the courage to lift your eyes for a single glance. For then you will no longer be able to conceal the tears in your eyes.

With a small sigh, the old woman will say, 'You will take Yamini, won't you? Unless you give me your word, I will have no peace even in death.'

All you will be able to say hoarsely is, 'I promise you. Nothing can shake my resolve.'

Then the bullock cart will draw up at the door again that afternoon. The three of you will get in, one by one. Yamini will come up to you as you are about to leave, raise her wistful eyes to your face and say, 'You forgot your fishing rod.'

Smiling, you will say, 'Let it remain here. I may not have been successful this time, but the fish of Telenapota cannot elude me forever.'

Yamini will not look away. Not from her lips, the grateful smile will come from her eyes, floating like white autumnal clouds across the horizon of your heart, gracing it with their beauty.

The cart will begin to roll. A hundred or a hundred and fifty years ago, the first malaria epidemic here had swept Telenapota away like an irresistible flood to this forgotten extremity of life, abandoning it there— perhaps this will be the subject of your friends' discussion. All this will not penetrate your hearing. The constricted space in the cart will no longer trouble you, the monotonous whining of its wheels will not sound harsh to your ears any more. Only a single phrase will resonate in time with your heartbeat—'I shall return, I shall return.'

When you reach the crowded, brightly-lit avenues of the metropolis, the memory of Telenapota will still be burning bright in your heart. The days will pass, punctuated by minor obstacles. You will not be aware of whether a fog is gathering in your head or not. Then, the day that you will have overcome all hindrances to prepare to return to Telenapota, you will have to burrow under a quilt because of a sudden headache, shivers and chills. The thermometer will signal one hundred and five degrees, the doctor will ask, 'Where did you get malaria?' You will sink into a feverish haze.

Much later, when you drag your weakened body into the sunlight on tottering steps, you will find a good deal of your mind and body wiped clean, unknown to yourself. Like a star that has set, the memory of Telenapota will appear to you as a blurred dream. It will seem as though there isn't really a place named Telenapota anywhere in the world. With her stern, serious expression and her distant, pensive eyes, the young woman, just like the derelict building, will feel like nothing but a misty figment of your imagination, conjured up in an idle moment of vulnerability.

Having been discovered for a fleeting moment, Telenapota will once again become submerged in the depths of eternal night.

THE SOLUTION

GOPINATH MOHANTY

*Translated from the Odia by Leelawati Mohapatra,
Paul St-Pierre, and K. K. Mohapatra*

Dadhibaman stared off into the darkening horizon, eyes dilated, face crushed by humiliation as he recalled the turbulent day at the office. He felt angry, hot, tired, and worried. Night was falling and he had just got home. A dog's day, toiling from ten to five, practically the whole time, unrelenting pressure at work, file upon file, no end in sight. And on top of all that, calls for explanations, reprimands, insults.

All for a measly salary of seventy-five rupees a month—not even the cost of three large sacks of rice in these hard times. Out of that, the house rent, the doctor's fees.... Laundry alone came to seven rupees, and firewood to fifteen, and so much else too. It was tough to make ends meet. Delicious food was only a dream; patched rags worn at home; skimp and save, skimp and save. How he and his family managed to hang on was a mystery. Ten years in the job, yet nothing more to show for it. His debts had only grown larger and the sheer pressure of work was nearly splitting his skull. The insults, the reprimands, the threats were only the final straw.

There—that was his life. Looking at the sahada tree at the back of the house he mulled things over. What more was there than work and reprimands? The future seemed as bleak as the past. They were his life; nothing more.

'Mein...mein...mein....' A tug at the hem of the rag wrapped around his waist and Dadhibaman came out of his reverie. His pet goat was demanding attention, producing a sound closely resembling 'I' in the national language: 'Mein...mein...mein....'

Dadhibaman bent over and patted the animal on the back. The soothing contact reduced his bitterness by half. His voice dripped with affection as he murmured his name: 'Betu! Betu!'

Betu twitched his tail, raised himself up on his forelegs, shoved his nose into his master's face, and expressed himself in his native tongue. Then he moved away and scampered around a bit, the bells around his neck tinkling. He circled Dadhibaman, rubbed against him and bleated: 'Mein...mein...mein....'

Just one year old, but how he had grown! Dadhibaman hadn't been able to put off his young son when he had asked for a kid goat as a pet. In the twelve months since then, Betu had grown a goatee, while Dadhibaman wondered whether or not to have him castrated.

Dadhibaman touched the goat. He ought to get a she-goat so they could raise some kids. The price of goat meat had soared; already three rupees a seer! Meat—curried, roasted, fried! The intimate relationship between the eater and the eaten always came to Dadhibaman as a revelation, increasing his desire to stroke the goat.

Dadhibaman continued to pet him.

As Dadhibaman's three young children came bounding out of the house, Betu began to prance around again, his bells tinkling. 'Betu!' The children chanted. 'Betu!'

Dadhibaman stood watching his life's main achievements. He had stuck to his damned job for the sake of his children. Why else would he have done it? Even a cobbler made five rupees a day, and a rickshaw puller, three—the coolie carrying sand and bricks made a rupee and a half. If he had had a paan shop he could have built a house for himself! Feyda Miyan, who had just a bicycle repair shop, had managed to buy four houses in just twelve years, with still enough money to lend out at a high interest rate. Couldn't Dadhibaman have done the same?

He was afraid on account of his children, he realized as he watched them. What if a business took two years to take off? How would he manage during that time? How would he earn at least a steady seventy-five a month? And if he didn't, what then?

No friend in the future, and none in the past! If he were about to starve to death, no one would come to his rescue. This is what made him hesitant. Shutting the unfulfilled dreams out of his mind, he sighed—business wasn't for him, it was not his destiny! Though those who succeeded in business weren't necessarily better than him. Many a time he had been about to give up his job, only to back out at the last moment—what would his children live on the first few years?

If not for this fear he'd gladly have left his bloody job—today, this very moment. The insults, reprimands, and jibes were becoming intolerable. Just today the big boss had clucked and tut-tutted for an hour, as if Dadhibaman had set fire to his house or something. And as if that weren't enough, the boss had then demanded a written explanation why Dadhibaman hadn't attended to such-and-such files.

Dadhibaman fished the boss's letter out of his pocket. The overpowering urge to read it yet again was like trying to find out if a wound had healed by picking its scab. He had almost learned the words by heart. What thundering language—demeaning, insulting, soul-killing! How would he reply? What reply would work? The pressure of work? No one would buy that. That he didn't get two square meals a day? That he didn't get enough sleep on account of his children constantly falling ill? No one would buy these either. If Lord Brahma had to work as hard as Dadhibaman, even he would make mistakes! Would anyone accept such an explanation? No one was willing to recognize the truth, but the same people would be content with clever lies! But what clever lies could Dadhibaman cook up? He was sadly lacking in imagination.

Dadhibaman smoothed the boss's letter out on the ground and went through it once again. Tears welled up in his eyes. What a life, what a wretched life!

'Mein...mein...mein....'

Dadhibaman lowered his head and gently pressed his eyelids to Betu's lips. The goat turned away, shook his ears, rubbed his head against his master's knees, and looked up at him in bewilderment.

A goat's life was fine, Dadhibaman reflected. Everyone's life was fine. Everyone's except his.

All of a sudden Betu snatched the letter from Dadhibaman's hand, and the folds of skin over his jaws started moving up and down furiously. Before Dadhibaman could stop him, the piece of paper was already inside his tummy.

'What—you gobbled it up, Betu? Now what explanation will I give?'

'Mein...mein...mein...' bleated Betu, shaking his beard. 'Don't worry,' he seemed to be reassuring him. 'I'm here for you.'

All this took some time to sink in, but when it did Dadhibaman was dumbstruck. This was the last straw. Instead of providing an explanation he would have to ask the head clerk for another copy of the boss's letter—an unpleasant prospect, at the very least. He thought he knew the letter verbatim, but now that it was gone, so was his memory of it.

The words seemed to have faded into oblivion, even as he wondered what is remembered and what is quickly forgotten.

Damn it, what's gone is gone! Suddenly resolute, Dadhibaman stood up. Betu's round eyes seemed to have become bloodshot. Dadhibaman suddenly remembered the enormity of the problem, and smoke seemed to come out of his eyes. When people had made up their minds not to be convinced by a genuine explanation, why provide any? No, he wouldn't bother; let them do as they pleased. Dadhibaman's self-control had crumbled. He was on fire.

He strode inside, Betu in tow. Heaped on the table were some office files. Picking up Betu he brought him near the table. Betu seemed to show great interest. All worked up, Dadhibaman pushed a file towards Betu's mouth. The goat wagged its short tail and gratefully fell on the task of disposing of the file at hand. The taste of the local newspapers and the papers the children did their homework on was familiar, but office work clearly had a distinct flavour! He placed his forelegs on the edge of the table and propped himself up. 'These files are so delicious,' he bleated from time to time, 'but there's so little to sate my hunger.'

Dadhibaman gently nudged another fat file towards Betu.

The next day, at around ten o'clock, the office watchman saw Dadhibaman coming from his house, just a stone's throw from the office, followed by a goat. There was a red ribbon with bells tied around the animal's neck. The bells were tinkling.

'Shoo! Scram! Beat it!' the watchman yelled at the goat. 'Look at the damned goat, it's trying to get in!'

'Stop, don't do that,' Dadhibaman said. 'He's a pet; he won't do any harm: he's just like a person.' Dadhibaman turned to the goat. 'Come on, Betu. Follow me.' Betu did, most obediently.

'So well-trained!' commented the watchman.

'Yes, just like a human; understands everything. Goats are like that. Haven't you seen how well they perform in circuses?'

In the office, Betu was introduced around.

'Well, well, a damn healthy specimen,' commented Ram. 'About ten seers of quality meat, don't you think?'

'But what's the use?' remarked Gopal. 'The meat would have a god-awful stink. Pity, Betu wasn't castrated when he was a kid.'

'Mein?' bleated Betu, looking askance.

'There'd be no foul smell to the meat, I tell you,' said Feyda Miyan, 'if, as I do, you knew the secret of how to slit its throat!'

A lively discussion ensued about various meat dishes and their preparation. Betu took a leisurely stroll around the office and came back to his master. Butting his feet with his head, he seemed to ask, 'Mein?'

Dadhibaman turned over the wastepaper basket for Betu. The goat settled down at his feet and set about disposing of the scraps of paper.

Betu went about his job at a lively pace. Hour after hour passed. Done with all the wastepaper baskets, Betu turned his attention to the files sitting on the shelves. It didn't take him long to go through one. Once he'd caught hold of it, he was finished in minutes. Sometimes he pulled down eight or ten at a time. After a little rest, he'd reach for someone else's. It was a feast day.

Finally, he reached the head clerk's table, loaded with piles of papers and files all marked 'urgent'. The head clerk had gone to see the big boss, and Betu set to lightening the poor fellow's load. After a bit of good work he ambled off, but not before depositing by the table a few precious droppings—a particularly good fertilizer.

'Betu,' Dadhibaman called out.

The goat came running back, his bells ringing.

'Come, lie down here.'

Betu wedged himself between Dadhibaman's legs.

The head clerk returned. 'You all have so many pending files that the boss is boiling. Now, tell me frankly—and I want your word on this—are you going to dispose of the files before the end of the day? What about you, Dadhibaman?'

'All done, sir.'

'Really? That's very good.'

'Mein?' Betu bleated, getting up. 'Mein?'

'Hey, look, look, a bloody goat has strayed inside,' the head clerk shouted. 'Watchman!'

'The goat's my pet, sir,' Dadhibaman said. 'He's followed me to the office. He's no nuisance, sir; just let him be. The smell of a goat fights tuberculosis, you must know that, sir. At least that's what doctors say. And considering the dark, dingy halls in which we work....'

'Oh yes,' answered the head clerk, seeming to think out loud, his eyes riveted on the goat. 'Could easily make eight or ten seers of lovely meat. But why on earth didn't you get it castrated, Dadhibaman?'

'Mein!' Betu shook his beard, nimbly stepping up to the head clerk's table, with still a large stack of 'urgent' files on it. Betu's work was far from finished: there were plenty of disposals pending.

A LETTER

K. M. MUNSHI

Translated from the Gujarati by Rita Kothari

My lord, my master! I wish to lay my head in your lap once again, while I am on my deathbed. I had considered not writing this letter. Thousands of my heart-rending entreaties amounted to nothing, why would this one have any effect now? I have no doubt that nothing is going to change. But voicing my thoughts, my experiences, will liberate me from pain. Also, if your future wife turns out to be lucky because you finally grow wiser, she will be spared the suffering I went through, and not wither away before blossoming.

In my lifetime of sixteen years, there's so much I have gone through. God alone knows who might be responsible for my miseries, but I do need to say this at least once—abandoning shame, or the maryada of the older generation—if at all there was one person responsible for my suffering, and one person who could have alleviated it—then that person was you, my master, my lord. The world handed you an inexperienced, delicate little girl, but you didn't even think about her. This is what happened to me. I am about to lose my life, my very breath is ebbing away from me.

Do you remember the time I came into your house as your wife? Despite being the adored child of loving parents, it was you I sought and pined for. Even when I went to school before we were married, just looking at you made me feel things I hadn't felt before, and I couldn't wait to meet you. I couldn't wait to serve you and feel fulfilled. Later, you found many faults with me; you even laid the cruel charge of my being indifferent to you. How could that even be possible? In a Hindu universe, the lordship of the husband is considered greater than that of even God.

Little girls start worshipping their husbands even before they meet them. The difference, however, is this: that this husband, lord of the lords, has even more pretensions than God and much less affection for his devotees.

When I came into your home, how small I was! A month before that, I was going to school and prancing about like a deer in a forest. A mother-in-law's rage and slavery to the husband were unknown concepts to me. I did not have the foggiest notion that in six months' time I was going to feel muffled and lacerated. No matter what I said or did, it became an unnecessary opportunity to accuse my parents. Why? If I did not know certain things, it was Sasuji's duty to teach me. I was hardly a demoness who refused to learn. If a man is expected to have regard for his parents, should a girl not have any towards those who gave birth to her, raised and nurtured her? If someone were to say to you, 'Your mother and your father and your kind', you would slap that person. But an innocent young girl listens to all the aspersions cast on her parents and merely suffers in silence.

After a few months, when I finally braced myself to endure these comments, a new thing began. Dear one, what kind of strength did you expect from the body of a thirteen-year-old? How did you expect a naïve child to know what the customs of your house were? Just as your sister was dear to your mother, so was I to mine. Your sister, however, was simply not bothered about my fragility. Are you saying that a twenty-year-old sister would be damaged by work while I, a thirteen-year-old, would not?

Does Hindu culture not teach the mother-in-law and husband to have any sense of fairness? I, too, was a body, not a log of wood. And after a day's arduous labour, what care did I receive from my husband? None, right?

I have endured all my life, but I shall speak today. Did you not know that I was also a young, foolish, and fragile child? That I slogged like a beast of burden every day? That I could neither sleep nor sit? You played cricket and went to office. Do you think people like us sleep at home? We worked every minute, endured abuse, filled our stomachs with leftovers, spent our lives longing for more. At the end of a hard day, when I came to you expecting a word of affection, you couldn't manage any. I was immediately made responsible for fetching every small thing you needed. A moment's delay and you began yelling. Your strong, manly feet ached from sitting in one place in your office, and you needed my weak hands to press them. If you perspired at night, I had to fan you with my small, trembling hands. Did you not think at that time, even for a moment, how was this young girl to withstand such burden? But why would you? I was a slave, wasn't I?

A daughter-in-law is like a mere cat in the house. But a cat gets to sleep and eat twice a day. What do you men know of what we go through? There were so many days when after back-breaking work I could barely sit; I also had to be deprived of sleep. Yet, I served you even during such times. Silently, I stole a wink here and there, only to be reprimanded, threatened, and even slapped. But shedding tears was also a crime.

Forbidden from going to my natal home, victimized by a perpetually enraged mother-in-law, you lording over me, cruel and heartless. You made a fifteen-year-old go through all this? I did what thousands of my kind do.

I inadvertently blurted out something to my mother one day. She sent word to your mother, who made a mountain out of a molehill and instigated you. That night, you beat me up. Do you remember? I sobbed into the pillow and asked for death. Let those women of earlier days—who filled pots with water from the river and carried them on their heads, or those dumb, thick-headed women who helplessly went through life—suffer if they will. But how could a delicate, young, educated girl have to go through this?

Had you shown affection, some concern for the courtesan who entertained you, the slave that fed you—some sense of fairness—then I would have made you the sovereign of my soul, not merely my husband, the owner of my body. I would have sprinkled your path with flowers and made you experience heaven. But all that remained unspoken and undone. I did not find justice, affection, nor happiness with you. I withered and wilted inside—so did my body. Finally, your words and actions managed to murder me.

At least for a day you could have talked to me about something other than your concerns. For one moment, couldn't you have allowed me to taste genuine love? At least after your meal you could have asked me, 'Is there food left for you, or mere crumbs?' At least for a day you could have exposed me to some aesthetic pleasure or a higher plane of being. But what was I expecting? Why would you care beyond gorging on food and fattening yourself? Those ideal women, the satis, prayed to have the same husband in their next birth. I could pray, too, but have you proven yourself worthy of that prayer? Those pious women had husbands who were worthy of their sacrifice. I am done with you in this birth. May God never bring us together.

Do tell Sasuji not to bring an educated daughter-in-law into her home again.

The Unfortunate Woman.

REPLY-PAID CARD

DINANATH NADIM

Translated from the Kashmiri by Neerja Mattoo

1

'Zoon Ded! Zoon Ded! Aren't you up yet?' Announcing his arrival loudly, Jamal Mir walked in and sat down on the doorstep. He pulled out a snuff-box from a pocket somewhere in the folds of his tattered pheran and, taking a large pinch from it, rubbed it all over his teeth and gums. There was a little stick in his hand and with it he began to draw shapes in the dust. After about fifteen minutes had passed, there was a creaking sound to his left. He was startled and looked towards the noise. It was the door to the barn, which had begun to open, revealing the figure of Zoon Ded. Seeing her standing there, he felt as if he had sighted the full moon and his lips parted in a broad grin. He then gave a full-throated laugh.

'Oh, you slime, it's you, is it? I wondered who it could be so early in the morning! How loudly you shouted!' Zoon Ded said with a smile.

Zoon Ded, grandmother to everyone in the village and mother to the whole world, her hair white as snow, with deep eyes, full as brimming cups of wine, a high, commanding nose, long arms, dressed in a spotless white under-pheran, standing at the door like a queen from the wild forests.

'Why, Ded, the sun has risen so high and you still seem reluctant to give up your sleep?' said Jamal Mir through a mouthful of snuff-stained saliva.

'When will you learn some manners? I don't know what to say to you,' said Zoon Ded. 'Didn't you see me coming out of the barn? How could I be sleeping?'

Jamal Mir looked a bit sheepish, but still went on, 'No, Ded, I thought maybe because of Gula sahib, perhaps....'

This brought a thoughtful look to Zoon Ded's brow. Jamal Mir ate the rest of his words. For a while, they both kept their eyes on the ground. Then Zoon Ded said with a sigh, 'You are right in a way, but I have actually been spending most of my time attending to Badri since dawn. She neither touches grass nor her feed.'

Meanwhile, some others had turned up and as usual a regular circle formed around Zoon Ded and everyone began chattering away.

Who was Zoon Ded? Where had she come from? How old was she? No one in the village knew the answer to any of these questions. Even the oldest among them did not remember her looking any different from what she looked like today. But Zoon Ded was everything to them—she ruled the village, she was judge, maulvi, police officer, nambardar, chowkidar, patwari. In fact, all authority rested with her. She was counsellor to the old and a friend to the young, a listener to mothers-in-law, and a repository of daughters-in-law's secrets. When the panchayat met, it was Zoon Ded who delivered the verdict. If somebody had to be sent for forced labour, it was Zoon Ded who decided whether to send him or not. When marriages had to be fixed, Zoon Ded was the one to act as a go-between. When someone fell ill, Zoon Ded provided medical assistance. The whole area knew that what Zoon Ded declared must prevail, her word was law and could not be challenged. Not even the viceroy could change her writ. That is why Zoon Ded's home was open to all villagers—they treated it as their own grandmother's place. Whenever they were in any trouble, even if it was merely a thorn that had pricked them, they would rush to her for comfort.

2

Bonapore is known as Kaav Maalyun or Kawpore, the home of crows, among the people here. The reason is that all the crows in the area spend their nights here among the high branches of the chinars, where many of them have built their nests. Today, too, the crows had started making a huge racket at sunset, so much so that even the rumble of the mountain stream had been drowned in it. Suddenly, there was the sound of a gunshot and all the crows flew away from their perches in the chinar, cawing loudly in panic. Who could have fired the shot? There, look, see that soldier advancing—it must be his doing, the crows thought, perched on the branches of fruit trees, turning their necks this way and that. A jawan, well built, with a broad chest, well-rounded shoulders, handsome face, imposing stride, looking like an officer from a foreign army. How he swaggers along without a care in the world!

As soon as he reached the village, all the children gathered around him, some hugging his legs, some putting their hands in his pockets, some scratching his gun with their nails and all of them setting up a shout of welcome, 'Gula sahib! It is Gula sahib. Zoon Dedi, it is Gula sahib. He has come home to you…it is our own Captain Gula sahib!' Singing this refrain, the procession of children reached Zoon Ded's doorstep. Throwing her door open with a bang, Zoon Ded came out. Her eyes were smiling, though she tried to keep a serious expression on her face. 'Oh yes, "Gula Chaab"' indeed! A captain, did you say? A cockatoo sahib, I say…if they make fools like him a captain, I don't know what they will do next!' But even as she said this the mother and son were hugging each other.

How was Gula sahib related to Zoon Ded? Nobody knew for certain—there are always as many stories as there are mouths to tell them. Some said he was her sister-in-law's daughter's son, some declared that he was her own grandson, while some others were sure he had been found by her on the stairs to the shrine of Makhdoom Sahib. But why are we concerned about their real relationship? The fact was obvious to everyone that Gula sahib was her life, Zoon Ded lived for him. Since he had joined the army, his name was always on her lips, she would talk of nothing else. His name figured in all her conversations.

'Did you hear, Vaasa? I received a letter from Gula today. He says that he killed seventeen tribal raiders in one single day!'

'Do you know, Sonamali? Gula sahib, may God bless him, has sent me a reply-paid postcard! It is beautiful, as though not words, but pearls have been studded on this paper.'

'Jamal Mir, our seven generations have been blessed, such glory has been brought by a son like Gula! Today he is defending the honour of the whole of Kashmir.'

3

The day Gula sahib left for the frontline, the whole village was on its feet. At the first light of day, their kitchen hearths had been lit and by the time the sun rose they were all—men and women, the elderly, and the young—at Zoon Ded's door. Some carried sanctified food from holy places, some brought talismans with powerful spells in them. Ordinary peasant women came with gifts of little packets of pickles or chutney tied to the ends of their veils. Some even brought bundles of dried vegetables like turnips and haak leaves with them. As soon as Zoon Ded opened her door, they all rushed in, jostling for space, each visitor eager to be the first to give their gift.

'Here, Zoon Ded, take this bunch of dried turnips. These grew from pure farm seeds,' said Rahti, the milkmaid, shyly holding out her gift. 'I had saved it for Gula sahib all these days.' 'Take this bunch of dried greens too, they are from the famous kohlrabi produce of Khashipore,' said Ramzu Begari. 'Tell Gula sahib that finding such stuff is not possible in the city!'

'Would you please take this little portion of pickle, too, Ded? Tell him it is from genuine Kashmiri kohlrabi of Bonapore.'

'Zoon Ded! Please call Gula sahib. Why doesn't he come out? Is he still in his nightcap?' said Vaasa Bhat, hesitantly.

'Didn't I say that you had become senile? Would he be still sleeping at this hour? He has gone to the stream to wash himself. He must be on his way here now. Why, are you getting late for something?' said Zoon Ded jokingly.

'How you dote on him! It is just that I got this powerful talisman for him with potent mantras from Kanth Guruji and I wanted him to wear it in my presence,' responded Vaasa Bhat.

As soon as Gula sahib walked in after his ablutions at the stream, they all crowded around him, some hugging him, some kissing his forehead. When he came out dressed in his uniform and picked up his gun, their hearts swelled with pride. The women showered blessings on him, 'God be with you, Gula! May you reach even greater heights, may good fortune follow your steps!' The whole village walked along with him up for many miles into his journey. They only retraced their steps when they lost sight of him behind the trees.

4

The sky had been hazy since the day dawned. Before the sun could show itself, clouds had enveloped the whole sky. The cloud cover was so thick that it reached down from the high crags to the foothills. Blinding forks of lightning accompanied by loud, terrifying thunder came from the east. It looked like there was about to be a huge downpour. Generally, on a day like this, the villagers preferred to stay indoors. But today they were all gathered in groups at the bank of the stream, talking in whispers. No one seemed to be their normal self. A little distance from the groups of men, the cluster of women seemed to be silently writhing in agony. Bareheaded, half-dressed, and breathless, Vaasa Bhat ran up to them, clenching his fists as though to control his emotions, and burst into a loud wail. 'What is this I hear, Karim Joo? Oh God, what calamity is this? A disaster... disaster....' he lost his voice.

'Quiet! Be silent,' Karim Kral put his hand on his lips, 'this won't do. Take heart. Think of Zoon Ded. For her sake we have to be brave. We have to think of how we should inform her.'

'But how did it happen? Who brought the news? Who could have wished for it! Oh no....' Vaasa Bhat said through sobs.

'Who could wish it? Only our wretched luck! Last night Jabbar postman came and handed this card from Gula sahib to me—it was blank, just as it was when Zoon Ded had sent it from here. He must have...on the battlefront....' Karim Kral fell silent.

5

Broken in spirit and body, one after another they all reached Zoon Ded's house. Today, too, as usual, she was in the barn giving her cow her feed and talking to her. 'You have lost your mind, you have! Do you expect him to stay at your bedside all the time? Since he went to the front to fight, you seem to have been struck by paralysis! This won't do at all, don't you realize?' Then she heard a suppressed cough. 'Is it you, Vaasa? How come so early in the morning?' she said as she came out of the barn.

'You know this Badri has been ruined by Gula.... But, no, something has happened...is all well?' Seeing the crowd gathered before her, she was taken aback and asked, 'Have you all fought over something? Tell me, why don't you speak to me?' They all stood there, mute, choked into silence, unable even to give vent to a sigh. 'Go on, say something, why don't you? Has a mouse stolen your tongue?' she asked, but the colour seemed to be draining from her face. 'What has happened? Has something happened to me?'

At last, his face averted, Vaasa spoke in a low, hesitant voice, 'Zoon Dedi, we would die for you....' He couldn't go on, his voice broke and he wept loudly. Everyone sobbed, tears streaming down their cheeks, overcome by uncontrollable grief. Zoon Ded stood still, uncomprehending and began to speak as though to herself, 'Is my Gula all right? Of course, he is all right. Doesn't He know, with how many sacrifices, in exchange for how many...?'

Vaasa Bhat took courage and handed her the reply-paid postcard to, 'It came yesterday, this postcard. It is a reply-paid one, but it is blank. I don't know....'

Zoon Ded seemed paralysed, but she stood there erect like a rock. The postcard, having been touched and handled by so many of them, was crumpled. She spread it out carefully and began to scrutinize it, back and front. Silence once again fell on the scene, a deathly silence. Not a sound was heard except for the murmur of the stream, which sounded like somebody was mourning a dear one at his graveside on Eid.

Within a few minutes, it seemed that Zoon Ded's face was covered in as fine a dust as rises when one winnows rice. All the wrinkles on it suddenly became visible. Tears appeared in her eyes, but were drawn back before they could fall.

'Hahahaha!' Zoon Ded laughed. They were all dumbfounded.

'Didn't I tell you Vaasa that you have become senile? If you had any brains, wouldn't you have been a tehsildar by now?' Zoon addressed them all. 'See, it is all written here clearly. Have you all lost your sight, too?' She spread out the card. The creases on it did look like pencilled writing from a distance. 'See, what my Gula has written to me. He asks me to go and join the women's militia,' Zoon Ded declared with great authority.

∞

The day Zoon Ded left, a wooden gun in hand, dressed in her white under-pheran tied with a sash, a pall of gloom fell over the whole village. No child made a sound, nor did a single crow caw in the trees of Kawpore that day.

VISION

M. T. VASUDEVAN NAIR

Translated from the Malayalam by A. J. Thomas

From time to time Sudha would go home from Madras to her village to visit her mother. But she shouldn't have assumed that news of her marital woes wouldn't have reached the village. She had eaten her breakfast, and was relaxing on the veranda of the house, when Amma came over and said abruptly:

'Is what we have been hearing true, Sudha kutty?'

'What have you heard?'

'That you and Prabhakaran have separated.'

Amma was blinking hard, a nervous tic that came over her whenever she was trying to talk about difficult matters. Sudha looked at her mother severely. She decided to go on the offensive rather than try to explain herself.

'How did you hear all this? Over the radio?'

Amma said: 'Sreedevi from Narayanankutty's house had come over the day before yesterday. Her Devu's husband also lives in Madras.'

Sudha's older sister was also responsible for spreading the news. 'Visalam wrote. Her letter got here yesterday.' She had no doubt her other sister Chandri too would hear about this from her older sister and write to Amma as well.

Wanting some respite from the interrogation, Sudha walked into the yard. Although it was still quite early in the day, it was already very hot. She went for a walk in the shade of the compound wall. She could hear the sound of her rubber slippers echoing off the yard as she walked.

Amma lived alone in this old house. She kept visiting not only to see her mother but also for the calm these visits brought her. No telephones ringing. No parties to dress up for. No need to wear a fixed smile when she hosted parties. No need to listen to the creepy jokes of colleagues. Her visits would have been more frequent but she didn't always get permission to go on leave. And even when they were approved, they were rarely for more than three or four days. After a brief walk, as Sudha returned to the veranda, Amma said: 'People are saying all sorts of things. What actually happened?'

She did not reply.

'From what I heard....'

Amma stopped midway.

'That's right, Amma. It was better for both of us to part ways....'

Amma looked away into the yard.

When the girl who helped in the kitchen came out to ask about something, Amma rose and went inside.

Sudha had taken fifteen days' leave from the bank to make this trip home. She needed to escape the gossip and tension at work. Her colleagues had begun alluding to her troubled marriage even though she had only really opened up to the cashier, Nirmala Sreenivasan. It was Nirmala who had arranged a room for her in the YWCA.

∽

Amma liked to live alone. She did not encourage relatives and others to visit. She had no complaints if her children did not visit. Every month, she would write an inland letter card to all three of her offspring, whether she received replies or not. She always had a girl from the neighbourhood to help out in the kitchen. On Sudha's last visit, Amma had told her about the impending wedding of the girl who had been working in the house. She was planning to give her a gold chain worth a sovereign.

'The three of you must help out as much as you can. Send a money order in the name of Kuttiraman. It's all right even if you send it in my name.'

Her older sister, Visalam, and Chandri, the younger one, were to give three hundred rupees each. Sudha was to give four hundred, because she and her husband were working, and they did not have children.

When the girl who worked for her got married, her younger sister replaced her.

Not all her children were comfortable with Amma living alone. Visalam who lived in a huge house in Thiruvananthapuram with a number of servants was the most vocal about her concern. At one family gathering, she had said: 'There isn't even a doctor nearby if she were to fall ill suddenly.'

'I won't fall ill,' was Amma's response.

A clump of banana trees grew near the compound wall, which had crumbled here and there. Through one of these gaps, a black hen and her brood entered the courtyard, hesitantly. They cautiously began foraging for food.

'It's a junglefowl and her chicks. They come around at the same time every day,' she heard Amma say.

Sudha looked at them amusedly. The mother hen kept looking around warily, clearly nervous at being so close to human habitation. Trying not to startle her, Sudha cautiously moved a little closer to get a better look at the junglefowl. But her actions spooked the hen and she scurried away with her brood.

Amma did not bring up her marriage at lunch. That evening, Sreedharan ettan arrived. The older brother of her younger sister's husband. He was a high school headmaster and a local leader.

Mentally bracing herself for questions about her marriage, outwardly Sudha remained calm. She asked after his wife and children. She spoke about the weather, how hot it was.

'How many days' leave do you have, Sudha kutty?'

'A week.'

Amma butted in, 'There isn't a drop of milk to make tea for you, Sreedharan.'

'No need.'

Sreedharan then began chatting generally about things in Madras, the blazing sun of Madras, Jayalalithaa's assets, Karunanidhi's rule, etc. Sudha sat listening. There was nothing to add. She had heard that at the time when marriage proposals were coming her way, his horoscope was also under consideration by the family. Sreedharan left after a while.

In the evening, a host of dragonflies hovered in the wind. She had heard it said in her childhood that if dragonflies flew low, it indicated the onset of rains. She wished it would rain at least once. The scorching heat of the month of Meenam here was no less than the Vaikasi sun of Madras. There were no fans inside the house, and none of them had been able to agree on who would pay to have fans installed.

'You can sleep in the room in the southern wing. You'll get some breeze there,' Amma said, as she ladled out supper.

'I'm fine anywhere.'

In Amma's room, there was an old, rusty table fan which Father had bought a long time ago. Sudha hadn't brought along anything to read, nor had she bought anything on the way. On the round table in Amma's room, Father's old books remained as they were years ago. Amma used to read at night. But there were no new books. She looked at the book that Amma had placed above *A Concise History of the World*. It was *Himagiriviharam*, a book by a guru.

Amma had made up a bed for her in a room on the south side of the house. Sudha changed into a nightie. She looked at her watch. Eight forty-five. This was when Prabhakaran would return home after playing rummy and finishing two beers.

Amma came in.

'You can bring that table fan and put it here. Though it makes a sound, it still works.'

'No need.'

Wishing that Amma would go away, she made as if to go to sleep.

'And yet....'

Amma wanted to say something.

'Go on, Amma!'

'To part ways after living together for five years....'

She didn't say anything.

'What will people think?'

She turned away. Now she could avoid seeing Amma's face.

She changed the subject.

'What does one do to make a phone call here, should the necessity arise?'

'There is a booth now in the room next to the medical store. You can make a call to any place now.'

Sudha couldn't think of anything else to say.

'What have you decided?' Amma asked.

'I am thinking about it.'

'Should I come to Madras? Have a talk with Prabhakaran?'

'No. No.' She said quickly.

Amma looked at her with pity. Sudha said, trying not to lose her temper, 'There is no need for any mediation in this matter, Amma.'

Without a word, Amma left the room. Sudha knew that Amma wouldn't raise this issue any more. Amma's nature was to suffer silently. Father had died after one and a half years of being bedridden, having suffered a paralytic stroke. Amma never complained in all that time. She refused to say anything even when people were whispering about his kept woman who had swindled them of all his savings.

In the morning, Amma said, 'Valyamma of Cholayil said she wants to meet you. Janu told Valyamma that you were expected. She met her when she went to buy milk from her neighbour.'

'I will go and meet her.'

'You said you would go during your last visit, too, but you didn't.'

'Right.'

'She is going on eighty-four. We don't know how long she'll live. Her eyesight is almost gone. But, she doesn't fuss about anything.'

Valyamma of Cholayil was the older sister of their grandmother. They had called her 'Valyamma' hearing Amma call her that. Valyamma had lived in the house as her younger sister's guest long ago. In the mornings, she would often braid and tie up Visaledatthi's hair. In the evening, she would gather the girls together to recite the evening prayer.

Grandma would sleep on the floor and leave the cot for her big sister, Valyamma. She was fond of telling stories at bedtime. Night after night, Sudha kutty was her only avid listener. Visalam would avoid getting caught in that situation and Chandri would be dozing off. Grandma listened, half-nodding, she recollected. The story of Unniyamma who shielded Palat Koman behind her thick, long hair, and the legend of Kannaki and Kovalan were imprinted on her mind. When they had visited Madurai for the first time, they recalled how Valyamma told the story of Kannaki. She would narrate it as if she had been an eyewitness to Kannaki plucking out her breast and burning the city with it.

Sudha had met Valyamma last when she had gone to get her blessings before her wedding. That was more than five years ago. Even when their grandma was alive, they were fonder of Valyamma for some reason. In the last five years, she had visited Amma seven times. Yes, seven times. Prabhakaran was with her on two of these visits. Valyamma had asked after her on all those occasions. Her house was not even three furlongs away, yet she hadn't gone to see her even once, something or the other had always cropped up. The last time around she had planned to get her something. But on the day fixed for shopping, she and Prabhakaran had quarrelled. She had ended up spending the day lying down quietly in the hotel room until it was time to catch the train.

⁂

The junglefowl family came out to the front yard again the next day. They did not seem as afraid this time. Sudha slowly walked up to the hen and her brood; their black feathers were shining in the sun.

Just then she heard someone calling out: 'Guests have arrived.' The hen and her chicks scurried away in alarm.

She turned to see Sreedevi Amma and her younger sister standing in the courtyard.

Amma invited them to sit down as was customary and asked Janu to make tea. Then, after giving Sudha a disapproving look, she went inside.

The look conveyed something like, 'Listen to a mouthful from her!'

Sreedevi Amma said: 'Sit down, Sudha. Let me talk. Don't be annoyed.'

Sudha did not sit down. She tried to smile, but failed.

'Go on,' she said.

'Why beat around the bush? I can't help but talk. If what I heard is correct, it is in bad taste.'

Sudha made as if to smile. And then, as if it were a simple matter, she replied, 'Yes, it's bad. But there's no other way.'

Sreedevi Amma's face turned dark. She glanced at her younger sister as if to prompt her to speak. The younger sister picked up from there, 'If there's something to what Narayanan kutty was saying, it'll be a matter of shame for our family.'

Sudha didn't respond.

'To say that you want to separate after living together for five years....' She looked at Sreedevi Amma, 'Why don't you tell her what you were thinking.'

'Certainly, things go wrong sometimes; there may be problems but one must put up with them. That's what marriage is all about. Your Amma put up with so much, don't you know?'

Sudha tried to stay calm. The first thing she felt like blurting out was, 'O Sreedevi Amma! The fault is not Prabhakaran's, but mine!' Then she decided against speaking her mind.

They went on talking.

She had, from early childhood, developed a miraculous ability to tune out unwanted conversations. She would start to think of other things—the names she had forgotten, the characters in novels, the topography of the places she had seen in childhood, the faces of her classmates from elementary school—and the voices would go away at once.

As she was leaving, Sreedevi Amma said, 'Do you think shouting myself hoarse has been utterly useless?'

'No,' she said.

'Don't you think there's at least some sense in what I said?'

'Yes.' Sreedevi Amma heaved a sigh of relief. 'What's your decision, then?'

'Let me think about it,' she said, laughing.

With the satisfaction of having succeeded in their mission, Sreedevi Amma and her younger sister left in good spirits.

Amma asked, 'When are you going to see Valyamma of Cholayil?'

'I'll go soon.'

Valyamma too would be waiting for her, wanting to give her advice.

At midday, Sumathi, who was her classmate in high school, visited with her three-year-old daughter. She used to wait for her at the boundary wall of the carpenter family's house every day when they went to school together. The wart below her nose looked as if it had grown bigger. She had married before she had completed Class X.

Sumathi did not sit down, although Sudha urged her to take a seat.

'How are you, Sumathi? Happy?'

'Just going on.'

She wore a shiny sari on which blue, violet, and red stood out loudly. Her husband, who worked in the Gulf, must have bought it for her. Every two years, he would visit on two months' leave. A pungent perfume encased her. Her neck and her hands were covered in gold ornaments leaving not an inch uncovered.

'I heard that you had come. Are you going to be here for a few more days?'

'Yes. For a few more days.'

Next Monday would be the housewarming of Sumathi's new house.

'Sudha kutty, you must certainly come!'

'I will, if I am around.'

Tousling the hair of the girl who stood tracing the flowers on Amma's sari, Sudha said, 'I'm sorry, I've forgotten her name.'

'Karthika.'

She tried to get hold of Karthika's hands and draw her near. The child snivelled and stood by her mother, winding her tiny hands around her body.

Sumathi whispered: 'I heard something is amiss....'

'O, did you hear it too?'

'When the wife of Sankar ettan who does the mosaic work told me, I didn't believe it.'

Sudha hummed under her breath.

'Is it true, Sudha kutty?'

Sudha laughed, 'Somewhat....'

Widening her eyes in alarm, Sumathi leaned forward and said softly: 'Please don't think that I am advising someone who has more education and wisdom than me but it's better to live together whichever way you look at it.'

Sudha stroked her hand.

'Hmmm. Let me think about it.'

'Your first mistake was to decide to not have children immediately. If there are children, there wouldn't be any unwelcome thoughts in the man or woman.'

Sudha looked at Sumathi wonderingly. A local phrase she should inscribe on her mind was 'unwelcome thoughts'.

Sumathi left. Later, Janu who had gone out to buy milk, said upon her return that Valyamma of Cholayil had once again enquired after her. Amma said, 'Go and meet her once, please!'

'Hmmm. I will go tomorrow.'

'She does not need any money. Nevertheless, give her something. When Visalam went to see her, she gave her fifty rupees and the old lady wouldn't stop talking about it.'

Amma laughed. This was the first time that Sudha saw Amma's face brighten up ever since she had arrived.

Sudha thought of countering, 'I am not going to compete with Visaledatthi.'

She decided that she would return to Madras on Monday. There was no way she was going to spend all the two weeks of her vacation in the village. There has already been so much commotion within three days of her arrival.

Should she call the one in Hyderabad, she wondered. She had jotted down his mobile number in her diary. His direct number in the office, she had inscribed in her mind.

There's no one who could book a ticket for her. Never mind. She could get into the ladies' compartment. It's just a matter of a night.

He had told her to call him when she got to her ancestral home.

'If possible,' he had added.

The next day, after breakfast, she said, 'I'll go meet Valyamma now.'

'Take Janu along with you.'

'No need.'

First, she went to the newly-built house of the Asaripparambil family. Sumathi was beside herself with wonder and joy. She belonged to a lower sub-caste and had not expected Sudha to visit her at home. She was at a loss as to how to entertain her guest. Two workers were varnishing the window shutters, under the supervision of the carpenter Narayanan.

She was taken on a tour of the house.

'Both rooms have attached baths,' Sumathi said with pride.

She struggled to sidestep Sumathi's request to drink something before she left.

'My husband has written that he'll come on leave in July.'

'Ask him to take you along the next time he returns to Dubai. That way you too can see the city.'

'That's not possible. Only those with high salaries can manage that, he says.'

Yet, Sumathi was very happy.

'I'm off, Sumathi. I have to visit Valyamma of Cholayil.'

'You remember what I said, don't you?'

'Yes.'

She laughed.

On the way to Valyamma's house she passed a clump of bamboo by a dried-up stream. Earlier, there were thickets on either side of the stream. In those days, it used to be full of water in all seasons. During the monsoons, it would brim over the banks. Farther down, it would become broader and become a small tributary of the river downstream.

Valyamma's house had been built in her father's elder brother's time. There was a bamboo stile in place of the old gatehouse now. When she climbed the steps and reached the courtyard, there was no one around. Black pepper had been spread out to dry on the bamboo mat in the yard.

She stood there hesitantly. It was Thankedatthi, the cousin who lived with Valyamma, when she came out on the veranda.

'What a surprise to see you here! Grandma had mentioned you just this morning. She was worried that you'd go away without meeting her.'

Thankedatthi sat her down on a chair placed next to the woodwork railing.

She began to talk about her family. Both her boys were studying. They had returned to the hostel the previous week because they had to prepare for their practical exams. Her daughter, the youngest, was in Class IX. Thankedatthi's younger sisters had divided the property when their mother died. They had sold their shares and built houses on their husbands' land and were living there.

'This tottering, mouldering old house fell to my lot. There was no one to take my side....'

She choked on her words as she remembered the passing of her husband, as she was expected to. She went through the motions of wiping her eyes.

'Where's Valyamma?'

'In the vadakkiny, the northern wing of the house. Her eyesight is almost gone but she resents anyone holding her hand to help her. Who knows when she's going to stumble and fall...!'

Just then she heard Valyamma saying: 'No one will have to face any trouble on account of me.'

When Valyamma held out her hands to feel the frame of the door opening on to the veranda, and carefully stepped on the threshold to the veranda, Sudha hurried over to her. Even at eighty-four, she stood ramrod straight. The rauka, traditional blouse, and the upper cloth she wore over it were dazzling white. The mundu with a decorative border that she had draped around her waist was stiffly starched. Her luminous face that Sudha had seen in her childhood had not dimmed even a bit. She took special note of the thickness of her snow-white hair, done up in the classical style. When she had heard the tale about Komappan of the *Northern Ballads*, she would imagine it was Valyamma herself who had hidden him behind her hair, while bathing in the pond.

When Thankedatthi tried to bring a chair for her, Valyamma said, 'No, I'll sit here. Sit down, Sudha kutty!'

She extended her hand towards Sudha's.

Sudha sat next to Valyamma and leaned against the parapet of the veranda.

'Haven't you put on weight, Sudha kutty?'

She looked at her own hands. Yes, Valyamma was right. She had indeed put on weight.

'You were gasping when you walked four steps towards me? I could make out that you had put on weight just by listening to your breathing, without actually seeing your body.'

Valyamma laughed.

There were lifeless spots in her ashen eyes, but her face was smooth. Only a few folds on her neck were indicative of ageing.

'Thankam! Make some tea. Fry some jackfruit kernels too.'

'No! I don't want anything. Just half a glass of tea will do,' Sudha said.

Valyamma waited for Thankedatthi to go inside the house and then said: 'What did you decide, my child?' Valyamma's abrupt question made her flinch.

'Don't be afraid. I didn't call you here to shout at you or admonish you. Hasn't it been four or five years since I saw you last?'

She felt relieved.

'The ones around here merely grin when I speak my mind about anything. They think, "What does this old one, with both her eyes blinded with cataract, see?" But are they able to see what I see?'

She guessed that it was for the benefit of Thankedatthi in the kitchen that Valyamma raised her voice as she said this.

Valyamma lowered her voice again, 'What have you decided?'

Her breathing quickened.

'If you feel that you are through with him, get rid of him. This arrangement called marriage is for our convenience. There's no point in engaging in an act for the benefit of others.'

Valyamma sighed deeply, crossed her legs, and leaned forward.

'None of you met my first husband.'

'Amma has seen him. He was a Bhagavathar, a vocalist, wasn't he?'

'That's how the trouble started. Music classes were held at the sharathu, household of a Pisharoty, a higher sect Sannyasi Brahmin; he would eat at our house. His singing was excellent. He wore gold earrings in which red gemstones were embedded, sandal paste on his forehead, and looked so striking. I was infatuated with him.'

Valyamma laughed quietly, running her fingers through her hair.

'He went away before the year was out.'

'Amma said so.'

Valyamma whispered, 'He didn't go away on his own. I asked him to leave.'

Valyamma kept smiling, her sightless gaze fixed on nothing in particular.

'He wasn't able to provide for me. I let that be. But he had a kind of lisping affectation in his speech and coquettish gestures! Mannerisms of women. Shouldn't men be at least a bit manly and smart? I told him bluntly that he would have to leave, that our marriage was over. What else was there to do?'

Although she had heard about Valyamma's first marriage with the Bhagavathar, she didn't know much about it. She had then married Valyachchan. He was a peon in the government salt depot. The couple had three children. Valyachchan died. Then the children died too. Valyamma was left alone.

'Hadn't you seen him? Valyachchan was not that handsome or anything. Was he?'

'I saw him when I was a child. He was on his deathbed at that time.'

'There wasn't anyone like him in this entire land. He'd always be there right in front of the temple festival procession.'

Thankedatthi brought tea.

When Thankedatthi was standing nearby, Valyamma sat with a serious mien without saying anything. When she went back into the house, Valyamma began to smile, as she remembered Valyachchan.

'Those who saw only his exterior would say he was a boor. He would shout and create a ruckus most of the time. But only I knew how gentle a soul he was. Even if I so much as caught a cold, he would fuss about it.'

Valyamma suddenly laughed out aloud.

Sudha forgot about her troubles. She sat waiting with the same eagerness she'd had as a child for whatever Valyamma was going to say next.

'Everything was going smoothly, suddenly some trouble arose. It was just after I had given birth to Kuttinarayanan.'

'What?'

'Imagine...I was attracted to another man. I told myself, "You wretch; control yourself, forget about this." So, things didn't go out of hand. Still....'

Without completing the sentence, Valyamma laughed out loud, open-mouthed. She saw that Valyamma had lost only her wisdom teeth.

'I was exactly your age, then,' Valyamma heaved a sigh.

'Is he still around, Valyamma?'

Valyamma's face clouded over.

'Gone. Everyone's gone. I am the only one left. Till I'm called, when the time comes, I'll just lie here. I can't kill myself!'

She shook her head.

'Who is the other one, Sudha kutty?'

She was startled, 'Eh?'

'You met someone. You like him. And you decided that you are going to be with him. Isn't this what has happened?'

'Who told you?'

Valyamma pulled up her legs.

'There's no need for anyone to tell me. Who is it, my dear girl?'

She tried to control her agitation.

'Is it someone who you work with?'

'No.'

She could not explain it to Valyamma. She had met him at a farewell dinner that was being given for the manager of the branch where he'd been transferred. Late in the evening the chief guest, the organizers of the party, other guests were all quite drunk. It was then that she had spotted him, standing by himself at one end of the hall. She had not heard him earlier. He held a glass of orange juice. He stood looking at her now and again and then finally moved towards her. As he walked towards her, she thought to herself in a frenzy of excitement: "My Lord! He is coming towards me. Please God, what am I going to say?"'

She was so happy when he told her that he would be in Madras for ten days every month. Watching other people move towards them, he said, 'Can I call you at the bank?'

She nodded quietly.

Valyamma said, 'Does he have a wife?'

'No.'

'Does Prabhakaran know?'

Her reply was a bit delayed, 'I think he suspects.'

'Then, you must separate immediately. Prabhakaran will also get another girl. Don't bother too much about such things. Get rid of him.'

Sudha was amused. 'It's not that easy to get rid of him like in the old days, Valyamma.'

'If you don't want him, you don't want him. Doesn't it end there?'

'No, it doesn't end there. First, there needs to be a joint petition. The judge will then summon both of us after six months and ask us whether we are still bent on parting. Even if we say yes, we have to wait another six months.'

She watched agitation spreading over Valyamma's face.

'Does it need the judge's consent if two people meet, like each other, and decide to live together?'

'That's the law, Valyamma.'

Valyamma was not at all satisfied.

'If there are children, their expenses and other things have to be settled, yes. That's the proper way. But what has the judge got to do with two people who like each other living together?'

'That's the law.'

'What law...?'

Thankedatthi came over to pick up the empty glass. Valyamma mumbled something to herself. Thankedatthi said, 'Till last year, Grandma could still see things faintly. Now she's completely blind.'

Sudha said, 'She can regain her eyesight with surgery, even at such an advanced age. I can take her to Madras.'

Valyamma laughed bitterly.

'No, no. Why should I have eyesight at this stage? I'm done with all that I've seen so far!'

Sudha prepared to leave.

Thankedatthi said, 'You can leave after lunch.'

'Oh no! Amma would've prepared lunch for me.'

'The rice is cooking. When you come next, visit us, please, Sudha kutty.'

Thankedatthi went inside. Her fourteen-year-old daughter arrived at the gate just then. Valyamma looked over to the gate. Removing her chappals and leaving them below the veranda, the girl looked at Sudha and smiled. Lowering her head, she walked inside without making any noise. When she reached the door, Valyamma asked, 'Hey! Where have you been?'

The girl was startled.

'To the Sharath. To get a book from Sarada.'

'Why should you wear a silk skirt to the Sharath, like a vamp?'

The girl went pale and quickly escaped inside.

Valyamma turned her face towards Sudha.

'There was no book in her hands, was there?'

'Aye, no.'

'I knew that it was silk by the rustling of the skirt.'
'She is a child, Valyamma.'
'Hmm…mm. The girl is flirtatious beyond her age. I can see everything.'
'May I get going?'
Valyamma stood up.
Remembering what Amma had said, she opened the purse in her hand.
Valyamma said, 'No need. It seems you are going to give me some money. Don't. What need does this Valyamma have for money?'
She closed the purse in amazement.
'When you come…next time….'
Valyamma's voice faltered.
'…if I am around, just come and meet me. I need only that….'
She saw Valyamma's lightless eyes tear up. Her eyes, too, were brimming. She bent down, touched Valyamma's feet, paying obeisance. She remembered having done exactly the same thing five years ago.
Valyamma placed her hand softly on Sudha's head.
'Let the best happen to you, at least this time around.'
She walked out. When she reached the market, she saw the signboard of the STD booth from a distance.
She turned the two phone numbers she had memorized over in her mind. She reminded herself that she should look up her diary and confirm the mobile number. If, after making the call, she was able to reach home quickly, she would not miss the junglefowl and its brood entering the courtyard.
She quickened her steps.

A HORSE AND TWO GOATS
R. K. NARAYAN

Of the seven hundred thousand villages dotting the map of India, in which the majority of India's five hundred million live, flourish, and die, Kritam was probably the tiniest, indicated on the district survey map by a microscopic dot, the map being meant more for the revenue official out to collect tax than for the guidance of the motorist, who in any case could not hope to reach it since it sprawled far from the highway at the end of a rough track furrowed up by the iron-hooped wheels of bullock carts. But its size did not prevent its giving itself the grandiose name Kritam, which meant in Tamil 'coronet' or 'crown' on the brow of this subcontinent. The village consisted of less than thirty houses, only one of them built with brick and cement. Painted a brilliant yellow and blue all over with gorgeous carvings of gods and gargoyles on its balustrade, it was known as the Big House. The other houses, distributed in four streets, were generally of bamboo thatch, straw, mud, and other unspecified material. Muni's was the last house in the fourth street, beyond which stretched the fields. In his prosperous days Muni had owned a flock of forty sheep and goats and sallied forth every morning, driving the flock to the highway a couple of miles away. There he would sit on the pedestal of a clay statue of a horse while his cattle grazed around. He carried a crook at the end of a bamboo pole and snapped foliage from the avenue trees to feed his flock; he also gathered faggots and dry sticks, bundled them, and carried them home for fuel at sunset.

His wife lit the domestic fire at dawn, boiled water in a mud pot, threw into it a handful of millet flour, added salt, and gave him his first nourishment for the day. When he started out, she would put in his hand a packed lunch, once again the same millet cooked into a little ball, which he could swallow with a raw onion at midday. She was old, but he was older and needed all the attention she could give him in order to be kept alive.

His fortunes had declined gradually, unnoticed. From a flock of forty, which he drove into a pen at night, his stock had now come down to two goats which were not worth the rent of a half-rupee a month the Big House charged for the use of the pen in their backyard. And so the two goats were tethered to the trunk of a drumstick tree which grew in front of his hut and from which occasionally Muni could shake down drumsticks. This morning he got six. He carried them in with a sense of triumph. Although no one could say precisely who owned the tree, it was his because he lived in its shadow.

She said, 'If you were content with the drumstick leaves alone, I could boil and salt some for you.'

'Oh, I am tired of eating those leaves. I have a craving to chew the drumstick out of sauce, I tell you.'

'You have only four teeth in your jaw, but your craving is for big things. All right, get the stuff for the sauce, and I will prepare it for you. After all, next year you may not be alive to ask for anything. But first get me all the stuff, including a measure of rice or millet, and I will satisfy your unholy craving. Our store is empty today. Dal, chilli, curry leaves, mustard, coriander, gingelly oil, and one large potato. Go out and get all this.' He repeated the list after her in order not to miss any item and walked off to the shop in the third street.

He sat on an upturned packing case below the platform of the shop. The shopman paid no attention to him. Muni kept clearing his throat, coughing and sneezing until the shopman could not stand it any more and demanded, 'What ails you? You will fly off that seat into the gutter if you sneeze so hard, young man.' Muni laughed inordinately, in order to please the shopman, at being called 'young man'. The shopman softened and said, 'You have enough of the imp inside to keep a second wife busy, but for the fact the old lady is still alive.' Muni laughed appropriately again at this joke. It completely won the shopman over; he liked his sense of humour to be appreciated. Muni engaged his attention in local gossip for a few minutes, which always ended with a reference to the postman's wife who had eloped to the city some months before.

The shopman felt most pleased to hear the worst of the postman, who had cheated him. Being an itinerant postman, he returned home to Kritam only once in ten days and every time managed to slip away again without passing the shop in the third street. By thus humouring the shopman, Muni could always ask for one or two items of food, promising repayment later. Some days the shopman was in a good mood and gave in, and sometimes he would lose his temper suddenly and bark at Muni for daring to ask for credit. This was such a day, and Muni could not progress beyond two items listed as essential components. The shopman was also displaying a remarkable memory for old facts and figures and took out an oblong ledger to support his observations. Muni felt impelled to rise and flee but his self-respect kept him in his seat and made him listen to the worst things about himself. The shopman concluded, 'If you could find five rupees and a quarter, you would pay off an ancient debt and then could apply for admission to swarga. How much have you got now?'

'I will pay you everything on the first of the next month.'

'As always, and whom do you expect to rob by then?'

Muni felt caught and mumbled, 'My daughter has sent word that she will be sending me money.'

'Have you a daughter?' sneered the shopman. 'And she is sending you money! For what purpose, may I know?'

'Birthday, fiftieth birthday,' said Muni quietly.

'Birthday! How old are you?'

Muni repeated weakly, not being sure of it himself, 'fifty'. He always calculated his age from the time of the great famine when he stood as high as the parapet around the village well, but who could calculate such things accurately nowadays with so many famines occurring? The shopman felt encouraged when other customers stood around to watch and comment. Muni thought helplessly, my poverty is exposed to everybody. But what can I do?

'More likely you are seventy,' said the shopman. 'You also forget that you mentioned a birthday five weeks ago when you wanted castor oil for your holy bath.'

'Bath! Who can dream of a bath when you have to scratch the tank-bed for a bowl of water? We would all be parched and dead but for the Big House, where they let us take a pot of water from their well.' After saying this, Muni unobtrusively rose and moved off.

He told his wife, 'That scoundrel would not give me anything.'

'So go out and sell the drumsticks for what they are worth.'

He flung himself down in a corner to recoup from the fatigue of his visit to the shop. His wife said, 'You are getting no sauce today, nor anything else. I can't find anything to give you to eat. Fast till the evening, it'll do you good. Take the goats and be gone now,' she cried and added, 'Don't come back before the sun is down.' He knew that if he obeyed her she would somehow conjure up some food for him in the evening. Only he must be careful not to argue and irritate her. Her temper was undependable in the morning but improved by evening time. She was sure to go out and work—grind corn in the Big House, sweep or scrub somewhere, and earn enough to buy foodstuff and keep a dinner ready for him in the evening.

Unleashing the goats from the drumstick tree, Muni started out, driving them ahead and uttering weird cries from time to time in order to urge them on. He passed through the village with his head bowed in thought. He did not want to look at anyone or be accosted. A couple of his cronies lounging in the temple corridor hailed him, but he ignored their call. They had known him in the days of affluence when he lorded over a flock of fleecy sheep, not the miserable, gawky goats that he had today. Of course, he also used to have a few goats for those who fancied them, but real wealth lay in sheep; they bred fast and people came and bought the fleece in the shearing season; and then that famous butcher from the town came over on the weekly market days bringing him betel leaves, tobacco, and often enough some bhang, which they smoked in a hut in the coconut grove, undisturbed by wives and well-wishers. After a smoke, one felt light and elated and inclined to forgive everyone including that brother-in-law of his who had once tried to set fire to his home. But all this seemed like the memoirs of a previous birth. Some pestilence afflicted his cattle (he could, of course, guess who had laid his animals under a curse) and even the friendly butcher would not touch one at half the price...and now here he was left with the two scraggy creatures. He wished someone would rid him of their company too. The shopman had said that he was seventy. At seventy, one only waited to be summoned by God. When he was dead what would his wife do? They had lived in each other's company since they were children. He was told on the day of their wedding that he was ten years old and she was eight. During the wedding ceremony they had had to recite their respective ages and names. He had thrashed her only a few times in their marriage, and later she had the upper hand. Progeny, none. Perhaps numerous progeny would have brought him the blessing of the gods.

Fertility brought merit. People with fourteen sons were always so prosperous and at peace with the world and themselves. He recollected the thrill he had felt when he mentioned a daughter to that shopman; although it was not believed, what if he did not have a daughter?

His cousin in the next village had many daughters, and any one of them was as good as his; he was fond of them all and would buy them sweets if he could afford it. Still, everyone in the village whispered behind their backs that Muni and his wife were a barren couple. He avoided looking at anyone; they all professed to be so high up, and everyone else in the village had more money than he. 'I am the poorest fellow in our caste and no wonder that they spurn me, but I won't look at them either,' and so he passed on with his eyes downcast along the edge of the street, and people left him also very much alone, commenting only to the extent, 'Ah, there he goes with his two great goats; if he slits their throats, he may have more peace of mind.' 'What has he to worry about anyway? They live on nothing and have nobody to worry about.' Thus people commented when he passed through the village. Only on the outskirts did he lift his head and look up. He urged and bullied the goats until they meandered along to the foot of the horse statue on the edge of the village. He sat on its pedestal for the rest of the day. The advantage of this was that he could watch the highway and see the lorries and buses pass through to the hills, and it gave him a sense of belonging to a larger world. The pedestal of the statue was broad enough for him to move around as the sun travelled up and westwards; or he could also crouch under the belly of the horse, for shade.

The horse was nearly life-size, moulded out of clay, baked, burnt and brightly coloured, and reared its head proudly, prancing with its forelegs in the air and flourishing its tail in a loop. Beside the horse stood a warrior with scythe-like mustachios, bulging eyes, and aquiline nose. The old image-makers believed in indicating a man of strength by bulging out his eyes and sharpening his moustache tips. They had also decorated the man's chest with beads which looked today like blobs of mud through the ravages of sun and wind and rain (when it came), but Muni would insist that he had known the beads to sparkle like the nine gems at one time in his life. The horse itself was said to have been as white as a dhobi-washed sheet, and had had on its back a cover of pure brocade of red-and-black lace, matching the multicoloured sash around the waist of the warrior. But none in the village remembered the splendour as no one noticed its existence. Even Muni, who spent all his waking hours at its foot, never bothered to look up. It was untouched by the young vandals of the village who gashed tree trunks with knives and tried to topple off milestones and inscribed lewd designs on all the walls. This statue had been closer to the population of the village at one time, when this spot bordered the village; but when the highway was laid through (or perhaps when the tank and wells dried up completely here) the village moved a couple of miles inland.

Muni sat at the foot of the statue, watching his two goats graze in the arid soil among the cactus and lantana bushes. He looked at the sun; it had tilted westwards no doubt, but it was not the time yet to go back home; if he went too early, his wife would have no food for him. Also he must give her time to cool off her temper and feel sympathetic, and then she would scrounge and manage to get some food. He watched the mountain road for a time signal. When the green bus appeared around the bend he could leave, and his wife would feel pleased that he had let the goats feed long enough. He noticed now a new sort of vehicle coming down at full speed.

It looked both like a motor car and a bus. He used to be intrigued by the novelty of such spectacles, but of late work was going on at the source of the river on the mountain and an assortment of people and traffic went past him, and he took it all casually and described to his wife, later in the day, not everything as he once did, but only some things, only if he noticed anything special. Today, while he observed the yellow vehicle coming down, he was wondering how to describe it later when it sputtered and stopped in front of him. A red-faced foreigner who had been driving it got down and went round it, stooping, looking, and poking under the vehicle; then he straightened himself up, looked at the dashboard, stared in Muni's direction, and approached him. 'Excuse me, is there a gas station nearby, or do I have to wait until another car comes—' He suddenly looked up at the clay horse and cried, 'Marvellous!' without completing his sentence. Muni felt he should get up and run away, and cursed his age. He could not readily put his limbs into action; some years ago he could outrun a cheetah, as happened once when he went to the forest to cut fuel and it was then that two of his sheep were mauled—a sign that bad times were coming. Though he tried, he could not easily extricate himself from his seat, and then there was also the problem of the goats. He could not leave them behind.

The red-faced man wore khaki clothes—evidently a policeman or a soldier. Muni said to himself, 'He will chase or shoot if I start running. Sometimes dogs chase only those who run—O Shiva, protect me. I don't know why this man should be after me.' Meanwhile, the foreigner cried, 'Marvellous!' again, nodding his head. He paced around the statue with his eyes fixed on it. Muni sat frozen for a while, and then fidgeted and tried to edge away. Now the other man suddenly pressed his palms together in a salute, smiled, and said, 'Namaste! How do you do?'

At which Muni spoke the only English expressions he had learnt, 'Yes, no.' Having exhausted his English vocabulary, he started in Tamil: 'My name is Muni. These two goats are mine, and no one can gainsay it—though our village is full of slanderers these days who will not hesitate to say that what belongs to a man doesn't belong to him.' He rolled his eyes and shuddered at the thought of the evil-minded men and women peopling his village.

The foreigner faithfully looked in the direction indicated by Muni's fingers, gazed for a while at the two goats and the rocks, and with a puzzled expression took out his silver cigarette case and lit a cigarette. Suddenly remembering the courtesies of the season, he asked, 'Do you smoke?' Muni answered, 'Yes, no.' Whereupon the red-faced man took a cigarette and gave it to Muni, who received it with surprise, having had no offer of a smoke from anyone for years now. Those days when he smoked bhang were gone with his sheep and the large-hearted butcher. Nowadays, he was not able to find even matches, let alone bhang. (His wife went across and borrowed a fire at dawn from a neighbour.) He had always wanted to smoke a cigarette; only once had the shopman given him one on credit, and he remembered how good it had tasted. The other flicked the lighter open and offered a light to Muni. Muni felt so confused about how to act that he blew on it and put it out. The other, puzzled but undaunted, flourished his lighter, presented it again, and lit Muni's cigarette. Muni drew a deep puff and started coughing; it was racking, no doubt, but extremely pleasant. When his cough subsided he wiped his eyes and took stock of the situation, understanding that the other man was not an inquisitor of any kind. Yet, in order to make sure, he remained wary. No need to run away from a man who gave him such a potent smoke. His head was reeling from the effect of one of those strong American cigarettes made with roasted tobacco. The man said, 'I come from New York,' took out a wallet from his hip pocket, and presented his card.

Muni shrank away from the card. Perhaps he was trying to present a warrant and arrest him. Beware of khaki, one part of his mind warned. Take all the cigarettes or bhang or whatever is offered, but don't get caught. Beware of khaki. He wished he weren't seventy as the shopman had said. At seventy one didn't run but surrendered to whatever came. He could only ward off trouble by talk. So he went on, all in the chaste Tamil for which Kritam was famous. (Even the worst detractors could not deny that the famous poetess Avvaiyar was born in this area, although no one could say whether it was in Kritam or Kuppam, the adjoining village.) Out of this heritage the Tamil language gushed through Muni in an unimpeded flow. He said, 'Before God, sir, Bhagwan, who sees everything, I tell you, sir, that we know nothing of the case. If the murder was committed, whoever did it will not escape. Bhagwan is all-seeing. Don't ask me about it. I know nothing.' A body had been found mutilated and thrown under a tamarind tree at the border between Kritam and Kuppam a few weeks before, giving rise to much gossip and speculation. Muni added an explanation, 'Anything is possible there. People over there will stop at nothing.' The foreigner nodded his head and listened courteously though he understood nothing.

'I am sure you know when this horse was made,' said the red man and smiled ingratiatingly.

Muni reacted to the relaxed atmosphere by smiling himself, and pleaded, 'Please go away, sir, I know nothing. I promise we will hold him for you if we see any bad character around, and we will bury him up to his neck in a coconut pit if he tries to escape; but our village has always had a clean record. Must definitely be the other village.'

Now the red man implored, 'Please, please, I will speak slowly, please try to understand me. Can't you understand even a simple word of English? Everyone in this country seems to know English. I have got along with English everywhere in this country, but you don't speak it. Have you any religious or spiritual scruples for avoiding the English speech?'

Muni made some indistinct sounds in his throat and shook his head. Encouraged, the other went on to explain at length, uttering each syllable with care and deliberation. Presently he sidled over and took a seat beside the old man, explaining, 'You see, last August, we probably had the hottest summer in history, and I was working in shirtsleeves in my office on the fortieth floor of the Empire State Building. You must have heard of the power failure, and there I was stuck for four hours, no elevator, no air conditioning. All the way in the train I kept thinking, and the minute I reached home in Connecticut, I told my wife Ruth, "We will visit India this winter, it's time to look at other civilizations." Next day she called the travel agent first thing and told him to fix it, and so here I am. Ruth came with me but is staying back at Srinagar, and I am the one doing the rounds and joining her later.'

Muni looked reflective at the end of this long peroration and said, rather feebly, 'Yes, no,' as a concession to the other's language, and went on in Tamil, 'When I was this high,' he indicated a foot high, 'I heard my uncle say....'

No one can tell what he was planning to say as the other interrupted him at this stage to ask, 'Boy, what is the secret of your teeth? How old are you?'

The old man forgot what he had started to say and remarked, 'Sometimes we too lose our cattle. Jackals or cheetahs may carry them off, but sometimes it is just theft from over in the next village, and then we will know who has done it. Our priest at the temple can see in the camphor flame the face of the thief, and when he is caught....' He gestured with his hands a perfect mincing of meat.

The American watched his hands intently and said, 'I know what you mean. Chop something? Maybe I am holding you up and you want to chop wood? Where is your axe? Hand it to me and show me what to chop. I do enjoy it, you know, just a hobby. We get a lot of driftwood along the backwater near my house, and on Sundays I do nothing but chop wood for the fireplace. I really feel different when I watch the fire in the fireplace, although it may take all the sections of the Sunday *New York Times* to get a fire started,' and he smiled at this reference.

Muni felt totally confused but decided the best thing would be to make an attempt to get away from this place. He tried to edge out, saying, 'Must go home,' and turned to go. The other seized his shoulder and said desperately, 'Is there no one, absolutely no one here, to translate for me?' He looked up and down the road, which was deserted in this hot afternoon; a sudden gust of wind churned up the dust and dead leaves on the roadside into a ghostly column and propelled it towards the mountain road. The stranger almost pinioned Muni's back to the statue and asked,

'Isn't this statue yours? Why don't you sell it to me?'

The old man now understood the reference to the horse, thought for a second, and said in his own language, 'I was an urchin this high when I heard my grandfather explain this horse and warrior, and my grandfather himself was this high when he heard his grandfather, whose grandfather....'

The other man interrupted him with, 'I don't want to seem to have stopped here for nothing. I will offer you a good price for this,' he said, indicating the horse. He had concluded without the least doubt that Muni owned this mud horse. Perhaps he guessed by the way he sat at its pedestal, like other souvenir sellers in this country presiding over their wares.

Muni followed the man's eyes and pointing fingers and dimly understood the subject matter and, feeling relieved that the theme of the mutilated body had been abandoned at least for the time being, said again, enthusiastically, 'I was this high when my grandfather told me about this horse and the warrior, and my grandfather was this high when he himself....' and he was getting into a deeper bog of reminiscence each time he tried to indicate the antiquity of the statue.

The Tamil that Muni spoke was stimulating even as pure sound, and the foreigner listened with fascination. 'I wish I had my tape recorder here,' he said, assuming the pleasantest expression. 'Your language sounds wonderful. I get a kick out of every word you utter, here'—he indicated his ears—'but you don't have to waste your breath in sales talk. I appreciate the article. You don't have to explain its points.'

'I never went to a school, in those days only Brahmins went to schools, but we had to go out and work in the fields morning till night, from sowing to harvest time...and when Pongal came and we had cut the harvest, my father allowed me to go out and play with others at the tank, and so I don't know the Parangi language you speak, even little fellows in your country probably speak the Parangi language, but here only learned men and officers know it. We had a postman in our village who could speak to you boldly in your language, but his wife ran away with someone and he does not speak to anyone at all nowadays. Who would if a wife did what she did? Women must be watched; otherwise they will sell themselves and the home,' and he laughed at his own quip.

The foreigner laughed heartily, took out another cigarette, and offered it to Muni, who now smoked with ease, deciding to stay on if the fellow was going to be so good as to keep up his cigarette supply. The American now stood up on the pedestal in the attitude of a demonstrative lecturer and said, running his finger along some of the carved decorations around the horse's neck, speaking slowly and uttering his words syllable by syllable, 'I could give a sales talk for this better than anyone else.... This is a marvellous combination of yellow and indigo, though faded now.... How do you people of this country achieve these flaming colours?'

Muni, now assured that the subject was still the horse and not the dead body, said, 'This is our guardian, it means death to our adversaries. At the end of Kali Yuga, this world and all other worlds will be destroyed, and the Redeemer will come in the shape of a horse called Kalki; this horse will come to life and gallop and trample down all bad men.' As he spoke of bad men the figures of his shopman and his brother-in-law assumed concrete forms in his mind, and he revelled for a moment in the predicament of the fellow under the horse's hoof: served him right for trying to set fire to his home....

While he was brooding on this pleasant vision, the foreigner utilized the pause to say, 'I assure you that this will have the best home in the USA. I'll push away the bookcase, you know I love books and am a member of five book clubs, and the choice and bonus volumes really mount up to a pile in our living room, as high as this horse itself. But they'll have to go. Ruth may disapprove, but I will convince her. The TV may have to be shifted too. We can't have everything in the living room. Ruth will probably say, "What about when we have a party?" I'm going to keep him right in the middle of the room. I don't see how that can interfere with the party—we'll stand around him and have our drinks.'

Muni continued his description of the end of the world. 'Our pandit discoursed at the temple once how the oceans are going to close over the earth in a huge wave and swallow us—this horse will grow bigger than the biggest wave and carry on its back only the good people and kick into the floods the evil ones—plenty of them about,' he said reflectively. 'Do you know when it is going to happen?' he asked.

The foreigner now understood by the tone of the other that a question was being asked and said, 'How am I transporting it? I can push the seat back and make room in the rear. That van can take in an elephant'—waving precisely at the back of the seat.

Muni was still hovering on visions of avatars and said again, 'I never missed our pandit's discourses at the temple in those days during every bright half of the month, although he'd go on all night, and he told us that Vishnu is the highest god. Whenever evil men trouble us, he comes down to save us. He has come many times. The first time he incarnated as a great fish, and lifted the scriptures on his back when the floods and sea waves....'

'I am not a millionaire, but a modest businessman. My trade is coffee.'

Amidst all this wilderness of obscure sound Muni caught the word 'coffee' and said, 'If you want to drink "kapi", drive further up, in the next town, they have Friday market, and there they open "kapi-otels"—so I learn from passers-by. Don't think I wander about. I go nowhere and look for nothing.' His thoughts went back to the avatars. 'The first avatar was in the shape of a little fish in a bowl of water, but every hour it grew bigger and bigger and became in the end a huge whale which the seas could not contain, and on the back of the whale the holy books were supported, saved, and carried.' Having launched on the first avatar it was inevitable that he should go on to the next, a wild boar on whose tusks the earth was lifted when a vicious conqueror of the earth carried it off and hid it at the bottom of the sea. After describing this avatar Muni concluded, 'God will always save us whenever we are troubled by evil beings. When we were young we staged at full moon the story of the avatars. That's how I know the stories; we played them all night until the sun rose, and sometimes the European collector would come to watch, bringing his own chair. I had a good voice and so they always taught me songs and gave me the women's roles. I was always Goddess Lakshmi, and they dressed me in a brocade sari, loaned from the Big House....'

The foreigner said, 'I repeat, I am not a millionaire. Ours is a modest business; after all, we can't afford to buy more than sixty minutes' TV time in a month, which works out to two minutes a day, that's all, although in the course of time we'll maybe sponsor a one-hour show regularly if our sales graph continues to go up....'

Muni was intoxicated by the memory of his theatrical days and was about to explain how he had painted his face and worn a wig and diamond earrings when the visitor, feeling that he had spent too much time already, said, 'Tell me, will you accept a hundred rupees or not for the horse? I'd love to take the whiskered soldier also but I've no space for him this year. I'll have to cancel my air ticket and take a boat home, I suppose. Ruth can go by air if she likes, but I will go with the horse and keep him in my cabin all the way if necessary,' and he smiled at the picture of himself voyaging across the seas hugging this horse. He added, 'I will have to pad it with straw so that it doesn't break....'

'When we played Ramayana, they dressed me as Sita,' added Muni. 'A teacher came and taught us the songs for the drama and we gave him fifty rupees. He incarnated himself as Rama, and he alone could destroy Ravana, the demon with ten heads who shook all the worlds; do you know the story of Ramayana?'

'I have my station wagon as you see. I can push the seat back and take the horse in if you will just lend me a hand with it.'

'Do you know Mahabharata? Krishna was the eighth avatar of Vishnu, incarnated to help the Five Brothers regain their kingdom. When Krishna was a baby he danced on the thousand-hooded giant serpent and trampled it to death; and then he suckled the breasts of the demoness and left them flat as a disc though when she came to him her bosoms were large, like mounds of earth on the banks of a dug-up canal.' He indicated two mounds with his hands. The stranger was completely mystified by the gesture. For the first time he said, 'I really wonder what you are saying because your answer is crucial. We have come to the point when we should be ready to talk business.'

'When the tenth avatar comes, do you know where you and I will be?' asked the old man.

'Lend me a hand and I can lift off the horse from its pedestal after picking out the cement at the joints. We can do anything if we have a basis of understanding.'

At this stage the mutual mystification was complete, and there was no need even to carry on a guessing game at the meaning of words. The old man chattered away in a spirit of balancing off the credits and debits of conversational exchange, and said in order to be on the credit side, 'O, honourable one, I hope God has blessed you with numerous progeny. I say this because you seem to be a good man, willing to stay beside an old man and talk to him, while all day I have none to talk to except when somebody stops by to ask for a piece of tobacco. But I seldom have it, tobacco is not what it used to be at one time, and I have given up chewing. I cannot afford it nowadays.' Noting the other's interest in his speech, Muni felt encouraged to ask, 'How many children have you?' with appropriate gestures with his hands. Realizing that a question was being asked, the red man replied, 'I said a hundred,' which encouraged Muni to go into details, 'How many of your children are boys and how many girls? Where are they? Is your daughter married? Is it difficult to find a son-in-law in your country also?'

In answer to these questions the red man dashed his hand into his pocket and brought forth his wallet in order to take immediate advantage of the bearish trend in the market. He flourished a hundred-rupee currency note and asked, 'Well, this is what I meant.'

The old man now realized that some financial element was entering their talk. He peered closely at the currency note, the like of which he had never seen in his life; he knew the five and ten by their colours although always in other people's hands, while his own earning at any time was in coppers and nickels. What was this man flourishing the note for? Perhaps asking for change. He laughed to himself at the notion of anyone coming to him for changing a thousand or ten-thousand-rupee note. He said with a grin, 'Ask our village headman, who is also a moneylender; he can change even a lakh of rupees in gold sovereigns if you prefer it that way; he thinks nobody knows, but dig the floor of his puja room and your head will reel at the sight of the hoard. The man disguises himself in rags just to mislead the public. Talk to the headman yourself because he goes mad at the sight of me. Someone took away his pumpkins with the creeper and he, for some reason, thinks it was me and my goats...that's why I never let my goats be seen anywhere near the farms.' His eyes travelled to his goats nosing about, attempting to wrest nutrition from minute greenery peeping out of rock and dry earth.

The foreigner followed his look and decided that it would be a sound policy to show an interest in the old man's pets. He went up casually to them and stroked their backs with every show of courteous attention. Now the truth dawned on the old man. His dream of a lifetime was about to be realized. He understood that the red man was actually making an offer for the goats. He had reared them up in the hope of selling them some day and, with the capital, opening a small shop on this very spot. Sitting here, watching the hills, he had often dreamt how he would put up a thatched roof here, spread a gunny sack out on the ground, and display on it fried nuts, coloured sweets, and green coconut for the thirsty and famished wayfarers on the highway, which was sometimes very busy. The animals were not prize ones for a cattle show, but he had spent his occasional savings to provide them some fancy diet now and then, and they did not look too bad. While he was reflecting thus, the red man shook his hand and left on his palm one hundred rupees in tens now. 'It is all for you or you may share it if you have a partner.'

The old man pointed at the station wagon and asked, 'Are you carrying them off in that?'

'Yes, of course,' said the other, understanding the transportation part of it.

The old man said, 'This will be their first ride in a motor car. Carry them off after I get out of sight, otherwise they will never follow you, but only me even if I am travelling on the path to Yama Loka.' He laughed at his own joke, brought his palms together in a salute, turned round and went off, and was soon out of sight beyond a clump of thicket.

The red man looked at the goats grazing peacefully. Perched on the pedestal of the horse, as the westerly sun touched the ancient faded colours of the statue with a fresh splendour, he ruminated, 'He must be gone to fetch some help, I suppose!' and settled down to wait. When a truck came downhill, he stopped it and got the help of a couple of men to detach the horse from its pedestal and place it in his station wagon. He gave them five rupees each, and for a further payment they siphoned off gas from the truck and helped him to start his engine.

Muni hurried homewards with the cash securely tucked away at his waist in his dhoti. He shut the street door and stole up softly to his wife as she squatted before the lit oven wondering if by a miracle food would drop from the sky. Muni displayed his fortune for the day. She snatched the notes from him, counted them by the glow of the fire, and cried, 'One hundred rupees! How did you come by it? Have you been stealing?'

'I have sold our goats to a red-faced man. He was absolutely crazy to have them, gave me all this money and carried them off in his motor car!'

Hardly had these words left his lips when they heard bleating outside. She opened the door and saw the two goats at her door. 'Here they are!' she said. 'What's the meaning of all this?'

He muttered a great curse and seized one of the goats by its ears and shouted, 'Where is that man? Don't you know you are his? Why did you come back?' The goat only wriggled in his grip. He asked the same question of the other too. The goat shook itself off. His wife glared at him and declared, 'If you have thieved, the police will come tonight and break your bones. Don't involve me. I will go away to my parents....'

THE SEARCH

DHEEBA NAZIR

Translated from the Kashmiri by Neerja Mattoo

Dusk was falling as I arrived at the SRTC stand in Srinagar. I was a stranger to the city. I saw an auto and asked its driver whether there was a hotel nearby. Asking me to get into his auto, he drove me to what was called the Jahangir Hotel.

I had two jobs to do in this city.

The next morning, I rose early. The hotel being in the middle of the city, the loud noise of traffic was inevitable. I lifted a corner of the curtain and looked out—big vehicles, a flyover, children in uniform being dragged along by their mothers carrying their satchels. I was reminded of my own childhood. Every day I used to....

I walked out of the hotel and asked a passer-by to guide me to a bus that would take me to the Safakadal and Habbakadal—that is where I was going. He pointed to a crossing in the distance, and said that was where I would find the right bus.

I found a seat on the bus. The passenger next to me was speaking on his mobile phone, telling somebody that he was going to 'downtown'... maybe it was the name of a locality in the city.

The conductor called out 'Safakadal', and I got down. There was a bridge in front of me. Crossing it, I looked over the side and thought it must be the Vyeth flowing underneath. 'Yes...it is the Vyeth,' I said aloud. 'What is it that you said?' a man dressed in a suit and tie was asking me. 'It is the Jhelum, my son,' he corrected me.

I smiled and said, 'Jhelum it may be to you, but for us it is the Vyeth.'

I looked at the banks of the Vyeth, at the shrines and temples dotting them. My eyes travelled to other bridges on the river in the distance. I spotted a temple close by and a thought occurred to me—why not pay my obeisance to the deity? Maybe that will help me in accomplishing my job. After crossing the bridge, I turned right and kept walking. There was a house in front of me built of bricks with projecting balconies, a veritable mansion. There was a huge mulberry tree in the yard and I froze in my tracks staring at it. But the people living in that house now were different.

I found myself standing in front of the temple, bowed my head down, and suddenly felt like I had lost my bearings. Who was I? Where was I going? Nothing was familiar, everything had changed. Something seemed to push me along on my feet. Next to the temple stood another house, with gaping spaces in place of doors and windows, and a collapsed fencing wall. A double door faced a veranda occupied by stray dogs. A huge walnut tree still stood in the compound. The dilapidated house seemed to tell its own story. Who had reduced it to this hollow shell I could not say, my tongue would not dare.

On my right were steps going down to the river. Perhaps the people used the boats moored alongside the banks to ferry themselves across. I saw more houses in ruins, some with broken doors and windows, others mere burnt-out shells covered in layers of grime and dust and festooned with cobwebs, the yards choked with weeds and nettles, the chinars and fruit trees in their compounds all stuck by an unseasonal autumn. I stood, irresolute, having quite forgotten the purpose of my visit to this place. Where was I going? Where had I come from?

Suddenly, I recalled that it was Friday. She and I had also been born on a Friday. I had heard from my grandfather that Muslims make yellow rice on Fridays. At a turning, I saw a woman come out of her house with a platter of yellow rice. All the children around rushed to her, holding out their bowls. She beckoned to me and I too went forward and took the yellow rice in my spread-out palms. It somewhat appeased my hunger. But I remained hungry, starving for everything in this place. I took a few more steps and found myself before a shrine of Sharifuddin Abdul Rehman alias Bulbul Shah. It also stood on the Vyeth riverbank.

It was as if these lanes, welcoming me with festive arches, had been waiting just for me all these long years. A small group of people, dressed in pherans, were sitting in a shop, smoking a hookah. Women walked by, their heads covered with long veils. Suddenly, a whiff of an aroma hit my nose. It was the smell of freshly baked unleavened bread from a baker's shop. Ah, the stacks of lavasas and girdas! I looked up and heard the cooing of pigeons perched on the wires of an electric pole. I stopped at every step, as though I wanted to drink in all the sights, relishing them with all my senses, everything that had been lost to us. Hence, the anguish in my heart.

Now, I was truly lost. What place was this, I wondered. Just then, I spotted a milkman's shop. I asked him what this locality was called. He answered this place was mockingly named 'downtown', but actually it was the 'Shehr-i-Khas'. I recalled the words of that passenger on the bus. The milkman continued, 'You are standing at the door of Shah-i-Hamadan.' I looked ahead and saw the shrine before me. 'Where are you headed to, son?' he asked me. I replied that I wanted to go to Safakadal and Habbakadal, but seemed to have lost my way. He asked me not to worry and to take a seat in his shop and rest for a while. I took my seat and he placed a blob of thick yogurt from his pot on my palm. I was somewhat bewildered, but then thought, 'This must be a custom, perhaps.' He said, 'You are quite close to Habbakadal. Take this road in front of the shop and you will come to a crossroads. There you must go straight ahead and you will find yourself in Habbakadal.' I felt a wave of relief wash over me.

I took the road he had pointed me to and did reach Habbakadal. My father had told me that I should look out for a lane with a public water tap at its entrance and that the house to the left in that lane was once our home. I saw a house exactly where he had suggested. I moved forward but my legs turned to lead—I just could not walk any further. Somehow, I dragged myself towards it. The house had a double door in the front, with a large iron ring hanging from it. In the yard full of irises in bloom, there were a couple of pomegranate trees. The outer wall had fallen in and the windows hung loose on their hinges. The walls of the house closed in on me, to hold me in a deadly embrace. The din and clamour of my family as they fled this place, their home, in the middle of that fateful night, seemed to resound all around me. The house held out an appeal, 'Come back, all of you. Don't you see my plight? I totter, barely able to stand, hiding my face, as though ashamed of my existence.'

The veranda was made of divri stone. I saw my grandmother sitting on it, a pile of greens before her, picking out and discarding the yellowed leaves, preparing them for dinner. And there was my mother, holding me in her arms, singing a lullaby. And my brother hiding under the pomegranate tree, ignoring my grandmother's call. And Rahti calling out, peering over the wall, 'Tulsi! Is the cooking done?'

All of a sudden, I felt somebody's hand on my shoulder and came out of my reverie. A voice was asking me, 'Who are you? What are you looking for?' And I answered, 'I am Motilal's grandson—he was my mother's father.' His eyes filled with tears as he held out his arms and hugged me tight. 'The whole of Habbakadal has been bereft since you all left. It has not been the same....' Saying this, he took me home. He told his family that I was Sunil's son. They all crowded around me, some crying, others wanting to know everything about my family.

They brought salt tea for me, made rice flour rotis and saw to it that I ate at least two of them. They begged me to stay. I told them that I had to go to Safakadal. They insisted that I stay with them for a couple of days, and then I could go wherever I wanted to. I said, 'I have seen what I had come to see. If I linger on and see more, I shall no longer be who I am.' Their son took out his scooter from the garage and asked me where exactly in Safakadal I had to go. I told him that it was a place known as Dyers' Lane. My mother had told me that it was the third house on the left. I stood before it and knocked at the door. A woman came out and I asked her, 'Does Masterji live here?'

'They left this place fourteen years ago. We are the owners of this house now,' she announced and my hopes crumbled. She asked me to step inside, but I stood frozen in my tracks—where was I to look for her now?

I asked her whether they had left an address with her. She said if they had, she would certainly have given it to me. Then she asked what my purpose in looking for them was. I replied 'I have a very strong connection with them.'

'What might that be?' she asked.

'It was the February of 1986 when a relationship was formed in ward number 12 of the Lal Ded Hospital. My mother's bed was number 201, while Masterji's wife occupied the adjacent bed, 202. My mother had just given birth to me and then fallen seriously ill. Masterji's wife had delivered a baby girl. My mother, because of her illness, could not suckle me, but, for two whole days, Masterji's wife fed me at her breast. I am told when a pen was put between my fingers according to the custom in our community, and a mantra was whispered in my ear, the same was done to her, too, for my sister. She was born at half past eight in the evening while

I had been born at two o'clock in the afternoon. Today, I am in desperate need of my sister. I am getting married next month. A sister's presence is essential at her brother's wedding. It is she who performs the ritual of welcoming the new bride and the ceremony is incomplete without her receiving the gifts due to her on the occasion. My blood yearns to meet my foster mother and sister.'

'Why did it take you so long to remember their existence? Did you think of them all these years? Why didn't you come earlier?' she wanted to know.

'We have lost so much—our very identity is lost. Houses and mansions may be rebuilt, but the loss of one's near and dear ones is tough to bear. I do remember my sister, and miss her on every Raksha Bandhan day....

'Whether she remembers me or not is something I do not know. But I do know that she will remember me, particularly on the day when they deck her hands with henna.'

My final words to her were, 'If you ever happen to see her, tell her that her brother is searching for her, and yearning to meet her.'

THE FLOOD
THAKAZHI SIVASANKARA PILLAI

Translated from the Malayalam by O. V. Usha

The temple stood on a rise, the highest ground for miles around. Despite this, its deity was submerged in water up to its neck. There was water everywhere you looked. In the three-roomed uppermost storey of the building, sixty-seven children, three hundred and fifty-seven adults, and assorted dogs, cats, goats, and fowl had taken refuge from the floodwaters.

Most of the locals had fled their homes, and made their way to dry land. If the family owned a boat, one of them would remain behind to guard their house and their possessions.

Chennan, the pariah, had been standing in water an entire night and day. It had been three days since his master had escaped to safety. Chennan did not own a rowboat so inside his hut he had built an elevated platform out of coconut fronds and twigs that jutted above the level of the floodwaters. The family spent two days in this primitive loft, hoping the floodwaters would recede soon. Chennan was concerned that if they left the hut, his five banana trees that were heavy with fruit and his hayrick would be stolen. The waters continued to rise. Chennan was now knee-deep in water as he stood on his platform. A couple of rows of thatch on the roof slipped under water. Chennan shouted for help, but who was there to hear him? He was convinced that he and his dependents—his pregnant wife, four children, a cat, and a dog—would die within the next twelve hours, as, by then, the waters would have risen above the roof. The downpour, which had started three days ago, showed no signs of abating.

Undoing a portion of the thatch from inside the hut, Chennan somehow scrambled on to the roof and looked around. He saw a big boat moving north. He yelled to the men in the boat for help. They heard him, and began rowing towards his hut. Chennan pulled out his children, his wife, the dog and the cat through the opening he had made in the roof. When the boat came alongside the hut, the children began climbing into it. Just then they heard a voice.

'Chennacho... Poohay...!'

It was Matiyathara Kunheippan, calling out from the roof of his house.

Chennan hastily helped his wife into the boat. The cat also jumped in. No one remembered the dog. It was sniffing at something on the western edge of the roof when the boat began to move away from the house.

When the dog eventually returned to the spot on the roof from which the family had made its escape, the boat was far away. The animal began to run around frantically on the roof, sniffing here and there, whining all the while. A frog which had been sitting on the roof was alarmed by the commotion the dog was creating and jumped into the flood as the dog drew close. The movement frightened the dog; it reared back, then stared intently at the ripples caused by the frog when it had dived into the water.

The dog was hungry now, and began sniffing around for food. It disturbed another frog, which urinated on its nose, before jumping into the water. The dog sneezed and snorted, shook its head violently, began cleaning its face with its forepaws.

The rain, which had stopped for a while, began lashing down again, and the dog crouched down miserably under its onslaught. Meanwhile, its master and family had got to safety in Ambalappuzha.

Night fell. An enormous crocodile, half submerged in the water, drifted by the hut. The dog put its tail between its legs in terror and howled, but the crocodile paid no attention to it and was soon out of sight.

Starving, terrified, tired, and without any protection from the driving rain, the dog crouched on the roof of the hut. It howled piteously and the gusting wind carried its cries of distress across great distances. The few people who remained in that flooded wilderness guarding their huts probably felt sorry for the dog when they heard its anguished howls.

Its master was probably eating his dinner. He was probably rolling a ball of rice for the dog between his fingers, as was his practice at the end of a meal. The dog's howls began to weaken, then died away. It pricked up its ears when it heard a man reciting the Ramayana. It remained silent for a while, almost as if it was listening to the chanting of the verse, and then began barking again as loudly as it could manage. The melodious chanting of the Ramayana rose clear and strong into the still night. The rain had stopped. The dog listened intently to the sound of that human voice. The voice died away into the cold air. Now there was no sound except that of the gusting of the wind, and the lapping of waves against the hut.

The dog lay down on the roof. It snuffled miserably. A fish splashed in the dark water. A frog jumped. The dog barked once or twice, then fell quiet.

❦

When the sun came up, the dog began a low howling, almost as if it were keening. Rows of frogs, lined up on the roof of the house, would eye the dog, and if it made a move, would jump into the water. The dog looked at the thatched roofs poking out of the floodwater in the vicinity, hoping that they would contain food; but there was no food to be had. It began nuzzling at its fur, feeding on the fleas it found there; it scratched the flea bites with its hind legs, and then it briefly fell asleep in the feeble warmth of the sun.

Dark clouds enveloped the sun. The wind rose, and with it the waves. The carcasses of drowned animals floated past the hut. The dog looked longingly at them, and barked once or twice.

❦

Every now and again small rowboats would come into view and the dog would look at them hopefully. One of them went past in the distance and disappeared behind a thick clump of ketaki shrubs. It began to drizzle again. Sitting on the roof, the dog presented a picture of utter helplessness.

The rain stopped. A small boat appeared in the distance and steadily drew closer. It moored under a coconut tree close to the hut. The dog wagged its tail, stretched, yawned, growled under its breath. The man in the boat climbed the tree, lopped off a coconut, sliced it open, drank its contents, and then rowed away.

A crow flew down and landed on the huge rotting carcass of a dead buffalo that was floating by, and began to rip and tear at the flesh. Chennan's dog barked longingly at the prospect of a meal. The crow ate its fill and flew away. A green bird landed on a banana trunk and chirped. An ant's nest that had become dislodged from somewhere upriver snagged on the eaves of the hut. Thinking that it was something it could eat, the dog nosed at the nest, and got bitten for its pains. It jumped away, snorting and sneezing, its tender nose flushed and swollen.

That afternoon, a small rowboat drifted by, with two men in it. The dog began barking joyfully, jumping up and down in its happiness. Its demeanour, the way it was trying to express itself, seemed almost human. It went down to the water's edge, ready to jump into the boat.

'Look, a dog,' one of the men said. The dog began to whimper in a peculiar key—it was almost as though it was responding to the compassion in the man's voice.

'Let it be,' said the second man.

The dog whimpered, opened and closed its mouth, it seemed as though it was praying to the men to rescue it. It tried twice to jump into the boat, and was rebuffed both times. The boat began to move away from the house. The dog howled. It was heart-rending. One of the men looked back.

'Ayyooo....' The sound wasn't from either of the men but the dog.

'Ayyooo....' It was an exhausted, pitiful sound. It was almost as if the animal was bidding goodbye to the world.

The men did not look back again. The boat drew steadily away, and the dog remained where it was on the roof, watching it go. Its moaning and the expression on its face seemed to say that it would love human beings no more.

The boat disappeared from sight.

The dog lapped up some water, looked at some birds flying overhead. A water snake was borne along by the flood at great speed towards the hut. Startled, the dog retreated along the roof. The snake slipped into the opening in the thatch through which Chennan and his family had made their escape. The dog peered into the opening and began to bark furiously.

The barking gradually tapered away into a whimpering. It was a sound of lament, full of the hunger the animal hadn't been able to sate, its despair at the hopelessness of its situation, and its fear that it might not survive. What it was trying to express would have been clear to anyone—even to a man from Mars.

With nightfall, a storm picked up. The roof of the hut began to shake as waves battered against it. The dog nearly fell off—twice. A long, sinister head rose out of the dark water. The dog began to bark frantically when it saw the crocodile. From somewhere close by came the sound of chickens squawking.

Another boat came into view, heavily loaded with coconuts and bunches of bananas. It stopped beside a banana tree close to the hut.

'Where is that barking coming from? Hasn't the hut been vacated?' one of the men in the boat asked.

The dog turned towards the sound of the men's voices and began barking. As one of the men began to climb the banana tree, the dog's barking grew in fury and menace.

'Better watch out, that dog sounds really angry, it might bite you,' the man who had remained in the boat warned his companion who had climbed the tree. No sooner had he spoken than the dog leapt at the thief who was trying to steal Chennan's bananas. The man tumbled down into the water, the dog with him. The thief's companion pulled him into the boat, while the dog swam back to the rooftop. It clambered back on, and shook the water off its coat, barking furiously all the while. The thieves lopped all the bananas off the trees, and loaded them on to the boat.

The men goaded the angry animal on to even greater rage. 'Just you wait, we've got something to show you,' they said grimly.

They transferred as much hay as they could from Chennan's hayrick on to their boat. Then one of the men got on to the roof and advanced threateningly towards the dog. It attacked him immediately, and sank its teeth into his leg. Howling in agony, the man jumped back into the boat, while his companion took hold of an oar and brought it crashing down on the dog's head. The animal yelped, and retreated.

The man who had been bitten lay in the bottom of the boat tossing and turning in agony. As the boat receded into the distance, the dog sent it on its way with a volley of barks. It was close to midnight by then. An enormous bloated carcass of a cow drifted up to the house, and snagged on the roof. The dog kept an eye on the carcass. After a while, pushed by the current, the carcass began to move away slowly. Galvanized into activity, its tail wagging, grunting, the dog rushed down the roof to where the carcass was still within reach, and began tearing at the flesh, sating its terrible hunger. Just then, with a loud cracking noise, the entire carcass was dislodged from the roof, and the dog, which was eating from it, went with it. The carcass rolled over in the current, and the dog disappeared from view. Now one could only hear the sound of the wind, the cacophony of frogs, and the sibilant whisper of the waves. There was no other sound.

Those who still stood guard in some of the flooded homes could no longer hear the dog's piteous whining, or heart-rending moaning. Every so often, another bloated carcass of some drowned animal would float by on the flood. Crows fed on some of them. Everywhere you looked there was nothing but desolation. And the only people who thrived in this wilderness of water and destruction were thieves and looters.

The hut collapsed after a while, and sank out of sight. And the loyal animal, which had stood guard over its master's property for as long as it could, was gone as well. The crocodiles had it now. It was all over, the waters covered everything.

The flood receded slowly. One day, Chennan swam across to the spot where his hut had once stood, looking for his dog. Under one of the coconut trees, he saw the corpse of a dog, gently rocking in the eddies of the shallow water. Chennan turned it over with his foot to check if it was his dog, he thought it might be. One of the animal's ears was missing. You couldn't even tell what colour the dog was, for its skin had rotted and sloughed away.

THE SHROUD

MUNSHI PREMCHAND

Translated from the Hindi by Arshia Sattar

Outside the hut, father and son sat before the dying embers in silence. Inside, the son's young wife, Budhiya, was thrashing about in labour. Every now and then, a blood-curdling shriek emerged from her mouth and they felt their hearts stop. It was a winter night, the earth was sunk in silence, and the whole village had dissolved into the darkness.

Ghisu said, 'Looks like she's not going to make it. She's been like this all day. Go take a look.'

Madhav replied irritably, 'If she's going to die, why doesn't she do it quickly? What's the point of taking a look?'

'You're pretty harsh. You've had a good time with her all year, and now? Such callousness?'

'Well, I can't stand to see her suffer and thrash about like this.'

This clan of cobblers was notorious in the village. If Ghisu worked a day, he would rest for three. Madhav was such a shirker that if he worked for half an hour, he'd smoke dope for one. Which was why they were never hired. If there was even a fistful of grain in the house, they took it to mean they didn't have to work. When they'd been starving for a few days, Ghisu would climb a tree and break off some branches and Madhav would sell them in the bazaar. As long as the money lasted, they'd loaf around here and there. And when starvation hit them they would break off more branches or look for work. There was no shortage of work in the village, it was a village of farmers and there were at least fifty jobs for a hard-working man. But these two were called in only when you had to be satisfied with two men doing the work of one.

Had they been renunciants, they would have had no need to exercise control or practise discipline in order to experience contentment and fortitude. Theirs was an unusual existence—apart from a few mud pots, there were no material possessions in their house. They went on with their lives, covering their nakedness with rags, free of worldly cares, burdened with debt. They'd suffer abuse, they'd suffer blows, but they had not a care in the world. They were so wretched that even though there was no hope of being repaid, people always loaned them something. During the potato harvest, they'd pull up peas or potatoes from other people's fields, cook them in some fashion, and eat them. Or, they'd uproot a few stalks of sugar cane and suck on them at night. Ghisu had lived out sixty years with such supreme detachment and now Madhav, his worthy son, walked in his father's footsteps, determined to become even more illustrious.

At this moment, too, they were roasting potatoes, which they had dug up from someone else's field, in the embers. Ghisu's wife had died many years ago. Madhav had married only the previous year. After the woman had come, she had laid the foundations for some kind of discipline in the household and managed to fill those shameless stomachs. And since she'd arrived, the two had become even more inclined to relax and had even started acting pricey. If someone called them in to work, they'd ask for double wages without batting an eyelid. Today, that woman was dying in childbirth and it was quite likely the pair was waiting for her to die so that they could get a good night's sleep.

Ghisu pulled out a potato and, peeling it, he said, 'Go and see what's happening to her. There'll be the business of a witch, you can bet on it.'

Madhav was afraid that, if he went into the hut, Ghisu would grab a larger share of the potatoes. He said, 'I'm scared to go in there.'

'What's there to be scared of? I'm right here.'

'So, why don't you go and see, then?'

'When my wife was dying, I didn't move from her side for three days. This one, she'll be embarrassed in front of me, won't she? I've never even seen her face. Now to look at her uncovered body! She'll be uncomfortable. If she sees me, she won't be able to throw her arms and legs around so freely.'

'I'm wondering what will happen if there's a child—ginger, jaggery, oil—there's nothing in the house.'

'Everything will come when God is good and ready. This lot, who aren't giving us any money now, these same people will call us tomorrow and give us cash. I've had nine sons, there was never anything in the house, but God got us through the mess somehow.'

In a society where people who toil day and night are not much better off than these two, and instead of farmers it's those who exploit them that grow rich, it's no surprise that attitudes like this develop. Let's say that Ghisu was cleverer than the farmers, that instead of joining those simple-minded peasants, he'd joined the company of conmen. Of course, he did not have the capacity to follow that company's rules and regulations, which was why others of his ilk had become chiefs and headmen in the village while he remained the one at whom fingers were pointed. Still, he had the consolation that, however badly off he was, he didn't have to work as achingly hard as the others and that people could not take undue advantage of his simplicity and helplessness.

The two of them pulled out the potatoes and devoured them, hot as they were. They had eaten nothing since the previous day. They didn't even have the patience to let them cool so, every now and then, they scalded their tongues. When it was peeled, the outer part of the potato did not seem that hot but, as soon as it was bitten into, the inner part burned the tongue, the throat, and the palate. Instead of holding that burning coal in one's mouth, it seemed wiser to send it down as soon as possible so it could cool down in the stomach. That's why they were swallowing so quickly, although the effort made their eyes water.

Ghisu thought back to a landlord's wedding feast that he had been to twenty years ago. The contentment he had felt at that feast was worth remembering for a lifetime and, even today, the memory was fresh. He said, 'I'll never forget that meal. I've never eaten that kind of food—or that much of it—ever again. The girl's family fed everyone as many puris as they could eat. Everyone. The rich, the poor—everyone ate those puris. And they were made with pure ghee, mind you. Chutney, raita, three kinds of greens, one curried vegetable, curds—I can't tell you how delicious that food was. There was no holding back. Ask for whatever your heart desired; eat as much as you want. People ate and ate, so much that they couldn't even drink water. But those who were serving, they kept putting freshly cooked, perfectly round, fragrant kachoris on to our plates. We refused, we covered our plates with our hands, but they just kept serving! And when we were done, we even got paan and cardamom. I was in no shape to take the paan, I could barely stand. I went off immediately and wrapped myself in my blanket and lay down. That's how big-hearted he was, that landlord. Like an ocean!'

Madhav savoured those delicacies in his mind and said, 'No one gives us a meal like that now.'

'There's no one to feed us like that any more. That was a different time. Now everyone's counting pennies—don't spend on weddings, don't spend on religious festivals. Ask them, where will they stash all the money they take from the poor? There's no problem stashing the money, but when it comes to spending, then they think of thrift.'

'You must have eaten about twenty puris, no?'

'I ate more than twenty.'

'I would have eaten fifty.'

'I ate no less than fifty. I was pretty sturdy those days. You're not half of what I used to be.'

They ate the potatoes, drank some water, curled up, covered themselves with their dhotis and fell asleep right there by the embers, like two enormous pythons that had eaten their fill.

And still, Budhiya moaned.

In the morning, when Madhav looked inside the hut, his wife lay there, stone cold, flies buzzing around her face, her expressionless eyes rolled upwards. Her body was covered with dust, the child had died in her womb. Madhav ran to Ghisu. They started to wail loudly and beat their chests. The neighbours heard the weeping and wailing and came and, as was customary, began to console the two unfortunates. But this was not the time for full-throated lament, the shroud and the wood had to be considered. Money disappeared from that house like a piece of meat in a kite's nest. Father and son went, wailing, to the village landlord who could not stand the sight of them. He'd beaten them himself often enough, for stealing, for not showing up for work after they had promised to. He asked, 'What is it, Ghisua, why are you crying? I don't see you around much these days, seems like you don't want to live in this village any more.'

His eyes filled with tears, Ghisu touched his head to the ground and said, 'Master, I am ruined. Madhav's wife died last night. She suffered all night, master. The two of us sat by her side half the night, we gave her all the medicines we could. But she has abandoned us. And now there's no one to give us even a piece of bread, master. We've been destroyed, our home has been uprooted. I am your slave! There's no one but you—who will organize her funeral? Who else can I turn to except you?'

The landlord was a compassionate man but having pity on Ghisu was like trying to dye a black blanket. In his heart, he felt like saying, 'Get away from here! You don't come when you are called and now, when you need me, you come here and flatter me! Bastard! Rascal!' But this was not the moment for anger or for retribution. He tossed a reluctant two rupees at him but not a single word of consolation escaped his lips. He did not even look at Ghisu, as if he'd rid himself of a burden.

Once the landlord had given two rupees, how could the village merchants and traders have the courage to refuse? And Ghisu knew how to use the landlord's name to his advantage. Some gave two annas, others gave four. Within an hour, Ghisu had collected the healthy sum of five rupees. Grain came from one place, wood from another. In the afternoon, Ghisu and Madhav went off to the bazaar to buy the shroud. People began to cut bamboo poles and the soft-hearted women of the village would come and stare at the corpse and shed a few tears at Budhiya's misfortune.

What a sad custom, that the woman who didn't even have rags to cover her body while she was alive now needed a shroud. After all, the shroud burned with the body. And then what's left? If the same five rupees had come earlier, there might have been some medicine. Ghisu and Madhav were trying to gauge each other's thoughts. They wandered around the bazaar, from this cloth shop to the next. They looked at all kinds of fabric, from silk to cotton, but nothing seemed right. Eventually, it became evening. And who knows by what divine inspiration the pair landed up in front of a bar and, as if they'd planned it earlier, sauntered in. They stood around uncertainly for a while. Then Ghisu went up to the counter and said, 'Mister, give us a bottle.' Soon, snacks arrived and then some fried fish, and the two of them sat on the porch, drinking calmly. After knocking back a few rather quickly, their spirits rose.

Ghisu said, 'What's the point of the shroud? It only gets burned, it's not as if goes with her.'

Madhav looked at the sky, as if calling the gods to witness his innocence, and said, 'It's the way of the world. Otherwise, why would people spend thousands feeding Brahmins? Who knows whether you benefit in the other world? Rich people have money, let them blow it. What do we have to waste? But we're still answerable to others. They're sure to ask, "Where's the shroud?"'

Ghisu laughed. 'Let's say I dropped the money. That we looked and looked but could not find it anywhere. They won't believe a word, but the same lot will give again.'

Madhav also laughed at this unexpected good luck. He said, 'She was a good woman, poor thing. She's dead, but she's given us food and drink.'

More than half the bottle was gone. Ghisu ordered two rounds of puris and chutneys and pickles and liver. There was an eating place just in front of the bar. Madhav leapt across and brought all the food back on two leaf plates. Another one and a half rupees well spent. There was only a little change left. The two of them sat eating their puris, as grandly as if they were lions hunting in the jungle. They were not afraid of being responsible to anyone, nor did they worry about their reputations. They had conquered those virtues long ago.

Ghisu said philosophically, 'We're feeling good. She'll get some credit for that, won't she?'

Madhav bowed his head piously and said, 'Of course. Definitely. Lord, you are present in each of us, let her go to the highest of heavens. We're both blessing her from the bottom of our hearts. The meal we've had today! We've never eaten like this in our lives.'

A moment later, a tiny doubt rose in Madhav's mind. He said, 'We'll go there one day, too, won't we, Father?'

Ghisu ignored the naïve question. He wasn't going to ruin the pleasure of the moment with thoughts of the world beyond.

'She's there. If she asks us why we didn't provide her with a shroud, what are we going to say?'

'We'll say, go to hell!'

'She's sure to ask.'

'And you're sure that she's not going to have a shroud? You think I'm an ass? You think I've spent sixty years on earth just digging up grass? She'll have a shroud. And a finer one than this.'

Madhav was still doubtful. He said, 'Who's going to give it? You've spent all the money. And I'm the one she'll ask, I'm the one that married her.'

Hotly, Ghisu said, 'I'm telling you, she'll have a shroud. Why don't you trust me?'

'Why don't you tell me who's going to give it?'

'The same people who gave us this one! Though, this time, we're not going to see the cash.'

As the darkness deepened and the light of the stars grew brighter so the bar grew more radiant. Some sang, some prattled, some embraced their companions, some pressed a cup to their friends' lips. The atmosphere was heady, the air intoxicating. So many came here and got high on a single sip. More than the drink, it was the air that got them drunk. They came, drawn there by the drudgery of living and, for a short while, they forgot whether they were alive or dead. Or neither.

Meanwhile, father and son tippled away happily. Everyone was staring at them. How favoured by fortune they were—they had an entire bottle between them. Having eaten his fill, Madhav gave the leftover puris to a beggar who had been watching them with hungry eyes. And, for the first time in his life, he felt the pride, the pleasure, the exultation of giving.

Ghisu said, 'Here. Eat it all. And bless us! The one who earned this is dead. But your blessings will surely reach her. Bless her with every part of your being, this is hard-earned money.'

Madhav gazed up at the sky again and said, 'She'll go to heaven, Father. She'll be the queen of heaven!'

Ghisu stood up and, swimming as he was through waves of joy, said, 'Son, she's going to heaven. She never bothered anyone, never hassled anyone. She's fulfilled the biggest wish of our lives by dying. If she doesn't go to heaven, you think those fat cats will, those fellows who loot the poor with both hands and then bathe in the Ganga and make offerings of holy water in temples to wash off their sins?'

But this rush of piety soon passed, for impermanence is the essence of intoxication. Sadness and despair crept in. Madhav said, 'But, Father, she suffered a lot in her life. She endured so much before she died.' He covered his eyes with his hands and began to weep, shrieking more and more loudly.

Ghisu reassured him, 'Why are you crying, son? Be glad for her—she's been freed from this world of illusion, she's been released from the cage. She's the lucky one, she's already broken the bonds that tie us to the world.'

And then, they stood there, both of them, and started to sing loudly, 'Liar! Why do you lower your eyes, you liar?' They began to dance. They leaped, they jumped, they wriggled their hips, they even fell. They expressed emotion with their eyes, they acted out feelings and, finally, they surrendered to their drunkenness and slumped down in a heap.

STENCH OF KEROSENE
AMRITA PRITAM

Translated from the Punjabi by Khushwant Singh

Outside, a mare neighed. Guleri recognized the neighing and ran out of the house. The mare was from her parents' village. She put her head against its neck as if it were the door of her father's house.

Guleri's parents lived in Chamba. A few miles from her husband's village, which was on high ground, the road curved and descended steeply downhill. From this point one could see Chamba lying a long way away at one's feet. Whenever Guleri was homesick, she would take her husband Manak and go up to this point. She would see the homes of Chamba twinkling in the sunlight and would come back with her heart aglow with pride.

Once every year, after the harvest had been gathered in, Guleri was allowed to spend a few days with her parents. They sent a man to Lakarmandi to bring her back to Chamba. Two of her friends, who were also married to boys outside Chamba, came home at the same time of the year. The girls looked forward to this annual meeting when they spent many hours every day talking about their experiences, their joys and sorrows. They went about the streets together. Then there was the harvest festival. The girls would have new dresses made for the occasion. They would have their dupattas dyed, starched, and sprinkled with mica. They would buy glass bangles and silver earrings.

Guleri always counted the days to the harvest. When autumn breezes cleared the skies of the monsoon clouds she thought of little besides her home in Chamba. She went about her daily chores—fed the cattle, cooked food for her husband's parents, and then sat back to work out how long it would be before someone would come for her from her parents' village.

And now, once again, it was time for her annual visit. She caressed the mare joyfully, greeted her father's servant, Natu, and made ready to leave the next day.

Guleri did not have to put her excitement into words: the expression on her face was enough. Her husband, Manak, pulled at his chillum and closed his eyes. It seemed either as if he did not like the tobacco, or that he could not bear to face his wife.

'You will come to the fair at Chamba, won't you? Come even if it is only for the day,' she pleaded.

Manak put aside his chillum but did not reply.

'Why don't you answer me?' asked Guleri in a temper. 'Shall I tell you something?'

'I know what you are going to say: "I only go to my parents once in the year!" Well, you have never been stopped before.'

'Then why do you want to stop me this time?' she demanded.

'Just this time,' pleaded Manak.

'Your mother has not said anything. Why do you stand in my way?' Guleri was childishly stubborn.

'My mother....' Manak did not finish his sentence.

On the long-awaited morning, Guleri was ready long before dawn. She had no children and, therefore, no problem of either having to leave them with her husband's parents or taking them with her. Natu saddled the mare as she took leave of Manak's parents. They patted her head and blessed her.

'I will come with you for a part of the way,' said Manak.

Guleri was happy as they set out. Under her dupatta she hid Manak's flute.

After the village of Khajiar, the road descended steeply to Chamba. There Guleri took out the flute from beneath her dupatta and gave it to Manak. She took Manak's hand in hers and said, 'Come now, play your flute!' But Manak, lost in his thoughts, paid no heed. 'Why don't you play your flute?' asked Guleri coaxingly. Manak looked at her sadly. Then, putting the flute to his lips, he blew a strange anguished wail of sound.

'Guleri, do not go away,' he begged her. 'I ask you again, do not go this time.' He handed her back the flute, unable to continue.

'But why?' she asked. 'You come over on the day of the fair and we will return together. I promise you, I will not stay behind.'

Manak did not ask again.

They stopped by the roadside. Natu took the mare a few paces ahead to leave the couple alone. It crossed Manak's mind that it was at this time of year, seven years ago, that he and his friends had come on this very road to go to the harvest festival in Chamba. And it was at this fair that Manak had first seen Guleri and they had bartered their hearts to each other. Later, managing to meet alone, Manak remembered taking her hand and telling her, 'You are like unripe corn—full of milk.'

'Cattle go for unripe corn,' Guleri had replied, freeing her hand with a jerk. 'Human beings like it better roasted. If you want me, go and ask for my hand from my father.'

Amongst Manak's kinsmen it was customary to settle the bride price before the wedding. Manak was nervous because he did not know the price Guleri's father would demand from him. But Guleri's father was prosperous and had lived in cities. He had sworn that he would not take money for his daughter, but would give her to a worthy young man of a good family. Manak, he had decided, answered these requirements and very soon after, Guleri and Manak were married. Deep in memories, Manak was roused by Guleri's hand on his shoulder.

'What are you dreaming of?' she teased him.

Manak did not answer. The mare neighed impatiently and Guleri, thinking of the journey ahead of her, rose to leave. 'Do you know the bluebell wood a couple of miles from here?' she asked. 'It is said that anyone who goes through it becomes deaf.'

'Yes.'

'It seems to me that you have passed through the bluebell wood; you do not hear anything that I say.'

'You are right, Guleri. I cannot hear anything that you are saying to me,' replied Manak with a deep sigh.

Both of them looked at each other. Neither understood the other's thoughts.

'I will go now. You had better return home. You have come a long way,' said Guleri gently.

'You have walked all this distance. Better get on the mare,' replied Manak.

'Here, take your flute.'

'You take it with you.'

'Will you come and play it on the day of the fair?' asked Guleri with a smile. The sun shone in her eyes. Manak turned his face away. Guleri, perplexed, shrugged her shoulders and took the road to Chamba. Manak returned to his home.

Entering the house, he slumped listless on his charpai. 'You have been away a long time,' exclaimed his mother. 'Did you go all the way to Chamba?'

'Not all the way; only to the top of the hill,' Manak's voice was heavy.

'Why do you croak like an old woman?' asked his mother severely. 'Be a man.'

Manak wanted to retort, 'You are a woman; why don't you cry like one for a change!' But he remained silent.

Manak and Guleri had been married seven years, but she had not borne a child and Manak's mother had made a secret resolve: 'I will not let it go beyond the eighth year.'

This year, true to her decision, she had paid 500 rupees to get him a second wife and now, she had waited, as Manak knew, for the time when Guleri went to her parents' to bring in the new bride.

Obedient to his mother, and to custom, Manak's body responded to the new woman. But his heart was dead within him.

In the early hours of one morning, he was smoking his chillum when an old friend happened to pass by. 'Ho Bhavani, where are you going so early in the morning?'

Bhavani stopped. He had a small bundle on his shoulder: 'Nowhere in particular,' he replied evasively.

'You must be on your way to some place or the other,' exclaimed Manak. 'What about a smoke?'

Bhavani sat down on his haunches and took the chillum from Manak's hands. 'I am going to Chamba for the fair,' he replied at last.

Bhavani's words pierced through Manak's heart like a needle.

'Is the fair today?'

'It is the same day every year,' replied Bhavani drily.

'Don't you remember, we were in the same party seven years ago?' Bhavani did not say any more but Manak was conscious of the other man's rebuke and he felt uneasy. Bhavani put down the chillum and picked up his bundle. His flute was sticking out of the bundle. Bidding Manak farewell, he walked away. Manak's eyes remained on the flute till Bhavani disappeared from view.

Next afternoon, when Manak was in his fields he saw Bhavani coming back but deliberately he looked the other way. He did not want to talk to Bhavani or hear anything about the fair. But Bhavani came round the other side and sat down in front of Manak. His face was sad, lightless as a cinder.

'Guleri is dead,' said Bhavani in a flat voice.

'What?'

'When she heard of your second marriage, she soaked her clothes in kerosene and set fire to them.'

Manak, mute with pain, could only stare and feel his own life burning out.

∞

The days went by, Manak resumed his work in the fields, and ate his meals when they were given to him. But he was like a man dead, his face quite blank, his eyes empty.

'I am not his spouse,' complained his second wife. 'I am just someone he happened to marry.'

But quite soon she was pregnant and Manak's mother was well pleased with her new daughter-in-law. She told Manak about his wife's condition, but he looked as if he did not understand, and his eyes were still empty.

His mother encouraged her daughter-in-law to bear with her husband's moods for a few days. As soon as the child was born and placed in his father's lap, she said, Manak would change.

A son was duly born to Manak's wife; and his mother, rejoicing, bathed the boy, dressed him in fine clothes, and put him in Manak's lap. Manak stared at the newborn baby in his lap. He stared a long time, uncomprehending, his face as usual, expressionless. Then suddenly the blank eyes filled with horror, and Manak began to scream. 'Take him away!' he shrieked hysterically. 'Take him away! He stinks of kerosene.'

NAADAR SIR

SUNDARA RAMASWAMY

Translated from the Tamil by Malini Seshadri

These days I often remember Naadar Sir. I am getting to be quite old, and I have this nagging feeling that Death, which came by and snatched him up, actually brushed me too in passing and is now lurking somewhere nearby, biding its time. I have lost many loved ones over the years...relatives, friends. I have always been nagged by guilt for never visiting Naadar Sir, although he lived barely half an hour away. Yet, the thought that he was still there, living in the village, had given me some solace. Now it's just me, my loneliness, and memories of the past....

These events are from fifty years ago. I was in the tenth class in Sethu Parvathy Bai School. Our maths teacher was E. R. S. (our nickname for him was Kaaraboondhi). That month, thirteen students, including me, scored zero in the maths test. 'Good-for-nothing idiots! After this week I'll wash my hands off you fellows! Ekambara Naadar will take my place. From now on, he is the one who will have to put up with you fellows....' shouted E. R. S.

We started imagining this new teacher, creating mental images of this Naadar Sir. He will be riding a bicycle, said one of the boys. The rest of us couldn't believe this. Our teachers had always arrived walking and carrying an umbrella. In fact, it seemed they were incapable of walking except under an open umbrella. True, a few of the scrawnier teachers did arrive in jutkas. And S. P. Sir, with a huge bandage on his leg, like someone who had recently been wounded in war, would roll up in a cart drawn by a single bullock. He would crawl onto the veranda and then clamber into a chair with a great deal of effort. Wouldn't it be beneath the dignity of a schoolteacher to be pedalling a bicycle along the road? How come Naadar Sir didn't know this?

Naadar Sir entered the classroom. His appearance was comical.

Our mental images of the new teacher bore no resemblance to the real man. We had imagined cropped hair or a tuft; some sandal paste on his forehead, or a smear of sacred ash; a coat and the traditional panchakachham dhoti, or maybe a double-length dhoti; a turban; a watch on the inner wrist, or perhaps a pocket watch on a chain. A severe expression, wounding words, refusal to be satisfied even with high test scores. And the power to make us cower under his thumb.

As it was, the whole class burst into laughter the moment Naadar Sir entered. Even the girls giggled, covering their mouths with their hands, heads bent. It was as if someone who happened to be passing by on the street had inadvertently wandered in, unaware of the reputation of the premises into which he was trespassing. The hair on his head stood up like stubble. When he placed the thumb and forefinger of his right hand on either side of his forehead and pressed upwards, the stubbly hair would stand up straighter and then ripple forward when released. He seemed totally unaware of what a comical sight he presented. The pointed ends of his twisted moustache arched upwards, and Sir would try to get a glimpse of them by squinting his eyes inwards. Khadi dhoti, khadi jibba, rough rubber sandals. His bare wrist was a curious, unsettling sight. Instead of a pen in his pocket, he sported a pencil sharpened at both ends. (How often our teachers had whacked us for breaking a classroom taboo and doing exactly this!)

'Without any warning they've thrust the maths class on me,' Naadar Sir informed us. 'I've forgotten everything. So now I have to learn it first.' And he laughed.

We laughed too.

'Take out your maths notebook, ma,' he said, holding a hand out towards Vilasini who was in the front row.

His use of 'amma' to address a student sounded bizarre to us. It set off a fresh wave of laughter.

'So, the very sight of me amuses you all so much?' remarked Naadar Sir, joining in the laughter.

He turned the pages of the maths notebook one at a time. 'Enna de, each is more frightening than the last,' he remarked.

Laughter rose in billows and crashed against the four walls. Sir stood staring at us with a bemused expression.

'It's not all that difficult, Sir. You can easily work them out with some practice,' Nagarajan reassured him.

Sir observed Nagarajan's face closely. 'How many marks do you score in maths, thambi?' he asked.

'A hundred,' said Nagarajan.

'Always?'

'Yes, always.'

'He has never got less than hundred, Sir,' shouted Thirumalai.

'Then naturally you would find it easy,' said Sir.

We were beginning to feel a strange sensation, as if the whole class was being dissolved in some strange fluid.

'How many marks did you get when you were in the tenth class, Sir?' asked Chakrapani.

Now, this Chakrapani was the most cowardly fellow in the class. And yet, here he was asking Sir a bold question like this! Did a whole yuga somehow go by in an instant? The student was questioning the teacher about the marks he secured. And that too in Sethu Parvathy Bai School, where Headmaster Rajam Iyer, ruled with an iron fist!

'Too low to announce publicly,' said Sir.

Again the students laughed.

'I don't think I will start teaching maths today. I will tell you about some games instead. Tomorrow we will get started with maths.'

'But are we allowed to talk about games in class, Sir?' Seshan wanted to know.

'Nothing wrong with that. After all, sports are also a kind of education.'

He started talking to us about football. He spoke with great involvement and passion. As he went on, he seemed to forget he was in a classroom. His hands were waving about. He headed away an imaginary ball. As though it had rolled down the stairs and into the garden, he stared into emptiness. He scored goal after imaginary goal, kicking the invisible ball through the goalposts repeatedly, while we sat watching in tension, wondering if his khadi dhoti might get ripped in the process.

We students could not contain our excitement. 'Goal! Goal!' we yelled. Sir sidled towards the classroom door like a child, and peeped around the edge cautiously.

Upstairs, at the front of the building, was an imposing structure resting on a stone foundation supported by massive pillars—the Headmaster's room—

flaunting its grandeur and proclaiming its importance to the universe. On three sides, wide windows displayed sturdy curved grilles, each of them having dark green curtains. It even had a tall, wide, green bamboo screen just in front of the entrance door; placed so close to it in fact that one had to slide in sideways to enter.

Sir took in the scene outside our classroom door with a keen eye. Then he looked at us and smiled a mischievous smile.

'De, don't make such a noise. He will pluck out your eyes,' he said, pointing upwards in the direction of the Headmaster's office.

'We couldn't beat Carmel School in the football match, Sir,' said Govindan Kutty.

'Why, de, what's so special about them. Do they have horns growing on their heads or something?' Sir mimed the horns by holding the back of his right hand against his forehead and extending the forefinger and little finger upwards.

'What's needed is coaching. And a strong will to succeed,' he told us.

'Sir, do you think it's possible for us to defeat Carmel School?'

'De, any game requires intelligence and discipline. What do you boys have? Do you have the brains for it? Do you have physical strength? Discipline? Determination?' asked Sir.

Each of his questions fell like blows on our skulls.

'If you show us how, we will play beautifully, Sir,' said Vallinaayagam.

'You all have to get permission from above, de,' said Sir, pointing at the ceiling above which sat the Headmaster's room.

'We're scared, Sir,' shouted all the boys in one voice.

'If that's so, then go and find a game that cowards can play. Then we will see,' declared Sir.

It suddenly dawned on us that Sir was capable of anger. The bell rang. Sir waved at us and strode out briskly.

Naadar Sir had stirred our minds deeply. Time and again, we had been made to swallow humiliations. In a school full of teachers who saw red at the very mention of sports, how could we ever learn a game? We saw that we had lost all sense of pride and self-respect. That is what rankled the most in our hearts.

Every year, on the day before Christmas break began, a familiar humiliation would await us. Carmel School challenged us every year to a football match, because they had the competence and skill to play. But why did our Headmaster have to accept their invitation? That was the question for which none of us had an answer. We went to Kumaravel Sir and pleaded with him.

'Let's not accept the invitation this time, Sir. We can't stand the repeated humiliation.'

'How is that possible? Our school is the largest one in the whole of Thiruvithangur. The Rani Amma, out of affection, sends the silver cup to our school. Isn't it proper that we should present it to the winning team?' asked Kumaravel Sir.

'But does that mean we should accept and then lose dismally year after year just so that Carmel School can win the cup?'

'They play beautifully, they win the cup. You scrawny fellows...are you capable of playing at all?'

'We are not going to play this year, Sir,' we declared.

'The Headmaster has already announced your names on the noticeboard. Is there any among you who has the guts to defy him?' shouted Sir.

'We are too scared to tell him, Sir. Please tell him on our behalf,' we pleaded.

'If I do, he'll ask me "So, then will you take the silver cup home with you or what?"'

The next thing we knew, the date of the match had been announced.

'Sir, Sir, wha-a-t's this?' we protested to Kumaravel Sir.

'I will coach you fellows for three days, de. Enough?'

'But there's no ball, Sir.'

Kumaravel Sir was angry. His voice rose.

'Balls are there aplenty. But the room key is lost. The Headmaster has written to the Inspector's office in Thiruvananthapuram for permission to break the lock, but the wretched people there haven't bothered to reply. You fellows are not even smart enough to get a ball on loan from somewhere and you're standing here arguing.'

'The rival team has had five years of coaching. You're telling us you will give us three days of coaching, Sir. Year after year they come and score goal upon goal, and taunt us by shouting "One more, one more" each time they score.'

'De, I will tell you something and I want you fellows to listen carefully. Those who are good at studies cannot be good at games. And those who play sports well will be hopeless at studies. In the whole of Thiruvithangur, which school tops in academics? Our school!' declared Kumaravel.

We were stumped for a suitable response to this, so were momentarily silenced.

Kumaravel Sir continued: 'Look, I have an idea. Go stealthily to Carmel School, observe the coaching they're receiving there and learn the techniques, de. You fellows can't get anything done, but still you want to win. Hmmhh!'

The next day three of us set off on our quest. Me, Subramania Sarma, and Emanuel. The moment we entered Carmel School, we were confronted by five or six students. The very sight of them brought fear to our minds. Each of the boys was about a foot taller than any of us. We had to crane our necks to look at their faces. Their chests were so broad that their vests were in imminent danger of giving way. Big, muscled thighs like mature banana plant stems. Knees moulded in solid iron. They were wearing special boots. We had heard that the soles of these boots were studded with nails.

'Aren't you the fellows from the Keerathandu school?' demanded one of them who seemed to be their leader.

We remained silent.

'Did you come to watch our football coaching?' he asked. Sarcasm spread over his face and scorn dripped from his voice.

How did he know? Who could have revealed to this accursed fellow what was in our minds?

He cleared his throat. Then he made a pronouncement: 'I will tear you limb from limb. I will disconnect all your joints. Be wise and run away from here.'

Sarma and I looked at Emanuel. Emanuel had some acquaintance with boxing techniques. His face was flushed.

'Some day you will be at my mercy. Then you will find out what I am capable of,' retorted Emanuel.

'Oh, get lost, you son of a bitch!' responded the Carmel School fellow.

I tugged Emanuel's shirt gently. The three of us shuffled away.

The failure of our mission brought us further humiliation.

'You hopeless fellows…you can't get even the simplest task done. But you want to win the silver cup,' scolded Kumaravel Sir.

∞

There were six or seven football fields on our school grounds. They were the best in the whole of Thiruvithangur. We also had a lot of footballs.

But because the key to the storage room had been lost, we had not seen a football for a very long time.

We managed to borrow a football, and practised for three days. Even our Sanskrit teacher turned up one day to watch us at practice. He continuously twirled the tuft on his head as he watched us, like someone trying to unscrew the lid of a ghee pot. When we ran he would shout out, 'Careful! Careful! Don't fall and break an arm or leg!' It seemed even the teachers were beginning to empathize with us. Kumaravel Sir stayed with us the entire three days. Because of his blood pressure condition, he couldn't join us on the field. But he supplied instructions and admonitions aplenty. 'Slice kick...now tap...no, no, idiot, not there, kick it into the goal...the goal!' Joseph Sir also came by. He had received football coaching at Carmel School in his student days. His football exploits and his goal count were among his favourite talking points. And—surprise of surprises—even the Headmaster watched our training session. Except that he watched from the veranda. When we had finished our practice we went up to the Headmaster.

'You all played well,' said the Headmaster in English.

Grabbing the unexpected opportunity that had presented itself, we said, 'We need a ball, Sir.'

The headmaster turned to Joseph Sir. 'Tomorrow itself we should write a reminder letter to the Inspector about the locked room. Don't forget,' he said.

We had been instructed by Kumaravel Sir that each of us should eat a nendran banana before turning up for the evening match. He explained that this input was essential to ensure that we were able to kick the ball hard and well. So we bought a whole bunch of nendran bananas and ate two each before heading for the football field. Just abutting the field was a spacious raised area of ground. The peons Arunachalam and Chokkalingam were arranging chairs on it. The Sanskrit teacher, Joseph Sir, Kumaravel Sir, Malayalam teacher Unnikrishnan Nair, E. R. S. Veerabhadran Chettiar, Sivaramakrishna Iyer, R. L. Kesava Iyer, the Arabic teacher, Sarvottam Rao, Sivan Pillai, Pannirugai Perumal, Achamma Thomas, Kanthimathi Teacher... many of the teachers were there. Near the front gate of the school, the Carmel School team players were standing together in a bunch. They were in uniform outfits: blue shorts and yellow jerseys. As we watched them, their formidable combined strength seemed to leap across from where they stood, turning our insides to mush.

'Only ten minutes left for the game to start. Why are they still hanging around over there?' the Headmaster asked sternly.

'They will come only after Father Xavier arrives. He is their coach,' explained Kumaravel Sir.

'What a big hoo-haa,' remarked the Headmaster, frowning. A motorcycle was heard approaching. It came in through the front gate and onto the raised area, and stopped under the neem tree. From it alighted Father Xavier, the hem of his cassock billowing stylishly in the breeze. His slender frame darted rapidly towards the Headmaster. The latter was still in the process of raising his arms with the intention of greeting the visitor with folded palms, when the visitor grabbed the Headmaster's half-raised right hand and shook it heartily. The Carmel School team fell into line and walked in. The awesome discipline that emanated from the group further impressed us.

'Please be seated, Father,' invited the Headmaster. The two sat down next to each other. We team members stood next to each of them. The student leader we had encountered during our humiliating visit to Carmel School was present, his expression full of menace. But no way would he have the courage even to lay his little finger on us with our teachers watching.

'Shall we have the first whistle now?' asked Kumaravel Sir.

'Go ahead,' said the Headmaster.

The Carmel School fellow turned towards Father Xavier and asked, 'Father, how many goals would you like us to score?'

Father Xavier lifted his head slightly and asked, 'How many did we score last year?'

'Nine,' replied the team leader.

'Then let's make it the same this time also. No more and no less,' advised Father Xavier.

We looked at the Headmaster. We looked at our teachers. The Headmaster wore a sheepish smile. His lips twitched slightly as though a mosquito had settled on them. The rest of the teachers stood with heads bowed, whispering among themselves.

Eight goals were scored against us before half-time. In the interval, the Carmel School heroes opened a large leather suitcase and took out soft freshly-laundered towels, one each, and wiped their faces and hands. They took out juice bottles, flipped open their caps, and gulped down the coloured drinks. As for us, we only had a tin bucket of water. As we dipped a tin mug into the bucket and took turns drinking water, the Carmel team captain came over to us. He said, 'We will score our last goal exactly three minutes before the final whistle. You poor weaklings, don't run around too much and kill yourselves.' He sauntered away.

One must praise his commitment towards keeping his promises. When the game was over and we looked around, the Headmaster's chair was empty. So were all the other chairs. All the teachers had left. Even Kumaravel Sir was nowhere to be seen.

'We must destroy our school, flatten it,' fumed Emanuel. 'My heart won't know any peace till it is reduced to rubble.'

❦

One day in class, Naadar Sir showed us some photographs and certificates. Each photo featured a team he had represented in his college days; and in each photo, Sir held a trophy. One, particularly, which showed him standing next to the Rani and holding a huge cup, made us rub our eyes in disbelief. What a radiant smile on the Rani's face!

Sir said, 'This afternoon, at three o'clock, the H. M. has agreed to meet me. Whoever is interested in playing football, give me your names.'

'What are the requirements, Sir?' we asked him.

'Both legs should be normal, with no knock knees. You should be prepared to work hard. You should have a determination to succeed. Tell yourself, if we lose the match this year, our life is over right there and then on that field. Those of you who can do all this may submit your names.'

Sir arrived in front of the H. M.'s front door screen at 2.45 p.m. We were already waiting. Through the side of the screen, we could see that the blades of the ceiling fan were turning hesitantly, as though expecting a reprimand any moment. On the wall hung a large clock with no pendulum, its second hand twitching as it moved around its face. None of us had ever been inside the H. M.'s room before. Before long, our feet would tread its floor; and as we stood with hands respectfully clasped together, the full majesty of the room would disclose itself to us. The momentousness of the anticipated event evoked emotions in us that we could barely control.

At exactly three o'clock, a peremptory summons was heard: 'Ekambaram! Ekambaram!'

'Sir, sir,' said our Sir, as he inserted himself sideways through the narrow opening between screen and wall. Then, turning back to us for a moment, he warned, 'Not a word from any of you in there.'

The Headmaster said, 'Ekambaram, we must win the silver cup this year. I don't know what you will do or how you will do it, but it must be done. Money is not a constraint. I will stand behind you and support you all the way.'

'Sir, I have brought some photos and certificates to show you,' said Naadar Sir.

'I don't need to see any evidence. I know football means Ekambara Naadar and Ekambara Naadar means football. The whole of Thiruvithangur knows this.' Then, turning towards us, the Headmaster said, 'If you don't listen to sir and play the way he tells you to, I will break your legs.'

Naadar Sir turned his gaze towards us. 'They are all very fond of football, Sir,' he said. Then, he added: 'Sir, I have a request.'

'What is it?'

'If you look up an auspicious day for us, I will start the coaching on that day.'

'Auspicious…inauspicious…no such thing. Start right now, this very minute.' The Headmaster turned to us and asked, 'What do you have in the last period, da?'

'History.'

'Who's the teacher? Sarvottam Rao, right?'

'Yes.'

'I will talk to him. You boys run to the playing field, right now. If you lose the match this year, I won't allow any of you donkeys to take the exams.'

Naadar Sir strode unhurriedly along the veranda. We followed in his wake. We descended the big staircase. Sir came to a halt at a tiny room that stood near the foot of a ladder. He tugged at the padlock. Then Sir took a few steps back, ran forward, and delivered a mighty kick to the bottom of the door. The hasp of the latch shattered. 'Collect all the footballs and throw them out of the room, de,' said Sir. And that is what we did. Big and small, there were seventeen balls in all.

Naadar Sir's house was on the route from my home to school. Before sunrise every morning, Emanuel would come up to Saanthaan Chetty Circle and signal for me with a shrill whistle (which he managed to produce by inserting a couple of fingers in his mouth and blowing hard). Primed for his signal and raring to go, I would leap out. Sir would be standing at the door of his house in khaki shorts and a white vest. The moment he saw us approaching from a distance, he would descend his front steps and start jogging away slowly. This was our running practice. Once in a way he would turn back and look at us to see whether we were using the proper running technique he had taught us. 'Heads up!' he would shout.

By the time we reached the school playing field, seven or eight bicycles would already be parked under the neem tree. At least twenty boys would be present. Sir would join the game and play with us. Sometimes, to get a better view of our on-field performance, he would station himself at the goalmouth.

How that remarkable brain of his could itemize and codify every single movement made by every single one of us remains a mystery to which only God above holds the key. Once our practice session was over we would move over to the wide steps leading down to another field at a lower level. We would sit down on these steps in a neat row. Sir would stand in front of us and talk to us non-stop for half an hour; and during all that time he would keep tossing the ball between his hands. He explained every mistake that each of us had made, and he followed it up with instructions on how to avoid these. No scolding, no censure.

'It's not only the legs that come into play, de,' he said. 'Your whole body has to play. The eyes play, the brain plays, the ears play...everything must join in the game. And another thing. You must anticipate what will happen next. Your mind must work out the strategy...the angles, the approaches, in a split second. De, the ball is willing and ready to carry out your instructions. Finally, always keep some of your strength in reserve. Keep the opposition guessing about your capabilities.'

Solid, powerful words, flowed towards us in a stream from Naadar Sir.

From Christmas right up to the Pongal vacation we did not miss a single day of practice. Morning and evening. Plus training sessions three times during the week. Physical exercises, running. We ourselves couldn't believe how much we had improved. Our relationship with our physical selves was rapidly and noticeably growing more intimate, as was our relationship with the football itself. Sir was fond of saying that the ball was the most emotionally responsive creation of the Almighty. We were beginning to understand what he meant. But whenever we thought we had attained great heights in football, Sir would say, 'De, we have only now placed our feet on the first step. Don't become overconfident. There's still a long way to go.' As a team, we were beginning to instinctively understand one another without actually speaking, and this intimacy strengthened day by day. If one of us tackled an oncoming player and got possession of the ball, we could be sure that the appropriate person would be in place, ready to accept our pass, and take it forward to the danger zone near the goal. There another of us would be in just the right spot to send the ball into the goal with a well-directed header.

On one occasion, Seshan said, 'Sir, this game is not just a game.... It is something else, something more.' He couldn't quite explain what exactly he felt.

'A sport is like a gold mine. You can keep digging, layer after layer, deeper and deeper, and continue to take out treasure,' said Sir.

His words seemed to lend shape to our muddled thoughts.

Sir would invite several of the teachers to come and watch our evening practice sessions. The teachers were astonished at what they were witnessing. They were full of praise and encouragement for us. The Sanskrit teacher told Sir, 'Ekambaram, you have transformed these reedy fellows into the swift arrows of Lord Ram! This is truly some kind of magic.'

Because it was the twenty-fifth anniversary of the school, the Headmaster was busy with preparations for the silver anniversary celebrations. He had already decided to invite the Rani, and was going ahead with the necessary arrangements. On the auspicious occasion, our school team should receive the winner's trophy from the Rani's hands. What could give the school greater pride than reaching that pinnacle of glory?

The day of the football competition dawned! That afternoon, Naadar Sir asked us to assemble in one of the vacant classrooms, and started talking to us. We felt detached from our bodies, as though soon some spirit would possess us and we would be able to walk on fire. Sir continued to encourage us. 'Today, you are definitely going to win, de. I don't have even an iota of doubt about that,' he declared. 'Let me remind you again. Strength of mind is the most important thing. Never waver. Within five minutes of the start of the game you should score a goal. It is do or die.'

As we stepped on to the playing field, we had no worries at all about our bodies. We felt we were walking on air. Electricity was coursing through us, from the soles of our feet to the hair on our heads. If we lose, let me die here and now, said the mind.

Within three minutes of the commencement of the match, we scored our first goal. At that moment it felt as if all the things around us...

trees, buildings, people, even the sky...were leaping around wildly. Father Xavier, who had been sitting in a chair, jumped up, shouted something in English, and ran around the edge of the field. Our rivals were mere broken cobwebs in our path. They tried their utmost to somehow respond with a goal of their own. But they couldn't even get the ball to our half of the field. Their frantic efforts revealed their desperation. Our hearts were like cores of steel in our chests, and the vapours that emanated from them were overpowering, enfeebling our rivals. Every time their bodies brushed against ours in the course of play, we sensed their weakness.

During the half-time break, Sir was so overcome with emotion that he couldn't utter a word. His eyes were brimming. Stammering a little, he managed to say, 'You played well, de. But you must score one more goal. They mustn't wriggle away by somehow managing to score an equalizer.'

'We are sure we can score another goal, Sir,' said Emanuel.

Sir looked at our faces. It seemed to us that he was reassured by the confidence he read in our eyes.

In the fifth minute after resumption of play, we scored another goal.

The crowd erupted with a roar. Our teachers, oblivious to decorum and dignity, were prancing around in glee. Like small children, they clambered on to chairs and cheered. The Headmaster raised both hands and waved wildly. The moment the game was over, the Headmaster and the teachers rushed onto the field. Totally unembarrassed, they embraced each of us.

'Ekambaram, the entire credit goes to you,' shouted the Headmaster in English.

'The boys played well,' replied Sir.

From wherever they stood, our school students began chanting 'Jai to Ekambaram Sir! Jai to Ekambaram Sir!' The chanting group broke up, fell into line, and approached the field in a procession. Ekambara Sir looked at the Headmaster and at the teachers. Then, in a loud voice, he shouted, 'Jai to Sethu Parvathy Bai School!' But his words did not reach the students, and they continued with their chants praising Ekambara Sir.

That week, school inspectors came from Thiruvananthapuram. Our teachers had given us two or three days of preparation ahead of their arrival. The school was clean enough already; how could we make it even cleaner? The teachers went around looking for tiny bits of dust on window grilles and in the corners of the rooms, and asked us to wipe harder. In the evenings we tidied the garden beds and removed every weed. The black paint on the wooden fence of the garden was fresh enough, but the Headmaster decided it was not an auspicious colour. So we had to paint it green instead.

Our class teacher E. R. S. was in a state of great agitation that day. He told us that the inspectors would be visiting our class in the first period of the day, which happened to be English. But the bell rang after English class and they had not yet come. When they did come, Pannirugai Perumal's Tamil class was going on. None of the three inspectors knew any Tamil. One of them asked in English, 'Do you study Thiruvalluvar's *Thirukkural* properly?' 'Yes,' we chorused. We had exactly three kurals in our syllabus. 'Right,' said the inspectors, and walked away.

That afternoon, during Ekambara Sir's maths class, the three inspectors paid us another visit. Neither Sir nor we had anticipated that this would happen. Along with the inspectors, the Headmaster had also arrived.

'We have come to tell you a few things,' said an inspector, addressing Ekambara Sir. His tone was stern and disapproving.

'Why is it that all the students are scoring so poorly in maths?' asked the inspector.

'But that's not so, Sir,' said our teacher.

The third inspector was holding a large sheet of white paper. He placed it on the table and unfolded it. He continued to consult the contents of the paper as he spoke, 'Earlier there were seven students in this class who usually scored a centum; now there are only six.'

All three inspectors turned their gazes on Ekambara Sir. The Headmaster was staring at Ekambara Sir in total surprise.

'Earlier the average mark was fifty-four; it is now fifty-one,' added the inspector.

Sir was looking at the Headmaster, waiting for him to intercede. Nothing. Why was the Headmaster silent? Did he have nothing to say?

'Many of the students who were scoring above ninety are now managing not more than eighty-five marks.'

Sir stood silent, head bowed.

The first inspector told Ekambara Sir, 'You must do your job more responsibly and teach better.'

Sir raised his head. Humiliation was writ large on his face. The Headmaster was still silent. Why did he have nothing to say?

'We will give you two months of grace time. You must bring the students back to their previous level,' ordered the first Inspector.

Sir nodded.

After the Inspectors had left, Sir was not in a state of mind to conduct the class as usual.

'De, do you all think I don't do a good job of teaching you?' he asked us, in a pathetic tone of voice.

'No, no, Sir. You are teaching us well,' we said in unison.

Our attempt to reassure him seemed to have made him more despondent. He stood gazing at nothingness through the open window.

That whole day, Ekambara Sir was the topic of discussion among all the teachers. We heard that the Headmaster had sent for him that evening. He seems to have told our Sir, 'The Inspectors have written good reports about all the teachers except you. You are the only one who has received an adverse report.'

Hearing this, Ekambara Sir apparently asked the Headmaster, 'What is your own opinion of me, Sir?'

'When the Inspectors base their comments on some data, we have no choice but to accept it, Ekambaram,' was the Headmaster's response.

The school building was resplendent. Garlands of coloured lights, elaborate festoons of leaves and flowers, arches flanked by lush banana plant stems, not a speck of dust or dirt anywhere. A huge pandal had been put up on the football field. Inside, a wide dais had been erected. The Rani sat smiling in a chair on the dais. The Headmaster stood close to his chair. More than once the Rani had urged him to sit down, but still he stood, lost in his thoughts, unaware of his surroundings.

The items followed one another as per the agenda. Music competitions. Dances. Fancy dress competitions. Debates. Prize distribution to the children. Suddenly, the Rani turned to the Headmaster and asked in Malayalam, 'Where is Sri Ekambara Naadar?'

The Headmaster looked around here and there. 'Mr Ekambaram! Mr Ekambaram!' he called aloud. He spoke to the teachers seated in the front row. 'Where is Ekambaram?' he demanded sternly. The teachers looked around. Ekambara Sir was nowhere to be seen. The Headmaster spoke directly to E. R. S. Sir. 'I want Ekambaram here in the next one minute,' he ordered. E. R. S. Sir rushed over to where we were gathered. He told Emanuel, 'Go quickly on your cycle and fetch Sir.' When Emanuel got on his cycle, I clambered on too and sat behind him. 'Give the cycle to Sir and ask him to get here at once,' shouted E. R. S. Sir.

We entered Sir's home. He was lying shirtless on a coir rope cot.

'Sir, what's the matter?' asked Emanuel.

'Headache. That's why I couldn't come,' said Sir.

'Who will receive the trophy, Sir?'

'H. M. can receive it. Nothing wrong in that.'

'Sir, the Rani asked for you,' I told him.

'Oh, so she remembers me,' remarked Sir.

Emanuel's voice was all choked up when he pleaded again: 'Sir, without you there...how...?'

'Just study hard, de, that's the most important thing,' was Sir's response.

We both studied Sir's expression. His face looked different, wrapped in gloom. It was as if he was in his own world.

'Sir, even if not for anyone else, please come for our sake,' urged Emanuel.

New shadows danced across the doorway. We turned to look. Seshan, Vallinaayagam, Govindan Kutty, Manikandan...all of them were there. We could see more faces through the window. Disappointment was writ large across all their faces.

Sir's wife stood leaning against the kitchen doorway.

'You toiled day and night for the sake of these boys, and now they are asking you to come,' she told her husband.

Sir made no move to get up.

'Then we won't go either,' declared Emanuel.

Sir looked into our faces, one by one.

His wife went over, removed Sir's jibba from where it was hanging from a nail on the wall, and handed it to him.

Naadar Sir rose from the cot.

RATS

BHABENDRA NATH SAIKIA

Translated from the Assamese by Gayatri Bhattacharyya

All the women who lived in the huts rushed out. They tried to find out what exactly was happening. They behaved very much like a blind man resting with his cane propped up nearby does, when he suddenly hears some commotion. His first reaction is to seek out and grasp his cane, and only then does he try to find out the reason for the turmoil. Normally, these women did not bother to find out where their children were or what they were doing, their attitude being that they would turn up when hungry. So, they did not worry. But today, as soon as they became aware of the tumult and confusion, all the women ran out of their huts, frightened and anxious. They began to rush around, each one screaming out her children's names. One woman could see her son standing nearby but this did not calm her anxiety. She went up to where the boy stood, dragged him out of the crowd of onlookers, and clasped him tightly to her. Only when her son was safe in her arms did she try to find out the details of what had happened. Within two minutes more of the women had found their children, and the shrill voices that were screaming out their names stopped.

Only the voice of Moti's mother gradually got louder. And louder. Her high-pitched voice could be heard clearly over the tumultuous din created by the crowd. In the beginning, she had called out to her son, Moti, like the other mothers, and had run hither and thither looking for him. But, as time passed, and there was no sign of him, she grew more and more panicky. She started running around anxiously, calling out his name in distress.

His companions said that Moti had been with them right there.
'He was here?'
'Then where is he now?'
'Are you sure he was here?'
'Exactly where, where was he exactly?'

She went around asking every boy and every girl the questions in an agitated voice. She was hoping to hear that Moti might have strayed away without their knowing. But the children told her categorically that Moti had been right here with them—in the place that was now full of heavy sacks, two and a half maunds each.

The open place abutted a narrow lane leading to huge warehouses. The narrow road emerged from another slightly wider dirt road. A long wall of corrugated sheets, marking the compound of a soap company bordered one side of the narrow lane, and on the other side was this open space. A bit further on, this lane split up and spread out among the many large warehouses. These were the storehouses that fed thousands of people in the city. The relationship of these to the city was as vital as the relationship of a handsome youth to the horrible-looking entrails of his stomach. They were ugly, but inevitable and unavoidable. Numerous huge trucks roared into that narrow lane, carrying hundreds of tonnes of produce and food products. These they unloaded into the warehouses. Some of the empty trucks would then load up other consignments from the godowns to transport elsewhere. Most rickshaw drivers found it difficult to turn their small vehicles on this lane. The truck drivers alone knew what they had to conjure up as they manoeuvred their trucks within that cramped space. Sometimes, if one vehicle created chaos by not being driven with the requisite skill, there would be a traffic jam in the lane, and the filthy, stinking environment would be overwhelmed with the riotous shouting of drivers and their assistants.

The appearance and size of the drivers matched the size of their trucks. Indeed, it seemed as though the truck-building companies had taken the measurements of the drivers first, and then fitted the vehicles to suit their bodies! Their eyes were always red, perhaps due to driving through the night, or maybe because of something they had imbibed. As far as possible, these drivers preferred to sit comfortably and quietly in their seats and rest; it was the handymen, their assistants, who created noise and confusion. These handymen would sit on top of their loaded trucks, yelling at each other, trying to find out who was to blame for the roadblock. Sometimes, the traffic jam would continue for hours together. That narrow space would become overcrowded with trucks and vehicles lined up, one after the other, all the way up the main road. No one would agree to shift his own vehicle even a little bit to help break the jam. 'Why should I? Let them do what they like!' each driver would say. Each of them would leave his truck and go to spend his time in the tea shop nearby. Sometimes, the trucks would enter the lane at midnight, heavily loaded, but the warehouses opened their doors only in the morning. On such days, the area would become still more filthy and smelly and sometimes both drivers and handymen would sleep, like babies in their cradles, inside their trucks.

A peculiar thick, slimy green and black liquid covered about half of this open space. Originally, this was probably plain rainwater. But over time the liquid had got mixed with green moss, motor oil, and such other substances, and turned into this peculiar colour and consistency. When the small children got dirty playing, they cleaned themselves in this water.

The line of shacks built with bits of bamboo, straw, sacks, packing boxes, and so on, that stood on one side of the open space had been occupied in the past by a few daily wagers employed to load and unload the trucks. But now the owners of the warehouses employed labourers on a regular basis, and no one from these huts got those jobs. So, they had left. Now, there were women living here with their children. There were no men living here permanently, and the few men seen around, at times, were not the fathers of these children. Most of the women, except a few like Moti's mother, were old. Some of them went out in the morning to beg; two of them worked in the hotels nearby, cleaning rice and grinding spices; and one of them kept herself busy selling snacks of puffed rice mixed with salt, oil, onions, and chillies.

But it was the children who helped the women most in earning their daily bread. They spent almost the entire day on the roadside, armed with woven bamboo baskets of various sizes and shapes. When there was no serious work to be done, they spent their time playing, screaming, and crying. But when the empty trucks returned after unloading their consignments in the warehouses, and when they were held up due to a traffic jam, and were forced to stop right here, then these children immediately jumped onto the trucks. Quickly they swept the floor of the vehicles, put the sweepings into their bamboo baskets, and ran home to their mothers. When these sweepings were carefully cleaned, the women would be able to collect quite an amount of rice, lentils, and other commodities. The drivers and handymen were quite happy to let the children do the sweeping because their vehicles were cleaned in a trice. And the boys and girls were happy when there were traffic jams. If the traffic jams were long-drawn out, they were still happier, because they got time to sweep all the trucks, and every child got a chance to share in the spoils.

Each child had managed to obtain an iron rod, one end of which was sharpened. If loaded trucks happened to get held up in a traffic jam, children would jump onto the trucks and pierce the sacks with their rods. They would push their fingers through the holes made by the rods, and take out rice, lentils, sugar, and other such goods. If the handymen saw them and gave chase, they would laugh with great merriment and run away. But, after a little while, they would come scampering back again and fearlessly resume their work.

If the drivers and handymen happened to go to the tea shops, the children had a field day. They, therefore, prayed that there would be many more such jams. Whenever they saw two vehicles approaching from opposite directions, they would clap and shout, 'Come on, come on, get into a traffic jam!'

But today, there was no such big traffic snarl. What had happened was this: a truck was coming towards a godown heavily loaded with huge, plump sacks of rice. Another truck belonging to some cooperative store was leaving the godown loaded just as heavily with sacks of rice, lentils, sugar, flour, salt, and other food items. Both drivers were aware of the truck approaching from the opposite side but each hoped that the other would give way, allowing him to proceed. Therefore, neither of them stopped, and ultimately both vehicles came to a standstill facing each other. The two drivers started to quarrel and shout at each other. This went on for some time, and the children started yelling: 'Come on, come on, get into a jam!'

Normally, when only two trucks were involved, the drivers took advantage of the open space, and managed to use their skill to manoeuvre their vehicles past each other and go on their way. And indeed, after arguing for some time, the drivers did start to do just that. But they were both still rather angry, and saw no reason why they should give way to the other driver. After backing up just a little, with a huge roar and emitting a great deal of smoke, both vehicles again advanced. The children, seeing the situation, started screaming out their infernal refrain.

And the trucks did get into a jam. The trucker from the cooperative society did not give as much leeway as he could have; and the trucker carrying the sacks of rice was forced to move to his side of the road than he would have liked to. The vehicle, loaded very high with heavy sacks, slid off the road and into soft mud. It leaned dangerously to the left—and, in an instant, the tragedy had occurred. As the truck veered to the left, one by one, many of the sacks it was carrying toppled over heavily and fell to the ground. The children ran away in confusion from the scene of the accident. Moti screamed in terror, and tried to run, but a sack fell on top of him, and squashed him under it. Then another sack fell on top of that...then another and another....

A large crowd gathered to witness the accident. They started to look for Moti only after his mother had gone almost mad with anxiety and grief. One by one, the sacks were removed. At first, one of Moti's feet appeared. The foot looked quite normal and natural. But after the last sack had been removed, they all looked the other way. The only thing that could be seen was blood, a lot of blood. No one had the heart to even try to remember what the boy had looked like before the accident.

The police came. And for that day, all loading and unloading was stopped in the warehouses. It was getting darker anyway, and the trucks lined up on the main road to wait for daybreak. The women surrounded Moti's mother and consoled her while the police collected the boy's body and took it away to the police hospital.

Gradually, night fell. The two trucks that were involved in the accident were taken to the police station. The sacks of rice lay where they had fallen. A few loaded sacks had fallen from the other truck also, on the opposite side of the road, against the corrugated sheet wall. These were laden with salt and lentils.

Most of the children had become quiet and still, and were sitting despondently in the common courtyard, situated at the centre of their huddle of huts. The older ones occasionally talked quietly with each other. None of them could sleep much that night, and although they went to bed quite late, most of them woke up very early the next morning. Probably they had been awake since before dawn. The older ones came out at daybreak armed with their rods and bamboo baskets, and went up to the fallen sacks. They collected rice, salt, lentils, and sugar. But they were careful not to go near the sack covered with Moti's blood.

Later that morning, some labourers arrived, along with a few well-dressed men, and started removing the sacks under the supervision of the latter. It was not known which of these well-dressed persons took the decision, but it was noticed that two of the labourers took the blood-stained sack to Moti's mother's hut. She, who had spent the night sitting on her string cot, jumped up in distress, and cried out, 'No, no! I don't want it!' She clasped the sack, and started wailing in grief and in helplessness. The labourers leaned the blood-stained side of the sack against one of the hut's walls. When they let go of the sack, the weak wall trembled under the weight of the sack.

For quite a few days, Moti's mother continued to shout, 'Take it out, take it away. I do not want it!' The neighbouring women grieved for her, understanding her sorrow.

This woman had no parents. She had lived in her paternal uncle's house and helped with the cultivation of lentils and gram. A man had said he would marry her and had brought her here, but he was not a good man. After Moti was born, hearing of a drug smuggling operation, he had abandoned Moti and his mother and gone away to try to make some money working with drug smugglers. Moti's mother waited for a long time for him to return. The drivers and handymen who came to buy puffed rice snacks at the next hut would say to her, 'Stop hoping he will come back. He will never return. And what sort of woman are you, sitting here thinking of him, when there are so many other men here!' The others would laugh when they heard this, and Moti's mother would get angry.

True, she was a bit scared of living alone. But she was afraid, not of other people, but of herself. Indeed, sometimes the natural needs and instincts of her body and age troubled her greatly, and threatened to overwhelm her. But she had always been able to overcome these feelings by clasping Moti to her breast. If, somehow, she could manage to pass a few more years like this, she thought, she would approach the age of 'beggarhood'. She could then transform herself into a beggar by wearing dirty, torn clothes like the older beggar women. And even if she could not beg, it would not matter, as long as she had Moti with her. A son was a far more important possession than a husband! She just wanted the words, 'Ma, Ma', ringing in her ears always, that was all.

But this sudden loss, this loneliness, and the empty hut almost drove her mad. She would sit alone, staring at the heavy, full sack and quietly weep her heart out. As time passed, all she would do is sit still and silent all day, not even weeping. Some neighbour would sometimes bring her a little rice and lentils gathered from the sweepings, or from what they had got from begging. She would cook them, but leave them untouched. Sometimes, she did not even bother to cook. The handyman of the truck from which the sacks had fallen on Moti, often came to visit her. He would bring her a packet of sweets, jalebis and other sweets, too, from the nearby tea shop. But she would never talk to him.

More time passed. Moti's mother was always hungry. Some days the neighbours would not bring rice and lentils. Gradually, she started becoming tormented by hunger pangs. She had noticed as she lay on her string cot that some rats had started making holes in the sack leaning against the wall, and every morning, the floor near it would be strewn with a few grains of rice. Sometimes, her eyes would become moist as she swept away the grains of rice. One day, after lying for a long time on her cot, hungry and desperate, she slowly got up. She brought a bamboo tray and held it against the sack. Poking her finger through the hole made by the rats, she slowly teased out a little rice. The hole was small, and it took a long time to collect enough for one meal.

The hole in the sack got bigger with the constant poking of her fingers. Or perhaps the rats themselves had made it larger. Whatever the reason, after a few days there was quite a lot of rice strewn on the floor. Moti's mother did not like the idea of rats spoiling the rice, so she folded a piece of torn cloth, and placed it over the sack, and placed her bamboo tray against the sack so that it pressed against the hole. Later, she took to getting up whenever she heard a scraping sound. Maybe the rats had made another hole in the sack?

Sometimes the handyman would come and say to her, 'How can anyone eat only rice? Let me get you some lentils or something.' But she would refuse.

In time, the sack became lighter and thinner. It was becoming difficult to bring out much rice with her fingers, even though the hole had become much wider. After some time, Moti's mother could put her entire hand through the hole. Then, after some more time had passed, she found that she could find no rice even after pushing her arm in, right up to her elbow. Whatever rice was still there had become embedded in the stitching of the sack.

One morning, Moti's mother undid the stitches at the top of the sack, and, holding it upside down on the floor, gave it a few good shakes. She was able to collect sufficient rice for the night meal. She swept up the grains, and putting the rice in her bamboo tray, cleaned it properly. She then put the sack out in the sun. The side of the sack which had been leaning for such a long time against the wall now fell flat on the ground. In the evening, she took the sack, shook it out, and placed it on her cot.

After eating her meal that night, she lay down on the cot. It had become quite chilly, and Moti's mother always felt cold at night. In past winters, Moti used to curl up to her in bed, and she had not felt the chill. Today, too, she did not feel the cold seeping in from below because of the warmth of the piece of sacking. As she lay there feeling warm and comfortable, she felt something gnawing at her. It was as if the rats were biting her. She felt at the instant that if the handyman came to her and asked if he could get her 'lentils or something', perhaps she would say, 'Yes. Bring me some.'

If not for herself, at least for the sake of the Moti who would come along in the future.

KALLURI'S RADIO

VILAS SARANG

Translated from the Marathi by Shanta Gokhale

Jattu did not know what to do with himself after Kalluri left. He would slip away from home, making sure his mother did not see him, and loaf around the village. He would fling stones at trees to knock down fruits or birds. The other boys in the village would do chores for their mothers. Occasionally, Jattu's mother, Illha would ask him, too, to do something and shout at him. But he paid her no heed. Jattu's father had died four years earlier. People said with no father, there was nobody to control Jattu.

Jattu often walked to the end of the village. There was a huge rock out there. He would sit on it for hours, his back to the village, looking out into the distance. The slope below him was bare, then came a hill and trees and bushes. There was nothing anywhere that could be called a path. Hardly anybody came to the village or went out. So who would make a path? Once a year an itinerant trader would come, walking beside a donkey laden with goods. He would exchange oil, salt, sugar, cloth, and stuff like that for grain. Nobody else came or went. So all you did was point and say that is the way out of the village. Jattu would sit looking at the hill that stood in that direction. Beyond the hill lay the world. Nobody knew how far away it was, or how many days it would take to get there. Behind the village, in the opposite direction, stood a tall hill covered with dense vegetation. Nobody had ever gone that way.

Jattu often wondered whether Kalluri would ever come back. When he was in the village, Jattu would be around him all the time. Kalluri knew things that nobody else in the village knew.

He knew of things that grew underground. He knew about birds' eggs. He could tell stories about gods and ghosts. Jattu found them particularly mesmerizing.

The villagers said Kalluri would never return. To reach the world from the village was a difficult thing. Once out there, to get back was even more difficult. But one day when Jattu was on his way to the stream to fetch water, he heard that Kalluri was back. Abandoning his water pot, Jattu raced towards Kalluri's hut.

Kalluri smiled at him. Jattu was his favourite. Kalluri had always been thin. He looked even thinner now. His dark skin had grown darker and drier. But his movements were as brisk as ever. And his eyes still shone. Jattu began bombarding him with questions one after the other. He asked if Kalluri had seen vehicles that moved automatically. He asked if he had seen that thing of many linked compartments that ran over iron rails belching smoke. Soon Jattu realized that Kalluri was not giving clear answers to his questions. He was fobbing off questions about where he had been, how he had got there, what he had seen. Kalluri had always been secretive. He was even more so now.

Soon people from the village began to gather around. Many were disappointed to see how little Kalluri had brought back. The general opinion in the village was that Kalluri lacked common sense. Just then Illha came shouting, carrying the water pot Jattu had left behind. Jattu got up with a grimace. As he left, Kalluri whispered in his ear, 'Come in the morning. I'll show you something.'

Jattu could not sleep that night. He was tormented by the thought of what Kalluri was going to show him. As soon as day broke, he ran to Kalluri's hut.

Kalluri pulled a thing out from the bottom of his bundle. He held the thing before Jattu. His teeth shone bright.

Jattu took the thing. It was a black box nestled in a black leather case. Jattu held it up to his eyes. It was a small box, about a span long and half a span tall. He ran his hand over the case. This is not leather, he said to himself. It looks like leather but it is something else. The false leather case did not cover the front of the box. If you flicked your nail on the uncovered part, it made a hollow tiktik sound. It was clearly not metal. Perhaps it was some metal that he had not seen. A transparent band ran across the face of the box. A nail flicked on it produced an unfamiliar sound. It was not glass. Jattu thought the whole thing was strange. Something that looked like leather but was not leather. Something that looked like metal but was not metal. Something that looked like glass but was not glass. Behind the false glass band there were a whole lot of marks crowded together. The box was punctured on one side and fitted with two discs. Jattu decided they were there to help open the box. He dug his fingers behind them and tried to open the box. It would not open.

'How do you open this thing?' he asked.

Kalluri took the box from his hands and said, 'It's not meant to be opened.' Then he twirled one disc. Jattu noticed that twirling the disc made a vertical white line behind the transparent band move. Instantly the box was filled with a crackling sound, and soon after by what sounded like speech. Kalluri stopped twirling the disc. The white line stopped travelling, but the speaking did not. Jattu listened in wonder.

To begin with, Jattu thought the speech was in some unknown language. But then he began to recognize some words. As he continued to listen attentively, he heard more words that were familiar. It occurred to him then that the speaker was speaking in Jattu's language but with a different accent and pronunciation, using several unfamiliar words. It was impossible to make out what he was saying. Jattu asked Kalluri. Kalluri could understand the speech a little better than Jattu. But that did not help him understand what the speaker was talking about. And so the two sat listening to something they could not understand.

A long time passed. Then the voice in the box changed. The first voice stopped and a woman's voice took its place. Jattu found it sweet. No woman in the village had a voice like that. The woman spoke briefly and then a song began to play. Jattu leaned forward to hear better. He thought he understood more words in the song than he had in the speech. The song was beautiful, enchanting. It was so different from any song he had heard in the village, even during festivals. The instrumental accompaniment was equally wondrous. Jattu could make out the familiar sound of the big drum. But the other sounds were quite unrecognizable.

After that Jattu began to spend practically the whole day in Kalluri's hut. News of the talking box had spread through the village. Villagers came in ones and twos, listened for a while, and went away. A handful would come after work in the evening and sit listening. Initially, like Jattu, they understood little of what was said. But gradually they began to understand more.

Two places in the talking box produced speech. When the white line travelled left, it hit one spot. When it travelled right, it hit the other. Kalluri discussed this with a few visitors. They realized that the voices spoke in a distant place and entered the box by magic. What flummoxed them was whether the two voices at the two ends of the box came from the same place or from different places. Voices from both sides spoke the same language, but the villagers found that they felt closer to the voices that came from the left. They were clearer and easier to understand than the ones that came from the right. Generally, people preferred listening to the voices talking and singing on the left.

One day, old Itanna came to listen. Many years ago, Itanna had gone away from the village and returned after a long time. He revealed that the two voices came from two different places. The voice from the right belonged to Astipur, the capital of our country. The voice from the left belonged to Hakimabad, the capital of neighbouring Shufristan. Others present instantly objected, saying that the voice from the left was clearer and sounded closer to how we spoke. How could it come from another country? Surely, the voice from our capital city would be clearer? To this Itanna said our village was on the very border of Khaurdesh, our country, and was nearer to Shufristan. Their territory started just beyond the hill at the back of our village. Shufristan was a small country. That's why its capital was nearer to us than our own capital. Naturally, the language we spoke was closer to theirs and we could hear the voice from there more clearly.

People had nothing to say to Itanna's clarification because nobody knew enough about these things to challenge him. Indeed nobody knew the names of either Shufristan's capital or their own.

A young man named Komva said, 'I always thought different countries spoke different languages. They are two different countries because their languages are different. That sounds right. If our Khaurdesh and Shufristan speak the same language, why should they be two separate countries? Wouldn't it be more convenient to make one country of places where the same language is spoken?'

Old Itanna laughed and said, 'In a way you're right. But these things are not so simple. It is difficult for backward people like us to understand how educated, developed people think.' After a pause, he said, 'I'll tell you something stranger than that. The languages spoken in our Khaurdesh and Shufristan are the same, isn't it? But we call our language Khaur and they call theirs Rufidi. Now, tell me, would you believe that?'

At this the gathering laughed as though to say, 'What a strange world this is.'

Gradually the village got used to the talking box. Jattu now knew at what time of day the box played songs. He would arrive at exactly that time. Like him, others in the village also found the talking boring. Only a couple of them would drop in once in a while and listen to it with thoughtful expressions.

One day, Kalluri showed Jattu a little secret about the talking box. He removed a plate at the back. Out came two red cylindrical objects. Jattu felt them in the palm of his hand. They were small but heavy. Kalluri demonstrated that when they were out, the box stopped talking. You could move the white line inside the transparent band as much as you liked, there would be no sound. But the minute you popped the cylinders in, the box began to talk. Jattu was surprised and curious. Kalluri said, 'The magic of the box is in these cylinders.' Feeling the cylinders, he said, 'A man's manhood is in his marbles. That's how it is with the box. Take them out and the box is neutered. It's like what we do. We pick smooth stones from the riverbank, smear them with paint, and turn them into gods. So someone who knows mantras has painted these cylinders and put a powerful spell on them. Nobody in our village has so much knowledge of spells as to be able to make a box like this. This mantra scholar from the big world must be a powerful man indeed.'

Kalluri stared at the box with wide-open eyes. He had some knowledge of spells and charms. He had occasionally been able to heal some villagers of their illness. Jattu was watching him, wondering whether Kalluri was asking himself how he could acquire this powerful knowledge of spells.

Although the sound from the left side of the box was clearer, Jattu preferred the right side. The left produced mostly talk, and little song. The right played a lot of songs. Meanwhile Kalluri had found something else that was even more engrossing. If you brought the white line just a little this side or that side of the point where you could hear talk clearly, the box made peculiar sounds—whistling sounds and gibberish. Jattu found those sounds amusing to begin with, but then they bored him. With Kalluri the opposite happened. He got more and more drawn towards those sounds. When he was alone, he listened to those sounds, not songs, and was overwhelmed by them.

Kalluri wondered now where those sounds came from. They did not come from this or that city. They were not human sounds. They sounded more like the sounds that the villager Turakkal made when he was possessed. A thought struck Kalluri. There was a burial ground between two hills at the back of the village.

Generations of villagers had been buried there. Kalluri would occasionally visit this place of earth mounds with large and small stones placed on them, aiming to explore the world of charms and spells. He recalled that the sounds from the box were quite like the sounds he heard there, whistling and gibberish. Those were the sounds that the dead and supernatural creatures made. It was clear to him that there was a connection between the sounds that came from the box and from the dead souls and supernatural spirits of the burial ground.

To sit listening to these sounds became a daily practice with Kalluri. These sounds did not come regularly as did the voices from the right and left in the box. There were times when you could hear them, times when you could not. Times when they came loud and clear, times when they came faintly in little bursts. After all, they were made by ghouls and spirits who were not bound to a fixed timetable. They began their gibberish when the mood took them. Kalluri discovered something else. Whereas the voices from right and left in the box would fall silent after a certain time at night, these sounds continued through the night. In fact their volume increased at night. There was nothing surprising about that. Nights were their very own time for spirits. When human beings quit the box and went home to sleep, ghouls took charge of it. The more he listened to their gibberish, the more Kalluri was convinced that it was a proper language. He recognized certain recurrent sounds. Kalluri was certain that if he could only connect the sounds in their syntax and structures, he would begin to understand the language. Kalluri's blood ran fast to think of the enormous treasure he would be the master of if that happened. He began to listen to the sounds with even greater concentration now and grew restless when he could not hear them.

Then the rains came. One day, the sky was densely overcast. Lightning flashed along the horizon. The ghoulish voices in the box grew in volume, speed, and frequency. Kalluri thought the spirits must have descended to the lower clouds because the upper sky had become stormy. And now they were chattering frenziedly. Kalluri listened to them with his heart and

...ind in his ears. After days of listening, he had begun to feel he stood on the very threshold of understanding the language. He had become familiar with the stresses and cadences of the language. One of these days, without warning, the riddle would be solved. Right now the spirits that have gathered below the stormy sky are chattering at the tops of their voices trying to tell me something; and here I am, a miserable wretch, unable to understand what it is.

As he sat listening, his despair grew. Tears gathered in his eyes. Holding the talking box in both his hands, he stared through the door of his hut at the world outside. A clap of thunder burst through the sky and the first showers came. The constant clatter of the pouring rain blocked all other sounds. Kalluri could barely hear the chattering in the box. He twirled the disc and shut them off. He put the box aside. He rose and stepped out of the hut. Standing in the rain, he spread his empty hands wide, getting drenched.

All through the season of rains the voices of the spirits continued to chatter in the box. It was the other voices, both from the right and left, that made listening difficult. The voices of the spirits appeared to have dominated and defeated human voices. Jattu could not hear the songs clearly and lost interest in the box. To make matters worse, Kalluri was so engrossed in the chattering sounds that he had become oblivious to everything else. He had withdrawn into his own world. He hardly ate or drank. His face had begun to look drawn. His eyes had changed. Forget talking to others, he barely talked to Jattu. Jattu stopped going to his hut.

The rains came to an end. The weather grew cooler. As was his practice during this season, the old trader arrived in the village with his donkey laden with goods. Along with salt and sugar, he would also bring colourful beads. The village women were very keen on them. But he did not bring them this year. The reason he gave was this: 'I used to buy the beads from a town in Shufristan called Tasariya. Earlier you could cross these mountains and enter the town whenever you pleased. We were free to cross the border as and when we liked. But this year I found soldiers posted at the border. They stop you from crossing the border. They even patrol the mountains.'

The story of Kalluri's talking box reached the trader's ears. He went over to see it. After the rains the voices of the spirits had grown faint. Kalluri was busy twirling the disc back and forth to see if he could locate them anywhere at all. But the white line produced no sounds till it reached the place on the left from where human voices came. The trader looked at the box and said, 'This is called a radio. So you are listening to speeches from Hakimabad, I see. These days people from our towns and cities don't listen to programmes from Hakimabad. Our government doesn't like it. But that shouldn't affect you in this remote place.'

One day after the trader had left, Jattu went over to see Kalluri. He saw him looking very worried. He started the box; but however frantically he twirled the disc, all they heard were faint voices. Kalluri said the force of the spell was wearing out. The box was dying.

As days passed, the force of the spell became weaker and the voices progressively fainter. Kalluri grieved. The box was losing its life before his eyes. He saw clearly that those otherworldly voices too would soon fall silent forever. He felt completely helpless and took to sitting around the hut despondently.

These days Jattu, rather than go to Kalluri's, would loaf around and sometimes sit on the rock at the edge of the village. One of those days, when he was sitting on the rock, he saw men in the distance approaching the village. He was thunderstruck. Men coming to the village was nothing less than a miracle. He narrowed his eyes and looked. The men were coming on horseback. They were all dressed in khaki and each one carried something on his shoulder that looked like a metal pipe. Jattu watched them till they were halfway up. Then he leapt off the rock and raced to the village.

The villagers were surprised to see the men, policemen or soldiers whatever they were. Very seldom would they come, once every five or six years. Now their leader asked a question. Nobody understood it. Then a man from the back stepped forward and asked the question another way. They were looking for the man who owned the talking box. The villagers took them to Kalluri's hut.

The soldiers dismounted. Kalluri was led out of the hut. The soldiers' leader looked boyish and had the face of a rich man. He took the talking box from Kalluri's hands and turned it around this way and that. 'This radio has been made in a communist country,' he said to one of his companions. 'Naturally, we don't import this make. He obviously bought it in Shufristan.'

Then he began to question Kalluri. Where had he gone last year? What had he done there? Kalluri decided that they suspected him of listening to otherworldly voices in the talking box. They must expect him to have amassed an enormous amount of spell power. It would therefore be prudent to hide the fact that he had been listening to those voices. 'Oh no. I wasn't listening to the spirits' voices at all. I would listen to the voices coming from here,' he said, pointing to the white line which was standing on the left side.

The soldiers' leader proceeded to ask him questions about what he had heard from there. Turning to some of his men in the back he directed them to ask around the village what they had heard over the radio. Three or four soldiers began to question the men in the village. They returned half an hour later to report that the villagers did not appear to have heard any propaganda from Shufristan. 'The people are quite stupid. They don't seem to have understood a thing of what they heard.'

'They could well be ignorant and stupid. But we have to act with caution. Shufristan is infiltrating these parts.'

He then ordered all able-bodied men in the village to be rounded up. They were brought to an open space. The soldiers mounted their horses and the leader began to address the villagers.

'People of the Urufikal Valley. Do not forget that you are citizens of Khaurdesh.' Waving Kalluri's radio before them, he said, 'If you hear anything on this radio or on any other brought here by anyone else, do not believe what you hear. Shufristan has been carrying out a vitriolic propaganda against our nation. Oil has been discovered in these mountains.' He swept his arm over the range behind the village. 'This is a great treasure bestowed on our nation. This place which has been neglected till now, will soon be developed. Shufristan had never said a thing about this territory until now. But suddenly, since oil was discovered here, they have raised their voice claiming that this entire territory that belongs to our native tribals, actually belongs to them. They say they want to reclaim it. They have been carrying out this propaganda consistently over the Hakimabad radio station. They are trying to incite you. They promise to liberate you. It is nothing but a sham. They call themselves socialists, champions of the poor. But, in fact, they are a ruthless dictatorship. Your radiant future lies in Khaurdesh and nowhere else. Jai Khaurdesh!'

'Jai Khaurdesh,' the soldiers chorused after him. Some villagers tried to join the chorus. Nobody had followed much of what the soldiers' leader had said. But none of them said anything about it. Women and children sat in a circle around the group of men in the centre. Jattu was standing among them looking first at the mounted leader and then at Kalluri.

The soldiers now got ready to leave. Kalluri was hoisted onto one of the horses. The village children ran behind the horsemen for a while, shouting. Jattu was among them. Then the others fell behind and Jattu continued to run behind the horsemen alone. He stared at Kalluri as he ran, but not once did Kalluri turn around to look at him. He sat erect on the horse, staring into space.

The soldiers were almost at the village border. The leader dipped into his pocket and pulled out the radio. Holding it out to one of his men he said, 'Keep this with you.'

The soldier took the radio, looked at it carefully, twirled the disc, held it up to his ear, and said, 'The battery is practically down.'

Then he opened the lid at the back and removed both its battery cells. He glanced at them once and threw them away. He shut the lid and put the radio away in his knapsack.

Jattu stopped in his tracks. He stared after the horsemen as they trotted further and further away. Soon they had gone past the rock at the village border and left the village. He saw their figures as they descended the hill and their smaller figures as they came up the hill on the other side. Then the hill rose between them and him. Their heads had dipped below the hilltop. Jattu moved quickly then. He stepped forward and picked up the two cells that lay gleaming in the grass. Grasping them tight in his hands, he raced home.

THE GOLD COIN
LAXMANRAO SARDESSAI

Translated from the Portuguese by Paul Melo e Castro

FIFTY YEARS AGO

Before leaving home, Narain Rao stepped into the deva kood, knelt before an image of the goddess, Shantadurga, and began to pray. Lakshmibai, his wife, joined him in his devotions and implored with pious fervour: 'Shantadurga Devi! At least this time allow us to succeed. Give us the strength not to give in....'

After their prayers, Narain Rao opened a cupboard and retrieved the mohar, the family coin, from a jewellery box. With great reverence he held it up to the light. It had belonged to his glorious ancestors, who had inherited that gold coin, the symbol of a magnanimous tradition sanctified by hundreds of blessed hands.

His father, before breathing his last, had summoned him to his bedside. Placing the gold coin in Narain Rao's hand, he murmured solemnly: 'Here is the family Lakshmi. No emergency will ever deprive you of it.' These were the venerable old man's final words.

As Narain Rao crossed the threshold of their home he cast a compassionate glance behind him at his dear wife, the only ray of light in the murk surrounding him.

It was at her urging that Narain Rao had decided to visit the noble Purxottam-bab, estimable representative of the Quencró family, whose son he coveted as a son-in-law.

That same day, at dawn, Lakshmibai had whispered in his ear, 'Last night our goddess appeared in my dreams and gave this advice: go to

Purxottam-bab and your wish will be granted.'

IN SEARCH OF A GROOM

Moved by the iron faith of his trustful wife, Narain Rao yielded to her entreaties. He knew that his task was not an easy one. Over the previous four months, he had called upon a dozen noble families. Each had rejected him. Their excuses were varied, but behind them all lay his poverty. Twenty-five years earlier the maidens of his house had been sought in marriage by all the wealthy men of the district. Today, his fate was to wander from house to house in search of a groom for his gracious daughter, Tulsi. But where would he find the dowry? Nothing remained of their past opulence but the thick walls of their house. Yet his family's traditional nobility had set thorns in his path. His household received many visitors and guests and often he and his family went without in order to feed them. That was the order of the day. In honour of the meritorious past of his forebears, no one left dissatisfied. And this was enough for Narain Rao to offer up thanks to his patron goddess.

Purxottam-bab was held to be a singular man, for whom the material things of life counted less than humanity. His generous hands had silently eased the pain of many people. This trait was a beacon of hope to the desolate Narain Rao.

Just then Tulsi approached her father. What a lovely creature she was! Her eyes like altar lamps, her brow so gentle and innocent. Only twelve springs old but shimmering with life. It glowed through her simple dress. Yet, for this tiny, precious being, how many difficulties must her father surmount? Her appearance alone dispelled the shadows, infused the very light with new splendour, sparked endless bliss, lent purity to glory itself. How anxious he was to offer this precious girl's hand to a noble and worthy young man. But the prestige of a family is measured by its wealth. No sooner does poverty peek out than scandal flourishes. Were another year to pass without his daughter's marriage, ill-intentioned tongues would begin to wag.

But how had they ended up in this woeful situation? Neither they nor their forebears had been libertines, sinners, or reprobates. Yet the noble character of the family had led, little by little, to their material decline.

Before leaving the house, Narain Rao caressed his daughter's cheek and asked, 'My dear! Do you also want to leave this house?' Then he trudged down the steps with a pained heart.

Lakshmibai looked on in sad silence at the rapidly departing figure of her husband. She recalled times now past when her father-in-law would leave the house on a palanquin flanked by servants. At this memory her eyes brimmed with tears.

When Narain Rao arrived at his destination after a journey of some hours, he was informed that Purxottam-bab had left for Manguexi, where he was to stay for several days, and that he had been accompanied by his youngest son. Nonetheless, Narain Rao was cordially welcomed.

After dinner he went to repose in the guest room. He was not quite asleep when he heard an uproar amongst the children playing in the corner of the front room. He got up immediately to investigate. The children told him that Purxottam-bab's grandson had just lost the gold coin with which he was playing. Taken aback by this unexpected news, Narain Rao reached down with his left hand to pat the coin he had wedged into the waistband of his dhoti. Shortly after, the house servants and members of the family rushed to the scene to begin searching for the lost coin.

VICTIM OF HONESTY

Narain Rao was in despair. He had seen the precious coin, as had the people of the house, but just as the mohar went missing he had been alone with the children in the front room. To the bystanders Narain Rao appeared to be a man in desperate straits. The search turned up nothing. How could a three-year-old explain what he had done with the coin?

Narain Rao noticed the servants glancing at him suspiciously, saw them whisper to one another and gesture knowingly. The idea that he was under suspicion was unbearable. God had seen fit to take away his wealth—now he was stripping away the good name of his family. A great tribulation? His forbears had protected their honour with such zeal; was he going to let it be stained? He recalled his dying father's solemn words. Over the centuries had his family not striven for honour over wealth? This question pierced his mind like a bullet.

The huddle dispersed. With a tremulous hand Narain Rao removed his coin and hid it beneath a broom, his heart torn to shreds. He didn't tarry, or even reveal to the family of the house the reason for his visit. Instead, under the malicious gaze of the servants, he walked crestfallen out of the room.

Two days later, Purxottam-bab returned home and was informed of the incident. He took little heed, as, according to the members of his household, the coin had been found a day later in the corner of the front room. What did disturb his peace of mind was the sudden visit and abrupt departure of Narain Rao. Why had he come? To ask some favour? But he knew Narain Rao and his noble family well. His pride would certainly not have allowed him to make such a petition. For a long while these doubts plagued the soul of Purxottam-bab, a man too caught up in his own business affairs to take note of those, like Narain Rao, who scrupulously avoided revealing their indigence.

Another matter occupied his mind during those days: he sought a bride for his son, Vishnu. It was a vexed issue, as it was no easy thing to find a maiden who met his requirements. For his son he wanted a girl who had abundant affection for all, who took delight in compassion, who was hardworking and cheery yet resolute, who, in sum, would continue the glorious tradition of their family. How was he to find such a bride in an environment so full of egotism, vanity, and dissimulation?

As Purxottam-bab had no time to call upon Narain Rao, he decided to write him a letter asking for the reasons behind his unexpected visit. He wrote it out with his own hand. In those days it was customary to dry the ink with a sprinkling of sand. Purxottam-bab groped for some inside the clay pot that stood on the table. What a shock it was when his fingers felt the cold touch of the coin!

MYSTERY UNRAVELLED

Where could this coin have come from, if the one his grandson had lost had already been found? The treasurer was summoned and an investigation was launched straight away. It proved that the coin buried in the sand of the pot had been stuck there by the little grandson of Purxottam-bab.

Another doubt emerged. Where could the coin found in the corner of the room have come from since it was not his? The investigations shed light on this conundrum. The staff of the house, confusedly and haltingly, revealed that the only stranger present in the room had been Narain Rao.

Thus, the enigma was resolved. Purxottam-bab could guess what torments the virtuous Narain-bab had suffered. The idea of this pure and innocent man beset by moments of great anguish, through no fault of his own, filled Purxottam-bab's soul with pain. He decided to leave his house immediately, to find and embrace that great man, Narain Rao.

Purxottam-bab ordered his treasurer to fetch a beautiful jewel case studded with pearls and rubies. He placed within it, reverently, that rare artefact which symbolized the glorious tradition of a noble family. With no further delay, accompanied by his retinue, he departed by palanquin for the village. The announcement of Purxottam-bab's visit left Narain Rao in a fluster. Had his secret been revealed? He hurried to the patio where the old philanthropist awaited. Without uttering a word Purxottam-bab embraced him. Both struggled to contain their emotions.

They entered the house in silence. The illustrious visitor was shown to the parlour he knew so well from his youth. Looking around, the old man saw only evidence of decline. Even the Kashmiri rug that had once borne witness to opulence had been reduced to tatters.

Seated on that rug, unable to hold back his emotions, Purxottam-bab tightly embraced the virtuous man, as a bird takes its young under its wing. Narain Rao, magnetized by the curious touch of those strong arms, began to sob.

VIRTUE REWARDED

The men then looked one another in the eye. In an instant Narain Rao realized that the slightest place in this man's affection would ensure life and prosperity for his family.

A few moments passed. Purxottam-bab removed the scintillating jewellery box from one of his pockets, opened it, and spoke thus as he presented Narain Rao the coin: 'Here it is, the Lakshmi of your house! The excellence of your family! You made a grave sacrifice to save your honour. You are, without doubt, a blessed man!'

The emotions he felt at that moment were so intense that Narain Rao was unable to utter a word. His mind was awhirl. He bowed his head and, with great difficulty, replied, 'Please do not embarrass me with these words. I am not worthy of such great honour.'

At that precise moment his daughter Tulsi appeared in the doorway. Her loving father said, 'Come here, my daughter, and ask Purxottam-bab for his blessing.'

And so Tulsi, maiden and modest, twelve years old, sincere and splendid, the image of virtue and modesty, of beauty and gentleness, stepped gracefully forward. She bowed before the venerable figure of Purxottam-bab and pressed her hands together in homage.

Purxottam-bab gazed at her. He felt he had just found what for months he had sought in vain.

He drew her to him affectionately. Running his fingers through her hair, he exclaimed, 'You shall be happy, my child.'

Purxottam-bab offered her a precious necklace of pearls from Hormuz, then turned to her poor father and, in a pleading voice, said, 'In truth, you are great. I wish my house to match yours in nobility. Thus, I beseech, your daughter's hand in marriage for my Vishnu.'

The eyes of Lakshmibai filled with delighted tears as she watched on from a window. Her mother's heart, weary of so much suffering, leapt for joy.

Deeply touched, Narain Rao pronounced these words: 'Purxottam-bab, I respect and honour your will. Our Tulsi shall be your daughter-in-law.'

As he spoke, Narain Rao opened the jewellery box and gazed with reverence at the ancient coin. In it he saw reflected the virtue and generosity of twenty generations. Two tears ran from his eyes and fell upon the shining gold piece.

HOUSE NUMBER

KAVANA SARMA

Translated from the Telugu by Dasu Krishnamoorty and Tamraparni Dasu

Dr Appalraju surveyed the neatly appointed rooms and nodded. It had taken him a week of house-hunting to find the place. He signed the lease of the two-room tenement for five hundred rupees in Dwaraka Nagar district of the Steel City. Now, all he had to do was to write home asking Her Excellency to come join him. With that, the day's to-do list would have been accomplished.

He bathed with half a bucket of water, saving the other half for any need that might arise before the next day's quota of water arrived. He wrapped a white lungi around his waist, and sat down close to the table fan to write to his wife:

Oh, my queen, my sweetness,

Found a place at last! Pack your things and ask your dad to put you on the next train; I'll receive you here. I've spruced up the rooms, though not as well as they do in America. But India is not America. When you were there you used to complain: 'There is no NTR or ANR. Every weekend, all we do is crowd into some friend's basement and see a movie. How about watching it in the comfort of cushioned seats in air-conditioned luxury for just half a dollar in a grand Indian multiplex? A city without Telugu films is a godforsaken place, my Appalraju darling. No jasmines here, only those pathetic surrogates for jasmines; no fragrance of any kind!' Well, we're back in our country. No houses to rent, no state-of-the-art kitchens or sparkling sinks. Daily power cuts for ten hours.

The faucets are always dry. But, you have Simhachalam selling you sampangi flowers at your door, paan cones made of betel leaves, and bottled soda. Today's temperature here is 42°C. I've lost count of the sodas I've downed. Without you, Vizag is a bore. Hurry home to me!

After he'd signed the letter, he went out to check the house number on the front door. 48-12-15. What a quirky number! Four and eight add up to twelve, one and two add up to three. The grand total is fifteen. He wondered if there was anyone other than him who could crack such a complicated code. He was a genius, an intellectual. Anyway, self-adulation is not a virtue, he reminded himself. Srinivasa Ramanujan could decipher such cryptograms in his sleep. Who would win if he, Dr Appalraju, and Ramanujan were locked in a battle of wits? Ramanujan perhaps, he conceded. There are R and J in his name too. Like Ramanujan, he too understood the uniqueness of numbers. An unseen bond existed between him and the world of numbers—once he saw a number he never forgot it.

Well, he'd better write the house number to help his wife to write back. She might write to his office address, God forbid. That was the last thing he wanted. First, he wrote his name with the care of a calligrapher on the envelope. Then he wrote Dwaraka Nagar, Visakhapatnam. Postal code? He couldn't remember. He hadn't paid attention. Oh well, it was not the end of the world. But he'd have to write the house number. What was it? Was it 12-3-15? No, he was not sure. His genius having deserted him, he thought it better to go out again and confirm. For all you know, Srinivasa Ramanujan might have riffled through the books stealthily when Hardy was not around! No shame in taking a second look, he decided.

So, Appalraju went out and checked the door number once again. It was now clear: two ones, one two, one four, one five, one eight. Simple! 48-12-15. He scribbled the number on the envelope.

What next? Find a mailbox. It was eight o'clock. 'Enough time to go to Ooty restaurant for a meal and chuck the letter into the mailbox on the way back,' he calculated. He was not in a mood to change into pants. One could step out of the house in America wearing unpresentable clothes. No one cared. Any rag would do. No questions asked. Why should it be different in India? We just don't try. And what had happened on the one occasion he *did* try? That was the time he'd visited Kakinada to look up his wife's folks. One day, the entire household set out for a drive because it was too stuffy inside the house. He took off his shirt and drove in an undershirt. On the way, his wife, Rani, had spotted a boy selling iced sodas on the sidewalk. She pointed to the soda cart, and cooed into Appalraju's ear, 'I want one, my love.' The dutiful husband that he was, he stopped the cart and asked the soda boy to uncork four iced sodas.

He thought he'd drink one at the cart itself so that he need carry only three cold bottles back to the car. The boy stopped him mid-gulp and yelled, 'What are you doing, man! First take the sodas to your boss and the lady. What impudence! You louts from the countryside are infesting the place and bringing your boorish ways here.' Appalraju couldn't understand why the soda boy took him for a chauffeur. His brother-in-law stepped in hurriedly and said, 'Bava Garu, pass the sodas to me please, I'll take them to my sister.'

The soda boy realized his mistake and turned his ire on Appalraju's brother-in-law, 'What sir, you couldn't buy a decent shirt for your brother-in-law? What happens to the image of our city if our sons-in-law wander the city shirtless?' he said. The vendor didn't know that not only had the young man not bothered to get a respectable shirt for his brother-in-law but had borrowed his Levi's pants instead.

After that experience, Appalraju made up his mind to change the values of this country. Stirred by such reformist zeal, he pulled out from the closet a red undershirt with a pocket but no collar. He thrust a ten-rupee note into the pocket, locked the house, and marched out. He arrived at Emporium Point and flagged down a rickshaw for Ooty restaurant. He got off near a red mailbox and gently slid in the letter to his Queen.

The rickshaw driver shouted after him, 'Sir, you haven't paid the fare!'

'I'm sorry,' Appalraju said and paid him.

Appalraju bought a meal ticket at the restaurant cash register and put the change in his pocket. The food tray arrived and, eating, he slipped into a reverie. Prices in India had shot up into the stratosphere during his stay in America. By the time he'd returned to India, the Janata Party was in power. The Emergency had been lifted. 'It has restored our esteem abroad,' his friends in the USA had argued, sipping whisky. Irritated, he'd asked, 'If India's prestige is so dear to you, why don't you go home and restore it?' The patriotism of these expatriates was limited to boasting about the greatness of their country. They mocked Appalraju for enjoying the comforts of the US even as he criticized the Emergency. He should return to India and protest, they said.

He had returned, but not to protest the Emergency. He wanted to share in the poverty and prosperity of the country, and act on his faith that India was great. Such noble thoughts enriched his meal. By nine o'clock, he had finished his meal, stepped outside the restaurant and bought a betel leaf cone from the paan bunk. As he walked back home, monstrous wall posters warned him in large fonts, 'Naughty Krishna and Cheeky Rama. Hurry up lest you should regret later.' For good measure, at the bottom of the poster blared another admonition 'Delay means Disappointment'.

'I should respect these posters,' he thought. 'The movie seems to have a good cast. I should give it a try. Rani had said she had seen the film in Kakinada and recommended it. I don't even have to get up early. Tomorrow is Sunday, ha!'

He'd passed a theatre on his way to Ooty. His watch showed that he had fifteen minutes to get there. The film had been running for more than hundred days. So, he had no problem getting a ticket. 'Ah, this theatre is air-conditioned,' he chuckled. But the euphoria was short-lived. The management had switched the AC off. Obviously, they'd not taken a vow at Raj Ghat in Gandhiji's holy presence to keep it running during the entire duration of the movie.

Halfway through the film, Raju got bored and stood up to leave. The audience tried to persuade him to stay, telling him about the fight scenes and dances yet to come. As Raju made his way out, he came between the women and their heroes on the screen. They bristled and cursed him. 'Why should such an impatient man come to see a movie, he should stay at home and not spoil other people's fun!' They yelled at him to sit down.

Raju scurried out of the movie hall and approached the metal gate of the compound. It was locked. The gatekeeper was engrossed in watching the fight scenes from the cheap seats closest to the screen. Raju requested him to come out and open the gate but he said he needed the permission of the manager. 'If you leave the hall in the middle what will the people at the box office think, sir?' the manager chided him.

'This is the last show,' Raju said.

'Last show? There is a morning show in a few hours. People are already lining up because tomorrow is a Sunday. Is it fair of you to leave the hall in their presence?'

Finally, the manager relented and had the gatekeeper open the gate.

Raju stumbled out and wiped the sweat off. He shredded the ticket stub and blew the pieces into the air. Despite everything, he was in a good mood and decided to walk back home. As the old saying goes, the miles go by quickly if we walk with a song on our lips and a hop in our step.

Walking with a jaunty stride, he began belting out, '*Raindrops keep falling on my head…my head….*'

Constable Appalsaami was on patrol. He eyed Raju with suspicion. 'Is this fellow really mad or is he a burglar pretending to be mad?'

He needed to book at least two arrests to keep up with his quota. He took a good look at Raju's flip-flops, the satchel slung across his chest, the red undershirt over a lungi secured by a belt.

'Here's a pickpocket,' he decided.

Appalsaami stopped Raju and asked with mock politeness, 'Where is it raining, sir?'

'My head…my head,' said Raju and stopped singing.

'On your head? Look at the sky and tell me where it is raining from, you drunk.'

'Sergeant, mind your language!' said Raju angrily.

'What, you think I don't know *Ingilis*? I'll thrash you. Where are you coming from at this late hour?'

'From the second show,' Raju said.

'Which movie?'

'*Naughty Krishna and Cheeky Rama.*'

'That show is not over yet.'

'I came away in the middle,' said Raju.

The cop laughed. This was the first time he had heard of anyone walking out from that movie in the middle. Appalsaami saw himself in the role of Naughty Krishna. I certainly look the part, he thought. Wasn't that why he'd been honoured by the theatre owners with the responsibility of being on duty on the opening night?

'Really? You walked out halfway through such a good film?'

'Of course,' said Raju.

'Where's the stub then?'

Raju looked for it in his pocket and remembered that he had thrown it away. Nice touch, the policeman thought.

'Okay, where are you going?'

'Home.'

'Where is it?'

'Dwaraka Nagar.'

'What's your house number?'

Raju smiled. He was sure he could handle this challenge without a problem, thanks to his special relationship with numbers. There are two ones, one two, one four, one five, one eight.

He thanked Ramanujan and said, '11-24-58.'

'There is no such number in Dwaraka Nagar,' snapped Appalsaami.

Raju came up with another number. '21-15-84.' He worked it out in his head. Two plus one is three. Five plus one is six. Two times three is six. That is, the sum of the second set of digits is twice the sum of the first set of digits. Now, eight plus four is twelve. Twelve is two times six, the sum of one and five. So, the rule applied to the second and third set of numbers as well. He was thrilled by his own brilliance. That had to be his house number and so he told the policeman.

'Come,' said Appalsaami.

'Where?'

'To the police station.'

'I'm allowed a phone call, according to the rules. You have to produce me before a magistrate if you take me into custody.'

'Will you follow me, or do I have to give you a taste of the baton?'

'Third degree is prohibited by law, officer.'

'Follow me quietly,' the policeman said flourishing his baton. It whipped through the air with a crack like a bullet.

Raju accompanied the policeman docilely to the station.

'What's the matter?' the writer at the station asked.

Raju was shocked that there was nothing like the statutory warning usually heard in American police precincts, the Miranda rights, which warned the suspect that whatever he said could be used against him.

'Caught him prowling around, I think he was planning to burgle a house. Let's put him inside and inform the sub-inspector.'

'I want to make a call and it is your duty to allow me,' Raju asserted his rights.

'You can receive a call, but not make it,' the writer corrected him.

'The guy is firing away in English, man,' he told the constable.

'Who doesn't speak English these days, sir?' Appalsaami said and pushed Appalraju into the lock-up.

That was the last straw.

'I'm Dr Appalraju. You'll regret your actions. There is no Emergency now. The magistrate will take you to task tomorrow. What crime have I committed?' Raju began shouting from behind bars.

'You should inform the SI,' the writer told the constable.

Appalsaami hesitated for an instant, but he walked down anyway to the SI's home, though he feared the boss might resent being disturbed at that late hour.

Luckily for Appalsaami, the SI was awake but in a bad mood. His son had sneaked out to watch a late-night film. He looked up at the cop.

'Not my fault, sir. I just did what you told me to and put the guy in the slammer. He says he will make us pay for this because there is no Emergency. Please tell me what to do.'

The SI told his wife to send his son to the station as soon as he came home from the movie and followed Appalsaami to the station.

'Where is your officer, where's the boss?' Appalraju was shouting when the SI walked in.

'You, there! I'm the boss. What's the problem?' the SI asked.

'Look at the address, sir. All wrong. There is no such number. He was singing that the rain is falling. He claims that he is going home from the theatre but he couldn't even produce the stub,' Appalsaami reeled off an account of what had happened.

'You know you shouldn't go by what a man wears. For that matter, look at what you are wearing. Let me see your ID,' Raju demanded.

The SI was taken aback by this audacity. He'd left home in a hurry, clad in a lungi and banian.

'In case he acts up,' he told the constable, 'just use the stick.'

Appalsaami made no such attempt because the bars of the lock-up grille got in the way.

'You have no right to torture me. It is for the court to punish me.... Provided I'm guilty,' Raju said.

An orderly interrupted the exchanges. He had a sixteen-year-old boy in tow.

'So, you thought you could do things behind my back and get away with it?' the SI snarled and slapped the boy hard.

The boy began to cry.

'Why is he pummelling the boy? I'll tell his father to file a case, and I'll testify with pleasure!' Appalraju yelled.

'You mean to say our boss can't thrash his own son?' asked the writer.

'Who gave him the right to do that?' Appalraju demanded and bawled out a slogan 'Police violence!'

The boy promptly supplemented, 'Down, down!'

'Where did you find this guy? What a nuisance this bum is, throw him out on the street,' the SI barked.

Once out of the lock-up, Raju asked the SI, 'Do you remember the house number of your relatives in Hyderabad?'

As the SI struggled to answer, his son bolted.

'See, just like you, I too can't remember house numbers...but that doesn't make me a thief,' Raju said and walked out onto the street.

SAVAGE HARVEST

MOHINDER SINGH SARNA

Translated from the Punjabi by Navtej Sarna

As he bent over the furnace stuffed with hard coal, Dina's iron-black body shone with the sheen of bronze; in fact, he seemed to be moulded in bronze, resembling a statue of a healthy labourer. The muscles of his well-exercised torso rippled as he swung the hammer around his head, and a great blow fell on the red-hot bits of iron.

The blows continued to fall and echo. Immersed in his work, Dina was lost to the world until the hot sun of late August, streaming in through the open window, began to lick at his very bones. With a start, he looked out. Already the sun was at its height and his work was not even half done. He shut the window to keep out the heat but then found it difficult to breathe. A clammy sweat broke out on his forehead. It had rained furiously all night, as if the skies had opened up, and then continued to drizzle all morning. But now the sun shone brightly and a suffocating humidity had built up. He threw the window open again and bent over the furnace. The sweat was flowing down his ears on to his body in little rivulets. He wiped it off his forehead with his forearm. Thick drops fell on the fire. There was a little hiss and for a split second, a piece of coal found some relief.

He seemed to be on fire with the combined heat from the sun and the furnace. This fire had dissolved into his blood and was now roasting the marrow of his bones. The sharp, roaring flames made his eyes burn. Every hair on his body had become a wick and it seemed to him that one of these wicks would catch fire any moment and blow up his body like a huge firecracker.

Suddenly he dropped his tools and went to the window. The sky was lit up by the screaming sharp sunshine. His eyes could not adjust to the brightness and he winced. When he could see, he gazed at the fields that spread far before him, and at the sandy path that cut through them and went all the way to the horizon like a straight white line. On the right of the path stood the cotton crop, and the puddles of water in the fields occasionally flashed silver. On the left, the ploughed furrows awaited the seed. The scent of the earth, wet from the recent rain, made him nostalgic and he wanted to jump out of the window. He wanted to roll in the fields and let the pores of his burning body soak in the moisture from the wet earth.

He loved the fields. During the sowing and harvesting, his blood would tingle and a strange freedom would enliven his limbs. He was the village blacksmith, but there wasn't much work for him in the village and he would spend a lot of time helping out the peasants in the fields. There wasn't a man in seven villages that could match him during the harvest or lift a larger load than him. Suddenly his hands yearned for the feel of a sickle.

Sickles, harvests, the sugar cane swaying gently in the moonlight. The call of the golden earth and the lilt in the songs born of this earth.... He forgot, for a moment, that a hellish fire raged behind him and that for the last twenty days he had done nothing but mould metal into axes and spears. The season of sickles and scrapers had passed; this was the time of axes and spears. And it had been a strange harvest. Instead of the wheat, those who had planted it had been chopped up.

What kind of a mess had he gotten himself into? It was as if he was shouldering the entire responsibility of arming the warriors of the newly born Pakistan. Pakistan already existed, but to complete that reality it seemed necessary to kill all the Hindus and the Sikhs.

He did not understand this fully, but this was what everybody said, from the village heads to the imams of mosques. And this jihad would succeed only if his furnace kept raging and spitting out fierce instruments of death.

He turned again to the fire. The sharp bits of metal in the furnace were brighter than the coals. His head began to swim. A sharp, hot pain rose inside him and he gripped his side. Hunger! He hadn't taken even a drop of water since the morning. Now hunger was ravaging his insides and thirst had turned his lips to wood.

'Oh! Bashir's mother!' he shouted towards the house. 'Give me water, quick.' A woman of about forty-five brought water in a jug. She wore a nose ring and her silver earrings swayed as she walked. She stared at her husband. He was panting with thirst. She had offered him food and water three times already since the morning, but he hadn't responded and had continued to blow at his fire. What had made him think of food and water now? She looked at the torrid fire, at the bits of iron scattered all over the floor, and at the evil pile of axes and spears. Then she stared at her husband's face for a long time, as if she didn't recognize him. Dina drained the jug at a go. 'More,' he panted. She brought more water and watched him as he drank. 'That's all,' he said.

The taut veins of his body and forehead relaxed. His breathing eased. And then a shadow of discomfort crossed his face. 'Why are you staring at me like that? Why don't you talk to me? And why do you stand away from me, as if I have the plague?' She didn't reply. Instead she went into the house and brought him food. 'I'm talking to you,' Dina shouted, shaking her by the shoulders. 'Why don't you speak to me? Have you put rice to boil in your mouth that you can't speak?'

The woman remained silent. Dina tore at a roti and tried to swallow a few large mouthfuls. But the food wouldn't go down his throat. He took a few bitter gulps of water and pushed away the basket of rotis. 'Not talking to me, just staring as if I've been possessed by demons.'

'Allah forbid,' she said, 'but it does appear so to me.' Dina's mouth fell open in surprise. He had lost all hope that Bashir's mother would ever speak, that she would break the stubborn silence of so many days.

When he recovered somewhat from his surprise, he said, 'I know what's on your mind, but what can I do? Your sons won't let me be. Now Bashir wants fifty axes ready by tomorrow night. He'll be at my neck if they aren't ready. I know you think otherwise but if I don't obey them they'll cut me into pieces.'

'Are they your sons or someone else's?' she asked, a little ashamed of her own question.

'Mine,' he replied, somewhat foolishly.

'Then should they fear you, or should you fear them?'

'You talk as if you don't know your own sons, what savages they are. Can I say anything to them? As if they wouldn't skin me alive....' said Dina.

'They are my sons, too.' His wife's tone was softer now. 'You know they shout at me and curse me. But I don't go making axes for them.'

'I only make the axes,' he replied. 'I don't kill people with them.'

'It's worse than killing,' she said. 'The killer kills one or two or at most, a handful of people. Each axe made by your hands kills dozens.'

A tremor passed through Dina's spine. Then this trembling touched every pore of his body. For a long time he was silent. And then, 'You are blaming me! Why don't you talk to your sons, the great warriors who burn two villages every night!'

'Nobody listens to me.' Her tone had grown even softer now. 'How can I tell anyone what to do? Everyone will have to answer for their own sins; why should I say anything to anyone?'

For some time, both of them stared at the floor, silently. Suddenly the woman said, 'And why don't you eat your food? Do you want to starve?' She slid the basket in front of him.

A soft knock on the front door shook Dina. He stood up in fright. It must be Bashir or his companions. They had come to threaten him. He hesitated with his hand on the latch and looked around. The fire in the furnace was raging; everything was in place. He opened the door. Rusted with the season's rain, it screeched on its hinges.

He jumped back several steps in fear, just missing the furnace. His wife's face drained of blood and a scream escaped her lips. At the door stood the old wife of the Brahmin of the thakurdwar, a net of wrinkles spread across the turmeric powdered on her face. Her head of snow-white hair shook uncontrollably. Their eyes filled with fear, Dina and his wife stared at the old woman. She seemed to be alive, even though she was most certainly a ghost.

At long last, Dina's wife took courage and said, 'Aunt, you are still alive?' The old woman did not reply. Dina's wife recalled that she had been hard of hearing. Perhaps the affliction had pursued her in death too. She went closer to the old woman and, loudly, repeated her question.

Understanding flashed in the old woman's eyes and she said, 'Can't you see that I am alive? Seven days was I racked with fever. There was no one to give me even a sip of water there. Tulsi has been away for many days. I could've died in his absence.... One can go anytime.... My fever went down today. I hardly had the strength to get up but somehow I have pushed myself till here. Why are the two of you staring at me so?'

The old woman was drenched in sweat from the effort of speaking and her breath came in uneven bursts. Holding her temples she sat down on the floor on her haunches. The light seemed to be fading in her pupils and every breath came as if it were her last.

Dina and his wife exchanged looks of immense relief. She really was the Brahmin's wife and not a ghost. The fever had saved her from the fate of the rest of the village. Her deafness had prevented her from hearing of the great sorrow that had befallen the village on Thursday night. She hadn't realized that her village was now in Pakistan. She did not know that Pakistan was now in her village. That not one Hindu or Sikh was alive except for a few girls in the hands of the rioters.

Suddenly, the old woman asked, 'Dina, have you seen my goat anywhere?'

Goat, thought Dina, her goat! In these days, when the rioters had cooked and eaten even the looted cattle, this old woman was bothered about a goat?

'I don't know where she has run off to,' the old woman continued, 'and she's due. I can't even look after myself now. I can't go looking for her, and how can I catch her anyway? If you see her anywhere, tie her up, God bless you. You know she's due. I hope she doesn't give birth somewhere outside.'

Dina said, 'Old woman, your goat is not there. She has been eaten up and has been digested by now.' But the old woman heard nothing. He was about to repeat himself loudly but a glance from his wife silenced him.

'And look at this,' the old woman said, 'I found this chain near the door of the thakurdwar. I don't know how this goat managed to loosen the chain. This link, where the lock goes, has been eaten through and through. I thought I'd ask you to fix it for me.'

For some time, Dina's wife had been staring at the old woman in a strange manner. She seemed to be wrestling with something.

And then, as if everything had suddenly become clear, she said, 'Aunt, why don't you stay here? You will be alone in the thakurdwar. And your fever has just abated. Cook your food here, and bring your own utensils, since you are a Hindu. Let Tulsi return, then you can go back.'

The old woman seemed to have grown even more deaf. Maybe it was the effect of the fever. She only caught Tulsi's name.

'I'm telling you, he's gone out of the village. He's gone with Ram Shah's daughter's betrothal party to Nawachak. On the first of next month, Preeto is to be married. I told Shah to gift me a cow. It's not every day that there are celebrations in the houses of the rich. And you know, Tulsi needs the milk and the curd for his health.'

Ignoring the old woman's talk, Dina's wife was trying to catch her husband's eye. She wanted to say something but before she could, Dina was already speaking.

'I know what's on your mind, but we can't do it. I have no objection, but where will we hide her? Soon your sons will be here, their nostrils sniffing out human flesh, and we won't be able to conceal her. They will figure it out instantly, and what will they do to us then?'

'She's old,' beseeched Dina's wife, 'the last of our village's Hindus. A God-fearing old woman. It's only a matter of a few days. Let her son return and then we will send her to some other village.'

'Which village will you send her to?' Dina was almost screaming now. 'Is there a village left where she will be safe? And her son: he'll never return. This time he has been sent to a place from where there is no return. All the Hindus of Nawachak have been killed. Not one of them is left.'

His wife's face fell. She put a trembling finger to her lips, begging him to lower his tone. 'Can't you speak softly? Or won't you be satisfied until she knows that her son has been murdered?'

Except for Dina's outburst, they'd been talking in whispers. But it was unnecessary, for even their loudest tones would not have reached the old woman through her deafness. She stared at them with her fevered eyes.

'What are you two whispering away about? And, Dina, why won't you look at me? Just repair this cursed chain. It's not that I'm asking for much.'

'Come tomorrow,' Dina shouted into the old woman's ear. 'I don't have any time today. And go home now.'

'All right,' the old woman croaked, putting her hands on her knees to steady herself as she rose. 'I'll go. If you say tomorrow, then let it be so, but keep an eye out for my goat. I've told you, just tie her up if you see her. Wretched thing. God knows where she has run away to.' And, before Dina's wife could stop her, the old woman had lurched out into the lane.

How much time this old woman had wasted, Dina fumed. He could have made five axes in that much time. And Bashir was not going to listen to any excuses; he would want his fifty.

But he could not put his heart into the work. Something began to gnaw at his heart. He could not dismiss the vision of fever-ridden eyes and snow-white hair. Those eyes were burning holes in his head like two red-hot embers. Most of all, it was her ignorance that bothered him. She knew nothing. That Tulsi was never to return, that Preeto was never to get married, that Bashir had already taken Preeto, along with her rich father's estate.

It was a rotten thing that Bashir had done. Defending the honour of the women of the village was a common burden. Everyone's daughters were just like your own. The loss of any woman's honour was a catastrophe for all.

A horrible scene appeared before his eyes—Preeto, wailing and clutching at her father's corpse; Bashir pulling her away by her hair. Imploring him, wailing and screaming, she had been dragged away. And then she had gone silent, just like a lamb in the moment before its slaughter.

And he, Bashir's father, had watched this evil sight unfold from the threshold. He had not stopped Bashir, or pulled him away by the scruff of his neck and thrown him on the ground. He had done nothing to save the honour of this daughter.

The pale, childlike face of Preeto began to swim before his eyes and her plaintive cries echoed in his ears. He was seized by a shiver, a cold and uncontrollable shiver that seemed a precursor to certain death. The shivering, he felt, could be stopped only if he picked up the red-hot iron from the fire and clasped it against his heart. But why was his head on fire? The entire blazing furnace seemed to have entered his head. He pressed his head with both hands and the fire came on to his palms.

He was going mad. He would end up doing something terrible. He must run away, far away from all this. He opened the window and jumped out. For a long time he wandered aimlessly in the fields. The afternoon had now become evening. On the horizon, someone had murdered the sun. The blood of innocents had spread across the sky and had dissolved into the waters of the streams and canals. Would anybody eat the sugar cane that had been sprayed with blood? Or wear the cotton which had been irrigated by blood? What kind of wheat would grow in this blood-drenched soil? And what kind of a harvest would it be after this bloody season? The shower of blood that had reddened everything had been caused by the axes he had fashioned. This crop of bones and flesh had been sown by spears made by his hands. And he had just finished making axes for the handful of villages that were still left. Those, too, would, be gone by tomorrow night.

He was guilty. Heavily, deeply guilty. Bashir's mother had been right. At least he should not let them lay their hands on the new axes. His sins would not be wiped out even if he prevented that. But what else could he do?

And then he started running, like a man possessed, towards the village. He wanted to reach home before Bashir's men. He wanted to throw the axes in some well or canal from where they would never be found.

When he reached the village, it was dark. The indifferent light of a hazy moon threw faint shadows on to the lane. The previous night's rain had left a muddy slush everywhere. Again and again his feet caught in the thick slush, but he kept walking quickly through the lanes. Suddenly, he stopped. He could hear voices coming from a short distance away. In fact, they were coming from his house. Had they already come, then? Was he too late? He could clearly hear Bashir's vulgar laughter.

He stumbled against some heavy object near his house and fell on his face. He tried to get up, but couldn't. An icy-cold grip had clasped his feet. He tried to free them but the grip only seemed to get tighter. A terrible fear clutched at his heart and a cold sweat covered his forehead. With a strong jerk, he turned to look back. In the dim moonlight, he saw a thatch of white hair rippling in the wind. The old woman's wrinkled forehead bore a long gash from an axe. And there was a curse in the wide open, frightened eyes. He looked at his feet. They were caught in the chain that was entangled around her forearms.

He screamed once and fainted. That night he was gripped by a high fever. All night he tossed wildly on the bed; all night his delirious shouts echoed in the silence of the village. 'Don't kill me, don't kill me with those axes! Get this chain off my neck! Oh, my daughter! Don't harm my daughter! Don't harm Preeto! Oh, these chains! In Allah's name, don't use those axes! Don't kill me!'

GOLD FROM THE GRAVES
ANNA BHAU SATHE

Translated from the Marathi by Vernon Gonsalves

Hearing that a powerful moneylender had died in a nearby village, Bhima sprang to his feet. He was exhilarated. His joy wouldn't subside. Looking in the direction of the village, he suddenly turned to glare at the sun in the sky.

The sun was setting. Rain clouds crowded the sky. They had the rough, battered look of freshly ploughed land. The retreating light, filtering through those nasty looking clouds, streamed down over Mumbai.

There was a gentle breeze. The fifty or so huts in this suburb in the jungle began to creak in the breeze. The huts were made of old tin sheets, mats, planks, and sacks. And those houses contained people. Cast-off things sheltering a cast-off people. Burnt out after the day's fight for food, they now rested. The kitchen fires were alight. White smoke loitered through the green trees. Children were playing.

Bhima sat lost in thought beneath a massive tamarind tree. He was terribly agitated. Drawn relentlessly towards that dead moneylender, his spirit was racing back and forth between that village's cemetery and the tamarind tree. He repeatedly glanced at the sun and then at that village. He needed the dark, so he was getting all fidgety. His beloved daughter Narbada was playing close by and his wife was in the house, patting bhakars into shape. Bhima looked awe-inspiring. His Satara outfit comprised a long red turban, a yellow dhoti, and a shirt of thick, coarse cloth. He looked a proper wrestler. His massive forehead, thick neck, dark eyebrows, flamboyant moustache, and broad yet fiery features had struck fear into many a ruffian.

Bhima's village was a long way off, on the banks of the Warna. However, seeing that even his bull-like strength could not fill his stomach there, he had moved to Mumbai. He had combed the entire city in search of work. But he hadn't found any. As his many dreams of getting a job, becoming a worker, bringing home a pay packet, making his wife a coin necklace were shattered, Bhima had lost hope and had moved to this suburb in the jungle. Mumbai had everything, except work and shelter. So he had got upset with Mumbai. However, just after shifting to the suburb, he had found work in the quarry on a nearby hill.

On finding work and shelter, Bhima was happy. As he put all his bull-like might to work, he seemed to almost challenge the hill. He lifted his pickaxe and the hill would recoil. As his sledgehammer rose, the dark rock face would flinch. The contractor was happy with him. Bhima too was contented, as he was getting a wage.

But, within a space of just six months, the quarry closed down. When he got to work one day, he learned that the quarry had shut. Hearing that he had lost his job, Bhima was thrown into a daze. Hunger danced before his eyes. Anxiety and indecision gripped him. What was he going to do, he wondered despondently.

Clothes under his arm, Bhima turned back from the quarry. On the way, he stopped at a stream. He bathed there and prepared to make his way home, devastated beyond belief. It was then that his eyes fell on a mound of ashes. They were the ashes of a dead body. As he looked at the charred human bones Bhima grew even more despondent. Must be some jobless wretch; poor chap must have given up on life. I'll also die like this! Starvation will start in a couple of days, then Narbada will sit crying. My wife will fall into a deep depression and there'll be nothing I can do about it....

Suddenly, he saw something sparkling in the heap of ashes. When he looked closely he discovered that the sparkle came from a gold ring of about a tola. Overjoyed, he grabbed hold of the ring. One tola of gold and that too from a corpse's ashes! He was delighted by his discovery—there was gold to be found in the ashes of a corpse. He had found a new means by which to live.

From the next day onwards Bhima began visiting crematoriums and cemeteries on the banks of rivers and streams. He would sift through the ashes of bodies and pick up a fragment of gold here, an ornament there—earrings, nose rings, a gold coin, bracelet or anklet; he would find something of value every day.

Bhima's new venture began to flourish. He discovered that gold ornaments which were left on bodies that were being cremated would melt with the heat of the fire and enter the bones. So he would crush burnt bones and remove the gold. He'd break skulls. He'd crush wrists. But he'd get the gold.

In the evening he would go to Kurla, sell the gold, and collect cash. On the way home he would get dates for Narbada. Business was steady.

                                            ∽

Bhima lived by sifting through the ashes of corpses. He soon lost sight of the difference between life and death. What he understood was that if there was gold in the ash it was the ash of the rich and if there was no gold it was that of the poor. Sometimes he would rave to whoever was within earshot—so it is the rich who should die and the rich who should live; the poor should never die. Continuing with his rant, he would loudly proclaim that the lowly lot had absolutely no right to live or to die. Happy was the man who died with a gold tola in his molars, is what he believed.

The brutal reality of unemployment had made him brutal. Night and day he hovered around cremation grounds and graveyards. Corpses had become his means of existence. His life had become one with the dead.

Before long, people began to notice that bizarre things were happening in those parts. Buried bodies were rising from their graves. The corpse of the young daughter-in-law of a moneylender had moved mysteriously from the burial ground to the riverbank. People living in the area were terrified by all this. Suspecting that somebody was digging up the bodies, the police began keeping watch. But keeping watch on corpses is no easy task.

                                            ∽

The sun had set. Darkness covered the land. As his wife served his meal, Bhima ate in grim silence. When she realized that he was preparing to go out, she said softly, 'You're going somewhere, aren't you? I don't think what you are doing is right. You should find some other way to make a living. Corpses, corpses' ashes, gold, this existence, it's all wrong. People brand—'

Bhima was upset by what his wife was saying. 'Be quiet,' he said irritably. 'How does it matter what I do? If my home fires go cold who's going to come and light them up?'

'It's not like that...' she said quietly, noticing her husband's angry face, 'It's not good to roam around like some ghoul or ghost. I'm saying whatever it is I'm saying because I'm afraid.'

'Who told you that there are ghosts in the graveyards? Listen, this Mumbai is a ghosts' bazaar. The real ghosts stay in houses and the dead ones rot in those graveyards. Ghosts take birth in the village—not in the wild,' raved Bhima.

In the face of his anger she kept her mouth shut as he made preparations to leave. He growled, 'I didn't get work even after going to Mumbai. But sifting through corpses' ashes, I've got gold. When I broke hills they gave me two rupees. But now that ash easily gives me even ten rupees....' Saying this, he left the house. It was quite late by then. It was quiet and peaceful outside.

⚮

Bhima had tied a muffler around his head. Over that he had put on a hooded cloak-like covering made of sackcloth, which he cinched at the waist. Carrying a pointed crowbar, he was walking with big strides. It was pitch-dark but he felt no fear. A sari, one petticoat, and a blouse, dates in the morning was all he had on his mind. He was in a wild mood today.

There seemed to be a certain amount of tension in the air and it was getting tenser by the moment. A pack of jackals ran past him. A snake crossed the path and slithered away. An owl hooted in the distance adding to the eerie atmosphere. Nothing moved in the desolate jungle. Straining to catch every sound, Bhima drew near the village in which the moneylender had died. He sat down and surveyed the surroundings. All was silent in the village. Occasionally, someone would cough. A lamp winked in a hut. When he saw that there was nothing to be worried about he slipped swiftly into the cemetery and started searching for the new grave of the moneylender. Pushing aside shattered pots and battered biers he jumped from this grave to that. He advanced from row to row looking carefully for the moneylender's grave. Clouds filled the sky. They deepened the darkness. Then abruptly lightning shone, dancing in the nooks and crannies of the clouds. It looked like it would rain. That made Bhima panic. Worried that he'd not be able to find the new grave if it rained, his search grew frenzied. He began to sweat, he felt he was losing his mind. By midnight he had searched the whole burial ground. From one end he reached the other end and slumped to the ground, distraught and confused. The wind was building up. It rattled the old poles of broken biers. It was almost as if someone were gnashing his teeth. Then a fearsome snarling erupted out of the night. Something was snarling, sobbing, and scraping at the mud. Fearfully, he moved towards the sound. It died out at once. But almost immediately he felt as if someone was dusting his hands and feet, and he got startled. He stopped abruptly. Fear ran like an electric current through his body and struck him right inside his head. For the first time in his life he was afraid.

In the next instant he got a grip on himself when he realized what was actually happening. He felt somewhat ashamed that he had been so scared. The new grave was close by. Ten to fifteen jackals were busy digging it up as they had scented the dead body. As stones had been placed on top of the grave, they had started tunnelling into it from all sides. As they scraped away the earth, they snarled and snapped at each other; each one was desperate to be the first to get at the corpse. Bhima was enraged by the sight of the jackals.

He took a giant leap and landed right on top of the grave. He began lifting the stones on the grave and hurled them at the pack of jackals. In the face of this sudden onslaught the jackals retreated. Determined to dig up the grave before the jackals renewed their assault on it, Bhima began scraping away the mud. The jackals, only momentarily deterred, attacked him. In a fit of madness one of the jackals pounced on Bhima. It bit him and leaped back. Excitement and anger surged through Bhima's body. He had wrapped his hand in the sacking he had brought with him. He removed the sacking and grabbed hold of the crowbar. When the jackal that had bitten him returned to the attack, he brought the crowbar down on its body with all his tremendous strength. The jackal yelped and died. Bhima began digging up the grave once more. The remaining jackals attacked in a solid, snapping mass. A desperate fight broke out. Bhima lunged at the snarling animals with his crowbar. The jackals were coming at him from every side, and he was getting bitten all over his body. But his flailing crowbar was finding its mark as well and he was wounding the jackals every time he connected.

And so battle was joined between this modern Bhima, heir to the legacy of Kunti's son Bhima, and the jackals. He struggled with all his strength—if he was going to have a meal tomorrow he needed to get to that corpse. Nature was asleep. Mumbai was resting. The village was quiet. And in that burial ground the clash over gold and corpse was reaching its climax. Bhima was attacking and felling the jackals, who yelped in agony every time they were hit. Even as some were wounded, others dodged the blows and bit Bhima, who moaned and cursed every time a bite was taken out of his flesh. Curses, growls, screams, the sound of the crowbar making contact with the jackals—all this mayhem sent tremors through the cemetery.

After a really long time, the jackals stopped attacking and retreated into the darkness. Taking advantage of this, Bhima removed the remaining mud from the grave. He wiped the sweat from his face. He jumped into the grave. At that the jackals charged him again. He began furiously lashing out at them once more, and finally managed to drive them off. As the last of the animals scurried away, Bhima got hold of the body, shoved his hands under its armpits and scooped it out of the straw in which it had been wrapped. As the man had been dead for a while, his body was stiff and unyielding. He leaned it upright in the grave, and began examining it for loot. He found a ring on its finger and pulled it off. It had an earring in one ear, which he clawed off. There would definitely be some gold in the mouth. He tried to insert his fingers into the corpse's mouth but its jaws were clenched tight. Quickly, Bhima took the crowbar and pried open the dead man's mouth. Propping it open with the crowbar he inserted his fingers into the open jaws. Just then, the jackals, which had been skulking unseen in the darkness, began howling in unison. Their wailing and howling woke up the village dogs, which began barking, and running around. The commotion woke up the villagers. Someone yelled: 'The jackals are eating the body, come on....'

Afraid that the villagers would find him robbing the corpse, Bhima hurriedly put the ring he had stolen inside his pocket and began rooting around inside the corpse's mouth. He yanked out the crowbar that he had used to prop open the mouth, without remembering to extract his fingers first. The dead man's teeth clamped down on his fingers like a nutcracker on a betel nut. Bhima writhed in pain.

He could see the men from the village approaching with lanterns. Desperately he tried to extricate his fingers. When they wouldn't move, he became furious with the corpse. He swung the crowbar at the dead man's jaw. The blow only succeeded in jamming his hand deeper into the dead man's mouth. He felt the corpse's teeth cut into his fingers. He froze, thinking: this is a real ghost, today it will catch me and hand me over to the people who will kill me because I am desecrating this body. Or they will hand me over to the police. As all this went through his head, Bhima lost control and began to savagely attack the corpse. 'Pimp, let me go...' he began to yell, before he realized any noise would give away his position; he struggled on in silence. The villagers were drawing close. Bhima forced himself to calm down, to think. He realized what he must do. He pushed the crowbar back into the jaws of the corpse, levered them apart, and slowly pulled out his fingers. They had been almost bitten through. Cradling his wounded hand with the other one, he leaped out of the grave and ran into the night.

When he reached home he had a high fever. His wife and daughter wept when they saw the state he was in. A doctor was summoned and he amputated two of Bhima's fingers. The same day, news arrived that the quarry was resuming operations. Hearing this, the elephant-like Bhima started sobbing like a small child. He had lost two of his 'hill-breaker fingers' for the sake of gold from the grave.

REBATI

FAKIR MOHAN SENAPATI

*Translated from the Odia by Leelawati Mohapatra,
Paul St-Pierre, and K. K. Mohapatra*

'But oft some shining April morn is darkened in an hour, And blackest griefs o'er joyous home, Alas! unseen may lower.'
—Rev. J. H. Gurney

'Rebati! Rebi! You fire that turns all to ashes.'

Patapur—a sleepy little village in Hariharpur subdivision, district of Cuttack. At one end stood Shyambandhu Mohanty's house: two rows of rooms, front and back, with an inner courtyard centring around a well, and a shed for husking rice behind the house, along with a vegetable patch, and a garden in front. It was in the outer room that visitors and farmers waiting to pay their taxes gathered and made themselves comfortable. Shyambandhu Mohanty, the zamindar's accountant, was responsible for collecting taxes. His salary was two rupees a month, but he could earn a little more by adjusting rent receipts and land records; all told, this added up to at least four rupees. With this he could make ends meet. And not just barely; no, to tell the truth, he was quite comfortable. His family never complained of wanting for anything. They had all they needed: two drumstick trees in the backyard, and a patch of land always full of greens and vegetables; two cows, which never went dry at the same time, so there was always a little curd and milk in the pails. Mohanty's old mother made fuel cakes from cow dung and husks, so they rarely had to buy firewood. The zamindar had given him three and a half acres of rent-free land to cultivate, and it produced just about enough to meet their needs.

Shyambandhu was a straightforward person, and the tenants respected, even liked, him. He went from door to door cajoling and coaxing them to pay their taxes; he never demanded a paisa extra from anyone. On his own initiative, and without their asking, he would slip four-finger-wide palm-leaf receipts into the underside thatch of their houses. He never let the zamindar's muscleman cast his shadow over the village; he'd pump the fellow's palm, fondle his chin, tuck two paise into the folds of his dhoti to buy a plug of tobacco, and see him off.

In his own home, Shyambandhu had four stomachs to fill—his own, his wife's, his old mother's, and his ten-year-old daughter's. The daughter's name was Rebati. In the evenings, Shyambandhu would sit on his veranda and sing 'Krupasindhu Badan' and other prayer songs; at times, he would light an oil lamp, place it on a wooden stand, and read aloud passages from the Bhagavata. Rebati always sat next to him, listening with rapt attention; soon she had learnt a few songs by heart. Her melodious voice lent them more appeal, and people would stop by to listen. There was one hymn which gave Shyambandhu the greatest joy, and every evening he would unfailingly ask Rebati to sing it:

> *Whither shall I take my prayers, Lord,*
> *If Thou turnest a blind eye?*
> *Surely shall I be finished.*
> *Be it salvation or damnation,*
> *To Thee this life a dedication,*
> *To Thee, this soul laden.*
> *Empty, empty, all the three worlds*
> *When I am without Thee.*
> *True refreshment, when I thirst,*
> *Only Thy love can be.*

Two years earlier, in the course of his visit to the countryside, the deputy inspector of schools had happened to spend a night at Patapur. At the request of the village elders he had written to the inspector of schools, Orissa Division, and an upper-primary school had been established in the village. The government paid the teacher's salary of four rupees a month to which each student contributed an additional anna.

The teacher, Basudev, a young man of twenty, had attended the teacher-training course at Cuttack Normal School. Urbane and polite, he never took on superior airs. He had been orphaned at an early age and had been brought up by his uncle. True to his name, he was a fine human being. Charming and handsome—the indelible mark of a bottle's mouth on his forehead applied by his mother to treat diphtheria during childhood enhanced rather than marred his looks. He seemed to have been sculpted out of a single block.

From the time he arrived in the village, Shyambandhu had taken a fancy to him: they belonged to the same caste.

Occasionally, on the day of a full moon or a Thursday, when cakes and savouries were made at home, Shyambandhu would call at the school: 'Son, come to our place this evening; your aunt has invited you.' A bond of affection had naturally developed between them after these visits. Even Rebati's mother, filled with concern, would sometimes exclaim: 'Ah, the poor orphan! What does he eat, who looks after his meals?' As the visits became regular, with Basu dropping in practically every evening, Rebati would wait at the door to announce his arrival. As soon as she spotted him at a distance she would call out to her father, 'Here comes Basubhai, here he comes!' Then she would sit beside him and sing all the prayer songs she knew. To Basu's ears, the songs were fresh and ever new.

One day, as they chatted about this and that, Shyambandhu learnt from Basu there was a school at Cuttack where girls could study and also learn crafts; instantly, the desire to give Rebati an education welled up in his heart. When he confided this to Basu, the young teacher, who had already begun to look upon him as a father, answered: 'I was about to suggest that myself.'

Rebati listened to the conversation and rushed inside. 'I'm going to study,' she announced excitedly to her mother and grandmother. 'I'm going to learn to read.'

Her mother smiled. 'Go ahead,' she said, but her grandmother's reaction was sharp: 'What good will it do you? How does book learning help a girl? It's enough to know how to cook, bake, churn butter, and make patterns on walls using rice paste.'

That night, when Shyambandhu sat down to dinner on a low wooden stool with Rebati beside him, the old lady sat opposite them, restive and itching to speak her mind: 'Serve him a little more rice, daughter-in-law, give him a second helping of dal and a pinch of salt,' and so on. Then she brought up the topic: 'Shyam, is Rebi going to study? Why should she, son? What good is that for a girl?'

'Never mind, Ma,' said Shyambandhu. 'Let her study if she wants to. Haven't you heard Jhankar Pattanaik's daughters can read the Bhagavata and *Baidehisa Bilas*?'

Rebati was furious at her grandmother. 'You silly old fool!' she snorted. Turning to her father, she begged him, 'Father, I do want to study.'

'And so you will,' said Shyambandhu.

The matter was left there.

The following afternoon Basu brought Rebati a copy of Sitanath Babu's *First Lessons*. She was so overjoyed she leafed through the book from cover to cover. The pictures of elephants, houses, and cows thrilled her no end. Kings could be happy to own elephants and horses, others perhaps derived joy from riding them, but for Rebati it was enough merely to gaze at their pictures. She could hardly wait to show them to her mother and grandmother.

The grandmother did not hide her irritation. 'Take that silly thing away from me,' she shouted.

'Silly you!' the girl retorted.

The auspicious day of Sri Panchami dawned. Rebati took an early bath, put on new clothes, and flitted in and out of the house, waiting impatiently for Basu. The usual pomp associated with beginning one's studies was played down out of fear of the grandmother. Six hours into the morning Basu arrived and taught her the alphabet: a, aa, e, ee, u, uu....

The lessons went on. Basu never missed a day.

Over the next two years Rebati studied a great deal. All the rhymes of Madhu Rao were on the tip of her tongue and she could reel them off without faltering.

At dinner one night, Shyambandhu asked his mother, as if rounding off a discussion they had been having, 'Well, Ma, what do you think?'

'Nothing could be better,' said the old lady. 'But are you certain what his caste is?'

'That's what I was trying to find out. He may be poor but he comes from a good family. And he's a pucca Karan to boot.'

'Good. Caste counts more than wealth. But will he agree to live with us?'

'Why not? After all, his only relatives are his uncle and aunt. He probably won't insist on living with them.'

What Rebati made of all this she alone knew, but a change certainly came over her. She became noticeably coy with Basu. In the evening she would hang around the front door, as though waiting for someone, which riled her grandmother no end, but when Basu arrived she would hide inside the house. It took Basu quite an effort before she would come out for her studies. Blushing and smiling for no apparent reason, she would refuse to read her lessons aloud and would answer him in monosyllables. As soon as the day's lesson was done she would rush inside, struggling to stifle her giggles.

∞

One Sri Panchami followed another, and two years passed. Providence's designs are strange and inscrutable; no two days are alike. One fine Phalguna day, like a bolt out of the blue, a cholera epidemic struck.

Early in the morning the news of Shyambandhu coming down with cholera spread through the village. As always, the immediate response was to bolt the doors and windows, and keep out of the path of the demonic deity, as though the evil old hag was out with her basket and broom sweeping up heads.

Shyambandhu's wife and mother were soon driven out of their minds by worry and anxiety. Rebati ran in and out of the house, crying for help. When the news reached Basu, he hurried from the school and, without fear for his own life, sat at the bedside, massaging Shyambandhu's hands and legs and forcing drops of water between his parched lips.

Three hours passed.

Suddenly, Shyambandhu looked up at Basu and stammered: 'Take care of my family, I leave them to you....'

Basu could not hold back his tears.

Shyambandhu passed away that evening.

The women wailed. Rebati rolled on the floor.

How could the two grief-stricken women and the inexperienced Basu make arrangements for the cremation? Bana Sethi, the village washerman, a veteran of fifty or sixty cremations, saved the day, turning up with a towel around his waist and an axe on his shoulder. Bana was rather philosophical about it: cholera or not, if your time's up you've got to go, whether today or tomorrow, but why miss out on a set of new clothes? Shyambandhu's was the only Karan family in the village, and help was neither expected nor forthcoming; the two women and Basudev had to carry the body to the cremation grounds and perform the last rites.

The morning star was shining in the eastern sky by the time they were done. No sooner had they got home than Rebati's mother came down with cholera. By midday the news of her death had spread through the village.

Providence works in mysterious ways—while one man is blessed with a regal umbrella atop his palanquin, another receives lashes on his fettered hands. Within three months of Shyambandhu's demise, the zamindar expropriated Shyambandhu's cows—apparently he had not deposited the last tax collection. This was hard to believe, however. Shyambandhu had always regarded depositing the money as sacred and would not rest in peace until every paisa of the collection was in the zamindar's treasury. The truth was that for a long time the zamindar had had his eyes on the cows. He also took back the three and a half acres he had given Shyambandhu. There was no work for the farmhand, and he left on the full moon day of the Dola festival. The team of bullocks had already been sold off for seventeen and a half rupees; with what remained after the funeral expenses, the grandmother and Rebati hung on for a month. In the month following they began to pawn household items—a brass bowl one day, a plate the next.

Basu visited them every evening and stayed until bedtime. He offered them money, but they would not touch it. Once or twice he pressed some on them, but the coins lay idle on the shelf. He had no choice but to accept the couple of paise the old woman produced every eight or ten days to buy them provisions. The house was falling apart, the straw roof had worn thin, but try as he might Basu couldn't get it rethatched; the bales of hay he bought with two rupees of his own money rotted in the backyard.

The grandmother no longer cried day and night; she now confined her wailing to the evenings. But she put so much of herself into it that it left her slumped in a heap on the floor for the night. Rebati, convulsing in sobs, would lie down next to her. The old woman's vision had declined and she had a wild look about her. She no longer cried as much and took to heaping curses and abuse on Rebati: the wretched girl was at the root of all her misery and misfortune; her education had caused it all—first, her son had died, then her daughter-in-law; the bullocks had been sold off; the farmhand had left; the cows had been taken by the zamindar; and now her eyes had gone bad. Rebati was the evil eye, the she-devil, the ill-omened.

The moment the curses started coming thick and fast, Rebati would shrink from her grandmother and hide in a corner of the house or the backyard, tears streaming down her cheeks.

The grandmother held Basu equally to blame. If he had not been so eager to teach the girl, she could not possibly have gone and taught herself! But the grandmother could not take Basu to task, because she couldn't do without him. The zamindar kept seeking flimsy clarifications, and almost every second day a messenger came asking for this account or that. Basu alone could fish them out from the clutter of papers Shyambandhu had left behind. Yet, behind Basu's back, the old woman sometimes gave vent to her feelings.

Rebati's presence no longer filled the house; gone were the days when she would be heard mourning loudly. Nobody heard her voice, nobody saw her out of doors. Her large brooding eyes, awash with silent tears, looked like blue lilies floating in water. Her heart and mind broken, day and night were alike to her. The sun brought her no light, the night no darkness; the world was an aching void. The memories of her parents overwhelmed her, their faces hung before her glazed eyes. She could not bring herself to believe they were truly dead and gone. Hunger no longer stirred her stomach; slumber no longer closed her eyes. She went through the pretence of eating only out of fear of her grandmother; she grew thin and emaciated, her skin hung loose on her bones, and she could barely lift herself off the floor where she lay day and night. The only time she revived a little was when Basu visited them. She would sit up and fasten her gaze on him, lowering her eyes with a sigh when their glances met. But the next moment she'd feverishly stare at him again. For those brief hours of the day when he was around, Basu completely possessed her eyes, her mind and her heart.

Roughly five months had passed. On a hot Jaistha Saturday afternoon, Basu knocked on their door. Never before had he ever called at such an unusual hour. The old woman was full of foreboding as she let him in.

'Grandmother,' said Basu. 'The deputy inspector of schools will be camping at the Hariharpur police station and giving the students an oral test. All the schools have been informed; I received the order today. Tomorrow morning I'll have to start off and be away for about five days.'

Listening to the conversation from behind the door, Rebati felt her legs give way. Her hold on the door was barely tight enough to stop herself from falling.

Basu bought them enough rice, oil, salt, and vegetables for five days, and bade them goodbye.

'Son,' said the old woman with a sigh. 'Don't walk about in the sun for too long. Take care of yourself; eat your meals on time.'

Rebati could not take her eyes off him. Before, she would look away when their eyes met, but today she stared unblinkingly, unabashedly into his eyes. A change seemed to have come over Basu, too. For a long time he had contented himself with stolen glances, but today he did not turn away. They stared deeply into each other's eyes.

Evening came; darkness filled the house and covered the earth. Rebati remained rooted to the ground until her grandmother's piercing screams jolted her to her senses. Basu had left much earlier.

Rebati counted the days.

On the morning of the sixth she even rushed a couple of times to the front door, which she had avoided since her parents' death. Six hours had passed when the schoolboys arrived back from Hariharpur, bringing the news of Basu's death. He had succumbed to cholera under the big banyan tree near Gopalpur on his return journey. The village folk mourned; the women and children shed copious tears. 'What a handsome fellow!' said one. 'So polite,' said another. 'Never hurt a fly,' remarked yet another.

The grandmother cried so much she choked. 'Poor boy!' she repeated between sobs. 'You only brought it on yourself!' Implying that he had perished in his prime because he had been foolish enough to want to teach Rebati.

Rebati sank to the floor and lay there without a whine or a whimper.

The grandmother woke up the following morning without Rebati beside her and shouted out in anger: 'Rebati! Rebi! You fire that turns all to ashes.' She worked herself into a froth, and passers-by heard these terrible words repeated all morning long.

Half-blind and angry, she groped her way through the entire house. When she finally found the girl, she was shocked. Rebati, burning with fever, was unconscious. Worry and fear gnawed at the old woman's heart. She couldn't decide what to do, who to turn to for help. Exasperated, out of breath, and without hope, she tartly commented: 'What medicine can there be for an illness of one's own making!' Rebati had brought the fever on herself by daring to study.

One, two, three, four, five days passed. Rebati remained glued to the ground, her eyes and lips shut. On the sixth morning she let out a whimper or two. The old woman ran her hand over the girl's body. It was cool to the touch; perhaps the fever had left. She called out to her, and Rebati mumbled a reply, then asked for water, stared wildly around, and broke into incoherent babble. One quick look and even a country doctor could have quoted from his text: 'Thirst, fever, delirium; of imminent collapse these are the symptoms.' But the poor grandmother was overcome with a sense of relief. The fever had left, the girl was able to open her eyes and speak two words, to ask for water. A little gruel was all she needed to regain her strength and get back on her feet.

'Don't get up,' the grandmother said. 'Stay where you are. I'm going to cook you a bit of food.' She left the room and rummaged in vain among the earthen pots for a handful of rice. Her head became clouded with despair and she sat down with a sigh. If only her eyesight had been better she would have realized the provisions meant for five days had already lasted for ten.

But there was a flicker of hope in her yet. She picked up the only object of value left—an old brass bowl with a hole in the bottom—and set out for Hari Sa's store. The so-called store was in Hari's residence, in the middle of the village, and he kept a paltry stock of rice, salt, lentils, and oil to sell to travellers passing by.

Hari saw the old woman with the bowl. He understood immediately, but let her first make her plea. He then took the bowl and examined it minutely, turning it from side to side. 'There's no rice,' he said, handing it back. 'Who's going to give you anything for a bowl like this?' Of course, he had both rice and the inclination to sell it, but getting the brass bowl for a song was what interested him the most. The grandmother staggered at his words, as though lightning had hit her. What would she do if she didn't get any rice, what would she cook for Rebati, how would the girl fight her weakness? She sat there for hours, depressed and silent, still as a log, casting imploring glances at the shopkeeper.

The day wore on. Realizing she had left the sick girl alone for a long time, fear stirred her old heart. 'Time I got back home,' she mumbled to herself, picking up the bowl. 'God knows how that girl of mine is doing.'

'Never mind,' said Hari grudgingly. 'Give me the bowl. Let's see if I can scrape up a little something for you.' He gave her four measures of rice, half a measure of lentils, and a handful of salt. The old woman hobbled back home, resting every four steps or so to catch her breath. She hadn't even washed her face since morning, and her mind was in a whirl.

She reached home hoping Rebati was better. She thought she'd ask the girl to draw water from the well. The rice wouldn't take long to cook. She called out to Rebati once, twice, three times, but got no response. Then she yelled at the top of her voice: 'Rebati! Rebi! You fire that turns all to ashes.'

By now, Rebati was sinking fast. Her body, already feeble from spasms of excruciating pain, had turned ice-cold. Her thirst was so terrible she felt as if her tongue was being sucked back into her throat. She found the room unbearably hot and crawled out to the inner courtyard. Even that brought no relief. She rolled out to the veranda at the back and propped herself up against the wall.

Dusk had fallen and a gentle breeze was blowing. A bunch of bananas hung from the plant her father had planted before his death. The guava sapling her mother had planted two years ago had grown to a considerable height and was covered with blossoms. Rebati remembered how she had drawn water from the well in a small jug and tended the sapling. This brought back a rush of memories of her mother. Her head was in a whirl, her thoughts jumbled, but the image of her mother clung to her.

Night slowly descended. Darkness stole out from the boughs of the trees and shrouded the garden. Rebati tilted her head back and watched the sky. The lone evening star was gleaming brightly. She could not take her eyes off it; and it grew and grew and grew, bigger and brighter, invading the whole sky, and behold! Her loving mother sat in the heart of it, her face glowing with love and kindness, her arms extended towards Rebati in invitation. Rebati was overwhelmed. Two shafts of light pierced her eyes and moved down to her heart. Her breathing, heavy and laboured, rose and fell, breaking the stillness of the night. She wheezed, choked, and cried out to her mother twice. Then there was silence.

The grandmother crawled around the house, going from the living room to the courtyard to the rice-husking shed, but Rebati was nowhere to be found. Then it occurred to the old woman that with the fever abating the girl might be taking a stroll in the garden at the back.

'Rebati!' she screamed. 'Rebi! You fire that turns all to ashes.'

She crawled out to the narrow veranda, which was only one hand wide and two high, and bumped into the girl. 'Death to you!' she cried. 'Sitting here, are you?' She wanted to shake her up, but she could sense something was amiss.

She ran her hand over the length of the girl's body and then held a finger close to her nostrils. The night's silence was rent by her eerie wail. Two bodies fell from the veranda and thudded to the ground.

That was the end of Shyambandhu Mohanty's family.

The last words which had emanated from his house were: 'Rebati! Rebi! You fire that turns all to ashes.'

SHARAVANA SERVICES
VIVEK SHANBHAG

Translated from the Kannada by Jayanth Kodkani

1

When Sharavana told me, 'Not today, sir.... Today is Tuesday', I agreed because it was convenient for me. I had a lot of work to do by evening and it wouldn't have been possible to go with him and check out a plot. Since the Tuesday factor came in as a handy pretext, I agreed at once. And to sound as if I had indeed meant it, said: 'Arre, it is Tuesday! I had forgotten too amidst all the work.'

Even after two days, Sharavana didn't talk about going to see the site. Otherwise, his business would start with office hours in the morning—from the moment he came in and placed a cup of tea on the table. He had joined this office as a peon some years ago, but of late had managed to retain his job by handling additional chores such as running errands in the bank as well as helping with office upkeep. Everyone in the office has had some personal dealing with him. For any service you wanted—be it buying a second-hand fridge, disposing of an old fan, getting the dented rear of your car fixed for a low price, looking for a carpenter to drill holes in the walls of your house for nails and hang pictures at five rupees per nail—you could get in touch with him and the work was done. If you wanted a site in Bangalore and a lawyer to scrutinize the property papers, a contractor to build the house and a priest for the Bhoomi Puja, he was at your disposal. If you wanted pandits of Nadi Shastra or Vastu Shastra, wished to go for a darshan of the baba, wanted a priest of your own sub-caste for puja as laid down in the scriptures, you could tell him and he would readily arrange for it. He could speak Kannada, Telugu, Tamil, and Hindi so fluently that one couldn't figure out what his mother tongue was. And his English, though faltering and faulty, could be understood.

After two days when my work pressure had eased a bit, I said, 'Let us go and check out the site today, Sharavana.'

'Just wait for one more day, sir.... Let's go on Friday.'

'Why? Are you looking for an auspicious time?' I said in jest.

'Take it that way. You'll see how smoothly the work gets done....'

That Friday, we went and saw the site. Hardly had we taken a look, when he got a bit restive and said, 'Ayyo, had I known that it faces the south, I wouldn't have brought you here at all.' I quite liked the plot. But Sharavana, said, 'This is certainly not for you, sir. If you wish, I can find you another site in the same layout.'

'I don't care which direction it faces. Tell me if there is any other problem....' My tone suggested, 'Do what you're told. Don't act smart!'

But Sharavana wouldn't be cowed down. 'As you say, sir. Your belief alone matters....' he said.

'Are you doing business or are you in the job of reading people's horoscopes?'

'If those who buy through me don't thrive, it is my business that will suffer, right? If everything goes smoothly, they will bring me half a dozen other customers. Otherwise, they'll say, we bought it from him and look what we've had to face.'

'If you wish, I can give it in writing that I won't complain. Even if we had come here on Tuesday, this site would be facing the south, wouldn't it?'

'Sir, I don't say this for the sake of argument. It isn't that easy to remove the tangled knot between thought, belief, and experience. Even if we don't believe in astrology, don't our eyes pause for a moment at the horoscope column while flipping through a newspaper? Even a pseudo-palmist's words about our private lives stay in our mind, no, sir? I'll tell you a secret. Your views make me feel like sharing it. It's to do with our Shahane saheb....'

I hadn't expected such skillful language from him. Yet, I composed myself and said, 'Let me hear what you have to say. What about Shahane saheb? Isn't he enjoying a happy retired life?'

'He bought a site and built a house too. I myself found a Maharashtrian priest for his housewarming ceremony. When I met him after two months, he told me, 'What do I do, Sharavana? My wife, who never raised her voice against me, has begun to pick quarrels with me every day for no reason. And, with a lump in his throat, he said he couldn't bear to see her grind her teeth during the fights. He had also secretly seen some doctors about this.

'....I felt this must be the handiwork of bad Vastu. I knew a person called Chennappa, who is well-versed in Vastu. I took him to Shahane's house. Chennappa said the direction of the water inflow into the house was not in order. Shahane didn't heed the advice. Just two days later, another mishap occurred. Leaving the front door wide open, his wife went out to buy vegetables. He was sitting on the sofa engrossed in the balance sheet of some company and thinking about the stock market. All of a sudden, a strong wind pushed the open door. To stop the door from slamming the frame, he rose swiftly, one hand still clutching the papers and the other stretched out. At that instant, he felt as if the devil had possessed him. The evil Vastu was acting again. Something strange happened as he forcefully bent his sixty-year-old body forward like a bow. He managed to prevent the door from banging but leaned on it and collapsed, unable to bear a shooting pain in his back. He was rushed to the hospital. They said it was a case of a slipped disc. And then one after another, he suffered a series of aches.

'....I visited him at the hospital. "You needn't get anything done, I'll set everything right," I said. He told me, "I leave it all to you." That very day I got the nozzle of the water pipe in his house turned towards another side. Just that, sir. That was all. As if it was some miracle, peace returned to the household. Then onwards, I bet, the woman didn't quarrel at all.'

After listening to his story, I had no intention of devaluing its entertainment bit. Still, unable to stomach it all, I said, 'Haven't you heard of the proverb: The crow sat on the branch and the tree snapped?'

'Take it as coincidence if you want. For a big tree to crash, even the weight of a crow can suffice. You see, the world is said to hang in balance. But a piece of straw is enough to disturb the equilibrium. Or, a flutter of a butterfly's wings. Call it a Vastu defect or simply bad fortune, a slight change in the time you wake up in the morning might ruin your day.'

I did not argue with him further. The site was lost. 'Nothing to worry. Good riddance, in fact,' Sharavana told me after two days.

2

'I've seen a house. It belongs to some people in the movie business. The owner needs money urgently and wants to sell it. All it needs are some minor changes. It's a first-class house!' Sharavana continued to badger me.

I wasn't sure whether I wanted a site or a house. And then, I wasn't confident of taking a big leap in life by buying a house. When I told him that I would think it over for a day or two, he said: 'Ayyo, sir, it'll be sold by then. These matters are such—if you keep pondering about them, you'll lose the one you have in hand. You can't get a house so dirt cheap,' Sharavana persuaded me.

We decided to see the house that evening. Sharavana told me that we would have to start at two minutes before five o'clock, suggesting that the time after five would be inauspicious. I didn't respond.

We stepped out of the office. Crossing the scooters and motorcycles parked outside, we reached the edge of the road and stood there waiting to hail an autorickshaw. Sharavana, who stood facing me, had launched into a detailed description of the house we were going to see and the excessive vanity and opulence of film folk. He spoke of one who fell from the heights of prosperity to the depths of destitution and another—names that I had never heard of—who rose like a meteor.

That very moment....

A speeding bus lost control and hurtled towards us. Sharavana was standing with his back to the road, engrossed in his talk. All that was recorded in my memory was that the bus turned towards us. My dragging him aside, both of us falling on to the pavement after losing balance, and because of the fall, escaping the wheels of the bus by inches—all had happened outside of my will and intent. Like in a film sequence, the bus had crashed into the parking lot, smashing the scooters and motorcycles much like a sickle scything through a corn field. Earlier, it had mowed down a drowsy dog even before it could finish howling. Sharavana was terrified, having glimpsed his death amidst the piles of wrecked vehicles. As if he had imagined his own body in the heaps of mangled metal, Sharavana held my hand and squatted on the ground without uttering a word. His hands were trembling. So were mine. I sat down too. Our clothes were dusty and people who had gathered around us within no time were talking of our providential escape. The sight of the motionless corpse of the dog, which only a while ago had crossed us, reminded me for the first time of the transience of life. I too was horrified. And I didn't realize that I had kept his hand pressed in my palms. As we sat there comforting each other like brothers, our colleagues who had rushed there on hearing the noise, gathered around us.

From that day, Sharavana began to regard me as God. And with utmost trust, like confessing before God, recounted to me some providential and jinxed happenings in his life. He didn't unburden himself in one sitting. The incidents were unravelled in the span of a month, as different situations arose, in bits and snatches. All told in the ups and downs of his moods. When incidents are narrated by one person to another, many details pass through a sieve. If I tell them in his words, at least the emotional intensity might remain.

3

Sir, my name is Shravana. I come from a small village near Srirangapatna. When I started my business, I ironed out the consonant conjuncts in my name so that my customers could roll out the letters easily on their tongues. Since it sounded like a Tamil name, I didn't lose anything in terms of business. My father kept accounts in the temple. He also read horoscopes and could tell one's lakshana or characteristics. Lakshana was the word he used, he preferred not to say fortune-telling. After he quarrelled with the temple management committee, lakshana-reading became the only source of the family's income. But then, in such a small place, how many people come every day to know about their future? What could they do even if they knew? At least in this city, one sees ups and downs every day. A slight change in the price of oil or in the percentage of tax can lead to such ebbs and flows. As the day breaks, either there is a windfall or one goes stone broke. Fortune-telling or knowing may be a useful occupation in this city where uncertainty rules. But why would people of our village want to rack their brains about tomorrow? Their questions revolve around a daughter's marriage or a son gone astray. And if they heard the answers to that once, it was enough. They didn't feel the need to visit my father ever again. Managing a square meal at home became difficult at times.

I completed my pre-university commuting to and from Mysore every day. Left with no option, I later took a job with the cooperative society in our village. I was required to do all kinds of work. Although the pay was low, I carried out every task diligently because the president of the society was genial. Years later, when life seemed to be getting into a groove, and believing that the job was there to stay, I contemplated marriage.

Lavanya was born and brought up in Bangalore; she is a distant relative of ours. Her family was of modest means. Yet, she is said to have balked at the thought of shifting to a smaller place. The elders had to convince her to agree to the marriage. All this, we learnt later. When she wept bitterly on the day of the marriage, we presumed it was because of the sorrow of leaving her parents' home. Later I suspected the grief might also have been about moving to a village. She had done her pre-university course. And in her talk, demeanour, and likes and dislikes, she tended to go the extra mile. In the beginning I liked that. But as days passed, the attitude annoyed me. I felt the show of her refinement was an expression of disgust towards our household. It would begin with what brand of tea leaves we must use. Even if she found fault with the cinema theatre in our village, I would take offence and get agitated. In the face of all this, when I recollect the first happy year of our life, all the romance seemed to belong to somebody else. It slowly dawned upon her that even if I toiled for my entire life, there wouldn't be any change in my job or in my status. Perhaps she had resigned herself to it. But I, who hadn't questioned it for so long, started to behave as though I was determined to transform everything.

One day my aunt's son came to our house from Bangalore. Shrikant was of my age, gaunt, and a dud at studies. We had nicknamed him Buddi because he wore spectacles as thick as that of a soda bottle. When he came this time, Buddi started talking about grandiose things in the share market. That was when the winds of change were blowing across the country and wherever you went, people were talking of business and money. That night after dinner, Buddi began to tell me thrilling stories of how people who bought stocks were making money. I am unable to say even now what happened in the room that night when this grand narration was on. But the heady sense of success and affluence gripped everybody there, at least a wee bit. The glance that Buddi threw at Lavanya as he spoke is still fresh in my mind. I wondered from where he had suddenly gathered that self-confidence. Almost the next instant, Lavanya looked at me. His glance followed by her look at me might seem casual to you. But it shot a message through me and I feel that it was then that my life forked in two directions. Sir, isn't it after such ordinary instances that the devil or spirit enters your life? My father, who had been listening to him in silence, said at last: 'Take care, son. Beware of this wealth that grows only on paper and doesn't come after hard work.'

I felt that unless I left my village, my life wouldn't change one bit. Before hitting the bed at night, I started dreaming about going abroad and returning with immense prosperity. Look at history, or consider the tales in *Chandamama*: the man chasing success goes away to a far-off land, doesn't he, sir? I felt Lavanya had spurred this dream indirectly. I told myself that her glance that day suggested that. I felt she was convinced that I had it in me to pursue the dream. But I didn't know where to go after leaving the village. I pestered Buddi and got myself a job in Bangalore. My parents were frightened. They sobbed and kicked up a ruckus. They taunted me saying that I was looking after them too well for having named me Sharavana Kumar. They called their daughter-in-law a sorceress and hurled abuse. Not heeding anybody, I left.

Only two months after I came to Bangalore I lost my first job. For about six months after that I struggled a lot. Nobody came forward to help me. With the market scam exposed, the share prices had nosedived, putting even Buddi to great hardship. Helpless, I took up any job I could get. The person who got me my present job used to be my client. His name was Kannan. Along with this, I took up real estate and other miscellaneous services. Gradually I started Sharavana Services. What is it about, you may ask. This is a business I conceived and set up. As you know, sir, Bangalore has grown in the last ten years. People have come here from different places. They can't handle things as they did in their places. They can't find priests for auspicious events. They are all at sea when they have to organize a house-warming ceremony. In a place where they have no acquaintances at all, if the mother, who had come to live with her son, dies all of a sudden, who is to perform the rites? How do they find support and succour in times of mental agony? Who do they look to for solace? They are tormented by the guilt that they haven't done anything right. Worse, they can't spare time to go in search of all these. And they feel they can buy anything for a price. More importantly, they are ready to accept new-fangled rituals. What do smokers do if they can't find their brand? They settle for some other. Likewise, the addiction of faith and rituals. I provide them such beliefs.

I don't regret having disclosed to you the secrets of my business. A broker ought to have faith in everything, sir. But then he shouldn't have excessive faith in anything. If he does, his job is ruined. It would smack of prejudice. My clients don't have a deep faith in caste and such matters. Nor can they renounce it. Their faith isn't deep-rooted but they would like to believe it is. Sharavana Services provides such people a crutch, you may say. I have converted a man from Uttar Pradesh into a devotee of Goddess Banashankari. I have turned Seth—who is in the lorry business—into a devotee of Auto Maramma, initiated Chatterjee into Nadi Shastra and driven the Vastu addiction into IIT engineer Singh. Don't laugh, sir... That's a kind of intoxication. Those who are too intelligent don't relish simple things. The more complex life gets, the happier they are. Nothing better than Vastu for that. It gets more intricate as you involve yourself. My job is to provide those with what they need. Baba for those who want him, UG for some, and so on. Call my vocation selling contentment, if you may.

The man who climbs trees for a job must be wide-hipped, no? So, my language too had to change. I don't use any word that hurts one's belief. Hence my language became dignified. I didn't learn astrology from my father. But from him, I learnt the art of expression. I haven't forgotten some of his words: 'People don't like it if you say "quarrel between husband and wife". They'll be satisfied if you say conflict in a marital relationship. They must feel the problem belongs to someone else but the solution is ours. In this profession, if you talk any other language, nobody will trust you....'

As I continued to engage in this business, my earnings rose. Even the real estate business may not fetch you the kind of money that this profession gets. Nobody hesitates to pay even if he is in trouble. Vastu, Nadi Shastra, Astrology, Yoga, Unani, Baba, Ayurveda, Kanaka Yajna—I offered what people needed. People began to tell me their problems. Then I became aware of this massive populace in Bangalore's belly, a community which belonged nowhere. They are prepared to accept anything. All they want is a foothold in this city. Even if roots can't be struck, the customary watering must be done so that hope doesn't dry up. You'll be surprised to know, sir, not just outsiders but this is the fate of people from our Malnad region. Sir, there is hardly any soil left to plant our feet in this city. There's nothing which we can call ours. How does a place that doesn't have a single unwritten code find its identity? I work magic, sir, magic. If I can't find flowers, I'll conduct the shastras with plastic flowers. All this calls for faith. Even frequenting pubs to drink and dance is related to faith; the belief there is that they are enjoying life. When I was a student, going to the cinema on the very day we finished our examinations was a way of rejoicing. Of course, it didn't offer me any great joy. Still, I used to believe that I was enjoying life. What was more significant was that others believed that to be so.

Within three years, money began to flow. But I didn't find time to spend with Lavanya. My relationship with her changed altogether. You may find this amusing: back in our village, every morning when my father went out to pick flowers for the puja, Amma would go for her bath. The privacy obtained then with Lavanya, used to turn me on. Although we shared the bed through the night, I couldn't imagine the kind of titillation those moments in the morning offered. Sir, that's how lovely our relationship was. I won't lie to you, sir. What was critical was that I sensed that my love for her had diminished. For her sake, I had left my village and my parents. There was a time when I would do anything to please her. But now my mind was fixed on something else. Nothing seemed more joyful than making money. She sensed this. She began to say we should go back to our village. I shut my ears to those requests.

One summer vacation, I left my daughter at my father's house and returned to the city. Two days later Lavanya told me, 'I'm running a fever. Don't go to work today.' I didn't even touch her to check the body temperature. I had to attend to some urgent work. So I left home. But the thought that she had never pleaded with me like that before tormented me all through the day. When I returned that night, she was sleeping as though she was unconscious. Her body was burning hot. Beside her bed was a bowl of porridge. The neighbour had brought it to her, made her drink some of it, and left. When I sat on the bed, my hand felt a few dried, hardened rice grains from the porridge. Parts of the sheets where some porridge had spilled had dried stiff. As my fingers ran up the marks left on the sheets, I felt something between us had snapped. And I decided then that there was no point in returning to our village. I cannot forget those moments I spent by her side, sir, never.... The message was as strong as the one carried by her glance the day Buddi had visited us one day.

Without informing anybody, she left behind a note and went away. At times I feel sad wondering whether she did not feel any remorse about leaving behind her daughter.

From that day my daughter has adopted a strange silence. She speaks only when it is absolutely necessary. Otherwise she stays mum. None of us can muster the courage to persuade her to speak.

4

After Sharavana's narrow escape from the accident, his mother insisted upon performing Shanthi, Mrityunjaya, and other japas. He pressed me to attend the ceremony. I joked, 'I don't believe that I staked my life to save you. That happened beyond my will. Don't be obliged to me for the rest of your life for having dragged you to the side on seeing the bus.'

'Why do you say so, sir? Because you had it in you, you could save my life. You must come to this poor man's house at least today....' And he persuaded me to agree saying that I would be the only guest.

That Sunday I went to his house. It wasn't difficult locating the address. In the same street, two houses away, a crowd had gathered. Sharavana was waiting for me at the door of his house. He drew open the gate to welcome me and said, 'Sir, do you know why so many people have gathered there? UG is here.'

I was curious. 'Can anybody go and see him?' I said.

'Oh-ho.... I know the household very well. We can go see him right now if you want.' I was eager. 'Yes, let's go,' I said and we set out.

I met Prabha, my colleague, in front of that house. She is from Hyderabad. She was professionally very ambitious. She would do nothing without any definite purpose. 'What brings you here?' I asked. She said, 'I am a UG follower. As soon as he arrives in town, Mr Sharavana informs me. And I land here.' Then, as if she had noticed my surprise, added: 'He has been able to look at life without the help of any filter. In that lies his greatness.' Those words remained in my mind.

When we entered the house, it was eleven o'clock. By then many persons had gathered there. A heap of chappals was lying outside. Inside, people were leaning on a divan on the floor. Some others stood where they could find space. Everyone was listening to him in deep silence.

I found a corner for myself. All was still. Then my arm touched the TV there. Though it was me alone who felt the touch, UG suddenly turned towards me as if there was a big noise. He looked at the TV and my arm. Only then did I sense his power and the burden of carrying it, and felt a bit strange. I recollected what Prabha told me about the filter. How much can one person see without the medium of a filter? If one begins to seek the intricacies of the world in this manner, wouldn't the mind explode into thousands of pieces?

All kinds of people were asking questions. And UG would reply to them. It seemed as if he would have replied even without the questions, he was so fluent and relentless in his response. I stood listening. Terms like a son of a bitch, bastard, motherfucker, sister's paramour were pouring out incessantly. My presence there must have embarrassed Prabha. After a while I left that place. Prabha came out with me and tried to offer some sort of an explanation. She was opposed to such language, she told me.

'You like UG because he seeks his experiences without a mediating filter, isn't it? Now, while receiving his words, too, see them without the screen in the middle,' I tried to reason.

Hearing a roar of laughter from inside the house, Prabha took leave of us and went inside again.

I went to Sharavana's place with him. He said he had bought this house. It had a big, long hall. A glass showcase lined a part of it. In it were school photos of his daughter, some toys, and some glass articles. His aged mother was seated in a broad chair, observing the rituals closely as the priest conducted the homa, raising a lot of smoke. His daughter's name was Revathi. When her father called out, she emerged from an inner room, greeted me with folded hands, and went back in.

'I thought you arranged these rituals only for others,' I said in jest.

'Even the cook has to eat, doesn't he, sir?' he laughed. Then, for the first time, I observed wrinkles on his cheek at the corner of his eyes.

Though his mother appeared to be too old to walk, her vision, hearing, and speech were quite sound. She sat me next to her and recollected the days when they were in the village.

The question arose in my mind whether this was the house Sharavana's wife had run away from and immediately cursed my wretched curiosity.

After the meal, as I rose to leave, Sharavana walked in and told me, 'Please wait for a minute.' His mother got up from her seat with an effort, came to me and holding my arm, said: 'Ask him to forget that slut and marry again. He attends to a hundred tasks for other people. But there is no one to look after him. I am too old to venture out. Please don't think that I'm entrusting to you the work of a marriage broker. You have saved his life. He has survived a certain death. Let him consider this as a new life, and erase the old memories....' And then she walked back slowly to her seat.

Knowing that I was about to leave, his daughter came and stretched out an autograph book towards me. I told her I was no big name to put my signature in the book. Still, she stood in front of me without uttering a word.

PORTRAIT OF A LADY
KHUSHWANT SINGH

My grandmother, like everybody's grandmother, was an old woman. She had been old and wrinkled for the twenty years that I had known her. People said that she had once been young and pretty and had even had a husband, but that was hard to believe. My grandfather's portrait hung above the mantelpiece in the drawing room. He wore a big turban, and loose-fitting clothes. His long white beard covered the best part of his chest and he looked at least a hundred years old. He did not look the sort of person who would have a wife or children. He looked as if he could only have lots and lots of grandchildren. As for my grandmother being young and pretty, the thought was almost revolting. She often told us of the games she used to play as a child. That seemed quite absurd and undignified on her part and we treated them like the fables of the prophets she used to tell us.

She had always been short and fat and slightly bent. Her face was a criss-cross of wrinkles running from everywhere to everywhere. No, we were certain she had always been as we had known her. Old, so terribly old that she could not have grown older, and had stayed at the same age for twenty years. She could never have been pretty; but she was always beautiful. She hobbled about the house in spotless white, with one hand resting on her waist to balance her stoop and the other telling the beads of her rosary. Her silver locks were scattered untidily over her pale, puckered face, and her lips constantly moved in inaudible prayer. Yes, she was beautiful. She was like the winter landscape in the mountains, an expanse of pure white serenity breathing peace and contentment.

My grandmother and I were good friends. My parents left me with her when they went to live in the city and we were constantly together. She used to wake me up in the morning and get me ready for school.

She said her morning prayer in a monotonous sing-song while she bathed and dressed me in the hope that I would listen and get to know it by heart. I listened because I loved her voice but never bothered to learn it. Then she would fetch my wooden slate which she had already washed and plastered with yellow chalk, a tiny earthen ink pot, and a reed pen, tie them all in a bundle and hand it to me. After a breakfast of a thick, stale chapatti with a little butter and sugar spread on it, we went to school. She carried several stale chapattis with her for the village dogs.

My grandmother always went to school with me because the school was attached to the temple. The priest taught us the alphabet and the morning prayer. While the children sat in rows on either side of the veranda singing the alphabet, or the prayer in a chorus, my grandmother sat inside reading the scriptures. When we had both finished, we would walk back together. This time the village dogs would meet us at the temple door. They followed us to our home, growling and fighting each other for the chapattis we threw to them.

When my parents were comfortably settled in the city, they sent for us. That was a turning point in our friendship. Although we shared the same room, my grandmother no longer came to school with me. I used to go to an English school in a motor bus. There were no dogs in the streets and she took to feeding sparrows in the courtyard of our city house.

As the years rolled by, we saw less of each other. For some time, she continued to wake me up and get me ready for school. When I came back, she would ask me what the teacher had taught me. I would tell her English words and little things of Western science and learning, the law of gravity, Archimedes' principle, the world being round, etc. This made her unhappy. She could not help me with my lessons. She did not believe in the things they taught at the English school and was distressed that there was no teaching about God and the scriptures. One day I announced that we were being given music lessons. She was very disturbed. To her music had lewd associations. It was the monopoly of harlots and beggars and not meant for gentlefolk. She rarely talked to me after that.

When I went up to university, I was given a room of my own. The common link of friendship was snapped. My grandmother accepted her seclusion with resignation. She rarely left her spinning wheel to talk to anyone. From sunrise to sunset she sat by her wheel, spinning and reciting prayers. Only in the afternoon she relaxed for a while to feed the sparrows.

While she sat in the veranda breaking the bread into little bits, hundreds of little birds collected around her, creating a veritable bedlam of chirrupings. Some came and perched on her legs, others on her shoulders. Some even sat on her head. She smiled but never shooed them away. It used to be the happiest half-hour of the day for her.

When I decided to go abroad for further studies, I was sure my grandmother would be upset. I would be away for five years, and at her age one could never tell. But my grandmother could. She was not even sentimental. She came to leave me at the railway station but did not talk or show any emotion. Her lips moved in prayer, her mind was lost in prayer. Her fingers were busy telling the beads of her rosary. Silently she kissed my forehead, and when I left I cherished the moist imprint as perhaps the last sign of physical contact between us.

But that was not so. After five years I came back home and was met by her at the station. She did not look a day older. She still had no time for words, and while she clasped me in her arms I could hear her reciting her prayer. Even on the first day of my arrival, her happiest moments were with her sparrows, whom she fed longer and with frivolous rebukes.

In the evening a change came over her. She did not pray. She collected the women of the neighbourhood, got an old drum, and started to sing. For several hours she thumped the sagging skins of the dilapidated drum and sang of the homecoming of warriors. We had to persuade her to stop to avoid overstraining. That was the first time since I had known her that she did not pray.

The next morning she was taken ill. It was a mild fever and the doctor told us that it would go. But my grandmother thought differently. She told us that her end was near. She said that since only a few hours before the close of the last chapter of her life she had omitted to pray, she was not going to waste any more time talking to us.

We protested. But she ignored our protests. She lay peacefully in bed, praying and telling her beads. Even before we could suspect, her lips stopped moving and the rosary fell from her lifeless fingers. A peaceful pallor spread on her face and we knew that she was dead.

We lifted her off the bed and, as is customary, laid her on the ground and covered her with a red shroud. After a few hours of mourning we left her alone to make arrangements for her funeral.

In the evening we went to her room with a crude stretcher to take her to be cremated. The sun was setting and had lit her room and veranda with a blaze of golden light. We stopped halfway in the courtyard. All over the veranda and in her room right up to where she lay dead and stiff, wrapped in the red shroud, thousands of sparrows sat scattered on the floor. There was no chirping. We felt sorry for the birds and my mother fetched some bread for them. She broke it into little crumbs, the way my grandmother used to, and threw it to them. The sparrows took no notice of the bread. When we carried my grandmother's corpse off, they flew away quietly. Next morning the sweeper swept the breadcrumbs into the dustbin.

THE TIMES HAVE CHANGED
KRISHNA SOBTI

Translated from the Hindi by Poonam Saxena

Dawn was breaking by the time Shahni, wrapped in a thick cotton shawl, rosary clasped in her hands, reached the banks of the river. A rosy hue was spreading far above on the curtain of the sky. Shahni took off her clothes, placed them to one side and, saying 'Shri Ram, Shri Ram', stepped into the water. She filled her cupped hands with water, saluted the sun god, splashing a little water on her sleepy eyes.

The waters of the Chenab were as cold as before, and the waves were kissing each other. Far away, in the mountains of Kashmir, the ice was melting. Bouncing, rolling waves smashed against the overhanging banks, but somehow that day, the sand that stretched far into the distance seemed silent and still! Shahni put on her clothes, looked around, there wasn't even a shadow to be seen. But below, on the sand, were countless footprints. She shivered a little with fear!

She had a sense of danger and fear in the sweet silence of dawn. She had bathed here for the last fifty years. What a long time! This was the same riverbank where she had first stepped foot as a bride. And today there was no Shahji, nor her educated son. She was alone, alone in Shahji's enormous haveli. But no! What was she thinking so early in the morning? Why was she unable to turn away from worldly matters! Shahni took a deep breath and, chanting 'Shri Ram, Shri Ram', made her way home through the bajra fields. Smoke rose from some of the whitewashed courtyards. Tann-tann rang the bells of the bullocks. Even so...even so, there was a feeling of suffocation. Even the Jammiwala well wasn't working that day. All the people here were Shahji's tenants. Shahni looked up. These fields, stretching for miles, are ours. Looking at the full, abundant, fresh harvest, Shahni was swamped with a love born out of a sense of belonging. This was all because of Shahji's blessings. Lands extending right up to far-off villages, dotted with wells—they owned all of it. Three harvests in a year, the land bequeathed gold. Shahni moved towards the well and called out, 'Shera, Shera! Hussaina, Hussaina....'

Shera recognized Shahni's voice. He would, wouldn't he! After the death of his mother, Jaina, Shera had grown up in Shahni's care. He picked up the chopper and pushed it under the pile of grass lying nearby. Holding the hookah in his hand, he said, 'Ai Hussaina, Hussaina....' How Shahni's voice affected him! He had been thinking about taking the trunks full of silver and gold lying in that dark, little room in Shahni's grand haveli.... And that's when he heard, 'Shera, Shera....' Shera was enraged. Who should he vent his anger on? On Shahni? He screamed, 'Ai, are you dead!... May God give you death....'

Hussaina put aside the platter she was using for kneading dough and hurried outside, 'Coming, coming, why are you so irritated early in the morning?'

By now Shahni had come closer. She had heard Shera's angry outburst. Lovingly she said, 'Hussaina, is this any time to quarrel? He is mad. But you should be more strong of heart.'

'Strong-hearted!' Hussaina said, her voice full of pride, 'Shahni, boys will be boys, after all. Have you asked Shera why he only curses so early in the morning?'

Shahni patted Hussaina's back fondly and said with a laugh, 'Silly girl, I like the bride more than the boy! Shera....'

'Yes, Shahni?'

'I believe those people from Kulluvaal came here at night?' Shahni asked in a grave voice.

A little rattled, Shera said hesitantly, 'No, Shahni....' Without listening to Shera's answer, Shahni continued in a worried voice, 'Whatever is happening is not good. Shera, if Shahji were here today, he might have done something. But—' Shahni stopped mid-sentence. What is happening today! Shahni felt choked with emotion. Shahji had been gone many years, but—but something was melting inside her that day—perhaps memories of the past.... In an attempt to control her tears, she looked towards Hussaina and laughed gently. And Shera wondered, what was Shahni saying! No one could do anything today, not even Shahji. What had to happen would happen and why shouldn't it? Shahji could weigh his sacks of gold only because he made money from the interest he took from our brothers and friends. Shera's eyes burned with the flames of vengeance. He thought of the long-handled chopper. He looked at Shahni. No-no, in the last few days Shera had already committed thirty-forty murders. But...but he wasn't such a degenerate.... Shahni's hands floated in front of his eyes. Those winter nights.... Sometimes, after being scolded by Shahji, he would be lying in some corner of the haveli. Then, in the light of the lantern, he would see Shahni's tender hands holding a bowl of milk, 'Shera, Shera, get up, drink this.' Shera looked at Shahni's wrinkled face and found that she was smiling gently. He felt unsettled and moved. After all, what wrong had Shahni ever done to him? Whatever Shahji had done had gone with his death. He would definitely protect Shahni. But what about last night's conference! How had he agreed with what Feroz had suggested? Everything would be all right...they would distribute all the belongings!

'Come, Shahni, let me see you home.'

Shahni got up. Shera followed Shahni with firm steps as she walked ahead, deep in thought. He kept looking around uneasily. The words of his companions echoed in his ears. But what would they get from killing Shahni?

'Shahni.'

'Yes, Shera.'

He wanted to warn Shahni of the impending danger, but how?

'Shahni....'

Shahni lifted her head. The sky was full of smoke. 'Shera....'

Shera knew this fire. A fire was to be lit in Jalalpur that day, and it had been lit! Shahni was unable to say anything. All her relatives lived there.

They reached the haveli. Shahni stepped across the threshold, her mind empty. She had no idea when Shera left. Her body was frail, she was alone, without any support! She had no idea how long she lay there. Afternoon came and went. The haveli stood, its doors open. Shahni couldn't get up. As if her authority was, of its own volition, slipping away from her! The mistress of Shahji's house...but no, today, she felt no attachment. As if she had turned to stone. It was twilight but she still lay there, unable to get up. She was startled by the sound of Rasooli's voice.

'Shahni, Shahni, we've heard the trucks are coming to pick up people.'

'Trucks...?' Shahni couldn't say anything else. She clasped her hands together. In no time, the news spread all over the village. Lah bibi said in a choked voice, 'Shahni, this has never happened before, it's never been heard of before. It's a disaster, there's darkness and violence all around.'

Shahni stood still as a statue. Said Nawab bibi, her sorrowful voice full of love, 'Shahni, we never thought it would come to this.'

What could Shahni say. She herself had thought of this! She heard Patwari Begu and Jailldar talking below. Shahni understood that the time had come. She walked down like an automaton but couldn't cross the threshold. In a hollow, barely-there voice, she asked, 'Who? Who all are there?'

Who wasn't there that day? The whole village was there, the village that had once done her bidding unquestioningly. They included her tenants whom she had never considered any less than her close relatives. But, no, that day no one was hers, that day she was alone! The Jats of Kulluval were there in the huge crowd. She'd understood this in the morning itself!

Who knew what Patwari Begu and the mosque's Mulla Ismail thought. They came and stood next to Shahni. Begu couldn't bring himself to look at her. Clearing his throat softly, he said, 'Shahni, this is what God has willed.'

Shahni's feet faltered. She felt dizzy and held on to the wall. Had Shahji left her alone to see this day? Looking at the lifeless, inert Shahni, Begu thought, 'See what Shahni is going through! But what can be done! The times have changed.'

Shahni's leaving the house was not an insignificant event. The entire village was there, standing at the door of the haveli, all the way up to the gate built by Shahji when his son got married. All the consultations and decisions in the village were taken here. Discussions about looting the haveli had also taken place here. It's not as if Shahni didn't know anything. She knew but pretended she didn't. She had never known enmity, never wronged anyone. But she didn't know that the times had changed....

It was getting late. Thanedar Dawood Khan stepped forward arrogantly but seeing the motionless, lifeless shadow standing at the door, he hesitated. This was the same Shahni whose Shahji had had tents set up near the river for him. This was the same Shahni who had given his fiancée flower-shaped gold earrings when she saw his bride-to-be for the first time. When he had come to see her in connection with the 'League' the other day, he had said in a high-handed manner, 'Shahni, a mosque has to be built at Bhaagovaal, you'll have to give three hundred rupees.' With her usual simplicity, Shahni had placed three hundred rupees in front of him. And today?

'Shahni!' Dawood Khan called out. He was a policeman, otherwise he might have teared up.

Shahni was lost, silent, unable to say anything.

'Shahni!' he came near the door and spoke softly, 'it's getting late, Shahni! Take something with you if you want to. Have you put away something or not? Any gold, silver....'

In a muffled voice, Shahni said, 'Gold, silver!' She paused for a moment and then said simply, 'Gold, silver! All that is for you people, child. My gold is spread out on every inch of this land.'

A shamefaced Dawood Khan said, 'Shahni, you are alone, you should keep something with you. At least keep some cash with you. Who knows what could happen at any time....'

'Time?' Shahni laughed, her eyes wet with tears. 'Dawood Khan, will I be alive to see a better time than this!' she said, her voice a mix of anguish and censure.

Dawood Khan had no answer. Gathering his courage, he said, 'Shahni...a little cash is necessary.'

'No child, this house...' Shahni's throat choked with tears, 'is more beloved to me than any money. The money that is here will stay here.'

At that moment Shera came and stood nearby. From a distance he had seen Dawood Khan next to Shahni and suspected that Dawood was probably extracting something or the other from her. 'Khan sahib, it's getting late....'

Shahni started. Getting late.... I'm getting late in my own house! Rebellion emerged from her whirlpool of tears. I am the queen of this house made by my ancestors and these people have grown up under my care. No, this is too much. All right, it's getting late. It's getting late. That was the only thing echoing in her ears: it's getting late, but, no, Shahni would not leave her ancestral home in tears, she would leave with pride, she would cross the threshold with her head held high, the same threshold where she had once arrived and stood like a queen. Steadying her wobbling legs, Shahni wiped her eyes with her dupatta and crossed the threshold. The old women in the crowd broke down. The one who had been their friend and companion in both happy and sad times was leaving. Who could be compared to her! God had given everything, but, fortunes changed, times changed....

Shahni covered her head with her dupatta and looked at the haveli one last time, her eyes blurred with tears. Even after Shahji's death, she had looked after the legacy entrusted to her so carefully, now that legacy itself had betrayed her. Shahni folded her hands. This was the last sight, the last salutation. Shahni's eyes would never again see this great haveli. Her love made her think: why don't I walk through the entire house one more time? She was feeling disheartened, but she wouldn't let it show in front of the people before whom she had always stood tall. This was enough. Everything was done. She lowered her head. After crossing the threshold, a few tears trickled out of the eyes of the daughter-in-law of this noble house. Shahni set off, the grand mansion was left behind. Dawood Khan, Shera, Patwari, Jailldaar, children, the very old, women, men, all followed in her wake.

The trucks were full by now. Shahni dragged herself forward. The assembled villagers were moved. Shera, the bloodthirsty Shera's heart was breaking. Dawood Khan stepped forward and opened the door of the truck. Shahni moved ahead. Ismail stepped forward and said in a heavy voice, 'Shahni, say something before leaving. Any blessing from you will come true!' And he wiped the tears from his eyes with his turban. Suppressing her sobs, her throat full of unshed tears, Shahni said, 'May God keep you well, my child, may you have joy and happiness….'

That small mass of people wept. There was not a grain of bitterness in Shahni's heart. But we—we couldn't keep Shahni with us. Shera stepped forward and touched Shahni's feet. 'Shahni, nobody could do anything, the ruling power changed….' Shahni placed a trembling hand on Shera's head and said falteringly, 'Live long, my dearest one.' Dawood Khan gestured with his hand. Some of the old women embraced Shahni and the truck set off.

It was time to move on. The haveli, the new sitting room, the high chamber, the big veranda—one by one, all of them spun in front of Shahni's eyes! She knew nothing—whether the truck was moving or whether she herself was moving. Her eyes rained tears. A shaken, unsettled Dawood Khan looked at the old Shahni. Where would she go now?

'Shahni, don't keep any bitterness in your heart. If we could have done something, wouldn't we have kept you with us? The times are what they are. The government has changed, the times have changed….'

Shahni reached the camp at night and, lying on the ground, she thought in her wounded heart, 'The government has changed… but how can money change, I've left it behind anyway, what does it matter to me….'

And Shahni's eyes filled with tears.
It rained blood that night on the villages around the green fields.
Perhaps the government was changing, the times were changing.

THE KABULIWALLAH

RABINDRANATH TAGORE

Translated from the Bengali by Arunava Sinha

My five-year-old daughter talked all the time. It had taken her a year after her birth to master the language, and since then she has not wasted a second of her waking hours in silence. Although her mother often hushed her, this was beyond me. A silent Mini was so unnatural a being that I could not bear it for long. So I always encouraged her to prattle on.

I had barely started the seventeenth chapter of my novel that morning when Mini appeared by my side and began chattering at once, 'Ramdayal, the doorman, calls the crow kauwa instead of kaak, Baba, he just doesn't know anything, does he?'

Before I could talk about linguistic diversity, she had moved to another subject. 'Baba, Bhola says it rains because elephants spray water with their trunks from the sky. He talks such rubbish, my god. He keeps talking, talks all the time.'

Without pausing for my opinion, Mini suddenly asked, 'What relation is Ma to you, Baba?'

'Shaali,' I answered to myself. To Mini I said, 'Go play with Bhola, Mini. I'm busy.'

Flopping down by my feet, next to the desk, she began to play a game involving her knees and hands, accompanied by a rhyme uttered at express velocity. In the seventeenth chapter of my novel, Pratap Singh was about to leap with Kanchanmala in his arms from the high window of the prison into the river flowing below.

My room looked out on the street. Mini abruptly stopped her game to rush to the window and began to shout, 'Kabuliwallah, Kabuliwallah.'

A tall Kabuliwallah—one of those hawkers of dry fruits who came all the way from Afghanistan to make a living in Calcutta—was walking slowly up the road, a turban on his head, a bag slung over his shoulder, holding two or three boxes of grapes. It was difficult to say what emotions he aroused in my daughter, but she continued to call out to him breathlessly. I was afraid that if the wily peddler, with a bag of things to sell, came into my room, I could bid goodbye to any prospect of finishing chapter seventeen that day.

The Kabuliwallah turned and smiled at Mini's shouts and began walking towards our house. Her courage gave way and she ran from the room at great speed, vanishing into the house. She was convinced that if the Kabuliwallah's bag was opened and examined it would reveal three or four children, just like her.

Meanwhile, the man himself appeared, offering me a smiling salute. Although Pratap Singh and Kanchanmala were in dire straits, I reflected that it would be discourteous to invite him into the house and buy nothing.

I bought a few things and we began chatting. We exchanged notes on frontier policies involving Abdur Rahman, the Russians, and the English.

When he was about to leave, the Kabuliwallah finally asked, 'Where did your daughter go, Babu?'

I sent for Mini in order to dispel her fears. Pressing herself to me, Mini cast suspicious glances at the Kabuliwallah and his large bag. He offered her some raisins and dry fruit, but she simply wouldn't accept them, holding my knee tightly. And there the first meeting between them ended.

A few days later, about to leave the house on an errand, I discovered my daughter seated on the bench next to the front door, chattering away to the Kabuliwallah who sat at her feet, listening smilingly, and occasionally saying something in broken Bengali. Mini had never encountered such an attentive listener in the five years of her life, besides her father. I even found nuts and raisins bundled into the aanchal of her tiny sari. 'Why have you given her all this?' I asked the Kabuliwallah. 'Don't do it again.' Taking an eight-anna coin out of my pocket, I handed it to him. He accepted it without demur, putting it in his bag.

I returned home to find the eight-anna coin at the heart of a hundred rupees worth of trouble.

Holding a circular, silvery object in her hand, Mini's mother was asking her daughter disapprovingly, 'Where did you get this?'

'The Kabuliwallah gave it to me,' Mini told her.

'Why did you have to take it from him?' Mini's mother inquired.

'I didn't want to, he gave it on his own,' Mini said, on the verge of tears.

I rescued Mini from imminent danger and took her outside.

There I learnt that it wasn't as though this was only Mini's second meeting with Rahmat, the Kabuliwallah. He had been coming to see her almost every day, bribing her with almonds and raisins to conquer her tiny, greedy five-year-old heart.

I observed that the two friends had established an easy familiarity between themselves, sharing private jokes and quips. For instance, on spotting Rahmat, my daughter would ask, laughing, 'What's in that bag of yours, Kabuliwallah?'

In an exaggeratedly nasal tone Rahmat would answer, also laughing, 'An elephant.'

The joke could not be termed particularly subtle, but nevertheless it kept both in splits—and the artless laughter of a middle-aged man and a child on an autumn morning brought me some joy, too.

They had another ritual exchange. Rahmat would tell Mini, 'Khnokhi, tomi sasurbaari kakhanu jaabena. Little girl, you must never get married and go to your father-in-law's house.'

Most girls from traditional Bengali families would be familiar with the word shoshurbaari almost from the time they were born, but because we were somewhat modern, we hadn't taught our daughter the meaning of the term. So, she did not know what to make of Rahmat's request, but because it was against her nature to be silent and unresponsive, she would fire a counter-question. 'Will you go there?'

Rahmat would brandish his enormous fist against an imaginary father-in-law, and say, 'I will kill the sasur first.'

Imagining the terrible fate awaiting this unknown creature, Mini would laugh her head off.

∞

It was the clear season of autumn. In ancient times, this was when kings set off to conquer other lands. I had never been anywhere outside Calcutta, but precisely for that reason my mind wandered all over the world. In the quiet corner of my room, I was like an eternal traveller, pining for places around the globe. My heart began to race as soon as another country was mentioned, the sight of a foreigner conjured up a vision of a cottage amidst rivers and mountains and forests, and thoughts of a joyful, free way of life captured my imagination.

But I was so retiring by nature that the very notion of abandoning my corner and stepping out into the world made me have visions of the sky crashing down on my head. That was why my conversations with this man from Kabul, this Kabuliwallah, every morning by the desk in my tiny room served the purpose of travel for me. Rugged and inaccessible, the scorched, red-hued mountain ranges rose high on either side of the road, a laden caravan of camels winding along the narrow trail between them; turbaned traders and travellers, some of them on the backs of camels, some on foot, some with spears, others with old-fashioned flint guns...with a voice like the rumbling of clouds, the Kabuliwallah would recount tales from his homeland in broken Bengali, and these images would float past my eyes.

Mini's mother was perpetually jumpy, her mind alive with imaginary fears. The slightest noise on the streets would lead her to believe that all the inebriated individuals in the world were rushing towards our house, bent on making mischief. Despite all the years (not too many actually) she had lived on earth, she had still not rid herself of the conviction that the universe was populated only by thieves and robbers and drunkards and snakes and tigers and malaria and earthworms and cockroaches and white men all intent on striking terror into her heart.

She was not entirely free of doubt about Rahmat, the Kabuliwallah, requesting me repeatedly to keep an eye on him. When I attempted to laugh away her suspicions, she would ask me probing questions. 'Aren't children ever kidnapped? Don't they have slaves in Afghanistan? Is it entirely impossible for a gigantic Kabuliwallah to kidnap a small child?'

I had to acknowledge that it was not entirely impossible but unlikely. The capacity for trust was not the same in everyone, which was why my wife remained suspicious of the Kabuliwallah. But I could not stop Rahmat from visiting our house for no fault of his.

Rahmat usually went home around the end of January every year. He would be very busy collecting his dues at this time. He had to go from house to house, but still he made it a point to visit Mini once a day. There did seem to be a conspiracy between them. If he could not visit in the morning, he made his way to our house in the evening. It was true that I experienced a sudden surge of fear at the sight of the large man in his loose shalwar and kurta, standing in a dark corner of the room with his bags. But when a laughing Mini ran up to him, saying, 'Kabuliwallah, Kabuliwallah,' and the simple banter of old was resumed between the two friends of unequal age, my heart was filled with delight once more.

∽

I was correcting proofs one day in my tiny room. The cold had grown sharper; as winter was about to bid farewell, there was a severe chill. The morning sunshine filtering through the window warmed my feet; it was a most pleasant sensation. It was about eight o'clock—most of those who had ventured out for their morning constitutionals, their heads and throats wrapped in mufflers, were already back home. Suddenly, there was an uproar in the street.

Looking out of the window I saw two policemen frogmarching our Rahmat, bound with ropes, up the road, followed by a group of curious urchins. Rahmat's clothes were bloodstained, and one of the policemen held a dagger dripping with blood. Going out, I stopped the policemen to enquire what the matter was.

The story was related partly by a policeman and partly by Rahmat himself. One of our neighbours owed Rahmat some money for a shawl from Rampur. When he disclaimed the debt, an altercation broke out, in the course of which Rahmat had stabbed him with his dagger.

The Kabuliwallah was showering expletives on the liar when Mini emerged from the house, calling out, 'Kabuliwallah, Kabuliwallah.'

Rahmat's expression changed in an instant to a cheerful smile. Since there was no bag slung from his shoulder today, they could not have their usual discussion about its magical contents. Mini asked him directly, 'Will you go to your father-in-law's house?'

'That's exactly where I am going,' Rahmat smiled back at her.

When he saw Mini wasn't amused, he showed her his arms bound with rope. 'I would have killed the sasur, but my hands are tied.'

Rahmat was in jail for several years for causing grievous bodily harm.

We forgot him, more or less. Going about our everyday routines it didn't even occur to us how difficult it must be for a man used to roaming free in the mountains to cope with years of imprisonment.

Even Mini's father had to accept that his fickle-hearted daughter's behaviour was truly shameful. She effortlessly forgot her old friend, and struck up a new friendship with Nabi, who groomed horses. Then, as she grew older, male friends were replaced by girls her age. Now, we seldom saw each other any more.

Many years passed. Another autumn arrived. My Mini's wedding had been arranged. She would be married during the Durga Puja holidays. Along with the goddess from Kailash, the joy of my house would also depart for her husband's home, robbing her father's house of its light.

A beautiful morning had dawned. After the monsoon, the freshly-rinsed autumn sunlight had taken on the colour of pure, molten gold. Its glow washed over the crumbling houses of exposed brick in the neighbourhood, making them exquisitely beautiful.

The shehnai had begun playing in my house before the night had ended. Its notes were like the sound of my heart weeping. The plaintive melody of Bhairavi was spreading the imminent pain of parting all over the world. My Mini was to be married today.

There had been a great to-do since the morning, with crowds of people going in and out of the house. In the courtyard a marquee was being set up with bamboo posts; the clinking of chandeliers being hung up in the rooms and the veranda could be heard. It was very noisy.

I was going over the accounts in my room when Rahmat appeared and saluted me.

I did not recognize him at first. He had neither his bags nor his long hair—his body was not as strapping as it once used to be. It was his smile that eventually told me who he was.

'Why, it's Rahmat,' I said. 'When did you get back?'

'I was released from jail yesterday evening,' he answered.

His reply made me uncomfortable. Until now, I had never seen a murderer in the flesh, his presence here made me shrink back. On this auspicious day, I wished he would go away.

I told him, 'There's something important going on at home, I am busy. You'd better go today.'

At this he made ready to leave at once, but when he had reached the door, he said hesitantly, 'Can't I meet Khnokhi?'

He probably thought that Mini had not changed. Perhaps he expected her to come running up as before, chanting, 'Kabuliwallah, Kabuliwallah,' as she always had. To honour the old friendship he had even gone to the trouble of collecting a box of grapes and some nuts and raisins wrapped in paper from a fellow Afghan as he no longer had his own sack of goods to sell.

'There are some ceremonies at home today,' I told him, 'meeting Mini is impossible.'

He looked very disappointed. He looked at me wordlessly for a few moments, then said, 'Salaam, Babu,' and left.

No sooner had he left than I felt bad and was considering calling him back when I found him returning of his own accord.

Coming up to me, he said, 'I have some grapes and nuts and raisins for Khnokhi, please give them to her.'

As I was about to pay for them, he caught hold of my hand firmly and said, 'Please don't pay me. You have always been so kind, I will never forget your kindness....

'I have a daughter back home just like yours, Babu. It was thinking of her that I brought some fruit for Khnokhi, this isn't business.'

Putting his hand inside his long, loose shalwar, he pulled out a dirty piece of paper. Unfolding it carefully, he spread it out on my desk for me. It had the print of a tiny pair of hands. Not a photograph, not an oil painting, just some lampblack smeared on the palms to make a print on paper. Rahmat travelled to Calcutta's streets every year to sell his dry fruits, holding this remembrance of his daughter close to his breast—as though the touch of those tiny tender hands comforted the heart inside his broad chest, a heart wracked by the pain of separation.

Tears sprang to my eyes. I forgot that he was a seller of dry fruits from Kabul and I, a member of a Kulin Bengali family. I realized that he was a father, just as I was. The handprint of his little Parbati from his home in the mountains reminded me of Mini.

I sent for my daughter at once. They raised objections in the ladies' chambers, but I paid no attention. Mini appeared shyly in my room, dressed as a bride in her red wedding garb.

The Kabuliwallah was taken aback when he saw her. Unable to revive their old banter, he said nothing for a while. Finally, he said with a smile, 'Khnokhi, tomi sasurbaari jaabis?'

Mini knew now what the words meant, she could not respond as before. Blushing at Rahmat's question, she stood with her face averted. I remembered the day Mini and the Kabuliwallah had met for the first time, and felt a twinge of sadness.

After Mini left, Rahmat slumped to the floor with a sigh. He had suddenly realized that his own daughter must have grown up and that he would have to get to know her all over again—she would no longer be the way he remembered her. Who knew what might have happened to her over these past eight years? The shehnai kept playing in the calming sunlight of the autumn morning, but inside a house in a Calcutta lane all that Rahmat could see were the mountains and cold deserts of Afghanistan.

I gave him some money. 'Go back home to your daughter, Rahmat,' I told him. 'Let the happiness of your reunion with her be a blessing for my Mini.'

Giving Rahmat the money meant pruning one or two things from the celebrations. The electric lights display was not as lavish as I had wanted it to be, nor were the musical arrangements as elaborate as planned. The ladies as usual objected strongly but, for me, the festivities were brightened by the benediction of a father's love.

ELEPHANT AT SEA
KANISHK THAROOR

In the late summer of 1979, the Second Secretary of the Indian embassy to Morocco received a cable that undid his considerable years of training and left him floundering. The message read simply: 'Elephant en route'. Was it some sort of code? Further investigation only deepened his confusion. The cable had come from the customs office in Cochin, a port in the south of India. No, the customs officials reported back to him, it wasn't code. It was an elephant—an elephant, that along with its mahout, was now very much headed by ship to Casablanca. The Second Secretary probed: why send an elephant? Here at the customs office, the reply came, we handle only the movement of goods; for the movement of reasons, please refer your enquiry to the Ministry of External Affairs.

The Second Secretary telegrammed his colleagues in the ministry in Delhi. With telegrams to the ministry, it was important, first, to be terse so that you were considered economical and, second, to be sharp so that in the midst of reams of communication from outposts around the world, your message would be noticed. WHY SHIP ELEPHANT STOP EMBASSY ALREADY HAS CARS STOP. No one in the ministry seemed to know anything about the elephant. A flummoxed telegram returned to the embassy. WHAT ELEPHANT STOP IS THIS CODE STOP. Embarrassed, the Second Secretary finally consulted the Ambassador, who knew through long experience that it was pointless to question the whims of the capital. Marvellous, the ambassador said, smoothing his moustache, an elephant, just what we need, and they couldn't even send it to us, no, they're sending it to Casablanca. You'll have to arrange for the thing to be met and picked up. He sprayed himself with cologne and mused: if an elephant can even be picked up.

That night the Second Secretary lay awake in bed, resenting the sheets, resenting the pillow, resenting the indifference of his work, resenting Morocco, resenting Arabic for its impossible, secret throatiness, and resenting, with what little bitterness was left to him, the unknown buffoon who would make diplomacy out of elephants.

The buffoon was not, as he imagined, some self-satisfied civil servant in South Block, but the princess of Morocco. Explanation arrived via telex from a friend in the ministry who owed him a few favours and so mustered the initiative to ask around.

The story of the elephant had begun six years earlier in the same Indian embassy in Rabat. At one of those habitual functions whose purpose seems so obvious in the preparation but disappears in the operation, the little Moroccan princess had come to the embassy and frozen before a picture of an elephant. It was among the many stock images—all approved by the ministry of tourism—that lined the lobby of the embassy: dawn over the Himalayan ranges; houseboats on the backwaters; the Taj Mahal rosy in its cushion of smog; a bright tractor devastating a field of wheat. The princess only had eyes for the elephant. Her wordless arm extended towards the picture, pointing. C'est un éléphant, said the embassy official tasked with escorting the princess. She remained transfixed. Vous aimez les éléphants? the unlucky man suggested. It seemed the princess did love elephants because she wouldn't move. The official, who had in previous posts offered counsel on trade policy with Indonesia and arms deals with the Soviet Union, looked around for help before lowering himself to her level. Mademoiselle, vous voulez un éléphant? he asked with the desperation stoked in him by all children—never mind the princess of Morocco. She turned, smiled, and gave him the smallest gift of a nod. It was enough. The official eventually spoke to the then ambassador who put in the request to Delhi, recommending the delivery of an elephant to satisfy the princess and to strengthen a bilateral friendship. The request passed through the appropriate channels at the usual speeds. Six years later, the creature was irrevocably on its way.

The Second Secretary received updates about the elephant's progress from various consular staff. In Yemen, it posed for photographs in front of the oldest coffee house in Aden. It bumped a football back and forth with boys on the beach in Alexandria. In Algiers, veterans of the war against the French held a reception in its honour; the Indian elephant was, in their words, a symbol of the ancient wisdom of a civilization that had inspired the global struggle against Western imperialism. After it passed through Gibraltar, the Second Secretary got an excited telegram from the British naval high command. BRILLIANT STOP TOP PACHYDERM STOP.

The Moroccans were less enthused. What are we to do with it? they said. Casablanca's zoo has enough African elephants and there's no space for an Indian one. The Second Secretary protested. It's for the princess, he reminded them, she asked for it. Well, she may have, the Moroccans said, but she's away studying sociology in Paris now and has no interest in elephants. So, you might have to take the thing back.

Only the Indian ambassador's persistence at a cocktail party won their grudging cooperation. It was agreed that the elephant would be specially housed in a portion of the royal gardens in Rabat. How it would get there was another matter altogether. The Moroccans insisted they had no trucks big enough to carry the creature between the two cities. This was a time of war and their heaviest military vehicles were all rumbling around the south. Worse, thanks to the mischief of Polisario terrorists, the single rail line between Casablanca and the capital was broken. But these inconveniences, the Moroccans claimed, shouldn't be a problem. After all, the elephant is its own means of transportation.

The Second Secretary was sent to Casablanca to escort the elephant back to Rabat. It took some time to find an appropriate launch in which to ferry the creature to port. When it finally disembarked, the small police band awaiting its arrival had grown sour in the heat. They rushed through the welcoming ditty and swiftly packed away their trombones. The reporters also sped through their work. They found the mahout altogether too clothed. As he perched on the elephant's back, they had him remove his shirt and roll up his trousers to look more convincing for the cameras, all knobby knees and gleaming skin. Instead of asking the mahout questions about the elephant, they surrounded the Second Secretary—he was wearing a suit. We are proud to share the joy of elephants with the people of Morocco, he said. The haathi belongs not to one nation, but to all.

What little the Second Secretary knew about elephants came from an urban childhood of zoos and encyclopaedias. As a measure of their robust memories, elephants hold grudges and harbour very finely developed notions of revenge. Elephants have sensitive feet capable of feeling through the earth, from long distances away, the approach of other elephants, or of rainstorms, or of bulldozers. Studies have shown that they can recognize their own reflections, suggesting that, however rudimentary, there may exist among elephants an amorphous theory of mind.

In sum, these scraps formed an altogether surreal idea of the elephant, one incommensurate with the full being in front of him, dappled with cooling splashes of mud, blinking restlessly and curling its trunk around the legs of its mahout. The mahout supplied more practical information. In its present ship-weary condition, the elephant could walk at most forty kilometres at a single stretch, probably no more than twenty-five. How far is it to the capital? he asked. He spoke no Hindi and the Second Secretary spoke no Malayalam, so they talked in a manner of English. A little more than ninety kilometres to Rabat, the Second Secretary said. Hoisting himself on to the elephant, the mahout surveyed the road leading out from the docks through the flat outskirts of Casablanca. For all the immensity of this unknown continent, the world always seemed more manageable from the back of an elephant. He smiled at the Second Secretary. Ninety of their Moroccan kilometres or ninety of ours? What are you talking about, the Second Secretary said, there's no difference. The mahout shook his head. You and I may not be able to tell the difference, but the elephant can.

In consultation with the two Moroccan gendarmes assigned to them, they agreed to break journey several times en route to Rabat. The convoy set out from Casablanca in the middle of the afternoon. The gendarmes led in their battered white car, its red lettering chipped and peeling. The Second Secretary brought up the rear in the embassy's sedan. In the middle, the mahout set a gentle tempo. The elephant wore an anklet that, wrapped around a man, would have had all the thickness of chains. Its every step tinkled with the jewellery of another land.

Perhaps because it was on its way to await the uncertain pleasure of a princess, or perhaps because it had already travelled so far, the elephant chose not to exert itself. But it quickened its pace whenever the coastal road veered west towards the Atlantic. The change would have been imperceptible to observers—and there were many on the busy highway—but the mahout felt it in his thighs. Each time the cobalt ocean wheeled into view, the creature's muscles seemed to quiver with new desire. It was an urge all the more palpable in its restraint; elephants are polite creatures of typically conservative temperament. Yet it was enough of a rumble and churn for the mahout to sense that his mount was already missing the sea.

At dusk, the elephant drank from a pond in the golf course of

Mohammedia, a pleasant enough beach town that brushed up against Morocco's only oil refinery. The last of the day's players lofted their balls in long arcs overhead before descending on the fairway and finding the creature asleep in a bunker. It lay on its side, flanked by the apologetic guards, its heavy breathing raising little tempests of sand. Nobody protested. Golf can only be improved by the intrusion of an elephant, even a snoring one.

The Second Secretary was given accommodation in the clubhouse, in a room glowing with trophies and the lidless glare of the nearby refinery. He smoked and dipped at a plate of zaalouk. The mahout came in but declined the invitation to share in the dish. He had already eaten with the policemen. The Second Secretary gestured to a couch for the mahout to sleep on. The man looked restless. No, I'll stay with the elephant, he said, this is our first night back on land after weeks.... It will rest poorly without me, and I without it. The Second Secretary shrugged and returned to his puréed eggplant, only to be surprised by the touch of the mahout's hand on his shoulder. In the parallel universe of their own country, such contact would be almost unimaginable, a movement far too intimate to cross the wide gulf of rank. Indians turn into more equal beings when not at home.

Tell me truthfully, the mahout leaned forward, are there no other elephants in Rabat? The Second Secretary sighed. I've told you already, it will have to be kept by itself. The royal gardeners can only manage one elephant. It will have all its creature comforts...don't worry. The mahout listened, see-sawing his head from side to side. This was the strongest and happiest elephant he had ever known, but he feared that it would struggle with its solitude. Like humans, elephants yearn for other elephants. It will be lonely, he said, it will need distractions. Annoyed, the Second Secretary promised they would make sure that it was the most distracted elephant in Africa. He unlaced his shoes and stretched out to sleep.

A few hours later, with the red and orange light of the refinery's towers angling upon his face, he awoke to find the mahout sitting cross-legged in front of him. I'm sorry to disturb you, the mahout said, but promise me something: that you won't let them use it in the circus. In the circus? The Second Secretary said. The mahout climbed to his feet and paced about the room. In the circus, yes.... I have heard about the way the firangs treat elephants, like dolls, like puppets, like cartoons. He grew more animated still. They make them dance, they make them ride cycles, they make them stand on their heads.... Sometimes, they think it is amusing to have the animals sit down to tea as if elephants were old women...this can't be its fate. The Second Secretary sat up. We won't let that happen, he said. Besides, you have nothing to worry about; these people aren't firangs, they're Moroccans, they're so much like us...just go to sleep.

But mahouts sleep as fitfully as elephants, and when the Second Secretary rose at dawn to perform his ablutions, he found the man at the door of the clubhouse, standing in a pose of total stillness, at war with the anxious writhing of his eyebrows. The mahout burst into speech at the sight of the secretary. These royal gardens, are they near the water? The water? The Second Secretary blinked. Yes, the water, the ocean. I have no idea, the Second Secretary replied. The mahout held the Second Secretary's hand in both of his. The elephant...for it to be happy, it must be near the sea.

As he shaved, the Second Secretary muttered to himself about the mahout. All the man has to do is deliver the elephant to Rabat and then the government will give him a tidy cheque and send him home by plane. How many mahouts ever see the inside of a plane? He'll never again get to be in a plane. He can tell his parents, his wife, his children, if he has any, his grandchildren in the future, that he was in a plane. And they'll tell all their friends and enemies and the mahout will be famous forever throughout his village. Yet this madman keeps me awake all night with his ridiculous demands for an elephant nobody actually wants. If he fusses any more, we'll return him by boat. What glory is there in a boat?

What the Second Secretary did not know—and what the mahout found impossible to explain—was that, for the elephant at least, travel by boat was utterly glorious. Before they left India, the mahout had worried about the creature's well-being. How would it cope in steerage for all those cramped weeks? Would it endure the din of the ship's innards, the engines and pipes pumping at all times, soot-faced engineers swinging like monkeys from the levers? Surely, the clamour of a mechanical universe would depress a creature that loved nothing more at the end of the day than lowering itself into mud. The only consolation the mahout could find was that he too was terrified of the ship. There was a solidarity to be had between two beings who had never travelled further than Kozhikode, two beings for whom the rusting expanse of an ocean-going ship was only ever something to behold, not enter. In its salty dark, the mahout imagined, they would comfort each other, leaning close, pressing head to trunk.

It was not to be. While the mahout lurched from deck to deck vomiting, the elephant thrilled to life at sea. It trumpeted every time the captain sounded the great foghorn. The ship's sailors fawned over the creature, playing it music, showering it with nuts and chocolate. There were pleasures to be had even in its hold in the cargo bay, which rattled with the vigour of the ship's machinery. One morning, the mahout discovered the elephant rumbling. Serenely, it produced a low and eerie noise that seemed to come from its most interior parts. The mahout rushed to its side and held it as best as he could, trying to calm the animal. A moment's listening dispelled his fears; in perfect pitch, the elephant was merely mimicking the sound of the engines, as if through imitation it could bridge the divide between thought and matter and speak with the grey monstrosity of the ship.

On deck, the elephant stormed from side to side, relishing the heave of the ship, the rise and prostration of the bow as it carved its mass through the blue. The mahout studied the joy of the elephant with awe. He thought the elephant would grow bored—as he swiftly did—of the sea, but the wonder never wore off. As the wind sprayed it with foam, the creature seemed to admire the uninterrupted ocean in a kind of a rapture, a dervish-like ecstasy. It once occurred to the mahout that this might be the closest he would ever get to touching the divine: the elephant forgetting its elephantness in the vista of the sea, the veils of moksha parted, the creature poking its trunk into the beyond and feeling its way towards cosmic oneness. Then the motion of the vessel shook the mahout's insides loose. He staggered to the rim of the stern and emptied himself into the deep.

The sailors also felt the magic of the elephant's presence. Once, in the Indian Ocean, a solitary whale bobbed into view. This was hardly an unusual sight for the tanker's crew but they watched as the whale crested the surface and snorted through its blowhole. They hoped at that moment for a response from the elephant, a trumpet, a bellow, a spout of water from its trunk, some little signal of recognition. After all, what was the whale but the elephant of the sea? These two creatures were kin in bulk and grace, breathing the most air through the largest lungs in a world rightfully made for them. There could be no better omen than that shared understanding. For men who commit their bodies to the ocean, who surrender childhoods on paddy fields and factory floors for the education of currents and gales on the shipways, the communion of these beasts would be a vindication of their lives. But the sailors were disappointed. Standing on the starboard side, the elephant had not seen the whale at all, or if it had, it chose to ignore it, keeping its eyes fixed instead in contemplation of the water.

On the golf course, the mahout found the elephant by the pond, its trunk lingering at its feet. He massaged the hard knot of muscle on its lower back, the corbelled arch that lifted the creature's mass from the earth. As he readied the elephant for the onward march, he wondered whether a journey across the seas had the ability to change us. When the elephant regarded its reflection in the still water, did it see a being transformed? Could it? Maybe it was presumptuous of the mahout to think so grandly of the elephant's capacities, its self-awareness, its very sense of the possibility of a self. Perhaps this sad-eyed creature merely looked at the pond and thought: what a miserable excuse for a sea.

The convoy reached Skhirat in the early evening. On the way, the mahout had suggested to Adil, one of the Moroccan gendarmes (he had learned their names; the other was Marouane), that he come sit on the back of the elephant. Adil stripped off his uniform jacket, approached the elephant from the front, hesitated, crept around the side and kept creeping till he made a full circle, and looked imploringly up at the mahout. The mahout laughed. He scratched the back of the elephant's head and pressed one knee against its neck. It dipped to the ground. Adil tried to look the creature in the eye for reassurance, but it stared beyond him up the road, its ears flapping like fans. He grasped the mahout's forearm and heaved himself up, gripping the hairy hide with both hands as the elephant rose to its feet and lurched on.

Elephants respond to confidence, the mahout said, to certainty. You do not need to charm them so much as direct them.... Like us, they are logical creatures, and like us, they understand that the order of the universe dictates to them a certain place, a certain rank, a certain dependence on the demands of others. The mahout spoke in Malayalam, but Adil listened to the tumbling words anyway, trying his best not to look at the road swaying beneath him. The truth is, the mahout continued, that driving an elephant does not require intuition or special intelligence, only a willingness to command...more than that, a belief in your command.

Command was in his blood. The mahout was raised to ride elephants, as was his father, and his father's father, and as far as he knew all the males of their line snaking back to some letterless past when man first wrestled the beast into obedience. No better life had presented itself to him than that of ordering elephants. He was aware that many in his village were jealous of his trade, the princely work that saved him from the drudgery of the fields. When the news arrived that he would be sent with the elephant to Morocco, his family lit many candles to fend off the evil eye. You'll come back a big man, they said, and nobody wishes well for big men. What nonsense, he laughed them off, I'll come back just the same...this isn't my journey, it's the journey of the elephant, I'm only an appendage of flesh. Adil squirmed behind him and cars passed, honking. How true, the mahout thought, I am commanded to command. I am an instrument of command. I am an instrument.

From the trailing sedan, the Second Secretary watched the spectacle of the Moroccan gendarme clinging to the elephant. He was surprised to feel a degree of envy. No invitation to mount the elephant had been extended to him. If anyone should first get a turn on the elephant, he thought, it should be me, not that fellow. He filed this grievance away as yet more proof of the strangeness of the mahout and as further evidence, if he needed any more, of the unending injustice that was the daily life of a Second Secretary.

At Skhirat, Adil slumped nauseous from the back of the elephant, attempted a few steps, and tumbled to his knees. The children of the village roared at his collapse and flocked about the elephant. Marouane, the other gendarme, dispersed them as best he could, but they remained bubbling in the corners of the village square, pantomiming the elephant and its minders. Skhirat's mayor, who was also its lead cleric, came to shake hands with the visitors and admire the elephant. In normal circumstances, the village was used to strangers passing through; it was a stop on the Casablanca–Rabat rail line. But since the interruption of rail service, the place had grown dustier and quieter. Its people were happy to produce a welcome fit for any occasion. They brought trellised tables into the square. Pitchers of fresh juices, cups of tea, and miraculous tagines came steaming from nearby houses. All the village's luminaries—its post office clerk, its librarian, its accountant, its letter-writer, its chief constable (its only constable), its doctor, its farm veterinarian (who kept his distance from the elephant, eyeing the creature with trepidation), and so on—assembled to have a meal with the Second Secretary, who was made to repeat, over and over again, in slow French, the basic facts of his life and of his world. The children cheered as the elephant munched carrots dipped in harissa. The gathering continued till late in the evening. When the day's last azaan interrupted proceedings, the elephant raised its trunk towards the minaret and bellowed in its own fashion the call to prayer. All the men of the village made their way to the mosque except for the librarian, who patted the Second Secretary on the back and smuggled him home to share a bottle of arak.

During the night, the Second Secretary snored drunk on the librarian's sofa. Adil slept on a bench. The mahout tucked his chin into his knees and dozed against the slumbering bulk of the elephant. Marouane stood awake, vigilant for any mischievous children lurking at the edges of the square. Nothing happened until an hour before the morning azaan. A shape formed in the provincial gloom and drifted towards the elephant. It was the cleric-mayor. Peace be upon you, Marouane said. And you, the cleric-mayor returned. He rolled up the sleeves of his robe and worked his way around the horizontal elephant. I just want to check, he said half to himself, I just want to check. Marouane watched him dubiously. Check what? The cleric-mayor had already knelt by the elephant's loins. He startled. Well, I'm just curious if the creature is Muslim. In three strides, Marouane had grabbed him by the collar, dragged him away, and dropped him to the ground. You fool, he looked down on the older man, you bumpkin.... Be decent and keep your crazy ideas to yourself. Does a donkey have religion? Can a donkey be Muslim? How can this animal be Muslim? The cleric-mayor straightened up and jabbed a finger into Marouane's uniform. Boy, he snarled, have some respect...that peaceful creature is more of a man than any of your kind will ever be.

The commotion woke the elephant and the mahout. Alarmed by the animal's surging to its feet, the cleric-mayor made apologetic noises and ghosted away. The mahout saw Marouane's agitation. He pointed at Adil sleeping on the bench, urging the gendarme to follow his colleague's example. Marouane nodded and tried to get to sleep. The elephant snorted. It stamped. It wrapped its trunk around the mahout's waist, hugging the man close. Whatever beliefs it did possess, it certainly disliked being roused from its dreams.

The mahout stood for a little while, stroking the elephant's trunk until it subsided once more to its knees, then rolled on to its side. They were alone in the village square. At this time before dawn in the mahout's own village, the roosters would be outdoing one another, the potholed roads would already be clanging with traffic, his family in their multitude would be scratching and groaning and clucking in the shared sleeping space. Morocco had so much room, so much silence. The mahout watched Skhirat take shape in the leavening dark. There was an enviable modesty to the even spread of low buildings, the humble bakery warming its ovens at the edge of the square, the grace of the mosque's silhouetted minaret, the peace of all its obscurity. He knew that this was a tiny country pinned between desert and sea. He knew that his own country was large by any estimation. And yet the calm of this small place felt infinite.

The elephant nuzzled his hand and murmured in its sleep. He buried his face in its ear. He whispered: sleep well, my beauty, sleep well, my prince. If you dream, don't dream of home and don't dream of me. Dream of the sea. You and I are now so alone in this world... Dream of the sea, my life, dream of the sea. The elephant slept, but its trunk remained wrapped around the body of the mahout. It refused to release him. Only as light began to escape down from the eastern mountains did the elephant loosen its grip and let the mahout go.

Dawn came with the first azaan. Adil shook awake, as did Marouane. The village crawled into its quiet, habitual motion, making the small adjustment for the sleeping elephant at its centre. The Second Secretary staggered to his sedan for his toiletries. By the time he finished brushing his teeth next to the well, both the gendarmes stood before him, delivering the news as best they could that the mahout had disappeared.

The Second Secretary was incredulous. Disappeared? Impossible. Skhirat was mobilized to find the mahout. Children swarmed over the rooftops. Scooters buzzed down the road in both directions. Farmers turned over their cauliflowers. The chief constable furiously blew his whistle. There was no trace of the man. At the post office, the Second Secretary sent a message to the embassy. MAHOUT ABSCONDED STOP PLEASE ADVISE STOP. The Indian ambassador rang the post office. He's vanished, has he? The Second Secretary said he had. That's a real pity, the ambassador lamented, but what to do. It's pure physics.... You propel an object a certain distance and you just can't expect it to come to rest, it will keep going forward. You take a man this far from his benighted village and he'll lose all interest in going back...so it goes. But, sir, the Second Secretary interjected, what do we do about the elephant? I don't know, the ambassador said, Rabat isn't all that far. Yes, the Second Secretary agreed, but how do we move the elephant? Why are you asking me? The ambassador snapped. If I were a mahout, I wouldn't be having this bloody conversation with you, would I?

Just do whatever it is you need to do.

The Second Secretary sat on the hood of his sedan, staring at the elephant. It looked back at him, long-lashed and indifferent. He imagined the various means at his disposal that would convince this mass of flesh to proceed down the last stretch of highway to the capital. Perhaps he could lay down a trail of carrots all the way to Rabat. Or maybe if all the children pushed hard enough together, they could inch the elephant up the road. Or better yet, why not just leave the elephant here for the people of Skhirat? Why not be generous and gift them the problem?

Pitying the glum resignation of the Second Secretary, Adil was stirred to provide the solution himself. He came forward to the elephant and placed his hand behind its head, speaking to the creature in Arabic. It bent down. Gingerly, he clambered on top. The elephant returned to its feet. Adil's prodding steered it on to the road. For the first time in two days, the Second Secretary smiled. Allons-y! he cried. Allons-y!

It was imperative to get going before Adil's luck ran out and the elephant decided to stop cooperating. The convoy reassembled and bid a hasty goodbye to Skhirat. All the villagers waved, except for the cleric-mayor. From the window of the mosque, he had seen the mahout slink away in the early hours, seen the alien gleam in his eyes, the rootless abandon of the wanderer. It was a sad spirit, one the cleric-mayor could not comprehend and dared not interfere with; who was he—who had never seriously left his village nor contemplated doing so—to judge the actions of a stranger come to a strange place? So he kept his peace. God be with you, the cleric-mayor said to the departing rump of the elephant, God be with you.

They had reached the outskirts of Rabat when the handlers from the royal gardens finally emerged and relieved them of the elephant. For the cameras, the ambassador posed in front of the creature with Adil, the hero who saved the day and strengthened the bonds between the people of India and Morocco. It was reported to the newspapers that the mahout had been incubating a mysterious tropical disease that had killed him en route to Rabat. The ambassador asked the Second Secretary to ensure that Adil's wife received a very tasteful flower arrangement. The Second Secretary did as he was told.

When the princess returned during her holidays, she was enchanted by the elephant. She would lie next to it and read aloud her books of philosophy and critical theory. She introduced it to champagne. The princess was so enamoured of the creature that she insisted it accompany her on a trip to the beach. The elephant hurried over the dunes at the sight of the ocean, the clarion call of its trunk warning the waves. Everybody laughed as it played in the surf. It seemed to enjoy being knocked over in the shallows, finding its feet, retreating to the beach, and then wheeling its bulk around for another charge against the sea. It all seemed a pleasure, but the elephant was sad that no matter how earnestly it plunged into the water, the tide always drove it back to shore.

CHARLIS AND I
SHASHI THAROOR

I was about eight or nine when I first came across Charlis. A few of us children were kicking a ball around the dusty courtyard of my grandmother's house in rural Kerala, where my parents took me annually on what they called a holiday and I regarded as a cross between a penance and a pilgrimage. (Their pilgrimage, my penance.) Bal-ettan, my oldest cousin, who was all of thirteen and had a bobbing Adam's apple to prove it, had just streaked across me and kicked the ball with more force than he realized he possessed. It soared upwards like a startled bird, curved perversely away from us, and disappeared over our high brick wall into the rubbish heap at the back of the neighbour's house.

'Damn,' I said. I had grown up in Bombay where one said things like that.

'Go and get it, da,' Bal-ettan commanded one of the younger cousins. Da was a term of great familiarity, used especially when ordering young boys around.

A couple of the kids, stifling groans, dutifully set off towards the wall. But before they could reach it the ball came sailing back over their heads towards us, soon followed over the wall by a skinny, sallow youth with a pockmarked face and an anxious grin. He seemed vaguely familiar, someone I'd seen in the background on previous holidays but not really noticed, though I wasn't sure why.

'Charlis!' a couple of the kids called out. 'Charlis got the ball!'

Charlis sat on the wall, managing to look both unsure and pleased with himself. Bits of muck from the rubbish heap clung to his shirt and skin. 'Can I play?' he asked diffidently.

Bal-ettan gave him a look that would have desiccated a coconut. 'No, you can't, Charlis,' he said shortly, kicking the ball towards me, away from the interloper who'd rescued it.

Charlis's face lost its grin, leaving only the look of anxiety across it like a shadow. He remained seated on the wall, his legs—bare and thin below the grubby mundu he tied around his waist—dangling nervously. The game resumed, and Charlis watched, his eyes liquid with wistfulness.

He would kick the brick wall aimlessly with his foot, then catch himself doing it and stop, looking furtively at us to see whether anyone had noticed. But no one paid any attention to him, except me, and I was the curious outsider.

'Why can't he play?' I finally found the courage to ask Bal-ettan.

'Because he can't, that's all,' replied my eldest cousin.

'But why? We can always use another player,' I protested.

'We can't use him,' Bal-ettan said curtly. 'Don't you understand anything, stupid?'

That was enough to silence me, because I had learned early on that there was a great deal about the village I didn't understand. A city upbringing didn't prepare you for your parents' annual return to their roots, to the world they'd left behind and failed to equip you for. Everything, pretty much, was different in my grandmother's house: there were hurricane lamps instead of electric lights, breezes instead of ceiling fans, a cow in the barn rather than a car in the garage. Water didn't come out of taps but from a well, in buckets laboriously raised by rope pulleys; you poured it over yourself out of metal vessels, hoping the maidservant who'd heated the bathwater over a charcoal fire had not made it so hot you'd scald yourself. There were the obscure indignities of having to be accompanied to the outhouse by an adult with a gleaming stainless-steel flashlight and of needing to hold his hand while you squatted in the privy, because the chair-like commodes of the city had made you unfit to discharge your waste as an Indian should, on his haunches. But it wasn't just a question of these inconveniences; there was the sense of being in a different world. Bombay was busy, bustling, unpredictable; there were children of every imaginable appearance, colour, language, and religion in my school; it was a city of strangers jostling one another all the time. In my grandmother's village everyone I met seemed to know one another and be related. They dressed alike, did the same things day after day, shared the same concerns, celebrated the same festivals. Their lives were ordered, predictable; things were either done or not done, according to rules and assumptions I'd never been taught in the city.

Some of the rules were easier than others to grasp. There were, for instance, complicated hierarchies that everyone seemed to take for granted. The ones I first understood were those relating to age. This was absolute, like an unspoken commandment: everyone older had to be respected and obeyed, even if they sent you off on trivial errands they should really have done themselves. Then there was gender: the women existed to serve the men, fetching and carrying and stitching and hurrying for them, eating only after they had fed the men first. Even my mother, who could hold her own at a Bombay party with a cocktail in her hand, was transformed in Kerala into a dutiful drudge, blowing into the wood fire to make the endless stacks of thin, soft, crisp-edged dosas we all wolfed down. None of this had to be spelled out, no explicit orders given; people simply seemed to adjust naturally to an immutable pattern of expectations, where everyone knew his place and understood what he had to do. As someone who came from Bombay for a month's vacation every year, spoke the language badly, hated the bathrooms, and swelled up with insect bites, I adjusted less than most. I sensed dimly that the problem with Charlis, too, had something to do with hierarchy, but since he was neither female nor particularly young, I couldn't fit him into what I thought I already knew of Kerala village life.

We finished the game soon enough, and everyone began heading indoors. Charlis jumped off the wall. Instinctively, but acting with the casual hospitality I usually saw around me, I went up to him and said, 'My mother'll be making dosas for tea. Want some?'

I was puzzled by the look of near panic that flooded his face. 'No, no, that's all right,' he said, practically backing away from me. I could see Bal-ettan advancing towards us. 'I've got to go,' Charlis added, casting me a strange look as he fled.

'What's the matter with him?' I asked Bal-ettan.

'What's the matter with you?' he retorted. 'What were you saying to him?'

'I just asked him to join us for some dosas, that's all,' I replied. Seeing his expression, I added lamely, 'you know, with all the other kids.'

Bal-ettan shook his head in a combination of disgust and dismay, as if he didn't know whether to be angry or sad. 'You know what this little foreigner did?' he announced loudly as soon as we entered the house. 'He asked Charlis to come and have dosas with us!'

This was greeted with guffaws by some and clucks of disapproval by others. 'Poor little boy, what does he know?' said my favourite aunt, the widowed Rani-valiamma, gathering me to her ample bosom to offer a consolation I hadn't realized I needed. 'It's not his fault.'

'What's not my fault?' I asked, struggling free of her embrace. The Cuticura talcum powder in her cleavage tickled my nose, and the effort not to sneeze made me sound even more incoherent than usual. 'Why shouldn't I invite him? He got our ball back for us. And you invite half the village anyway if they happen to pass by.'

'Yes, but which half?' chortled Kunjunni-mama, a local layabout and distant relative who was a constant presence at our dining table and considered himself a great wit. 'Which half, I say?' He laughed heartily at his own question, his eyes rolling, a honking sound emerging from the back of his nose.

I couldn't see why anyone else found this funny, but I was soon sent off to wash my hands. I sat down to my dosas feeling as frustrated as a vegetarian at a kebab shop.

'Who is Charlis, anyway?' I asked as my mother served me the mild chutney she made specially since I couldn't handle the fiery, spiced version everyone else ate.

'I don't know, dear, just a boy from the village,' she responded. 'Now finish your dosas, the adults have to eat.'

'Charlis is the Prince of Wales, didn't you know?' honked Kunjunni-mama, enjoying himself hugely. 'I thought you went to a convent school, Neel.'

'First of all, only girls go to convent schools,' I responded hotly. 'And, anyway, the Prince of Wales is called Charles, not Charlis.' I shot him a look of pure hatred, but he was completely unfazed. He soaked it in as a paddy field would a rainstorm, and honked some more.

'Charlis, Charles, what's the difference to an illiterate Untouchable with airs above his station? Anyway, that's how it sounded in Malayalam, and that's how he wrote it. Charlis. So, you see how the Prince of Wales was born in Vanganassery.' He exploded into self-satisfied mirth, his honks suggesting he was inhaling his own pencil-line moustache. I hadn't understood what he meant, but I vowed not to seek any further clarification from him.

My mother came to my rescue. I could see that her interest was piqued. 'But why Charles?' she paused in her serving and asked Kunjunni-mama. 'Are they Christians?'

'Christians?' Kunjunni-mama honked again. 'My dear chechi, what do these people know of religion? Do they have any culture, any traditions? One of them, that cobbler fellow, Mandan, named his sons Mahatma Gandhi and Jawaharlal Nehru. Can you imagine? The fellow didn't even know that Mahatma was a title and Nehru a family surname. His brats were actually registered in school as M. Mahatma Gandhi and M. Jawaharlal Nehru. So, of course, when this upstart scavenger shopkeeper had to name his offspring, he went one better. Forget nationalism, he turned to the British royal family. So what if they had Christian names? So what if he couldn't pronounce them? You think Charlis is bad enough? He has two sisters, Elizabeth and Anne. Of course, everyone in the village calls them Eli and Ana.'

This time even I joined in the laughter: I had enough Malayalam to know that Eli meant 'rat' and Ana meant 'elephant'. But a Bombayite sense of fairness asserted itself.

'It doesn't matter what his name is,' I said firmly. 'Charlis seems a nice boy. He went into the rubbish heap to get our ball. I liked him.'

'Nice boy!' Kunjunni-mama's tone was dismissive, and this time there was no laughter in his honk. 'Rubbish heaps are where they belong. They're not clean. They don't wash. They have dirty habits.'

'What dirty habits?' I asked, shaking off my mother's restraining hand. 'Who's they?'

'Eat your food,' Kunjunni-mama said to me, adding to no one in particular, 'and now this communist government wants to put them in our schools. With our children.' He snorted. 'They'll be drinking out of our wells next.'

∽

A few days later, the kids at home all decided to go to the local stream for a dip. On earlier Kerala holidays, my mother had firmly denied me permission to go along, sure that if I didn't drown I'd catch a cold; but now I was older, I'd learned to swim, and I was capable of towelling myself dry, so I was allowed the choice. It seemed a fun idea, and, in any case, there was nothing better to do at home: I'd long since finished reading the couple of Biggles books I'd brought along. I set out with a sense of adventure.

We walked through dusty, narrow lanes, through the village, Bal-ettan in the lead, half a dozen of the cousins following. For a while the houses we passed seemed to be those of relatives and friends; the kids waved cheerful greetings to women hanging up their washing, girls plaiting or picking lice out of each other's hair, bare-chested men in white mundus sitting magisterially in easy chairs, perusing the day's *Mathrubhumi*. Then the lane narrowed and the whitewashed, tile-roofed houses with verdant backyards gave way to thatched huts squeezed tightly together, their interiors shrouded in a darkness from which wizened crones emerged stooping through low-ceilinged doorways, the holes in their alarmingly stretched earlobes gaping like open mouths. The ground beneath our feet, uneven and stony, hurt to walk on, and a stale odour hung in the air, a compound of rotting vegetation and decaying flesh. Despair choked my breath like smoke. I began to wish I hadn't come along.

At last we left the village behind, and picked our way down a rocky, moss-covered slope to the stream. I didn't know what I'd expected, but it wasn't this, a meandering rivulet that flowed muddily through the fields. At the water's edge, on a large rock nearby, women were beating the dirt out of their saris; in the distance, a man squatted at a bend in the stream, picking his teeth and defecating. My cousins peeled off their shirts and ran into the water.

'Come on, Neel,' Bal-ettan exhorted me with a peremptory wave of the hand. 'Don't be a sissy. It's not cold.'

'Just don't feel like it,' I mumbled. 'It's okay. You go ahead. I'll watch.'

They tried briefly to persuade me to change my mind, then left me to my own devices. I stood on the shore looking at them, heard their squeals of laughter, then looked away at the man who had completed his ablutions and was scooping water from the river to wash himself. Downstream from him, my cousins ducked their heads underwater. I quickly averted my gaze.

That was when I saw him. Charlis was sitting on a rocky overhang, a clean shirt over his mundu, a book in his hand. But his eyes weren't on it. He was looking down at the stream, where my cousins were playing.

I clambered over the rocks to him. When he spotted me, he seemed to smile in recognition, then look around anxiously. But there was no one else about, and he relaxed visibly. 'Neel,' he said, smiling. 'Aren't you swimming today?'

I shook my head. 'Water's dirty,' I said.

'Not dirty,' he replied in Malayalam. 'The stream comes from a sacred river. Removes all pollution.'

I started to retort, then changed my mind. 'So, why don't you swim?' I asked.

'Ah, I do,' he said. 'But not here.' His eyes avoided mine, but seemed to take in the stream, the washerwomen, my cousins. 'Not now.'

Bits of the half-understood conversation from the dining table floated awkwardly back into my mind. I changed the subject. 'It was nice of you to get our ball back for us that day,' I said.

'Ah, it was nothing.' He smiled unexpectedly, his pockmarks creasing across his face. 'My father beat me for it when I got home, though. I had ruined a clean shirt. Just after my bath.'

'But I thought you people didn't—' I found myself saying. 'I'm sorry,' I finished lamely.

'Didn't what?' he asked evenly, but without looking at me. He was clearly some years older than me, but not much bigger. I wondered whether he was scared of me, and why.

'Nothing,' I replied. 'I'm really sorry your father beat you.'

'Ah, that's all right. He does it all the time. It's for my own good.'

'What does your father do?'

Charlis became animated by my interest. 'He has a shop,' he said, a light in his eyes. 'In our part of the village. The Nair families don't come there, but he sells all sorts of nice things. Provisions and things. And on Thursdays, you know what he has? The best halwa in Vanganassery.'

'Really? I like halwa.' It was, in fact, the only Indian dessert I liked; Bombay had given me a taste for ice cream and chocolate rather than the deep-fried laddoos and brick-like Mysore paak that were the Kerala favourites.

'You like halwa?' Charlis clambered to his feet. 'Come on, I'll get you some.'

This time it was my turn to hesitate. 'No, thanks,' I said, looking at my cousins cavorting in the water. 'I don't think I should. They'll worry about me. And besides, I don't know my way about the village.'

'That's okay,' Charlis said. 'I'll take you home. Come on.' He saw the expression on my face. 'It's really good halwa,' he added.

That was enough for a nine-year-old. 'Wait for me,' I said, and ran down to the water's edge. 'See you at home!' I called out to the others.

Bal-ettan was the only one who noticed me. 'Sure you can find your way back?' he asked, as my cousins splashed around him, one leaping onto his shoulders.

'I'll be okay,' I replied, and ran back up the slope as Bal-ettan went under.

※

Charlis left me at the bend in our lane, where all I had to do was to walk through a relative's yard to reach my grandmother's house. He would not come any farther, and I knew better than to insist. I walked slowly to the house, my mind full of the astonishment with which his father had greeted my presence in his shop, the taste of his sugary, milky tea still lingering on my palate, my hands full of the wobbling, orange-coloured slabs of halwa he had thrust upon me.

'Neel, my darling!' my mother exclaimed as I walked in. 'Where have you been? I've been so worried about you.'

'Look what I've got!' I said proudly, holding out the halwa. 'And there's enough for everyone.'

'Where did you get that?' Bal-ettan asked, a white thorthumundu, a thin Kerala towel, in his hand, his hair still wet from his recent swim.

'Charlis gave it to me,' I said. 'I went to his father's shop. They—'

'You did what?' Bal-ettan's rage was frightening. He advanced towards me.

'I—I—'

'Went to Charlis's shop?' He loomed over me, the towel draped over his shoulder making him look even older and more threatening. 'Took food from Untouchables?' I began to shrink back from him. 'Give that to me!'

'I won't!' I snatched the halwa away from his hands, and as he lunged, I turned and ran, the precious sweet sticky in my grasp. But he was too fast for me; I had barely reached the yard when he caught up, seized me roughly by the shoulders, and turned me around to face him.

'We don't do this here, understand?' he breathed fiercely. 'This isn't Bombay.' He pried my hands apart. The halwa gleamed in my palms. 'Drop it,' he commanded.

'No,' I wanted to say, but the word would not emerge. I wanted to cry out for my mother, but she did not come out of the house.

'Drop it,' Bal-ettan repeated, his voice a whiplash across what remained of my resistance.

Slowly, I opened my hands outwards in a gesture of submission. The orange slabs slid reluctantly off them. It seemed to me they took an age to fall, their gelatinous surfaces clinging to the soft skin of my palms until the last possible moment. Then they were gone, fallen into the dust.

Bal-ettan looked at them on the ground for a moment, then at me, and spat upon them where they lay. 'The dogs can have them,' he barked. He kicked more dust over them, then pulled me by the arm back towards the house. 'Don't you ever do this again.'

I burst into tears then, and at last the words came, tripping over themselves as I stumbled back into the house. 'I hate you! All of you! You're horrible and mean and cruel and I'll never come back here as long as I live!'

∞

But, of course, I was back the next year; I hardly had any choice in the matter. For my parents, first-generation migrants to the big city, this was the vital visit home, to their own parents and siblings, to the friends and family they had left behind; it renewed them, it returned them to a sense of themselves, it maintained their connection to the past. I just came along because I was too young to be left behind, indeed too young to be allowed the choice.

In the year that had passed since my last visit, there had been much ferment in Kerala. Education was now universal and compulsory and free, so all sorts of children were flocking to school who had never been able to go before. There was talk of land reform, and giving title to tenant farmers; I understood nothing of this, but saw the throngs around men with microphones on the roadside, declaiming angry harangues I could not comprehend. None of this seemed, however, to have much to do with us, or to affect the unchanging rhythms of life at my grandmother's house.

My cousins were numerous and varied, the children of my mother's brothers and sisters, and also of her cousins, who lived in the neighbouring houses; sometimes, the relationship was less clear than that, but as they all ran about together and slept side by side like a camping army on mats on the floor of my grandmother's thalam, it was difficult to tell who was a first cousin and who an uncle's father-in-law's sister's grandson. After all, it was also their holiday season, and my parents' return was an occasion for everyone to congregate in the big house. On any given day, with my cousins joined by other children from the village, there could be as many as a dozen kids playing in the courtyard or going to the stream or breaking up for cards on the back porch. Sometimes I joined them, but sometimes, taking advantage of the general confusion, I would slip away unnoticed, declining to make the effort to scale the barriers of language and education and attitude that separated us, and sit alone with a book. Occasionally, someone would come and look for me. Most often, that someone was my aunt Rani-valiamma.

As a young widow, she didn't have much of a life. Deprived of the status that a husband would have given her, she seemed to walk on the fringes of the house; it had been whispered by her late husband's family that only the bad luck her stars had brought into his life could account for his fatal heart attack at the age of thirty-six, and a whiff of stigma clung to her like a cloying perfume she could never quite wash off. Remarriage was out of the question, nor could the family allow her to make her own way in the world; so, she returned to the village house she had left as a bride, and tried to lose herself in the routines of my grandmother's household. She sublimated her misfortune in random and frequent acts of kindness, of which I was a favoured beneficiary. She would bring me well-sugared lime-and-water from the kitchen without being asked, and whenever one of us brought down a green mango from the ancient tree with a lucky throw of a stone, she could be counted upon to return with it chopped up and marinated in just the right combination of salt and red chilli powder to drive my taste buds to ecstasy.

One day, Rani-valiamma and I were upstairs, eating devilled raw mango and looking out on the kids playing soccer below, when I saw something and nearly choked. 'Isn't that Charlis?' I asked, pointing to the skinny boy who had just failed to save a goal.

'Could be,' she replied indifferently. 'Let me see—yes, that's Charlis.'

'But he's playing in our yard! I remember last year—'

'That was last year,' Rani-valiamma said, and I knew that change had come to the village.

But not enough of it. When the game was over, the Nair kids trooped in as usual to eat, without Charlis. When I asked innocently where he was, it was Bal-ettan, inevitably, who replied. 'We play with him at school, and we play with him outside,' he said. 'But playing stops at the front door.'

I didn't pursue the matter. I had learned that whenever any of the Untouchable tradespeople came to the house, they were dealt with outside.

With each passing vacation, though, the changes became more and more apparent. For years, my grandmother, continuing a tradition handed down over generations, had dispensed free medication (mainly aspirins and cough syrup) once a week to the poor villagers who queued for it; then, a real clinic was established in the village by the government, and her amateur charity was no longer needed. Electricity came to Vanganassery; my uncle strung up a brilliant neon light above the dining table, and the hurricane lamps began to disappear, along with the tin cans of kerosene from which they were fuelled. The metal vessels in the bathroom were replaced by shiny red plastic mugs. A toilet was installed in the outhouse for my father's, and my, convenience. And one year, one day, quite naturally, Charlis stepped into the house with the other kids after a game.

No one skipped a beat; it was as if everyone had agreed to pretend there was nothing unusual. Charlis stood around casually, laughing and chatting; some of the kids sat to eat, others awaited their turn. No one invited Charlis to sit or to eat, and he made no move himself to do either. Then those who had eaten rose and washed their hands and joined the chatter, while those who had been with Charlis took their places at the table. Still, Charlis stood and talked, his manner modest and respectful, until everyone but he had finished eating, and then they all strolled out again to continue their game.

'Charlis hasn't eaten,' I pointed out to the womenfolk.

'I know, child, but what can we do?' Rani-valiamma asked. 'He can't sit at our table or be fed on our plates. Even you know that.'

'It isn't fair,' I said, but without belligerence. What she had stated was, I knew, like a law of nature. Even the servants would not wash a plate off which an Untouchable had eaten.

'You know,' honked Kunjunni-mama, tucking into his third helping, 'they say that boy is doing quite well at school. Very well, in fact.'

'He stood first in class last term,' a younger cousin chimed in.

'First!' I exclaimed. 'And Bal-ettan failed the year, didn't he?'

'Now, why would you be asking that?' chortled Kunjunni-mama meaningfully, slapping his thigh with his free hand.

I ignored the question and turned to my aunt. 'He's smarter than all of us, and we can't even give him something to eat?'

Rani-valiamma saw the expression on my face and squeezed my hand. 'Don't worry,' she whispered. 'I'll think of something.'

She did; and the next time Charlis walked in, he was served food on a plantain leaf on the floor, near the back door. I was too embarrassed to hover near him as I had intended to, but he seemed to eat willingly enough on his own.

'It's just not right!' I whispered to her as we watched him from a discreet distance.

'He doesn't mind,' she whispered back. 'Why should you?'

And it was true that Charlis probably ate on the floor in his own home.

When he had finished, a mug of water was given to him on the back porch, so that he could wash his hands without stepping into our bathroom. And the plantain leaf was thrown away: no plate to wash.

We returned to the game, and now it was my turn to miskick. The ball cleared the low wall at one end of the courtyard, hit the side of the well, teetered briefly on the edge, and fell in with a splash.

It had happened before. 'Go and get it, da,' Bal-ettan languidly commanded one of the kids. The well was designed to be climbed into: bricks jutted out from the inside wall at regular intervals, and others had been removed to provide strategic footholds. But this was a slippery business: since the water levels in the well rose and fell, the inside surface was pretty slimy, and many of those who'd gone in to retrieve a floating object, or a bucket that had slipped its rope, had ended up taking an unplanned dip. The young cousin who had received Bal-ettan's instruction hesitated, staring apprehensively into the depths of the well.

'Don't worry,' Charlis said quietly. 'I'll get it.' He moved towards the edge of the well.

'No!' There was nothing languid now about Bal-ettan's tone; we could all hear the alarm in his voice. 'I'll do it myself.' And Charlis, one half-raised foot poised to climb onto the well, looked at him, his face drained of expression, comprehension slowly burning into his cheeks. Bal-ettan ran forward, roughly pushing aside the boy who had been afraid to go, and vaulted into the well.

I looked at Rani-valiamma, who had been watching the game.

'Bal-ettan's right,' she said. 'Do you think anyone would have drunk water at our house again if Charlis had gone into our well?'

∞

Years passed; school holidays, and trips to Kerala, came and went. Governments fell and were replaced in Kerala, farm labourers were earning the highest daily wage in the country, and my almost toothless grandmother was sporting a chalk-white set of new dentures under her smile. Yet, the house seemed much the same as before. A pair of ceiling fans had been installed, in the two rooms where family members congregated; a radio crackled with the news from Delhi; a tap made its appearance in the bathroom, though the pipe attached to it led from the same old well. These improvements, and the familiarity that came from repeated visits, made the old privations bearable. Kerala seemed less of a penance with each passing year.

Charlis was a regular member of the group now, admitted to our card-playing sessions on the porch outside, joining us on our expeditions to the cinema in the nearest town. But fun and games seemed to hold a decreasing attraction for Charlis. He was developing a reputation as something of an intellectual. He would ask me, in painstaking textbook English, about something he had read about the great wide world outside, and listen attentively to my reply. I was, in the quaint vocabulary of the villagers, 'convent-educated', a label they applied to anyone who emerged from the elite schools in which Christian missionaries served their foreign Lord by teaching the children of the Indian lordly. It was assumed that I knew more about practically everything than anyone in the village; but all I knew was what I had been taught from books, whereas they had learned from life. Even as I wallowed in their admiration, I couldn't help feeling their lessons were the more difficult, and the more valuable.

Bal-ettan dropped out of school and began turning his attention to what remained of the family lands. It seemed to me that his rough edges became rougher as the calluses grew hard on his hands and feet. He had less time for us now; in his late teens, he was already a full-fledged farmer, sitting sucking a straw between his teeth and watching the boys kick a ball around. If he disapproved of Charlis's growing familiarity with all of us, though, he did not show it—not even when Charlis asked me one day to go into town with him to see the latest Bombay blockbuster.

I thought Charlis might have hoped I could explain the Hindi dialogues to him, since Keralites learned Hindi only as a third language from teachers who knew it, at best, as a second. But when we got to the movie theatre, Charlis was not disappointed to discover the next two screenings were fully sold out. 'I am really wanting to talk,' he said in English, leading me to an eatery across the street.

The Star of India, as the board outside proclaimed, was a 'military hotel'; in other words, it served meat, which my grandmother did not. 'I am thinking you might be missing it,' Charlis said, ushering me to a chair. It was only when the main dish arrived that I realized that I was actually sitting and eating at the same table with Charlis for the first time.

If he was conscious of this, Charlis didn't show it. He began talking, hesitantly at first, then with growing fluency and determination, about his life and his ambitions. His face shone when he talked of his father, who beat him with a belt whenever he showed signs of neglecting his books. 'You can do better than I did,' he would say, before bringing the whip down on Charlis. 'You will do better.'

And now Charlis was aiming higher than anyone in his family, in his entire community, had ever done before. He was planning to go to university.

'Listen, Charlis,' I said gently, not wanting to discourage him. 'You know it's not going to be easy. I know you're first in class and everything, but that's in the village. Don't forget you'll be competing for places with kids from the big cities. From the—convents.'

'I am knowing that,' Charlis replied simply. Then, from the front pocket of his shirt, he drew out a battered notebook filled with small, tightly packed curlicues of Malayalam lettering in blue ink, interspersed with phrases and sentences in English in the same precise hand. 'Look,' he said, jabbing at a page. 'The miserable hath no other medicine / But only hope.—Shakespeare, *Measure for Measure*, III.i.2,' I read. And a little lower down, 'Men at some time are masters of their fates; / The fault, dear Brutus, is not in our stars, / But in ourselves, that we are underlings.' Charlis had underlined these words.

'Whenever I am reading something that inspires me, I am writing it down in this book,' Charlis said proudly. 'Shakespeare is great man, isn't it?'

His Malayalam was, of course, much better, but in English Charlis seemed to cast off an invisible burden that had less to do with the language than with its social assumptions. In speaking it, in quoting it, Charlis seemed to be entering another world, a heady place of foreign ideas and unfamiliar expressions, a strange land in which the old rules no longer applied.

'For the Colonel's Lady an' Judy O'Grady,' he declaimed at one point, "are sisters under their skins!"—Rudyard Kipling,' he added. 'Is that how you are pronouncing it?'

'Rudyard, Roodyard, I haven't a clue,' I confessed. 'But who cares, Charlis? He's just an old imperialist fart. What does anything he ever wrote have to do with any of us today, in independent India?'

Charlis looked surprised, then slightly averted his eyes. 'But are we not,' he asked softly, 'are we not brothers under our skins?'

'Of course,' I replied, too quickly. And it was I who couldn't meet his gaze.

The following summer, I was sitting down to my first meal of the holiday at my grandmother's dining table when Rani-valiamma said, 'Charlis was looking for you.'

'Really?' I was genuinely pleased, as much by Charlis's effort as by the fact that it could be mentioned so casually. 'What did he want?'

'He came to give you the news personally,' Rani-valiamma said. 'He's been admitted to Trivandrum University.'

'Wow!' I exclaimed. 'That's something, isn't it?'

'Untouchable quota,' honked the ever-present Kunjunni-mama, whose pencil-line moustache had gone from bold black to sleek silver without his ever having done a stroke of work in his life.

'Reserved seats for the Children of God. Why, Chandrasekhara Menon's son couldn't get in after all the money they spent on sending him to boarding school, and here Charlis is on his way to university.'

'The village panchayat council is organizing a felicitation for him tomorrow,' Rani-valiamma said. 'Charlis wanted you to come, Neel.'

'Of course, I will,' I responded. 'We must all go.'

'All?' snorted Kunjunni-mama, who was incapable of any action that could be called affirmative. 'To felicitate Charlis? Speak for yourself, boy. If you want to attend an Untouchable love-in organized by the communists who claim to represent our village, more's the pity. But don't expect to drag any members of the Nair community with you.'

'I'll come with you, Neel,' said a quiet voice by my side. It was Rani-valiamma, her ever-obliging manner transformed into something approaching determination.

'And me,' chirped a younger cousin, emboldened. 'May I go too, Amma?' asked another. And, by the next evening, I had assembled a sizeable delegation from our extended family to attend the celebration for Charlis.

Kunjunni-mama and Bal-ettan sat at the table, nursing their cups of tea, and watched us all troop out. Bal-ettan was silent, his manner distant rather than disapproving. As I passed them, I heard the familiar honk: 'Felicitation, my foot.'

The speeches had begun when we arrived, and our entry sparked something of a commotion in the meeting hall, as Charlis's relatives and the throng of well-wishers from his community made way for us, whispers of excitement and consternation rippling like a current through the room. I thought I saw a look of sheer delight shine like a sunburst on Charlis's face, but that may merely have been a reaction to hearing the panchayat president say, 'The presence of all of you here today proves that Charlis's achievement is one of which the entire village is proud.' We applauded that, knowing our arrival had given some meaning to that trite declaration.

After the speeches, and the garlanding, and Charlis's modest reply, the meeting broke up. I wanted to congratulate Charlis myself, but he was surrounded by his own people, all proud and happy and laughing. We made our way towards the door, and then I heard his voice.

'Neel! Wait!' he called out. I turned to see him pulling himself away from the crush and advancing towards me with a packet in his hands. 'You mustn't leave without this.'

He stretched out the packet towards me, beaming. I opened it and peered in. Orange slabs of halwa quivered inside.

'It's the last bag,' Charlis said, the smile never fading from his face. 'My father sold the shop to pay for me to go to university. We're all moving to Trivandrum.' I looked at him, finding no words. He pushed the halwa at me. 'I wanted you to have it.'

I took the bag from him without a word. We finished the halwa before we got home.

⁂

Years passed. Men landed on the moon, a woman became prime minister, wars were fought; in other countries, coups and revolutions brought change (or attempted to), while in India elections were won and lost and things changed (or didn't). I couldn't go down to Kerala every time my parents did; my college holidays didn't always coincide with Dad's leave from the office. When I did manage a visit, it wasn't the same as before. I would come for a few days, be indulged by Rani-valiamma, and move on. There was not that much to do. Rani-valiamma had started studying for a teacher's training diploma. My grandmother spent most of her time reading the scriptures and chewing areca, usually simultaneously. Bal-ettan, tough and taciturn, was the man of the house; now that agriculture was his entire life, we had even less to say to each other than ever. My cousins were scattered in several directions; a new generation of kids played football in the yard. No one had news of Charlis.

I began working in an advertising agency in Bombay, circulating in a brittle, showy world that could not have had less in common with Vanganassery. When I went to the village the talk was of pesticides and irrigation, of the old rice levy and the new government-subsidized fertilizer, and, inevitably, of the relentless pace of land reform, which was taking away the holdings of traditional landlords and giving them to their tenants. It was clear that Bal-ettan did not understand much of this, and that he had not paid a great deal of attention to what was happening.

'Haven't you received any notification from the authorities, Bal-ettan?' I asked him one day, when his usual reticence seemed only to mask ineffectually the mounting level of anxiety in his eyes.

'Some papers came,' he said in a tone the aggressiveness of which betrayed his deep shame at his own inadequacy. 'But do I have time to read them? I'm a busy man. Do I run a farm or push papers like a clerk?'

'Show them to Neel,' Kunjunni-mama suggested, and as soon as I opened the first envelope I realized Bal-ettan, high-school dropout and traditionalist, had left it too late.

'What are these lands here, near Kollengode?'

'They're ours, of course.'

'Not any more, Bal-ettan. Who's T. Krishnan Nair, son of Kandath Narayananunni Nair?'

'He farms them for us, ever since Grandfather died. I farm here at Vanganassery, and Krishnan Nair takes care of Kollengode, giving us his dues after each harvest. It's the only way. I can't be at both places at the same time, can I?'

'Well, it says here he's just been registered as the owner of those lands. You were given fourteen days to show cause as to why his claim should not have been admitted. Why didn't you file an objection, Bal-ettan?'

We were all looking at him.

'How can they say Krishnan Nair owns our land? Why, everybody knows it's our land. It's been ours ever since anyone can remember. It was ours before Grandmother was born.'

'It's not ours any more, Bal-ettan. The government has just taken it away.'

Bal-ettan shifted uneasily in his chair, a haunted, uncomprehending look on his face. 'But they can't do that,' he said. 'Can they?'

'They can, Bal-ettan,' I told him sadly. 'You know they can.'

'We've got to do something,' honked Kunjunni-mama with uncharacteristic urgency. 'Neel, you've got to do something.'

'Me? What can I do? I'm a Bombaywallah. I know less about all this than any of you.'

'Perhaps,' admitted Kunjunni-mama, 'but you're an educated man. You can read and understand these documents. You can speak to the Collector. He's the top IAS man in the district, probably another city type like you, convent educated. You can speak to him in English and explain what has happened. Come on, Neel. You've got to do it.'

'I don't know,' I said dubiously. The advertising life had not brought me into contact with any senior Indian Administrative Service officers. I hadn't the slightest idea what I would say to the Collector when I met him.

And then I saw the look in Bal-ettan's eyes. He had grown up knowing instinctively the rules and rituals of village society, the cycles of the harvest, how to do the right thing and what was never done. He could, without a second thought, climb trees that would make most of us dizzy, descend into wells, stand knee-deep in the slushy water of a paddy field to sprout grain into the world. But all these were skills he was born with, rhythms that sang in his blood like the whisper of his mother's breath. He wore a mundu around his waist, coaxed his buffalo across the fields, and treated his labourers and his family as his ancestors had done for thousands of years. He was good at the timeless realities of village India; but India, even village India, was no longer a timeless place. 'Don't you understand anything, stupid?' he had asked me all those years ago; and in his eyes I saw what I imagined he must have seen, at that time, in mine.

'I'll go,' I said, as Bal-ettan averted his eyes. In relief, perhaps, or in gratitude. It didn't matter which.

·◊·

The Collector's office in Palghat, the district capital, was already besieged by supplicants when I arrived. Two greasy clerks presided over his antechamber, their desks overflowing with papers loosely bound in crumbling files held together with string. Three phones rang intermittently, and were answered in a wide variety of tones, ranging from the uncooperative to the unctuous, depending on who was calling. People crowded around the desks, seeking attention, thrusting slips of paper forward, folding hands in entreaty, shouting to be heard. Occasionally a paper was dealt with, and a khaki-uniformed peon sent for to carry it somewhere; sometimes, people were sent away, though most seemed to be waved towards the walls where dozens were already waiting, weary resignation on their faces, for their problems to be dealt with. All eyes were on the closed teak door at the corner, bearing the brass nameplate M. C. THEKKOTE, IAS., behind which their destinies were no doubt being determined.

'It's hopeless,' I said to Bal-ettan, who had accompanied me. 'I told you we should have tried to get an appointment. We'll be here all day.'

'How would we have got an appointment?' Bal-ettan asked, reasonably, since we did not yet have a phone in the village. 'No, this is the only way. You go and give them your card.'

I did not share Bal-ettan's faith in the magical properties of this small rectangular advertisement of my status, but I battled my way to the front of one of the desks and thrust it at an indifferent clerk.

'Please take this to the Collector-saare,' I said, trying to look both important and imploring. 'I must see him.'

The clerk seemed unimpressed by the colourful swirls and curlicues that proclaimed my employment by AdAge, Bombay's smartest new agency. 'You and everyone else,' he said sceptically, putting the card aside. 'Collector-saare very busy today. You come back tomorrow, we will see.'

At this point Bal-ettan's native wisdom asserted itself. He insinuated a five-rupee note into the clerk's palm. 'Send the card in,' he said. 'It's important.'

The clerk was instantly responsive. 'I am doing as you wish,' he said grudgingly, 'but you will still have to wait. Collector-saare is so so very busy today.'

'You've told us that already,' I replied. 'We'll wait.'

A peon wandered in, bearing tea for the clerks. Once the man at the desk had satisfied himself that his tea was sugared to his taste, he added my card to the pile of papers he gave the peon to take in to the Collector. 'It will take some time,' he added curtly.

It didn't. Soon after the door had closed behind the peon, the black phone on the clerk's desk jangled peremptorily. 'Yes, saar. Yes, saar,' he said, perspiring. 'No, saar. Not long. Yes, saar. At once, saar.' He had stood up to attention during this exchange, and when he replaced the receiver there was a new look of respect in his eyes. 'Collector-saare will be seeing you now, saar,' he said, with a salaam. 'You didn't explain who you were, saar.' The five-rupee note re-emerged in his hand. 'You seem to have dropped this by mistake, saar,' he said shamefacedly, handing it to Bal-ettan.

'Keep it,' Bal-ettan said, as mystified as I by the transformation in the man's attitude. But the clerk begged him to take it back, and bowed and scraped us towards the imposing doorway.

'Obviously Bombay's ad world counts for more than I thought with these governmentwallahs,' I whispered to Bal-ettan.

'He's just happy to be able to speak English with someone,' Bal-ettan suggested.

The clerk opened the door into a high-ceilinged office. The Collector rose from behind a mahogany desk the size of a ping-pong table, and stretched out a hand. 'It's so good to see you again, Neel,' he said.

It was Charlis.

'Charlis!' I exclaimed, astonishment overcoming delight. 'B—but—the name—the IAS—'

'You never did know my family name, did you? After all these years.' Charlis spoke without reproach. 'And, yes, I've been in the IAS for some time now.' The Administrative Service, too, I found myself thinking unworthily, offered one more of the quotas Kunjunni-mama liked to complain about. 'But this is the first time I've been posted so close to Vanganassery. I've barely got here, but once I've settled in, I'm planning to visit the village again soon.' He added casually, 'It's part of my district, after all. That'd make it an official visit, you see.'

He seemed to enjoy the thought, and I found myself looking at Bal-ettan. I didn't know what I expected to find in his expression, but it certainly wasn't the combination of hope, respect, and, yes, admiration with which he now regarded the man across the desk.

Charlis seemed to catch it, too. 'But what is this? We haven't even asked Bal-ettan to sit down.' He waved us to chairs, as tea appeared. 'Tell me, what can I do for you?'

We explained the problem, and Charlis was sympathetic but grave.

The law was the law; it was also just, undoing centuries of absentee landlordism. In our case, though, thanks to Bal-ettan's inattention (though Charlis didn't even imply that), it had been applied unfairly, leaving Bal-ettan with less land than his former tenant. Some of this could be undone, and Charlis would help, but we would not be able to get back all the land that had been confiscated. Charlis explained all this carefully, patiently, speaking principally to Bal-ettan rather than to me. 'Some changes are good, some are bad,' he concluded, 'but very few changes can be reversed.'

'Shakespeare or Rudyard Kipling?' I asked, only half in jest, remembering his little notebook.

'Neither,' he replied quite seriously. 'Charlis Thekkote. But you can quote me if you like.'

Charlis was as good as his word. He helped Bal-ettan file the necessary papers to reclaim some of his land, and made sure the files were not lost in the bureaucratic maze. And the week after our visit, knowing I would not be staying in Vanganassery long, Charlis came to the village.

I will never forget the sight of Charlis seated at our dining table with the entire family bustling attentively around him: Rani-valiamma, on leave from the school where she was now vice-principal, serving him her soft, crisp-edged dosas on Grandmother's best stainless-steel thali; Kunjunni-mama, honking gregariously, pouring him more tea; and half the neighbours, standing at a respectful distance, gawking at the dignitary.

But the image that will linger longest in my memory is from even before that, from the moment of Charlis's arrival at the village. His official car cannot drive the last half-mile to our house, on the narrow paths across the paddy fields, so Charlis steps down, in his off-white safari suit and open-toed sandals, and walks to our front door, through the dust. We greet him there and begin to usher him into the house, but Bal-ettan stops us outside. For a minute, all the old fears come flooding back into my mind and Charlis's, but it is only for a minute, because Bal-ettan is shouting out to the servant, 'Can't you see the Collector-saare is waiting? Hurry up!'

I catch Charlis's eye; he smiles. The servant pulls a bucketful of water out of the well to wash Charlis's feet.

AFTER THE HANGING

O. V. VIJAYAN

Translated from the Malayalam by the author

As Vellayiappan set out on his journey, the sound of ritual mourning rose from his hut, and from Ammini's hut, and beyond those huts, the village listened in grief. Vellayiappan was going to Cannanore. Had they the money, each one of them would have accompanied him on the journey, it was as though he was journeying for the village. Vellayiappan now passed the last of the huts and took the long ridge across the paddies. The crying receded behind him. From the ridge he stepped on pasture land across which the footpath meandered.

Gods, my lords, Vellayiappan cried within himself.

The black palms rose on either side and the wind clattered in their fronds. The wind, ever so familiar, was strange this day—the gods of his clan and departed elders were talking to him through the wind-blown fronds. Slung over his shoulder was a bundle of cooked rice, its wetness seeped through the threadbare cloth onto his arm. His wife had bent long over the rice, kneading it for the journey, and as she had cried the while, her tears must have soaked into the sour curd. Vellayiappan walked on. The railway station was four miles away. Further down the path he saw Kuttihassan walking towards him. Kuttihassan stepped aside from the path, in tender reverence.

'Vellayi,' said Kuttihassan.

'Kuttihassan,' replied Vellayiappan.

That was all, just two words, two names, yet it was like a long conversation in which there was lament and consolation. *O Kuttihassan*, said the unspoken words, *I have a debt to pay you, fifteen silvers.*

Let that not burden you, O Vellayi, on this journey.
Kuttihassan, I may never be able to pay you, never after this.
We consign our unredeemed debts to God's keeping. Let His will be done.
I burn within myself, my life is being prised away.
May the Prophet guard you on this journey, may the gods bless your gods and mine.

The dithyramb of the gods was now a torrent in the palms. Vellayiappan passed Kuttihassan and walked on. Four miles to go to the train station. Again, an encounter on the way. Neeli, the laundress, with her bundles of washing. She too stepped aside reverentially.

'Vellayiappan,' she said.

'Neeli,' said Vellayiappan.

Just these two words, and yet between them the abundant colloquy. Vellayiappan walked on. The footpath joined the mud road, and Vellayiappan looked for the milestone and continued on his way. Presently, he came to where the rough-hewn track descended into the river. Across the river, beyond a rise and a stretch of sere grass, was the railway. Vellayiappan stepped onto the sands, then into the knee-deep water. Schools of little fish, gleaming silver, rubbed against his calves and swam on. As he reached the middle of the river Vellayiappan was overwhelmed by the expanse of water, it reminded him of sad and loving rituals, of the bathing of his father's dead body and how he taught his own son to swim in the river; all this he remembered and, pausing on the riverbank, wept in memory.

He reached the railway station and made his way to the ticket counter and with great care undid the knot in the corner of his unsewn cloth to take out the money for the fare.

'Cannanore,' Vellayiappan said. The clerk behind the counter pulled out a ticket, franked it, and tossed it towards him. *One stage in my journey is over,* thought Vellayiappan. He secured the ticket in the corner of his unsewn cloth and, crossing over to the platform, sat on a bench, waiting patiently for his train. He watched the sun sink and the palms darken far away, and the birds flit homewards. Vellayiappan remembered walking with his son to the fields at sundown, he remembered how his son had looked up at the birds in wonder. Then he remembered himself as a child, holding onto his father's little finger, and walking down the same fields. Two images, but between them as between two reticent words, an abundance of many things. Soon another aged traveller came over and sat beside him on the bench.

'Going to Coimbatore, are you?' the stranger asked.

'Cannanore,' Vellayiappan said.

'The Cannanore train is at ten in the night.'

'Is that so?'

'What work do you do in Cannanore?'

'Nothing much.'

'Just travelling, are you?'

The stranger's converse, inane and rasping, tensed around Vellayiappan like a hangman's noose. Once you left the village and walked over the long ridge, it was a world full of strangers, and their disinterested words were like a multitude of nooses. The train to Coimbatore came, and the old stranger rose and left. Vellayiappan was again alone on the bench. He had no desire to untie the bundle of rice, instead he kept a hand on the threadbare wrap, he felt its moisture. He sat thus and slept. And dreamt. In his dream he called out, 'Kandunni, my son!'

Vellayiappan was woken up from his sleep by the din and clatter of the train to Cannanore. He felt for the ticket tied into the corner of his cloth and was reassured. He looked for an open door, he tried to board the compartment nearest to him.

'This is first class, O elder.'

'Is that so?'

He peered into the next compartment.

'This is reserved.'

'Is that so?'

'Try further down, O elder.'

The voice of strangers.

Vellayiappan got into a compartment where there was no sitting space left. He could barely stand. *I shall stand, I don't need to sleep, this night my son sits awake.* The rhythm of the train changed with the changing layers of the earth, the fleeting trackside lamps, sand banks, trees. Long ago he had travelled in a train, but that was in the day. This was a night train. It sped through the tunnel of darkness, whose arching walls were painted with dim murals. The day had not broken when he reached Cannanore. The bundle of kneaded rice still hung from his shoulder, oozing its wetness. He passed through the gate into the station yard, the dark now livened with the first touch of dawn. The horse-cart men clumsily parked together did not accost him.

Vellayiappan asked them, 'Which is the way to the jail?' Someone laughed. *Here is an old man asking the way to the jail at daybreak.* Someone laughed again, *O elder, all you have to do is to steal, they will take you there.* The converse of strangers tightened around his neck. Vellayiappan felt suffocated.

Then someone showed him the way and Vellayiappan began to walk. The sky lightened to the orchestration of crows cawing.

At the gate of the jail a guard stopped him, 'What brings you here this early?'

Vellayiappan shrank back like a child, nervous. Then slowly he undid the corner of his cloth and took out a crumpled and yellowing piece of paper.

'What is that?' the guard enquired.

Vellayiappan handed him the paper; the guard glanced through it without reading.

Vellayiappan said, 'My child is here.'

'Who told you to come so early?' the guard asked, his voice irritable and harsh. 'Wait till the office is open.'

Then his eyes fell on the paper again, and became riveted to its contents. His face softened in sudden compassion.

'Tomorrow, is it?' the guard asked, almost consoling.

'I don't know. It is all written down there.'

The guard read and re-read the order. 'Yes,' he said, 'It's tomorrow morning at five.'

Vellayiappan nodded in acknowledgement, and slumped on a bench at the entrance of the jail. There he waited for the dark sanctum to open.

'O elder, may I offer you a cup of tea?' the guard asked solicitously.

'No.'

My son has not slept this night, and not having slept, would not have woken. Neither asleep nor awake, how can he break his fast this morning? Vellayiappan's hand rested on the bundle of rice. *My son, this rice was kneaded by your mother for me. I saved it during all the hours of my journey, and brought it here. Now this is all I have to bequeath to you.* The rice inside the threadbare wrap, food of the traveller, turned stale. Outside, the day brightened. The day grew hot.

The offices opened, and staid men took their places behind the tables. In the prison yard there was the grind of a parade. The prison came alive. The officers got to work, bending over yellowing papers in tedious scrutiny. From behind the tables, and where the column of the guards waited in formation, came rasping orders, words of command. Nooses without contempt or vengeance, gently strangulating the traveller. The day grew hotter.

Someone told him, *sit down and wait.* Vellayiappan sat down; he waited. After a wait, the length of which he could not reckon, a guard led him into the corridors of the prison. The corridors were cool with the damp of the prison. *We're here, O elder.*

Behind the bars of a locked cell stood Kandunni. He looked at his father like a stranger, through the awesome filter of a mind that could no longer receive nor give consolation. The guard opened the door and let Vellayiappan into the cell. Father and son stood facing each other, petrified. Then Vellayiappan leaned forward to take his son in an embrace. From Kandunni came a cry that pierced beyond hearing and when it died down, Vellayiappan said, 'My son!'

'Father!' said Kandunni.

Just these words, but in them father and son communed in the fullness of sorrow.

Son, what did you do?

I have no memory, father.

Son, did you kill?

It does not matter, my son, there is nothing to remember any more.

Will the guards remember? I have no memory.

No, my son.

Father, will you remember my pain?

Then again the cry that pierced beyond hearing issued from Kandunni, *Father, don't let them hang me!*

'Come out, O elder,' the guard said, 'time's up.'

Vellayiappan came away and the door clanged shut.

One last look back, and Vellayiappan saw his son like a stranger met during a journey. Kandunni was peering through the bars as a traveller might through the window of a hurtling train.

Vellayiappan wandered idly around the jail. The sun rose to its zenith, then began the climb down. *Will my son sleep this night?* The night came, and moved to dawn again. Within the walls Kandunni still lived.

Vellayiappan heard the sound of bugles at dawn, little knowing that this was death's ceremonial. But the guard had told him that it was at five in the morning and though he wore no watch, Vellayiappan knew the time with the peasant's unerring instinct.

∞

Vellayiappan received the body of his son from the guards like a midwife a baby.
O elder, what plans do you have for the funeral?
I have no plans.
Don't you want the body?
Masters, I have no money.
Vellayiappan walked along with the scavengers who pushed the trolley carrying the body. Outside the town, over the deserted marshes, the vultures wheeled patiently. Before the scavengers filled the pit Vellayiappan saw his son's face just once more. He pressed his palm on the cold forehead in blessing.

After the last shovelful of earth had levelled the pit, Vellayiappan wandered in the gathering heat and eventually came to the seashore. He had never seen the ocean before. Then he became aware of something cold and wet in his hands, the rice his wife had kneaded for his journey. Vellayiappan undid the bundle. He scattered the rice on the sand, in sacrifice and requiescat. From the crystal reaches of the sunlight, crows descended on the rice, like incarnate souls of the dead come to receive the offering.

GOBYAER*

SADAF WANI

While I exist as a spirit in this cold grey valley, sometimes I get tired of not being seen and perceived, not being heard, and not being able to leave my footprints on the snow as I pass by mountains, towns, and villages. However, in this valley marred by grief, complaining about these little inconveniences seems a bit absurd and, at times, quite selfish. Selfish even for someone like me, whose entire sense of self is unresolved and perpetually in doubt. This valley that I have grown to call my home, I don't call it by its name, for it makes me uneasy. Every time I hear its name being said out loud, I fear something bad might happen. The thought of leaving this place and its disquiet crosses my mind often. In the past, I have acted upon this impulse, but every time I left, I found myself making the arduous journey back.

I leave this valley, which is my home, because I get tired of being invisible here. Sometimes, I long to participate in the events that are taking place in the streets, rivers, and markets. However, people pass through me as I reach out for them. I am ridiculed by other spirits for these frivolous desires. They mock my longing for home by saying that spirits do not have homes. I disagree. I say home is only a place, and a place is its people. So, doesn't that make these people my people, and this valley my home?

I speak about these people in the valley as 'my people' like I know them or like they know me. I speak of them as if I like them and as if they like me. In fact, I do not know them, and they do not know me. We are mutually oblivious to each other's existence for the most part. However, something cuts through this relationship of oblivion and ties us to each

---

*Heaviness or weight in Kashmiri. In the everyday vernacular, gobyaer is also used to refer to the state of being possessed by djinns or other supernatural forces.

other. There is a gobyaer on our being. It is amusing that a phenomenon as physical as weight and heaviness connects me, who is supposed to have transcended the physical realm, to these people and this place.

At first, I did not understand how a word representing something so physical could describe what I was feeling. So, I started paying attention to how humans across the valley were using this word. Once, I was passing through a cluster of villages by a small hill near the south of Jhelum. There, I saw that a crowd had gathered around a young boy who had fainted, just as he had reached his village, after spending a long day in the deep forest. The boy was speaking gibberish and appeared to have a concussion. It was intriguing, for I knew at first sight that it was the work of my distant cousins. The older djinns are known to take offence at humans disturbing the quiet of the deep forest. They get enraged when humans shamelessly relieve themselves under the old chinar trees that they've made their home. To teach them a lesson, and dissuade the rest of the villagers from venturing into the forest, they possess the bodies of people who've invoked their wrath. Having seen that it was just another young boy possessed by the djinns, I lost interest and started moving away from the crowd where the imam was inspecting the boy. However, as I started moving away, the imam suddenly got up, walking quickly in my direction. He stopped right before he could pass through me. It's the closest I've come to being perceived. I swear I thought he was talking to me when he said, 'Ye chu gobyaer' (It's the heaviness).

After this incident, I started getting drawn to this word, to every conversation where it was mentioned. One night I was passing by an old street towards the south of the valley, and I saw a grim-looking young man smoking cigarettes, standing outside the house of his lover from long ago. The sound of the tumbaknari, the Kashmiri drum, from the house filled up the street, where he stood for a while. There was nothing he could do and nothing he wanted to do to stop the event, but the loss he experienced throughout that night of anticipation he also called gobyaer. Similarly, towards the east of the valley, I was once roaming through an apple orchard enjoying the blossoms when I noticed an older woman in the middle of the orchard. She looked up at the May sky, overcast with dark clouds, and knew they were the clouds of misfortune and hailstones. She looked around her apple trees, knowing very well that, in a few hours, the blossoms and the promise of a good harvest would be gone. The heavy footsteps she took towards her home, as she waited for the rains to intensify, she called gobyaer, too.

However, this gobyaer prompted by personal grievances is not what connects me to these people. Since I don't have loved ones who I yearn for, or land that I cultivate, or a future to prepare for, I cannot relate to these emotions. There is an overarching feeling of impending loss and terror that goes far beyond the everyday affairs of my people, something that everyone here is always waiting for. Sometimes it is realized sooner than at other times, but each cycle of loss confirms that our fears are not unfounded. The fear grows in hearts, as does the gobyaer. I cannot tell exactly what this gobyaer does to humans, for they don't seem to hear me, so I cannot ask them anything. I am only telling you what I have overheard in open markets and closed rooms.

Having heard about it from so many people over decades, I have started seeing it as well, even though I don't experience it like humans do. I have started seeing that gobyaer has a personhood as abstract as mine. I say this because I have seen how gobyaer surrounds and seeps into people and what it does to them. When I look at my people, I see that this strange presence has engulfed their lives, the gobyaer has attached itself to their skin, sedimented in their bones, and it feeds off the hope in their hearts. It lives in their homes now, sits in their hamams, and shares their rice with them. And when they are watching TV late at night, it occupies the cosiest spot in the room, and my people pretend not to see it.

The old people in the valley seem to have found a dedicated corner in their lives for this gobyaer. They put it in the deepest pocket of their baend, which they always wear under their pherans, carrying it around with them wherever they go. The younger ones, however, are more ambitious. 'Why should we carry this burden with us all our lives? Why should we give in like you cowards did?' they ask the old ones, who do not smile, and only smoke their jijeers. Spurred on by their ambitions, some young ones travel to far-off lands, hoping they could leave this gobyaer behind. Some go to the tallest mountains, some to distant deserts, and others towards seas because it was rumoured that seawater could melt it.

One time when I ran away from the valley to travel the world and find a new home, I was surprised at how easily I could spot my people wherever I went. I had thought everybody carried this gobyaer with them until I met people who are not my people. It was then that I realized that it is something that only people of the valley have, and I also found the answer to what differentiated my people from the crowds in cities, riversides, and deserts. Naturally, I followed some of my people when I saw them outside the valley. I found some of them running through icy alleyways. Some were plodding through desert towns, and others were hiding in muddy lanes by the sea. I found a few walking briskly on the wide roads and dingy streets of big cities visiting pirs, faqirs, and shamans seeking foreign remedies for their very indigenous disease. Some of them kept running for years and years, and when they thought enough time had passed, they came back home. However, to their horror, they found this gobyaer waiting on their dastarkhwan to share their razma dal with them.

Some people who have got tired of running have now realized that the gobyaer always finds a way home. So, they have started building houses with a spare room. They make it big and cosy so that they can scream and wail in it. Men who have only one room and not enough razma dal to share cannot find a quiet place to sit with their fears. The children are always crying, and the creditors are always knocking on their doors. They deal with the gobyaer by bringing it up all the time and to everyone they can find. In the fields, in the bus, at the shop, on their verandas. They repeat the same stories every day with minor additions and deletions, of how they first encountered this feeling, how they tried to run away from it, and how there is no place like home, so they come back. 'Gari wandihai gari saasah, bari nyerihai ni zanh' (There is no place like home), they keep repeating all day. I often see women peeling vegetables on the verandas of their houses sigh in exasperation and put their hands on both their ears as they run inside. They seem to be sick of hearing the same stories every day. Women have their versions of how they encountered gobyaer and how they live with it. But the men never stop talking, and so the women always leave the room in frustration.

One of the reasons I keep coming back to this valley from faraway places is my belief that the cure of this indigenous disease cannot be found outside the valley. So, I pass through the valley looking for comfort, if not the ultimate answer. There is a small, lonesome house in an apricot orchard in the valley's northern end, where an old woman puts her granddaughter and daughter to sleep every night. In this house, there are no men, so women talk out loud without interruptions. But that's not the only reason I come back here. Every night, before putting them to sleep, the grandmother whispers a six-letter word into their ears as they fall asleep. A six-letter charm that gets you in trouble if you say it out loud in the valley, but the only known charm that puts the gobyaer to rest, at least for some time. The old woman tells them stories of the day when the charm will manifest itself, cutting through the grey cloudy sky, falling softly on the valley like morning sunlight on all its living and non-living things. It will slowly melt away what occupies the heart and weighs it down. It is said that after that day the spare rooms in the houses will be filled with the aroma of sun-dried tomatoes, the young ones will not need to run off to deserts, mountains, seas, and cities, and men will finally let the women narrate their own stories.

After the lights in the entire valley are dimmed, the last batch of soldiers and rebels have gone off to sleep, and the placards and flags have been locked in for the night, I come back to hear the same story night after night. I feel comforted watching the little girl fall asleep to this reassurance. Last night, as she fell asleep, her little fist unclenched at some point to reveal the charm she had just learned to write: Azaadi.

BHASKARA PATTELAR AND MY LIFE
PAUL ZACHARIA

Translated from the Malayalam by Gita Krishnankutty

I first saw Bhaskara Pattelar one evening in Udina Bazaar. Squatting on the edge of a shop veranda, I was brooding upon my sorrows. The sound my frayed mundu made as it gave way little by little kept pace with my thoughts. Suddenly, I heard someone call out to me.

'Hey!'

I looked up to see who it was.

The man who had hailed me sat on a chair in the veranda of a shop across the road. He must have been about thirty-five years old. He was as tall as he was large. He wore a silk jubba and was fair-skinned. His eyes and hair had a coppery tint. He had a big moustache which curved downwards and his lips were stained red with betel juice. His big body barely fitted into the chair. Half a dozen people stood around him respectfully.

'Come here, you whore's son!' Pattelar called out in Kannada. I sprang up, my palms joined together. Who could this be? What did such a great man want of me?

As I jumped down from the veranda, my mundu tore along its entire length. With one hand, I held the torn ends of the garment together behind me, covered my mouth respectfully with the other, and crossed the road.

The giant got up from the chair and came to the edge of the veranda.

'What is that in your hand, rascal?'

'Nothing, master,' I said.

'Why then, dog, are you holding one hand behind you? Do you want to shit? Don't you know how to show respect to those who deserve respect? Come closer, you rascal.'

I quickly took away the hand that held the mundu together, joined my palms, bowed deeply, and moved closer. My torn mundu fell apart like the halves of a stage curtain. Laughing loudly, Pattelar gave me a kick. I fell backwards, naked and staring skywards. Pattelar spat betel juice at me. 'Thoo!'

I rolled on my stomach, pressed my face into the sand, joined my palms together, and begged. 'Show me mercy, yejamanare!'

It was then that I saw the gun leaning against Pattelar's chair. It was as large and terrifying as Pattelar himself. The people around him said something in Malayalam and laughed. What! They were Malayalis!

'Get up, dog,' said Pattelar.

I got up and tied one of the pieces of the mundu around my waist.

'Where are you from, rascal?'

'From Kochi, master.'

He switched to Malayalam. 'Where do you live?'

'In Ichilampadi, master.'

'How many acres have you encroached upon?'

'Only five, master!'

'Are you married?'

'Yes, master.'

'How old is your wife?'

'Twenty-one, master.'

'Good,' said Pattelar. 'Is she pretty?'

I said nothing.

'Speak, son of a dog, is she a beauty?'

'No,' I managed to say.

'Ha, ha, ha,' laughed Pattelar. His men laughed with him. I could hear people in the other shops laugh as well.

'You liar!' Pattelar took his gun and aimed it at me in jest.

He said, 'I'll have a look and see if she's pretty, and give her a certificate.' The betel-juice-stained teeth smiled through the stubble on his pink face.

'Run!' he said.

I began to run in the direction of Ichilampadi.

'Not that way! This way.' Pattelar pointed with his gun in the opposite direction. I gathered my mundu with one hand and ran along the road in the direction he was pointing. The sun was setting. I looked back once.

'Don't look back, rascal!' Behind me, I heard the loud report of the gun.

I sobbed aloud and kept running towards a bend in the road some distance away. When I had rounded it, I stopped and leaned against a tree, gasping. Then I clambered down the slope to the riverbank and lay on a big, flat rock. I saw a star fall from the sky. When I got my breath back, I rolled down into the water, shivering, and washed away the betel-flecked spittle from my body. I wrung out my torn mundu and wiped myself dry with it. Then I crossed the river and ran to Ichilampadi. Even as I neared my hut, I heard Omana sobbing. On the other side of the hut, torch beams went down to the river and crossed it.

∞

Pattelar sent for me the next day. He bought me a mundu and Omana a sari from the jauli shop. He said to me, 'From today you can work in the toddy shop as a server—I've spoken to Varkey chettan. Omana is pretty. You lied to me. Will you tell lies again?'

'No, yejamanare,' I said.

Everyone knew that it was the Malayali hangers-on who had corrupted Pattelar. He had been just another proud janmi and a man of pleasure. When he sat on the shop veranda, the hangers-on would sometimes point to a woman and say, 'Yejamanare, look at that one, she's so beautiful! Why don't we have a word with her?'

Pattelar would say in Kannada, 'Why bother? It's not worth it.'

They would then say, 'Maja madana, let's have fun, Pattelare! We are with you!'

'All right.' Pattelar would get up and go after the woman.

If someone walked through the bazaar unmindful of Pattelar and his group, they would whisper. 'Pattelar, look at him, he's behaving as if you're not here. What cheek! Should we give him one?'

Pattelar would gulp down his toddy and say, 'No. Let's not have trouble. Galatta beda.'

'We are with you! Give him one, Pattelare. Teach him to show respect.'

'All right!' Pattelar would then get up.

In time, Pattelar came to believe in all this and to go along with it. When I think of it, I feel sad for him. What a pity that such a good man should have come to this! Whose sins was he paying the price for, by sinning over and over again? And what bond from a previous birth was it that brought me to him all the way from the land of my birth?

And so I became Pattelar's servant. As soon as he took his seat on the shop veranda, I would bring him a pot of toddy and then wait in the yard, bowing respectfully, hands folded across my chest. Whenever he went woman-hunting, he would ask me to go with him. In a narrow, deserted gully somewhere, he would cover some whimpering Gowda girl's mouth with one hand and grip her hands with the other, before pushing her down on the dry leaves. Once in a while, he would ask me, 'Want her, rascal?'

'No, yejamanare,' I would say.

Without letting go of the girl, Pattelar would aim a friendly kick in my direction.

'Go away, scoundrel; go where I can't see you.'

I would move away and while waiting for Pattelar to finish, look up at the sky and at the mountains in the distance. If someone came by, I would signal to them, 'Pattelar is here!' At once they would take another path. Indeed, people understood what was going on as soon as they saw me. Whenever I heard a girl cry out, I would think of Omana, of that first day. Omana had stopped crying as time went by. That was a great relief to me. Omana is such a simple soul. So am I. How good it is not to have to cry.

One day, at dusk, Pattelar was seated in his armchair on the shop veranda in Udina Bazaar, drinking toddy tapped that evening. I stood in the yard and filled his glass from the pot. Every now and then I ran across the street to the tea shop and brought him vadas and bolis. The usual group stood around Pattelar, some on the veranda and some down in the yard. I brought glasses for them too from the toddy shop and poured them drinks.

It was then that the last bus from Dharmasthala to Hassan groaned and slid to a stop in the bazaar. One or two people got off. Spreading a reddish glow behind it, the bus disappeared into the darkness to make its way up the Shiradi hills past Sakaleshpuram, determined to reach Hassan somehow before midnight. One of the passengers who had alighted crossed the road and approached us. I recognized him at once. He was a dhani—a rich merchant from Arshanamukki. He had areca nut groves and, with his younger brother, owned a lorry. He looked very worried. I ran up to him, joined my palms together respectfully, and said, 'Ayyo, dhani! Why have you come by bus today and why are you looking so worried?'

He said, 'My brother went to Yenijira early this morning with the lorry and is not back yet. He should have returned at noon. Have any of you seen him? Did you hear of an accident anywhere?'

Suddenly, Pattelar pointed with his foot at the newcomer from his armchair and asked me, 'Who is this, rascal? Why are you grovelling? Is he your father, dog?'

I stood between them on the roadside, in the huge shadows cast by the Petromax lamp, beginning to perspire and aware that my joined palms were growing limp with fear. I said, 'Yejamanare, this is Yousappicha from Arshanamukki. He's a dhani. His younger brother is missing.'

Pattelar flung the toddy from the glass in his hand on Yousappicha's face.

He said, 'Do we keep your brother here? Look at the bloody dhani!'

The shops were closing for the day and everyone was going home. Only a few people lingered in the tea shop and the toddy shop. They were listening silently. No one came out.

Pattelar jumped down into the yard, swaying a little. My voice trembled as I begged him to spare Yousappicha. 'Please forgive me, yejamanare! Yousappicha is one of our own.'

Pattelar gave me a terrible blow across my right cheek and ear. I slumped to the ground; my ears filled with the noise of a world splitting apart. When I raised my head, Pattelar had Yousappicha on the ground and was kicking him. He kicked him in the head, stomach, and spine.

'This dog of a dhani comes to look for his brother here! So late in the evening!' shouted Pattelar. I was too scared to get up from where I cowered.

My god, I thought, Pattelar is beating Yousappicha to a pulp. A man he is seeing for the first time! Why hit a man who had come to look for his brother?

Yousappicha lay still on the roadside, in the shadows of Udina Bazaar, like a muddy bundle of rags. Not moving and hardly daring to breathe, I stared at the sprawled figure.

Pattelar climbed back on to the veranda, sat down on his chair and summoned me. My head buzzed violently as I jumped up and rushed to him.

In the dark I stumbled over one of Yousappicha's outstretched legs and fell. He knew nothing of all this. I scrambled up again, ran and poured toddy for Pattelar from the pot. Pattelar said, 'A dhani, is he? And he comes at dusk, like a bad omen. You be careful, too! Next time you invite people like this, you'll get the same treatment.'

'Ayyo, yejamanare.' I wailed, 'I didn't invite Yousappicha. His younger brother—'

'Shut your mouth, dog!' shouted Pattelar.

I shut my mouth.

∞

It was late when Pattelar finally got up to go home. He said to us, 'Put him in the back of the jeep.'

We carried Yousappicha and put him in the jeep. It was I who held his hands. The pulse is beating, I said to myself.

Pattelar's wife, Sarojakka, did not like noisy gatherings in the house at night. So Pattelar usually went to play cards in the watchman's hut in the yard where areca nuts are dried. Tonight, there were six or seven people with him. Yousappicha was dumped in a corner. Blood oozed from his mouth in a long thread and vanished into the dusty floor. I sat near him and watched the card game, dozing off occasionally. Now and then, when I woke up and saw the way Yousappicha lay, I felt sorry. Once, I almost whispered, 'Yejamanare, may I give Yousappicha a drop of water?' But my voice stayed trapped in my throat. Sometime near dawn, Yousappicha groaned once. Then I fell asleep. When I woke up, it was daylight and only Yousappicha and I were in the hut. He was cold and dead. 'Ayyo, my Yousappicha, that you had to die this way,' I said sadly, looking at his corpse. Suddenly, I thought of Sarojakka. Ayyo, Yousappicha must be moved before she finds out.

Shivering in the morning cold, I ran, slipping and sliding on the areca nuts, to the window of Pattelar's room. I knocked on it softly.

It was Sarojakka who opened the window.

'What is it?' she asked.

'Nothing, nothing, yejamanathi,' I stammered.

Then Pattelar got up, came to the window and asked, 'What is it?'

I said, 'Nothing, master.'

Pattelar looked searchingly at me and said, 'I see. Go back now; I'll come.'

I waited near Yousappicha, trembling in the cold. Pattelar came, wearing a shawl, his ears covered with a monkey cap, and said, 'Get two or three people, tie him up in a sack and bury him in Arabi Majal before Sarojakka comes out to milk the cow. I'll take care of the police.'

I felt very relieved.

One day, Pattelar said to me. 'Listen, I'm going to kill Sarojakka. I need you to help me.'

I shook with fear. Sarojakka was such a good person. She gave me something to eat or drink every day. She was aware of Pattelar's wayward ways but treated him with affection. She gave him good advice and never quarrelled with him.

I felt very sad. I said. 'Why do you want to do that, yejamanare? She is such a good akka. Please don't....'

Pattelar said, 'I shall make it look like an accident. You will be the witness. You will call her out to the veranda. I will sit there pretending to load my gun. It will look as if the gun went off by mistake. She must not know that I shot her. I do not want her to die with that sorrow. There's no need for you to feel sad either. Just think of it as an accident, that's all. You'll have to give proper evidence. Her brothers are nasty fellows.'

I thought sadly: Pattelar wants to kill Sarojakka to get hold of her share of the property.

'Yejamanare,' I said, 'we don't need Sarojakka's share.'

He gave me a long look.

That afternoon, Pattelar sat on his chair on the veranda, put the gun on his lap, opened the bag of gunpowder and pretended to load his gun. I squatted on the edge of the veranda some distance away. The gun turned slowly in my direction. I told myself, Pattelar is just loading his gun, that's all he's doing. There's nothing to worry about.

When Pattelar signalled with his eyes, I looked towards the kitchen and called, 'Sarojakka!'

She answered.

I said, 'Please give me something to drink.'

'Shall I give you some kanji?' she asked.

'All right.' I said. Poor Sarojakka, I thought to myself. She will bring me kanji to satisfy a hunger I do not feel. And she will die.

With sudden fear, I called out again, 'Sarojakka, please don't add salt!' I did not look at Pattelar.

Sarojakka came out. She had the bowl of kanji in one hand and a glass of buttermilk in the other. She gave Pattelar the buttermilk and said. 'Drink this. You did not eat anything this morning.'

Pattelar flinched, but took the glass from her.

Sarojakka walked towards me with the bowl of kanji. My eyes were on Pattelar. He tried hurriedly to put down the glass of buttermilk in one hand.

At the same time, he tried to point the gun with the other at Sarojakka. I saw him pull the trigger. The glass fell down and broke. At the same moment, I heard the shot…. I was staring at Sarojakka, wanting to cry for her, when suddenly I felt a searing pain in my stomach, as if someone had stabbed me with a red-hot stick. It felt like a fire beginning to blaze inside me. I could not bear the pain and jumped up. Blood spurted from my stomach! Ayyo! Is it I who've been shot! Pattelar was staring at me wide-eyed. Sarojakka screamed.

I shouted, 'Yejamanare, save me. It's I who have been shot!'

'Shut your mouth, scoundrel,' shouted Pattelar, 'or I'll finish you off right now!'

Sarojakka went out into the courtyard and called for help. People came running. I fainted then. When I regained consciousness, I was lying on the floor of the grain shed, with a cloth tied around my stomach.

I heard Pattelar say to the others. 'Don't waste time. He's finished. Carry him to Arabi Majal. I'll bring my gun. We can bury him there.'

I whimpered, 'Yejamanare, Omana will have no one. Don't kill me, please.'

Pattelar looked at me in astonishment. While he watched me uncertainly, Sarojakka suddenly came in and said, 'What are you saying? I'll not allow it. Take him to the hospital!'

∽

I lay unconscious in the hospital for a week. I had many dreams about Sarojakka and Omana. It was while I dreamt that I was lying with my head on Sarojakka's lap that I woke up. My head swam in a wave of happiness. The warmth and softness of Sarojakka's lap clung to me for a long time. I put my hand on my wounded stomach, feeling very happy that Sarojakka was alive.

After I was discharged from the hospital, I said to Omana, 'Do you know, I had a dream that I lay with my head on Sarojakka's lap?' Omana did not believe me.

∽

Pattelar came to my house one night, woke me up and said, 'Come. We're going to catch the fish in the temple ghat at Arshanamukki.'

'Ayyo! My yejamanare!' I said, trembling with fear.

'Why are you scared?' asked Pattelar. 'I am here.' He held up a cloth bag which contained dynamite sticks, and shook it. 'You and I will do it. No one else has the courage. Cowardly dogs!'

I looked out fearfully. Moonlight filtered faintly through the Makara mist. This was the time the yakshi of the Arshanamukki temple came out to stroll around. The fish that lived in the ghat belonged to the yakshi. The Udina River flowed wide in front of the temple, looking like a lake. Even in summer, the current was strong enough to make your legs totter. In the rainy season the roaring floodwaters resembled a stormy sea. But the five thousand fish in the bathing ghat by the temple always lay there undisturbed. They were huge, sleek, gleaming fish, with knowing eyes. They did not fear men, but allowed no one to touch them. They splashed and writhed in the water, clustered together as if they were in a fish basket. If you threw them puffed rice, you could not see the water for the thrashing of the giant fish as they fought to get to the food. When they jumped and fell back, the sound was like coconuts falling.

I have often felt frightened as I watched them. What if I were to fall among them? Wouldn't they eat me up in a flash? I would edge backwards a couple of steps before throwing them more puffed rice. At other times, my mouth would water as I looked at the fish. If Omana could get just one of them, it would last her a whole week—to make curry, deep-fry, make roast chutney and also pickle some. Just one fish would be enough. But they belonged to the yakshi. The yakshi caught and ate anyone who caught and ate her fish. She would tear him open, bring her fish back to life from where it lay in his greedy intestines, give it a loving kiss on its pouting lips and, her laughter filling the night like the tinkle of crystal balls, shoot it back into the river like a silver arrow flashing through the darkness. Then, smacking her lips, she would bend down to savour slowly the one who had eaten her fish.

'Ayyo, yejamanare,' I wailed. 'Ayyo! Ayyo!'

Pattelar took the headlamp out of his shoulder bag and strapped it on to his forehead. He gave me the cloth bag of dynamite sticks and said, 'Carry it carefully.' Then he picked up his gun. As we went down into the courtyard, Pattelar said, 'Bring two or three baskets with you.'

All along the way, in the meadows and valleys filled with moonlight, I sensed a restless wariness. I heard the tinkling of anklets. The yakshi was pursuing us to protect her fish. Carefully placing my feet in Pattelar's footprints, and trembling with fear, I walked under the eye of the moon, to the river by the Arshanamukki temple.

Once, I mustered enough courage to say, 'Yejamanare, the yakshi....' Pattelar brandished the gun and said, without turning around, 'Fool, the yakshi is afraid of guns. Don't you know a gun is made of iron? She's afraid of you as well. You're from another religion and because of that she doesn't like your blood!'

In the darkness, Pattelar shook with laughter.

When we had gone quite a way, I whispered, 'Yejamanare, if anything happens to me...Omana....'

Pattelar laughed again. 'Don't I look after Omana even when you are here? If you're not here, you don't have to worry at all. Ha, ha, ha!'

We reached the river even as I was asking myself whether Omana would grieve if something happened to me. There was only the soft sound of the summer waters. And the moonlight. And the mist drifting over the water. And the stillness of the temple. Shivering with terror, I looked up at the sky, standing on the steps of the bathing ghat. The moon was only a faint glow in the foggy sky. Veils of mist and cloud floated in its shadowy light. In the waters of the river, all was quiet. Where were all the fish, I wondered. Were they asleep? Do fish sleep? Were we going to kill the fish when they were sleeping? Ayyo! That would be so sad. Ayyo, my fish, I said to myself, you doze and dream in still corners under the moving sheet of water. But now you will not be able to complete your dreams. The thunder of these dynamite sticks will, like a hammer, shatter your dreams and your hearts. Then I will jump into the water with my basket. I will stack your gleaming bodies in it till it is full. The moonlight will fill your unclosing eyes. The mist will kiss your gasping mouths. I will weave through the water like an otter, lift up your corpses and stack my basket high, over and over again. The shreds of your broken dreams will cling to me like your white scales. And then, while the yakshi is devouring me, you will fly out of these baskets with throbbing hearts and return to the river through the mist. I will drip from the yakshi's mouth as blood and marrow, dribble down her thighs, and become manure for the earth.

I said to Pattelar, 'Yejamanare, I am afraid.'

I looked once towards the temple, took a stick of dynamite, and held it out to Pattelar. He said, 'Shitting coward, throw it yourself!' He pressed the switch on the battery box tied to his waist and bent his head so that his headlamp shone directly into the water. I lit the stick of dynamite and threw it into the centre of the patch of light. It sank and disappeared. Both of us waited for the explosion that would resound from the envelope of water. One! Two! Three: I counted. I counted to fifty and said, 'The stick did not explode, yejamanare!'

'Throw the next one, rascal,' said Pattelar.

I lit the next stick and threw it. When I had counted to fifty, Pattelar said, 'The next one!' I counted to fifty again.

Only the light from the lamp on Pattelar's forehead floated on the water.

I took the next stick in my hand and looked at Pattelar. 'Yejamanare,' I stammered, 'you throw this one, yejamanare.'

Pattelar looked at me and muttered something. The beam from his forehead wove its way through the night. I was terrified. Pattelar was growling obscenities.

His face was distorted as he hurled dirty words at the yakshi. Then he grabbed the stick of dynamite from me and, spilling light from his headlamp over the steps, he ran up to the temple yard.

'Baddimagale! You whore's daughter!' he screamed, lit the stick of dynamite and threw it with all his might at the closed door of the temple. I covered my ears with both hands and crouched down. Look at yejamanare, he's wrecking the temple. The explosion comes now! I closed my eyes tight, dug my fingers into my ears, and sat there, frozen. But there was only silence everywhere.

When light filtered through my closed eyes, I opened them and looked up. Pattelar was bending down and peering at me. I thought, Pattelar is mad with rage and is going to kill me. Ayyo! My Omana, I shall not see you again. My god, here I come. Was Pattelar picking up his gun? I stared into the blinding light. Suddenly, he switched off the lamp. He stood there without moving for some time. When the ghost light of the headlamp had faded from my eyes, I stood up. I picked up the cloth bag in which I had brought the dynamite. I put the baskets on my head.

'Shall we go, yejamanare?' I asked.

Pattelar said nothing. He walked up to the temple door and picked up the unexploded stick of dynamite lying there. Then, with a grunt, he threw it far into the river, as if aiming at the other bank. I heard it fall with a plop somewhere in the middle of the river, beyond where the fish lived. As we were going out through the temple yard, a sound came from the river, 'Bhum!'

The sound of the exploding dynamite pursued us like something awful the river had uttered, making me feel as if a world had ended.

'Bhum!' the river had said.

As we walked back under the whirling stars of the midnight sky, I heard footsteps around us and bells tinkling from the shadows, and I shivered in fear. Pattelar moved silently, like a sleepwalker, with the gun on his shoulder.

Shadowy forms of bats circled in the sky above us. For a moment I thought they were flying fish.

People regularly brought Pattelar gifts so that he would not harass them. They would prod me and say, 'Pattelar might forget who brought this. You must remind him.' I used to put away the balls of jaggery, the dried and salted chunks of deer meat, the rough boards of rosewood, ripe jackfruit, fowl, and big packets of pickled fish wrapped in spathes of the areca nut palm.

In the evening, I would usually give Pattelar the details of who had brought what. Pattelar would clear his throat loudly, spit and say, 'The spineless scoundrels!' I would carry all the gifts on my head to Pattelar's house, taking care not to leave anything behind.

Sarojakka would say, 'Do people give these things out of love? They give them because they're afraid. I don't like to keep such things at home.'

'Ayyo!' I would exclaim, looking towards the front veranda, where Pattelar was seated. Sarojakka always secretly gave me a portion of all the gifts. And I would take them in a basket to Omana. 'See, Sarojakka gave me these!'

One day, Pattelar said to me, 'You rascal, the fish pickle I ate at your house with the toddy yesterday tasted exactly like the pickle that Kuttapparai brought to my house. How did this happen? Does Kuttapparai also have an account in your house? Tell me the truth!'

I said, 'Ayyo, yejamanare. I don't know.'

Pattelar burst out laughing. 'So, you need my help to finish the pickle your Sarojakka gives you with such love, do you?' He shook with laughter.

Early one morning, I was lying with Omana, hugging her close. She was still enveloped in the fragrance of Pattelar's perfume. I took a deep breath of the scent which I loved and pressed Omana to me with great pleasure. I said to myself, although she smells of Pattelar's perfume, she belongs only to me. Some day, I'll buy her this perfume. It was then that I heard a knock. I jumped up, startled, opened the door a little and peered out. There were four or five people standing in front of the house. I made out Kuttapparai, Ahmed—the panchayat president's younger brother—and a couple of Malayalis. I began to tremble uncontrollably. They had come to kill me. Perhaps they had killed Pattelar before they came here. I stood there, unable to move. When Omana peered over my shoulder, her breasts brushed my back. I thought, I will never feel her breasts rub against me again. Kuttapparai said from the courtyard, 'Come out. We have come to ask you something.'

I closed the door without replying, hugged Omana, and said, 'If these people kill me, Omana, you must commit suicide. I think Pattelar is already dead.' Then I opened the door and went out.

They grabbed hold of me by the shoulder, took me under the elanji tree in the compound, and said, 'Look, don't be scared! Pattelar has to be killed. What is the best way to do it?'

I stared at them. Kill my yejamanare! Ayyo, who would I have then to turn to?

They said, 'Listen, everyone is fed up with Pattelar. You know that no man or woman can walk safely in the village because of him. Pattelar is useful to you, we know. But you're a good fellow, and a harmless one. If you help us, we'll help you. We'll give you a hundred rupees. And the job of a peon in the panchayat office.'

Sunrise had touched the sky. I thought, if Pattelar dies, the village and the villagers will benefit. I'll have a good job as well. But Omana, won't she feel sad? Or would she be happy? I had never asked her this question. Suddenly, I was afraid. If Pattelar died, would Omana then belong to me? And only me?

I was both thrilled and frightened by this thought.

My mind in a whirl, I asked Ahmed, 'What sort of help do you want, muthalali?' My words tumbled into my ears as if somebody else had spoken them. Ahmed said, 'It's not easy to kill Pattelar, you know. His companions are always with him. All we want you to do is to get Pattelar to sit for a while on your veranda this evening. We will shoot him from a hiding place. It will happen right in front of his men, so no one will suspect you.'

I stared at them, and said, 'Don't let them shoot me or Omana, please.'

They laughed soundlessly. 'We don't shoot as badly as your Pattelar, you fool.'

At noon, scratching my head, I asked Pattelar, 'I wonder if you're going to Ichilampadi this evening, yejamanare?'

Pattelar said, 'How does it matter to you whether I go or not?'

I said, 'Omana is preparing a meal specially for yejamanar. Yejamanar must come.'

'What is she making?'

'Mushrooms fried with coconut, roasted deer meat, fried fish, and arrack. She's frying eggs as well, yejamanare.'

'All right,' said Pattelar.

When Pattelar arrived at my house with his men that evening, the lamp had been lit. The men squatted here and there in the courtyard. Pattelar told me, 'I don't feel like drinking arrack. Go and bring me two bottles of fresh toddy.'

I heard suppressed laughter from the courtyard. It doesn't matter, I whispered, you won't laugh after today. Although I'm scared, Omana will soon be mine alone.

I was anxious about the people hiding somewhere in the darkness with their guns. What if Pattelar ate and left before I returned with the toddy? Who would get him to sit on the veranda?

I looked helplessly into the darkness, then left my house and started running down the road to the toddy shop. I then ran back again, a bottle of toddy in each hand. As I set foot in the courtyard, Pattelar opened the door and came out on to the veranda. 'Ah, you've come,' he said. 'I've just finished eating.'

His men were dozing in the shadows of the courtyard. I did not have the courage to look farther. What were the assassins going to do now? Would they do something in haste? As I climbed on to the veranda, I shrank into myself. Where would they shoot from? My god, don't let them shoot Omana. I kept trying to think of a way to make Pattelar sit down. But he stood on the upper veranda, waiting to wash his hands. I knew that the thatch of the hut hung so low that the killers would not be able to see him from where they were hiding.

Omana came to the veranda with a lamp in her hand. I put down the toddy and said, 'I'll draw water for you to wash your hands, yejamanare.'

The well was next to the lower veranda. It was a deep well; they had had to dig right down to the netherworld to find water. Pattelar stepped down to the lower veranda and walked to the well. I lowered the bucket into the well, drew water and straightened up. As Pattelar bent and extended his hands to wash them, I heard the shot. I wept silently, and looked at Pattelar. Then I looked at Omana. She was running into the house, crying. Pattelar covered his right ear and cheek with one hand, and tried to jump to safety. The second shot came then, and dislodged earth and stones from the wall of my hut. I dropped the bucket and rope. Pattelar had fallen on the well's rim and was beginning to slip in. He was silently clawing at the earth, desperately trying to hold on. In a moment he would be gone. 'My yejamanare!' I shouted. I leaped forward, caught hold of both his hands, stretched myself out on the ground for support and pulled him from the mouth of the well. Pattelar lay on the wet earth and breathed through his open mouth like a fish that has been thrown on land. I saw Pattelar's men crashing through the shrubbery, flashing their torches. Shots rang out and there were shouts. I helped Pattelar get up, took him into my hut and made him sit down on a mat spread on the floor. There was a wound on his ear. His right cheek looked black and blue and he could not open his right eye properly. Omana leaned against the wall, weeping. I poured a glass of toddy from the bottle I had brought from the shop and said, 'Drink this, yejamanare.'

I stood looking at Pattelar and thought, why did I save this man? A small push with these hands of mine would have been enough. I stared at Omana. Was this really my Omana? Who was I? Who was this wounded man, sitting on my torn mat? In the shadows thrown by the flame of the kerosene lamp that was flaring in the breeze, it seemed to me that Pattelar and Omana were turning into shapeless, writhing forms. My head reeled. I fainted.

As I lay in a swoon, I remember seeing, like a picture in a calendar, Sarojakka and Omana flying somewhere through the clouds, looking like white cranes.

∞

A few days after the failed attempt to kill Pattelar, I was squatting on the veranda of the toddy shop on a rainy evening. The shop was closed because the toddy had not yet arrived. Suddenly, Pattelar came by in his jeep and asked me to get in. I got into the back and he drove off like a madman. Now and then, the jeep grazed against culverts. At one of the bends, it skidded and nearly overturned. I leaned forward, full of fear, and forcing my voice against the screaming wind, I cried, 'Yejamanare, please go slow; otherwise we'll be killed!' Pattelar did not answer. The jeep roared on, soaking the forests on either side of the road in the blaze of its headlights. Eventually it rattled over the stones of the rough pathway to his house, and stopped. Pattelar turned to me and said, 'I've killed Saroja. We have to make it look like suicide. You have to help me.'

I stared at Pattelar, unable to take my eyes off his face. 'Ayyo, my yejamanare!'

I said. 'My Sarojakka! My Sarojakka!' Crying silently in my heart, I stumbled out of the jeep and started running. Pattelar got into the jeep and gave chase through the peringalam groves and the thickets of weeds. I heard the jeep growling behind me, its eyes glittering in the dark. The headlights threw enormous shadows that writhed through the bushes and pursued me. I was sure Pattelar was going to run me over and kill me too. Sarojakka, I cried to myself, here I come! Omana, what will you do? Suddenly I was blocked by an embankment. I put my back against it and looked at the shining eyes of the jeep racing towards me. I did not want to die! I screamed, 'My yejamanare, please don't kill me!'

Pattelar stopped the jeep, got down, took me by the hand, pushed me inside the vehicle and said, 'Don't run away, you wretched rascal. What are you afraid of? I need you. Be a little brave.'

∽

Sarojakka lay on her back on a cot. She had been strangled. Her tongue was hanging out. Her neck was black and blue. Her face was distorted. I put a trembling hand to my chin and gazed at Sarojakka.

Sarojakka, who had fed me sweets and kanji, given me old clothes. Sarojakka, whom I had once betrayed, but whom I loved. Sarojakka, who had refused to let me be killed. And now she was dead. At the moment of death, what thoughts had gone through her head as she looked at Pattelar's face. Had she pleaded for her life? No, she would have looked at Pattelar with eyes full of astonishment and sorrow.

Then Pattelar said, 'She didn't know I killed her. I covered my face with a towel, came in through the window in the darkness and caught hold of her. But she gripped my hands. That's what worries me. Would she have known they were my hands when she touched them?'

I did not say anything.

Pattelar was quiet for a while and stood looking at Sarojakka.

Then he said to me, 'I've run through all my money. So I had to kill her. Don't you know that I have nothing against Sarojakka?'

He then bent down and gazed at Sarojakka's face. He said, 'Saroja, I didn't kill you.'

I drew back, afraid. I thought Sarojakka was going to get up to answer Pattelar with her tongue hanging out.

Then Pattelar turned to me and said, 'Never mind. Come here and take hold of her legs.'

I caught hold of her ankles in both my hands. It was the first time I had touched Sarojakka. Holding her slim, pale, soft ankles tightly in my hands, I looked at Sarojakka's face. That distorted face was not my Sarojakka's. I looked once at Pattelar, and then I bent down, pressed my face into the soles of her feet and kissed them.

Pattelar said softly, 'You liked Sarojakka.'

I climbed on the bed without saying anything, hoisted Sarojakka on to my shoulders, then put my arms around her and lifted her up as one would a child. Pattelar tightened a rope around her neck and pulled her up. I squatted on the bed, pressed my face to her cold feet and sobbed aloud. Pattelar did not scold me. He stood quietly, looking out of the window.

I looked back once, as we left the room. My Sarojakka hung from the rafters like a broken reed.

Pattelar said again, 'She wouldn't have known, would she?' I followed him without replying. All I wanted to do was to get back to Omana. I wanted to embrace her feet and weep all night, to overcome my sin and sorrow.

As we walked to the jeep. Pattelar said, 'I'm going to the police and to her brothers now to tell them that she killed herself. Remember, you are the witness.'

He stopped near the jeep. I waited in front of him in the dark. Suddenly Pattelar flashed his torch into my face. With dazzled eyes, I searched confusedly for his face behind the torch. Pattelar shone the light into my blinking eyes and asked in a small voice. 'Tell me, look at my face, and tell me, can one recognize a person by just touching his hands?'

I said, 'Who knows, yejamanare?'

Pattelar spat out an obscenity and threw the torch on the ground. Its light came rolling towards my feet. I bent, picked it up and switched it off.

I heard Pattelar gasp. In the darkness, stretching both his hands towards my blinded eyes, Pattelar said. 'Touch my hands.'

My fingers brushed his outstretched hands.

'Is this me?' he whispered.

'Yes, yejamanare,' I said and drew my hands back. Pattelar growled in a voice that came from deep within him. 'I made a mistake. I should have asked you to kill her.'

The next day I heard that Sarojakka's brothers had got some people together and attacked Pattelar's house. I ran there, crept up behind the crowd, and peered over their shoulders. The house had been set on fire, but the fire had been put out. Shattered household items were strewn all over the courtyard. The jeep looked battered. I did not wait to see more but ran back home before anyone could recognize me. When I got home, I shut the door, and said to Omana, 'It's all over. Pattelar's house has been attacked and burned. I don't know where Pattelar has gone. They are sure to come looking for me now.'

'What will you do?' Omana asked, holding on to my shoulder and weeping.

∞

No one came looking for me. All that day and the next I sat at home not knowing what to do. When I was certain that no one was interested in me, I asked a passer-by, 'Do you have any news of Pattelar?' He gave me a hard stare, then said, 'Yes. They say he's gone into hiding. But why are you asking me, it is you who should know.' Worried, I sat on the veranda and thought, what do I do now?

At midnight, as soon as I heard a knock on the door, I said to Omana, 'That's Pattelar.' I got up and opened the door. Pattelar stood on the veranda.

The rain had drenched him. He did not have a torch. He had his gun and a bag of gunpowder. All he wore was a mundu. There were bruises on his body.

'My yejamanare!' I said. I brought him into the hut and shut the door.

Pattelar squatted on the ground. I felt very sad, looking at him. I sat next to him with folded hands and said, 'My yejamanare, to think that this should have happened to you! Tell me what I must do.'

Omana brought some hot kanji for Pattelar. As I stood by the well in the dark, pouring water for Pattelar to wash his hands and feet, I remembered many things. Pattelar had his kanji, then he asked me, 'Will you go with me?'

'Where to, yejamanare?'

Pattelar said, 'We'll go to Kodagu. I can hide in my nephew's house.'

He took some money out of the fold of his mundu, put it on the mat and said to Omana, 'This is for your expenses until this fellow comes back.' Then he raised his head and looked at Omana. Her face was in the shadows thrown by the lantern.

Would Omana feel sad, I wondered. It seemed to me that the fragrance of Pattelar's perfume filled the room. Omana came up to me, held my hands, and began to cry. She put her face between my palms and sobbed. Pattelar sat staring at the ground. Omana's crying made me feel suffocated. Trying to lift her face, I said, 'Omana, I am there for yejamanar.'

∽

Slinking through the night, we reached the main road, hailed a night lorry passing by, and arrived in Madikere. As soon as we entered the courtyard of Pattelar's nephew's house, he hurried us into the shed used for distilling lemon grass oil, closed the door, and said, 'It's dangerous for you here as well. I've just heard that Aunt's brothers are in town with gunmen; you had better go into the forest, Uncle.'

Pattelar's face fell. 'Who told you?'

'People who saw them in town. The story has spread to these parts, Uncle.' His face showed pity and fear.

We stayed in the shed till nightfall. Pattelar spoke to his nephew about the possibility of coming to an understanding with Sarojakka's relatives.

The nephew replied, 'What I heard is that they have already taken over Aunt's share. In which case, they'll hardly be interested in making the peace.' Pity touched his face once more. I could not bear it. I squatted in my corner and shut my eyes tight.

At night, we packed up the roast meat, salt, chillies, and coconuts that Pattelar's nephew gave us. I put the bundle on my head. Pattelar took the gun, the bag of gunpowder, and a torch. We entered the forest. It was peaceful and quiet. My fears vanished as we moved like two ants beneath the shade of the sky-high trees. Walking briskly and enthusiastically, I said, 'Yejamanare, this is like our old hunting trips.' Pattelar didn't reply. He just turned and looked at me.

That night and the following day we ate our dried meat and coconut chutney, rested now and then, and walked. I followed Pattelar, with the load on my head, thinking in wonder of the paths my life had taken.

The hiding place that Pattelar had in mind was on the far side of a river. We heard the murmur of the river from quite a distance. We were then walking under a wild champakam tree full of flowers. I paused beneath the tree. 'Yejamanare,' I called, 'the fragrance of your perfume!'

Pattelar turned. He called me by my name, 'Thommi.'

'Yejamanare,' I answered.

Pattelar stood on the fallen wild champakam blossoms, gun in hand. The roar of the river filled my ears. Pattelar said, 'You must never again make Omana cry.'

'My yejamanare,' I said, 'Omana is my life. Will I ever make her cry?'

Once again, there was only the sound of the rushing river. Pattelar leaned against the champakam tree. He said softly, not looking at me, 'Saroja would not have known, would she?' For a moment, the sunlight drifting through the leaves cast a net over Pattelar's face. I looked into his eyes, which were caught in the meshes of the net, and said, 'No! No! No, yejamanare.' We walked to the river.

∞

The river hissed amongst the rocks. From the hills on the other side, a brook sprang down a rocky slope, descending as a waterfall. Pattelar began crossing the river, gun and bag held high over his head. I followed with the bundle on my head, through the chest-deep foaming water. Pattelar was more than halfway across the river when I suddenly saw something strike a protruding rock, making splinters fly. A shot! I had not heard the sound of the shot above the roar of the water. I counted six gunmen running down the hill on the other bank. Pattelar was thrashing through the water towards the same bank. More shots hit the river, flinging up water and bits of rock. 'My god,' I said, 'they are using big rifles!' I turned and waded back like a madman. I stumbled, fell, went under and, flailing about, somehow reached the riverbank we had started out from. Crouching behind the thickets at the water's edge, I looked back. Pattelar had reached the far shore and was now running, bent double, under cover of the bushes. Two of the gunmen were just behind him.

I saw two others running through the trees to cut him off in front. Suddenly, Pattelar stopped. He held the gun above his head in both hands and stood still. I cried, 'My yejamanare!' Shots came one by one, then together. I saw blood gush from Pattelar's chest, forehead, and stomach. He fell over and lay still. I then proclaimed my great sorrow—my voice carrying across the white expanse of the river, 'My yejamanare! Ayyo! My yejamanare!'

Someone shouted, 'Don't let him go!' A few gunmen jumped across the rocks, waded through the water, and rushed to the bank where I was hiding. I left the shelter of the thickets and ran for my life. 'Ayyo! I don't want to die!' Panting like a dog, I raced headlong, the fear of death in me. I heard the gunmen somewhere behind me.

Beyond the wild champakam, there was a steep slope. I rolled down the slope into a grove of enormous trees. I clambered up one, clinging to it like a chameleon. The dusk-like darkness beneath the branches wrapped itself around me. I stopped climbing only when I felt as if my arms and legs were being torn off. I looked down. Where was I? My head reeled. I closed my eyes and wound my arms tight around the tree. The gentle warmth of urine flowed down my legs. Pressing my face into the moss-covered bark, I became yet another shadow amongst the dim branches. I stayed there like a lizard that had forgotten to move. Even when everything had become silent and quiet below, I did not move. After a long time I grabbed hold of a branch and straddled it. In the evening, it rained. Even after the rain stopped, the leaves dripped on me all night long.

In the morning I limped, shivering, to the river. I saw no one. Only Pattelar lay there. I crossed the river, walked up to his body, and looked at his face wonderingly: it was Bhaskara Pattelar who lay on the grass by the river! The body had begun to smell. I held my nose with one hand and asked, 'Yejamanare, is this really you?' Pattelar lay cold on the grass with his eyes closed. Bhaskara Pattelar was dead! Bhaskara Pattelar, who had bought me mundus, who had found me a job, who had loved my wife, was dead! I squatted there and wept. Forgive me, master, for having once betrayed you! I looked at his swollen, discoloured face and continued to weep.

I opened his dead fingers and took the gun from his hand. For a moment, I held his wrist. I said, 'Get up, yejamanare. Sarojakka might be waiting for us.'

I covered Pattelar with grass and twigs. Then I took his gun, walked along the bank of the river, climbed on to a rock and threw it into the rainbows that fluttered in the waterfall beneath me. I felt a kind of relief. And also, a kind of courage. Crossing the river, I ran to Ichilampadi to tell Omana that Pattelar was dead.

ACKNOWLEDGEMENTS

Grateful acknowledgement is made to the following copyright holders for permission to reprint copyrighted material in this volume. While every effort has been made to locate and contact copyright holders and obtain permission, this has not always been possible; any inadvertent omissions brought to our notice will be remedied in future editions.

'Two Old Kippers' by Siddiq Aalam, translated by Muhammad Umar Memon, was first published in *The Greatest Urdu Stories Ever Told*, 2017, by Aleph Book Company. Reprinted by permission of the publisher.

'Gangrene' by Agyeya, translated by Poonam Saxena, was first published in *The Greatest Hindi Stories Ever Told*, 2020, by Aleph Book Company. Reprinted by permission of Om Thanvi and the publisher.

'The Blue Light' by Vaikom Muhammad Basheer, translated by O. V. Usha. Reprinted by permission of the translator.

'The Gravestone' by Shahnaz Bashir. Reprinted by permission of the author.

'Trishanku' by Mannu Bhandari, translated by Poonam Saxena, was first published in *The Greatest Hindi Stories Ever Told*, 2020, by Aleph Book Company. Reprinted by permission of Rachana Yadav and the publisher.

'The Story of a Crow Learning Prosody' by Subramania Bharati, translated by P. Raja. Reprinted by permission of the translator.

'The Blue Umbrella' by Ruskin Bond. Reprinted by permission of the author.

'The Madiga Girl' by Chalam, translated by Dasu Krishnamoorty and Tamraparni Dasu. Reprinted by permission of the translators.

'Mahesh' by Sarat Chandra Chattopadhyay, translated by Arunava Sinha, was first published in *The Greatest Bengali Stories Ever Told*, 2016, by Aleph Book Company. Reprinted by permission of the publisher.

'Of Fists and Rubs' by Ismat Chughtai, translated by Muhammad Umar Memon, was published in *The Greatest Urdu Stories Ever Told*, 2017, by Aleph Book Company. Reprinted by permission of Ashish Sawhny and the publisher.

'The Booking Counter' by Mamang Dai. Reprinted by permission of the author.

'Countless Hitlers' by Vijaydan Detha, translated by Christi A. Merrill and Kailash Kabir. Reprinted by permission of Kailash Kabir.

'Urvashi and Johnny' by Mahasweta Devi, translated by Arunava Sinha, was first published in *The Greatest Bengali Stories Ever Told*, 2016, by Aleph Book Company. Reprinted by permission of Seagull Books and the publisher.

'Jumo Bhishti' by Dhumketu, translated by Rita Kothari. Reprinted by permission of Gurjar Prakashan and the translator.

'The Night of the Full Moon' by K. S. Duggal, translated by Khushwant Singh. Reprinted by permission of Suhel Duggal and Mala Dayal.

'The Alligator of Aligarh' by A. M. Gautam was first published in the *Bombay Review* (May 2020). Reprinted by permission of the author.

'Tale of a Toilet' by Ramnath Gajanan Gawade, translated by Vidya Pai. Reprinted by permission of the author and the translator.

'Values' by Mamoni Raisom Goswami, translated by Gayatri Bhattacharyya. Reprinted by permission of South East Asia Ramayana Research Centre and the translator.

'Beyond the Fog' by Qurratulain Hyder, translated by Muhammad Umar Memon, was published in *The Greatest Urdu Stories Ever Told*, 2017, by Aleph Book Company. Reprinted by permission of the publisher.

'The Governor's Visit' by Kalki, translated by Gowri Ramnarayan. Reprinted by permission of the translator.

'A Death in Delhi' by Kamleshwar, translated by Poonam Saxena, was first published in *The Greatest Hindi Stories Ever Told*, 2020, by Aleph Book Company. Reprinted by permission of Penguin Random House, India, and the publisher.

'Coinsanv's Cattle' by Damodar Mauzo, translated by Xavier Cota. Reprinted by permission of the author and the translator.

'The Holy Banyan' by Bamacharan Mitra, translated by Leelawati Mohapatra, Paul St-Pierre, and K. K. Mohapatra. Reprinted by permission of the translators.

'The Discovery of Telenapota' by Premendra Mitra, translated by Arunava Sinha, was first published in *The Greatest Bengali Stories Ever Told*, 2016, by Aleph Book Company. Reprinted by permission of Mrinmoy Mitra and the publisher.

'The Solution' by Gopinath Mohanty, translated by Leelawati Mohapatra, Paul St-Pierre, and K. K. Mohapatra. Reprinted by permission of Omkar Nath Mohanty and the translators.

'A Letter' by K. M. Munshi, translated by Rita Kothari. The English version of 'Ek Patra' ('A Letter') of K. M. Munshi is reproduced with the permission of Bharatiya Vidya Bhavan, Mumbai, and the translator.

'Reply-paid Card' by Dinanath Nadim, translated by Neerja Mattoo. Reprinted by permission of Shantiveer Kaul and the translator.

'Vision' by M. T. Vasudevan Nair, translated by A. J. Thomas. Reprinted by permission of the translator.

'A Horse and Two Goats' by R. K. Narayan. Reprinted by permission of Indian Thought Publications.

'The Search' by Dheeba Nazir, translated by Neerja Mattoo. Reprinted by permission of the author and the translator.

'The Flood' by Thakazhi Sivasankara Pillai, translated by O. V. Usha. Reprinted by permission of the translator.

'The Shroud' by Munshi Premchand, translated by Arshia Sattar. Reprinted by permission of the translator.

'Stench of Kerosene' by Amrita Pritam, translated by Khushwant Singh. Reprinted by permission of the author's estate and Mala Dayal.

'Naadar Sir' by Sundara Ramaswamy, translated by Malini Seshadri. First published in the collection *Kagankal* (Sundara Ramaswamy, 2000, Kalachuvadu Publications). Reprinted by permission of the publisher and the translator.

'Rats' by Bhabendra Nath Saikia, translated by Gayatri Bhattacharyya. Reprinted by permission of Preeti Saikia and the translator.

'Kalluri's Radio' by Vilas Sarang, translated by Shanta Gokhale. Reprinted by permission of Shabdalay Prakashan and the translator.

'The Gold Coin' by Laxmanrao Sardessai, translated by Paul Melo e Castro. Reprinted by permission of the translator.

'House Number' by Kavana Sarma, translated by Dasu Krishnamoorty and Tamraparni Dasu. Reprinted by permission of Vijayalakshmi Kandula and the translators.

'Savage Harvest' by Mohinder Singh Sarna, translated by Navtej Sarna. Reprinted by permission of Rupa Publications.

'Gold from the Graves' by Anna Bhau Sathe, translated by Vernon Gonsalves. Reprinted by permission of Savitri Sathe.

'Rebati' by Fakir Mohan Senapati, translated by Leelawati Mohapatra, Paul St-Pierre, and K. K. Mohapatra. Reprinted by permission of the translators.

'Sharavana Services' by Vivek Shanbhag, translated by Jayanth Kodkani. Reprinted by permission of the author and the translator.

'Portrait of a Lady' by Khuswant Singh. Reprinted by permission of Mala Dayal.

'The Times Have Changed' by Krishna Sobti, translated by Poonam Saxena, was first published in *The Greatest Hindi Stories Ever Told*, 2020, by Aleph Book Company. Reprinted by permission of Rajkamal Prakashan and the publisher.

'The Kabuliwallah' by Rabindranath Tagore, translated by Arunava Sinha, was first published in *The Greatest Bengali Stories Ever Told*, 2016, by Aleph Book Company. Reprinted by permission of the publisher.

'Elephant at Sea' by Kanishk Tharoor. Reprinted by permission of the author.

'Charlis and I' by Shashi Tharoor. Reprinted by permission of Penguin Random House, India.

'After the Hanging' by O. V. Vijayan, translated by the author. Reprinted by permission of Penguin Random House, India.

'Gobyaer' by Sadaf Wani. Reprinted by permission of the author.

'Bhaskara Pattelar and My Life' by Paul Zacharia, translated by Gita Krishnankutty. Reprinted by permission of the author and the translator.

NOTES ON THE AUTHORS

Siddiq Aalam (b. 1952) was born in a small town, Purulia, in West Bengal and since 1983 has lived in Calcutta, a city which is the background of his first novel, *Charnock ki Kashti*. He holds an MA in English and a degree in law. He has published three collections of short stories, *Aakhri Chhaa'on*, *Lamp Jaalaney Vaaley*, and *Bain*.

Agyeya (1911–1987) was the nom de plume of Sachchidananda Hirananda Vatsyayan, an Indian writer, poet, novelist, literary critic, journalist, translator, and revolutionary. He pioneered modern trends in Hindi poetry, fiction, criticism, and journalism. His novel, *Shekhar: Ek Jeevani*, based on his experiences in prison, is considered a literary masterpiece. He won the Sahitya Akademi Award, 1964, for his collection of poems, *Prison Days and Other Poems*, and the Jnanpith Award, 1978.

Vaikom Muhammad Basheer (1908–1994) was a humanist, freedom fighter, novelist, and short story writer who revolutionized Malayalam literature through sarcasm, satire, and black humour. His notable works include *Balyakalasakhi*, *Shabdangal*, *Pathummayude Aadu*, *Mathilukal*, *Ntuppuppakkoranendarnnu*, *Janmadinam*, and *Anargha Nimisham*. He was awarded the Padma Shri in 1982.

Shahnaz Bashir (b. 1980) teaches creative journalism and literary reportage at the Central University of Kashmir, where he is the coordinator of the media studies programme. His debut novel, *The Half Mother*, was published in 2014.

Mannu Bhandari (1931–2021) was an eminent Hindi novelist. She was one of the founders of the Nayi Kahani movement alongside Nirmal Verma, Rajendra Yadav, and others, and wrote extensively on the realities of urban life. Her major works include *Aap ka Bunty* (1971) and *Mahabhoj* (1976).

Subramania Bharati (1882–1921) was a freedom fighter, social informer, translator, editor and, above all, a great poet. His timeless expressions indelibly mark Tamil phraseology. His prodigious output included poems, songs, essays, articles, translations, and children's writings.

Ruskin Bond (b. 1934) has been writing for over sixty years, and now has over 120 titles in print—novels, collections of stories, poetry, essays, anthologies and books for children. His first novel, *The Room on the Roof*, received the prestigious John Llewellyn Rhys award in 1957. He has also received the Padma Shri, and two awards from the Sahitya Akademi—one for his short stories and another for his writing for children. In 2012, the Delhi government awarded him its Lifetime Achievement Award.

Chalam (1894–1979), as Gudipati Venkata Chalam was popularly known, typically wrote on themes related to the unconsummated passions of women, the social consequences of the repression of women's desires, and their real and fantasy lives. His novels include *Maidanam, Sasirekha, Dyvamicchina Bharya, Jeevitadarsam, Brahmanikam,* and *Bujjigadu.* Prominent among his fifteen short story collections are *Jealousy, Aa Raathri, Prema Paryavasanam,* and *Satyam Sivam Sundaram.*

Sarat Chandra Chattopadhyay (1876–1938) was a novelist and short story writer. He was born into poverty in Debanandapur and received very little formal education. He began to write in his teens, and went on to become an extremely prolific writer producing many novels, novellas, short stories, essays, and plays, including *Parineeta* (1914), *Palli Samaj* (1916), *Charitraheen* (1917), *Devdas* (1917), and *Griha Daha* (1920).

Ismat Chughtai (1915–91), counted among the earliest and foremost women Urdu writers, was born in Badayun, UP, in 1915 and was educated at Agra, Aligarh, and Lucknow. Her published work includes several collections of short stories, three novellas, and two novels, including *Terhi Lakir* (The Crooked Line). 'Lihaf' (The Quilt) is considered her most controversial short story, as it deals with the plight of a married woman thirsting for her husband's love and embrace which, when denied, drive her to the affections of another woman.

Mamang Dai (b. 1957) is a poet, novelist, and journalist based in Itanagar, Arunachal Pradesh. Her published works include a poetry collection, *River Poems*; a book of interlinked stories, *The Legends of Pensam*, and a novella *Stupid Cupid*. She received the Sahitya Akademi Award for her novel *The Black Hill* in 2017, Verrier Elwin Award for her book *Arunachal Pradesh:*

The Hidden Land in 2003, and was awarded the Padma Shri in 2011 in recognition of her contributions in the fields of literature and education.

Vijaydan Detha (1926–2013), also known as Bijji and 'the Shakespeare of Rajasthan', has more than 800 short stories to his credit, including *Bataan ri Phulwadi* (A Garden of Tales), a fourteen-volume collection of stories that draws on folklore and the spoken dialects of Rajasthan. His stories and novels have been adapted for many plays and movies including Habib Tanvir's *Charandas Chor*, Amol Palekar's *Paheli* and *Duvidha* by Mani Kaul. He was co-founder of Rupayan Sansthan, an institute that documents Rajasthani folklore, arts, and music; he was a recipient of the Padma Shri and Sahitya Akademi awards.

Mahasweta Devi (1926–2016) was born in Dhaka. She was educated at Vishva-Bharati and Calcutta University. She then became a writer, journalist, and professor. Her first book, *Jhansir Rani*, was published in 1956. She retired from her professorship in 1984 and became a full-time writer of fiction and a champion of Adivasi rights. For her achievements as a writer and human rights worker, she has been given several awards and honours, among them the Ramon Magsaysay Award and the Jnanpith Award. Her works *Rudaali* and *Hajar Churashir Maa* have been adapted into films.

Dhumketu (1892–1965) was the nom de plume of Gaurishankar Goverdhanram Joshi. His first collection *Tankha* (1926) is an enduring masterpiece. His stories have been translated into English by Jenny Bhatt and published in a collection called *Ratno Dholi*.

K. S. Duggal (1917–2012) wrote in both Urdu and Punjabi and published over fifty books in his lifetime. He won several major awards including the Sahitya Akademi Award and the Padma Bhushan.

A. M. Gautam (b. 1994) is an internationally published author whose work explores and examines India's sociopolitical curiosities through the lenses of speculative fiction and magical realism. A short story by him was included in the *Best Asian Fiction Anthology* by Kitaab, Singapore, in 2018, and most recently his work has appeared in the April 2022 issue of the literary journal *Orca*.

Ramnath Gajanan Gawade (b. 1969) is a short story writer, novelist, and playwright writing in Konkani. His works include six short story collections, seven novels (including three for children), and two plays. He has been felicitated with many awards during his career such as the Bal Sahitya Puraskar in 2015 for *Sadu Ani Jadugar Mhadu*, two state awards from Goa Konkani Academy (in 2009 and 2011), and a state award from Goa Kala Academy in 2010.

Mamoni Raisom Goswami (1942–2011), also known as Indira Goswami, is a Jnanpith awardee, a Sahitya Akademi awardee, and a noted Ramayan scholar whose work was recognized and lauded worldwide. Though awarded a Padma Shri, she declined the award. She was also the recipient of the Principal Prince Claus Laureate Award of the Netherlands, the monetary component of which she donated to charitable causes. Among the numerous other awards she received were the Kamal Kumari Award, the Mahiyoshi Joymoti Award, the Katha National Award, a honorary D. Litt degree from Rabindra Bharati University, West Bengal, The International Tulsi Award, and also the highest civilian award of the Government of Assam, the Assam Ratna. Her popular novels are *Chenabor Srot* (The Chenab's Current), *Neelkanthi Braja, Mamore Dhora Torowal, Dontal Hatir Uiyey Khowa Howdah, Tej aru Dhulirey Dhuxorito Prishtha, Thengphakhri Tehsildaror Tamor Tarowal* as also several collections of short stories and autobiographical works.

Qurratulain Hyder (1927–2007) ranked among the foremost women writers of Urdu fiction, produced seven novels, several collections of short stories, and translations into Urdu of such writers as Henry James, T. S. Eliot, and Truman Capote. Her critically acclaimed, but no less controversial, novel *Aag kaa Daryaa* has been translated into fifteen Indian languages, and was published in 1999 as *River of Fire*, transcreated by the author herself. She was the recipient of many honours and awards, among them the Sahitya Akademi Award for her collection of short stories *Patjhar ki Aavaaz*, and the Jnanpith Award. She was conferred the Padma Shri in 1984 and the Padma Bhushan in 2005 by the Government of India for her contribution to Urdu literature and education.

Kalki (1899–1954) was the pen name of R. Krishnamurthy, a writer known for his humorous and satirical articles and nationalist and historical novels, serialized in popular magazines and cherished by generations of readers. A nationalist and freedom fighter, he was jailed thrice during the freedom struggle. He launched and edited the magazine *Kalki* after having worked in *Ananda Vikatan*, another weekly, for several years.

Kamleshwar (1932–2007) was one of post-Independence India's most prominent Hindi writers, having published over thirty novels and several short story collections. He won the Sahitya Akademi Award in 2003 for his book *Kitney Pakistani* and the Padma Bhushan in 2005. He was also editor of *Dainik Jagran, Dainik Bhaskar,* the now-defunct *Sarika,* and worked as a scriptwriter for Hindi movies and TV serials.

Damodar Mauzo (b. 1944) is a short story writer, novelist, critic, and scriptwriter who lives in Goa and writes in Konkani. He received India's highest literary honour, the Jnanpith Award, in 2022. His most recent published book is *The Wait: And Other Stories*. He was awarded the Sahitya Akademi Award in 1983, for his novel *Karmelin*, and the Vimala V. Pai Vishwa Konkani Sahitya Puraskar in 2011, for his novel *Tsunami Simon*. His collection of short stories, *Teresa's Man and Other Stories from Goa*, was nominated for the Frank O'Connor International Short Story Award in 2015. He has served as a member of the executive board of the Sahitya Akademi, New Delhi.

Bamacharan Mitra (1915–70) was lauded by critics for his extraordinary depth and perception, and his diverse interests ranging from classical music to swimming to football and detective fiction. He published three novels and more than a hundred short stories, which have been collected in eight volumes.

Premendra Mitra (1904–88) was a novelist, short story writer, poet, scriptwriter, and film director of the 'Kallol' era in Bengali literature. He also wrote thrillers, fairy tales, ghost stories, and science fiction, and was associated with the journal *Kalikalam*. Born in Varanasi and brought up in Uttar Pradesh, he later lived in Dhaka and Calcutta. He created the beloved children's book character, Ghanada. He was awarded the Sahitya Akademi Award, the Rabindra Puraskar, and the Padma Shri, among many other honours.

Gopinath Mohanty (1914–91) was the winner of the inaugural Sahitya Akademi Award in 1955 and the Jnanpith Award in 1974. His novels include *Paraja, Danapani, Amrutara Santana, Laya Bilaya,* and *Dadi Budha,* all of which have also been translated into English. He was also awarded the Padma Bhushan in 1991. His prodigious output in a literary career spanning almost half a century included twenty novels and sixteen collections of short stories, an incomplete autobiography in three volumes, and several translations, including Leo Tolstoy's *War and Peace* and Maxim Gorky's *My University*.

K. M. Munshi (1887–1971) is synonymous with regional pride in Gujarat, for he popularized the idea of 'Gujarati ni Asmita' or 'Gujarat's pride'. His trilogy of Patan novels (*The Glory of Patan*; *The Lord and Master of Gujarat*; and *The King of Kings*) has recently been translated by Rita and Abhijit Kothari. Munshi contributed to every genre of Gujarati literature. He established numerous institutions including the Bharatiya Vidya Bhawan. He also participated in the Gandhian movement for Independence and served as a Member of the Rajya Sabha as well as the Constitution Committee of India.

Dinanath Nadim (1916–88) was a celebrated poet, and wrote the first Kashmiri short story. Poetry, however, was his chosen medium and he experimented with different forms, including operas, with great success. He was the recipient of many awards, including the Sahitya Akademi Award for his opera *Shihul Kul* in 1986.

M. T. Vasudevan Nair (b. 1933) is an author, screenplay writer, and film director. He has won many prestigious literary awards including the Kerala Sahitya Akademi Award for his novel *Naalukettu* in 1958, Kerala Sahitya Akademi Award for his short story 'Swargam Thurakkunna Samayan' in 1986, and the Jnanpith Award in 1995 for his contribution to Malayalam literature.

R. K. Narayan (1906–2001) was one of the country's greatest writers, illuminating the human condition through small-town life. He created the fictional town of Malgudi, which he introduced in his first work of fiction, *Swami and Friends*; it was the setting for many of his works. In 1958 Narayan's work *The Guide* won the Sahitya Akademi Award and was adapted for film and Broadway. He won numerous awards, including the Padma Vibhushan, and was nominated to the Rajya Sabha.

Dheeba Nazir (b. 1988) is a research scholar and teacher. She has translated three books from Kashmiri into Urdu: *Gul Bakawali Dastan*, *Kuliyaat Abdul Ahad Azad*, and *Kuliyaat Ropi Bhawani*. In 2008, she received the Sahitya Akademi Yuva Puraskar for her collection of Kashmiri short stories, *Zareen Zakham*.

Thakazhi Sivasankara Pillai (1912–99) was a Malayalam novelist and short story writer, popularly known as Thakazhi, after his place of birth. He wrote several novels and over 600 short stories. His most famous works are the epic novel *Kayar* (Coir, 1978), for which he won India's highest literary award, the Jnanpith; and *Chemmeen* (Prawns, 1956).

Munshi Premchand (1880–1936) is regarded as one of the most important writers of Urdu fiction not just in view of his phenomenal output, but also for his passionate belief in the transformative agency of literature in ridding society of its myriad social and religious ills. Premchand was born in the small village of Lamhi near Benares in 1880. Here, he received his early education in Persian and Urdu under a maulvi in a madrasa. He first wrote in Urdu, but later switched to Hindi in view of the poor market for Urdu books, too small to support him. He is the author of more than a dozen novels, over two hundred short stories, several essays, and translations of foreign literary works.

Amrita Pritam (1919–2005) is acclaimed as a doyenne of Punjabi literature. Her best-known works are the poem 'Aaj Aakhan Waris Shan Nu' and the novel *Pinjar* (The Skeleton), which was made into an award-winning film in 2003. In 1956, she became the first woman to win the Sahitya Akademi Award for her magnum opus, a long poem, *Sunehe* (Messages); she received the Jnanpith in 1982 for *Kagaz Te Canvas* (The Paper and the Canvas). In 2004, she was awarded the Padma Vibhushan, as well as the Sahitya Akademi's Lifetime Achievement Award.

Sundara Ramaswamy (1931–2005) was an influential Tamil writer. As a native of Nagercoil in Tamil Nadu, in close proximity to Kerala, he represented the bilingual felicity of Tamil and Malayalam. His literary career, spanning over five decades, included short stories, novels, translations, poetry, and criticism. He published poetry under the name Pasuvayya. His novel, *Oru Puliya Maraththin Kathai* was a classic, presenting contemporary life in the dialect of the region. The University of Toronto conferred on him the inaugural Iyal Award in 2001.

Bhabendra Nath Saikia (1932–2003) filmmaker, playwright, and writer, was a recipient of the Sahitya Akademi Award for fiction. He was also a Padma Shri awardee, as well as a recipient of seven Rajat Kamal awards for his films, several of which are based on his own stories. Besides this, he was a recipient of the Srimanta Sankardeva Award and the Assam Valley

Literary Award. A teacher of Physics at Gauhati University, he was also a member of the Sangeet Natak Akademi, New Delhi. Among his works are three novels, eleven short story collections, twenty-eight plays, several books for children, and collections of essays. His short stories are known for their delineation of character and their psychological motivations, as well as their powers of observation and plotting.

Vilas Sarang (1942–2015) was born in Karwar, a coastal town in Karnataka. As a bilingual writer, Sarang had stories, novels, and poetry in both English and Marathi to his credit. His Marathi short story collections were *Soledad* (1975) and *Atank* (1999) and translations of his stories in English were collected in *A Fair Tree of the Void* (1990) and more recently *The Women in the Cages* (2006). His other works included the English novel was *The Dinosaur Ship* (2005) and the Marathi novel *Enkichya Rajyat* (1983). His Marathi collection of poems was published under the title *Kavita* (1969–84) and his collection of English poems was published as *A Kind of Silence* (1978).

Laxmanrao Sardessai (1904–86) was born in Savoi-Verem in Ponda. Considered one of the territory's finest writers in the Marathi language, he also wrote prose and verse in Konkani and Portuguese. His first short story, 'Sasurvani', was published in *Yeshwant* magazine. He wrote about 700 short stories in Marathi; these provide a spectrum of Goa over the twentieth century. Towards the end of his life, he began writing in Portuguese and Konkani. His book of essays *Khabri* won the Sahitya Akademi Award in Konkani in 1982.

Kavana Sarma (1939–2018) is known to Telugu readers both as a storyteller and as a man of science. A former professor at the Indian Institute of Science, Bengaluru, he taught and lectured at universities in the US, the UK, Iraq, Australia, and the West Indies. *Vyangya Kavanalu*, *Kavana Sarma Kathalu*, *America Majili Kathalu*, and *Sangha Puranam* are prominent among his short story collections. He won the Jyeshta Award and Telugu University Award.

Mohinder Singh Sarna (1923–2001) moved to Delhi from Rawalpindi after the tumultuous partition of India, and joined the Indian Audit and Accounts Service in 1950. In a writing career spanning six decades, Sarna produced several volumes of poetry, short stories, and novels, many of which have been widely translated into other Indian languages and made into telefilms. Sarna's work has received critical acclaim, and is prescribed in university syllabi in India and abroad. He was the recipient of the Sahitya Akademi Award, the Sahitya Kala Parishad Award, the Balraj Sahni Trust Award, the Nanak Singh Fiction Award on four occasions, the Katha Award, the Bhai Santokh Singh Poetry Award, the Giani Gurmukh Singh Poetry Award, the Sewa Sifti International Award, the Zehne Jadid Award, the Bawa Balwant Trust Award and the Waris Shah Samman. He was recognized as the Shiromani Punjabi Sahitkar by the Government of Punjab in 1989.

Anna Bhau Sathe (1920–1969) was a writer and social reformer. Despite a lack of formal education, he wrote thirty-five novels in Marathi, of which the most famous—*Fakira*—is in its nineteenth edition. He also wrote numerous collections of short stories, screenplays, ballads, and a travelogue on Russia. Much like his life, his stories embody the human struggle against immense odds.

Fakir Mohan Senapati (1843–1918) is widely acknowledged as the father of modern Odia prose. He wrote four novels, including the iconic *Chha Mana Atha Guntha*, considered a foundational text of Indian literature, two collections of short stories, an autobiography and several essays, besides textbooks and a book of verse. He had earlier translated the Ramayana and the Mahabharata into Odia.

Vivek Shanbhag (b. 1962) is a novelist, playwright, short story writer, and editor who writes in Kannada. He has published thirteen works of fiction and edited two anthologies. He is the founding editor of the literary journal *Desha Kaala*. His critically-acclaimed novel *Ghachar Ghochar* has been translated into nineteen languages worldwide. Shanbhag is the co-translator of U. R. Ananthamurthy's book *Hindutva or Hind Swaraj* into English. He is a Visiting Professor at Ashoka University teaching Creative Writing. An engineer by training, Shanbhag lives in Bengaluru.

Khushwant Singh (1915–2014) was, arguably, India's best-known and most widely read author, columnist, and journalist in his lifetime. He was the founder-editor of *Yojana*, and editor of the *Illustrated Weekly of India*, *National Herald,* and the *Hindustan Times*. He wrote several books, including the novels *Train to Pakistan, I Shall Not Hear the Nightingale,* and *Delhi*; his autobiography, *Truth, Love & a Little Malice*; and the two-volume *A History of the Sikhs*. He also translated from Hindi, Urdu, and Punjabi. Khushwant Singh was a member of the Rajya Sabha from 1980 to 1986. In 2007, he was awarded India's second highest civilian honour, the Padma Vibhushan.

Krishna Sobti (1925–2019) is regarded as the grande dame of Hindi literature. Her novels *E Ladaki* and *Mitro Marjani* are cult classics and known for their inventive formal approach and strong female characters. Her first short story, 'Sikka Badal Gaya', was notably published without a single change in the prestigious Hindi magazine, *Pratap*, edited by Agyeya. In her last novel, *Gujarat Pakistan Se Gujarat Hindustan* (A Gujarat Here, A Gujarat There), she wrote about her painful memories of Partition. She won the Sahitya Akademi Award in 1980 for *Zindaginama* (1979) and the Jnanpith Award in 2017.

Rabindranath Tagore (1861–1941) was the fourteenth son of Debendranath Tagore and Sarada Devi, and started writing early in his life. He joined the Swadeshi Movement against the British in the 1900s. He won the Nobel Prize for Literature in 1913, and used his earnings to partly fund his school and university Visva-Bharati in Santiniketan. His influence on Bengali culture extends far beyond his highly regarded poetry and prose, into music, visual art, and theatre.

Kanishk Tharoor (b. 1984) is the author of *Swimmer Among the Stars*, an award-winning collection of short stories. His writing has appeared in publications around the world, including the *New York Times*, *The Guardian*, *The Caravan*, and the *Times of India*. He is the presenter of the BBC radio series *Museum of Lost Objects*. He is a senior editor of *Foreign Affairs* magazine. He grew up in and currently lives in New York City with his wife and two children.

Shashi Tharoor (b. 1956) is the bestselling author of twenty-five books, both fiction and non-fiction, besides being a noted critic and columnist, a former Under Secretary-General of the United Nations and a former Minister of State for Human Resource Development and Minister of State for External Affairs in the Government of India. In his third term, he is the longest-serving member of the Lok Sabha from Thiruvananthapuram and has chaired Parliament's Standing Committees on External Affairs and on Information Technology. He has won numerous literary awards, including the Sahitya Akademi Award, the Ramnath Goenka Award for Excellence in Books (non-fiction), the Commonwealth Writers' Prize, and the Crossword Lifetime Achievement Award. He was honoured as New Age Politician of the Year by NDTV in 2010 and won the Pravasi Bharatiya Samman, India's highest honour for overseas Indians, in 2004.

O. V. Vijayan (1931–2005) was an Indian author and cartoonist, and an important figure in modern Malayalam language literature. Best known for his first novel *Khasakkinte Itihasam* (1969), Vijayan was the author of six novels, nine short story collections, and nine collections of essays, memoirs, and reflections.

Sadaf Wani (b. 1993) is a Kashmiri writer and researcher. Her work has been published in *Himal Southasian*, *Scroll*, *Wande* Magazine, and *Inverse Journal*, among others.

Paul Zacharia (b. 1945) is an eminent Malayalam fiction writer and essayist. He was awarded the Kendra Sahitya Akademi Award in 2005 for his short-story collection, *Zachariyayute Kathakal*. His works that have been translated into English include *Bhaskara Pattelar and Other Stories*, *Reflections of a Hen in Her Last Hour and Other Stories*, and *Paul Zacharia: Two Novellas*.

NOTES ON THE TRANSLATORS

Gayatri Bhattacharyya worked in St. Edmund's College, Shillong, before joining Gauhati University. After retirement, she took up translation as a hobby, and has since translated many anthologies of short stories and novels written by eminent Assamese writers, into English, including works by Sarat Chandra Goswami, Bhabendra Nath Saikia, Mamoni Raisom Goswami, Anuradha Sarma Pujari, Dipak Barkakati, and Birinchi Kumar Barua. So far she has fifteen books to her credit, besides many short stories and articles published in anthologies and newspapers.

Paul Melo e Castro teaches comparative literature and Portuguese at the University of Glasgow. He is a regular translator of short stories from across the Portuguese-speaking world.

Xavier Cota has worked as a teacher, banker, and sports administrator, and translates fiction from Konkani to English and non-fiction from Portuguese to English. His translated fiction and other articles have appeared in publications like *The Week*, *Man's World*, *Katha Prize Stories*, and Sahitya Akademi's journal. He has won the 2005 Katha Award for Translation. His Konkani-to-English translations of Damodar Mauzo's works include the short story collections *The Wait: And Other Stories*, *These Are My Children*, and *Teresa's Man and Other Stories from Goa*, and the novel *Tsunami Simon*. He lives in Betalbatim, Goa.

Tamraparni Dasu, along with her father, Dasu Krishnamoorty, founded the literary non-profit organization IndiaWrites Publishers Inc. to support high quality translation and the dissemination of short fiction written in Indian languages. The non-profit supported *Literary Voices of India* (2006–2012), an online magazine, culminating in the anthology *1947 Santoshabad Passenger and Other Stories*. Dasu publishes genre fiction under the name T. Dasu. Her works include *Spy, Interrupted: The Waiting Wife* and *Spy, Interrupted: The Perfect Candidate*. She has a PhD in Statistics from the University of Rochester and specializes in computational statistics, machine learning, data quality, and stream analytics. She was a Lead Inventive Scientist at AT&T and has numerous patents and academic publications to her credit.

Shanta Gokhale is an accomplished translator and writer of novels, plays, short stories, film scripts, and innumerable newspaper articles. She has translated essays, short fiction, novels, autobiographies, and plays from Marathi into English and a play and a novel from English into Marathi. Gokhale has a volume on the history of Marathi theatre and edited books on the works of theatre directors Satyadev Dubey, Veenapani Chawla, and oral history experimental theatre in Mumbai to her credit.

Vernon Gonsalves is a social and political activist. He was on the editorial board of *Thingi Kamgar Masik*, a Marathi-language monthly magazine for workers, from 1981 to 1986. He has been associated with the Marathi magazine *Jahirnama* since the eighties; until his arrest in August 2007 (on charges of being a Naxalite), he was also involved with a bilingual Hindi-Marathi magazine, *Kamgar*. He was released from prison in 2013.

Kailash Kabir is an award-winning translator and poet of Hindi and Rajasthani who makes his home in Jodhpur, India.

Jayanth Kodkani is a writer and journalist based in Bengaluru. He has written extensively on social and cultural topics, besides trying his hand at fiction and translation. His stories and essays have been part of anthologies like the *Puffin Book of Funny Stories*, *Where the Rain is Born*, *Dots and Lines*, and *Playback: Sports Legends of Bangalore*. He has co-edited an anthology entitled *Beantown Boomtown: Bangalore in the World of Words*. Among his English translations of Kannada are K. V. Akshara's *Two Plays*.

Rita Kothari is the Vani Foundation Distinguished Translator and has translated widely from Gujarati and Sindhi. A multilingual scholar, Kothari speaks and writes on language politics, translation theory, Partition, and border studies. She is the author of *Translating India*, *The Burden of Refuge*, and numerous other publications. She teaches at Ashoka University, Sonepat, India.

Dasu Krishnamoorty is an anthologist, translator, and storyteller based in New Jersey. He was educated at Andhra University, the University of Bombay (LLB), and Osmania University (Journalism), before becoming an influential Indian print media journalist. He has worked in an editorial capacity at the *Indian Express*, *Times of India*, and *Patriot*. He was a senior political commentator with All India Radio and taught mass communications at Osmania University, the Indian Institute of Mass Communications in New Delhi, and the University of Hyderabad. His works include *1947 Santoshabad Passenger and Other Stories,* and *The Seaside Bride and Other Stories.*

Gita Krishnankutty is a scholar, critic, and a well-known translator of Malayalam and French literature.

Neerja Mattoo is an eminent writer, teacher, and translator who has taught in Kashmir for over three decades. She has published five books, the most recent being the critically acclaimed *The Mystic and the Lyric: Four Women Poets from Kashmir.* Her works have been published by the Sahitya Akademi, and she has been awarded a Fellowship and a Visitorship to Oxford, by the Ministry of Education and the British Council respectively. She lives in Srinagar, Kashmir.

Muhammad Umar Memon was professor emeritus of Urdu literature and Islamic studies at the University of Wisconsin, Madison. He was a critic, short story writer, and translated numerous works of Urdu fiction. He was editor of the *Annual of Urdu Studies* (1993–2014). He passed away in June 2018 in Madison, Wisconsin.

Christi A. Merrill is an assistant professor of South Asian Literature and postcolonial studies at the University of Michigan. Her translations from Hindi, French, and Rajasthani and essays on translation have appeared in journals such as *Genre, Studies in Twentieth Century Literature, The Iowa Review, Modern Poetry in Translation,* and *Indian Literature,* the Sahitya Akademi's bi-monthly journal.

K. K. (Kamalakanta) Mohapatra has written three collections of short stories, a novel, a book of non-fiction, and an autobiography. He has also translated into Odia selected stories by Isaac Bashevis Singer, Jean-Paul Sartre, and Franz Kafka, as well as William Shakespeare's *King Lear,* and collaborated with Leelawati Mohapatra and Paul St-Pierre on numerous works of translation from Odia into English.

Leelawati Mohapatra published her debut novel, *Hanging by a Tail,* in 2008. She has co translated (with K. K. Mohapatra and Paul St-Pierre) extensively from Odia into English. Her books of translation include, among others, *The HarperCollins Book of Oriya Short Stories, Ants, Ghosts and Whispering Trees:*

An Anthology of Oriya Short Stories, J P Das: Sundardas, Fakir Mohan Senapati: The Brideprice and Other Stories, and *Laxmikanta Mahapatra: Uncle One Eye*.

Vidya Pai stumbled on to the field of translation after winning the Konkani award at the Katha-British Council Translation Contest in 1993. Her translated stories have appeared in several anthologies published by Penguin, Katha, Sahitya Akademi, *Govapuri, Goa Today*, and *Navhind Times*. She has translated seven Konkani novels; the most recent of them are: Mahableshwar Sail's *Forest Saga* (2014) and *Age of Frenzy* (2017), and Meena Kakodkar's *Abode of Joy* (2020). She has also translated and published *Kaleidoscope*, a collection of Ravindra Kelekar's essays, and *Mirage and Other Stories*, a collection of short stories by Damodar Mauzo.

Paul St-Pierre is a former professor of Translation Studies at Montreal University. He has co-edited several books on translation theory and practice and has spent nearly a quarter-century collaborating with, apart from the Mohapatras, several Odia translators such as Ganeswar Mishra, Basant Kumar Tripathy, Himansu Sekhar Mohapatra, Rabindra Swain, and Dipti Ranjan Patnaik. With the Mohapatras he has also recently finished a new translation of Fakir Mohan Senapati's iconic novel, *Chha Mana Atha Guntha*.

P. Raja formerly a professor of English, Kanchi Mamunivar Centre for Postgraduate Studies, Pondicherry, is a bilingual author. Dr Raja has published more than 5,000 articles, short fiction, poems, interviews, plays, reviews, skits, translations, and features in no less than 350 newspapers and magazines, both in India and abroad. He has authored thirty-two books in English and fourteen books in Tamil.

Gowri Ramnarayan is a playwright, theatre director, journalist (formerly deputy editor, *The Hindu*, now freelance writer), and was a vocal accompanist to legendary musician M. S. Subbulakshmi. Dr Ramnarayan's *Dark Horse & Other Plays* anthologizes her original plays. She has authored children's books and a biography of M. S. Subbulakshmi (*MS & Radha*), and translated two plays by Marathi playwright Vijay Tendulkar, and the Tamil short stories of Kalki Krishnamurthy.

Navtej Sarna was India's Ambassador to the United States, High Commissioner to the United Kingdom, and Ambassador to Israel. He has also served as Secretary to the Government of India and as the Foreign Office Spokesperson. His earlier diplomatic assignments were in Moscow,

Warsaw, Thimphu, Tehran, Geneva, and Washington DC. His literary work includes the novels *Crimson Spring*, *The Exile*, and *We Weren't Lovers Like That*, the short story collection *Winter Evenings*, non-fiction works *The Book of Nanak*, *Second Thoughts*, and *Indians at Herod's Gate*, as well as two translations, *Zafarnama* and *Savage Harvest*. He is a prolific columnist and commentator on foreign policy and literary matters, contributing regularly to media platforms in India and abroad.

Arshia Sattar's English translations include Valmiki's *Ramayana* and *Tales from the Kathasaritsagara*. She has a PhD from the Department of South Asian Languages and Civilizations at the University of Chicago and her interests are Indian epics, mythology, and the story traditions of the subcontinent.

Poonam Saxena is a journalist, writer, and translator. She worked with the *Hindustan Times* for several years, first as editor of *Brunch* and then of the weekend section. She has translated Dharamvir Bharati's *Gunahon ka Devta* from Hindi to English (*Chander & Sudha*), Rahi Masoom Raza's *Scene: 75*, and co-authored filmmaker Karan Johar's memoir, *An Unsuitable Boy*. She lives in Delhi.

Malini Seshadri is a freelance writer, editor, and translator based in Chennai. She has over three decades of experience writing newspaper columns and magazine articles on a wide variety of themes. Recently, she co-authored a series of value education books for schools entitled *Living in Harmony*. She has translated Bama's novel *Vanmam*, and also ten Tamil short stories by various authors as part of an anthology. She has also written a work of fiction for children, and co-edited a textbook for an undergraduate programme.

Arunava Sinha translates classic, modern, and contemporary Bengali fiction and non-fiction from Bangladesh and India into English. He also translates fiction from English into Bengali. Over seventy of his translations have been published so far in India, the UK, and the USA. He is the editor and translator of *The Greatest Bengali Stories Ever Told*. He has won India's top translation prize, the Crossword Award for translated books, twice. He teaches at Ashoka University, where he is also the co-director of the Ashoka Centre for Translation, and is the Books Editor at *Scroll.in*.

A. J. Thomas is a poet, editor, and translator who writes in English. He has more than twenty books to his credit and is the former editor of

Indian Literature, Sahitya Akademi's bi-monthly journal. Thomas taught English at Benghazi University, Libya, and worked as a Senior Consultant at IGNOU. He is a recipient of the Katha Award, AKMG Prize, and the Vodafone Crossword Award for Translation. Thomas holds a Senior Fellowship, Government of India, and was an Honorary Fellow, Department of Culture, Government of South Korea.

O. V. Usha is a Malayalam poet and novelist. She has published four volumes of poems and a novel. Her articles have appeared in various journals. She served the Mahatma Gandhi University, Kottayam, as its director of publications. She won the Kerala State Film Award for Best Lyrics for *Mazha*, a Malayalam film released in 2000.